Cutlass And Cudgel

by

George Manville Fenn

Cutlass And Cudgel
by George Manville Fenn

Copyright © 2023

ISBN: 978-93-60463-70-0

Published by

DOUBLE 9 BOOKS

2/13-B, Ansari Road
Daryaganj, New Delhi – 110002
info@double9books.com
www.double9books.com
Tel. 011-40042856

ABOUT THE AUTHOR

George Manville Fenn was a very productive author of novels, a writer, an editor, and an educator from England. He was born on January 3, 1831, in Pimlico, London. He mostly learned on his own; he taught himself Italian, French, and German. During the years 1851–1854, he went to Battersea Training College for Teachers and then became the head of a state school in Alford, Lincolnshire. In the early 1850s, Fenn started to write short stories and pieces for newspapers and magazines. The Old Forest Ranger, his first book, came out in 1856. Afterward, he wrote more than 100 books, many of them for teenagers and young adults. He was one of the most famous writers of his time, and his books were well-liked and read by many people. He also worked as a reporter and writer for Fenn. Among the newspapers and magazines, he worked for was The Boy's Own Paper, which he ran from 1866 to 1874. He worked hard to make children's books better and was a strong supporter of education and reading. The Englishman Fenn passed away on August 26, 1909, in Isleworth.

CONTENTS

Chapter One

"Heigh-Ho-Ha-Hum! Oh dear me!"

"What's matter, sir?"

"Matter, Dirty Dick? Nothing; only, heigh-ho-ha! Oh dear me, how sleepy I am!"

"Well, sir, I wouldn't open my mouth like that 'ere, 'fore the sun's up."

"Why not?"

"No knowing what you might swallow off this here nasty, cold, foggy, stony coast."

"There you go again, Dick; not so good as Lincolnshire coast, I suppose?"

"As good, sir? Why, how can it be?" said the broad, sturdy sailor addressed. "Nothin' but great high stony rocks, full o' beds of great flat periwinkles and whelks; nowhere to land, nothin' to see. I am surprised at you, sir. Why, there arn't a morsel o' sand."

"For not praising your nasty old flat sandy shore, with its marsh beyond, and its ague and bogs and fens."

"Wish I was 'mong 'em now, sir. Wild ducks there, as is fit to eat, not iley fishy things like these here."

"Oh, bother! Wish I could have had another hour or two's sleep. I say, Dirty Dick, are you sure the watch wasn't called too soon?"

"Nay, sir, not a bit; and, beggin' your pardon, sir, if you wouldn't mind easin' off the Dirty—Dick's much easier to say."

"Oh, very well, Dick. Don't be so thin-skinned about a nickname."

"That's it, sir. I arn't a bit thin-skinned. Why, my skin's as thick as one of our beasts. I can't help it lookin' brown. Washes myself deal more than some o' my mates as calls me dirty. Strange and curious how a name o' that kind sticks."

"Oh, I say, don't talk so," said the lad by the rough sailor's side; and after another yawn he began to stride up and down the deck of His Majesty's cutter *White Hawk*, lying about a mile from the Freestone coast of Wessex.

It was soon after daybreak, the sea was perfectly calm and a thick grey mist hung around, making the deck and cordage wet and the air chilly, while the coast, with its vast walls of perpendicular rocks, looked weird and distant where a peep could be obtained amongst the wreaths of vapour.

"Don't know when I felt so hungry," muttered the lad, as he thrust his hands into his breeches pockets, and stopped near the sailor, who smiled in the lad's frank-looking, handsome face.

"Ah, you always were a one to yeat, sir, ever since you first came aboard."

"You're a noodle, Dick. Who wouldn't be hungry, fetched out of his cot at this time of the morning to take the watch. Hang the watch! Bother the watch! Go and get me a biscuit, Dick, there's a good fellow."

The sailor showed his white teeth, and took out a brass box.

"Can't get no biscuit yet, sir. Have a bit o' this. Keeps off the gnawin's wonderful."

"Yah! Who's going to chew tobacco!" cried the lad with a look of disgust, as he buttoned up his uniform jacket. "Oh, hang it all, I wish the sun would come out!"

"Won't be long, sir; and then all this sea-haar will go."

"Why don't you say mist?" cried the lad contemptuously.

"'Acause it's sea-haar, and you can't make nowt else on it, sir!"

"They haven't seen anything of them in the night, I suppose?"

"No, sir; nowt. It scars me sometimes, the way they dodges us, and gets away. Don't think theer's anything queer about 'em, do you?"

"Queer? Yes, of course. They're smugglers, and as artful as can be."

"Nay, sir, bad, I mean—you know, sir."

"No, I don't, Dick," cried the young officer pettishly. "How can I know? Speak out."

"Nay, I wean't say a word, sir; I don't want to get more scarred than I am sometimes now."

"Get out! What do you mean? That old Bogey helps them to run their cargoes?"

"Nay, sir, I wean't say a word. It's all werry well for you to laugh, now it's daylight, and the sun coming out. It's when it's all black as pitch, as it takes howd on you worst."

"You're a great baby, Dick," cried the midshipman, as he went to the side of the cutter and looked over the low bulwark toward the east. "Hah! Here comes the sun."

His eyes brightened as he welcomed the coming of the bright orb, invisible yet from where he stood; but the cold grey mist that hung around was becoming here and there, in patches, shot with a soft delicious rosy hue, which made the grey around turn opalescent rapidly, beginning to flash out pale yellow, which, as the middy watched, deepened into orange and gold.

"Lovely!" he said aloud, as he forgot in the glory of the scene the discomfort he had felt.

"Tidy, sir, pooty tidy," said the sailor, who had come slowly up to where he stood. "And you should see the morning come over our coast, sir. Call this lovely? Why, if you'd sin the sun rise there, it would mak' you stand on your head."

"Rather see this on my feet, Dick," cried the lad. "Look at that! Hurrah! Up she comes!"

Up "she" —otherwise the sun—did come, rolling slowly above the mist-covered sea, red, swollen, huge, and sending blood-tinted rays through and through the haze to glorify the hull, sails, and rigging of the smart cutter, and make the faces of the man at the helm and the other watchers glow as with new health.

The effect was magical. Just before all was cold and grey, and the clinging mist sent a shiver through those on deck; now, their eyes brightened with pleasure, as the very sight of the glowing orb seemed to have a warming— as it certainly had an enlivening—effect.

The great wreaths of mist yielded rapidly as the sun rose higher, the rays shooting through and through, making clear roads which flashed with light, and, as the clouds rolled away like the grey smoke of the sun's fire, the distant cliffs, which towered up steep and straight, like some titanic wall, came peering out now in patches bright with green and golden grey.

Archibald Raystoke—midshipman aboard His Majesty the king's cutter, stationed off the Freestone coast, to put a stop to the doings of a smuggler whose career the Government had thought it high time to notice—drew in a long breath, and forgot all about hunger and cold in the promise of a glorious day.

It was impossible to think of such trifling things in the full burst of so much beauty, for, as the sun rose higher, the sea, which had been blood-red and golden, began to turn of a vivid blue deeper than the clear sky overhead; the mist wreaths grew thinner and more transparent, and the pearly glistening foam, which followed the breaking of each wave at the foot of the mighty cliffs, added fresh beauty to the glorious scene.

"Look here, Dirty Dick," began the middy, who burst out into a hearty fit of laughter as he saw the broad-shouldered sailor give his face a rub with the back of his hands, and look at them one after the other.

"Does it come off, Dick?" he said.

"Nay, sir; nothin' comes off," said the man dolefully. "'Tis my natur too, but it seems werry hard to be called dirty, when you arn't."

"There, I beg pardon, Dick, and I will not call you so any more."

"Thankye, sir; I s'pose you mean it, but you'll let it out again soon as you forget."

"No, I will not, Dick. But, I say, look here: you are a cheat, though, are you not?"

"Me, sir? No!" cried the man excitedly.

"I mean about the Lincolnshire coast. Confess it isn't half so beautiful as this."

"Oh, yes it is, sir. It's so much flatter. Why, you can't hardly find a place to land here, without getting your boat stove in."

"If all's true, the smugglers know how to land things," said Archibald, as he gazed thoughtfully at the cliffs.

"Oh, them! O' course, sir, they can go up the cliffs, and over 'em like flies in sugar basins. They get a spar over the edge, with a reg'lar pulley, and lets down over the boats, and then up the kegs and bales comes."

"Ah, well, we must catch them at it some day, Dick, and then there'll be lots o' prize-money for you all."

"And for you too, sir; officers comes first. But we arn't got the prize yet, and it's my belief as we shan't get it."

"Why?"

"Because it seems to me as there's something not all right about these here craft."

"Of course there is, they are smugglers."

"Yes, sir, and worse too. If they was all right, we shouldn't ha' been cruising 'bout here seven weeks, and never got a sight o' one of 'em, when we know they've been here all the time."

"I don't understand you, Dick," said the middy, as he watched the going and coming of the rock pigeons which flew straight for the cliff, seemed to pass right in, and then dashed out.

"Well, sir, I can't explain it. Them there's things as you can't explain, nor nobody else can't."

He wrinkled up his face and shook his head, as if there were a great deal more behind.

"Now, what are you talking about, Dick?" cried the lad. "You don't mean that the smuggler's a sort of ghost, and his lugger's all fancy?"

"Well, not exactly, sir, because if they was, they couldn't carry real cargoes, which wouldn't be like the smuggler and his lugger, sir, and, of course, then the kegs and lace wouldn't be no good. But there's a bit something wrong about these here people, and all the men thinks so too."

"More shame for them!" said the middy quickly. "Hi! Look there, Dick; what's that?"

He seized the sailor by the shoulder, and pointed where, some five hundred yards away, close under the cliff, but on the rise of the line of breakers, there was something swimming slowly along.

Dick shaded his eyes, for no reason whatever, the sun being at his back, and gazed at the object in the water.

"'Tarnt a porpus," he said thoughtfully.

"As if I didn't know that," cried the lad; and, running aft, he descended into the cabin, and returned with a glass, which he focussed and gazed through at the object rising steadily and falling with the heave of the sea.

"See her, sir?"

"Yes," answered the middy, with his glass at his eye. "It's a bullock or a cow."

"Werry like, sir. There is sea-cows, I've heared."

"Oh, but this isn't one of them. I believe it's a real cow, Dick."

"Not she, sir. Real cows lives in Lincolnshire, and feeds on grass. I never see 'em go in the sea, only halfway up their legs in ponds, and stand a-waggin' their tails to keep off the flies. This here's a sea-cow, sir, sartin."

"It's a cow, Dick; and it has tumbled off the cliff, and is swimming for its life," said the lad, closing the glass.

The sailor chuckled.

"What are you laughing at?"

"At you, sir, beggin' your pardon. But you don't think as how a cow would be such a fool as to tumble off a cliff. Humans might, but cows is too cunning."

"I don't believe you would be," cried the lad smartly. "Put you up there in such a fog as we've had, and where would you be?"

"Fast asleep in the first snug corner I could find," said the sailor, as the midshipman ran aft, and descended into the cabin, to go to the end and tap on a door.

There was no answer, and he tapped again.

"Hullo!"

"Beg pardon, sir," began the midshipman.

"Granted! Be off, and don't bother me again."

There was a rustling sound, and a deep-toned breathing, that some rude people would have called a snore. The midshipman looked puzzled, hesitated, and then knocked again.

There came a smothered roar, like that of an angry beast.

"Beg pardon, sir."

"Who's that?"

"Raystoke, sir."

"What do you want? Am I never to have a night's rest again?"

All this in smothered tones, as if the speaker was shut up in a cupboard with a blanket over his head.

"Wouldn't have troubled you, sir, but—"

"Smugglers in sight?"

"No, sir; it's a cow."

"A what?"

"Cow, sir, overboard."

"Quite right. Milk and water," came in muffled tones.

"Beg pardon, sir, what shall I do?"

"Go and milk her, and don't bother me."

"But she's swimming under the cliff, sir."

"Go and ask her on board, then. Be off!"

Archy Raystoke knew his commanding officer's ways, and after waiting a few moments, he said softly, after giving a tap or two on the panel—

"Shall I take the boat and get her aboard?"

There was a loud rustle; a bang as if some one had struck the bulkhead with his elbow, and then a voice roared—

"Look here, sir, if you don't be off and let me finish my sleep, I'll let go at you through the door. You're in charge of the deck. Go and do what's right, and don't bother me."

Bang!

Another blow on the bulkhead, and rustling noise, and, as well as if he had seen it all, Archy knew that his officer had snuggled down under the clothes, and gone to sleep.

But he had the permission, and calling to a couple of the crew, he soon had the small boat in the water, with Dick and another man pulling towards where the cow was slowly swimming here and there, with its wet nose and two horns a very short distance above the surface.

"Now, then, Dick, is it a sea-cow?" cried Archy, as they drew nearer.

"Well, sir, what else can it be?"

"Ah, you obstinate!" cried the lad. "Now, then, what are we going to do? We can't land her," he continued, looking up at the towering cliff, "and, of course, we can't take her in the boat."

"I'll soon manage that," said Dick, leaving his rowing to take up a coil of rope he had thrown into the boat, and make a running noose.

"Yes, but—"

"It's all right, sir. Get this over her horns, and we can tow her alongside, and hyste her on deck in no time."

The cow proved that she was accustomed to man, for, as the boat approached, she swam slowly to meet it, raising her nose a little to utter a loud bellow, as if glad to welcome the help. So quiet and gentle was the poor creature, that there was no difficulty in passing the noose over her horns, making the line fast to a ring-bolt, so as to keep her head well above the surface, and then Dick resumed his oar; and after a glance round to make sure that there was no place where the poor beast could be landed, Archie gave the order for them to row back to where the cutter lay in the bright sunshine, five hundred yards from the shore.

He looked in vain, for at the lowest part the green edge of the cliff was a couple of hundred feet above the level of the sea, and right and left of him the mighty walls of rock rose up, four, five, and even six hundred feet, and for the most part with a sheer descent to the water which washed their feet.

The cow took to her journey very kindly, helping the progress by swimming till they were alongside the cutter, where the men on deck were looking over the low side, and grinning with amusement.

"Pull her horns off, sir!" said Dick, in answer to a question, as he proceeded to pass the rope through a block, "not it."

"But hadn't we better have a line round her?"

"If you want to cut her 'most in two, sir. We'll soon have her on board."

Dick was as good as his word, for the task was easy with a vessel so low in the water as the cutter; and in a few minutes the unfortunate cow was standing dripping on deck.

Chapter Two

"Can any one of you men milk?" said Lieutenant Brough, a little plump-looking man, of about five and thirty, as he stood in naval uniform staring at the new addition to His Majesty's cutter *White Hawk*, a well-fed dun cow, which stood steadily swinging her long tail to and fro, where she was tethered to the bulwarks, after vainly trying to make a meal off the well holystoned deck.

There was no reply, the men grinning one at the other, on hearing so novel a question. "Do you men mean to say that not one amongst you can milk?" cried the lieutenant.

No one had spoken; but now, in a half-shrinking foolish way, Dick pulled his forelock, and made a kick out behind.

"You can?" cried the lieutenant, "that's right; get a bucket and milk her. I'll have some for breakfast."

"Didn't say as I could milk, sir," said Dick. "Seen 'em milk, though, down in Linkyshire, and know how it's done."

"Then, of course, you can do it," said the lieutenant shortly; "look sharp!"

The men grinned, and Dirty Dick by no means looked sharp, but exceedingly blunt and foolish as he shuffled along the deck, provided himself with a bucket, and then approached the cow, which had suddenly began chewing the cud.

"Look at her, mate," said one of the sailors.

"What for?" said the man addressed.

"Some one's been giving her a quid o' bacca."

"Go on."

"But some one has. Look at her chewing."

"Why, so she is!" said the sailor, scratching his head, as he watched the regular actions of the cow's jaw, as she stood blinking her eyes, and swinging her tail to and fro, apparently quite content; the more so, that the sun was shining upon her warmly, and the sea water rapidly quitting her skin for the deck, where it made a rivulet into one of the scuppers.

Jack the sailor is easily pleased, for the simple reason that anything is a relief from the tedium of life on ship-board; consequently the coming of the cow was like a half-holiday to them at the wrong end of the day, and they stood about nudging each other, as Dirty Dick trotted up with his bucket, Archy looking on as much amused as the men.

The cow blinked her eyes, and turned her head to smell at the bucket which Dick set down on the deck, and stood scratching his head.

"Well, sir, go on," said the lieutenant—"Seems to me, now, Mr Raystoke, that we ought to have cream and fresh butter. Capital prize you've taken.— Do you hear, sir? Go on."

"Yes, sir. Beg pardon, sir, but you see I wants something to sit on. 'Nother bucket."

"You, sir, fetch another bucket," said the lieutenant sharply; and another was brought, turned upside down, and, taking the first bucket, amidst the titterings of the men, Dick seated himself, leaned his head against the cow's side, placed the vessel between his legs, and began to operate in true dairyman style upon the cow.

Whack! Bang! Clatter!

There was a tremendous roar of laughter from every one on board except from Dirty Dick, who was down on his back a couple of yards away, staring at the cow as if wondering how she could have gone off as she did. For the quiet-looking, inoffensive beast was standing perfectly still again, blinking her eyes and chewing her cud, but writhing and twisting her tail about as if it were an eel, after, at Dick's first touch, raising one of her hind legs and sending the pail flying across the deck and the would-be milker backwards.

"Come, come," said the lieutenant, wiping his eyes and trying to look very important and stern, "that's not the right way, my man. Try again."

Dick rose unwillingly, planted the upturned bucket once more in its place, and took the milking bucket from one of the men who had picked it up. Then, sitting down again rather nervously, he once more placed the vessel between his legs, stuck his head against the cow's side, and prepared to milk.

Whack!

The bucket flew along the deck again, and Dick bounded away, saving himself from falling this time as he was prepared, and made a sudden leap backwards to stand wiping the perspiration from his forehead.

There was another roar of laughter, and the lieutenant bade Dick try again.

The man gave his officer an appealing look which seemed to say, "Tell me to board the enemy, sir, and I'll go, but don't ask me to do this."

"Come; be smart!"

Dick turned, glanced wistfully at Archy, shaking his head at him reproachfully, sighed, and, taking the bucket again, he looked into it with his rugged brown face full of despair.

"It's quite empty, Dick," said the middy, laughing.

"Yes, sir; there's nowt in it, and," he added to himself, "not like to be."

Again he settled himself into his place in as businesslike a way as a farm lad would who was accustomed to the cow-shed, but the moment he began the cow gave her tail a swing, lifted her leg, and planted it in the bucket, holding it down on the deck.

"Pail's full," cried Archy; and the men yelled with delight, their officer vainly trying to control his own mirth as Dick began to pat and apostrophise the cow.

"Coom, coom! Coosh, cow, then," he said soothingly. "Tak' thy leg oot o' the boocket, my bairn;" and to the astonishment of all present the cow lifted her leg and set it down again on deck.

"Well done, my lad," cried the lieutenant. "Now, then, look sharp with the milk."

Dick sighed, wiped his hands down the sides of his breeches, and began once more, but at the first touch of the big strong hands accustomed to handle capstan-bars and haul ropes, the cow gave a more vigorous kick than ever; away flew the bucket, and over went Dick on his back.

He sprung up angrily now in the midst of the laughter, and touched his forehead to his commanding officer.

"It arn't no good, sir; she's a beef cow, and not a milker."

"You don't know your business, my lad," said the lieutenant.

"But she's such a savage one, sir. Don't go anigh her, sir."

"Nonsense!" said the lieutenant, going up to the cow, patting her and handling her ears and horns; to all of which attentions the animal submitted calmly enough, blinking her eyes, and gently swinging her tail.

"I think I could milk her, sir," said Archy.

"Think so, Raystoke?" said the lieutenant. "I was just thinking I should have liked some new milk."

"So was I, sir. Shall I try?"

"Yes," said the lieutenant. "I believe I could do it myself. It always looks so easy. But no; won't do," he said firmly, as he drew himself up and tried to look stern and tall and big, an impossibility with a man of five feet two inches in height, and whose physique had always been against his advance in the profession. For as a short energetic little man he might have gained promotion; as a little fat rosy fellow the Lords of the Admiralty thought not; and so, after endless disappointments regarding better things, he had been appointed commander of the little *White Hawk*, and sent to cruise off the south coast and about the Channel, to catch the smugglers who were always too clever to be caught.

"No," he said shortly, as he drew himself up; "won't do, Raystoke, though you and I are condemned to live in this miserable little cutter, and on a contemptible kind of duty, we must not forget that we are officers and gentlemen in His Majesty's service. Milking cows won't do. No; we must draw the line at milking cows. But I should have liked a drop for my breakfast."

"Ahoy!" cried one of the men loudly.

"Ahoy yourself!" cried a voice from off the sea on the shore side, and all turned to see a boat approaching rowed by a rough-looking fisherman, and with a lad of about sixteen sitting astern, who now rose up to answer the man who shouted.

"Where did he come from?" said the lieutenant. "Anybody see him put off?"

"No, sir! No, sir!" came from all directions; and the lieutenant raised his glass to sweep the coast.

"What do you want?" cried the man at the side as the boat came on, and the lieutenant bade the man ask.

"Want?" shouted the lad, a sturdy-looking fellow with keen grey eyes and fair close curly hair all about his sunburned forehead. "I've come after our cow!"

Chapter Three

"How do, Sir Risdon?"

The speaker was a curious-looking man of fifty, rough, sunburned, and evidently as keen as a well-worn knife. He was dressed like a farmer who had taken to fishing or like a fisherman who had taken to farming, and his nautical appearance seemed strange to a man who was leading a very meditative grey horse attached to a heavy cart, made more weighty by the greatcoat of caked mud the vehicle wore.

He had been leading the horse along what was called in Freestone a road, though its only pretensions to being a road was that it led from Shackle's farm to the fields which bordered the cliff, and consisted of two deep channels made by the farm tumbril wheels, and a shallow track formed by horses' hoofs, the said channels being more often full of water than of mud, and boasting the quality of never even in the hottest weather being dry.

The person Blenheim Shackle—farmer and fisher, in his canvas sailor's breeches, big boots, striped shirt, and red tassel cap—had accosted, was a tall, thin, aristocratic-looking gentleman, in a broad-skirted, shabby brown velvet coat, who was daintily picking his way, cane in hand, over the soft turf of the field, evidently deep in thought, but sufficiently awake to what was around to make him stoop from time to time to pick up a glistening white-topped mushroom, and transfer it to one of his pockets with a satisfied smile.

"Ah, Master Shackle," he said, starting slightly on being addressed. "Well, thank you. A lovely morning, indeed."

"Ay, the morning's right enough, Sir Risdon. Picking a few mushrooms, sir?"

"I—er—yes, Master Shackle. I have picked a few," said the tall thin gentleman, colouring slightly. "I—beg your pardon, Master Shackle, for doing so. I ought to have asked your leave."

'Bah! Not a bit," said the fisher-farmer, with a chuckle. "You're welcome, squire."

"I thank you, Master Shackle—I thank you warmly. You see her ladyship is very fond of the taste of a fresh gathered mushroom, and if I see a few I like to take them to the Hoze."

"Ay, to be sure," said Shackle, as he thought to himself "And precious glad to get them, you two poor half-starved creatures, with your show and sham, and titles and keep up appearances."

"I—er—I have not got many, Master Shackle. Would you like to see?" continued the tall thin gentleman, raising the flap of one of his salt-box pockets.

"I don't want to see," growled the other, as he stood patting the neck of his old grey horse. "Been to the cliff edge?"

"I—yes, Master Shackle."

"See the cutter?"

"I think I saw a small vessel lying some distance off, with white sails."

"That's the *White Hawk*, Luff Brough. And I wanted to speak to you, Sir Risdon."

The gentleman started.

"Not about—about that—" he stammered.

"Tchah! Yes. It was about that, man," said the other. "Don't shy at it like a horse at a blue bogey in a windy lane."

"But I told you, man, last time, that I would have no more to do with that wretched smuggling."

"Don't call things by ugly names."

"My good man, it is terrible. It is dishonourable, and the act is a breaking of the laws of our country."

"Tchah! Not it, Sir Risdon," cried the other so sharply, that the grey horse started forward, and had to be checked. "Not the king's laws, but the laws of that Dutchman who has come and stuck himself on the throne. Why, sir, you ought to take a pleasure in breaking his laws, after the way he has robbed you, and turned you from a real gentleman, into a poor, hard-pressed country squire, who—"

"Hush! Hush, Master Shackle!" said the tall gentleman huskily. "Don't rake up my misfortunes."

"Not I, Sir Risdon. I'm full o' sorrow and respect for a noble gentleman, who has suffered for the cause of the real king, who, when he comes, will set us all right."

"Ah, Master Shackle, I'm losing heart."

"Nay, don't do that, Sir Risdon; and as to a few mushrooms, why, you're welcome enough; and I'd often be sending a chicken or a few eggs, or a kit o' butter, or drop o' milk, all to the Hoze, only we're feared her ladyship might think it rude."

"It's—it's very good of you, Master Shackle, and I shall never be able to repay you."

"Tchah! Who wants repaying, Sir Risdon? We have plenty at the farm, and it was on'y day 'fore yes'day as I was out in my little lugger, and we'd took a lot o' mackrel! 'Ram,' I says to my boy Ramillies, 'think Sir Risdon would mind if I sent him a few fish up to the Hoze?'

"'Ay, father,' he says, 'they don't want us to send them fish. My lady's too proud!'"

Sir Risdon sighed, and the man watched him narrowly.

"It's a pity too," the latter continued, "specially as we often have so much fish we puts it on the land."

"Er—if you would be good enough to send a little fish—of course very fresh, Master Shackle, and a few eggs, and a little butter to the Hoze, and let me have your bill by and by, I should be gratified."

"On'y too glad, Sir Risdon, I will.—Think any one's been telling tales?"

"Tales?"

"'Bout us, Sir Risdon."

"About *us*!"

"You see the revenue cutter's hanging about here a deal, and it looks bad."

"Surely no one would betray you, Master Shackle?"

"Hope not, Sir Risdon; but it's okkard. There's a three-masted lugger coming over from Ushant, and she may be in to-night. There's some nice thick fogs about now, and it's a quiet sea. Your cellars are quite empty, I s'pose?"

The last remark came so quickly, that the hearer started, and made no reply.

"You see, Sir Risdon, we might run the cargo, and stow it all up at my place, for we've plenty o' room; but if they got an idea of it aboard the cutter, she'd land some men somehow, and come and search me, but they wouldn't dare to come and search you. I've got a bad character, but you haven't."

"No, no, Master Shackle; I cannot; I will not."

"The lads could run it up the valley, and down into your cellar, Sir Risdon," whispered the man, as if afraid that the old grey horse would hear; "nobody would be a bit the wiser, and you'd be doing a neighbour a good turn."

"I—I cannot, Master Shackle; it is against the law."

"Dutchman's law, not the laws of Bonnie Prince Charlie. You will, Sir Risdon?"

"No—no, I dare not."

"And it gives a neighbour a chance to beg your acceptance of a little drop o' real cognac, Sir Risdon—so good in case o' sickness. And a bit of prime tay, such as would please her ladyship. Then think how pleasant a pipe is, Sir Risdon; I've got a bit o' lovely tobacco at my place, and a length or two of French silk."

"Master Shackle! Master Shackle!" cried the tall thin baronet piteously, "how can you tempt a poor suffering gentleman like this?"

"Because I want to do you a bit of good, Sir Risdon, and myself too. I tell you it's safe enough. You've only to leave your side door open, and go to bed; that's all."

"But I shall be as guilty as you."

"Guilty?" the man laughed. "I never could see a bit o' harm in doing what I do. Never feel shamed to look my boy Ramillies in the face. If a bit o' smuggling was wrong, Sir Risdon, think I'd do it? No, sir; I think o' them as was before me. My father was in Marlborough's wars, and he called me Blenheim, in honour of the battle he was in; and I called my boy Ramillies, and if ever he gets married, and has a son, he's to be Malplackey. I arn't ashamed to look him in the face."

"But I shall be afraid to look in the face of my dear child."

"Mistress Denise, Sir Risdon? Tchah! Bless her! I don' believe she'd like her father to miss getting a lot of things that would be good for him, and your madam. There, Sir Risdon; don't say another word about it. Leave the door open, and go to bed. You shan't hear anybody come or go away, and you're not obliged to look in the cellars for a few days."

"But, my child—the old servant—suppose they hear?"

"What? The rats? Tell 'em to take no notice, Sir Risdon. Good day, Sir Risdon. That's settled, then?"

"Ye–es—I suppose so. This once only, Master Shackle."

"Thank ye, Sir Risdon," said the man. "Jee, Dutchman!"

The horse tugged at the tumbril, and Sir Risdon went thoughtfully along the field, toward a clump of trees lying in a hollow, while Master Shackle went on chuckling to himself.

"Couldn't say me nay, poor fellow. Half-starved they are sometimes. Wonder he don't give up the old place, and go away. Hope he won't. Them cellars are too vallyble. Hallo! What now?"

This to the fair curly-headed lad, who came trotting up across the short turf.

"Been looking at the cutter, father?"

"Oh, she don't want no looking at. Who brought those cows down here?"

"Jemmy Dadd."

"He's a fool. We shall be having some of 'em going over the cliff. Go home and tell mother to put a clean napkin in a basket, and take two rolls of butter, a bit of honey, and a couple of chickens up to the Hoze."

"Yes, father."

"And see if there's any eggs to take too."

"Yes, father. But—"

"Well?"

"Think the lugger will come to-night?"

"No, I don't think anything, and don't you. Will you keep that rattle tongue of yours quiet? Never know me go chattering about luggers, do you?"

"No, father."

"Then set your teeth hard, or you'll never be a man worth your salt. Want to grow into a Jemmy Dadd?"

"No, father."

"Then be off."

The boy went off at a run, and the fisher-farmer led his horse along the two rutted tracks till he came down into the valley, and then went on and on, towards where a couple of men were at work in a field, doing nothing with all their might.

Chapter Four

Ramillies—commonly known by his father's men as Ram—Shackle trotted up over the hill, stopping once to flop down on the grass to gaze at the cutter, lying a mile out now from the shore, and thinking how different she was with her trim rigging and white sails to the rough lugger of his father, and the dirty three-masted vessels that ran to and fro across the Channel, and upon which he had more than once taken a trip.

He rose with a sigh, and continued his journey down into the hollow, and along a regular trough among the hills, to the low, white-washed stone building, roofed with thin pieces of the same material, and gaily dotted and splashed with lichen and moss.

He was met by a comfortable-looking, ruddy-faced woman, who shouted,—"What is it, Ram?" when he was fifty yards away.

The boy stated his errand.

"Father says you were to take all that?"

"Yes."

"Then there's a cargo coming ashore to-night, Ram."

"Yes, mother, and the cutter's lying a mile out."

"Oh, dear, dear, dear!" cried the woman; "I hope there won't be no trouble, boy."

She stood wiping her dry hands upon her apron, and gazed thoughtfully with wrinkled brow straight before her for a minute, as if conjuring up old scenes; then, taking down a basket as she moved inside, she began to pack up the various things in the dairy, while Ram looked on.

"Father didn't say anything about a bottle of cream, mother," said the boy, grinning.

"Then hear, see, and say nothing, my lad," cried his mother.

"And I don't think he said you was to send that piece of pickled pork, mother."

"He said chickens, didn't he?"

"Said a chickun."

"Chicken means chickens," cried Mrs Shackle, "and you can't eat chicken without pork or bacon. 'Tisn't natural."

"Father said two rolls of butter."

"Yes, and I've put three. There, these are all the eggs I've got, and you mind you don't break 'em!"

"Oh, I say, mother," cried Ram, "aren't it heavy!"

"Nonsense! I could carry it on my finger; there, run along like a good boy, and you must ask for her ladyship, and be very respectful, and say, Mother's humble duty to you, my lady, and hopes you won't mind her sending a bit o' farm fare."

"But she ought to be thankful to us, mother?"

"And so she will be, Ram?"

"But you make me speak as though we were to be much obliged to her for taking all these good things."

"You take the basket, and hold your tongue. Father's right, you chatter a deal too much."

Ram took the basket, grunted because it was so heavy, and then set off up the hill-slope towards where the patch of thick woodland capped one side of the deep valley, and at last came in sight of a grim-looking stone house, with its windows for the most part covered by their drawn-down blinds. Under other circumstances, with fairly kept gardens and trim borders, the old-fashioned building, dating from the days of Henry the Seventh, would have been attractive enough, with its background of trees, and fine view along the valley out to the far-stretching blue sea; but poverty seemed to have set its mark upon the place, and the boy was so impressed by the gloomy aspect of the house, that he ceased whistling as he went across the front, outside the low wall, and round to the back, where his progress was stopped by the scampering of feet, and a dog came up, barking loudly.

"Get out, or I'll jump on you—d'ye hear?" said Ram fiercely.

"Down, Grip, down!" cried a pleasant voice, and a girl of fifteen came running out, looking bright and animated with her flushed cheeks and long hair.

"Don't be afraid of him, Ram; he will not bite."

"I'm not afraid of him, Miss Celia; if he'd tried to bite me, I'd have kicked him into the back-garden."

"You would not dare to," cried the girl indignantly.

"Oh yes, I would," said Ram, showing his white teeth. "Wouldn't do for me to be 'fraid of no dogs."

The girl half turned away, but her eye caught the basket.

"What's that you came to sell?" she said.

"Sell? I don't come to sell. Father and mother sent this here. It's butter, and chickuns, and pork, and cream, and eggs."

"Oh!" cried the girl joyously, "my mother will be so—"

She stopped short, remembering sundry lessons she had received, and the tears came up into her eyes as she felt that she must be proud and not show her delight at the receipt of homely delicacies to which they were strangers.

"Take your basket to the side door, and deliver your message to Keziah," she said distantly.

"Yes, miss," said Ram, beginning to whistle, as he strode along with his basket, but he turned back directly and followed the girl.

"I say, Miss Celia," he cried.

"Yes, Ram."

"You like Grip, don't you?"

"Yes, of course."

"Then I won't never kick him, miss. Only I arn't fond on him. Here, mate," he continued, dropping on one knee, "give us your paw."

The dog, a sturdy-looking deerhound, growled, and closed up to his mistress.

"D'ye hear? Give's your paw. What yer growling about?"

The dog didn't say, but growled more fiercely.

"Grip, down! Give him your paw," cried the girl.

The dog turned his muzzle up to his mistress, and uttered a low whine.

"Says he don't like to shake hands with a lad like me," said Ram, laughing.

"But I say he is to, sir," cried the girl haughtily. "Give him your paw, Grip."

She took the dog by the ear and led him unwillingly toward the boy, whose eyes sparkled with delight while the hound whimpered and whined and protested, as if he had an unconquerable dislike to the act he was called upon to perform.

"Now," cried the girl, "directly, sir. Give him your paw."

What followed seemed ludicrous in the extreme to the boy, for, in obedience to his mistress's orders, the dog lifted his left paw and turned his head away to gaze up at his mistress.

"The wrong paw, sir," she cried. "Now, again."

"*Pow how!*" howled the dog, raising his paw now to have it seized by the boy, squeezed and then loosened, a termination which seemed to give the animal the most profound satisfaction. For now it was over, he barked madly and rushed round and round the boy in the most friendly way.

"There, miss," said Ram with a grin; "we shall be friends now. Nex' rats we ketch down home, I'll bring up here for him to kill. Hey, Grip! Rats! Rats!"

The dog bounded up to the boy, rose on his hind legs and placed his forepaws on the lad's chest, barking loudly.

"Good dog, then. Good-bye, miss; I must get back."

"Oh!"

"You call, miss?" cried the boy, turning as he went whistling away.

"Yes, yes, Ram," said the girl hesitatingly, and glancing behind her, then up at the house where all was perfectly still. "Do you remember coming up and bringing a basket about a month ago?"

"Yes, miss, I r'member. That all, miss?"

"No," said the girl, still hesitating. "Ram, are the men coming up to the house in the middle of the night?"

"Dunno what you mean, miss."

"You do, sir, for you were with them. I saw you and ever so many more come up with little barrels slung over their shoulders."

Ram's face was a study in the comic line as he shook his head.

"Yes you were, sir, and it was wicked smuggling. I order you to tell me directly. Are they coming up to-night?"

"Mustn't tell," said the boy slowly.

"Then they are," cried the girl, with her handsome young face puckering up with the trouble which oppressed her, and after standing looking thoughtful and anxious for a few moments, she went away toward the front of the house, while Ram went round to the side and delivered his basket.

"Course we are," he said to himself, as he went down the hill again. "But I warn't going to blab. What a fuss people do make about a bit o' smuggling! How pretty she looks!" and he stopped short to admire her—the *she* being the *White Hawk*, which lay motionless on the calm sea. "Wish I could sail aboard a boat like that, and be dressed like that young chap with his sword. I would like to wear a sword. I told father so, and he said I was a fool."

He threw himself down on the short turf, which was dotted with black and grey, as the rooks, jackdaws, and gulls marched about feeding together in the most friendly way, where the tiny striped snails hung upon the strands of grass by millions.

"It'll be a fog again to-night," he said thoughtfully, "and she's sure to come. Ha, ha, ha!" he laughed, as he made a derisive gesture towards the cutter; "watch away. You may wear your gold lace and cocked hats and swords, but you won't catch us, my lads; we're too sharp for that."

Chapter Five

Shackle was quite right; the fog did begin to gather over the sea soon after sundown, and the depressing weather seemed to have a curious effect on Farmer Shackle, who kept getting up from his supper to go and look out through the open door, and come back smiling and rubbing his hands.

Mrs Shackle was very quiet and grave-looking and silent for a time, but at last she ventured a question.

"Did you see her at sundown?"

"Ay, my lass. 'Bout eight mile out."

"But the cutter?"

"Well, what about the cutter?"

"Will it be safe?"

"Safe? Tchah! I know what I'm 'bout."

That being so, Mrs Shackle made no remark, but went on cutting chunks of bread and butter for her son, to which the boy added pieces of cold salt pork, and then turned himself into a mill which went on slowly grinding up material for the making of a man, this raw material being duly manipulated by nature, and apportioned by her for the future making of the human mill.

"Now, Ram," said his father, "ready?"

"Yes, father," said the boy, after getting his mouth into talking trim.

"Lanthorns! Off with you."

"Lanthorns won't be no good in the fog."

"Don't you be so mighty clever," growled Shackle. "How do you know that the fog reaches up far?"

"Did you signal s'afternoon, father?"

"Lanthorns! And look sharp, sir."

The boy went into the back kitchen, took down from a shelf three horn-lanthorns, which had the peculiarity of being painted black save in one narrow part. Into these he glanced to see that they were all fitted with thick candles before passing a piece of rope through the rings at the top.

This done he took down a much smaller lanthorn, painted black all round, lit the candle within, and, taking this one in his hand, he hung the others over his shoulder, and prepared to start.

"Mind and don't you slip over the cliff, Ram," said his mother.

"Tchah! Don't scare the boy with that nonsense," said the farmer angrily; "why should he want to slip over the cliff? Put 'em well back, boy. Stop 'bout half an hour, and then come down."

Ram nodded and went off whistling down along the hollow for some hundred yards toward the sea, and then, turning short off to the right, he began to climb a zigzag path which led higher and higher and more and more away to his left till it skirted the cliff, and he was climbing slowly up through the fog.

The lad's task was robbed of the appearance of peril by the darkness; but the danger never occurred to Ram, who had been up these cliff-paths too often for his pleasure to heed the breakneck nature of the rough sheep-track up and up the face of the cliff, leading to where it became a steep slope, which ran in and on some four hundred feet, forming one of the highest points in the neighbourhood.

"It's plaguey dark," said Ram to himself. "Wonder what they're going to bring to-night?"

He whistled softly as he climbed slowly on.

"Fog's thicker than it was last night. They won't see no lanthorns, I know."

"Dunno, though," he muttered a little higher up. "Not quite so thick up here. How old Grip growled! But he had to do it. Aren't afraid of a dog like him. Look at that!"

He had climbed up the zigzag track another fifty feet, and stopped short to gaze away at the bright stars of the clear night with the great layer of fog all below him now.

"Father was right, but I dunno whether they'll be able to see from the lugger. Don't matter. They know the way, and they'd see the signal s'afternoon."

He whistled softly as he went on higher, laughing all at once at an idea which struck him.

"Suppose they were to row right on to the cutter! Wouldn't it 'stonish them all? I know what I should do. Shove off directly into the fog. They wouldn't be able to see, and I wouldn't use the sweeps till I was out of hearing, and then—oh, here we are up atop!"

For the sheep-track had come to an end upon what was really the dangerous part of the journey. The zigzag and the cliff-path had been bad, but a fall there would not have been hopeless, for the unfortunate who lost his footing would go down to the next path, or the next, a dozen places perhaps offering the means of checking the downward course, but up where the boy now stood was a slope of short turf with long dry strands which made the grass terribly slippery, and once any one had fallen here, and was in motion, the slope was at so dangerous an elevation that he would rapidly gather impetus, and shoot right off into space to fall six hundred feet below on to the shore.

This danger did not check Ram's cheery whistle, and he climbed on, sticking his toes well into the short grass, and rising higher and higher till he reached some ragged shale with the grass, now very thin, and about a hundred feet back from the sea, in a spot which he felt would be well out of the sight of the cutter if those on board could see above the fog. He set down his lanthorns, two about five feet apart, lit them all, and held the third on the top of his head as he stood between the others, so that from seaward the lights would have appeared like a triangle.

It seemed all done in such a matter of course way that it was evident that Ram was accustomed to the task, and supporting the lanthorn on his head, first with one and then with the other hand, he went on whistling softly an old west country air, thinking the while about Sir Risdon and Lady Graeme, and about how poor they were, and how much better it was to live at a farmhouse where there was always plenty to eat, and where his father could go fishing in the lugger when he liked, and how he could farm and smuggle, and generally enjoy life.

"That's good half an hour," said Ram, lowering his lanthorn, opening the door, and puffing out the candle, afterwards serving the others the same.

Whew — whew — whew — whew!

A peculiar whishing of wings from far overhead, as a flock of birds flew on through the darkness of the night, following the wonderful instinct which made them take flight to other lands.

"Wasn't geese; and I don't think it was ducks," said the lad to himself, as he slung his darkened lanthorns together, and began to descend as coolly as if he had been provided by nature with wings to guard him against a fall down the cliff.

"Wonder whether they saw the lights," he said to himself. "Not much good showing them, if they were in the fog."

He went on, gradually approaching the mist which lay below him, and at last was descending the zigzag path with the stars blotted out, and the tiny drops of moisture gathering on his eyelashes, finding his way more by instinct than sight.

"Come in with the tide 'bout 'leven," said Ram, as he still descended the face of the cliff, then the path, and at last was well down in the little valley, whose mouth seemed to have been filled up in some convulsion of nature by a huge wall of cliff, under which the streamlet which ran from the hills had mined its way.

As soon as he was down on level ground, the boy started for home at a trot, gave the lanthorns into his mother's hands, and, after a brief inquiry as to his father's whereabouts, he started off once more.

The part of the cliff for which he made was exactly opposite Sir Risdon's old house, and to a stranger about the last place where it would be deemed possible for a smuggler to land his cargo.

Hence the successful landing of many a boat-load, which had been scattered the country through.

For there, at the foot of the cliff, lay a natural platform or pier, almost as level as if it had been formed for a landing stage. The deep water came right up to its edge, and here, at a chosen time of tide, a lugger could lie close in, and her busy crew and their helpmates land keg and bale upon the huge ledge,—a floor of intensely hard stone, full of great ammonites, many a couple of feet across, monsters of shell-fish, which had gradually settled down and died, when the stone in which they lay had been soft mud.

Revenue boats had of course, from time to time, as they explored the coast, noted this natural landing-place, but as there was only a broad step twenty feet above this to form another platform, and then the cliffs ran straight up two hundred feet slightly inclined over toward the sea, and the existence of even a moderate surf would have meant wreck, it was never even deemed likely that there was danger here, and consequently it was left unwatched.

The smugglers had a different opinion of the place, and on Ram reaching the spot he was in nowise surprised to find a group of about thirty men on the cliff, clustered about the end of a spar, whose butt was run down into a hole in the rock, which lay a foot beneath the turf, and at whose end, as it rose at an angle, was a pulley block and rope run through ready for use should the lugger come.

"Where's father?" whispered Ram to one of the men, who looked curiously indistinct amid the fog.

"Here, boy," was whispered close to his ear. "Going down to help?"

"May I, father?"

Shackle grunted; and, after speaking to one of the men, Ram took hold of the loop at the end of the rope, thrust a leg through, held on tightly, and, after the word was given, swung himself off into the fog.

The well-oiled wheel ran fast, and it was a strange experience that of gliding rapidly down and steadily turning round and round with the thick darkness all around, and nothing to show that he who descended was not stationary. The peril of such a run down would have appeared the greater, could he who descended have seen how the rope was allowed to run. For no careful hands held it to allow it to glide through fingers, which could at any moment clutch the line tightly and act as a check. The rope lay simply on the turf, and the man who watched over the descent, merely placed his boot over it, the hollow between sole and heel affording room for the rope to run, and a little extra pressure stopping its way.

Thus it was that Ram was allowed to glide rapidly down, till by experience the man knew that he was nearly at the bottom when the rope began to run more slowly, and then was checked exactly as the boy's feet touched the stone shelf, and he stepped from the loop on to the ammonite-studded rock.

Dimly seen about him was a group of a dozen men, whose faces looked mysterious and strange, and this was added to by the silence, for only one spoke, and he when he was addressed, for the first few minutes after Ram's arrival among them, every one there being listening attentively for the distant beat of oars.

"Think she'll come to-night, young Ram?" said the man close by him.

"Dunno."

"Been to show the lights?"

"Yes."

"Was there any fog up there?"

"No; clear as could be."

"Then she may come. Pst!"

Hardly a breath could be heard then as ears were strained, and after a good deal of doubt had been felt, a kind of thrill ran through the men who had taken hold of a line fastened to a stanchion and lowered themselves down to the broad ledge.

The low, regular, slow beat of great sweeps became now audible, but though Ram strained his eyes seaward, nothing was visible for quite another ten minutes, when, as the boy stood at the brink of the upper ledge he dimly saw something darker than the mist coming into view. Soon there came a faint crunching noise as of a fender being crushed against the rock, followed by the sound of ropes drawn over the bulwark, and Ram hesitated no longer, but ran to the loop, placed his leg through it, gave the signal by shaking the rope, and in an instant he was snatched from his feet, run up, the rope drawn in, and he was landed on the turf.

A small bag of stones was then attached to the loop, the wheel spun round, and the bag went whizzing down, while the group of men stood waiting and waiting, for they could see nothing below, hardly see each other, so dense was the mist now.

Sundry familiar sounds arose from time to time, and more than once the farmer uttered an ejaculation full of impatience at the length of time taken up in bringing the vessel below and taking precautions to keep her from grinding and bumping against the edge of the shelf, for though the sea was calm, there was the swell to contend with.

At last.

There was a murmur from below which those two hundred feet above knew well, and as two stood ready, another man by them took hold of the rope, and suddenly started off at a run, disappearing at once in the fog, while a peculiar whizzing sound was heard, as the little wheel in the block now ran round till all at once a couple of kegs and the bag of stones appeared level with the top of the cliff. These were seized, unhitched, and as the bag ran down, a man knelt, fitted a short rope about the kegs and hoisted them on his shoulder, just as the man who held the rope trotted up out of the fog into which the other with the kegs disappeared.

There was a faint hiss, and away ran the man again bringing the next two kegs up rapidly, to be set at liberty, slung, and hoisted on another man's back as the hauler came back out of the fog.

And so the unloading went on with marvellous rapidity, the hauler rushing off into the fog, a couple of kegs coming up into sight, being taken out of the loops, slung and hoisted just as the hauler came back and the bearer disappeared, till quite a line of men were trudging slowly up the hill, down into the valley, and up again toward Sir Risdon Graeme's old house, the Hoze, till all the bearers were gone, and the kegs still kept coming up out of the fog.

The silence was astonishing, considering the amount of work being done and the rapidity with which all went on. Away to left and right sentries were placed, from among the haulers who, as they grew tired by their exertions in running up the kegs, were placed there to rest and listen for danger from seaward; but hour after hour went on, the carriers, augmented by a dozen more, came and went in two bands now, so that part were returning as the others were going.

But still they were not in sufficient force, for the Hoze was some distance away, and the number of kegs kept increasing on the turf at the top of the cliff.

About half the cargo was landed when Shackle whispered an order to Ram, who at once stooped to pick up a keg.

"No, no; run without, and see that they store them all up well."

Ram was used to the business, and he went off at a trot, breasted the hill, dived down into the hollow, and then passing men going and coming, made for the Hoze, entered by the side door, made his way along a stone passage, and then down into a huge vault with groined roof lit by a couple of lanthorns hanging from hooks.

Here for the next three hours he worked hard, helping to stack the little brandy kegs at first, and afterwards the small tightly packed bales and chests which were brought more quickly now—a dozen of swarthy, dirty-looking men, with earrings and short loose canvass trousers which looked like petticoats, helping to bring up the cargo, and showed by their presence that all had been landed from the lugger—that which was now being brought up consisting of the accumulation on the ledges and at the top of the cliff.

"Much more?" Ram kept asking as he toiled away, wet now with perspiration.

"Ay, ay, lad, it's a long cargo," he kept hearing; and the lanthorns had to be shifted twice as the stacks of kegs and bales increased, till just as the boy began to think the loads would never end, he realised that the French sailors had not been up lately, and one of their own men suddenly said—

"Last!"

Ram drew a breath full of relief as the men came out silently, and he stopped behind with one lanthorn only alight to lock the door of the great vault, and then stood in the stone passage, thinking how quiet and still the house seemed.

He went out, closing the door after him, and stood in the garden.

"Wonder whether Miss Celia heard us," he said; "never thought of it before; they must have tied up old Grip."

He glanced up at the windows as he went out, then they seemed to disappear in the mist as he made for the track and went downwards, to hear low voices, and directly after he encountered his father.

"Got 'em all right, boy?"

"Yes, father," said Ram, handing the key. "Lugger gone?"

"Hour and a half ago, lad; just got her empty as the tide turned. Best run we've had."

He burst into a low fit of chuckling.

"What are you laughing at, father?"

"I was thinking how artful revenue cutters are, boy. I don't believe that *White Hawk's* more than half a mile away."

"But then see what a fog it was, father?"

"Tchah! To me it's just the same as a moonshiny night, boy. There, come on home and get to bed. Must be up early; lots to do to-day."

Seeing that it could not be long before morning, Ram asked himself what was the use of his going to bed; but he said nothing, only hurried to keep pace with his father; and soon after, feeling fagged out, he was fast asleep, and dreaming that whenever he piled the kegs up they kept on rolling down about him, and that the midshipman from the *White Hawk* stood looking on, and laughing at him for being clumsy, and then he awoke fancying he was called.

It was quite right, for Farmer Shackle was shouting—

"Now you, Ramillies, are you going to sleep there all day?"

Chapter Six

Ram had thrown himself down, dressed as he was, so that an interview with a bucket of water at the back door, and a good rub with the jack towel, were sufficient to brighten him up for the breakfast waiting, and the boy was not long before he was partaking heartily of the bowl of bread and milk his mother placed before him, his father muttering and grumbling the while to himself.

"I'm sure you needn't be so cross this morning, master," said Mrs Shackle reproachfully.

"If you had as much to fret you as I do, wife, you'd be cross."

"Why, you told me this morning that you carried your crop of sea hay without a drop of water on it."

Farmer Shackle shut one eye, tightened up his mouth, and looked with his other eye at his wife, which was his idea of laughing.

"Well, then," she said, "what makes you so cross?"

"Cross! Enough to make any man cross. I shall be ruined—such a set of careless people about me. Those cows left out on the cliff field all last night, and Tally must have gone over, for I can't see her anywhere."

"Oh, poor Tally! My kindest cow," cried Mrs Shackle.

"Yes, I shall set that down to you Ramillies. That's a flogging for you if she isn't found."

"No, no, master; don't be so hard. The poor boy was out all night looking after signals and—"

Bang! Down came the farmer's fist on the table making the plates and basins jump.

"Hay, woman, hay!" he roared. "Mind what you're talking about!"

"Don't do that, Blenheim!" cried Mrs Shackle. "You quite frightened me."

"Yes, I'll frighten the whole lot of you. Ten golden pounds gone over the cliff through that boy's neglect."

"Well, never mind, dear. You made ever so much more than that last night, I'll be bound!"

"Will you hold your tongue?" roared the farmer. "There, make haste and finish that food, boy. Take Jemmy Dadd and the boat and find her. Skin's worth a few shillings. I must have that."

"Did you look over the cliff, father?" asked Ram.

"I looked over? Of course, but how could I see in that fog?"

Ram was soon out and away, to hunt up Jemmy Dadd, whom he found at last with his eyes half-closed, yawning prodigiously. They went down to the boat, launched her, and rowed out along under the tremendous cliffs, and were about to give up in despair, convinced that the unfortunate cow had been swept right out to sea, when Ram exclaimed—

"Look yonder, Jem?"

"What for?" grumbled the man; "I'm half asleep, now."

"Never mind that! Look at the cutter."

"Shan't! I've seen un times enough."

"Yes, yes; but look on her deck."

"What for?" said Jemmy, who was steadily pulling homeward.

"Oh, what an obstinate chap you are, Jemmy! Look there; Tally's on deck."

"Ck!" ejaculated the man, this being meant for a derisive laugh. "Why don't you say she's having a ride in the Saxham coach."

"I tell you she is. They've got her there, and the sailors are trying to milk her."

"Then I wish 'em luck," said Jemmy. "There's only one man as can milk Tally, and that's me."

"Turn the boat's head, and let's go for her."

"Ck!" ejaculated Jemmy again. "What a one you are to joke, Ram Shackle; but it won't do this mornin'. I'm burst up with sleep."

"Open your stupid eyes, and look for once. I tell you they've got Tally on the deck of the cutter."

"And I tell you, you young Ram Shackle, I'm too sleepy to see fun anywhere. Won't do, my lad—won't do."

Ram jumped up, stepped over the thwart, seized the man's head, and screwed it round toward the cutter, where the scene previously described was plain in the sunshine.

"Well!" ejaculated Jemmy, "so she be."

"Why couldn't you believe me before, when I told you?"

"Thought you was gammoning me, my lad!"

"There, row away!" cried Ram; and as soon as they were well within hearing he answered the hail, and next shouted—

"I've come after our cow."

"Very undignified proceeding, Mr Raystoke," said the lieutenant, busily walking up and down as the boat with Ram in it was being rowed alongside. "It all comes of being appointed to a wretched, little cobble boat like this, and sent on smuggling duty. If I—if we had been aboard a frigate, or even a sloop-of-war, we shouldn't have had such an affair as this. Why, confound that boy's impudence, he has jumped on board. Go and speak to him; order him off; pitch him overboard; anything. How dare he!"

Archy drew himself up, laid one hand upon his dirk, and strutted up to Ram, looking "as big as a small ossifer," as Dirty Dick said afterwards; and gave him a smart slap on the shoulder as he was going after the cow.

"Here, you sir!" cried Archy, as the boy faced round. "What do you mean by coming aboard one of His Majesty's ships like that?"

"Eh?"

"Touch your hat, sir, when an officer speaks to you."

"Touch my hat to you like I do to Sir Risdon?"

"Like you do to any gentleman, sir."

"Oh, very well," said Ram giving one of his fair brown curls a tug, and showing his teeth.

"That's better. Now then, what do you want?"

"Our Tally."

"Your what?"

"Our cow, Tally."

"How do I know it's yours?"

"Why, it is. She must have walked over the cliff in the fog. Was your cutter close under so as she fell on deck?"

"Of course not, bumpkin," said Archy impatiently, as the men burst into a guffaw, and then looked horribly serious as if they had not smiled. "We saw her swimming and fetched her on board."

"Thank ye," said Ram. "I say, how am I to get her home? Can you lend us a rope?"

"Who are you, boy?" said the lieutenant, marching up.

Ram faced round, stared at the officer's rather shabby uniform, and gave his curl another tug before pulling his red cap over his brow.

"Ram Shackle, sir."

"Is—is that your name, sir," said the lieutenant pompously, "or are you trying to get a laugh at my expense?"

Ram stared.

"Do you hear what I say, sir?"

"Yes, but I dunno what you mean."

"Here, my man, what's that boy's name?" cried the lieutenant to Jemmy Dadd in the boat.

"Ram Shackle," said Jemmy gruffly. "Christen Rammylees!"

"And is this your cow?"

"No, sir!"

"Then, you young rascal, how dare you come and claim it," cried the lieutenant wrathfully.

"Because it's ours. My father's; I didn't mean it was my own."

"Can you give me some proof that it is yours?" said the lieutenant.

"Eh!" exclaimed Ram, staring.

"I say, show me that the cow is yours, and you shall have her."

"Oh," cried Ram, and he ran to the side, unfastened the rope used as a halter for the patient beast, ran right forward, and began to call, "Tally, Tally! Coosh-cow, coosh-cow!"

The effect was magical, the cow turned sharply round, stretched out her nose so as to make her windpipe straight, and uttered a low soft lowing, as she walked straight forward to where Ram stood, thrust her nose under his arm, and stood swinging her tail to and fro.

"Mr Raystoke!"

"Ay, ay, sir!" said Archy, going aft and saluting.

"It seems to be their cow; let them take it ashore."

"Ay, ay, sir!"

"Stop. Bring the boy here," said the lieutenant.

Archy marched forward.

"Come here, boy," he said importantly; and Ram followed him to where the little fat officer stood near the helm, frowning.

"Now, sir," said the lieutenant, "I want you to answer me a few questions. What is your name—no, no, stop, you told me before. Where do you live?"

"Yonder, at the farm."

"Oh! At the farm. Look here, boy, did you ever hear of smugglers?"

"What?"

"Did you ever hear of smugglers?"

"Yes, lots o' times," said Ram glibly. "They're chaps that goes across to France and foreign countries, and brings shipfuls o' things over here."

"Yes, that's right. Ever seen any about here?"

"Well," said Ram, taking off his red cap, and scratching his curly head, "I dessay I have. Father says you never know who may be a smuggler: they're all like any one else."

"Humph! Know where they land their cargoes?"

"Oh, yes; I've heard tell as they land 'em all along the cliff here."

"Bah! Impossible," shouted the lieutenant.

"Is it, sir?" said Ram vacantly. "My father said it was true."

"Seen any smugglers' craft about during the last few days?"

"No, sir; not one," cried the boy with perfect truth.

"That will do, boy. Mr Raystoke let him take his cow and go."

"Ay, ay, sir!"

"Then get the gig alongside, and we'll explore round more of the coast close in."

"Ay, ay, sir! Now, boy, this way."

Ram looked vacantly about him, but there was a very keen twinkle about his eyes, as he followed Archy forward to where the cow stood blinking her eyes, and swinging her tail amongst the men.

"I say," he said.

"Did you speak to me, sir?" cried Archy, facing round, and frowning.

"Yes. Is that little sword sharp?"

"Of course."

"Pull it out, and let's have a look."

Archy frowned.

"Take your cow and go," he said. "She is a miserable thing without a drop of milk in her."

"What?" cried Ram, with his face becoming animated. Then he shouted to the man in the boat, "Hi! Jemmy, he says Tally's got no milk in her."

"How do he know?" cried Jem scornfully.

"Why, I tried ever so long," said Dick, who could not refrain from joining in.

"Ck!" laughed Jemmy.

"Why, she's our best cow," cried Ram. "I say skipper."

"Here, you mustn't speak to an officer like that," whispered Archy.

"What does the boy want?" said the plump little lieutenant, marching forward.

"On'y want our cow."

"Then take her, sir, and go!"

"Have a drop of milk?"

"No," said the lieutenant, turning his back. "Perhaps Mr Raystoke here might like a little. Can you milk?"

"I can't," said Ram, shaking his head. "He can. Here, Jemmy, take hold of the painter and come aboard."

"Stop!" cried the lieutenant, "you must not speak like that. You must ask leave, sir."

"Ask who?" said Ram, vacantly.

"Touch your cap, and ask the lieutenant to let you."

"Why, I have touched it twice. Want me to pull my hair off? I say, skipper, if you'll let him come aboard—oh! He is aboard now,"—for Jemmy was already making the boat fast—"Here, give me a clean pail."

The little commander of the cutter tried to look important, and Archy more so, but they forgot everything disciplinarian the next moment, in the interest of the proceedings, as Jemmy Dadd took the bucket handed to him, turned another up beside the side of the cow, and as he was sitting down, Dirty Dick dug his elbows into his messmates' ribs right and left, whispered "Look out! And over he goes." Then he drew in a long breath, ready for a roar of laughter when the bucket went flying, and stood staring waiting to explode.

But, to Dick's great disappointment, Tally uttered a soft low, and began to swing her tail gently round, so as to give Jemmy a pat on the back. At regular intervals there was a whishing noise, then another whishing noise half a tone lower, then *whish—whosh—whish—whosh*, two streams of rich new milk began to pour into the bucket, whose bottom was soon covered, and a white froth began to appear on the top.

"I say!" cried Dick eagerly, "shall I lash her legs?"

"What for?" growled Jemmy.

"'Cause she'll kick it over directly."

"Not she. You wouldn't kick it over, would you, Tally, old cow?"

The cow waved her tail and whisked it about the man's neck as the milking went on, to the delight of the men, who began to see biscuit and milk in prospect, while the two officers, who were none the less eager for a draught as a change from their miserable ordinary fare, veiled their expectations under a severe aspect of importance.

"Here you are," said Jemmy, drawing back at last—while Dick seemed to be watching, in a state of agony, lest a kick should upset the soft white contents of the bucket—"More'n a gallon this time. How much are we to leave aboard?"

"All of it," said Ram generously; "they deserve it for saving the cow. I say, you," he continued, turning to Archy, "what do you say to her now?"

"Thank you," replied Archy. "Here, Dick, take that bucket aft, and you, my lads, open the side there, and help them to get the cow overboard."

"Thank ye, sir," said Ram, smiling. "I say, Jemmy, she'd stand in the boat, wouldn't she? Or would she put her feet through?"

"Let's try," was the laconic reply, and taking hold of the rope that had been used as a halter, the man stepped down into the boat, the cow, after a little coaxing, following, without putting her feet through, and showing great activity for so clumsy-looking a beast. Ram followed, and took one of the oars, settled down behind Jemmy, and the next minute, with the whole crew of the cutter standing grinning at the side, they began to row shoreward.

"How about the tide, Jemmy?" said Ram, when they had been rowing a few minutes, with the cow standing placidly in the boat.

"Too high, can't do it," said the man.

"Let's row to the ledge then, and land there till the tide goes down."

"Right," said Jemmy, and they bore off a little to the east, made straight for the shelf of rock, which was just awash; and as they rowed, they saw the lieutenant and the midshipman enter the light gig, four men dropped their oars in the water, and with the drops flashing from the blades, the gig came swiftly after them.

"Why, they're coming here too, Jemmy," said Ram, as they reached the ledge, and leaped on to the ammonite-studded stone, over which the water glided and then ran back.

"Well, let 'em," said Jemmy, following suit with the painter, the cow standing contentedly with her eyes half-closed. "Don't matter to us, lad, so long as they didn't come last night."

They made fast the hawser to an iron stanchion, one of several dotted about and pretty well hidden by the water, climbed up on the rock, and sat down in the warm sunshine to wait for the turn of the tide, while after a pull in one direction, the gig's course was altered, and they saw its course changed again.

"I liked that chap," said Ram, as he gazed across a few hundred yards of smooth water, at where Archy sat in his uniform, steering.

"What are they up to?" said Jemmy, shading his eyes. Then quite excitedly, "Say, lad, lookye yonder," he whispered.

"I was looking," cried Ram excitedly; "they've picked up a brandy keg."

There was no denying the fact; and as the dripping little barrel was placed by one of the men in the fore part of the gig, the others gave way, and the light vessel came rapidly now toward the ledge.

Archy was shading his eyes just then, and pointing out something to the lieutenant a little to the left of where Ram and his companion were seated, and the boy's eyes, trained by his nefarious habits, gazed sharply in search of danger or criminating evidence, in the direction the midshipman pointed.

A chill of horror ran through him, for there, with the wash of the tide half covering and then leaving them bare, were two more brandy kegs, which had been missed the previous night during the fog.

"Ah!" ejaculated Ram, as in imagination he saw the well-filled vault, and the crew of the cutter being marched up to make a seizure, and arrest his father perhaps.

If he could but get away and give the alarm!

Chapter Seven

"Get away, and give the alarm?"

How could we?

There was no rope and pulley up on the cliff now, and the boat was occupied by the cow; while, even if it had been empty, it would have meant a six mile row to reach a landing-place at that time of the tide, and an eight miles' walk back.

And here was the cutter's gig close to them, and the lieutenant ready to ask him the meaning of the smuggled spirits being there.

For there was no mistaking the fact that the kegs were full of smuggled spirit. The one the king's men had dragged dripping from the sea, bore certain unmistakable markings, and it was evidently brother to those on the rock.

Ram and Jemmy had no time for thinking; the gig was run quickly up alongside of the ledge, and Dick tossed in his oar, sprang out, sending the clear water splashing with his bare feet, as he crossed up to the kegs, and, taking one under each arm, went more slowly and cautiously back to the boat, where his messmates took them carefully, with many a chuckle and grin, to deposit them beside the others.

"Now, my lad, run her alongside of the cow—I mean of the other boat," cried the lieutenant.

This was quickly done, and the little officer turned sharply to where Ram and Jemmy Dadd were seated on the rock, looking on as stolidly as if nothing whatever was coming.

"Hi! You, sir; come here!" cried the lieutenant.

"Me, or him?" replied Ram coolly.

"You, sir."

Ram got up, whistled softly, and went down to the boat.

"Want some more milk?" he said, with a grin.

"Silence, sir! Do you see those?"

"What, them tubs?"

"Yes, sir."

"Not till you got 'em. Wish I had!"

"I dare say you do, sir. Now, then: how did they come there?"

"Why, your chaps put 'em there. I see 'em just now."

"No, no; I mean in the sea and on that rock."

"Come there?" said Ram, with a vacant look.

"Yes, sir! How did they come there? Now, no trifling; out with it at once."

"Been a wreck, p'r'aps, and they're washed up."

"Bah!" cried the lieutenant.

"Ah, you may say 'Bah!' but they might. Why, there was a big ship's boat and a jib-boom washed up here one day; warn't there, Jem?"

"Yes," growled the rough-looking fellow, half-fisherman half farm-labourer. "And don't you 'member the big tub o' sugar, as was all soaked with water, till she was like treacle?"

"Ay, and the—"

"That will do—that will do!" cried the lieutenant.

"Washed up, eh? What's in those kegs?"

"I know," cried Ram, showing his teeth, and looking at Archy. "Full o' hoysters! Give us one!"

"Come, sir; this won't do for me. You know as well as I do what's in those kegs. Where are the rest?"

"Rest?" said Ram, looking round. "Are there any more of 'em?"

"Yes, I'll be bound there are. Now, then, out with it, if you want to save your skin."

"Skin? That's what father said this morning about the cow; but she wasn't drowned."

"Look here, boy. All this sham innocency won't do for me. Now, then, if you will tell me where the other kegs are, you shall have a reward; if you don't, you'll go to prison as sure as you're there. Jump ashore, two of you, and arrest them before they run."

Ram turned, and stared at Jemmy Dadd with an ill-used countenance.

"What does he mean, Jemmy?"

The man shook his head.

"Do you know where the other little barrels are?"

"Wish I did," grumbled Jemmy. "Say, master, what would you give a man if he showed you where they were?"

"Ten guineas; perhaps twenty," said the lieutenant eagerly.

"Ten guineas! Twenty pounds!" said Jemmy, taking off his red worsted cap, and rubbing his head. "My! Was they your'n? Did you lose 'em?"

"No," roared the lieutenant; "it's plain enough, and you know. A cargo has been run here on this ledge. Now, then; it's no use to try and hide it. You know where it is; so will you gain a reward by giving evidence, or will you go to prison?"

Jemmy shook his head, and gave Ram a puzzled look.

"We came after our cow, sir, please," said the latter, looking up at the sailor, who stood with a hand upon his arm, while Jemmy did the same.

"Here, boy!" cried the lieutenant. "You know what a lot of money ten guineas would be?"

"Yes," said Ram grinning.

"Why, you could buy yourself a watch and chain, and be doing your duty to the king as well. Come, did you see a French boat down here last night?"

"No," said Ram. "It was so foggy."

"You are playing with me, sir. Now then, will you answer?"

"I did answer," said Ram meekly. "Didn't I, Jemmy?"

"Jump ashore, you two," said the lieutenant, "and have a good search all among those rocks. The cargo's there for certain. You two others," he continued, "draw cutlasses, and keep guard over the prisoners."

His orders were obeyed, and the two men stood by guarding Ram, Jemmy, and the cow, who blinked her eyes and smelt at the sea water from time to time, raised her head and uttered a soft low, which was answered from the green top of the cliff two hundred feet above them, where another cow stood gazing down.

The lieutenant and Archy stood up in the boat watching and directing as Dick and his companion searched about in all directions along the lower ledge, and then managed to climb up to the one twenty feet above, where the next minute Dick gave a shout.

"Hah!" cried the lieutenant joyfully. "He has found them."

Ram shut one of his eyes at Jemmy, who made a rumbling noise, but his face did not change.

"What is it, my lad?"

"Cave," cried Dick.

"What's in it?"

"Lobster-pots and old sail. All wore out."

"Nothing else?"

"No, sir."

"You go and look."

The second man disappeared, but returned directly.

"It's on'y a bit of a hole, sir, and there's nothin' else."

The search was continued and ended, for the ledge was shut in by the mighty wall of rock towering above their heads, and the lieutenant was soon convinced that it was impossible for any one to climb that without tackle from above.

"Come back aboard," he said. "You two stop and guard those prisoners."

The sailors stepped back into the boat and resumed their oars, to row steadily east for about half a mile, past several shallow caves, but they could not see one likely to become a hiding-place for smuggled goods, and the rock rose higher and higher above their heads, precluding all ascent.

The boat was rowed quickly back past where the prisoners sat contentedly enough; save the cow, which kept making the great rock wall echo with her lowings, while three more of her kind now stood on high, gazing down at her plight.

The lieutenant now had himself rowed west for about the same distance, but in this direction they did not pass a crack in the great rock wall, let alone a cave, and once more the gig was rowed back.

"Get back into your boat," said the little officer sharply.

"Thank ye, sir," cried Ram. "Come along, Jemmy. Find your little barrels?"

"Come aboard, my lads," continued the lieutenant, without replying to the question. "Make fast her painter to the ring-bolt here."

This was done, a fresh order given, and, with the rough boat and cow in tow, the gig began to make slowly for the cutter.

Ram bent his head down in the boat.

"Hist, Jemmy!" he whispered.

"Hallo!"

"Shall we jump over and swim ashore?"

"Nay; what's the good?—they'd come arter us, and there's no getting away."

"I say," shouted Ram, "what are you going to do?"

Archy turned to the lieutenant.

"Take no notice. A day or two aboard will make him speak."

"The cow wants turning out to grass," shouted Ram; but no heed being paid to his words, "Oh, very well," he said, "I don't care. She'll die, and you'll have to pay for her. I wish my father knew."

He need not have troubled himself to wish, for Farmer Shackle was lying down, hidden behind some stones on the top of the cliff, watching what was going on, with his brow rugged. He had heard enough of the conversation, after being attracted to the place by the action of his cows, to know that the kegs had been discovered, and he smiled as he made out that his boy and man were quite staunch, and would not say a word.

"Won't get anything out o' them," he muttered, as he watched the returning boats. "Shall I tell old Graeme? No; that would only scare him. They'll land a party, and come and search; but they won't dare to go to the Hoze, so I'll leave the stuff there and chance it."

Having made up his mind to this, he lay behind the stones watching till he had seen Ram, Jemmy, and the cow on board the cutter and the boats made fast; after which, as he could see that the lieutenant was busy with his glass, he waited his opportunity, got a cow between him and the sea, and then with raised stick began to drive the cattle from the neighbourhood of the precipice, his action seeming perfectly natural, and raising no suspicion in the officer's breast.

Farmer Shackle was quite right, for it was not long before a boat, well-filled with men, under the command of the midshipman and the master, put off from the cutter, and began to row west to the little cove, through whose narrow entrance a boat could pass to lie on the surface of a cup-shaped depression, at whose head a limpid stream of water gurgled over the cleanly-washed shingle below the great chalk cliffs.

Shackle saw them go, and, guessing their destination, chuckled; for in their ignorance the search party were going to make a journey of twelve or fourteen miles round each way, when any one accustomed to the place would have made the trip in less than two.

"Well, let 'em go," said Shackle; "but if they do find out, I'd better have my two boats out at sea," and he thought of his luggers lying in the little cup-like cove. "Nay there's no hurry; people won't be too eager to tell 'em whose boats they are, and I might want to get away."

He remained thinking about his son for a few minutes and then his countenance lightened.

"Tchah!" he said; "they won't eat him, and they can't do anything but keep him. They've found three kegs—that's all. Wish I'd been behind the man who forgot 'em! He wouldn't forget that in a hurry."

Farmer Shackle went home, and was saluted by the question—

"Found my Tally?"

"Yes, wife."

"Drowned?"

"No; all right."

That was sufficient for Mrs Shackle, who had some butter to make.

Meanwhile the boat containing Archy Raystoke and Gurr the master, with her crew, was rowed steadily along under the cliffs, the deep water being close up. It was a hot day and hard work, but the men pulled away cheerfully, for a run ashore was a change.

The opening into the cove was reached, and the boat run ashore, and one man being left as keeper, the little well-armed party of a dozen men were marched off along the narrow road toward the Hoze.

Archy was in the highest of spirits, and meant to search everywhere in the neighbourhood of the ledge, so as to cover himself with glory in the eyes of his superior officer. Old Gurr the master, who had been turned over to the cutter for two reasons, that he was a good officer and a man with a bad temper, found no pleasure in the walk whatever.

Now he grumbled about his corns, and said he never saw such a road; worse than an old sea beach. Then he limped with the pain of an old wound; and lastly, he forgot all about his troubles in the solace he found in a huge quid of tobacco, with whose juice he plentifully besprinkled the leaves of the brambles that were spread on either side.

The men tramped on, exciting the interest of the people of the little villages that were passed—clusters of white rough stone houses by the roadside, whose occupants looked innocence itself, but there was hardly one among them who could not have told tales about busy work on dark nights, carrying kegs and bales, or packages of tobacco from the cliff, to some hiding-place in barn or cave.

Old Gurr knew that, and he winked solemnly at the young midshipman.

"Nice chickens, Mr Raystoke," he said.

"Where, Gurr?" cried Archy, who was growing fast, and wanted material to help nature. "Let's get some eggs to take back."

"Eggs!" grumbled the weather-beaten officer; "I didn't mean fowls, I meant people."

"Oh!"

"Eggs, indeed! Their eggs is kegs o' brandy. Right Nantes; Hollands gin. I know them. They're all in the game. Keep on, my lads. Step together like the sogers do. This here road's not the cutter's deck."

The last order was not needed, for the men marched on cheerfully and well, till they had passed on the inner side of the high cliff where Ram had displayed his lanthorns, and following the rough road, came at last to the scattered cottages occupied by Shackle's men, and those who had once been servants at the Hoze, before it had sunk down in the world, consequent upon its master's having espoused the wrong side, and its servants were reduced to one old woman.

As they reached the tiny hamlet, a short conference was held between Archy and the master, the latter, in a surly way, giving the lad a few hints as to his proceedings, every suggestion, though, being full of common sense.

"We've no right to go searching their places, Mr Raystoke, but I shall make a mistake. They won't complain. They daren't."

"Why?"

"Hands are too dirty; if not with this job, with some other."

So they halted the men, posted one at each end of the little place, so as to command a good view of any one attempting to carry off contraband goods, and went from house to house, the people readily submitting to the intrusion and search, which in each case was without result.

Every one of the cottages being tried, the men were marched down hill after Archy, and stood for a few moments gazing out over the cliff, to where the cutter lay at anchor, with the farmer's boat trailing out astern, and the air so clear that he could even see the cow tethered to a belaying pin, just in front of the mast.

Five minutes after they came upon Fisherman-farmer Shackle himself, leaning over his gate and smoking a pipe, as he apparently contemplated a pig, and wondered whether he ought to make it fatter than it was.

"Mornin', gentlemen," he said, as Archy and the master came up, and halted their men.

"Good morning," said Archy shortly. "Stand aside, please; we must search all your places."

"Search my places, squire—capt'n, I mean? He aren't here."

"Who is not here? Are not you the master?"

"Ay, my lad, but I mean him you're searching for. Hi! Missus!"

"Yes," came from within, and Mrs Shackle appeared wiping her hands.

"Ain't seen a deserter, missus, have you? Capt'n here has lost one of his men."

"If you'll let me speak, I'll explain," said Archy sharply. "A cargo of contraband goods was landed on the rocks below the cliff last night, and—"

"You don't say so, master!" said Shackle earnestly.

"I do say so," cried Archy; "and you are suspected of having them concealed here."

"Me!" cried Shackle, bursting into a roar of laughter. "Me, Mr Orficer? Do you know what I am?"

"No."

"Why, I'm a farmer. Hi, missus, hear him! Young gent here thinks I'm a smuggler. That is a good un, and no mistake."

Archy was taken aback for the moment, but he caught the eye of the master, who was too old over the business to be easily hoodwinked.

"The young gentleman's made quite a mistake," said Mrs Shackle demurely. "P'r'aps he'd like a mug of our mead before he goes, and his men a drop of home-brewed."

"Ay, to be sure," cried Shackle. "Put out the bread and cheese, missus, and I'll go and draw a drink or two. You'll take something too, won't you, master?"

"Yes; don't mind," said Gurr, "but I'd rather take a tot o' right Nantes or Hollands."

"Ay, so would I," said Shackle, with a laugh, as his wife began to bustle about and get knives and plates; "but you've come to the wrong place, master. I have heared o' people getting a drop from 'em, after they've used their horses and carts, but that's never been my luck; has it, missus?"

"No, never," said Mrs Shackle; and to herself,—"That's quite true."

"You are very hospitable," said Archy shortly; "but I've got my duty to do, sir. It's an unpleasant one, that we must search your place for contraband goods."

"Sarch? Oh, I give you my word, squire, there's nothing here."

"We must see about that."

"Well, this here arn't werry pleasant, Mr Orficer, seeing as I'm a reg'lar loyal servant of the king. But theer, I don't mind if my missus don't object. You won't mind, old gal, so long as they don't rip open the beds and chuck the furniture all over the place?"

"I should like to see any of them doing it, that's all," cried Mrs Shackle, ruffling up like a great Dorking hen who saw a hawk.

"Nothing about the place shall be injured, madam," said Archy politely; "but we must search."

"Oh, very well then," said Mrs Shackle; "but I must say it's very rude."

"Pray, forgive us," said Archy, raising his hat; "we are His Majesty's servants, and we do it in the king's name."

Mrs Shackle responded with her best curtsey, and a smile came back in her face as the farmer said, —

"It's all right, missus; they're obliged to do it. Where will you begin first—what are you sarching for?"

"Brandy," said Archy.

"Oh, then, down in the cellar's the place," said Shackle, laughing, and taking three mugs from where his wife had placed them. "If it had been for silks and laces, I should have said go upstairs."

He led the way to a door at the top of some stone steps.

"One moment," said Archy, and, giving orders to the men to separate, surround the premises, and search the outbuildings, then stationing two more at the doors, and taking one, Gurr, to search upstairs, he followed the farmer into a fairly spacious stone cellar, where there was a cider barrel in company with two of ale, and little kegs of elder wine and mead.

"Sarch away, squire," said Shackle bluffly, as he placed the mugs on the floor and turned the wooden spigots.

"That's elder wine in the little barrel. Say, you haven't seen anything of a boy of mine in your travels? My lad and one of the men have gone after a stray cow. I'm fear'd she's gone over the cliff."

"They're all on board the cutter."

"What? Well, that is good news. Full up here. Done sarching, sir?"

"Yes," replied Archy, who began to feel more and more ashamed of being suspicious of so frank and bluffly hospitable a man.

"Come along then. Your lads will be as pleased as can be with a mug of my home-brewed."

As he led the way to the door the midshipman gave another glance round, seeing nothing in the slightest degree suspicious, and, a few minutes after, the whole party was being refreshed, both officers quite convinced that there was nothing contraband on the premises.

"What other houses are there near here?" asked Gurr at last.

"Only one. The Hoze."

"The Hoze?"

"Yes; Sir Risdon Graeme's. Yonder among the trees. Going up there?"

"Yes, of course," said Archy shortly.

"Yes, of course," said the farmer, in assent. "But I'd be a bit easy with him, sir. Don't hurt his feelings. Gentleman, you see."

"Don't be alarmed," said the midshipman quietly. "I hope we shall not be rude to any one."

He moved towards the door, after saluting Mrs Shackle, the farmer leading the way, and pointing out the nearest path up the steep slope.

"'Bout my cow," he said.

"I have no doubt that as soon as the lieutenant in command is satisfied that you had nothing to do with the smuggling, your people will be set at liberty."

"And the cow?"

"And the cow of course."

"Thank ye, sir; that's good news. I'll go and tell the missus. Straight on, sir; you can't miss it."

"Ah, my fine fellow," he continued, as he walked back, "if it hadn't been for your gang with you, how easily I could have turned the key and kept you down in that cellar, where I wish I had your skipper too."

"Oh, Blenheim!" said his wife, in an excited whisper, "how could you help them to go up to the Hoze? They'll find out everything now."

"P'r'aps not, missus. I sent 'em, because if I hadn't they'd have found the way. We may get off yet, and if we do—well, it won't be the first time; so, here's to luck."

As he spoke he opened a corner cupboard, took out a bottle of spirits which had never paid duty, poured out and drank a glass.

"Thank you," said a gruff voice. "I think, if you don't mind, farmer, I'll have a little taste of that. I came back to tell you that your cider is rather harsh and hard, not to say sour, and I'm a man accustomed to rum."

As he spoke, Gurr the master stepped into the room, took the bottle from the farmer's hand, helped himself to a glass, and poured out and smelt the spirit.

"I say, farmer," he said, as he tasted, "this is the right sort or the wrong sort, according to which side you are."

"Only a little drop given me by a friend."

"French friend, for any money," said the master, drinking the glass. "Yes, that's right Nantes. I thought so from the first, farmer, and I know now I was right."

He went off again, and Shackle stood shaking his fist after him.

"And we'd got off so well," he muttered. "I knew that rascal suspected us."

"Say me, Blenheim," retorted Mrs Shackle. "I've begged you hundreds of times not to meddle with the business, but you would, and I'm your wife and obliged to obey. Isn't Ram a long time bringing home that cow?"

"Yes," said Shackle drily. "Very."

Chapter Eight

Archy was some little distance ahead of his men, and he had just stepped into the patch of woodland which surrounded the Hoze, when he heard a pleasant little voice singing a snatch of a Jacobite song.

He stopped short to listen, it sounded so bird-like and sweet, and half-laughingly he sang the last line over aloud, thinking the while how disloyal he was.

Hardly had he finished, when there was a burst of barking, a rush, and a dog came hurrying toward him, followed by a voice crying—

"Grip, Grip, come here!"

The dog seemed to pay no heed to the call, and at a turn of the track, Archy saw him coming open-mouthed.

It was not a pleasant sight, and the youth felt disposed to take to his heels, and run for protection to his men.

But there were drawbacks to such a proceeding.

If he ran it would look cowardly, and he knew for certain that the dog would come after him, and take him at a disadvantage; so, making a virtue of necessity, he whipped out his dirk and ran hard at the dog, who checked his pace, hesitated, stopped, barked more furiously than ever, and then turned round, and was chased by the midshipman, who drew up on finding himself face to face with Sir Risdon's daughter, out for her daily walk.

The girl turned white, and was in the act of turning to run away, when Archy's words arrested her.

"No, no," he cried, "don't run away."

She stopped, and looked from his face to his dirk, and back.

"Oh, I see," he said, "that alarmed you. There," he continued, sheathing the little weapon, "I only drew it because your dog looked so fierce. Does he bite?"

"Sometimes, I'm afraid. But were you coming to see my father? Who are you?" she added uneasily, as she glanced at the lad's uniform.

"I am Archibald Raystoke, of His Majesty's cutter *White Hawk*."

"And you want to see my father?" cried the girl, beginning to tremble.

"Well, yes, I ought to see him. The fact is, we have landed to search for a quantity of smuggled things, and to make a capture of the smugglers if we can."

Celia looked at him wildly, and her face grew more and more white.

"Will you show me the way to the house? The Hoze you call it, do you not?"

Celia gave a quick, almost imperceptible nod, as she recalled how she had lain in her clothes, and listened to the busy coming and going of footsteps, for the greater part of the night.

As all this came to her mind, she felt at first as if she must run to warn her father. Then a giddy feeling of dread came over her, and she stood staring blankly at the frank-looking boy before her.

"I know the great vault is full of smuggled things," she said to herself, "and that they will think my father put them there. What shall I do?"

"Poor little lassie!" said Archy to himself, as he smiled complacently; "she has never seen an officer in uniform before, and I frightened her with my drawn sword."

At that moment, Gurr came up with the men, and Celia seemed as if turned to stone.

"This young lady lives at the house, Mr Gurr," said Archy aloud, "and she will show us the way."

Poor Celia felt as if she could neither move nor speak. It seemed horrible to her that she should have the task of guiding the king's men, perhaps to arrest her father. But just then she was brought to herself by the behaviour of the dog, who, on seeing his mistress talking in a friendly way to the stranger who had chased him, had condescended to be quiet, but now that a fresh party of the enemy was approaching, set up his bristles, and began to bark and growl furiously.

"Down, Grip! Quiet!" she cried, and feeling bound to act, she went on, with the midshipman keeping close up, and putting in an apologetic word about giving her so much trouble.

Celia could hardly keep down a hysterical cry, as she caught sight of her father and mother, the latter with her hand upon the former's arm. They had been taking their customary walk in the neglected garden, and Sir Risdon was about to lead his pale, careworn lady up the steps, when the snarling and subdued barking of Grip made him turn his head, and he stopped short with his lips almost white.

"What is it?" whispered Lady Graeme, as she saw the uniforms and weapons of the men.

"The end!" said the unhappy man, as he looked wildly at his wife. "The result of my weakness. They are on the scent of the smuggled goods, and I am to be called to account for their possession. Better that we had starved!"

Lady Graeme caught his hand, and pressed it hard.

"Be firm," she whispered; "you will betray yourself."

"Well," he replied bitterly, "why not? Better so than being the slave of that wretched man. I feel that I am worse than he. I do know better, he does not."

Recalling that he was in the presence of a gentleman, Archy raised his hat, advanced and said, apologetically, who and what they were. That his was a very unpleasant duty, but that as a gentleman, Sir Risdon would see that the king's officers had no alternative but to carry out their duty.

"Of course not, sir," said Sir Risdon. "I understand, sir, you wish to search. Very well, I shall raise no objection. Proceed."

"Shall we close the men all round the house?" said the master, coming up after halting the men.

"Wait a minute," replied Archy. "Really, I hardly think it is necessary for us to commit so serious an act of rudeness towards a gentleman. Perhaps Sir Risdon Graeme will be good enough to assure me."

"No, sir," said the baronet sternly; "I shall make no obstacle. You have your duty to do; pray proceed."

The midshipman hesitated, and looked from one to the other, seeing Lady Graeme standing pale, handsome, and statuesque by her husband's side, while on the other side was Celia, holding her father's hand, and resting her forehead against his arm.

"I won't do it, I can't," thought Archy. "Why didn't he say out at once he had no knowledge of the affair, and send us about our business?"

At that moment, he felt his sleeve plucked, and turning angrily round, he saw the elderly master, who had been standing hat in hand, greatly impressed by Lady Graeme's dignity.

"We're on the wrong tack, Mr Raystoke, sir," he whispered.

"Think so, Gurr?" said Archy joyfully.

"Oh, yes! These are not the sort o' folk to do that kind o' thing. Apologise, and I'll give the order to march. It goes through me like a knife."

Archy drew a long breath, and was about to retire his men, when he heard something which made him bound forward, for Celia, unable to bear the horror and alarm any longer had suddenly swooned away.

The midshipman was too late, for Sir Risdon had bent down, raised his child, and was about to carry her into the house.

He turned fiercely on the young officer.

"Well, sir," he said sternly, "you have your duty to do; pray go on, and then relieve my wife and child of the presence of your men."

"I beg your pardon, Sir Risdon," said Archy quickly. "No one could regret this more than I do. You see I am only a young officer, quite a boy, and was sent on this unpleasant duty."

"Go on, sir, go on!"

"Oh, no!" cried the lad; "I am unwilling to search the place. I'm sure if our lieutenant knew he would not wish it for a moment."

The baronet gazed at the boy wildly, as he clasped his child to his breast.

"You—you are not going to search?" he said hesitatingly.

"No, of course not. Pray forgive me. I'll lead my men back to the boat at once."

He raised his hat to Lady Graeme, an example followed by the master clumsily, as he backed away to the men, whom he faced round, the order was given, and they began to march back.

As they disappeared among the trees, Sir Risdon stooped down and kissed his child's forehead passionately.

"Wife," he said, in a deep, husky voice, "I never felt the misery and degradation of my position so cruelly before. Take her up to her room."

"What are you going to do, Risdon?" exclaimed the lady.

"Follow that poor lad, and let him know the truth. I will not let him fail in his duty, to rescue that old scoundrel down below."

"No, no! You must not. It would be too cruel," whispered Lady Graeme wildly. "Think of the consequences."

"I do," said Sir Risdon sternly. "I should have behaved like what I have a right to be called—a gentleman."

"And make our fortunes ten times worse. You would be torn from us. What are poverty and disgrace to that?"

"You are cruel," said Sir Risdon bitterly. "I must, woman; I tell you I must. If this poor child should ever know into what a pit I have allowed myself to be led, how can I ever look her in the face again?"

"It would kill her for you to be taken away, to be punished, perhaps, for that which you could hardly help."

"No, she would soon forget."

"And I should soon forget?" said Lady Graeme reproachfully.

Sir Risdon turned to her wildly, as she laid her head upon his breast.

"If you were taken from us, it would kill me too," she said tenderly; and then in silence, they bore their insensible child into the forbidding-looking house.

Chapter Nine

"Think we've done right, my lad?" said Gurr, after they had half way descended the slope.

"Yes, of course. How could we search the house of a gentleman like that?"

"Oh, easy enough."

"It was impossible."

"But suppose, after all, he has got all the stuff hid away. Some men's very artful, as you'll find out some day. Oughtn't we to go back?"

He paused as he said these words, and then laid his hand firmly on Archy's shoulder.

"I didn't tell you," he said, "what I saw when I went back to the farm."

"No! What?" cried the midshipman eagerly.

"That old chap having a glass of real smuggled spirits."

"How do you know it was?"

"Because I tasted it. No mistake about that, I can tell you. Then he was very eager to get me to go up yonder, and that looks bad. He knows all about it."

"Nonsense! If he knew that the smuggled goods were up there he wouldn't send us to find them."

"How do you know? That may have been his artfulness, to keep us from searching. If he'd as good as said don't go up there, and tried to stop us, we should have gone at once."

"But we can't go back and search, Gurr. Suppose we did go and ransacked the place, and hurt everybody's feelings, and then found nothing, what should we look like then?"

"Silly," said the master laconically, and for a time he was silent, marching on behind the men. "All comes of being sent on such dooty," he burst out with. "It isn't right to send gentlemen and officers to do such dirty work. I've been ashamed of myself ever since I've been on the cutter. Hallo! Here's the farmer again."

For they had suddenly come upon Shackle driving an old grey horse before him as if going on some farming business, and he started apparently from a fit of musing as he came abreast.

"Ah, gentlemen," he said; "going back?"

"Yes," said Gurr smartly.

"Found the stuff?"

"No."

"I say."

"Well?"

"Are you sure there was anything landed there last night?"

"Of course we are."

"Oh, I didn't know. Good day, gentlemen, good day."

He went on after his horse chuckling to himself, while the search party made for the track to get back to the cove and row back.

But before they were half way there, Archy who had been thinking deeply, suddenly said to Gurr—

"I say, though, isn't he right?"

"What about, my lad?"

"Are we sure that a cargo was landed last night?"

"Didn't you and the skipper find three kegs?"

"Yes, but they might have been there a month ago."

"Why, of course, my lad. Here, let's go and tell the skipper so. How I do hate being sent upon a wild-goose chase like this!"

The rest of the journey to the cove was performed almost in silence; they then embarked, heartily tired with their walk, and ready enough to take the rest of the burden of their journey on their hands and arms by rowing steadily and well, the tide being in their favour.

"Yes, I do hate these jobs," said the master after a long silence. "See that the people was nodding and winking to one another as we went by their cottages?"

"Yes, I did see something of the kind once or twice," replied Archy.

"Laughing at us, and knowing we should find out nothing, while they knew all the time."

The first thing plainly visible as the boat approached the cutter was the head of Tally gazing contemplatively at them over the side, as if anxious to know what news there was from home, and directly after Ram and Jemmy looked over in a quiet stolid way, as if not troubled in the least by the fact that they were prisoners.

"Well, Mr Raystoke," cried the lieutenant, as the young midshipman sprang over the side; "found the cargo and left two men in charge, eh?"

"No, sir."

"Tut—tut—tut! What is the use of having you for my first officer. You ought to have searched everywhere, and found it."

"We did search everywhere, sir, nearly, but didn't find it."

"Oh! What's that? Nearly? Then where didn't you search?"

Archy told him and his reasons.

"Humph! Ha! Well, I don't know: Government has no bowels of compassion, Mr Raystoke. I'm afraid you ought to have searched the Gloves."

"Hoze, sir, Hoze."

"Oh well, gloves, hose, gloves, all the same; only one's for downstairs, the other up. Stupid name for a place."

"You think, then, I haven't done my duty, sir."

"Yes, Mr Raystoke, as an officer I do; but as a gentleman I'm afraid I think I should have done just the same."

"I'm very sorry, sir. I wanted to do what is right."

"And you let your amiability step in the way, sir. That cargo must be run to earth."

"But is it quite certain, sir, that there was a cargo run?"

"My good fellow," cried the little lieutenant impatiently, "if you found a skin lying on the beach, wouldn't you feel sure that it had once had a sheep in it?"

"Yes, sir, if it was a sheepskin."

"Bah! Don't try to chop logic here; go below and get something to eat, while I make up my mind what I shall do."

Archy went into the cabin, not at all satisfied with the result of his run ashore, and he did not feel much better after his meal, when he went on deck just in time to find the lieutenant laying down the law to Ram and Jemmy Dadd.

"There," he was saying, "take your cow and go ashore. I'm not going to keep you prisoners, but the eye of the law is upon you, and this smuggling will be brought home to you both. Be off!"

"Shan't Jemmy milk the cow again before we go?" said Ram, with a grin, that might have been friendly or mocking.

"No!" thundered the lieutenant. "Here, Mr Gurr, see these smuggling scoundrels off the deck."

This was soon done, the cow being easily got into the boat, and just as it was growing dark Ram stood up to push from the side.

"I say," he cried again, addressing Archy, "is that thing sharp?"

The midshipman did not condescend to answer, but stood gazing thoughtfully over the side, till the boat gradually seemed to die away in the faint mist of the coming night.

"Well, Raystoke, what are you thinking?" said a voice behind him, and he started round.

"I was just thinking of coming to you, sir."

"Eh, what for?"

"It seems to me, sir, that if that cargo was run, and is hidden anywhere near, they'll be moving it to-night."

"Of course. Raystoke, you'll be a great man some day. I shouldn't have thought of that. Well, what do you propose?"

"To go ashore, and watch."

"Of course. My dear boy, if you can help me to capture a few of these wretched people, I shall get promoted to a better ship, and you shall come with me. I won't rest till I am post-captain, and as soon as you can pass, you shall be my lieutenant. There, select your crew and be off at once."

"No, sir; that will not do. They'll be on the watch, and if they see a boat's crew land, they'll do nothing to-night."

"Then what do you propose?"

"Don't laugh at me, sir, and call me stupid; but I've been thinking that if I could be set ashore, dressed as one of the boys, I might go about unnoticed.

And if they were moving the cargo, I could see where they took it, and then you could land the men."

"Oh, you'll be an admiral before I shall, boy. That's it; but will you do it?"

"If you'll let me, sir."

"Let you? Here, Mr Gurr, help Mr Raystoke, and—stop though; I don't think I can let you go alone, my lad."

"If I don't go alone, sir, it's of no use."

"You are right. Then we'll risk it; but if the smugglers kill you, don't come and blame me. Have the boat ready, Mr Gurr. Here, Raystoke, come down into the cabin at once."

Chapter Ten

Half an hour after, a dirty-looking sailor lad slipped down into the boat, with his worsted cap pulled well down over his eyes, and an uncomfortable feeling about his chest, as he sat back in the stern-sheets by Gurr the master.

"Lay your backs well into it, my lads," said the lieutenant, "and try and land him without being seen."

"Ay, ay, sir!" came from the men, the boat began to surge through the still water, and the boy tried to shift the lion's head which formed the top of his dirk handle.

This he had placed inside the breast of his woollen shirt, ready for use if wanted, but it promised to hurt him more than any enemy, and he wished he had left it on board.

"No talking, lads," said the master, "and don't splash."

The oars had been muffled, and they glided along through the faint mist, in a ghostly way, well in the shadow of the cliffs, Gurr keeping up a whispered conversation with the lad by his side.

"It's no use to ask you 'bout where you are going first, sir," whispered the master, "because I suppose it will all be chance. But you'll go up to the farm, eh?"

"Yes, I shall go there."

"And up to that big house?"

Archy was silent.

"Ah, well; it's your plan, and you must do what you think's best, only take care of yourself, and if they're after you, don't make for the sea, that's where they'll think you would go. Make inland for the woods, and hide there."

Archy nodded, and no more was said during the dark journey. They were so close to the huge wall of rocks that it seemed as if they were alive with strange marine creatures, which kept on writhing and whispering together, and making gasping and sucking noises, as the tide heaved and sank among the loose rocks and seaweed, while Archy could not divest himself of the idea that they were watched by people keeping pace with them higher up on the top of the cliff.

"Wonder whether those two have landed the cow by this time?" whispered Gurr, breaking in upon one of Archy's reveries, in which he saw himself following a band of smugglers laden with contraband goods.

"I don't know," he replied. "We must take care they do not see us."

"Not likely on a dark night like this. Won't be so foggy, though, as 'twas last."

Nothing was seen or heard of the late prisoners' boat, and for very good reasons; and at last they found themselves abreast of the opening into the cove, where they lay upon their oars for a time listening.

All was still. Not a sound to be heard on either of the luggers lying at their buoys, and no light was visible at the cottages at the head of the little bay.

"I might venture now," whispered Archy. "Have me rowed close in to the shingle beach on the right, not close ashore, but so that I can wade in. I shall drop over the side where it's about two feet deep. Let them back in and we can try the depth with the boat-hook."

The order was whispered, the boat glided in through the broad opening, was turned quickly, and then the men backed water till told to stop, Archy, who had the boat-hook over the side, suddenly finding it touch the shingly bottom at the depth of about a foot.

"Good-bye," he whispered, and, gliding over the side, he softly waded ashore and stood on the beach.

It looked light in front, where the limestone rocks had given place to chalk, but to right, left, and seaward, all was black as night, and stepping cautiously along, the lad approached the cottages, listening attentively, but not hearing a sound save the gurgling of water as it trickled under the stones on its way to the sea.

As he reached the track leading past the cottages he had a narrow escape from falling over a boat that was drawn up on the stones, but he saved himself with a jerk; and, feeling hot with the sudden start, he turned and crouched down, but there was not a sound to indicate that he had been heard, and drawing a long breath he stepped on to reach the hard earth where his feet were not among the water-worn pebbles, and in a few minutes he was on the road he had traversed twice that day, and walking fast toward the farm.

Once or twice he hesitated, for the way lay so low down in the valley, with the hills towering up to such a height on either side, that the night seemed as dark as during the fog of the previous night; but he got along over the ground pretty well in spite of its seeming more hilly and rough, till at the end of about an hour and a half he felt that he must be approaching the farm, and he advanced more cautiously, listening for footsteps and voices from time to time.

There was a good broad green marge to the lane about here, and he stepped on to it, the turf deadening his footsteps.

"But I don't recollect seeing this grass in the morning," he thought; and then he stopped short, for it suddenly occurred to him that he had not come upon the cluster of houses where the people smiled and nodded at one another as they passed.

"I can't have trailed off into another road, can I?" he said to himself, as he felt quite startled and turned hot.

He looked round, but it was too dark to make out anything, and he was about to start on again, comforting himself with the idea that he must be right, when he heard at a distance the *pat-pat* of feet on hard ground, and drew back close up to the side to stoop down among some brambles, which told him at once after their fashion what they were.

"If I only dared ask whoever this is," thought Archy, "I should do."

His thoughts took another direction directly, for, apparently about twenty yards away, he heard some one sneeze, and then mutter impatiently, followed by another sneeze.

And all the while the regular *pat-pat* of footsteps came from his right, but not as he had come, for the sound was as if some one was approaching by a road which came at right angles to the one he was in.

Archy crouched there, breathless and listening, wondering who the man could be who was perfectly silent now, but he had not moved away unless the turf had silenced his footprints.

"How lucky it was I stopped!" thought the midshipman. "I should have walked right on to him and been caught."

The steps came nearer, and at last it seemed as if they were going to pass on, when a gruff voice from close by said,—

"Well, lad?"

There was a sudden stoppage, and an exclamation, and—

"Made me jump, master."

"Don't talk foolery," said the first voice in impatient tones, and to Archy it was unmistakable. He had heard both voices before. "What have you made out?"

"Nothing."

"No boat landed?"

"Nor no sign o' one, master. Both lads swear as no one has passed along the lane."

"Wouldn't take the upper lane, would they?"

"Not likely."

"Upper lane!" thought Archy. Had he taken the upper lane in the darkness, and so missed the men on the watch?

"Didn't hear the sailors say nothing on the cutter, did you?"

"Not a word."

The middy's heart seemed to give a throb. He did know that voice then. It was that of the man who had been detained with the boy, and this other, he was sure, was the voice of the farmer.

"Going to keep on watching?"

"Of course. They'll be up to some game to trap us safe. Ought to get that stuff away."

"No, I wouldn't, master; it's safe enough now."

"You're a fool," came back in a savage growl. "Anybody but you and that mole-eyed boy would have seen the kegs before them sailors."

"Did see 'em—when it was too late," grumbled the other.

"Well, go back; and take off them boots, and hang 'em round your neck. I could hear you a mile away."

"Right."

"Go and tell 'em to keep a sharp look-out in the cove, and then to run the moment a boat comes in sight."

"No boat won't come in sight to-night. Dark."

"Then the moment you hear one."

"They won't come to-night, master."

"Go and do as I tell you," said the other savagely.

"It's the farmer and his man," thought the listener; "and there is something wrong."

He wondered what he had better do. Should he give notice to them on the cutter?

The answer came at once. How could he? He had made no plans for that.

"Off you go," was said roughly, and the rustling sound seemed to indicate that the man had gone back toward the cove.

Archy listened patiently for the next movement of the farmer, but he could detect nothing, and he was feeling sure that the man was still watching and listening, when he heard a sneeze at a distance followed by a muttering sound, and knew that he must have moved off.

Without a moment's hesitation the lad followed, keeping along the grassy marge of the road, and listening intently to make out at last the dull sound of steps, which told that the man who made them was walking barefoot.

As far as he could judge now, Archy was in the proper road, and as he walked along he tried to understand what was going on, coming at last to the conclusion at which he had at first jumped, that something would be done that night if the farmer and his people were certain that they would not be disturbed.

As he thought he walked cautiously on, wondering what he had better do, and seeing at last a bright light in front high up a slope, and another away to his right much higher.

A little consideration told him that the first was at the farm; the other high up, facing toward the sea, must be up at the Hoze.

Trusting more to chance than plan, the midshipman went on and on, following Farmer Shackle; the task becoming easy now, for as he neared the lights the man grew more careless, so that it was easy to trace his movements, which were evidently homeward, till a few minutes later Archy saw him pass the glowing window, swing open a door from which came a burst of light, pass in, and the door was closed.

Archy stood outside with a vague belief that before long the man would come out, and perhaps go to the spot where the cargo was hidden.

As he waited he could not help turning his eyes in the direction of the long, solitary house in the patch of woodland, and found himself wondering whether he should ever go up there again.

After waiting about a quarter of an hour outside the farm, with his back against one of the roughly piled-up stone walls of the district, Archy began to think it was very dull, and his expectations of a discovery or an adventure grew less and less. All was very quiet at the farm, so quiet that he determined at last to go and peer in at the window to see if the farmer was likely to come out again, because if this were not so he was wasting his time.

"But they are not likely to do anything without him," he thought.

Advancing cautiously, he entered the garden, and was just going up to the window, when the door was thrown open, and he dropped down behind a bush as the farmer strode out.

"He must see me," thought Archy. "What a position for an officer to be in!"

"Eh?" exclaimed Shackle, turning sharply round, as if to answer his wife. "Oh yes. Ought to have been here by now."

This gave the midshipman a moment's breathing time; and he had drawn himself up behind the bush by the time the farmer had closed the door, the sudden change from darkness to light preventing Shackle from seeing the spy upon his proceedings.

Just as he was passing he stopped short, uttering an ejaculation; and feeling that he was seen, the midshipman was about to leap up, jump over the low wall, and run, when he heard steps.

He lay still, hoping that this might have drawn forth the exclamation, but for the next few moments he was in agony.

Then came relief.

"That you, Ramillies?"

"Yes, father."

"Well?"

"I think it's all right. Carts are coming, and all the lads are down the roads."

"All?"

"No. Two of 'em's down by the cove, but they won't send anybody from the cutter to-night."

"Not so sure of it, my boy,—not so sure. Can't be too careful. 'Tain't as if we were obliged to move 'em to-night. Landing a cargo's one thing; getting it away another. Well, we'll try. You're sure they're keeping good watch at the cove?"

"Yes, father."

"What sort of an officer did he seem on the cutter?"

"Little, fat, sleepy chap."

"And the others?"

"Don't seem to be no others, only that cocky-hoopy middy, who came ashore with the men. I should like to ketch him ashore some day."

One of Archy's legs gave a twitch at the first remark about him, and the twitch occurred in his right arm at the second.

"Don't chatter. Not very sharp sort of officer, eh?"

"No, father. Sort of chap who'd go to sleep all night."

Archy began wondering. He had thought the boy a dull, stupid-looking bumpkin, and he was finding out how observing he had been.

"Well, we'll risk it, boy. Come along."

Archy's heart gave a bound.

Here was news! He had been growing dull and disheartened, thinking that his expedition was foolish and impossible, and here at once he had learned what he wanted. He knew that now all he had to do was to take advantage of every wall and tree, even to creep along the ground if necessary, and he would be able to follow the smugglers to the place where they had hidden the run cargo, watch them bring it out, and then track them to the fresh hiding-place.

He would thus learn everything, and be able at daybreak to make his way to the cliff, signal for a boat, and a grand capture would be made.

His heart beat high as he thought of the lieutenant's delight, and of the joy there would be amongst the men, for this would mean prize-money, and perhaps the means of deluding the vessel that had brought the cargo into a trap, so that it could be captured, and more prize-money as well as honour be the result.

It did not take him long to think all this; and then he rose cautiously and dropped down again, for the door was re-opened, and the light beamed out so that the watcher felt that he must be seen.

"That my Rammy?" cried Mrs Shackle.

"Yes," growled the farmer; "keep that door shut and your mouth too."

"But do be careful, master. I don't want him took prisoner again."

"It's all right, mother."

"Come along, boy."

Archy heard the departing steps, and began to suffer a fresh agony of suspense. He could not stir, for the farmer's wife stood at the open door, and the slightest movement would have caused a discovery; and all the time he could hear the footsteps growing more and more faint.

"Oh!" he said to himself; "and it's so dark I shan't be able to tell which way they have gone."

What should he do? Start up and run?

If he did the woman was certain to raise an alarm; and, knowing that, he could do nothing but wait till she went in, when he might chance to pick up the clue again.

His heart beat so loudly that he felt as if it must be heard, but Mrs Shackle was too intent upon listening to the departing footsteps, which grew more faint till they died out entirely, and as they passed away the midshipman's heart sank.

"Had all my trouble for nothing," he thought. "So near success, and yet to fail!"

"Ah, deary deary me!" said a voice from close at hand, "I'm very sick and tired of it all. I wish he'd be content with his cows and sheep."

Mrs Shackle drew back as she said this, the door closed, and Archy sprang up, darted out of the gateway, and hurried along the path as fast as the darkness would allow, stopping from time to time to listen.

For a long time he could hear nothing. He was descending the slope toward the road leading to the cove, as far as he could tell, for it seemed to him likely that the farmer and his son had gone in that direction; but as he went on and on, and was unable to detect a sound, he felt that he must be wrong, and stopped short, listening intently.

"Bother the woman!" he thought; "it's all through her. They'll go and get all the cargo from the hiding-place, and take it somewhere, and I shall know nothing."

He bit his lip with disappointment, and gave an angry stamp on the grass.

"I'll go back, and try some other way."

Easy to determine, but hard to carry out in the darkness, and in a place which seemed quite changed at night. There should be a lane or track leading down to the cliff he knew, but where it was he could not say; in fact, at that moment, in his confusion, he could hardly tell for certain that he was on the road leading right away to the cove.

"I may just as well be moving," he said at last despondently. "Oh, if I could only have followed them up!"

His heart gave a bound just then, for plainly on the night air came a dull sound, as of footsteps on grass. Then there was a whisper, and directly after he knew that a number of people were coming quickly toward him.

A moment or two later he heard a rattling noise, which he recognised as that made by a horse shaking his harness, and once more Archy's heart beat high.

There had not been time for them—if those people coming were the smugglers—to fetch the cargo, and they must be coming in his direction.

"What shall I do?" thought the watcher; "lie down and let them pass, or go on?"

He decided on the latter course, and finding that he was in a lane bounded by stone walls, he went on, pausing from time to time to make sure that he was being followed.

This proved to be the case, the people getting nearer and nearer, and it was a curious experience to hear the whispering of voices and trampling of feet coming out of the darkness.

"Walking on the side turf," said Archy to himself, as he kept on, to find after a few minutes that the stone wall on his left had ceased, but he could feel that the road went on, and heard the people coming.

A minute or two later he realised that he was going up hill; then the slope grew steeper, and he paused again to listen.

He was quite right. They were coming on steadily, and he knew that there must be twenty or thirty people; but he could hear no horses now.

"They've stopped at the foot of this steep place," he thought, as he went on and on, the people still advancing fast, and all at once, as he went on, a sudden thought ran through him like a stab. For he had guessed at least the direction in which he was going in the black darkness; he was once more ascending the slope toward the patch of woodland high up the hill, and the place of deposit of the smuggled goods must be the Hoze.

Chapter Eleven

A feeling of misery that he could not have explained came over Archy Raystoke as he grasped the position, and he wished that he had never undertaken the task he had in hand.

For it seemed so shocking that the noble-looking lady and gentleman he had seen that day should be in league with a gang of smugglers, and have lent their out-of-the-way house to be a depository for the contraband goods.

"Oh, it's impossible," he said to himself. "They could not. The scoundrels have hidden the things somewhere up in the wood by the house, thinking that nobody would come in there to search."

"The artful rascal!" said Archy to himself, feeling better now that he had put this interpretation upon the proceedings; and, knowing his way better now, and thinking of the dog the while, he hurried on, and had nearly reached the house, meaning to hide somewhere among the abundant shrubs which surrounded it till the smugglers had passed, when all doubt as to the party being those he was tracking was chased away by his hearing a voice just before him say,—

"All right, father. Here they come."

Archy stopped short, as he felt his position. The farmer and his son had come up here, and were waiting for the men to act as carriers.

"What shall I do?" he asked himself, for he was between two parties, and a step might mean discovery. In fact, if the last speaker had taken a step forward, he must have detected the spy's presence.

There was no time for thought Archy stood for a moment or two as if paralysed; then, as he heard the farmer's gruff voice, he dropped down, and began to crawl among the bushes.

"Been a long time coming; here, go in and get the lanthorns now."

At that moment Archy was brought up by a wall, over which he passed his hands, to find that he was directly after touching iron bars close to the ground.

It was some building, and then, as he crouched there, he was conscious of a peculiar odour, which told him not only that this was a cellar, but one in which brandy was stored.

Again he felt a strange sensation of misery. He had accidentally hit upon the place where the cargo had been hidden, and it must be in the cellar of the Hoze, and not in the wood.

He wished he had not made the discovery now, and felt ready to retreat, for it would be horrible to have to tell the lieutenant, giving him such information as would lead to the arrest of the tall, careworn man who had impressed him so strangely that day.

All at once he was conscious of a gleam of light, following a faint noise, and right before him he saw the fluttering blue flame of a brimstone match, which blue began to turn yellow and illumine the face of the boy who had been a prisoner, and two great stacks of kegs and bales, reaching nearly from floor to ceiling of a low vault.

The light shone out through the grated window, by which he was on hands and knees, and feeling that he would be at once recognised if his face was seen, he crept on under the wall a few yards, and lay flat listening, as he wished that there was time for him to get down to the cliff, and signal for help, to capture the smugglers and their store.

An impossibility, he knew, for the cargo might be all gone long before he could reach the cutter, even if a boat were waiting; beside which, he felt that he did not want to tell all he had seen, for if he did, what would follow with respect to those he had spoken with that day?

"Now, my lads, in with you," cried a familiar voice. "Load up carefully when you get down to the carts, and we shall get all snug before daylight."

A murmur of acquiescence followed, and they began to tramp very close to where the midshipman lay, expecting every moment to be seen.

He crouched down as low as he could, not daring to raise even his head, and wondering whether the bright hilt of his dirk would show, and he thrust it farther into his breast. Then he wondered whether he could back softly away; but that was impossible, for the light came from behind him, through the grated window, while escape forward was impossible, as he was close to a door through which shadowy forms were passing in.

There was nothing for it but to lie still, and trust to his not being seen, when the next minutes were made agreeable by a host of recollections regarding the treatment received by those who betrayed smugglers, of the desperate fights there had been, how many had been killed, and a shudder ran through the lad as he recalled the story of a man who had played the spy, somewhere about the south coast, being thrown from a cliff, and literally smashed.

"They'll see me, I know they'll see me," thought Archy; "but I'm a king's officer, young as I am, and I'll show them that I can fight for my life like a man."

As this thought struck him, his hand went involuntarily to his side to get a good grip of and draw his dirk.

The movement betrayed him, for, before he could quite realise that his dirk was hidden in his breast, he was seized by two great muscular hands, dragged into a standing position, and he could dimly see a face peering into his, as a voice, which he recognised as the farmer's, growled savagely—

"Who's this?"

Before he could struggle or answer, the man went on fiercely—

"Why, you lazy, shuffling, young villain! Sit there and skulk, while the others do the work, would you? Come on!"

Before the midshipman could recover from his surprise, he felt himself run forward by the two hands which had been dropped on his shoulders, thrust through the door, the farmer whispering savagely, "Work, or I'll break your neck;" and giving him a fierce push and a kick, which drove him along a passage, where on his left was the open doorway into the dimly lit cellar.

So great was the impetus given, that but for a desperate effort to keep his feet, and a bound or two, the lad would have gone down upon his face.

As it was, the actual first leap took him level with the door of the cellar, the second right on to a flight of steps beyond in the darkness, and as he stood panting there, he realised the meaning of the old smuggler's mistake; for he had forgotten that he was roughly dressed as a sailor boy, and had a red worsted tasselled cap, well drawn-down over his besmirched face.

As Archy stood there in the darkness, at the foot of the stair which he knew must lead up into the house, he looked back to see a man come out of the cellar, his figure just dimly seen by the light from within and below, and over the man's shoulders were swung a couple of kegs.

Archy held his breath, and felt that in all probability the farmer had contented himself with driving him in to work, for he made no further movement, and the coming out of this man, and another who followed directly, completely reassured him. It was evident, too, that they did not know of his presence, and with his heart beating with hopes of escape, as he more and more understood that he had been taken for one of the boys of the gang, he backed softly up the steps, more and more into the darkness, till further progress was stayed by a door.

Here he stopped, panting, and holding his hand upon his throbbing heart. Then feeling that he would be seen directly if a lanthorn were brought into the passage, he pressed the lock, it yielded, and he stepped softly up on to a stone floor.

Here all was blacker than before, but it was a haven of refuge, and he passed in and softly closed the door behind him, to stand listening.

All was still as death, and he began to ask himself what he should do next. He dared not stay where he was, for if the smugglers were so much at home at the Hoze that they could come like this by night, the farmer or some one else might at any moment come up those steps with a light, and then discovery was certain.

But what to do? A closet—a room—a staircase—an open window leading in another direction to that where the men were busy! If he could find any of these he might be safe, and he was about to try and search for some means of concealment or escape when a cold shudder of superstitious dread ran through him, and he began to recall all he had read of haunted houses, for from somewhere in the darkness in front of him, he heard a low, piteous cry.

Archy was as courageous as most boys of his age, as he was proving by his adventurous acts; but this sound, heard by a lad living in a generation wanting in our modern enlightenment, paralysed him. His blood seemed to run cold, his lips parted, his throat felt dry, and a peculiar shiver ran over his skin, accompanied by a sensation as if tiny fingers, cold as ice, were parting and turning his hair.

Again the sigh came, to be followed by a cold current of air, which swept across the boy's face, and then there was a low rustling sound, which hovered in front of him, and went up and up and up, and then slowly died away.

Archy's first impulse, as he recovered himself a little in the silence which followed, was to turn, open the door, and flee. But he hesitated. It would be right into the hands of the enemy. Besides, the terribly chilling sounds he had heard had ceased, and he felt less cowardly.

"Perhaps," he said to himself, "it was fancy, or nothing to be afraid of."

A heavy step on the other side of the door alarmed him more, and stretching out his hands, he stepped forward, went cautiously on and on, and at the end of a few yards touched what felt like panelling. The next moment he realised that he had reached a door, which was yielding, and he passed into a room, to scent the cool night air, and hear subdued sounds without and below.

He was in a room over the cellar, he was sure, and the window was wide open. He crept to it, guided by the cold air which came in, and had just reached it when he heard rapid footsteps, and some one panted,—

"Where's the skipper?"

"Here. What is it?" whispered Shackle, who seemed close to where the midshipman stood.

"Jemmy Dadd—came from the cove. Boat's crew landed."

"Run down and tell them all to come back," said Shackle hoarsely.

"I did, and they're coming. I met first man."

"Right! Get all back in quick!"

As he finished speaking, Archy could hear the dull, soft steps of laden men returning, and more and more kept coming, and it was soon evident that they were quickly and silently replacing the kegs they had been carrying down hill to where tumbrils were waiting for a load.

The midshipman stood a little way back from the window, seeing nothing, but drinking all this in, and in imagination grasping the whole scene which went on for the next quarter of an hour or so, by which time the last load seemed to have been brought back.

As he listened, he wondered what boat's crew it could be that had landed, as no arrangement had been made for any help to be sent till he either signalled from the cliff or went down to the cove at twelve the next day, where a boat would be about half a mile out, with two men in her fishing.

He could not understand it; all he could tell for certain was that the smugglers had been alarmed, and that they would not remove the cargo that night, for all at once he heard the sharp snap of a great lock beneath his feet; this was followed by the closing of a door, and directly after there was the shuffling of feet, and Shackle's voice was heard in a hoarse whisper,—

"Got the lanthorn, boy?"

"Yes, father."

"Off you go then—all. Scatter!"

"You won't try again to-night?"

"Try? No," said the farmer savagely. "Wish I had some of them here!"

There were retiring steps then, and Archy leaned forward towards the window, to utter a faint cry of pain, for his head had come in contact with something, and as he put up his hand he found that the window was protected by thick iron bars.

He stood listening till not a sound could be heard, and then he drew back from the window, thinking about his next course, gazing out into the darkness the while, and wishing he could have stepped out, leaped down, and fled at once.

"Made our plans badly," he thought to himself. "I can't signal even if I could find my way to the cliff, and I ought to be able to get back here at once to seize all this store, and—"

More unpleasant thoughts came back now about how hard it seemed to have to betray these people.

"Can't help it," he said to himself. "I am a king's officer, and I've got to do my duty."

Then to keep these thoughts from troubling him, he began to think again about the cutter.

They never expected that he would get valuable information so soon. He had been wonderfully fortunate, but what was to be his next course? Certainly to get back to the ship as soon as possible, but that was not possible till morning, and he was miles away from the cove.

What should he do? Two hours would be plenty for the work, and as he guessed it was not much past twelve now. How was he to pass all those weary hours? If he could find some barn or even a haystack he would not have cared, but it seemed to him that he would have to pass the remainder of the night in walking, and watching so that he did not encounter any of the smuggler gang on his way back and so raise their suspicions.

Better be off at once. Perhaps, after all, he thought as by an inspiration, the lieutenant had altered his plans, and was sending men to look after and protect him.

"Let's see," said Archy to himself. "I must go out of this door, and keep turning a little to the right till I feel the door at the top of the stairs."

Suppose any one should hear him, take him for a thief, and fire at him?

Suppose that door at the end of the passage had been locked by the smugglers?

It seemed so probable, that a nervous feeling attacked the lad. He would be a prisoner, and discovered by the inmates in the morning.

He would soon put that to the proof, he told himself; and he was about to step cautiously back toward the door when another thought sent a shudder through him.

Suppose as soon as he got into the hall, or whatever place it was, he should hear that sigh again and the rustling sound?

He shrank back as he recalled how it had affected him.

"Oh, what a coward I am!" he said softly; and he took a step forward, where very faintly, as if far distant, he heard the rustling sound again. It came nearer and nearer, then there was a low sigh, the door was pushed open, for the rustling came quite plainly now, accompanied by a faint breathing.

The door closed with a soft dull sound as Archy stood as if turned into stone, his hair again feeling as if moved by hands, and he would have spoken, but no words would come.

At last, as he stood there in front of the window, terrified too much to stir, he suddenly heard a faint sound as of catching breath, and a voice said in a hurried, frightened whisper,—

"Who's there? Is that you, Ram?"

Archy tried to speak but could not. Before he could draw a breath of relief, feeling as he did that this was nothing of which he need feel such fear, the voice said again,—

"You are trying to frighten me. I can see you plainly there by the window. How dare you come in here like this, sir? Go back home with your horrid men."

Chapter Twelve

"You are making a mistake," said Archy softly.

"Oh!"

There was a cry and a quick rustling toward the door.

"Don't—don't cry out; I did not come to frighten you."

"Who are you?"

"I am from the cutter lying off the coast. You saw me and spoke to me to-day when the dog came at me."

There was a low wailing sound which troubled the midshipman, and he said quickly,—

"Can you not believe me? I did not come to frighten you; you frightened me."

"Then, why are you here? How dare you break into our house. Oh, I know! I know!"

"Don't cry," he said. "I was obliged to come. It was by accident I came into this room. I was trying to find out about the smugglers."

"And—and—you have not found out anything?" came in quick, frightened tones.

Archy was silent.

"Why don't you speak, sir?"

"What am I to say? I am on duty. Yes, I have found out all I wanted to know."

"Ah!" came again out of the darkness, in a low wailing tone.

"I wish you would believe me, that I am in as great trouble about it as you are."

"But your men. They are close here, then, and they frightened these people away."

"I suppose so. I don't know," said Archy.

"Don't they know that you are here?"

"No."

"But you will go and tell all you have found out?"

"Yes," said Archy, slowly as he strained his eyes to try and make out the speaker.

"That my father, Sir Risdon Graeme, has smuggled goods here?"

"What else can I do?" replied Archy sadly.

There was a sound of breath being drawn sharply through the teeth, and then the voice seemed changed as the next words came,—

"Do you know what this means?"

Archy was silent.

"They will put him in prison, and—and—"

There was a low burst of sobbing, and the young midshipman felt his own breast swell.

Suddenly the sobbing ceased, and the girl said slowly,—

"You shall not tell. It is not my father's doing. He could not help it. He hates the smugglers. You shall not tell. Pray, pray, say you will not!"

Archy was silent.

"Do you not hear me?" came in imperious tones.

"Yes, I hear you," he replied; "but it is my duty, and—"

"Yes—yes—speak!"

"I must."

"Oh!"

The interjection came as if it were the outcome of sudden passion. There was a quick, rustling sound, and before the boy could realise what was to come, the door was closed, the lock shot into its socket, and he heard the grinding sound of bolts, top and bottom.

Then, as Archy stood in the dark, literally aghast with astonishment, he heard the faint rustling once more, and again all was silent.

"Well!" he exclaimed; "and I felt sorry for her as one might for one's sister at home, and hung back from getting her people into trouble. Of all the fierce little tartars! Oh, it's beyond anything! Why, she has locked me up!"

He laughed, but it was a curious kind of laugh, full of vexation, injured *amour propre*, as the French call our love of our own dignity, of which Archibald Raystoke, in the full flush of his young belief in his importance as a British officer, had a pretty good stock.

"I never did!" he exclaimed, after standing listening for a few minutes to see if the girl would repent and return. "It all comes of dressing up in this stupid way, like a rough fisher-lad. If I had been in uniform, she would not have dared."

Cold water came on this idea directly, as he recalled the fact that the darkness was intense, and Celia could not have seen him.

"And I meant to save them from trouble if I could, out of respect for them all, and did not believe that such people could stoop to be mixed up with rogues and smugglers. But, all right! I've got my duty to do, and I'll do it. I'll soon show them that I am not going to be played with. Looked such a nice, lady-like girl, and all the time she's a female smuggler, and must have been sitting up to let them in, and lock up after the rascals had done."

Rather hard measure, by the way, to deal out to the anxious girl, who could not rest while Shackle's gang were busy about the place, and had come stealthily down to open the little corner room window, and watch from time to time until they had gone.

"Well," said Archy, as there was no further sound heard, "I'm not going to put up with this. I'll soon rattle some one up;" and he went sharply to the door, felt for the handle, tried it, and was about to shake it and bang at the panels, when discretion got the better of valour.

For it suddenly occurred to him that he was not only a prisoner, but a prisoner in the power of a very reckless set of people, who would stop at nothing. They had a valuable cargo hidden in the cellar beneath where he stood, and themselves to save, and naturally they would not hesitate to deal hardly with him, when quite a young, apparently gentle girl treated him as she had done.

"No," he thought to himself, "I don't believe they would kill me, but they would knock me about."

On the whole, he decided that it would not be pleasant to be knocked about. The kick he had received was a foretaste of what he might expect, and after a little consideration he came to the conclusion that his duty was to escape, and get back to the cutter as quickly as he could.

To do this he must scheme, lie hid till morning, then make for the nearest point, and signal for help, unless a boat's crew were already searching for him.

How to escape?

The door was, he well knew, fast. The window was barred, but he went to it, and tried the bars one by one, to find them all solidly fitted into the stone sill.

Perhaps there was another way out, and to prove that he went softly round to feel the oak panelling which covered the walls, to come upon a door directly. His hopes began to rise, but they fell directly, for he found it was a closet.

Next moment, as he felt his way about, his hand touched an old-fashioned marble mantelpiece.

Fireplace—chimney! Yes, if other ways failed, he could escape up the chimney.

No, that was too bad. He could not do that. And if he did, it would only be to reach the roof of the house, and perhaps find no way down.

He went on, and found a closet to match the first on the other side of the fireplace. Then all round the room. Panels everywhere, but no means of escape, and he went again to stand at the window, to bemoan his stupidity for allowing a weak girl to make a prisoner of him in so absurd a way.

Sympathy and pity for the dwellers in the Hoze were completely gone now, and he set his teeth fast, and mentally called himself a weak idiot for ever thinking about such people. For the first few minutes he had felt something uncommonly like alarm, and had dwelt upon the consequences to himself if the smugglers found the spy upon their proceedings; but that dread had passed away in the idea that he had to do his duty, and before he could do that he must escape.

A chair or two. Then an easy-chair. A narrow table against the wall in two places. An awkwardly-shaped high-backed chair with elbows and cushions. A thick carpet in the centre. Nothing else in the room, as far as he could make out in the darkness, and if those wretched bars had only been away, how soon he could have escaped!

He went and tried to force his head through, recalling as he did that where a person's head would go the rest of the body would pass. But there was no chance for his body there, the head would not go first.

He returned, after listening intently, unable to hear a sound, and put his ear to the key-hole of the door to listen there; but all was still, and the faint hope that the girl might be near and open to an appeal for his liberty died away.

Again he felt all about the room, to satisfy himself afresh that there was no way out, and he paused by the chimney, half disposed to essay that means of escape, but he shook his head.

"A fellow who was shut up in prison for life might do it," he said, "but not in a case like this."

Then, utterly wearied out, with his long and arduous twenty-four hours' task, beginning with his watch on the cutter's deck, he felt his way to the big chair opposite to the window to rest his legs, and try and think out some plan.

"Nobody can think well when he's tired," he said; and he began to run over in his mind the whole of the incidents since he landed a few hours earlier.

Chapter Thirteen

"Sure you've looked round everywhere, boy?"

"Yes, father, quite."

"Nothing left nowhere? Sure none of the lads chucked anything aside the path when they ran up?"

"Yes, father. I looked well both sides."

"Humph! Worse lads than you if you knew where to find 'em."

"Thank ye, father."

"I'm going home to breakfast."

"Shall I come too, father?"

"No. Stop here till Sir Risdon comes down, and tell him I'm very sorry; that we should have cleared out last night, only a born fool saw Jerry Nandy's lobster-boat coming into the cove, and came running to say it was a party from the cutter."

"Yes, father."

"Tell him not to be uneasy; 'tis all right, and I'll have everything clear away to-night."

The dull sound of departing steps, and a low whistling sound coming down through the skylight window into the cabin where Archy Raystoke lay with his heavy eyelids pressed down by sleep.

"What a queer dream!" he thought to himself. "No; it couldn't be a dream. He must be awake. But how queer for Mr Gurr to be talking like that to Andrew Teal, the boy who helped the cook! And why did Andy call Mr Gurr father?"

There was an interval of thinking over this knotty question, during which the low whistling went on.

"If Mr Brough goes on deck and catches that boy whistling, there'll be someone to pay and no pitch hot," thought Archy nautically. "But what did Mr Gurr mean about going home to breakfast? And I'm hungry too. Time I was up, I suppose."

He gave himself a twist, and was about to turn out of his sleeping place, and then opened his eyes widely, and stared about him, too much overcome still by his heavy sleep to quite comprehend why it was that he was in a gloomy, oak-panelled, poorly furnished room, staring at an iron-barred open window.

No: he was not dreaming, for he was looking out on the sea, over which a faint mist hung like wreaths of smoke. It was just before sunrise too, for there were flecks of orange high up in the sky.

What did it mean?

The answer came like a flash. He recollected it all now, even to his sitting down in the chair, wearied out.

He had been fast asleep, and those words had awakened him.

What did they say?—false alarm—tell Sir Risdon they would clear all away to-night—see if anything had been left about—lobster-boat!

Then no boat had come from the cutter last night, and the lieutenant would wait for him to signal, and here he was a prisoner, with the information—locked up—the very news the lieutenant would give anything to know.

He jumped up from the chair feeling horribly stiff, and looked steadily round for a way to escape before it was too late. Once out of that room he could ran, and by daylight the smugglers dare not hunt him down.

"Oh, those bars!" he mentally exclaimed, and he was advancing toward them, when just as he drew near, there was a rustling noise under the window, a couple of hands seized the bars, there was a scratching of boot-toes against stone work, and Ram's face appeared to gaze into the room by intention, but into the astonished countenance of the young midshipman instead.

Ram was the first to recover from his surprise.

"Hullo!" he said, "who are you? I was wondering why that window was open."

"Here, quick! Go round and open the door. I was shut in last night by mistake."

"Oh!" said Ram looking puzzled. "I saw you last night, and wondered whose boy you was. It was you father kicked for shirking, and—My!—well: I hardly knowed you."

"Nonsense! Come round and open the door. I've been shut in all night."

"Won't do," said Ram grinning. "Think I don't know you, Mr Orficer? Where's your fine clothes and your sword? Here, what made you dress up like that?"

"You're mistaken," said Archy gruffly, as he made a feeble struggle to keep up the character he had assumed.

"Won't do," said Ram quickly. "I know you. Been playing the spy, that's what you've been doing. Who locked you in?"

"Will you come round and open the door?" said Archy in an angry whisper.

"Oh, of course," replied the boy grinning; and he dropped down, rushed through the bushes, and disappeared from view.

Archy stepped back to the door listening, but there was not a sound.

"He has gone to give the alarm," thought the prisoner, and he looked excitedly round for a way of escape.

Nothing but the chimney presented itself. The door was too strong to attack, and he remembered the three fastenings.

Should he try the chimney?

And be stuck there, and dragged out like a rabbit by the hind legs from his hole!

"No; I've degraded myself enough," he said angrily, "and there are sure to be bars across. Hah!"

A happy inspiration had come, and placing one hand upon his breast, he thrust in the other, gave a tug, and drew out his little curved dirk, glanced at the edge, ran to the window and began to cut at one of the bars.

Labour in vain. He divided the paint, and produced a few squeaks and grating sounds, as he realised that the attempt was madness.

Turning sharply, he looked about the room; then, after glancing ruefully at the bright little weapon, halfway up the blade of a rich deep blue, in which was figured a pattern in gold, he yielded to necessity, and began to chop at the top bar of the grate, so as to nick the edges of his weapon and make it saw-like.

The result was not very satisfactory, but sufficiently so to make him essay the bar of the window once more, producing a grating, ear-assailing sound, as he found that now he did make a little impression,—so little though, that the probability was, if he kept on working well for twenty-four hours, he would not get through.

But at the end of five minutes he stopped, and thrust back the dirk into its sheath.

He fancied he had heard steps outside the room door, and he ran to it and listened, in the faint hope that the boy might have come to open it and set him free.

It was a very faint hope, and one he felt not likely to be realised, and he returned once more to the window, with the intention of resuming his task, when he heard the bushes pressed aside by some one coming, and directly after the bars were seized as before. Ram sprang up, found a resting-place for his toes, and looked in, grinning at him.

"Hullo!" he cried, in a whisper, as if he did not wish to be heard; "here you are still."

"Yes. Come round and open the door."

"What'll yer give me?"

"Anything I can," cried Archy eagerly.

"Well, you give me that little sword o' your'n."

"No; I can't part with that."

"Ha! Ha! Ha!" laughed the boy jeeringly.

"But I'll—yes, I'll give you a guinea, if you will let me out."

"Guinea?" said the boy. "Think I'd do it for a guinea?"

"Well, then, two. Be quick, there's a good fellow. I want to get away at once."

"Not you," said the boy jeeringly. "It would be a pity. I say, do you know what you look like?"

"A fisher-boy."

"Not you. Only a sham. Why, your clothes don't fit you, and your cap's put on all skew-rew. Don't look a bit like a fisher-lad, and never will."

"Never mind about that; let me out of this place."

"What for?" cried Ram.

"Because I want my liberty."

"Not you. Looks comf'table enough as you are. I say, do you know what you are like now?"

"I told you, a fisher-boy!" cried Archy impatiently, but trying not to offend his visitor, who possessed the power of conferring freedom, by speaking sharply.

"Not you. Look like a wild beast in a cage. Like a monkey."

"You insolent—"

Archy checked himself, and the boy laughed.

"It was your turn yesterday, it's mine to-day. What a game! You laughed and fleered at me when I was on the cutter's deck. I can laugh and fleer at you now. I say, you do look a rum 'un. Just like a big monkey in a show."

"Look here, sir!" said Archy, losing his temper. "Gentlemen don't fight with low, common fellows like you, but if you do not come round and let me out, next time we meet I'll have a bit of rope's-end ready for you."

Ram showed his white teeth, as he burst out with a long, low fit of laughter.

"You rope's-end me!" he said. "Why, I could tie you up in a knot, and heave you off the cliff any day. What a game! Bit of a middy, fed on salt tack and weevilly biscuit, talk of giving me rope's-end! Dressed up with a dirty face and a bit o' canvas! Go back aboard, and put on your uniform. Ha! Ha! Ha!"

"Once more; will you come and let me out?"

"No. I'm going to keep you here till the gentlefolks get up, and then I'll bring 'em round to see the monkey in his cage, just like they do in the shows, when you pay a penny. See you for nothing, middy. I say, where's your sword? Why don't you draw it, and come out and fight? I'll fight you with a stick."

"You insolent young scoundrel!" cried Archy, darting his hand through between the bars, overcome now by his rage, and catching Ram by the collar.

To his astonishment the boy did not flinch, but thrust his own arms through, placing them about the middy's waist, clenching his hands behind, and uttering a sharp whistle.

It was a trap, and the midshipman understood it now. The boy had been baiting him to rouse him to attack, and he was doubly a prisoner now, held fast against the bars, so that he could not even wrench round his head as he heard the door behind him opened, while as he opened his mouth to cry for help, a great rough hand was placed over his eyes, pressing his head back, a handkerchief was jammed between his teeth, and as he heard a deep growling voice say, "Hold him tight!" a rope was drawn about his chest, pinioning his arms to his sides, and another secured his ankles.

"Now a handkerchief," said the gruff voice. "Fold it wide. Be ready!"

The midshipman gave his head a jerk, but the effort was vain, for the hand over his eyes gave place to a broad handkerchief, which was tightly tied behind, and then a fierce voice whispered in his ear,—

"Keep still, or you'll get your weasand slit. D'ye hear?"

But in spite of the threat the lad, frenzied now by rage and excitement, struggled so hard that a fresh rope was wound round him, and he was lifted up by two men, and carried away.

By this time there was a strange singing in his ears, a feeling as if the blood was flooding his eyes, a peculiar, hot, suffocating feeling in his breast, and then he seemed to go off into a painful, feverish sleep, for he knew no more.

Chapter Fourteen

Angry, but trembling with dread, Celia had hurried up to her own room, to try and think what was best to be done. She had secured the door of the room below to gain time, feeling as she did that, as the young midshipman knew of the storing of the smuggled goods, he would, the moment he was free, go back to the cutter, bring help, there would perhaps be a desperate fight, with men killed, and her father would be dragged away to prison.

Her first thought was to go to her father, but she shrank from doing this as her mother would probably be asleep, and in her delicate state the alarm might seriously affect her.

Having grown learned in the ways of the smugglers, from their having on several occasions made use of the great vault without asking permission—at times when Sir Risdon was away from home—Celia had sat up to watch that night to see if the men would fetch away the kegs and bales; hence her presence during the scene, and when she had awakened to the fact that the midshipman had played spy and was ready to denounce her father, she felt that all was over.

Three times over, after listening at the head of the stairs for sounds from below where her prisoner was confined, Celia had crept on tiptoe to her father's door, only to shrink away again not daring to speak.

For what would he say to her? She thought. She had no right to be downstairs watching the acts of the smugglers, and she dreaded to make a confession of her knowledge of these nocturnal proceedings.

At last, bewildered, anxious, and worn-out, she knelt down by her bed, to consider with her head in her hands, ready for kindly nature to bring her comfort, for when she started up again the sun was streaming brightly in at her window.

She pressed her hands to her temples, and tried to think about the business of the past night, and by degrees she collected her thoughts, and recalled that the smugglers had come to take up their kegs and bales from the temporary store to carry them further inland, that she had discovered the young midshipman watching, and to save her father she had shut their enemy in the lower corner room.

Celia stood with her cheeks burning, trembling and anxious, and after bathing her face and arranging her hair, she went out into the broad passage and listened at her father's door.

It was too soon for him to be stirring yet, and determining at last to go and declare his innocency, and make an appeal to the frank-looking lad, she crept timidly down the grand old flight of stairs, trying to think out what she would say.

There were two flights to descend, and the first took a long time; but she worked out a nice little speech, in which she would tell the cutter's officer that her father had once been rich, but he had espoused the young Pretender's cause, and the result had been that he had become so impoverished that there had been a time when they had had hardly enough to keep them and the old maid-servant who still clung to their fallen fortunes.

By the time she was at the bottom of the second flight she was ready and quite hopeful, and, with the tears standing in her eyes, she felt sure that the frank, gentlemanly lad would be merciful, forgive her, and save her father from a terrible disgrace.

She had, then, her speech all ready, but when she spoke everything was condensed in the one exclamation—

"Oh!"

For as she reached the hall where her coming and going had so startled the midshipman in the darkness, she found that the door was wide open and the window shut.

She looked about bewildered, but there was no sign of the room having been occupied.

"Did I dream it all?" she said in an awe-stricken whisper. "No: the men came to take away the brandy and silk, and I saw them here."

She pressed her hands to her temples, for the surprise had confused her, and in addition her head ached and throbbed.

"Could I have dreamed it?" she asked herself again. "No, I remember the men coming to fetch away the things and then I found him watching."

She stood gazing before her, with her puzzled feeling increasing, till a thought struck her.

She saw the men come to fetch the kegs. If she really did see that, the kegs would be gone.

The proof was easy. If the brandy and silk were gone, the door of the vault would be open. If the things were not fetched away, it would be locked up; and if she tapped on the door with her knuckles, there would be a dull sound instead of a hollow, echoing noise.

She ran quickly down, and the door was locked.

She tapped with her knuckles, and the sound indicated that the place was full, for all was dull and heavy and no reverberation in the place.

"I must have dreamed it all," she cried joyously. "I have thought so much about it that I have fancied all this, and made myself ill. Why, of course he could not have got in there to watch or the men would have seen him come."

It is very easy to place faith in that which you wish to believe.

Chapter Fifteen

Lieutenant brough was out for a long walk. That is to say, he had his glass tucked under his arm, and was trotting up and down his cleanly holystoned deck, pausing from time to time to raise his glass to his eye, and watch the top of the cliff, ending by gazing in the direction of the cove.

The men said he had been putting them through their facings that morning, and he had been finding more fault in two hours than in the previous week, for he was getting fidgety. He had not enjoyed his breakfast, and it was getting on toward the time for his mid-day meal.

Suddenly he stopped short by the master, who had also been using a glass, and was evidently waiting to be spoken to.

"Seemed in good spirits last night, Mr Gurr, eh?"

"Mr Raystoke, sir? Oh yes."

"I mean liked his job?"

"Yes, sir; determined on it."

"Humph! Time we had some news of him, eh?"

"Yes, sir; but he may turn up on the cliff at any moment."

"Yes. Men quite ready?"

"Yes, sir."

"That's right. Of course, well-armed?"

"Yes, sir; you did tell me. Soon as the signal comes, we shall push off. Awkward bit o' country, sir; six miles' row before you can find a place to land."

"Very awkward, but they have to find a place to land their spirits, Mr Gurr, and if we don't soon have something to show we shall be called to account."

"Very unlucky, sir. Seems to me like going eel-fishing with your bare hand."

"Worse. You might catch one by accident."

"So shall we yet, sir. These fellows are very cunning, but we shall be too many for them one of these days."

"Dear me! Dear me!" said the little lieutenant after a few more turns up and down. "I don't like this at all I don't think I ought to have let a boy like that go alone. You don't think, Mr Gurr, that they would dare to injure him if he was so unlucky as to be caught?"

"Well, sir," said the master, hesitating, "smugglers are smugglers."

"Mr Gurr," said the little lieutenant, raising himself up on his toes, so as to be as high as possible, "will you have the goodness to talk sense?"

"Certainly, sir."

"Smugglers are smugglers, indeed. What did you suppose I thought they were? Oysters?"

"Beg pardon, sir; didn't mean any harm."

"Getting very late!" said the little officer after another sweep of the top of the cliff, especially above where the French lugger landed the goods. "I shall be obliged to send you on shore, Mr Gurr. You must go and find him. I'm getting very anxious about Mr Raystoke."

"Start at once, sir?"

"No, wait another half-hour. Very ill-advised thing to do. I cannot think what you were doing, Mr Gurr, to advise me to do such a thing."

"Me, sir?" said the master, looking astonished.

"Yes. A great pity. I ought not to have listened to you; but in my anxiety to leave no stone unturned to capture some of these scoundrels, I was ready to do anything."

"Very true, sir."

"Now, my good fellow, what do you mean by that?"

"It was only an observation, sir."

"Then I must request that you will not make it again. 'Very true?' Of course, what I say is very true. Do you think I should say a thing that was false?"

"Beg pardon, sir. 'Fraid I picked up some awk'ard expressions aboard the old frigate."

"Awk-ward, Mr Gurr, awkward."

"Yes, sir; of course."

"You do not understand the drift of my remarks."

"'Fraid not, sir," said the master, smiling; "understand drift of the tide much better."

"Mr Gurr!"

"Yes, sir."

"I was trying to teach you to pronounce the king's English correctly, and you turn it off with a ribald remark."

"Beg pardon, sir. 'Nother o' my frigate bad habits."

"It is a great privilege, Mr Gurr, to be one of those who speak the English tongue, so do not abuse it. Say awk-ward in future, not awk'ard."

"Certainly, sir, I'll try," said the master; and then to himself, "Starboard, larboard, for'ard, back'ard, awk'ard. Why, what does he mean?"

By this time the little lieutenant was scanning the cliffs again, and the master took off his hat and wiped his forehead.

"Talk about thistles and stinging nettles," he muttered, "why there's no bearing him to-day, and all on account of a scamp of a middy such as there's a hundred times too many on in the R'yal Navy. Dunno though; bit cocky and nose in air when he's in full uniform, and don't know which is head and which is his heels, but he aren't such a very bad sort o' boy. Well, what's the matter with you?"

Dirty Dick screwed up his mouth as if to speak, but only stared.

"Don't turn yourself into a figurehead of an old wreck sir. What do you want?"

"Leave to go ashore, sir."

"Well, you're going soon as the skipper orders."

"I mean all alone by myself, sir."

"What for? There aren't a public-house for ten miles."

"Didn't mean that."

"Then what did you mean? Speak out, and don't do the double shuffle all over my clean deck."

"No, sir."

"Hopping about like a cat on hot bricks. Now, then, why do you want to go ashore?"

"Try and find Mr Raystoke, sir. Beginning to feel scarred about him."

"What's that?" said the lieutenant, who had come back from abaft unheard. "Scared about whom?"

"Beg pardon, didn't mean nowt, sir," said the sailor touching his forelock.

"Yes, you did, sir. Now look here," cried the lieutenant, shaking his glass at the man, "don't you try to deceive me. You meant that you were getting uneasy about Mr Raystoke's prolonged absence."

"Yes sir, that's it," said Dick eagerly.

"Then how dare you have the effrontery to tell me that you did not mean 'nowt' as you have the confounded north country insolence to call it? For two pins, sir,—women's pins, sir, not belaying pins,—I'd have you put ashore, with orders not to show your dirty face again till you had found Mr Raystoke."

Dirty Dick passed his hand over his face carefully, and then looked at the palm to see if any of the swarthy tan had come off.

"Do you hear me, sir?" cried the lieutenant.

"Yes, sir," said the man humbly. "Shall I go at once sir?"

"No. Wait. Keep a sharp look-out on the cliff to see if Mr Raystoke is making signals for a boat. I daresay he has been there all the time, only you took up my attention with your chatter."

He swung round, walked aft and began sweeping the shore again with his glass, while the master and Dick exchanged glances which meant a great deal.

"He is in a wax," said Dick to himself, as he walked to the side, and stood shading his eyes with his hands, looking carefully for the signals which did not come.

Two hours more passed away, during which it was a dead calm, and the sun beat down so hotly that the seams began to send out little black beads of pitch, and drops formed under some of the ropes ready to come off on the first hand which touched them.

At last the little lieutenant could bear the anxiety no longer.

"Pipe away the men to that boat there," he said; and as the crew sprang in. "Now, Mr Gurr," he said, "I'm only going to say one thing to you in the way of instructions."

"Yes, sir."

"Will you have the goodness to wait till I have done speaking, Mr Gurr, and not compel me to say all I wish over again?"

"Beg pardon, sir," said the master deprecatingly.

"I say, sir, I have only one order to give you. Get ashore as soon as you can, and find and bring back Mr Raystoke."

"Yes, sir," cried the master, and he walked over the side, glad to get into the boat and push off, muttering the while, "and I always thought him such a quiet, amiable little chap. He's a Tartar; that's what he is. Making all this fuss about a boy who, as like as not, is having a game with us. Don't see me getting out o' temper with everybody, and spitting and swearing like a mad Tom-cat. Hang the boy! He's on'y a middy.—Now, my lads,—now, my lads, put your backs into it, will you?"

The boat was already surging through the water faster than it had ever gone before, but the men bent lower and the longer, and the blades of the oars made the water flash and foam as they dipped and rose with the greatest of regularity.

For the lieutenant's anxiety about the young officer of the *White Hawk* was growing more and more contagious, and the men gave a cheer as they span the boat along, every smart sailor on board thinking about the frank, straightforward lad who had so bravely gone on the risky expedition.

"Look ye here, Jemmy," said one of the men to his nearest mate, "talk about 'tacking the enemy, if wrong's happened to our young gentleman, all I can say is, as I hopes it's orders to land every night to burn willages and sack everything we can."

"And so says all of us," came in a chorus from the rest of the crew.

"Steady! My lads, steady!" cried the master—"keep stroke;" and then he began to make plans as to his first proceedings on getting ashore.

He wasn't long in making these plans, and when the cove was reached, the two fishing luggers and another boat or two lying there were carefully overhauled, Gurr gazing at the men on board like a fierce dog, and literally worrying the different fishermen as cleverly as a cross-examining counsel would a witness ashore.

Chapter Sixteen

Always the same answer.

No, they hadn't seen no sailor lad in a red cap, only their own boys, and they were all at home. Had he lost one?

Yes; a boy had come ashore and not returned.

The different men questioned chuckled, and one oracular-looking old fellow spat, wiped his lips on the back of his hand, stared out to sea, and said gruffly, —

"Runned away."

"Ay," said another, "that's it. You won't see him again."

"Won't I?" muttered Gurr between his teeth. "I'll let some of you see about that, my fine fellows."

He led his men on, stopping at each cluster of cottages and shabby little farm to ask suspiciously, as if he felt certain the person he questioned was hiding the truth.

But he always came out again to his men with an anxious look in his eyes, and generally ranged up alongside of Dick.

"No, my lad," he would say, "they haven't seen 'im there;" and then with his head bent down, but his eyes eagerly searching the road from side to side, he went on towards Shackle's farm.

"Say, Mester Gurr," said Dick, after one of these searches, "he wouldn't run away?"

"What! Mr Raystoke, sir? Don't be a fool."

"No, sir," replied Dick humbly, and the men tramped on with a couple of open-mouthed, barefooted boys following them to stare at their cutlasses and pistols.

"Say, Mester Gurr," ventured Dick, after a pause, "none of 'em wouldn't ha' done that, would they?"

Dick had followed the master's look, as he shaded his eyes and stared over the green slope which led up to the cliffs.

"What?"

"Chucked him off yonder."

Gurr glanced round to see if the men were looking, and then said rather huskily but kindly, —

"In ord'nary, Dick, my lad, no; but when smugglers finds themselves up in corners where they can't get away, they turns and fights like rats, and when they fights they bites."

"Ah!" ejaculated Dick sadly.

"You're only a common sailor, Dick, and I'm your officer, but though I speak sharp unto you, I respect you, Dick, for you like that lad."

"Say, Mester Gurr, sir, which thankful I am to you for speaking so; but you don't really think as he has come to harm?"

"I hope not, Dick; I hope not; but smugglers don't stand at anything sometimes."

Dick sighed, and then all at once he spat in his fist, rubbed his hands together and clenched them, a hard, fierce aspect coming into his rough dark face, which seemed to promise severe retaliation if anything had happened to the young officer.

There was nowhere else to search as far as Gurr could see, save the little farm in the hollow, and the black-looking stone house up on the hill among the trees.

Gurr, who looked wonderfully bull-dog like in aspect, made straight for the farm, where the first person he encountered was Mrs Shackle, who, innocent enough, poor woman, came to the door to bob a curtsey to the king's men, while Jemmy Dadd, who was slowly loading a tumbril in whose shafts was the sleepy grey horse, stuck his fork down into the heap of manure from the cow-sheds, rested his hands on the top and his chin upon his hands, to stare and grin at the sailors he recognised.

"Morning, marm," said Gurr; "sorry to trouble you, but—"

"Oh, sir," interrupted Mrs Shackle, "surely you are not going to tumble over my house again! I do assure you there's nothing here but what you may see."

"If you'd let me finish, you'd know," said Gurr gruffly. "One of our boys is missing. Seen him up here? Boy 'bout seventeen with a red cap."

"No, sir; indeed I've not."

"Don't know as he has been seen about here, do you?" said Gurr, looking at her searchingly.

"No, sir."

"Haven't heard any one talking about him, eh? Come ashore yesterday."

Mrs Shackle shook her head.

"Thank ye!—No, Dick," continued the master, turning back to where the men were waiting, and unconsciously brushing against the bush behind which the middy had hidden himself, "that woman knows nothing. If she knew evil had come to the poor lad, her face would tell tales like print. Hi! You, sir," he said, going towards where Jemmy stood grinning.

"Mornin'," said Jemmy; "come arter some more milk?"

"No," growled Gurr.

"Don't want to take the cow away agen, do 'ee?"

"Look here, my lad, one of our boys is missing. Came ashore yesterday, lad of seventeen in a red cap."

"Oh!" said Jemmy with a vacant look. "Don't mean him as come with you, do you?"

"I said a lad 'bout seventeen, in a red cap like yours," said Gurr very shortly.

"Aren't seen no lads with no red caps up here," said the man with a vacant look. "Have he runned away?"

"Are you sure you haven't seen him, my lad?" growled Gurr; "because, look here, it may be a serious thing for some of you, if he is not found."

The man shook his head, and stared as if he didn't half understand the drift of what was said.

Gurr turned angrily away, and to find himself facing Dick.

"Well, seen anything suspicious?"

"No, sir," said Dick, "on'y my fingers is a itchin'."

"Scratch them then."

"Nay, you don't understand," grumbled Dick. "I mean to have a turn at that chap, Master Gurr, sir. I feel as if I had him for 'bout quarter hour I could knock something out of him."

"Nonsense! Come along. Now, my lads, forward!"

Jemmy Dadd's countenance changed from its vacant aspect to one full of cunning, as the party from the cutter moved off, but it became dull and semi-idiotic again, for Gurr turned sharply round.

"Here, my lad, where's your master?"

"Eh?"

"I say, where's your master?"

"Aren't in; mebbe he's out in the fields."

Gurr turned away impatiently again, and signing to his men to follow, they all began to tramp up the steep track leading toward the Hoze, with the rabbits scuttling away among the furze, and showing their white cottony tails for a moment as they darted down into their holes.

Dick followed last, shaking his head, and looking very much dissatisfied, or kept on looking back at Jemmy, who stood like a statue, resting his chin upon the shaft of his pitchfork, watching him go away.

"I dunno," muttered Dick, "and a man can't be sure. There was nowt to see and nowt to hear, and of course one couldn't smell it, but seems to me as that ugly-looking fisherman chap knows where our Mr Raystoke is. Yah, I hates half-bred uns! If a man's a labourer, let him be a labourer; and if he's a fisherman, let him be a fisherman. Man can't be two things, and it looks queer."

An argument which did not have much force when self-applied, for Dick suddenly recollected that he was very skilful with the scissors, and knew that he was the regular barber of the crew, and as this came to his mind he took off his cap and gave his head a vicious scratch.

"Never mind the rabbits, lads," cried Gurr angrily; "we want to find Mr Raystoke."

The men closed up together, and mastered their desire to go hunting, to make a change from the salt beef and pork fare, and soon after they came suddenly upon Sir Risdon and his lady, the latter, who looked weak and ill, leaning on her husband's arm.

Gurr saluted, and stated his business, while the baronet, who had turned sallower and more careworn than his lot drew a breath full of relief.

"One of your ship boys?" he said.

"A lad, looking like a common sailor, and wearing a red cap."

"No," said Sir Risdon. "I have seen no one answering to the description here."

"Beg pardon, sir, but can you, as a gentleman, assure me that he is not here?"

"Certainly," said Sir Risdon. "You have seen no one?" he continued, turning to Lady Graeme.

The lady shook her head.

"That's enough, sir; but may I ask you, if you do see or hear anything of such a lad, you will send a messenger off to the cutter?"

"It is hardly right to enlist me in the search for one of your deserters," said Sir Risdon coldly.

"Yes, sir, but he is not a deserter; and the fact is, we are afraid the lad has run alongside o' the smugglers, and come to grief."

"Surely!" cried Sir Risdon excitedly. "No, no,—you must be mistaken. A boyish prank. No one about here would injure a boy."

"Humph!" ejaculated Gurr, looking at the baronet searchingly. "Glad you think so well of 'em, sir. But I suppose you'll grant that the people about here would not be above a bit of smuggling?"

Sir Risdon was silent.

"And would run a cargo of brandy or silk?"

"I suppose there is a good deal of smuggling on the coast," said Sir Risdon coldly, as he thought of his vault.

"Yes sir, there is, and it will go hard with the people who are caught having any dealings with the smugglers."

Lady Graeme looked ghastly.

"What would you say, sir, if I were to order my men, in the king's name, to search your place?"

Sir Risdon dared not trust himself to speak, but darted an agonised glance at his wife.

"However, sir, I'm not on that sort of business now," continued Gurr sternly. "Want to find that boy. Good day. Now, my lads."

The men marched off, and Sir Risdon stood watching them.

"Ah, Risdon," and Lady Graeme, "how could you let yourself be dragged into these dreadful deeds!"

"Don't blame me," he said sadly. "I loathe the whole business, but when I saw my wife and child suffering almost from want of the very necessaries of life, and the temptation came in the shape of presents from that man, I could not resist—I was too weak. I listened to his insidious persuasion, and tried to make myself believe that I was guiltless, as I owned no fealty to King George. But I am justly punished, and never again will I allow myself to be made an accessory to these lawless deeds."

"But tell me," she whispered, "have they any of their goods secreted there now?"

"I do not know."

"You do not know?"

"No. The only way in which I could allow myself to act was to keep myself in complete ignorance of the going and coming of these people. I might suspect, but I would never satisfy myself by watching; and I can say now honestly, I do not know whether they have still goods lying there or have taken them away."

"But Celia—keep it from her."

"Of course."

"And about the missing boy. Surely, Risdon, they would not—"

Lady Graeme did not finish, but gave her husband a piercing look.

"Don't ask me," he said sadly. "Many of the men engaged in the smuggling are desperate wretches, and if they feared betrayal they would not scruple, I'm afraid, to strike down any one in the way of their escape."

Lady Graeme shuddered, and they went together into the house, just as Celia came across the wood at the back, in company with the dog.

Chapter Seventeen

Gurr continued his search till it was quite dark, and then tramped his men back to the cove, where the boat-keeper was summoned, and the boat with her crew, saving Dick, were sent back to the cutter, one of the men bearing a message from Gurr to say that he was going to stay ashore till he had found Mr Raystoke, and asking the lieutenant to send the boat back for him if he did not approve.

It was a very dark row back to the cutter, but her lights shone out clearly over the smooth sea, forming good beacons for the men to follow till the boat was run alongside.

"Got them, Mr Gurr?" came from the deck.

"No sir, and Mr Gurr's stopping at one of the fishermen's cottages ashore to keep on the search."

"Tut, tut!" ejaculated the lieutenant as he turned away and began to pace the deck.

"Beg'n' pardon, sir, Mr Gurr said—"

"Well, well, well, what did Mr Gurr say? Pity he did not do more and not say so much."

"Said as his dooty, sir, and would you send the boat for him if you did not think he'd done right."

"No, sir! His Majesty's boats are wanted for other purposes than running to and fro to fetch him aboard. Let him stay where he is till he finds Mr Raystoke and brings him back aboard."

"Dear, dear," muttered the lieutenant as he walked to and fro. "To think of the boy being missing like this.—Now you, sirs, in with that boat.—Where can he be? Not the lad to go off on any prank.—There, go below and get something to eat, my lads.—All comes of being sent into a miserable little boat like this to hunt smugglers."

"Ahoy!" came from forward.

"What's that?" cried the lieutenant, and an answer came from out of the blackness ahead.

"What boat's that?" shouted the man on the watch. "Mine," came in a low growl. "What is it?"

"Want to see the skipper."

There was a little bustle forward, in the midst of which a boat came up alongside, and the man in it was allowed to come on board.

He was a big, broad-shouldered, heavy fellow, with rough black beard and dark eyes, which glowered at those around as a lanthorn was held up by one of the men. "Where's the skipper?" he growled. "Bring the man aft," cried the lieutenant. "This way."

"All right, mate; I can find my way; I aren't a baby," said the man as he took three or four strides, lifting up his big fisherman's boots, and setting them heavily down upon the deck as if they were something separate from him which he had brought on board.

"Now, my man, brought news of him?" cried the lieutenant eagerly. "Eh?"

And the great fellow seemed to tower over the little commander.

"I say, have you brought news of the boy?"

"What boy?"

"Haven't you come to tell me where he is?"

"Here, what yer talking about?" growled the man. "I aren't come 'bout no boys."

"Then, pray, why have you come?"

"Send them away," said the man in a hoarse whisper.

He jerked his thumb over his shoulder, and the lieutenant was about to give an order but altered his mind, for he suspected the man's mission, not an unusual one in those days.

"Come into my cabin, sir," he said imperiously, and as he turned and strutted off, making the most of his inches, the giant—for such he was by comparison—stumbled after him, making the deck echo to the sound of his great boots.

"Now, sir," said the lieutenant haughtily, "what is your business?"

The man leaned forward, and there was a leer on his bearded face seen by the dull swinging oil-lamp, as, half covering his mouth, he whispered hoarsely behind his hands—

"Like Hollands gin, master?"

"What do you mean, sir?" cried the lieutenant. "Speak out, for I have no time to lose."

"Oh, I'll speak plainly enough," growled the man; "on'y do you like it?"

"Do you mean that a foreign vessel is going to land a quantity of Hollands to-night?"

"Never said nothing o' the sort, Master Orficer. Why, if I was to come and say a thing like that, and folks ashore knowed on it, there'd be a haxiden."

"What do you mean, sir?"

"Some un would run up agin me atop o' the cliff, and I should go over, and there'd be an end o' me."

"You mean to say that if it was known that you informed, you would be in peril of your life?"

"No, I don't mean to say nothing o' the kind, master. I only says to you that there's going to be a drop to be got in a place I knows, and if you care to say to a chap like me—never you mind who he is—show me where this drop of Hollands gin is to be got, and I'll give you—for him, you know—fifty pounds, it would be done."

"Look here, my lad, if you have got any valuable information to give, wouldn't it be better for you to speak out plainly?"

"Didn't come twenty mile in my boat and get here in the dark, for you to teach me how to ketch fish, Master Orficer."

"Twenty miles!" said the lieutenant sharply; "where are you from?"

"Out o' my boat as is made fast 'longside. Is it fifty pound or aren't it?"

"Fifty pound is a great deal of money, my man. Your information may not be worth fifty pence. Suppose the boat does not come?"

"Why, o' course, you wouldn't pay."

"Oh, now I understand you. If we take the boat with the spirits I am to give you fifty pounds?"

"Me? Think I'm goin' to be fool enough to risk gettin' my neck broke for fifty pound? Nay, not me. You'll give it to me to give to him."

"And where is he?"

"Never you mind, master."

"Oh, well, there then; I'll give you the fifty pounds if I take the boat. Dutch?"

"P'raps. Shake hands on it."

"Is that necessary?" said the lieutenant, glancing with distaste at the great outstretched palm.

"Ay, shake hands on it, and you being a gentleman, you'll say, 'pon your honour."

"Oh, very well. There, upon my honour, we'll pay you if we take the boat."

"Oh you'll take her, fast enough," said the man with a hoarse chuckle. "Yah! There's no fight in them. They'll chatter and jabber a bit, and their skipper'll swear he'll do all sorts o' things, but you stick to the boat as soon as your lads are on board."

"Trust me for that," said the lieutenant. "Now, then, when is the cargo to be run?"

"T'night."

"And where?"

"Never you mind wheer. Get up your anchor, and make sail; I'll take the helm."

"What, do you think I am going to let a strange man pilot my vessel?"

"Yah!" growled the man; "shan't you be there, and if I come any games, you've got pistols, aren't you? But just as you like."

"Come on deck," said the lieutenant. "But one minute. I have lost a boy—gone ashore. Have you seen one?"

"Not I; lots o' boys about, soon get another!"

The man went clumping on deck, and stepped over the side into his boat.

"What are you going to do?" said the lieutenant sharply.

"Make her fast astarn."

"Well, you need not have got into her, you could have led her round."

"This here's my way," said the man; and as the order was given to slip the anchor, with a small buoy left to mark its place, the informer secured his boat to one of the ringbolts astern, and then drew close in; and mounted over the bulwark to stand beside the man at the helm.

"What do you propose doing?" said the lieutenant.

"Tellin' o' you what I wants done, and then you tells your lads."

The lieutenant nodded, and in obedience to the suggestion of the man the stay-sail was hoisted; then up went the mainsail and jib, and the little cutter careened over to the soft land breeze as soon as she got a little way out from under the cliffs, which soon became invisible.

"Why, you aren't dowsed your lanthorns," whispered the man. "I'd have them down, and next time you have time just have down all your canvas, and get it tanned brown. Going about with lanthorns and white canvas is showing everybody where you are."

After a time, as they glided on, catching a glimpse of a twinkling light or two on the shore, the man grew a little more communicative, and began to whisper bits of information and advice to the lieutenant.

"Tells me," he said, "that she's choke full o' Hollands gin and lace."

"Indeed!" said the lieutenant eagerly.

"Ay, so that chap says. And there's plenty o' time, but after a bit I'd sarve out pistols and cutlasses to the lads; you won't have to use 'em, but it'll keep those Dutchies from showing fight."

"That will all be done, my man."

"Going to get out four or five mile, master, and then we can head round, and get clear o' the long race and the skerries. After that I shall run in, and we'll creep along under the land. Good deep water for five-and-twenty miles there close under the cliff."

"Then you are making for Clayblack Bay?"

"Ah, you'll see," said the man surlily. "As long as you get to where you can overhaul the boat when she comes in, you won't mind where it is, Mister Orficer. There's no rocks to get on, unless you run ashore, and 'tarn't so dark as you need do that, eh?"

"I can take care of that," said the lieutenant sharply; and the cutter, now well out in the north-east wind then blowing, leaned over, and skimmed rapidly towards the dark sea.

The reef that stretched out from a point, and formed the race where the tide struck against the submerged rocks, and then rushed out at right angles to the shore, had been passed, and the cutter was steered on again through the clear dark night, slowly drawing nearer the dark shore line, till she was well in under the cliffs; with the result that the speed was considerably checked, but she was able to glide along at a short distance from the land, and without doubt invisible to any vessel at sea.

"There," said the great rough fellow, after three hours' sailing; "we're getting pretty close now. Bay opens just beyond that rock."

"Where I'll lie close in, and wait for her," said the lieutenant.

The man laughed softly.

"Thought I—I mean him—was to get fifty pounds, if you took the boat?"

"Yes."

"Well, you must take her. Know what would happen if you went round that point into the bay?"

"Know what would happen?"

"I'll tell yer. Soon as you got round into the bay, some o' them ashore would see yer. Then up would go lights somewhere yonder on the hills, and the boat would go back."

"Of course. I ought to have known better. Wait here then?"

"Well, I should, if I wanted to take her," said the man coldly. "And I should have both my boats ready for my men to jump in, and cut her off as soon as she gets close in to the beach. She'll come on just as the tide's turning, so as to have no fear of being left aground."

"You seem to know a good deal about it, my lad?" said the little lieutenant.

"Good job for you," was the reply, as the sails were lowered, and the cutter lay close in under the cliff waiting. The boats were down, the men armed, and the guns loaded, ready in case the smuggler vessel should attempt to escape.

Then followed a long and patient watch, in the most utter silence; for, in the stillness of such a calm night a voice travels far, and the lieutenant knew that a strange sound would be sufficient to alarm those for whom he was waiting, and send the boat away again to sea. He might overtake her, but would more probably lose her in the darkness, and see her at daybreak perhaps well within reach of a port where he dare not follow.

It was darker now, for clouds had come like a veil over the bright stars, but the night was singularly clear and transparent, as soon after eight bells the informer crept silently up to where the lieutenant was trying to make out the approach of the expected vessel.

The little officer started as the man touched his elbow, so silently had he approached, and on looking down, he dimly made out that the man had divested himself of his heavy boots.

"Do be quiet, master," whispered the great fellow. "Can't 'ford to lose fifty pounds for fear o' getting one's feet cold. See anything?"

"No," whispered the lieutenant, after sweeping his glass round.

"Tide serves, and she can't be long now. But two o' your chaps keep whispering for'ard, and it comes back off the cliff. No, no—don't shout at 'em. We daren't have a sound."

"No," replied the lieutenant; and he went softly forward toward where a group of men were leaning over the bulwarks, peering into the darkness and listening to the tide as it gurgled in and out of the rocks, little more than a hundred yards away.

"Strict silence, my lads, and the moment you get the word, over into your boats and lay ready. Are those rowlocks muffled?"

"Ay, ay, sir!" said the boatswain, who was to be in command of one of the boats.

"No bloodshed, my lads. Knock any man down who resists. Five minutes after you leave the side here ought to make the smuggler ours. Hush! Keep your cheering till you've taken the boat."

A low murmur ran round the side of the cutter, and every eye was strained as the little officer whispered,—

"A crown for the first man who sights her."

After a while, the lieutenant mentally said,—

"I wish Mr Raystoke was here, he and Gurr could go in the other boat. I wonder where the lad can be!"

He went cautiously aft along the starboard side of his vessel, looking hard at the frowning mass of darkness under which they lay, and thinking how dangerous their position would have been had the wind blown from the opposite quarter. But now they were in complete shelter, with the little cutter rising and falling softly on the gentle swell and drifting slowly with the tide, so that the *White Hawk's* head was pointing seaward.

He glanced over the side to see that the boats were in readiness, and then went aft without a sound, till all at once he kicked against something in the darkness beneath the larboard bulwark, to which he had crossed, and nearly fell headlong.

"What's—here? Who was—Oh, it's those confounded boots. Hush, there; silence!"

He said the last words hastily, for the crew made noise enough to startle any one within range, and the sound: were being followed by the hurried whisper of those who came running aft.

"Back to your places, every one," he said; and then the men drew off, becoming invisible almost directly, for the darkness was now intense, the lanthorns carefully hidden below, and once more all was still, and the little office rested his glass on the bulwark and carefully swept the sea.

"Stupid idiot!" he said to himself. "Lucky for him he isn't one of the crew. No, not a sign of anything."

But knowing that seeing was limited enough, he put his hand to his ear and stood leaning over the side, listening for a full ten minutes, before, with an impatient ejaculation, he turned to speak to the informer, who was not aft but probably forward among the men.

He walked forward.

"Where's that man?" he whispered to the first sailor he encountered, who, like the rest, was eagerly watching seaward.

"Went aft, sir."

The little officer went aft, but the fisherman was not there, and he passed back along the starboard side, going right forward among the crew.

"Where is the fisherman?" he said.

"Went aft, sir," came from every one he encountered; and, feeling annoyed at the trouble it gave him, Mr Brough went aft again, to notice now that there was no man at the helm.

He walked forward again.

"Here!" he cried in an angry whisper, "who was at the helm?"

"I, your honour," said a voice.

"Then why are you here, sir?"

"That fisherman chap told me you said I was to go forward, sir, as he'd take a spell now, ready for running her round the head into the bay."

"Where is that man?"

There was no reply, and more quickly than he had moved for months, the lieutenant trotted aft, and looked over the stern for the fisherman's boat.

It was gone.

Chapter Eighteen

Lieutenant brough went into a fit of passion. Not a noisy, sea-going fit of passion, full of loud words, such as are not found in dictionaries, but a rising and falling, swelling and collapsing, silent fit of passion, as moment by moment he realised more and more that he had been victimised, and that he had been sent forward to quiet the men so as to give the big rough fellow an opportunity to creep over into his boat and cut the painter by which it was made fast, and let it glide away on the tide till it was safe to thrust an oar over astern, and, using it like a fish does its tail, paddle softly away close under the rocks to some hole, or perhaps round into the bay.

For a moment the lieutenant thought of manning the boats and sending in pursuit, but he knew that such an act would be madness; and, accepting his position, he suddenly gave the order for four men to go into each boat, and begin to tow the cutter, while a few of the crew put out the sweeps to get her a little farther from the cliff to catch the breeze.

Half an hour later the boats were ordered in, sail was being set, and the cutter was again moving swiftly through the water.

But the wind was dead ahead now, and though the *White Hawk* could use her wings well even in such a breeze, and sail very close, it was far different work getting back to coming away.

The men were not forbidden to talk, and they were not long in grasping the situation, while their commanding officer went up and down the deck, fuming and taking himself to task more seriously than any captain had done since he first went to sea.

"Only to think of me, after what I have learned of their shifts and tricks, letting myself be taken in by such a transparent dodge. Oh, it's maddening!"

He looked up at the sails, and longed to clap on more, but it was useless. The little craft was doing her best, and the water surged under her bow as she took a long stretch seaward, before tacking for the land.

"There's not a doubt of it," muttered the lieutenant. "I know it—I'm sure of it. I deserve to lose my rank. How could I have been such a blind, idiotic baby!"

He was obliged to confess, though, that the trick, if such it proved to be, had been well planned and executed, and the stipulation of the man that he should be paid fifty pounds if the boat was captured had completely thrown dust into his eyes.

More than once, as the cutter rushed on through the darkness, he found himself wondering whether, after all, he was wrong, and that the man had slipped away, so as to avoid being recognised when the smuggling vessel was captured, for, if seen, he would be a marked man.

"And, perhaps, in a few minutes, the smuggler would have been coming into the little bay, I should have taken her, redeemed my reputation, been looked upon as a smart officer, my crew would have got a nice bit of prize money, and the fellow would have come stealthily some night for his reward. — I've done wrong. Would there be time to go back?"

He was on the point of bidding the men "'bout ship," when a firm belief in his having been cheated came over him, and he kept on.

Then there was another season of doubt—and then of assurance—another of doubt, till the poor little fellow grew half bewildered, and gazed around, longing for the daylight and his old moorings, so that he might send a boat ashore, and carefully examine the ground, to see if he could trace any signs of landing having gone on.

At last, just at daybreak, the cutter was about to make a dash, and run right down for her old berth, when one of the men shouted "Sail ho!"

He raised his glass, and there, hull down, were the three masts of a lugger, a Frenchman without a doubt, and his suspicions had their just confirmation.

His immediate thought was to give chase, but the swift sailing vessel was well away with a favourable wind, and she would most probably get across the Channel before he could overtake her, and even if he were so lucky as to catch up to her, what then? She would not have a keg or bale on board which would give him an excuse for detaining her; and wrinkling up his brow, he went on more satisfied that he had been deluded away, so as to give the *chasse marée* an opportunity to come in and rapidly run her cargo.

He saw it all now. No sooner had he passed round the race, than lights had been shown, and the lugger was run in. He felt as certain as if he had seen everything, and he ground his teeth with vexation.

"Wait till I get my chance!" he muttered. "I'll sink the first smuggler I meet; and as to that blackavised scoundrel who came and cheated me as he did — oh, if I could only see him hung!"

A couple of hours later, after seeing the lugger's masts and sails slowly disappear, the cutter was once more at her old moorings, and leaving the boatswain in charge, the lieutenant had himself rowed ashore, to land upon the ledge, and carefully search the rocks for some sight of a cargo having been landed.

But the smugglers and their shore friends had been more careful this time, and search where they would, the cutter's men could find no traces of anything of the kind, and the lieutenant had himself rowed back to the cutter, keeping the boat alongside, ready to send along shore to the cove to seek for tidings of Gurr and Dick but altering his mind, he had the little vessel unmoored once more to run back the six miles along the coast till the cutter was abreast of the cove,—the first place where it seemed possible for a boat to land,—and here he sent a crew ashore to bring his two men off.

Chapter Nineteen

"How many horses has your father got?"

"Three."

"What colour are they?"

"Black, white, and grey."

"Turn round three times, and catch whom you may."

That, as everyone knows, is the classical way of beginning the game of Blind Man's Buff; and supposing that the blinded man *pro tem*, is properly bandaged, and cannot get a squint of light up by the side of his nose, and also supposing that he confuses himself by turning round the proper number of times honestly, he will be in profound darkness, and in utter ignorance of the direction of door, window, or the salient objects in the room.

Take another case. Suppose a lad to have eaten a hearty supper of some particularly hard pastry. The probabilities are that he will either have the peculiar form of dream known as nightmare, or some time in the night he will get out of bed, and go wandering about his room in the darkness, to awake at last, cold, confused, and asking himself where he is, without the slightest ability to give a reasonable answer to his question.

It has fallen to the lot of some people to be lost in a fog—words, these, which can only be appreciated by those who have passed through a similar experience.

The writer has gone through these experiences more than once, and fully realised the peculiar sensation of helplessness, confusion, and brain numbing which follows. Dark as pitch is mostly a figure of speech, for the obscurity is generally relieved by something in the form of dull light which does enable a person to see his hand before him; but the blackness around, when Archibald Raystoke began to come back to his senses, would have left pitch far behind as to depth of tint.

His head ached, and there was a feeling in it suggestive of the contents having been turned into brain-fritters in a pan—fritters which had bubbled and turned brown, and then been burned till they were quite black.

He opened his eyes, and then put his hands up to feel if they were open.

They were undoubtedly, and he hurt them in making the test, for he half fancied, and he had a confused notion, that a great handkerchief had been tied over them. But though they were undoubtedly open he could not see. In fact, when he closed them, strange as it may sound, he felt as if he could see better, for there were a number of little spots of light sailing up and down and round and round, like the tiny sparks seen in tinder before the fire which has consumed is quite extinct.

He lay still, not thinking but trying to think, for his mind was in the condition described by the little girl who, suffering from a cold, said, "Please, ma, one side of my nose won't go."

Archy Raystoke's mind would not go, and for a long time he lay motionless.

His memory began to work again in his back, for he gradually became conscious of feeling something there, and after suffering the inconvenience for a long time, he thrust his hand under his spine and drew out a piece of iron, sharp-edged and round like a hoop.

He felt better after that, and fell to wondering why he had brought his little hoop to bed with him, and also how it was that his little hoop, which he used to trundle, had become iron instead of wood.

The exertion of moving the hoop made him wince, for his back was sore and his arms felt strained as if he had been beaten.

His mind began "to go" a little more, and he had to turn back mentally; but he could not do that, so he made an effort to go forward, and wondered how soon it would be morning, and the window curtains at the foot of the bed would show streaks of sunshine between.

Time passed on and he still lay perfectly quiet, for he did not feel the slightest inclination to move after his late efforts, which had produced a sensation of the interior of his skull beginning to bubble up with fire or hot lead rolling about. But as that pain declined he felt cold, and after a great deal of hesitation he suddenly stretched out his hands to pull up the clothes.

There were none.

His natural inference had been, as he was lying there upon his back, that he must be in bed; but now he found that, though there were no bed-clothes, he was wearing his own, only upon feeling about with no little pain they did not seem like his clothes.

That was as far as he could get then, but some time after there came a gleam of light in his understanding, and he recalled the mists that hung about the Channel.

Of course he was in one of those thick mists, and he had gone to sleep on—on—what had he gone to sleep on?

The light died out, and it was a long time before, like a flash, came the answer.

The deck of the cutter!

He made a movement to start up in horror, for he knew that he must have gone to steep during his watch, and his pain and stiffness were like a punishment for doing so disgraceful a thing.

"What will Mr Brough say if he knows?" he thought, and then he groaned, for the pain caused by the movement was unbearable.

At last his mind began to clear, and he set himself to wonder with more force. This was not the deck, for he could feel that he was lying on what was like an old sail, and where his hand lay was not wood, but cold hard stone, with a big crack full of small scraps.

The lad shook his head and then uttered a low moan, for the pain was terrible.

It died off though as he lay, still trying hard to think, failing—trying in a half dreamy way, and finally thrilling all over, for he remembered everything now—the smugglers—the scene in the darkness of the room where he was imprisoned—the coming of that boy who jeered at him till they engaged in a fierce struggle, with the result all plainly pictured, till he was stunned or had swooned away.

These thoughts were almost enough to stun him again, and he lay there with a hot sensation of rage against the treacherous young scoundrel who had lured him on to that struggle, and held him so thoroughly fixed against the bars till he was secured and bound. Yes, and his eyes were bandaged. He could recall it now.

"Oh, only wait till I get my chance!" he muttered, and he involuntarily clenched his fists.

He lay perfectly quiet again though, for he found that any exertion brought on mental confusion as well as pain, and he wanted to think about his position.

It came by degrees more and more, and as he was able to think with greater clearness, he found an explanation of the fancy he had felt, that he must be ill and sea-sick again, and that somebody had been giving him brandy.

Part was fevered imagination, part was reality, for there could be no doubt about that faint odour of spirits. It was brandy, but brandy in smuggled kegs, and the scoundrels of smugglers had shut him up in the vault with their kegs.

"Well, they have not killed me," he said to himself with a little laugh. "They dared not try that, and all I have to do now is to escape, if Mr Brough does not send the lads to fetch me out."

He went through the whole time now since his landing; thought of what a disgraceful thing it was for a titled gentleman to mix himself up with smuggling, and what a revelation he would have for the lieutenant and the master who had been so easily deluded by Sir Risdon's bearing.

Then he thought of Celia, and how bright and innocent she had seemed; putting away all thoughts of her, however, directly as his angry feeling increased against Ram and this treacherous girl.

He must have been for hours thinking, often in a drowsy, half-confused way, but rousing up from time to time to feel his resentment growing against Ram, who seemed to him now to be the personification of the whole smuggling gang.

By degrees he grew conscious of a fresh pain, one that was certainly not produced by his late struggles, or by stiffness from lying upon an old sail stretched upon the damp floor of a vault.

As he thought this last, he asked himself why he called it the damp floor of a vault. For it was not damp, but perfectly dry, and below the scraps of stone in the seam there was fine dust.

But the said pain was increasing, and there was no mistaking it. He was hungry, decidedly hungry; and paradoxically, as he grew better he grew worse, the pain in the head being condensed in a more central region, where nature carries on a kind of factory of bone, muscle, flesh, blood, and generally health and strength.

Suddenly Archy recalled that his legs had been bound, and he sat up to find that they were free now, and if he liked he could rise and go to the grated window and call for help.

"If I do, they'll come down and stuff a handkerchief in my mouth again," he thought, "and it is no use to do that. I may as well wait till I hear our men's voices, and then I'll soon let them know where I am."

He got on his feet, feeling stiff and uncomfortable, and then tried to make out where the grated window was, but the darkness was absolute, and he stretched out one foot and his hands, as he began to move cautiously along, feeling his way till he kicked against a loose stone.

This arrested him, and he tried in another direction for his foot to come in contact with what seemed to be round, and proved to be a spar lying in company with some carefully folded and rope-bound sails.

"The old rascal!" thought Archy, as he mentally pictured the stern, sad countenance of Sir Risdon.

"Why, he must have a lugger of his own, and keep his stores in here."

A little feeling about convinced him that the window of the vault could not be behind the pile of boat-gear against which he had stumbled, and he moved slowly of! Again, to stop at the end of a yard or two, feeling about with one foot.

"Why, I'm not shut up!" he cried joyously. "I'm out on the ledge. They must have laid me here to be fetched off by the boat. Suppose the tide had risen while I was asleep!"

But the joyous feeling went off as he stared about him. It had been dark enough in a dense fog, but it did not feel dark and cold now, as if there was a dense fog. Everything seemed dry, and though he listened attentively, he could not hear the washing of the waves among the rocks, nor smell the cool, moist, sea-weedy odour of the coast. Instead of that a most unmistakable smell of brandy came into his nostrils.

And yet he seemed to be standing on that ledge close down to the water, for as he stooped down now he could trace with his hand one of the huge, curled-up shell-fish turned to the stone in which it was embedded, while, as he felt about, there was another and another larger still.

He listened again.

No; he was not on the seashore. He must be in the vault beneath Sir Risdon's house, and though he had not noticed it, the floor must be paved with a layer of stones similar to those found where the little kegs had been left.

He went cautiously on with outstretched hands through the intense darkness, and his feet traced the flat curls of stone again and again, but he did not find any wall, and now, as he made up his mind to go back to where he had been when he first awoke, he found that he had not the faintest idea as to which direction he ought to take.

As he grew more able to move and act, the sense of confusion which suddenly arrested him was terrible—almost maddening.

Where was he? What was here on all sides? It could not be the cellar, as he went in one direction or the other toward the walls, and he stood at last resting, in the most utter bewilderment of mind and helplessness of body possible to conceive, while a curious feeling of awe began to steal over him.

The smugglers had not dared to kill him or throw him into the sea, as he had heard of them doing on more than one occasion, but as far as he could make out they had cast him down into some terrible place to die.

The idea was terrible, and unable to contain himself he took a step or two in one direction, then in another, and stopped short, not daring to stir for fear some awful chasm such as he had seen among the rocks should be yawning at his feet, and he should fall headlong down.

He stopped to wipe the cold perspiration away that was gathering on his brow, and then, trying to keep himself cool, he stood thinking, and finally, in utter weariness, sat down.

"I wish I wasn't such a coward," said the young midshipman, half aloud. "It's like being a child to be frightened because it's dark. What's that!"

He started up.

"*That*" was a gleam of light some distance off, shining on the rugged walls of a vast chamber or set of chambers. He could only dimly see this, for the light was but feeble, and the bearer hidden behind the rugged pillars which supported the roof; but it was evidently coming nearer, and as it approached he could see that he was in a vast cavernous, flat-ceiled place, which appeared to have been a quarry, from which masses of stone had been hewn, the floor here and there being littered with refuse of all sorts and sizes.

As the light came on, the midshipman made out that quite a store of spars, ropes, and blocks lay at a short distance, and that more dimly seen was a large stack of tubs, from which doubtless emanated the odour of brandy.

Archy's first idea was to go and meet the bearers of the light, but on second thoughts he decided to stand upon his dignity and let them come to him, and as the thought occurred to him that the visit might be of an inimical nature, his hand stole into his breast in search of his dirk. Vainly though: the weapon was gone.

All this time, as if the bearers were coming very leisurely, the light slowly approached, and as the midshipman more fully grasped the fact that he must be either in a stone quarry or a mine, he saw that the light was an ordinary horn lanthorn, and from the shadows it cast he could see that there were two people, one of whom was carrying something weighty on his shoulders.

This soon resolved itself into four kegs, slung two and two, the bearer panting under their weight, while his companion held the light low down, so that he could see where to plant his feet and avoid the corners of the huge square pillars which supported the roof.

Neither of the pair seemed to pay any attention to him; in fact, the midshipman was doubtful whether he was seen as he stood back waiting till they had passed him, and then hesitated as to whether he should make for the entrance and escape.

Through the black darkness, not knowing which way he should go, perhaps to fall down some shaft such as was sure to be in a place like this? No; he could not risk the journey without a light, and he stood waiting and trying to make out the shadowy figures, one of whom looked strangely uncouth beneath his load, while the other was quite short.

Archy had not long to wait before the pair halted by the stack of kegs, to which the four carried by the man were added, and this done they turned and came toward him.

At this moment, after excitedly watching them, the midshipman became convinced.

The bearer of the lanthorn was his young enemy—the boy.

Chapter Twenty

Raystoke looked round him for a weapon, but the only thing visible was a stone, and not feeling disposed to descend to such a barbarous means of offence or defence, he drew himself up, burning with indignation, but waiting for the others to commence speaking.

He had not long to wait.

"Hullo, sailor!" cried Ram; "like some milk?"

"You rascal!" burst out Archy, taking a step toward the lad, but feeling directly a strong hand upon his arm to hold him back.

"What's the matter?" growled the owner of the hand.

"The matter will be that you two will be hung at the yardarm some fine morning. How dare you shut me up in this hole?"

"Hung for shutting you up here?" cried the boy. "We shall have to hang him then, Jemmy, after all."

"Ay, lad," said the man. "When'll we do it; now?"

"Now!" cried the midshipman. "Do you think you are going to frighten me with such talk? Show me the way out of this place directly."

"Ram, lad," said Jemmy Dadd, with a cackling laugh; "when yer ketches a wild thing, and puts him in a cage, he begins to bang hisself agen the sides, and knocks his head agen the bars, and if he could talk he'd go on just like that 'ere. Then you keeps quiet, and don't give him nothing to eat, and after a day or two you can do what you like with him."

"Then we'd better take back the basket, Jemmy, eh?"

"Ay, lad, that's it. Leave him in the dark a bit to cool him down."

"You scoundrels!" cried the lad in frenzy. "If you do not show me the way out, I'll shout for help, and when it does come, I'll take care your punishment shall be ten times worse."

"Ah, do," said Ram, laughing. "Won't bring the roof down, will it, Jemmy?"

"Nay, not it, lad. Come on."

"Wait a bit," said Ram.—"I say, didn't tell me whether you'd like a bottle o' milk?"

Archy felt as if he would like to fly at the boy, the very mention of the milk exasperating him to such an extent. But at every movement he felt himself more tightly held, and knowing from sad experience that it was waste of energy to contend with the iron-muscled fellow who gripped his arm, he smothered his anger.

He did not speak, but as Ram held up the light, Archy's countenance told tales of the passion struggling in his breast for exit, and the boy grinned.

"I say, do have a bottle o' milk," he said; "it's fresh and warm. Mother said it would do you good."

"Nay, lad, don't give him none till he's grow'd civil, and don't talk about hanging on us."

"I brought you a bottle o' new milk and some hot bread, on'y it's getting cold now, and some butter and cold ham. Do have some."

Archy ground his teeth: he felt as if he would give anything for some food, and the very mention of the tasty viands made his mouth water, but he only stamped his foot and tried to shake himself free.

"I am a king's officer," he shouted, "and order you to let me go!"

"Hear that, Jemmy? Hold him tight."

"Ay! He's tight enough!" cried the man, throwing a sturdy arm about the middy's waist, and holding him back as he tried to get at Ram.

"No good to give orders here," said the latter, grinning. "You're only a king's officer when you're aboard your little bit of a cutter."

"Will you let me out of this place?"

"If I let you go will you tell your skipper about what you've seen?"

"Yes," cried Archy fiercely.

"Then what a dumble head you must be to think we'll let you go. Won't do, little officer; will it, Jemmy?"

"Do! Better chuck him off the cliff."

"What!" cried the midshipman fiercely.

"Chuck you off the cliff. What do you mean by coming interfering here with honest men getting their living? We never did nothing to you."

"You scoundrel!" cried Archy, "how dare you say that? You know you are breaking the laws by smuggling, and you are doing worse by kidnapping me."

"Should have kep' away then," growled the man.

"Don't speak cross to him, Jemmy. He's very sorry he came now, and if I let him go he'll promise not to say a word about what he has seen; won't you now, mate?"

"No!" roared Archy.

"Oh, well then, Jemmy's right. We shall have to tame you down."

"Show me the way out of this."

"Come along then," said Ram with a sneering laugh. "But you'd better promise."

"Show me the way out."

"Won't you have some milk first?"

"Do you hear me?"

"And bread and butter, home-made?"

"Will you show me the way out."

"Nor no ham? You must be hungry!"

"You scoundrel!" cried Archy, who was exasperated almost beyond bearing. "Show me the way out."

"Oh, very well, this way, then. Hold him tight, Jemmy."

"Ay, ay, lad!"

"This way, my grand officer without your fine clothes," said Ram tauntingly, as he held down the lanthorn to show the rough stone floor. "Mind how you put your feet, and take care. Why don't you come?"

Archy made a start forward, but he was tightly held.

"Why don't you come, youngster?" cried Ram mockingly, as he held the lanthorn more closely. "There, now then, mind how you come."

Whang!

The dull sound was followed by a faint clatter, and all was black darkness again, for raging with hunger and annoyance as the boy was, tightly held, the light down just in front of him, without any warning Archy drew back slightly, delivered one quick, sharp kick full at the lanthorn, and it flew right away into the darkness.

"Well!" ejaculated Ram in his first moment of surprise. Then he burst into a roar of laughter which echoed from the roof.

"You're a nice un," growled Jemmy.

"Let him go, and come on," cried Ram.

A sudden thought struck the middy.

"No, you don't," he muttered, as he wrenched himself round and clung to the man. "If you are going from here, I go too."

"Got the lanthorn, Ram, lad?" cried Jemmy.

"No; and it's smashed now. Come away."

"Let go, will you?" growled Jemmy.

For answer the midshipman held on more tightly.

"Do you hear? Come on!" cried Ram.

"He won't let go. He's holding on legs, wings and teeth. Come and help."

"Get out: you can manage him. Put him on his back."

No sooner were the words uttered than, as he struggled there in the black darkness, Archy felt himself twisted up off his feet. There was a shake, a wrench, and as he clung tightly to the man, his arms were dragged, as it felt to him, half out of their sockets, and he was thrown, to come down fortunately on his hands and knees.

For a few moments he felt half stunned by the shake, but recovering himself he leaped up and began to follow the retiring footsteps which were faintly heard.

He knew the direction, and went on with outstretched hands to find the way, checked directly by their coming in contact with one of the great pillars of stone.

But he felt his way round this, got to the other side, listened, made out which way the footsteps were going, followed on, and caught his feet against something which threw him forward on to a pile of broken stone.

He got up again, and felt his way cautiously to the right, for the stones rose like a bank or barrier in his way, and he went many yards without finding a way through.

Then feeling that he had taken the wrong turning, he retraced his steps as quickly as he could, going on and on without avail and never stopping. He was just in time to save himself from another fall as he heard a dull bang as if a heavy door were closed, followed by a curious rattling sound, as of large pieces of slate falling down and banging against wood. Then came a dull echoing, which died off in whispers, and all was perfectly still.

"The cowards!" cried Archy, as he fully realised that his gaolers had escaped from him. "How brutal to leave a fellow shut up in a hole like this. 'Tis horrible; and enough to drive one mad. Ugh!" he now cried, "if I only could get out!"

He sat down upon the rough stones, feeling weak, and perspiring profusely. It was many hours now since he had tasted food, and in his misery and despair he felt that he should be starved to death before his gaolers came again.

"How dare they!" he cried passionately. "A king's officer too! Oh, if I could only be once more along with the lads, and with a chance to go at them! I think I should be able to fight."

Then as he sat on the stones he began to cool down and grow less fierce in his ideas. In other words, he came down from pistols and sharp-edged cutlasses to fists, and felt such an intense longing to get at Ram, that his fists involuntarily clenched and his fingers tingled.

"Wait a bit," he said fiercely, — "wait a bit."

"Yes, I shall have to wait a bit," he said sadly, as he rose from the stones. "Oh, how weak and hungry I am! It's as if I was going to be ill. I wonder whether I could track where they went out."

"Not now," he said, — "not now;" and with some faint hope of finding the place where he had been lying on the old sail, he began to move slowly and laboriously along, his mind dragged over, as it were, to the words of the boy as he taunted him about milk and bread and butter with ham. It was agonising in his literally starving condition to think of such things, and he tried to keep his mind upon finding the way out, meaning to work desperately after he had lain down for a bit to rest.

But it was impossible to control his thoughts, strive how he would. Hunger is an overmastering desire, and he crept on step by step with outstretched hands, picturing in the darkness slices of ham, yellow butter, brown crusted loaves, and pure sweet milk, till, as he dragged his feet slowly along, half-fainting now with pain, weariness, and despair, his foot suddenly kicked against something which rolled over and over away from him.

"The lanthorn!" he exclaimed eagerly, and planning at once how he could strike a light with a stone and his knife, and perhaps contrive some tinder, he went down on his hands and knees, feeling about in all directions till he touched the object which he had kicked, and uttered a cry of joy and excitement.

It was not the lanthorn, but a round cross-handled basket with lid, and he trembled as he recalled Ram's words about what his mother had sent.

Was there truth in them, or were they the utterances of a malicious mind which wished to torture one who was in its power?

Archy Raystoke hardly dared to think, and knelt there for a few minutes, with his trembling hands resting upon the basket, which he was afraid to open lest it should not contain that which he looked for.

"Out of my misery at all events," he cried; and he tore off the lid.

Chapter Twenty One

"They only want to keep me a prisoner," said the midshipman half an hour after, as he sat with his mouth full, steadily eating away as a boy of seventeen can eat—"a prisoner till they've got all their stuff safe away. They dare not hurt me. I'm not afraid of that, and it's a very strange thing if I can't prove myself as clever as that cunning young scoundrel who trapped me here. At all events, I'll try. They dare not starve me: not they. Wait a bit, and I'll show them that I'm not so stupid as they think. Shut me up here, would they? Well, we'll see!"

He went on munching a little longer, then felt for the bottle, took out the tight cork, had a good long draught of the milk it contained, recorked and put it away in the basket with the bread, butter, and ham he had not consumed, shut down the lid, and laughed.

There was nothing very cheerful about his prison to make him laugh, but the reaction was so great—he felt so different after his hearty meal—that he was ready to look any difficulty in the face, and full of wonder at his despondency of a short time before.

There's a good deal of magic in food to one who is fasting, and is blessed with health and a good appetite.

"Now then," he said, rising with the basket in his hand, "the first thing is to find a place to stow you;" and he had no difficulty in finding ledge after ledge that would have held the basket, but he wanted one that would be easily found in the darkness.

At last he felt his way to a great mass of rock, upon which, about level with his head, was a projection upon which the basket stood well enough, and trusting to being able to find it again by means of the great block, he turned his attention to the lanthorn.

"If I only had that," he said to himself.

He stood thinking in the darkness, wondering which way he had better try.

"Any way," he said at last, "for I will have it; and then if I don't find my way out of this hole, I'm as stupid as that fellow thinks."

Stretching out his hands to save himself from a blow against any obstacle, he stalked off in as straight a direction as he could go, feeling his way with his feet, and always making sure of firm foothold before he moved the one that was safe, for his one great dread in the vast cavern was lest he should suddenly find himself on the brink of some yawning shaft.

He knew little about the district, his ideas of the place being principally confined to what he had seen of the coast-line from the sea, but rugged piles of stone had been pointed out to him here and there as being the refuse of the stone that had been ages before dug and regularly mined by shafts and galleries out of the bowels of the earth; and a little thinking convinced him that he must be shut up in one of those old quarries which had been seized upon by the smugglers as a place to hide their stores.

It was a shrewd guess, and he could not help thinking afterwards that it was no wonder that so little success attended the efforts of the revenue cutter's crew to trace cargoes which had been landed when the smugglers had such lurking places as this.

As he crept slowly on, step by step, these and similar thoughts came rapidly through the prisoner's brain, and as he slowly mounted what seemed to be a pile of fragments, he began to wonder where his prison could be—whether it was close to the shore or some distance inland.

He stopped to listen, hoping to hear the breaking of the waves among the rocks, which would have proved what he wished to know at once; but though he listened again and again, he could not distinguish a sound. The only noises he heard were those he made in stepping on one side of some piece of stone, which gave forth a musical clink as it struck another.

He was climbing up now what appeared to be a steep slope, over great fragments of stone heavier than he would have been able to lift, and he seemed to creep up and up till he felt assured that the ceiling was just above him, and raising his hand he touched the roof, his fingers tracing out again the great cast of one of the old-world shell-fish—one of the great nautiluses of the geologist.

But fossils were unknown things in Archy Raystoke's day. He was hunting for a lanthorn, not for specimens.

As he stood on the highest part of this pile of stone, he hesitated about going farther, and bore off to his left, feeling that in all probability the object of his search had not come so far.

From time to time he paused to listen, and at last thought of trying to find the extent of the place by shouting; but he was satisfied with his first essay, his voice going echoing away apparently for a great distance, and the peculiar, dying, whispering sound was not pleasant to one alone in the darkness.

After a while, however, as he felt that he was walking over small fragments of stone, he picked up a piece and threw it, to try if he were near the end of the cavern in this direction, for he was growing tired and longed now to find his way to the sailcloth to lie down and rest.

The piece he held was about a pound weight, and, drawing back his hand as far as he could reach, he threw it with all his might, to start back in alarm, for it struck wood with a heavy thud, and dropped down almost at his feet.

Unknown to himself he had gradually found his way to the pile of kegs, and these he touched the next moment, thinking that, as he stood facing them, the place where he had first come to himself must lie off to his left; and so it proved after a long search, and he sank down so wearied out, that as he chose by preference to lie down, he was before many minutes had elapsed in a deep and dreamless sleep, forgetful of the darkness and any peril that might be ready to assail him next.

Chapter Twenty Two

Whether it was night or day when Archy awoke he could not tell, but he felt rested and refreshed, and ready to try and do something to make his escape.

There was a way into his prison, and that way, he vowed, should by some means or other be his way out.

The first thing to do was to find that lanthorn, of whose position he seemed to have some vague idea; but, after a little search, he found that all idea of locality had gone, and he had not the slightest idea of the direction to go next.

"I must leave it to chance," he said. "I shall find it when I'm not trying;" and, wearying of the search, he set himself now to try and make his way to the place where his visitors had come into the old quarry.

Here, again, he was utterly at fault, for the cavern was so big and irregular, and he was still so haunted by the thought that he might be at any moment on the brink of some deep hole, half full of water, that he dared not search so energetically as he would have liked.

He had many narrow escapes from falls and blows against projecting masses of stone, and he found himself, after hours of wandering, so tired and faint, that he would gladly have found the basket and the resting-place; but the more he searched the more convinced he grew of the ease with which he could lose himself entirely in the darkness, and when he did come upon any spot again which he recognised by touch as one that he had felt before, it seemed to him that he stumbled upon it quite by accident, and the moment he left it he was as helpless as before.

Wearied out at length, he determined to go in a straight line from where he was to the extremity of the vault; then to curve back, and from this point strike out to the left in search of his resting-place and the basket.

It took him just about an hour, and when he had done all this he could find no traces of his food, but he heard a noise close behind him which nailed him to the spot, and he stood motionless, listening.

According to his idea, he was at the end of the cave farthest from where his gaolers approached, but unless there were two entrances he was quite wrong, for he had wandered close up to the place whence Ram and Jemmy had come, and, the noise continuing, he stooped down to let whoever it was pass him, while he made for the entrance and slipped out.

Directly after there was the soft glow of a lanthorn, which suddenly came into view round a corner, high up by the ceiling, and the bearer began to descend a rough slope.

Archy saw no more, for he dropped down and hid behind a stone, watching the glare of light, and then, as it passed him going on toward the other end of the cave, he crept from behind the stone and made for the rough slope, which was thoroughly printed on his mind, so that he could almost picture every rock and inequality that might be in his way.

The door would be open, he thought; and, if he could, he would have a clever revenge, for he determined to turn the tables on his enemies, shut them in, and he hoped to make them prisoners till he could signal for help from the cutter, and get a boat's crew ashore.

As he crept on quietly he glanced over his shoulder once, saw the light disappearing behind the great square, squat pillars, and then with a feeling of triumph that thrilled through him, he went cautiously up the rest of the slope, his arms outstretched, his breath held, and in momentary expectation of hearing an exclamation from the other end of the cave.

"They'll think I'm somewhere about," he said to himself, as he crept on, expecting to pass through an opening into daylight the next moment; but it did not turn out as he anticipated, for he stopped short with his nose against some one's throat, his arms on each side of a sturdy body, and the arms belonging to that body gripped him tight.

"Steady, Ram, lad!" came in a gruff whisper. "Light out?"

Archy's heart beat heavily, and he felt that, to escape, he ought to try and imitate the boy's voice, and say "Yes."

But he could not only stand panting, and the next instant his opportunity, if opportunity it was, had gone. For Ram's real voice came from right at the other end, echoing along the roof.

"Look out, Jemmy. He aren't here."

"No, he aren't there, lad," said the smuggler with a laugh. "Bring your lanthorn, I've ketched a rat or some'at. Come and see."

Archy made a violent struggle to escape, but the man's arms were tight round his waist, he was lifted off the slope, and as he fully realised that, in a wrestling match, no matter how active and strong seventeen may be, it is no match for big, well-set seven-and-thirty.

"No good, youngster," growled the smuggler, as he carried the midshipman down the slope, and held him at the bottom. "Very good idea, but you see we didn't mean you to get out like that."

Feeling that he was exhausting himself for nothing, Archy ceased his struggling, and was held there motionless, as Ram came up with the lanthorn to begin grinning.

"Bring him along, Jemmy," he said. "His dinner's ready."

"Shall I carry him, lad?"

"Look here," cried Archy haughtily. "You two are, I suppose, quite ignorant of the consequences of keeping me here?"

"What's he talking about, Jemmy?" said Ram.

"Dunno, lad: something 'bout consequences."

"As soon as it is known that you have seized and kept me here, you will both be arrested, and have to suffer a long term of imprisonment, even if you get no worse off."

"But suppose no one knows you are here?" said Ram.

"But it will be known, so I give you both fair warning."

"Thank ye," said Ram mockingly.

"And thank ye for me too, my lad."

"So now, take my advice, open that door, and set me free. If you do this, I'll promise to intercede for you two, and I daresay I can save you from punishment."

"Well, that's handsome; isn't it, Jemmy?" said Ram mockingly.

"Do you hear me?" cried Archy.

"Oh, I can, quite plain," said Jemmy.

"So can I," said Ram; "but your dinner's ready, Mr Orficer; so come and have it."

"Enough of this," cried Archy, wrenching himself free. "Open that door, and let me go."

"Better carry him, Jemmy."

"If you dare!" cried the angry prisoner, beginning the struggle, but Jemmy Dadd's muscles were like steel, and he whipped the young midshipman off his feet, and carried him, kicking and struggling with all his might, right along the cave, Ram going first with the lanthorn; and in spite of its feeble, poor, dulled light, the prisoner was able to get a better idea of the shape and size of the place than he had had before.

The captive ceased struggling, and keenly watched the various pillars and heaps they passed, noting too how the cavern seemed to extend in a wide passage right on before them, and seemingly endless gloom.

"There you are," said Jemmy, as he set his burden down; "quite at home. Is he going to ask us to dinner, Ram, lad, and send for his skipper to jyne us?"

Archy paid no heed to the man's jeering words, for he was thinking of the place, and trying to fix it all in his memory, for use when these two had gone.

He knew that he must have been over the parts he had seen again and again in the darkness, but beyond the memory of the great pillars he had marked, the place had made no impression; but now he had seen the way out, and the way further in, and throwing himself down, he without apparent reason took up a long narrow piece of stone, handled it for a moment or two, and set it down carelessly, but not with so much indifference that he did not contrive that it should act as a rough pointer, ready to indicate the direction of the door.

Feeling that it was useless to say more to his gaolers, especially after his attempt to escape, he half lay on the old sail; while, as if the darkness were the same to him as the light, the smuggler said laconically, "Going back!" turned on his heel, and disappeared in the black gloom.

"Brought you some bacon and some fried eggs, this time," said Ram, looking at him attentively, but Archy made no reply.

"No use to rile," continued the boy, "and you can't get out, so take it easy. Father'll let you go some day."

"Where is the cutter?" said Archy sharply.

"I d'know. Gone."

"Gone?"

"Yes, she went off somewhere. To look for you, pr'aps," said the boy grinning, "or else they think you're drownded."

"Look here," said the midshipman suddenly, "you behaved very treacherously to me, but I'll forgive you if you'll let me go."

"Look here," replied the boy, "you behaved very treacherously to us, dressing up, and spying on us; but I've got you, and won't let you go."

"I was doing my duty, sir."

"And I'm doing my dooty—what father telled me."

"How much will you take to let me go?"

"How much will you give?" said Ram, grinning, and the midshipman's heart made a bound.

"You shall have five pounds, if you'll let me go now, at once."

"There's as much as you'll eat till I come agen," said Ram abruptly; "and if I don't forget you as I did my rabbits once, and they were starved to death, I'll bring you some more.—I say!"

Archy looked at him fiercely.

"Don't try to drink what's in them tubs. It's awful strong, and might kill you."

"Stop a moment; leave me a light."

"What do you want with a light? You kicked the last over, and thought you'd get out in the dark. You may have the one you kicked."

"But it is so dark here," said Archy, as the boy picked up the empty basket.

"Course it is when there's no light," said the boy coolly; and swinging the lanthorn as he rose, he continued, "You'll find the road to your mouth, I daresay. I did not bring you a knife, because you're such a savage one."

"Where is my dirk?"

"What d'yer mean? Your little sword?"

"Yes."

"Father's got it all right; said it was a dangerous thing for a boy!"

Ram gave his prisoner a nod, and went off whistling, the prisoner following at a distance, and getting pretty close up to the beginning of the slope as the lanthorn disappeared round a corner. Then, as he listened, it seemed to him that the boy climbed up somewhere, talking the while to his companion, their voices sounding hollow and rumbling, then there was a pause, the dull thud of a closing door, the drawing of bolts, and soon the rattling of heavy stones, and once more all was silent.

Chapter Twenty Three

A strange depressing sensation came over the young prisoner as he stood there once more alone, but he turned sharply round with his teeth set, thought for a few moments about his course back, and then, feeling more determined and firm, walked slowly on, and to his great delight found that it was possible to become educated to do without sight, for, each time that he thought he was near a pillar, he stretched out his hand to find that he touched it, and with very little difficulty he walked straight up to the old sail, felt about, and there was the basket of food, which he attacked at once, and soon after fell asleep.

Four more visits were paid him by Ram, but whether they were at intervals of days or half days, the prisoner could not tell, for any questions he asked were laughingly evaded, and all attempts at persuasion and bribery proved useless.

He did learn that the cutter had just returned and gone away again. And it seemed to him that he was forgotten, but he never thoroughly lost heart, and during this time he had accustomed himself to the darkness, and educated his feet wonderfully in the topography of the place.

Of one thing he had fully satisfied himself, and that was the hopelessness of getting out by the way his visitors came in. They were too cautious ever to leave the door unguarded; hence the prisoner felt that if he knocked down and stunned the frank, good-tempered boy who seemed disposed to be the best of friends in every way but that of helping him to escape, he would be no nearer freedom than before.

He had gone up the slope twice, and the last time crept near enough to see that Ram was climbing up a well-like shaft by means of rugged projections in the wall, that as he got about twenty feet up he handed the lanthorn to the man, climbed out through a square opening, and then a trap-door was shut down, locked, and bolted, and what sounded to be a number of heavy pieces of stone were drawn over.

As far as he could judge, after venturing up and nearly having a severe fall in the darkness, escape was impossible that way, so he returned after each trial to think, and come to the conclusion that if the place had been used for the purpose of digging out stone, of which there could be no doubt, there must be some other way by which the great pieces had been dragged up to daylight.

With a lanthorn or torch he might easily have satisfied himself upon this point. To achieve it without was a terribly risky task.

Still he determined to try, and after a hasty meal, directly his gaolers had paid their last visit, he started off in the opposite direction to that which led to the trap-door, and proceeding cautiously, taking the precaution to keep on throwing pieces of stone before him, to satisfy himself that there was no well or pit in his way, he went on and on.

Now he threw a piece of stone to his left hand, to his right, and after going many yards at what was but a snail's pace, he discovered that the place had suddenly contracted, and after creeping a little farther, the place was more contracted still, and ascended. So narrowed was it now that a couple of steps in either direction enabled him to touch a wall, while about twenty short paces farther on the ascent grew much more straight, and there was no fear of a pit or shaft in the way, for he found that roughly square blocks of stone were laid like a flight of steps, up which he clambered, and then sunk down, overcome by the feeling of joy which had flooded his brain.

He must have come up quite fifty feet after ascending the slope along which he had walked, and here he was at the top of the flight of clumsy stairs on a kind of platform of rugged stones, and straight before him there was a chink so narrow that he could not have thrust a hand through it, but wide enough to allow the passage of a gleam of light; there was a familiar odour, too, of salt air and seaweed, and as he placed his ear to the chink he could hear, as if far below, the wash of water.

"Why, this must be at the side of the cliff," he said joyously; and if he could enlarge that crack there would be a way out to the face of the rocks, where it would go hard with him indeed if he could not climb up to the grassy fields above, or down to the shore below.

"Why didn't I try this before?" he cried. "Oh, how foolish! Not get out, eh? I'll soon show them that;" and he began to feel about carefully all over the face of the stones before him, to satisfy himself before long that there had been a large roughly square opening here, which had been filled in with some pieces of stone, between which he could feel that there was mortar.

"Now, then, what I want is a good marlinspike or an iron bar. Oh, if I had my dirk here I could move them with that."

But he had neither bar, marlinspike, nor dirk, nothing but his hands and a small pocket-knife, so a depressing feeling of vexation humbled him for a time.

He soon cast that off though, for it was impossible to feel low spirited in the face of such a discovery, and before commencing the task he had in hand he knelt down with his face close to the chink to drink in the delicious sea air.

"I wonder how long I shall be a prisoner," he said aloud; and he laughed, for he could see no difficulties now. Still they began to appear soon after, and the first one he mentally saw was the coming of Ram with his food. He must know the place thoroughly, as he had shown by the care with which he threaded his way among the loose stones and pillars, and if he came with his lanthorn and missed him, he might walk up there and find him at work.

"I'll be careful," he said to himself; and taking out his knife forcing himself to believe that it was about twelve o'clock each day that the lad came, and if so, as it was about six hours, as near as he could guess, since the basket was brought, he had about a couple of hours more daylight, then the long night and all the morning, before his gaoler would come again.

He bitterly regretted now not having tried to time Ram's visits, forgetting that it would have been impossible to do so without light, and, unable to restrain his impatience to the extent of waiting till he came again, and watching for night from then, he went to work to try and loosen a stone by the side of the crevice, and toiled away till at the end of what seemed to be two hours, the light through the crevice paled, grew dull, then dark, and for the first time for many days he knew that it was night.

Cheered by his calculation being so far right, he worked and scraped out the mortar, satisfied even with getting away the tiniest scraps, feeling as he did that if he could only dislodge one stone he could bring up from below plenty of great and splinter-shaped pieces with which he could hammer, and take out the rest, or enough for his body to pass through.

So light-hearted did he feel, as guiding the point of his knife by his fingers, he picked and scraped away, that he began to hum a tune over softly. It was as black now as it was in the deepest part of the ancient quarry, but that did not seem to matter, for it was only the darkness of evening, and if he waited there and kept on working, he would see, first of all, a long pallid ray that would grow brighter, and bring as it were some light and hope, while as soon as he could get out a stone he would be able to see the sea, perhaps even make out the cutter, and signal.

No: the boy had said that it was gone. But it would come back, and they would see his signals; a boat would come ashore, he would be fetched out of this miserable black hole; the smugglers would be captured, and he would have such a revenge on that boy Ram. It would be glorious.

But all depended upon little *ifs*—*if* he could get out the stone, *if* the hole happened to be opposite the spot where the cutter was moored, *if* they could see his signals.

It was discouraging to have such thoughts as these, but Archy Raystoke had been for days condemned to inactivity, and the opportunity of working at something definite which proffered a way of escape made him toil on with all his his might.

In fact, he was obliged to check himself, for his task needed care. Too much exercise of the strength which had been growing latent might mean breaking his knife, and the destruction of his hopes.

So he toiled on well into the night, picking and loosening tiny scraps of mortar, which, hard though it was, had fortunately for him been made of an exceedingly coarse sand, or rather very fine shingle, whose tiny pebbles formed each a point to work upon till it was loosened and fell.

Archy's first thought was to work right on through the night, but the monotonous task in the darkness, and the fatigue and excitement, combined to produce their customary effect, and he found himself nodding and starting into wakefulness so many times over, that he resolved at last to go back to his starting-place, have a good meal, and then come back.

He left his task with reluctance, but nature would not be refused, and without much difficulty he found his way to the basket, ate heartily, sat still to think a few minutes, and thought too much, starting up suddenly and rubbing his eyes.

"How stupid of me!" he exclaimed. "I must have just nodded off to sleep. Nearly wasted a lot of time."

Afraid to remain where he was, lest he should yield to the temptation again and fall dead asleep, he eagerly made his way back to the slope and the rough steps, to stand there wondering as he got to the top.

For there, straight before him, was a pale ray of light, and the place smelt cool and fresh.

Surely a star or the moon must be up, he thought, as he knelt down and resumed his task, feeling somehow a good deal rested.

The explanation was not long in coming, for to his astonishment the ray of light grew brighter and brighter, and broadened out full of dancing motes when he had been an hour at work, teaching him that he had not dropped off to sleep for a minute or two, but long enough to give him a good night's rest sufficient to prepare him for the toil to come.

He felt vexed and called it laziness, working the harder to recover lost time, and as the hours glided by listening intently for the slightest sound from the quarry below that should indicate the coming of Ram with his daily portion of food.

On previous days he had looked forward to the lad's approach as something that would break the monotony of his captivity, but now he would have given anything to have known that by some accident the lad would be kept away.

Still Archy toiled on, the stone he had attacked as tight as ever, but quite a little heap of rough mortar increasing beneath where he knelt.

"It's only getting out the first one," he argued; "the others will come easily enough."

And so, full of hope, he kept on, till feeling that it must be near the time for the visit, he reluctantly closed his pocket-knife and went down, gazing back first at the tiny ray of light which pointed the way to liberty.

His arms ached and his fingers were sore. There was a blister too in the palm of his hand where the knife had pressed; but these were trifles now, and he seated himself in his old spot ready to receive his visitors, and so full of hope that he could hardly refrain from shouting for joy.

He could see it all, now. This was quite an ancient mine, one perhaps from which all the best stone had been worked. Where Ram came down was the land entrance, and the ray of light marked the opening in the face of the cliff, from which the pieces of stone had been lowered down into boats or ships below. After the smugglers had taken possession it seemed probable that they had filled up the hole in the cliff face, though it struck Archy that this would leave them a handy place to get their cargoes ashore if they had tackle to haul it up, and get it into their store at once.

The time seemed very long before the rattle and rumble of the stones on the trap-door struck upon Archy's listening ear, but at last, after he had convinced himself that he might have worked two or three hours longer, there it was, and then came the rattle of the bolts and the sharp sound of the lock. Directly afterwards there was a soft glare, the lanthorn appeared like some creature of light swaying and floating towards him in the darkness till it stopped close by, and Ram's now familiar voice exclaimed, —

"Hullo there! Getting hungry?"

"Yes," said Archy, in a voice he wished to sound surly and obstinate, but which in spite of his wishes had a cheerful ring, which affected Ram, who began to laugh and chatter.

"Nice to be you," he said. "Get all the good things, you do. Fried fish to-day, and pork pie. I say, midshipman, you have got into good quarters, you have."

Archy tried to seem sulky.

"Oh, you needn't talk without you like, but they didn't feed you up aboard ship like you're getting it now, I know; salt beef, then salt pork, and hard biscuits. Why, it's like fattening up one of our pigs for Christmas. I say, you are quiet. Haven't been at one of them little kegs, have you? Oh, very well; if you don't like to talk, I can't make you."

"Are you going to let me out of this place?" said the midshipman, so as to keep up the idea of his longing to be set free, and chase any suspicions of his having discovered a way out.

"When I get orders, Mr Orsifer, and not before. I aren't skipper, no more nor you are."

"Another piece of insolence," thought the prisoner. "Oh, how I will pay him out for this by and by!"

"Aren't you going to peck?"

Archy took no notice, and at last there came, in a deep, echoing growl through the place, —

"Say, lad, going to be all day?"

"Coming, Jemmy," Ram shouted. "Want anything else, midshipman?"

"Yes, you to go and not worry me," replied Archy, heartily repenting his words the next moment for fear that they should excite suspicion.

But they did not, for Ram only laughed and walked away.

Chapter Twenty Four

As the prisoner sat listening to the bang of the trap-door and the rattling of the bolts, he could hardly contain himself. But knowing the danger of the boy coming back and finding him gone, he forced himself to stay where he was; and to pass away the time he opened the basket Ram had now left in place of the other, and forced himself to eat.

But he could hardly swallow the food, which seemed tasteless in the extreme, and he was about to give up and hasten back to his work when his heart leaped, for there was the distant sound of the bolts being drawn, and a minute or two later the soft yellow light came slowly towards him and stopped.

"Just remembered," said its bearer. "Got half way home first, though. Mother said I was to be sure and take back that basket. Put the stuff out on the sail. Hullo, what you been doing to your hands?"

Archy started guiltily, and looked at them in the light to see that they were covered with blood, from injuries that he had made unconsciously in toiling with his knife against the stones.

"Tumbled down?" continued Ram without waiting for an answer. "Well, 'tis dark 'mong these stones. I used to trip over them, but I could go anywhere now in the dark. Seem to feel like when they are near. Never mind, tear up yer hankychy and wrap round. I'll bring you one o' mine next time I come. There we are. Haven't forgot the basket this time. I say?"

"Well?"

The lad was ten yards away now, holding the lanthorn above his head.

"You lost a chance."

"What do you mean?"

"Jemmy Dadd isn't up by the door. You might have given me a topper with a stone, and run away; too late now."

He ran off laughing, and holding the lanthorn down low to make sure of his way.

But Archy did not start up in pursuit. He saw a better way out now, and waiting till he felt convinced that the boy must be well on his way home, he jumped up, felt his way to the crevice, and was soon after hard at work picking the mortar from between the stones.

Now and then, as he grew faint and weary, it seemed to him that he had made no progress, but the little heap of mortar told different tales, and once more taking heart he toiled away.

It seemed a very easy thing to do, to loosen one stone in a rugged wall, draw it out, and then remove the other, but in practice it appeared almost impossible, and again going back into the quarry to partake of the food that was absolutely necessary, Archy returned to his task, and after working away again for about half an hour he fell fast asleep.

How long he slept he did not know, but he started awake again to find that it was quite dark, and he kept on like one in a dream.

The stone seemed as fast as ever, and his progress was getting very slow now, for he had cleared away the mortar as fast as he could reach in; but at last, seizing the stone and getting his fingers well in the joint, he gave it a vigorous shove, and then uttered a shout of triumph, for to his delight there came a sharp crack, and after giving a vigorous shove, the stone, which was about twenty inches long, was drawn out, and became the instrument for dislodging its fellows.

This was comparatively easy now, and in the course of the next two days the prisoner had loosened and drawn out stones till he had made a way through a rough piece of wall six feet thick, and had enlarged the hole so that there was room to creep into the opening he had made and look out.

Here came disappointment the first. The wall he had worked through did not face out to sea, but was one side of a chasm, and he gazed at the opposite side.

Soon after he learned that this had not been the place where the stones were carried out for landing in boats, but the hole through which all the refuse was discharged, to fall in a crumbling heap a tremendous distance below, to be washed away by the waves which curved over and over against the foot and rolled up into the chasm.

Still he worked on, enlarging the hole and sending the broken pieces and mortar, rattling down the face of the cliff into the sea, till there was nothing to hinder his crawling out at any time, and either getting to the top of the cliff or down below to the shore.

He decided for the former as the more easy and the less likely to suggest peril, and he spent the next few hours after cleansing himself as much as possible, so as not to excite the attention of his young gaoler, and in his efforts to do this he made use of a piece of sailcloth, and an end of a coil of rope which lay with some sea-going tackle hard by where he slept.

The day had come at last when the way was open, and he had but to creep out into the fresh bright sunshine and run for his liberty.

He could hardly refrain from doing so at once, but his long and arduous labour, which had taken the skin from his fingers and left his whole hands so tender that he hardly dared to touch anything, had taught him some wisdom, especially not to throw away the opportunity for which he had worked so hard.

And now he sat there in the darkness, wafting, so exultant that his seat might have been a throne, instead of a worn-out sail stretched over a mass of stone. He hugged the knees upon which his chin rested, and gazed straight before him into the blackness, watching for the first glow of Ram's lanthorn, and seeing as he watched the glorious sky, the blue sea all a-ripple; the shimmer and play of a passing shoal of fish; gulls floating without effort, now high up, now low down, their breasts of purest white, their backs of delicate grey, and their wondering eyes gazing at the rough-looking fisher-lad who crept out of a hole in the face of the cliff, made his way from shelf to shelf, ever up and up till he was on the grass at the top, where he lay down to wait till night for fear of being seen and dragged back.

The black darkness of the great cavern quarry was all alight now with the pictures his mind painted, and, in his delight and satisfaction, he laughed aloud as he thought of Ram's disappointment on coming one day and finding his prisoner flown.

It was hard work to keep from starting at once, but the midshipman felt that if he did, his escape would be discovered at any moment, and if it were, it was only a question of time before he would have the whole smuggling gang after him, and he would be hunted down to a lot ten times more bitter from the fact of his having failure to contemplate, and form his mental food.

The rattle at last. The door dragged up, and Ram was not alone, for his voice could be heard in conversation with Jemmy Dadd.

The boy was in capital spirits, and he was whistling merrily, his shrill notes echoing from the flat roof as he came on swinging his lanthorn in one hand, the basket in the other.

"Sleep?" he said, as he saw Archy's attitude. "There you are," he continued. "I know you weren't asleep, and if you don't like to talk it aren't my fault. Want anything else?"

No reply; Archy dare not speak.

"Oh, very well," he said, "you can do as you like. Where's t'other basket?"

A shiver ran through the prisoner as he recollected that which he had forgotten in his excitement: the basket which he had taken with some of the food therein, ready for his use as he worked, was standing by the opening at the top of the steps, and he cast an anxious glance sidewise in the direction of the passage, in dread lest the boy should detect the light shining down.

He need not have been alarmed, for there was not a ray visible, and even if there had been, the light cast by the opened lanthorn would have hidden it; but he sat there trembling all the same, and with a curious sensation of suffocation rising in his throat, as he softly altered his position and loosened his hands, ready to make a spring at his enemy if it should become necessary.

"Well, I do call that grumpy. Keeps on bringing you nuts, and you're so snarky that you won't so much as give one back the shells. Now, then, where's that basket?"

Archy felt that he must speak, or else the boy would go in search of it.

"I haven't done with it."

"But I want it to take back."

"It has some of the dinner in it."

"Well, then, let's empty it out."

"No," said Archy, sitting up angrily; "you can't have it now."

"Oh," said Ram, "that's it, is it? Suppose I say I will have it?"

"If you don't take yourself off," cried Archy, "I'll break your head with one of these pieces of stone."

"Two can play at that game."

"Be off."

"I shan't. I want our basket. Mother said I was to bring it back."

"Tell her you haven't got it."

"Now, look here," cried Ram, "if you don't give me that basket back, I won't bring you what I was going to bring to-morrow. Where is it?"

"Where I put it. You contemptible young smuggling thief! How dare you come worrying a gentleman about a dirty old basket!"

"Wasn't dirty, for mother scrubbed it out before she'd send it to you. Where is it?"

Desperate now in his fix, and feeling that his only resource to keep Ram from searching for the basket with his lanthorn was to keep up this show of anger, Archy made a snatch at a long splinter of stone, and started up menacingly.

"Oh, that's it, is it?" cried Ram, who stood upon his guard, but did not appear in the least bit alarmed. "Fed you too well, have I? Had too many oats, and you're beginning to kick up your heels and squeak and snort. Never mind, I'll soon make you civil again. Going to give me that basket?"

"No."

"Then you shan't have this. There!" cried Ram, and snatching up the one he had brought, he walked straight away, swinging his lanthorn after he had shut it with a snap.

"Going to give it to me?" he cried, as he stopped about half way to the trap-door.

"No."

"You'll want all this, and I've got some good tack inside."

"Be off, fellow, and don't bother me."

"Yah! Who want's to?" cried Ram; and he went off whistling merrily till he was at the opening, when he shouted back, —

"No oats to-day, pony. Good-bye."

Archy leaped up and stood listening with his heart beating fast, and his head bent in the direction taken by the boy.

"How unfortunate!" he said. "But I could not help it. Will he come back?"

He listened and listened and hesitated, but there was no sound, and still he hesitated, till quite a couple of hours must have passed, when he uttered a loud exultant cry, determined now to make one bold dash for liberty, and made straight through the darkness for the open way.

Chapter Twenty Five

The midshipman drew in a long breath of the salt air, as he stood at the opening in the cliff face. He tightened his belt, drew his red cap down on his head, wished that his hands were not so sore, and muttered the words, "Now for liberty!" He began to creep through the hole till his head was well out, and he could look round for enemies.

There was not one. The only thing that he could see was a gull sailing round and round between him and the sea, down to his right.

And now, for the first time, it struck him that the gull looked very small, and from that by degrees he began to realise that the hole out of which he had thrust his head was fully four hundred feet above where the waves broke, and that it must be two hundred more to the top of the cliff.

It looked more perilous too than it had seemed before, but the lad was in nowise daunted. The way was open to him to climb up or lower himself down apparently, but he chose the former way of escape, knowing as he did how very little at the base of the cliffs was left bare even in the lowest tides, and that if he got down he would either have to swim or to sit perched upon a shelf of rock till some boat came and picked him off.

There was no cutter in view, but he did not trouble about that. He stopped only to gaze down at the dazzling blue sea, and thought that if it came to the worst he could leap right off into deep water, and then he drew himself right out on to a rugged ledge, a few inches in width, and stood holding on by the stones round the opening, looking upward for the best way to get up.

"Don't seem easy," he said cheerily, "but every foot climbed will be one less to get up. So, here goes."

As he ceased speaking he drew a deep breath, and then feeling that safety depended upon his being firm, cool, and deliberate, he made his way from the mouth of the hole along the ledge upon which he stood, till he found a spot where he could ascend higher.

It was necessary that he should find such a spot, for the ledge had grown narrower and in another yard died completely away. So, raising his hands to their full extent, he found a place for one foot, then for the other, repeated the experiment, and was just going to draw himself up to a ledge similar to that which he had just left, when one foot slipped from the stone upon which it rested, and had the lad lost his nerve he must have fallen headlong.

But he held on tightly, waited a minute to let the jarring sensation pass away, depending upon his hands and one foot. Then calmly searching about he found firm foothold, raised himself, and the next moment he was on the green ledge.

"Wouldn't have done to tumble," he said with a hall laugh. "Fall's one thing, a dive another. I suppose the water's pretty deep down there."

The ledge he was now on was fully a foot wide, and the refuse and fish bones with which it was strewn told plainly enough that in the spring time it was the resting—perhaps nesting—place of the sea-birds which swarmed along the coast.

As he stood facing the rock he found directly that he could not get any farther to his right, and a little search proved that from this ledge he could get no higher, not even had he been provided with a ladder. Even if a rope had been lowered down to him from the top of the cliff, it would have been of no avail, for he realised now that which he could not see from the hole by which he had escaped, to wit, that the cliff projected above the opening, and a lowered down rope would have hung several feet right away clear.

"Get farther along," he said coolly; and he edged himself slowly along, taking hold of every prominence he found to steady himself, and passing cautiously along the rough ledge over the hole, and then onward for forty or fifty feet, where a rift ran upward, and, by cautious climbing, he mounted slowly till he was on a fresh ledge, a few feet above which was another rift, and he climbed again, to come to a depression or niche, where he stopped to rest.

"No occasion to hurry," he said to himself, and as there was plenty of room he sat down and gazed out to sea, noting a sail far away to the right, but the vessel was a schooner—it was not that which he sought.

He was apparently cool enough, but his pulses beat more rapidly than was consistent with the exertion through which he had gone, and being after a few minutes eager now to get his task at an end, he tried to the left, to find no way up there, to the right, but everywhere the rock was perpendicular, and offered no foothold; or else sloped outward, and concealed what was above.

He tried again and again, hoping against hope, but without result.

"Must be a way up," he said, evidently considering that there must be because he wanted it, and he took tightly hold of a rough corner and leaned out a little to gaze upward, to find, in whichever direction he looked, right or left, there was nothing but rugged limestone, which had been splintered and moulded by time till there was not a spot where the most venturesome climber could obtain foothold; in fact, above him he could not see a spot where even the sea-birds had been in the habit of finding a resting-place.

It was for liberty, and naturally enough the midshipman made no superficial search. His next plan was to lie flat down in the niche he had made his temporary resting-place, lean over, and try and map out a course by which he could descend a little way and then pass along for a distance, and resume his climb upward with better chances of success.

But no; he could see no sign to help him, and, as a keen sense of disappointment assailed him that he should have got so near liberty and have to give up, he decided that the way to freedom was downward.

And now, as he looked over the edge of the shelf on which he lay, it struck him for the first time that it was a very terrible descent, and, turning his eyes away, he looked up again for a way there.

All in vain. He was fully a hundred and twenty feet from the top of the huge cliff, and, half afraid now that he should be quite afraid, he determined to lose no time, and, going to the spot where he had crept on to the niche floor, he began to lower himself slowly down.

"Be a good thing," he said to himself, as he searched with his feet and made sure of his footing, "if one could leave all one's thoughts behind at a time like this, or only keep enough to think where to put one's feet."

"Glad I haven't got on my uniform," he said a few moments later, as his breast scraped over the rough rock.

Soon after, —

"Oh, how sore my hands are! That's better."

He was back in safety on the ledge over the hole, and, passing along, he had soon descended to the one beneath the exit.

"Now then," he said, as he paused for a few minutes before commencing his descent; "this will be easier."

Somehow he did not feel in any hurry to begin, and he sat down with his legs hanging over the ledge, to give his nerves time to calm down, for there was a strong tendency to throb about his pulses, and he was not sufficiently conversant with the house he lived in, to know that confinement, worry, want of fresh air, and excessive work during the past few days had not given him what the doctors call "tone."

So he sat there with his back to the rock, gazing out to sea again, and then watching the graceful curves made by a gull, which had risen higher and higher, and came nearer and nearer, till it was on a level with him, and watching him curiously.

"Wonder whether you think I am going to fall and let you have a pick at me," said Archy, with a forced laugh; "because I am not going to tumble, so you can be off."

All the same, though, he shuddered, and he had to exercise a little force to make his new start downward.

"Best way after all," he said, as he began to descend. "If you go up, it gets more dangerous every minute, because you have farther to fall. If you go down, it gets safer, because you have less."

He found the way now comparatively easy, for the rock sloped a little out, and he had even got down some sixty feet when he had a check.

"I don't know, though," he said, as he put a bleeding knuckle to his lips. "Don't make much difference, I should think, whether you fall one hundred feet or five. Bother! I wish I did not keep on thinking about tumbling."

He forced himself to study the next part of his descent, which was nearly perpendicular, but well broken up with ledges and cracks which offered good holding, and terminated a hundred feet below, upon a shelf, which naturally offered itself as his next resting-place, but beyond which it was impossible to see.

"Don't matter," he said more cheerfully. "Let's take difficulties a bit at a time. I'm free, and I can laugh at them now. I could jump into deep water and swim, if there were no way down from below there."

His spirits rose now, for, though a false step or slip of the foot would have sent him headlong down to the broad ledge, from which he would in all probability have bounded into the sea, the climbing was good, and, panting with the exertion, he got from projection to ledge, now straight down, now diagonally, and often along first one tiny ledge or cornice and then another, zig-zagging, till, at about twenty feet from the place he was making for, a slaty piece of the limestone rock by which he was holding parted, frost-loosened, from the parent rock, and he went down with a rush.

But it was only a slide. He alighted on his feet, and, scratched and startled a bit, stood panting and trying to recover his composure.

"No harm done," he said, as he looked up to where the hole from which he had escaped was beginning to look quite small. "Might have been worse.

Quite bad enough, though. Shakes one so. Now for a rest, and then down again."

He stepped to the edge and looked over in the middle, next to the left, then to the right, and always with the same result. He was now on a regular sea-birds' sanctuary, for the rock below him was not perpendicular; but sloped right under, and, try as he would, he could devise no plan for getting down lower, save by taking a header into the sea, where the water looked black and deep to his right, while to his left there was the chasm upon which, twenty feet or so out of the perpendicular line, was the hole from which he had come.

Heights of sea-cliffs are very deceptive, and slopes which look to the inexperienced eye only a hundred feet or so to the top, are often more than double. It was so here, for, in spite of the distance he had come down, the midshipman found that he must be fully two hundred feet above the sea.

"Oh, how vexatious!" he cried, as he ground his teeth. "After all that work, after being so sure, to be out here on this wretched shelf like an old cormorant, but without any wings."

"I don't care," he said aloud, after again and again convincing himself that there was no possible means of farther descent. "I won't go back to prison; I'll sit here and starve first. Not I," he added, after a few moments' thought; "the cutter will be sure to sail by, and they could see me if I made signals from just here."

Rather doubtful, as he knew, for he was only at the corner of the chasm or tiny gulf into which the sea rushed, and the chances were that unless he had something big and white to wave, he was not likely to get his signal seen.

For one moment only the recollection of the food he had left behind tempted him to return.

"I might get it, and bring the basket down," he said. "No, I won't try it again; it's too dangerous. I don't want another slip. Besides, there must be a way down farther, if I could find it. Of course! I knew it!" he cried, as he gazed over once more, farther in toward the head of the little chasm, which looked as though the rock had been split from top to bottom.

He rubbed his hands, for some thirty feet below there was certainly a narrow possible place, and from there perhaps another might be found.

"If one could get down," he said to himself; but it did not look possible; the rock was out even of the perpendicular, and no sane person would attempt to drop from the edge so great a distance as that.

At that moment a piece of slaty rock came sliding down from on high, to fall with a crash and splinter on the rock at his feet.

"Must have loosened that," he said; "good job I didn't get it on my head. Oh!"

It was a cry of rage as much as of alarm, for there, following his track exactly, was Ram, who had returned repentant, alone, with his basket, to miss his prisoner, search, find the opening, and without hesitation to come down the cliff in pursuit.

Chapter Twenty Six

For the moment Archy Raystoke was puzzled—completely taken aback. This was something upon which he had not counted; and he stood there looking up, as he saw the boy descending with a far greater show of activity than he could have displayed.

Naturally, the first thought was of further flight, but he had already convinced himself that he was again a prisoner, and as, after another glance down at the ledge below to his left, he looked up at Ram, he set his teeth, and laughed in a way that did not promise well for his pursuer.

"What is he coming down for?" he said to himself, as his teeth began to set fast and his hands involuntarily to clench. "Does he think he is going to drag me up there again? He had better not try."

Meanwhile Ram was descending rapidly, and sending little ambassadors down before him in the shape of pieces of rock and shale, all of which arrived at the ledge in a very inimical way, bounding off, scattering in fragments, or falling with a heavy thud.

From time to time Ram looked down at his escaped prisoner, and then devoted himself to the places where he should never plant his feet, achieving the whole in the most fearless manner, and finishing with a leap which landed him near where Archy stood gazing at him, regularly at bay.

Ram did not hesitate an instant, but dashed at the midshipman to seize him by the jacket, but Archy was on his mettle, and he struck out sharply, a blow in the chest and another in the right shoulder, sending the young smuggler staggering back.

"Oh, that's it, is it?" cried Ram furiously. "I give you one more chance, though—will you give in, and come back quietly?"

"If you attempt to come near me, you dog," said Archy slowly through his clenched teeth, "I'll knock you off here into the sea."

"Will you?" cried Ram, dashing at his late prisoner again, dodging the blow struck at him, closing with his adversary; and then began a struggle which would have made the blood of an onlooker curdle, so terribly narrow and dangerous was the place where the encounter took place.

Of the pair, Archy Raystoke was a little the bigger, but the smuggler's son fully made up for any deficiency by his activity, and the hardening his muscles had undergone for years.

No blows were struck, the efforts of Ram being apparently directed to throwing the midshipman down, when he meant to sit upon him till he had reduced him to obedience.

Archy's tactics were, of course, to prevent this, and rid himself of his adversary, as he felt all the time how horribly risky it was to struggle and wrestle there, for the ledge was six feet wide at the outside, and not much more than twice the length.

But in a few minutes, as the encounter grew more hot, and they held on to each other, and swayed here and there, all thought of the position they occupied was forgotten. One minute Ram, by entwining his leg within those of his adversary, nearly threw him; then, by a dexterous effort, Archy shook himself fairly free. Then they clasped again, swayed here and there, Archy getting far the worse of the encounter from weakness, but, with a final call upon himself, he strove desperately to recover lost ground, and made so fierce an effort to throw Ram in turn, that he succeeded.

His effort was not sufficiently well sustained, though, for success to have attended it, but for one fact. They had struggled to the extreme edge of the inward part of the shelf, and as the midshipman was at the end of his strength, and Ram realised it, the boy smiled, thrust back his right leg to give impetus to his next thrust, and his foot went down over the rock.

There was a cry, a jerk, and the midshipman was down on his chest, as he had fallen, clinging to the edge, for the young smuggler seemed to have been snatched from his arms, and was now lying thirty feet below on the edge of a sloping rock, part of his body without support, and apparently about to glide off into the waves below.

Chapter Twenty Seven

Archy shuddered, his eyes grew fixed, and his whole body seemed to be frozen. The minute before he had been burning with rage, and struggling to gain the mastery over his enemy; now he would have given anything to have undone the past.

"Ram!" he cried excitedly, — "Ram, my lad, turn over quickly, and lay hold, or you will be off."

There was no reply. Ram's face looked ghastly, and his eyes were closed.

"I've killed him! I know I have!" cried Archy excitedly; and he strained himself more over the edge of the rock, to gaze wildly about for a means of descent, but there was only one: if he wished to get down to where the boy lay, apparently about to slip off into the sea, there was only one way, and that was to jump. Thirty feet! And if he did jump, he could not do so without coming down in contact with the boy, perhaps right on him, when it seemed as if a touch of a finger would send him headlong into the sea.

"What shall I do?" thought the midshipman. "It is horrible. Ram!" he shouted. "Rouse up! For goodness' sake, speak! Try to creep farther on to the rock. Oh, help I help!"

He shouted this frantically, but a wild and mournful cry from a gull was the only response, and his voice seemed to be utterly lost in the vast space around.

"I shall have murdered the poor fellow," groaned Archy; and he stared about wildly again, in search of some means of getting to his adversary.

None — none whatever. It would have been madness to jump, and he knew it — death — certain death to both. No one could have leaped down that distance on to a shelf of rock without serious injury, and then it would have been impossible to save himself from the rebound which must have sent him headlong into the sea below. This even if the shelf had not already been occupied; and Ram lay there, evidently stunned, if not killed.

What did Mr Brough and old Gurr always say? *"Be cool in danger — never lose your nerve!"*

"Yes, that was it!" he said, as he recalled lessons that he had received again and again. But what could he do? Even as he gazed down, he momentarily expected to see Ram glide slowly off, and, with brow covered with great drops of perspiration and his hands wet and cold, the midshipman rose panting to his feet, looked round, and sent up shout after shout for help.

Again his voice seemed utterly lost in the air, and a peculiar, querulous cry from the gull, which came slowly sailing round, was all the response he got.

"Ram!" he cried at last. "Ram! Don't play tricks, lad. Speak to me. I want to help you. Tell me what to do—to get help. Can't you speak?"

There was no mistaking the state of affairs; the boy was either dead or completely stunned by his fall.

Archy put his hands to his temples, and stood looking down wildly for a few moments, to assure himself that he could not reach his late adversary; and then, perfectly satisfied of the impossibility of the task, he began resolutely to climb up the face of the cliff where he had come down, and, setting his teeth hard, went from crack to crevice and ledge, on and on, seeing nothing but the white face below him on the shelf, and praying the while that the poor lad might not fall before he came back with help.

The work was more dangerous than he had anticipated, and twice he slipped, once so badly that he was holding on merely by the sharp edge of a projecting piece of stone, but he found foothold again, drew himself up, and went on climbing again, till, with face streaming with perspiration and his fingers wet with blood, of which he left traces on the stone as he went on, he at last reached the opening he had fought so hard to make, climbed in, turned and leaned out as far as he could, to try and get a glimpse of Ram, and be sure that he had not glided into the sea.

He could see nothing; Ram was far below under the projecting rock; and, drawing back once more, the midshipman began to hurry down the steps and then the slope, into the black quarry that he had fancied he had quitted for ever.

To his great delight, there, right away before him, was Ram's lanthorn, burning brightly with the door open, and shining upon the old sails and shipping gear, stores, and remains of wrecks saved from the sea.

But he did not stay. He caught up the lanthorn, closed the door lest a puff again should extinguish the candle, and then hesitated a moment or two as a thought struck him.

"No," he said aloud, "I must get help;" and, hurrying toward the opening, he kicked against the basket of provisions the lad had brought back. He made his way to the top of the other slope and shouted,—

"Hi, Jemmy!—smuggler! Quick! Come down!"

There was no response, for, good-heartedly enough, Ram had, as before-said, repented, and come back alone.

What should he do? Climb out, and run for help?

No, he did not know where to find it; and by the time he had discovered some of Ram's people, it would be too late; so, with the way of escape open to him, and freedom ready to welcome him once again, he hurried back, lanthorn in hand, selected a coil of rope from the pile of stores, threw it over his shoulder, passing his left arm through, and, leaving the lanthorn where he had found it, he hurried back to the narrow passage, climbed the slope and the steps up to the opening; and, with the rope hanging like a sword-belt from his shoulder, impeding his movements, and getting caught in the projections over and over again, he once more began to descend.

How he got down he hardly knew, but long before he reached the great shelf, he was so incommoded by the rope that he contrived, spread-eagled as he was against the rock face, to get it over his head, and then carefully let it drop, uttering a cry of anguish as he saw it fall, catching against a piece of rock which diverted its course, so that it rested nearly half over the edge, and he clung there, gazing down wildly, expecting to see it disappear, in which case he would have had to climb again for another coil.

Fortunately it lodged, and in a few minutes he was down beside it, and close at the end of the great ledge, gazing over wonderingly, and with his eyes half blinded by a mist, expecting to see the narrow shelf below bare.

But no; Ram had not moved, and there was yet time.

Seizing the coil of rope, he shook it open, and selecting one of the biggest blocks of stone, which had at some time fallen from above, he made one end of the rope fast, tried it to make sure, lowered the other over the edge, and carefully slid down, swinging to and fro, and turning slowly round, to hang for a few moments, trying to plant his foot on the ledge without touching Ram, for he felt more than ever convinced he would glide off at the slightest shock.

It was impossible. The only way was to draw up his legs, give himself an impetus by kicking against the rock, swinging to and fro, and then letting himself, at a certain moment when he was well beyond the boy, drop on to the shelf.

He tried the experiment, and swung past Ram again and again, but dared not leave go for fear of missing the rock with his feet.

At last he ventured: swung well past the prostrate figure, loosened his grasp, alighted on the narrow ledge quite clear, but could not preserve his balance, and fell back, uttering a low cry, as he tightened his grasp upon the rope again, but not till he had slipped rapidly down a good twenty feet, where he began swinging to and fro again.

For a few moments it seemed all over; there was the sea at a terrible depth below him, and all that distance to climb up with his hands bleeding and giving him intense pain, while his arms felt half jerked out of their sockets.

But he had had plenty of experience in climbing ropes, and, muttering, "Don't lose your nerve," he got the line well twisted round his legs, and climbed up again sufficiently high to repeat his former experiment, this time with success, and he stood upon the ledge and loosely knotted the rope about his waist, to guard against letting the end go, before kneeling down tremulously, and getting one hand well in under the collar of the boy's rough coat.

For some minutes he felt giddy; there was a mist before his eyes, and he involuntarily pressed himself close to the rock, expecting to fall, and in a curious, dreamy way he saw himself hanging far below, swinging at the end of the rope.

But all this passed off, and, exerting his strength as far as he could in the terribly dangerous, crippled position in which he was, he gave three or four sharp jerks, and succeeded in drawing Ram well on to the shelf, when, in the revulsion of feeling, the dizziness came back, and he felt that he must faint.

"Leave off, will yer?" came roughly to his ears, and roused him, telling him that the boy was not dead. "D'yer hear, Jemmy Dadd? Great coward! Father know'd you'd hit me like that, he'd half kill you."

There was a pause, and a sob of relief struggled from Archy's breast.

Then Ram began to mutter again.

"Oh, my head!" he groaned. "Oh, my head! Oh, my—"

He opened his eyes, and began to stare wildly; then he seemed to recollect himself, and started up to gaze up, then over the side at the sea far below, and lastly at his companion in misfortune.

"I reck'lect now," he said. "We was fighting, and I put my foot over the side, and come down here, hitting my head on the stones, and then I turned sick, and I knew I was falling over, and then I went to sleep. I was half off, wasn't I, with my legs down?"

"Yes. In a horrible position."

"Yes, it wasn't nice. Oh, my head! But who— Why, you didn't go and get the rope and come down and pull me on?"

Archy nodded.

"Is Jemmy here?"

"No."

"But did you climb up and get a rope, and come down again and haul me on here?"

"Yes," said the midshipman.

Ram stared at him, holding his hand to the back of his head the while, and a couple of minutes must have elapsed before he said,—

"Well, you are a rum chap!"

Archy grew red. Curious gratitude this seemed for saving the lad's life.

"Didn't you know the door was open?"

"Yes."

"Why didn't yer run away?"

"How could I, and leave you to fall off that place?"

"Dunno. Wouldn't ha' been nice. Where did you get the rope?"

"From close to where I slept."

"Yes, there was a lot there. 'Tain't cut," he said, looking at the hand he drew from the back of his head. "What a whop it did come down on the rock!"

"Don't talk about it," said Archy, with a shiver.

"Why not? Father allus said I'd got the thickest head he ever see. I say, though, you—did you—course you did. You climbed up again, and went into the cave, got the rope come down again, and then got down here to help me?"

"Yes."

"When you might have run away?"

"Of course."

"Thank ye. Shake hands!"

Chapter Twenty Eight

Ram sat there holding out his hand to the midshipman, but it was not taken, and for a space they gazed into each other's eyes. The silence was broken by Ram.

"Well," he said at last, "won't you shake hands?"

"An officer and a gentleman cannot shake hands with one like you," replied Archy coldly.

"Oh, can't he?" said Ram quietly. "You're a gentleman. Was it being a gentleman made you come down and pull me on here."

"I don't know whether being a gentleman made me do it," said Archy coldly. "I saw you would lose your life if I did not get a rope and come to you, and so I did it."

"Yes; that's being a gentleman made you do that," said Ram thoughtfully. "None of our fellows would have done that."

"I suppose not."

"I know I wouldn't."

"Yes, you would."

Ram looked the midshipman hard in the face again.

"You mean, if I'd seen you lying down here like I was, I should have gone and fetched the rope and pulled you up?"

"Yes; I am sure you would."

Ram sat in his old position, with his hand to the back of his aching head.

"But it's being a gentleman made you do it."

"No; anybody who saw a person in danger would try and save his life; and you would have tried to save mine."

"But I might have slipped and gone over the cliff."

"You wouldn't have thought about that," said Archy quietly. "You did not think about the danger when you saw me trying to escape."

"No, I didn't, did I?" said Ram thoughtfully. "I knew how savage father would be if you got away and fetched the sailors; and he told me I was to see you didn't get out, so I come down after you."

"And you would have done as I said."

"Well, praps I should," said Ram, laughing; "but, as we didn't neither of us go over, it's no use to talk about it. My! How it does ache!"

He turned himself a little, so as to plant his back against the rock, and let his legs hang down over the edge.

"That's more comf'table. Bit of a rest. Hard work getting down here and wrastling."

Archy was in so cramped and awkward a position, half kneeling, that he followed his companion's example, shuddering slightly, though, as he let his legs go down, and put his hands beside him to press his back firmly against the rock.

"Frightened?" said Ram, who was watching him.

"I don't know about being frightened. It would be a terrible fall."

"Oh, I don't know," said Ram, leaning forward and gazing down into the void. "Water's precious deep here. Such lots of great conger eels, six foot long, 'bout the holes in the bottom. Jemmy Dadd and me's caught 'em before now. Most strong enough to pull you out of the boat. Dessay, if you went down, you'd come up again, but you couldn't get ashore."

"Why? A good swimmer could get round the point there, and make for the ledge where I saw you and that man land."

"No, you couldn't," said Ram; "it's hard work to get round there with a boat. You do have to pull. That's where the race is, and it would carry you out to—oh?"

The boy was looking down between his legs as he spoke; and the midshipman just had time to dart forward his hand, catch him by the shoulder, and drag him back, or he would have gone off the rock.

Ram lurched over sidewise, his sun-browned face mottled and strange-looking, as his head dropped slowly over on to the midshipman's shoulder, where it lay for a good ten minutes, Archy passing his arm round the boy, and supporting him as he lay there, breathing heavily, with his eyes half-closed.

It was a terrible position; and a cold, damp perspiration bedewed the midshipman's face, as he felt how near they both were to a terrible end. The deep water after that awful fall, the fierce current which would carry him out to sea—and then came shuddering thoughts of the great, long, serpent-like congers, of whose doings horrible stories were current among the sailors.

At last, to his great relief, Ram uttered a deep sigh, and sat up, smiling at his companion.

"I've felt like that before," he said. "Come over all at once sick and giddy, like you do if you lean down too much in the sun. I should have gone over, shouldn't I, if you hadn't ketched me?"

"Don't talk about it."

"Oh, very well; it was hitting my head such a crack, I suppose. I say, though, you never thought you could get away down here, did you?"

"Meant to try," said Archy laconically.

"Yah! What was the good, I knowed you wouldn't; but I meant to fetch you back. Me and Jemmy Dadd come down here once after birds' eggs, before father had the place up there quite blocked up. It used to be a hole just big enough to creep through. Jemmy stopped up on that patch where you and me wrastled, and let me down with a rope. There's no getting no farther than this."

"Not with a rope?"

"Well, with a very long one you might slide down to the water, but what's the good, without there was a boat waiting? You hadn't got the boat, and you didn't bring no rope. No use to try to get away."

The words seemed more and more the words of truth as the midshipman listened, and he was compelled to own in his own mind that he had failed in his attempt; but a question seemed to leap from his lips next moment, and he said sharply,—

"Perhaps there's no getting down, but any one might climb up right to the top of the cliff."

"Fly might, or a beedle," said the boy, laughing. "Why, a rabbit couldn't, and I've seen them do some rum things, cutting up the rocks where they've been straight up like a wall. Why, it comes right over up nigh the top. No, father's right; place is safe enough from the seaside, and so it is from the land. Now, then, let's go back."

"You can go," said Archy coldly. "I'm going to stop here."

"That you won't," said Ram sharply. "You're a-coming up with me. Yah! What's the good o' being obstinate? We don't want to have another fight. Don't you see you can't get away?"

"I will get away," said Archy sternly.

"Well, you won't get off this way, till your wings grow," said Ram, laughing. "Come on, mate, let's get back."

Archy hesitated, but was obliged to come to the conclusion that he was beaten this time, and he turned slowly to his companion and said, —

"Can you climb that rope?"

"Can I climb that rope? I should think I can!"

"But dare you venture now?"

Ram put his hand to his head, and gazed up thoughtfully.

"Well, it would be stoopid if I was to turn dizzy again. S'pose you untie the rope from round you, and let me tie it round my waist. Then you go up first, and when I come, you'll be ready to lend me a hand."

"Yes, that will be best," said Archy.

"Without you want to leave me?" said the boy, laughing.

The midshipman made no reply. There was an arduous task before him, and his nerves were unstrung. After he had unfastened the end of the rope and passed it to Ram, who did not secure the end about him, but the middle, after he had nearly drawn it tight, so that, if he did slip, the fall would not be so long. Then reluctantly, but feeling that it must be done, Archy climbed the thirty feet of rope between him and the great ledge, slowly and surely, glad to lie down and close his eyes as soon as he was in safety so far.

He tried to, but he dared not look over when the rope began to quiver again. He contented himself with taking hold near the edge, and crouched there, picturing the boy turning dizzy once more from his injury, letting go, and dropping with a terrible jerk to the extent of the rope where it was tied. Then, as he felt the strong hemp quiver in his hands, he found himself wondering if the strands would snap one by one with the terrible strain of the jerk, and whether the boy would drop down into the sea.

What should he do then?

What should he do if the rope did not part? He did not think he would have strength to draw the boy up, and, if he did, he was so unnerved now, that he did not believe he would be able to drag him over the edge on to the rock platform.

There! Ram must be turning giddy, he was so long; and, unable to bear the pressure longer, Archy opened his eyes and crept nearer to the edge, to face the horror of seeing the boy's wild upturned eyes.

But he saw nothing of the kind, save in the workings of his own disordered imagination. What he did see was Ram's frank-looking rustic face close up, and a hand was reached over the edge.

"You may get hold of me anywhere if you like," said the boy, "and give a hand. That's your style, orficer! Pull away, and up she comes. That's it!" he said, as he crept over the edge. "Thank'ee. I aren't smuggled."

They both sat down for a few minutes, while Ram untied the rope from his waist and from round the big block of stone, before beginning to coil it up.

"I say," he said, as he formed ring after ring of rope, "that rock isn't very safe. If I'd slipped, and the rope hadn't snapped, that big stone would have come down atop of me, and what a mess you'd have been in, if father had said you pitched me off!"

"Let's get back," said the midshipman, who felt sick at heart; and he moved toward the place where he had been down and up three times.

"Wait a moment," said Ram, securing the end of the rope, and throwing the coil over his shoulder. "That's right. I'll go first. Know the way?"

"Because you don't trust me," said Archy angrily.

"That's it," said Ram. "Door's open, and you might get out."

Archy's teeth grated together, but he said nothing, only began to climb, following the boy patiently till they were nearing the opening, when he started so violently that he nearly lost his hold.

For a voice came from above his head, —

"Got him, Ram?"

"Yes, father; here he is."

For the moment the midshipman felt disposed to descend again, but he kept on, and a minute later he looked up, to see Ram's frank face looking out of the hole, and the boy stretched out his hand.

"Want any help? Oh, all right then!"

"Did you think you'd get out that way, youngster?" said Shackle, as the midshipman stood erect at the top of the rough stairs.

"I thought I'd try," said the lad stiffly.

"Took a lot o' trouble for nothing, boy," said the smuggler. "I come to see what was amiss, Ram, boy, you was so long. Don't come again without Jemmy Dadd or some one."

"No, father."

"So you thought you'd get away, did you?" said the smuggler, with an ugly smile. "Ought to have known better, boy. You wouldn't be kept here, if there was a way for you to escape."

Archy felt too much depressed to make any sharp reply, and the smuggler turned to his son.

"What's the matter with you?"

"Bit of a tumble, father, that's all," said the boy cheerfully, as he placed his hand to the back of his head.

"You should take care, then; rocks are harder than heads. Hi! You Jemmy Dadd!"

"Hullo!" came out of the darkness.

"Get Tom to help you to-morrow. Bring a bushel or two o' lime stuff, and stop up this hole, all but a bit big enough for a pigeon to go in and out. It'll give him a taste o' light and air. Now, youngster, on with you. Show the lanthorn, Jemmy."

The man came forward, and Archy was made to follow him, the smuggler and his son coming on behind; and ten minutes later the prisoner was seated in his old place in the darkness, with Ram's basket of provisions for consolation. As he sat there, listening to the departing footsteps, and feeling more and more that it was quite true,—escape must be impossible down the cliff, or else they would not have left him with the opening unguarded,—there was the dull, heavy report of the closing trap-door, and the rattle and snap of bolts, and that followed by the rumbling down of the pieces of stone.

He had pretty well thought out the correct theory of this noise, that it was on purpose to hide the trap-door from any prying eyes which might pass, and prying eyes must be few, he felt, or else the smugglers would not have had recourse to so clumsy a contrivance.

He thought all this over again, as he sat there wearied out and despondent, for in the morning his task had seemed as good as achieved, and now he was face to face with the fact, after all that labour, that it had been in vain, and he was more a prisoner than ever.

"Not quite so badly off as some, though," he thought, as, moved thereto by the terrible hunger he felt, he stretched out his hand for the basket. Not bread and water, but good tasty provisions, and— "What's this in the bottle?" he asked himself, as he removed the cork.

It was good wholesome cider, and being seventeen, and growing fast, Archy forgot everything for the next half-hour in the enjoyment of a hearty meal.

An hour later, just as he was thinking of going to the opening to sit there and look out at the evening sky, he dropped off fast asleep, and was wakened by the coming of two of the smugglers, who busied themselves in the repairs of the broken wall.

Chapter Twenty Nine

That day Jemmy Dadd brought him his food, and the next day, and the next.

"What did it mean?" he asked himself. He could understand this man being the bearer while he was employed at the mason work; but when that was over, he felt puzzled at Ram not coming.

Then he began to wonder whether the boy was ill in consequence of his fall, and he longed to ask, but, as everything he said to Dadd was received in gloomy silence, he felt indisposed to question the man, and waited, patiently or impatiently, till there should be a change.

The change did come, Ram appearing the next day with the basket; but his father and several other men entered the quarry, and something was brought in—what he did not see.

Ram came up to him with his basket, but, just as he began speaking, Shackle called him away, and once more the prisoner was left alone.

He partook of his meal, feeling more dull and dispirited than ever, and a walk afterwards to the little opening, just big enough to allow of his arm being thrust in, afforded no relief. For he wanted, to talk to Ram about their adventures, and to try whether he could not win over the boy to help him to escape.

The next day arrived, and, as of old, Ram came, with Jemmy Dadd left at the door.

"He's grumbling," said the boy, "about having to help watch over you."

"Then why not put an end to it?" cried Archy, eagerly dashing into the question next his heart, for his confinement now grew unbearable.

"How?"

"Help me to escape."

The boy laughed.

"Aren't you going to ask me how I am?"

"No; why should I?"

"'Cause you made me have that fall, and my head's been trebble. I've been in bed three days."

"I am sorry for you," said Archy; "but I can only think of one thing—how to get away."

"No good to think about that. Father won't let you go; I asked him."

"You did, Ram?"

"Yes, I asked him—though you wouldn't be friends and shake hands."

"What did he say?" cried Archy, ignoring the latter part of his gaoler's remarks.

"Said I was a young fool, and he'd rope's-end me if I talked any more such stuff."

The midshipman did not notice it, but there was a quiet and softened air in Ram's behaviour toward him, and the boy seemed reluctant to go, but, in the midshipman's natural desire to get away, he could think of nothing else but self.

"It would not be the act of a fool to set one of the officers of the Royal Navy at liberty."

"He says it would, for it would be the end of us all here. The sailors would come and pretty well turn us out of house and home. No; he won't let you go."

"How long is he going to keep me here?"

"Don't know. Long as he likes."

That last sentence seemed to drive the prisoner into a fit of anger, which lasted till the boy's next coming.

The prisoner had been listening anxiously for the sound which betokened the visit of his young gaoler, and he was longing to have speech with him; but, telling himself that the boy was an enemy, he punished himself, as soon as the lanthorn came swaying through the darkness, by throwing himself down and turning away his head.

Ram came up and held the lanthorn over him.

"Morning. How are you?"

Archy made no reply.

"'Sleep?"

Still no answer.

"You aren't asleep. Come, look up. I've brought you four plum puffs, and a cream-cheese mother made."

"Hang your plum duffs and cream-cheeses!" cried Archy, starting up in a rage.

"Didn't say plum duff; said plum puffs."

"Take 'em away then. Bread and water's the proper thing for prisoners."

"Oh, I say, you wouldn't get fat on that."

"Will you let me out?"

"No."

"Then I warn you fairly. One of these days, or nights, or whatever they are, I'll lie wait for you, and break your head with a stone, and then get away."

Ram laughed.

"What?" cried the prisoner fiercely.

"I was only larfin'."

"What at?"

"You. Think I don't know better than that? You wouldn't be such a coward."

"Oh, wouldn't I?"

"Not you," said Ram, sitting down quietly, and making the lid of his basket squeak. "You know I can't help it."

"Yes, you can. You could let me out."

"Father would kill me if I did. Why, if I let you out, you'd come with a lot o' men, and there'd be a big fight, and some of our chaps wounded and some killed, and if we didn't whop you, our place would be all smashed up, and father and all of 'em in prison."

"And serve 'em right!"

"Ah, but we don't think so. That's what you'd do, isn't it?"

"Of course it is."

"Well, then, I can't let you go. 'Sides, if I said I would, there's always Jemmy Dadd, or big Tom Dunley, or father waiting outside, and they'd be sure to nab you."

"But you might come by night and get me out."

"No," said the boy sturdily, "I couldn't."

"Then you're a beast. Get out of my sight before I half kill you!"

"Have a puff."

"Take them away, you thieving scoundrel!" cried Archy, who was half mad with disappointment. "You come here professing to be civil, and yet you won't help me."

"Can't."

"You can, sir."

"And you wouldn't like me if I did."

"Yes, I should, and I never could be grateful enough."

"No, you wouldn't. You'd know I was a sneak and a traitor, as you call it, to father and all our chaps, and you'd never like me."

"Like you! I tell you I should consider you my best friend."

"Not you. I know better than that. Have a puff."

"Will you take your miserable stuff away?"

"Have some cream-cheese and new bread."

Archy made a blow at him, but Ram only drew back slightly.

"Don't be a coward," he said. "You're an officer and a gentleman, you told me one day, and you keep on trying to coax me into doing what you know would be making me a regular sneak. What should I say when you were gone?"

"Nothing," cried the prisoner. "Escape with me. Come on board, and the lieutenant will listen to what I say, and take you, and we'll make you a regular man-o'-war's-man."

"And set me to fight agen my father, and all my old mates?"

"No; you should not do that."

"And you'd call me a miserable sneak."

"I shouldn't."

"Then you'd think I was, and I should know it, so it would be all the same."

"Then you will not help me?"

"Can't."

"You will not, you mean," said Archy bitterly. "You'd sooner keep me here to rot in the darkness."

"No, I wouldn't, and I'd let you out if I could," cried Ram, with animation. "I like you, that I do, because you're such a brave chap, and not afraid of any of us. S'pose I was a prisoner in your boat, would you let me out?"

"That's a different thing," said Archy proudly. "I am a king's officer, and you are only a smuggler's boy."

"I can't help that," said Ram warmly. "You wouldn't let me go because you couldn't, and I won't let you go because I can't."

"Then get out of this place, and let me be."

"Shan't. It's horrid dull and dark here, and lonesome. I shouldn't like it, and that's why I get mother to give me all sorts o' good things to bring for you, and save 'em up. Father would make a row if he knew. I do like you."

"Get out!"

"Ah, you may say that, but I'd do anything for you now."

"Then let me go."

"'Cept that."

"Knock me on the head, then, and put me out of my misery."

"And 'cept that too. I say, don't be snarky with me. You must stop here as long as father likes, but why shouldn't you and me be friends? I've brought you a Jew's harp to learn to play when you're alone."

Archy uttered an ejaculation full of contempt, and snatched the proffered toy and hurled it as far as he could.

"It was a sixpenny one, and I walked all the way to Dunmouth and back to get it for you—twenty miles. It aren't much of a thing for an orficer and a gentleman, though, I know. But, I say, look here, would you like to learn to play the fiddle?"

"Will you take your chattering tongue somewhere else?"

"'Cause," continued Ram, without heeding the midshipman's petulant words, "I could borrow big Tom Dunley's old fiddle. He'd lend it to me, and I'd smuggle it here."

"Smuggle, of course," sneered Archy.

"In its green baize bag. I could teach you how to play one toon."

Archy remained silent, as he sat on a stone, listening contemptuously to the lad's words.

"I thought I could often come here, and sit and talk to you, and bring a light, and I brought these."

He opened the door of the horn lanthorn, and produced from his pocket a very dirty old pack of cards, at which Archy stared with profound disgust.

"You and me could play a game sometimes, and then you wouldn't feel half so dull. I say, have a puff now!"

There was no reply.

"Shall I bring you some apples?"

Archy threw himself down, and lay on his side, with his head resting upon his hand, gazing into the darkness.

"We've got lots o' fox-whelps as we make cider of, and some red-cheeks which are ever so much better. I'll bring you some."

"Don't," replied Archy coldly. "Bring me my liberty. I don't want anything else."

"Won't you have the Jew's harp, if I go and find it?"

"No."

"Nor yet the fiddle, if I borrow it?"

"No."

"I say, don't be so snarky with me. I can't help it. I was obliged to do what I did, same as you'd have been if it had been t'other way on. Look here; let you and me be friends, and I could come often and sit with you. I'll stay now if you like. Let's have a game at cards."

Archy made no reply, and Ram sighed.

"I'm very sorry," he said sadly; "and I'd leave you the lanthorn if you like to ask me."

"I'm not going to ask favours of such a set of thieves and scoundrels," cried the midshipman passionately; "and once more I warn you that, if you come pestering me with your proposals, I shall knock you down with a stone, and then escape."

"Not you," replied Ram, with a quiet laugh.

"Not escape?"

"I meant couldn't knock me down with a stone."

"And pray why?"

"'Cause I tell you agen you couldn't be such a coward. I'm going now."

No notice was taken of the remark.

"Like another blanket?"

No answer.

"I'm going to leave the basket and the puffs and cheese. Anything else I can get you?"

Archy was moved by the lad's friendly advances, but he felt as if he would rather die than show it, and he turned impatiently away from the light shed by the lanthorn.

"I'll bring you some apples next time I come, and p'r'aps then you'll have a game at cards."

There was no reply, so Ram slowly shut the door of the lanthorn, turning the bright light to a soft yellowish glow, and rising to his knees.

"Do let me stop and have a game."

"Let me stop and talk to you, then."

There was no reply to either proposal, and just then there came a hoarse —

"Ram ahoy!"

"A-hoy!" cried the lad. "I must go now. That's Jemmy Dadd shouting for me."

Archy made no reply, and the boy rose, set down the basket beside where he had been kneeling, and stood gazing down at the prisoner.

"Like some 'bacco to chew?" he said. Then, as there was no answer, he went slowly away, with the prisoner watching the dull glow of the lanthorn till it disappeared behind the great pillars, there was a faint suggestion of light farther on, then darkness again, the dull echoing bang of the heavy trap-door and rattle of the thin slabs of stone which seemed to be thrown over it to act as a cover or screen, and then once again the silence and utter darkness which sat upon the prisoner like lead.

He uttered a low groan.

"Am I never to see the bright sun and the sparkling sea again?" he said sadly. "I never used to think they were half so beautiful as they are, till I was shut up in this horrible hole. Oh, if I could only get away!"

He started up now, and began to walk up and down over a space clear of loose stones, which he seemed to know now by instinct, but he stopped short directly.

"If that young ruffian saw me, he'd say I was like a wild beast in a cage. He'd call me a monkey again, as he did before. Oh, I wish I had him here!"

The intention was for the administration of punishment, but just then Archy kicked against the basket, and that completely changed the current of his thoughts.

"The beggar wants to be civil," he said. "He is civil. It was kind of him to bring the things to amuse me, and better food. Wants to be friends! But who's going to be friends with a scoundrel like that? I don't want his rubbish— only to be able to keep strong and well, so as to escape first chance."

"Likes me, does he?" muttered the midshipman, after a pause. "I should think he does. Such impudence! Friends indeed! Oh, it's insufferable!"

Archy's words were very bitter, but, somehow, all the time he kept thinking about their adventure, and the lad's bravery, and then about his having saved him.

"I suppose he liked that," said Archy, after a time, talking aloud, for it was pleasant to hear a voice in the solemn darkness, even if it was only his own.

He grew a little more softened in his feelings, and, after resisting the temptation for three hours, and vowing that he would keep to bread and water and starve himself before he would let them think he received their gifts, he found himself thinking more and more of the friendly feeling of the boy and his show of gratitude. Then he recalled all that had passed about the proposal to escape—to set him at liberty—to be his companion; and he was obliged to own that Ram had behaved very well.

"For him," he said contemptuously, and then such a peculiarly strong suggestion of its being dinner-time reminded him that he ought to partake of food, that he opened the basket, and the temptation was resisted no longer.

Pride is all very well in places, but there is a strength in cold roast chicken, plum puffs, and cream-cheese, that will, or did in this case, sweep everything before it; and, after making a very hearty meal, the midshipman almost wished that he had Ram there to talk to as a humble companion in that weary solitude.

"He's a miserable, contemptible beggar," said Archy at last, "but I need not have been quite so rough with him as I was."

Chapter Thirty

Matters grew no better. There was a leaning toward the rough lad, who seemed never weary of trying to perform little acts of kindness for his father's prisoner; but there was only one thing which the midshipman desired, and, as that could not be accorded, the friendly feeling between the two lads stayed where it was. In fact, it seemed to be turning into positive dislike on one side, Archy fiercely rating his gaoler over and over again, and Ram bearing it all in the meekest way.

The gloom was so familiar to Archy now that he could go almost anywhere about the great place, without stumbling over the loose fragments of stone, or being in danger of running up against the great pillars. And, as he roved about the quarry, his busy fingers touched packages and bales; he knew which parcels contained tobacco; he handled bales which he felt sure were silk, and avoided the piled-up kegs of brandy, whose sickly odour would always remind him of being ill at sea.

All these things occupied his mind a little, and when he was extra dull, he would go and lie down by the hole which admitted the salt sea air, or else make his way right under the trap-door, and climb up to it, and sit and listen for the coming of Ram.

One morning he was there, wondering whether it was near the boy's hour, and he was listening most intently, so as to get full warning and insure time enough to go back to his place and wait, when he fancied he heard the bark of a dog.

It was not repeated, and he was beginning to think that it was fancy, when the sound came again nearer, then nearer still, till there was a prolonged volley of canine-words, let us call them, for they evidently meant something from their being so persistent.

"Why—hurrah! He has found me!" cried the prisoner excitedly; and he heard quite plainly, as he clung to the rough steps and pressed his ear against the trap-door, the eager scratching made by a dog, and the snuffling noise as it tried to thrust its nose down amongst the stones.

"Hi! Good dog then!" he shouted, and there was a furious burst of barking.

Then there was a sharp sound as if a heavy stone had fallen upon a heap, and he heard it rattle down to the side.

Then there was a fierce growl, a bark, and directly after silence.

The midshipman's heart, which had been throbbing with excitement a few minutes before, sank down now like lead, as he waited to hear the sounds again, but waited in vain.

If ever the loud baying of a dog sounded like music in his ear, it was during those brief moments, and as he sat there, longing to know what it meant, and whether his conjecture was right that the dog had scented him out, he faintly heard the gruff tones of a voice, and, hastily descending, he went down the slope and made for his usual place.

"That's what it was," said Archy to himself. "The dog scented me out, and was scratching there till that great brute of a smuggler saw him, and threw a stone and drove him away. There they are."

He was right, the rough pieces of stone were being removed, and a few minutes later he saw the swinging lamp coming through the gloom.

The prisoner was, as he said, quite right, for that day Celia Graeme had wandered down towards the edge of the huge line of cliffs in a different direction to that which it was her wont to take.

It was not often that she stirred far from the gloomy fir-wood at the back of the house, for her life had not been that of most young people of her age. Her father's disappointed and impoverished life, consequent upon his political opinions, and her mother's illness and depression, had made the Hoze always a mournful home, and naturally this had affected her, making her a serious, contemplative girl, older than her years, and one who found her pleasure in sitting on a fallen trunk in the sheltering woods, listening to the roar of the wind in the pine boughs, watching the birds and squirrels, and having for companion her dog Grip, who, when she took him for her walks, generally ran mad for the first hour, scampering round and round her, making charges at her feet, and pretending to worry her shoes or dress; running off to hide and dash out upon her in a mock savage way; bounding into furze bushes, chasing the rabbits into their holes; and then, as if apologising for this wild getting rid of a superabundance of animal spirits kept low in the mournful old house, he would come as soon as she sat quietly down, crouch close up to her, and lay his head on her knee, to gaze up in her face, blinking his eyes, and not moving again perhaps for an hour.

Celia seldom went seaward. The distance was short, but she was content to watch the beautiful changes on the far-spreading waste from high up on the hills. There had been wrecks on the Freestone Shore, which made her shudder as she recalled how the wild cries of the hapless mariners in their appeals for help had reached the shore; she had seen the huge waves come tumbling in, to send columns of spray high in the air, to be borne over the land in a salt rain, and, as a rule, the sea repelled her, and she shrank, too, from the great folds of the cliff, with their mysterious-looking grass-grown ledges and cracks, up which came the whispering and gurgling of water, and at times fierce hissings as if sea monsters lived below, and were threatening those who looked down and did not pause to think that these sounds must be caused by air compressed by the inrushing tide.

Then, too, there was something oppressing in the poorly protected shafts with their sloping descents, once, perhaps hundreds of years back, the busy spots where old hewers of stone worked their way down below the thinner and poorer strata to where the freestone was clean and solid.

These spots attracted and yet repelled her, as she peered cautiously down, to see that they were half hidden by long strands of bramble, with tufts of pink-headed hemp agrimony, and lower down the sides and archway infringed with the loveliest of ferns.

There was something very mysterious-looking in these ancient quarries where foot of man never trod now, and she shivered as she passed funnel-shaped holes which she knew were produced by the falling in of the surface to fill up passages and chambers in the stone whose roofs had given way far below.

She often thought, when tempted by Grip in the direction of these weird old places, how horrible it would be if some day the earth suddenly sank beneath her, and she should be buried alive.

At such times her hands grew wet, and she retraced her steps, fancying the while that the earth sounded hollow beneath her tread.

Upon this particular morning Grip had vanquished her. He was always tempting her in this direction by making rushes and looking back as if asking her to come, for the dark holes tempted him. The rabbit burrows were all very well, but he could never get in them beyond his shoulders, while in these holes he could penetrate as far as he liked in search of imaginary wild creatures which were never found. Then, too, there were the edges of the cliffs where he could stand and bark at the waves far below, and sometimes, where they were not perpendicular, descend from shelf to shelf.

The morning was glorious, and the sea of a lovely amethyst blue, as Celia wandered on and on toward the highest of the hills away west of the Hoze. Grip was frantic with delight, his tail stood straight out, and his ears literally rattled as he charged over the short turf after some rabbit, which dodged through the bushes, reached its hole, displayed a scrap of white cotton, and disappeared.

And still, smiling at the dog's antics, the girl wandered on, nearer and nearer to where the land suddenly ended and the cliff went sharply down to the sea.

As she went on, stopping to admire the beautiful purple thistles, which sent up one each a massive head on its small stalk, or admired the patches of dyer's rocket and the golden tufts of ragwort, the old fancies about the ancient quarries were forgotten for the time, and she seated herself at last upon a projecting piece of stone, away there in the solitude, to watch the grey gulls and listen to the faint beat of the waves hundreds of feet below.

There were a few sheep here and there, but the Hoze was hidden beyond a fold of the mighty hills, and Shackle's farm and the labourer's cottage were all down in one of the valleys.

It was very beautiful, but extremely lonely, and to right and left there were the great masses of cliff, which seemed like huge hills suddenly chopped off by the sea, and before her the wide-stretching amethystine plain, with a sail or two far away.

Celia sat watching a little snake which was wriggling rapidly along past her, a little creature whose scales looked like oxidised silver in the afternoon sunshine, and she was about to rise and try to capture the burnished reptile, knowing from old experience that it was harmless, when at one and the same moment she became aware that Grip was missing, and that Ram Shackle and the big labourer from the farm, Jemmy Dadd, were coming up a hollow away to the right, one by which they could reach the down-like fields that spread along the edge of the cliffs from the farm.

She saw them, and hardly realising that they did not see her, she went on watching the reptile as it glided with easy serpentine motion through the grass.

"Ram is going to gather blackberries," she said to herself, as she glanced at his basket; "and Dadd is going to count the sheep. I ought to have brought a basket for some blackberries."

She felt full of self-reproach, as she recalled how plentifully they grew there, and how useful they would be at home. "And I might get some mushrooms, too," she thought, "instead of coming out for nothing."

Just then she heard Grip again barking very faintly.

"Stupid dog!" she said to herself, with a little laugh. "He has followed a rabbit to its hole. If he would only catch a few more, how useful they would be!"

Then she moved a little to follow the slow-worm, which was making for a patch of heath, and she was still watching it when, some time after, Grip came running up quickly, snarling and growling, and pausing from time to time to look back.

"Oh, you coward!" she said, sitting down and pulling his ears, as he thrust his head into her lap. "Afraid of a fox! Was it a fox's hole, then, and not a rabbit's, Grip?"

The dog growled and barked.

"Poor old fellow, then. Where is it, then?"

The dog leaped up, barked, and ran a few yards, to stop, look back at her, and bark again.

"No, no, Grip; I don't want to see," she said; and she began idly to pick up scraps of wild thyme and toss at the dog, who vainly kept on making rushes toward the slope of the great cliff.

"No, sir," she said, shaking her finger at him. "I am not going to be led to one of your discoveries, to see nothing for my pains."

The dog barked again, angrily, and not until she spoke sharply did he obey, and followed her unwillingly up the slope and then down into a hollow that looked as if at one time it might have been the bed of some great glacier.

The dog tried again to lead her away toward the sea, but she was inexorable; and so he followed her along unwillingly, till, low down in the hollow, as she turned suddenly by a pile of great blocks of weather-worn and lichened stone, she came suddenly upon Dadd and Ram, the former flat on his back, with his hat drawn-down over his eyes, the latter busy with his knife cutting a rough stick smooth.

"How do, Miss Celia?" said Ram, showing his white teeth.

"Quite well, Ram. How is your head now?"

"Oh, it's all right agen now, miss. On'y a bit sore."

"You tumbled off the cliff, didn't you?"

"Off a bit of it," said Ram, grinning. "Not far."

"But how foolish of you! Mrs Shackle said you might have been killed."

"Yes, miss, but I wasn't."

"What were you doing in such a dangerous place?"

"Eh?" said Ram, changing colour; "what was I doing?"

"Yes, to run such a risk."

"I was—I was—"

Ram was completely taken aback, and sat staring, with his mouth open.

"Lookin' after a lost sheep," came in a deep growl from under Jemmy Dadd's hat.

"Oh! And did you find it?"

"Yes; he fun' it," said the man, "but it were in a very dangerous place. It's all dangerous 'long here; and Master Shackle wouldn't let young Ram here go along these here clift slopes without me to take care on him."

Ram grinned.

"And you take my advice, miss, don't you come 'bout here. We lost four sheep last year, and come nigh losing the missuses best cow not long ago. Didn't you hear?"

"Yes; old Mary told me, and Mrs Shackle mentioned it too."

"Ay," continued Jemmy, without removing his hat, "she fell slip-slap into the sea."

"Poor thing."

"Ay, little missus; and, if I were you, I wouldn't come along top o' they clifts at all. Grass is so short and slithery that, 'fore you knows where you are, your feet goes from under you, and you can't stop yourself, and over you goes. And that aren't the worst on it; most like you're never found."

"Yes, 'tis very slippy, Miss Celia," said Ram, beginning to hack again at his stick.

"I do not come here very often, Ram," she said, quietly. "It is a long time since I came."

"Ay, and I wouldn't come no more, little missus," continued Jemmy, from under his hat, "for if you did not go off, that there dog—"

Grip had been looking on uneasily, and turning his head from one to the other, as each spoke in turn; but the minute he heard himself mentioned, he showed his teeth, and began to growl fiercely at the man.

"Look ye here," cried Jemmy, sitting up quickly and snatching away his hat, "if you comes at me—see the heel o' that there boot?"

He held up the great heavy object named, ready to kick out, and Grip bared his teeth for an attack.

"Down, Grip! Come here, sir. How dare you?"

But Grip did dare, and he would have dashed at the labourer if Celia had not caught him by the loose skin of his neck, when he began to shake his head and whine in a way that sounded like protesting.

"And me giving a bit of advice too," said Jemmy in an ill-used tone.

Grip barked fiercely.

"Be quiet, sir!"

"And going to say, little missus, that if that there dog comes hanging about here, he'll go over them there cliffs as sure as buttons, and never be seen no more."

"Come away, Grip. Thank you, Mr Dadd," said Celia, hurrying the dog away, and giving him a run down along the hollow; while Jemmy Dadd threw himself back, rolled over on to his face, and laughed hoarsely.

"I say, young Ram," he cried, "what a game!"

"What's a game?" said the boy sharply.

"That there dog; he won't forget that whack I give him on the ribs for long enough."

"Needn't have thrown so hard."

"Why not?"

"Don't like to see dogs hurt," said Ram, who was dealing with an awkward knot.

"Oh, don't you! Why, if your father had been along here with that rusty old gun of hisn, that he shoots rabbits with, and seen that dog scratching among them stones, know what he'd have done?"

"No."

"Well, then, I do. He'd have shot him. And if I ketches him ferretin' about there again, I'll drop a big flat stone down on him, and then chuck him off the cliff."

"If you do, I'll chuck you down after him," said Ram.

"What?" cried the man, bursting into a fresh roar of laughter. "Oh, come, I likes that. Why, you pup! That's what you are—a pup."

This was uttered with what was meant to be a most contemptuous intonation of the voice.

"Pups can bite hard sometimes, Jemmy," said Ram slowly; "and I shan't have Miss Celia's dog touched."

"Ho! Then he's to come here when he likes, and show everybody the way into our store, is he? Well, we shall see."

"Yes; and you'd better go and see if they've gone."

"Ah, yes, lad, I'll go and see if they've gone; and we needn't quarrel 'bout it, for it strikes me as little missus won't come down here no more, I scared her too much."

Jemmy burst into another hoarse fit of laughing, and went lumping off in his big sea-boots to see if Celia and her dog were well out of sight, before rejoining Ram to take the prisoner his repast.

Chapter Thirty One

Three days passed, and the idea of losing her companion was so startling to Celia, that she made no further journey toward the cliffs, in spite of several efforts made by Grip to coax her in that direction. But on the fourth day there was so mean and unsatisfactory a dinner at the Hoze, of the paltry little rock fish caught by the labouring men, that, as Celia watched her mother partaking of the unsatisfactory fare, and thought how easily it might have been supplemented by a dish of mushrooms and a blackberry pudding, she made up her mind that the next day she would go.

"I could be very careful, and not go near any of the slopes running down to the cliff, and I could make Grip keep with me. Yes, I will go," she said.

The next morning she partook of her breakfast quite early—a simple enough meal, consisting of barley bread and a cup of fresh milk from the Shackles' farm, and, taking a basket, she called Grip, who came bounding about her in a state of the most exuberant delight.

The dog's satisfaction was a little damped as his mistress took her way toward the fir-wood, and he kept making rushes by another path. But it was of no use; Celia had made her own plans, and, as the dog could not coax her his way, and would not go alone, he had to follow her.

There was a reason for this route being chosen, for Celia did not care to be seen by Ram, or any of the men who might be pretending to work hard on Shackle's farm, which was ill tended, and consisted for the most part of cliff grazing land; but somehow seemed to need quite a large staff of labourers to keep it in such bad order.

By passing through the fir-wood, Celia meant to get out of sight of the cottages, and she went on, with the dog following sulkily behind, but reviving a little upon being given the basket to carry.

She trudged on for about a mile over the thin stony pastures, found a fair number of small, sweet, pink-gilled mushrooms where the turf was finest and richest, and gradually adding to her store of glistening bramble-berries till her finger-tips were purple with the stains.

The course she chose was down in the hollows between the hills, till at last she struck the one along which she had passed after leaving Ram and his companion, and turned down here, believing that, if the boy selected it, there would be good reason for his so doing. She walked steadily on, finding a button mushroom here and a bunch of blackberries there. For one minute she paused, struck by the peculiar sweet and sickly odour of a large-leaved herb which she had crushed, and admired its beautifully veined blossoms, in happy ignorance of the fact that it was the deadly poisonous henbane, and then all at once she missed Grip.

"Oh, how tiresome!" she cried excitedly; and she called him loudly, but there was no reply. A gull or two floated about and uttered their querulous calls, otherwise the silence was profound, and, though she swept the great curved sides of the hollow, whose end seemed filled up by the towering hill, all soft green slope toward her, but sheer scarped and projecting cliff toward the sea, there was not so much as a sheep in sight.

With a great horror coming upon her, she hurried along towards the cliff, thinking of what Dadd had said, and picturing in her mind's eye poor Grip racing along some seaward slope in chase of a rabbit, and going right over the cliff, she went on almost at a run, pausing, though, to call from time to time.

It was intensely hot in that hollow, for the sea breeze was completely shut off, but she did not pause, and rapidly neared the cliff now, her dread increasing, as she wondered whether Ram would be good enough to get a boat, and row along under the cliff to find the poor dog's body, so that she might bury it up in the fir-wood behind the house, in a particular spot close to where she had so often sat.

No sign of Grip: no sound. She called again, but there was no cheery bark in response, and with her despondent feeling on the increase, she began to climb the side of the hollow, passing unnoticed great clusters of blackberries, whose roots were fast in the stones, and the fruit looking like bunches of black grapes; past glistening white mushrooms, better than any she had yet seen, but they did not attract her; and at last she had climbed so high that she could see the blue waves spreading up and up to the horizon, and about a couple of miles out the white-sailed cutter, which was creeping slowly along the shore.

"I wonder where that midshipman is," she thought, forgetting the dog for the moment. "How strange that all was! Could it really have been a dream?"

"Yes, it must have been, or else he would have gone and told his captain, and they would have come and searched the cellar, and there would have been sad trouble."

She turned her eyes from the sea, and began to search the green slopes around, and then all at once she uttered a cry of joy as she could sight, on the highest slope right at the end of the valley, a white speck which suddenly appeared out of the earth, and then stood out clear on the green turf, and seemed to be looking about before turning and plunging down again.

It was quite half a mile away, and her call was in vain, and she began to descend diagonally into the hollow, the tears in her eyes, but a smile of content on her lips.

"Oh, you bad dog," she cried merrily, "how I will punish you!" and she stooped and picked a couple of mushrooms, quite happy again, and even sang a scrap of a country ditty in a pretty bird-like voice as she came to a bramble clump, and went on staining her fingers.

By degrees she passed the end of the hollow, leaving all the blackberries behind, and now, only pausing to pick a mushroom here and there, she began to ascend the slope toward where she had seen the dog.

"It is getting nearer the edge of the cliff," she said; "but it slopes up, and not down. Ah, I see you, sir. Come here directly! Grip! Grip!"

The dog had suddenly made his appearance about fifty yards in front, right as it were out of the grassy slope, to stand barking loudly for a few moments before turning tail and plunging down again.

"Oh, how tiresome!" she cried. "Grip! Grip!"

But, as the dog would not come to her, she went on, knowing perfectly well that he had gone down one of the old stone pits, and quite prepared to stand at last gazing into a hole which inclined rapidly into the hillside, but was as usual provided with rough stones placed step-wise, and leading the way into darkness beneath a fern-fringed arch, while the whole place was almost entirely choked-up with the luxuriantly growing brambles.

"He has found a rabbit," she thought to herself, as her eyes wandered about the sides of the pit, and brightened at the sight of the abundant clusters of blackberries, finer and riper than any she had yet secured.

"I wish I was not so frightened of these places," she said to herself. "Why, I could fill a basket here, and there can't be anything to mind, I know; it is only where they used to dig out the stone."

A sudden burst of barking took her attention to the dog, who came bounding up the rugged steps right to her feet, looked at her with his great intelligent eyes, and, before she could stop him, rushed down again, where she could hear him scratching, and there was a sound which she knew was caused by his moving a piece of stone such as she could see lying at the side in broken fragments, and of the kind dug in thin layers, and used in the neighbourhood instead of tiles.

"Oh, Grip, Grip! And you know you can't get at him. Come here."

"Ahoy!"

Celia was leaning over the rugged steps, gazing down into the darkness beneath the ferns, when, in a faint, smothered, distant way, there came this hail, making her nearly drop her basket as she started away from the pit.

The hail was followed by a sharp burst of barking, and the dog came bounding up again, to stand looking after her, barking again before once more descending.

Slowly, and with her eyes dilated and strained, the girl crept back step by step, as she withstood her desire to run away, for all at once the thought had come that perhaps some shepherd or labourer had fallen down to the bottom, and was perhaps lying here with a broken leg.

She had heard of such things, and it would be very terrible, but she must know now, and then go for help.

In this spirit she once more reached the entrance to the old quarry, and peered down, listening to the worrying sound made by the dog, who kept rattling one piece of stone over another, every now and then giving a short, snapping bark.

"Ahoy!" came again, as if from a distance, and a thrill ran through the girl, bringing with it a glow of courage.

"It is some poor fellow fallen down;" and, placing her basket by the side, she began to descend cautiously, with Grip rushing to meet her, barking now joyously, and uttering whine after whine.

The descent was not difficult, and after the first few steps the feeling of timidity began to wear off, and Celia descended more quickly till, about fifty feet from the top, some distance under where the fringe of ferns hung, and where it had seemed quite dark from above, but was really a pleasant greenish twilight, she found beneath her feet a few loose flat stones, part of a quantity lying before her in the archway that seemed to lead straight on into the quarry.

But here, right at her feet, the dog began to scratch, tossing one thin piece of stone over the others upon which it lay.

Celia looked before her wonderingly, for she had expected to see a fallen man at once, probably some one of the men whom she knew by sight; but, in spite of the dog's scratching, she could not imagine anything was there, and she was bending forward, gazing into the half choked-up level passage before her, when there came from under her feet the same smothered, —

"Ahoy!"

She started away, clinging to the side for support, and ready in her fear to rush back to the surface.

But the dog's action brought her to herself, as he began again to bark furiously, and tore at the stones.

"Hush! Quiet, Grip!" she said in an awe-stricken whisper, as she went down on her knees and listened, her heart beating wildly, and a horrible idea, all confused, of some one having been buried alive, making her face turn ashy pale.

"Ahoy! Any one there?" came in the same faint tones.

"Yes—yes," panted the girl. "What is it?"

"Help!"

And then, more loudly, —

"Let me out, pray."

"Oh," moaned the girl, "what does it mean?"

"Ahoy there!" came more plainly now. "Whoever you are, get a boat, and go off to the cutter *White Hawk*. Can you hear?"

"Yes, yes," said the girl huskily, as a horrible suspicion ran through her mind.

"Tell Lieutenant Brough that Mr Raystoke is a prisoner, kept by the smugglers, and then show his men the way here."

There was a pause, for Celia could make no reply; she knew who Mr Raystoke was, and it seemed horrible to her that the frank, good-looking young midshipman should be kept a prisoner in such a tomb-like place as that.

"Don't, don't say you will not go!" came up in the smothered tones. "You shall have a reward."

"As if I wanted a reward!" panted Celia. "What shall I do? What shall I do?"

"Help—pray help!" came from below; and Grip joined in.

"Yes, I will help you," cried Celia, placing her face close down to the stones.

"What!" came up. "I know you—the young—yes, Miss Graeme."

"Yes," she cried hastily.

"Pray help me."

"I want to," she said; "but—but you will go and—and tell—about what you have seen."

There was a pause, and then came faintly the words,—

"I—don't—want to; but—I must."

"But I cannot—I cannot help you if you are going to fetch the sailors here, perhaps to seize—Oh, what shall I do?"

There was a pause before the prisoner spoke again.

"Look here," he said; "I don't want to tell about your father being mixed up with the smugglers."

"You must not—you dare not!" cried Celia.

There was another pause, and then the prisoner's voice came again reproachfully.

"You ought to know it's my duty, and that I was sent ashore to find this out.—I say."

"Yes."

"Did you know I was shut up like this by those beasts?"

"Oh, no, no, no!"

"Your father did. He had me sent here, so that he should not get into trouble."

"Indeed no! He would not do so wicked a thing."

"But he is a smuggler."

"It is not true!" cried Celia passionately; "and if you dare to say such things of my dear, good, suffering father, I'll go away and never help you."

"I can't help saying it," said Archy sturdily. "I'd give anything to get out of this dreadful dark place; but I must speak."

"Not of him."

"I don't want to speak of him," said Archy, "but what can I do? I must tell about all those smuggled things there in the cellar that night when you found me in that room—out of uniform."

"Ah!" ejaculated Celia.

"I know it's hard on you, but I've been here a prisoner ever since, and it's enough to break one's heart."

The poor fellow's voice changed a little as he spoke, and he would have given way if he had seen Celia's head bowed down, and that she was crying bitterly.

"You will send for help?"

"I cannot," sobbed the girl, "unless you will promise not to tell."

There was a pause again.

"I can't promise," came up huskily, in faint smothered tones. "I say, is the door locked as well as bolted?"

"I cannot tell; it is covered with stones. Pray, pray promise me that you will not tell. I do want to help you to get away."

"I can't promise," said Archy at last, after a bitter struggle with self. "I must go straight to my officer and tell him as soon as I get out."

At that moment there was a sharp barking from the dog, who rushed up the steps to stand at the top for a few moments before coming down again.

"Won't you help me?"

"To send my poor innocent father to prison," said Celia in a low voice.

"I can't hear you," came from below.

"And I can't tell you," said Celia to herself. "What shall I do—what shall I do?"

She stole softly up the rugged steps, with her fingers in her ears, in dread lest she should be called upon to listen to the prisoner's piteous appeals for help; and, as soon as she reached the top, she set off running as hard as she could go, to find her father, tell him all, and appeal to him to try and save the poor fellow from the cruel trials he was called upon to bear.

Celia could hardly see the direction in which she was going, for her eyes were blinded with tears, and so it was that, when down in the lowest part of the hollow, as she hurried blindly along, she tripped over one of the many loose stones, fell heavily, striking her temple against a block projecting from the steep side of the little valley; and fell, to lie insensible for a time; and when she did come to her senses, it was to find Grip lying by her, with his head upon her chest, and his eyes looking inquiringly into hers, as if to ask what it all meant.

Her head ached, and she felt half stunned still, but she strove to rise to her feet, and sank back with a moan of pain.

For a worse trouble had discovered itself: her ankle was badly wrenched, so that she could not stand, and in the solitary place in which she had fallen, it was possible that she might lie for days and not be found, unless special search was made.

A sudden thought came—to tie her handkerchief about Grip's neck, and send him home.

The first was easily done, the latter impossible. Grip was an intelligent dog in his way, but nothing would make him leave his mistress there; and the poor girl lay all day in the hot sun, and at last saw that night was coming on, and that there was no help.

Chapter Thirty Two

Celia Graeme took sundry precautions to avoid being seen, but she was not so successful as she imagined.

Jemmy Dadd was an old servant of Farmer Shackle, one who always made a point of doing as little as was possible about the farm. He did not mind loading a cart, if he were allowed as much time as he liked, or feeding the pigs, because it afforded him an opportunity to lean over the sty and watch the pretty creatures eat, while their grunting and squeaking was sweet music in his ear. He generally fed the horses, too, and watched them graze. Calling up the cows from the cliff pastures he did not mind, because cows walked slowly; and he did the milking because he could sit down and rest his head; but to thump a churn and make butter was out of his line.

Mrs Shackle complained bitterly to her lord and master about different lots of cream being spoiled, but Farmer Shackle snubbed her.

"Can't expect a man to work night and day too," he grunted. "Set one of the women to churn."

In fact, the farmer never found any fault with Jemmy, for the simple reason that he was his best worker on dark nights, and as handy a sailor as could be found.

Jemmy knew it, felt that he was licensed, and laughed to himself as he followed his own bent, and spent a good deal of time every day in what he called seeing the crops grow.

When there were no crops growing, he went to see how the grass was getting on, and to do this properly, he put a piece of hard black tobacco in his cheek, and went and lay down on one of the hill-slopes.

He was seeing how the grass got on that particular morning with his eyes shut, when, happening to open them, he caught sight of Celia going along, a mile away, with her basket and dog.

He knew her by the dog, though even at that distance, as she moved almost imperceptibly over the short turf of the treeless expanse along by the sea, he would have been sure that it was Sir Risdon's child.

"What's the good of telling on her?" he growled to himself, as he lay back with his hands under his head; and in that attitude he rested for nearly three hours. Then, moved by the cogitations in which he had been indulging, he slowly and deliberately rose, something after the fashion of a cow, and began to go slowly in the direction taken by Celia hours before.

Jemmy Dadd seemed to be going nowhere, and as he slouched along, lifting up one heavy sea boot and putting it down before the other, he never turned his head in either direction. So stiff was he in his movements, that any one who watched him would have concluded that he was looking straight forward, and that was all.

A great mistake; for Jemmy, by long practice, had made his eyes work like a lobster's, and, as he went on, they were rolling slowly round and round, taking in everything, keeping a look-out to sea, and watching the revenue cutter, sweeping the offing, running over the fields and downs and hollows, missing nothing, in short, as he steadily trudged along, not even the few mushrooms that the pleasant showers had brought up, and placing them in his hat.

Slow as his pace was, the distance between the prints of the big boots was great, and the mushroom hunting took him, before very long, up the cliff beyond the entrance to the old quarry, then down below it, and then close up alongside, where he stooped over, and then went down a few steps out of sight.

He did not turn his head, for his lobster eyes had convinced him that no one was in sight, and, as he disappeared in the deep hole, he pounced upon the basket, and then went softly and quickly down to where the loose tile stones lay.

A rapid examination satisfied him that they had not been moved, and he went softly up again, basket in hand, stood still and rolled his eyes, but saw no sign of the basket's owner, and then, thrusting his arm through the handle, he went steadily back to the farm, where he thrust his head in at the door, stared at Farmer Shackle, who was innocently mending a net, and backed out and went into the rough stable.

Shackle followed him, net in one hand, wooden netting-needle in the other.

"Hullo!" he said.

Jemmy held out the basket.

"Well, I see brambrys and masheroons. What of 'em?"

"Little missus's basket. Fun' it."

"Take it home. No—I'll send Ramillies. Ladyship don't like to see you."

"Fun' it in number one!"

"What!"

"See her going along there with that dog. She must ha' smelled him out."

"Place been opened?"

"No."

Farmer Shackle scratched his nose on both sides with the netting-needle; then he poked his red worsted cap a little on one side with the same implement, and scratched the top of his head, and carefully arranged the red cap again.

"Mayn't have seen or heard anything, lad."

"Must, or wouldn't have left the basket."

"Right. Have big Tom Dunley, Badstock and two more, and be yonder at dark. Ramillies know?"

"Not yet."

"Don't tell him. He's waiting yonder for you. Here he comes. Go on just as usual, and don't tell him nothing. I'll meet you soon as it's dark."

"Pistols?"

"No. Sticks."

"Jemmy there, father? Ah, there you are! Come on. I've been waiting such a time."

Ram looked sharply from one to the other, and knew there was something particular on the way, but he said nothing.

"Get it out of Jemmy," he said to himself.

"I'm ready, lad; I'm ready."

"Look sharp, boy," said the farmer.

"Yes, father," said Ram. "I'll go and get the basket."

"Ay, do, boy. And look here—never mind more to-day; but take double 'lowance to-morrow, so as not to go every day."

"Very well, father. Look sharp, Jemmy!"

The boy ran back to the house, followed by his father, who went on netting, and a minute later Jemmy and Ram were off over the bare pastures in the direction from which the man had come.

"Find that basket you give to father, Jemmy?"

"Ay, lad, half full o' brambrys and masheroons. Wondered whose it was. Gaffer says it's little missus's, and you're to take it up."

"Oh," thought Ram, "that's what they were talking about;" and he began whistling, quite content, as they went wandering about mushrooming, till, apparently tired, they sat down close to the mouth of the quarry, where Jemmy's eyes rolled round for a good ten minutes before he said, "*Now.*"

Then the pair rolled over to left and right, down into the hole, and descended quickly to the bottom, where the man crept right on along the half choked passage, took a lanthorn from a great crevice; there was the nicking of flint and steel, a faint blue light, and the snap of the closing lanthorn as the dark passage showed a yellow glow.

Meanwhile Ram had been busy removing the pieces of stone, laying bare a trap-door upon which were a big wooden lock and a couple of bolts. These he unfastened, threw open the door, and descended with his basket; while, after handing down the lanthorn into the black well-like hole, Jemmy climbed up again to the surface and stood with his eyes just above the level, sheltered by blackberry strands and other growth, and slowly made his eyes revolve; till, at the end of half an hour, Ram reappeared, when the business of closing and bolting the door went on, while Jemmy blew out the light, closed the lanthorn, through whose crevices came forth an unpleasant odour, bore it back to its hiding-place; and then the pair departed as cautiously as they came.

"What did he say?" growled Jemmy.

"Oh, not much. Seemed all grumpy, and wouldn't answer a civil question."

"Should ha' kicked him," said Jemmy.

Very little more was said till they reached home, and Ram busied himself about the farm till after supper, wishing that he could help the midshipman to escape without getting his father into trouble.

He was thinking how horribly dark and miserable the old quarry must be, for the first time. The thought had not occurred to him before, through every hole and corner being so familiar, from the fact that scores of times he had held the lanthorn while his father's men carried in smuggled goods landed at the ledge, if there was plenty of time; for, if the landing had been hurried, and the danger near, the things were often carried up to the Hoze for temporary deposit till carts came to bear the things into the interior.

"I do wish he'd be friends," thought Ram, when his musings were interrupted by his father saying, —

"Ah, there's that basket Jemmy found's mornin'. Go and take it up to the Hoze."

"He needn't go to-night, need he?" said Mrs Shackle.

"You mind your own business," said the farmer fiercely. "Be off, boy."

Ram put on his red cap, took the basket, and trotted off toward the Hoze, while Mrs Shackle sighed, for she knew that something particular must be on the way, or Ram would not have been sent off, and her husband have prepared to go out directly after.

"Oh dear me, dear me, dear me!" said the plump, comfortable-looking woman, as the door closed on her husband's back. "If he would only keep to his cows and sheep!"

"Here," said the farmer, reopening the door, "be off to bed. Ramillies need not know that I'm gone out."

"No, dear. But do take care of yourself."

"Yah!"

Bang went the door, and Mrs Shackle, after putting a few things straight, went off obediently to bed, troubling in no wise about the door being left on the latch.

Chapter Thirty Three

Archy Raystoke was fast asleep, dreaming about being once more on board the cutter, with the sun shining full in his eyes, because he was lying on the deck, right in everybody's road, and Gurr the master was scolding him for it in a way which was very disrespectful to an officer and a gentleman, while the men grouped around grinned.

He was not surprised, for somehow Mr Brough was not there, and Gurr had assumed the command of the cutter, and was playing the part of smuggler and pirate, and insulting him, whom he addressed again: "Get up!"

Archy leaped to his feet, and saw at a glance that it was not the sun, but the light of a lanthorn shining in his eyes, while, before he could do more than realise that several men were standing close to him, half of a sack was drawn-down over his head and shoulders, and a thin rope was twisted round and round his arms, fastening him securely, and only leaving his hands free.

"What are you going to do?" he shouted, after a vain struggle to free himself, and his voice sounded muffled and thick through the heavy sack.

"Pitch you off the cliff if you make so much as a sound," said a gruff voice by his ear. "Keep quiet, and you won't be hurt."

The lad's heart beat heavily, and he felt hot and half suffocated.

"Do you want to smother me?" he said. "Can't breathe."

"Slit the back of the sack, lad," said the same gruff voice, and there was a sharp cutting noise heard, as a breathing-hole was cut right up behind his head.

"Now, then, bring him along."

His hand was grasped, and, as he felt himself led over ground that was quite familiar now, he knew that he was on the way to the entrance.

Were they going to take him out, and set him free?

No; if they had been going to do that, they would not have blindfolded his eyes.

Yes, they would, for, if they were going to set him free, they would do so in a way that would place it beyond his power to betray their secret store.

Quick immatured thoughts which shot through him as he was led along, and he knew directly after that it was only fancy. Of course. He could show the lieutenant where the opening was in the cliff, and by knowing that it would be easy to track out the land entrance.

"No," said the midshipman to himself sadly; "they are going to take me and imprison me somewhere else, for they must now know that I was holding communications with that girl."

"Now then, steady!" said a voice, as he felt that the cool air was coming down on to his head, and he breathed it through the thick sacking. "Make a rope fast round him."

"I must be at the foot of the way in," thought Archy, as he felt a rope passed round him, and the next minute it tightened, he was raised from his feet, and the rope cut into him painfully as he felt himself hauled up. Then hands seized him, and he was thrown down on the grass, while the last rope was cast off.

As he lay there being untied, though his eyes were blinded, his ears were busy, and he listened to the smothered sounds of the trap being fastened and the stones being drawn over it again.

"Trap-door—door into a trap," he thought. "Where am I going now? Surely they would not kill me."

A cold chill shot through him, but he mastered the feeling of terror as he felt himself dragged to his feet.

"Now, then, keep step," the same gruff voice said; and, with apparently half a dozen men close by him, as far as he could judge by their mutterings and the dull sound of their feet over the grass, he was marched on for over an hour—hearing nothing, seeing nothing, but all the while with his ears strained, waiting for an opportunity to appeal for help, in spite of the threats he had heard, as soon as he could tell by the voices that he was near people who were not of the smugglers' gang.

But no help seemed to be at hand, and, as far as he could judge, he was being taken along the fields and rough ground near the edge of the wild cliffs, now near the sea, now far away. At one time he could hear the dull thud and dash of waves, for a good brisk breeze was blowing, and he fancied that he had a glint of a star through the thick covering, but he was not sure. Then the sound of the waves on the shore was completely hushed, and he felt that they must either be down in a hollow, or going farther and farther away inland.

Twice this happened, and the third time, as all was still, and he could feel a hard road beneath his feet, he became sure. There was an echoing sound from their footsteps, dull to him, but still plain, and it seemed as if they were down in some narrow cutting or rift, when all at once! Just in front, after the men about him had been talking more loudly, as if clear of danger, there rang out a stern—

"Halt—stand!"

There was a hasty exclamation. Then came in the loud, gruff voice,—

"Back, lads, quick!"

He was seized, and retreat had begun, when again rang out:—

"Halt—stand!"

The smugglers were between two fires.

The midshipman was conscious of a familiar voice crying,—

"No shots, lads. Cutlashes!"

There was a rush; the sound of blows, men swayed and struggled about wildly, and the lad, bound, blindfolded, and helpless, was thrust here and there. Then he received a sharp blow from a cudgel, which sent him staggering forward, and directly after a dull cut from a steel weapon, which, fortunately for him, fell upon and across the rope which bound his arms to his sides. There were oaths, fierce cries, and the struggling grew hotter, till all at once there was a rush, Archy went down like a skittle, men seemed to perform a triumphal war-dance upon his body, and then they passed on with the fight, evidently consisting of a retreat and pursuit, till the sounds nearly died away.

A minute later, as Archy lay there perfectly helpless, the noises increased again. Men were evidently laughing and talking loudly, and the sounds seemed to come round a corner, to become plainer all at once.

"Pity we didn't go on after them? Nonsense, my lad! They know every hole and corner about here, and there's no knowing where they'd have led us," said a familiar voice.

"Well, it is precious dark," said another.

"Too dark to see what we are about. But I take you all to witness, my lads, they 'tacked us first."

"Ay, ay: they began it," came in chorus.

"And if it happens that they are not smugglers, and there's trouble about it, you know what to say."

Archy heard all this, and it seemed to him that the party were about to pass him, when a voice he well knew growled out, —

"Hit me an awful whack with a stick."

"Ay, I got one too, my lad; and I didn't like to use my cutlash."

"Wish we'd took a prisoner, or knocked one or two down. Why, here is one."

There was a buzz of voices, and Archy felt himself hoisted up.

"Can you stand? Not wounded, are you? Who cut him down?"

"Well, I'm 'fraid it was me," said one of the familiar voices. "Why, he is a prisoner ready made."

"What? Here, cut him loose, lads. Hullo, my lad, who are you?"

"Take this off," panted Archy in a stifled voice; and then, as the sack was dragged over his head, he uttered a sigh, and staggered, and would have fallen, had not one of the men caught him.

"Hold up, lad. Not hurt, are you?"

"No," said Archy hoarsely.

"Who are you? What were they going to do with you?"

"Don't you know me, Mr Gurr?"

"Mr Raystoke!"

The rest of his speech, if he said anything, was drowned in a hearty cheer as the men pressed round.

"Well, I am glad!" cried the master. "We've been ashore a dozen times, my lad, and searched everywhere, till the skipper thought you must have run away."

"Run away!" cried Archy huskily. "I've been a prisoner."

"Those were smugglers, then?"

"Yes," cried Archy; "but they shall smart for all this. I know where all their hiding-places are, and we'll hunt them down."

"Hooray!" shouted the men.

"Were you looking for me?"

"Well, not to-night, my lad. Making a bit of a patrol," said Gurr. "The skipper thought that perhaps we might run against something or another, and we have and no mistake. But what's the matter? Not hurt, are you?"

"No, not much. I got a blow on the shoulder, and then some one gave me a chop with a cutlass."

"That was you, Dirty Dick! I did see that," cried one of the men.

"Well, I don't say it warn't me. How was I to know it was a orsifer in the dark, and smothered up like that?"

"Are you wounded, then?" cried the master excitedly.

"No; it felt more like a blow, but people kept trampling on me after I was down."

"That's bad," said Gurr, giving vent to a low whistle. "Here, lads, let's carry him to the boat."

"No, no!" cried the midshipman. "I think I can walk. I could hardly breathe."

"Well, go steady, then. It's on'y 'bout half a mile to the cove. Where did they mean to take you, lad?"

"I don't know. Perhaps on board some ship to get me out of the way;" and he briefly explained his late position, as they walked steadily on, the men listening eagerly the while.

"Then you can take me right to the place, Mr Raystoke?" said Gurr.

Archy hesitated.

"I can point it out from the sea, but it will be all guess-work from the shore."

"Never mind; we'll find it. But you can't think about where they were taking you to-night?"

"I have no idea. Of course they blindfolded me, so that I should not see the way out of the place I left, nor the way into the other."

"Ah, well, come on, and the skipper will talk to you. He has been fine and mad about it, and I 'most think he's turned a bit thinner, eh, Dick?"

"Ay, that he have," said the latter. "Leastwise you might think so."

"One day he's been all in a fret, saying you've run away, and that you'd be dismissed the service, and it was what he quite expected; and then, so as not to put him out, when you agreed with him, he flew out at you, and called you a fool, and said he was sure the smugglers had murdered his officer, or else tumbled him off the cliff."

Archy was too weary with excitement to care to talk much, and he tramped on with the men, hardly able to realise the truth of his escape, and half expecting to wake up in the darkness and find it all a dream. But he was reminded that it was no dream, from time to time, by feeling a hand laid deprecatingly upon his bruised arm, and starting round to see in the darkness that it was Dirty Dick, who patted his injury gently, and then uttered a satisfied "Hah!"

"Pleased to see me back," thought the midshipman, "but I wish he wouldn't pat me as if I were a dog."

"Hullo!" exclaimed the master just then, as they came opposite a depression in the cliff which gave them a view out to sea. "What's going on? Forrard, my lads. Smart!"

The pace was increased, for away in the darkness there hung out a bright signal which all knew meant recall, and the midshipman's heart throbbed as he felt that before long he would be in a boat dancing over the waves, and soon after treading the deck of the smart little cutter.

"No," he said to himself, as after a hail a boat came out of the darkness, its keel grating on the pebbly shore, and he uttered a sigh of content on sinking back in the stern-sheets; "it isn't a dream."

Chapter Thirty Four

Archy Raystoke's sense of weariness rapidly passed off, as the oars splashed, and the boat glided softly out of the waters of the cove, between the two huge corners of rock which guarded the entrance, and then began to dance up and down as she reached out into the tideway. After the darkness of the old quarry, with its faint odour of spirits, the night seemed comparatively like noonday, and the pure, brisk air that fanned his cheek delicious. He seemed to drink it in, drawing down great draughts which made his bosom swell, his heart beat, and there were moments when, like a schoolboy upon whom has suddenly come the joys of an unexpected half-holiday, he felt ready to jump up, toss his cap in the air, and shout for joy.

"But it would be undignified in an officer," he felt; and he sat still, feeling the boat live almost in the water as she throbbed from end to end with the powerful strokes, and glide up the waves, hang for a moment, and slide down.

"Tidy swell on, Mr Raystoke," said Gurr.

"Oh, it's glorious!" replied the lad in a low voice.

"Glorious?"

"Yes. You don't know what it means to have been shut up in a place like a cellar, always black, and longing to see the blue sky and sunshine."

"Well, there aren't none now, my lad."

"No, Gurr, there is no blue sky and sunshine, but—but—this is delightful;" and he said to himself, with his breast swelling, "I feel stupid, and as if I could cry like a child."

They were nearing the cutter fast, her lights growing plainer, and the lad leaned forward with feelings that were almost ecstatic as he tried to scan her lines, and thought of leaping on her deck, and feeling the easy, yielding motion as she rose and fell to her cable where she lay at anchor. He even thought of how glorious it would be for there to come a storm, with the spray beating on his cheeks and then, as he involuntarily raised his hand to his face, a thought occurred to him which made him start.

"Oh!" he mentally ejaculated, as he thought of his long sojourn in the cave, and a feeling of satisfaction came over him that it was dark; "what a horribly dirty wretch I must look!"

A hail came from the cutter at last, and was answered from the boat, Archy's heart beating fast as he dimly saw the figures on board, and thought of the joy of being once more in his own cabin.

"Gurr," he whispered, "don't say a word to Mr Brough; let me tell him I have come on board."

"Right, my lad; but you'll say we found you, and all that. You see, I must make my report."

"Of course."

Just then the oars were thrown up and laid alongside, and, as the lieutenant came to the gangway, Archy sprang on to the cutter so sharply that he came rather roughly in contact with his commanding officer.

"How dare you! Why, you clumsy young—" Before he could say more, the midshipman touched his red cap.

"Come aboard, sir," he said.

"Why? What? Mr Ray—Oh, my dear boy!"

There was not a bit of official dignity in the greeting, for the plump little lieutenant, in his surprise and delight, caught Archy by the arms, then by the shoulders; stared in his face; seized his hands, shook them both, and was about to hug him, but, suddenly recollecting himself, he drew back.

"In with that boat," he cried sharply. Then, giving the orders to slip the cable, and prepare to make sail, he turned to Gurr.

"I'll take your report directly, Mr Gurr," he said. Then, very stiffly, "Take charge of the deck. Mr Raystoke, follow me, sir, to my cabin."

"Going to wig me," said the midshipman, as he followed his officer down into the cabin and shut the door.

"Now, sir," cried the lieutenant, turning upon him sharply, "have the goodness to explain your conduct. Stop—not a word yet. I entrusted you with an important commission. I dealt with you as if you were a man, an officer and a gentleman; and, instead of doing your duty, you went off like a contemptible cabin-boy on a shore-going game, sir—dissipation, sir— behaved like a blackguard till all your money was spent; and then you come sneaking back on board, insult me by blundering up against me, and all you've got to say for yourself is, 'Come aboard, sir.' Now, then, what else have you to say?"

"Well, sir!—"

"Stop. Let me tell you that, knowing as I did what a young scamp you were, I refrained from reporting your conduct at Portsmouth, to get you dismissed His Majesty's service; and knowing, too, that it would break your father's and mother's heart, I did not write and tell them. For I said to myself, 'He'll come back and ask forgiveness to-morrow, and I'll punish him and forgive him,' for I did not want to blast your career. But to-morrow has always been coming, and you haven't come till to-night. And now, what have you to say before—before I treat you—yes, I've a good mind to—like some mutinous scoundrel, and—What's that, sir, what's that? How dare you sit down in my presence, when—"

"I'm so done up, sir, and hungry and faint."

"And serve you right, you insolent young dog. I knew it, and—"

"Oh, I say, Mr Brough, you don't think I could have been such a beast."

"What?"

"I found out all about the smugglers, but they caught me, and I've been a prisoner ever since. Do give me something to eat and drink, and don't scold me any more, till I've got on my uniform and had a good wash."

"My dear boy! My dear Archy Raystoke!" cried the lieutenant, seizing his hands and pumping them up and down. "Of course I didn't think it! Knew you were too much of a gentleman, but I was stuffed full of thoughts like that, and they would come out. Here," he cried, "drink that, and here's some cake sent from Poole, and—tip it up, and eat away. I am glad to see you again. God bless you, my dear boy! I'm your officer, but you don't know how miserable I've been."

"Yes, I do, sir. I know you always liked me," cried the midshipman, between the mouthfuls he was taking. "But never mind the being prisoner, sir. I know all the scoundrels' secrets now, and you can capture them, and make some good hauls. You must send a strong party ashore as soon as it's day."

"But—but—"

Archy answered those buts to such an extent that Gurr's report was needless, and the master was terribly disappointed.

By that time the cutter was slowly gliding away seaward, with every eye on the watch, for, as the lieutenant explained, after telling his recovered officer how he had searched in all directions, he had that night seen lights shown far up on one of the cliffs—lights which might mean a warning to some vessel to keep off, or just as likely might have the other intention, and be an invite to some lugger to land her cargo.

In any case the lieutenant meant to be on the alert, and hence the sailing of the cutter.

The lieutenant had hesitated a little at first after hearing his midshipman's report, but he now decided how to act.

"No," he said; "not to-night, my lad. I'm inclined to think the signal was a warning to keep off. They may hide the cargo they leave ashore, and if we don't capture it, so much the worse, but our work is to crush up the gang more than to capture a few barrels and bales. We'll look out to-night, and, as soon as it is daylight, you shall make sure of the bearings of your prison, then we'll land a strong boat's crew, and go along the top of the cliff to the place, and put an end to that game. You shall make a good meal, and then have a sleep, ready for to-morrow's work. Hah!" cried the little lieutenant; "that ought to mean a good day's business, Mr Raystoke, and promotion to better jobs than this."

"I hope so, sir," said Archy, with his mouth full.

"No use to hope," said the lieutenant dismally. "I'm like poor old Gurr; they don't consider me fit for service in a crack ship; and when I make my report, and send in my despatches, and ask for an appointment, I shall be told I do my work too well on this important service, and that they cannot spare so valuable an officer from the station. Gammon, Mr Raystoke, gammon! It's all because I'm so little and so fat."

Archy was silent, for he knew it was the truth, and that such a quaint little fellow did not somehow quite command the men's respect.

Half an hour after, he was sleeping heavily, with the delightful sensation of being undressed and between blankets, to wake up with a start in the morning, by hearing Ram coming to the trap-door.

No, it was a noise on deck; and he sprang up and rapidly washed and dressed, to hurry up to see what was going on.

Chapter Thirty Five

As the midshipman reached the deck, it was to find that there was a light mist on the water, and that the lieutenant was at the side with Gurr, where they were watching a boat coming in from seaward.

The cutter was back not far from her old moorings, and the great cliffs of the shore were dimly visible.

"Lobster-boat, sir," said Gurr, as Archy came behind them.

"Never mind! I'll overhaul her. I'm going to be suspicious of everything now. Take the boat, and—Ah, to be sure. Mr Raystoke, take the boat, and see what those fellows mean. They're making straight for the ledge, and there is no one to buy lobsters there."

"Ay, ay, sir!"

That familiar sea-going reply seemed to ring out of the lad's throat, and afforded him a pure feeling of delight. No more groping about in the darkness, biting his nails, and feeling heart-sick with despondency, but the full delight of freedom and an active life.

No lad ever sprang to his work with more alacrity, and, as he leaped into the boat, and the men dropped their oars, there was a hearty look of welcome in each smiling face.

"She has just gone into the mist there, Mr Raystoke," said the lieutenant; "but she's making straight for that ledge, and you can't miss her. One moment. If the men seem all right and honest as to what they are going to do, see if you can get any information, but be on your guard, as they'll send you, perhaps, on some fool's errand."

"Ay, ay, sir!" cried Archy again, as he took the handle of the tiller. "Now, my lads, give way!"

The mist was patchy, thin here and thick there, but it seemed an easy task to overtake the boat, which had glided into the fog, going slowly, with her little sail set, and with only a man and boy for crew. She was about a mile away from the cutter, and about a quarter of that distance from the land when she passed out of sight, and the possibility of not overtaking her never entered the midshipman's head. All the same, though, he was well enough trained in his duties to make him keep a sharp look-out on either side, as they crept in, to make sure that the boat did not slip away under the cliffs to right or left unseen.

The mist grew more dense as they neared the towering cliffs. Then it seemed to become thinner, and, just as the midshipman was thinking to himself how glorious it would be if the man and boy in the boat should prove to be his old friends Ram and Jemmy Dadd, there came a peculiar squeaking sound from somewhere ahead.

"Lowering sail, sir," said Dirty Dick, who was pulling first oar.

"Then we have not missed them," thought Archy, as the men pulled steadily on, with the rushing, plunging noise of the waves beginning to be heard as they washed the foot of the cliffs. "I'll be bound to say it is Ram and that big scoundrel. Oh, what a chance to get them aboard in irons and under hatches, for them to have a taste of what they gave me!"

It seemed perfectly reasonable that those two should have been off somewhere in a boat, and were now returning. Who more likely to be making for the ledge, which, as far as he could judge, was a point or two off to the right.

All at once, after a few minutes' pulling, the boat glided right out of the bank of mist which hung between them like a soft grey veil, while in front, lit up by the first beams of the morning sun, was the great wall of cliff, the ledge over which the waves washed gently, the green pasture high up, and the ledges dotted with grey and white gulls. The picture was lovely in the extreme, but it wanted two things in Archy's eyes to make it perfect; and those two things were a background formed by the great cliff, down which he had crept, and the feature which would have given it life and interest — to wit, the fishing-boat containing Ram and Jemmy Dadd.

"Hold hard, my lads!" cried the midshipman, and the men ceased rowing, holding their oars balanced, with the diamond-like drops falling sparkling from their blades into the clear sea, while the boat glided slowly on towards the ledge, which was just in front.

"Why, where's the boat?" cried Archy excitedly, as he swept the face of the cliff with his eyes.

"She aren't here, sir," said Dick.

"Well, I can see that, my man. Can she have slipped aside and let us pass?"

"No," said one of the other men. "'Sides, sir, she was just afore us ten minutes ago, and we heard her lowering down her mast and sail."

"Could that have been a gull?"

"What, make a squeal like a wheel in a block? No, sir, not it."

"Then they have run her up on the ledge and dragged her into one of the holes. Give way!"

The men pulled in quickly, and at the end of a few minutes they were as close to the side of the ledge as it was safe to go, for, as the waves ran in, the larger ones leaped right over the broad level space, washing it from end to end. But there was no sign of the boat, and the midshipman hesitated about believing that the man and boy could have taken advantage of a good wave and run her right on.

"It's strange," said Archy aloud, as he sat there thinking that, if he chose his time right, he might make his men pull the boat in upon a wave, let them jump out and drag her up the rocks.

But he shook his head, for he knew that if everything was not done to the moment, the boat would be stove in.

"Hullo! What are you shaking your head about?" he said sharply to Dick.

"Nothing sir, only you said it was strange."

"Well, isn't it strange?"

"Ay, sir; so's the *Flying Dutchman*!"

"What? Why, you do not think any of that superstitious nonsense about the boat, do you?"

"Well, sir, I dunno. I only says, Where's the boat now? She couldn't have got away."

"No," said another of the men. "She couldn't have landed there."

"Nonsense!" cried Archy angrily. "Absurd! Who ever heard of a phantom lobster-boat?"

Dick shook his head, and then sat playing with the handle of his oar.

"You Dick," cried Archy, "you're a goose! There, it will not be safe to land, my lads. Here, you two jump ashore as we back in. Mind, just as the sea's off the ledge; and run up and have a good look round."

The boat was turned, backed in, and, seizing the right moment, the men jumped on to the rock just as the water was only ankle-deep, had a good search round, and came back, to be picked up again safely, though the boat was within an ace of being capsized.

But they had seen nothing. There was no boat, and they searched along some distance east, turned back to the ledge and went west, still without elucidation of the mystery; then they went as close under the cliffs as they dared go, in the hope of finding some cavern or passage through the rocks that escaped notice from outside.

All in vain, and, obeying the signal now flying on the cutter, the boat was rowed back.

"Well, Mr Raystoke, where's the boat?"

"Don't know, sir. We never got sight of her."

"Then you must have been asleep," cried the lieutenant angrily. "There, breakfast, my lads, and be smart."

After the meal, Gurr was left in the charge of the cutter, while the lieutenant accompanied Archy to search for the high cliff which contained the old quarry, and they rowed east for a couple of miles in vain. But, after pulling back to the starting-point, and making for the other direction, they had not gone four hundred yards under the cliff before the midshipman exclaimed excitedly, —

"There; that's the place: there!"

"Then why didn't you say so when we were on deck? You could have seen it there."

"I could not tell without seeing it close in, sir; and besides it looks so different from right out yonder."

"But are you sure this is right?"

"Oh yes, sir. Look, that's the place—where there is that narrow rift, and if you look high up there is a hole. There, I can see it plainly."

"Humph! Can you? Well, I cannot!"

"But you can see that broad ledge, sir, about two hundred feet up. That's where I climbed down to, and we had the struggle—that boy and I."

"No, I can't see any ledges, Mr Raystoke. There may be one there, but if you had not been upon it, I don't believe you would know that there was one."

Archy looked up at the towering pile of rock, and was obliged to own that he was right. He shivered slightly as he swept the face of the cliff for the various points that had helped him in his descent, and, as he gazed out there in cold blood, it seemed to have been an extremely mad idea to have attempted the descent.

"Well, it is impossible to land here," continued the lieutenant. "You are certain that this is the place?"

"Certain, sir."

"Good. Then we'll go back to the cutter, and this evening a strong party shall land. I'll lead them myself, and we'll try and surprise them. It's quite likely that the signals I saw last night may mean business for to-night. If so, we shall be on the spot."

"Won't you go at once?" Archy ventured to observe.

"No, certainly not; what would be the good? We would be watched, of course, and the scoundrels would signal from hill to hill, and our every step would be known. This evening, my lad, at dusk. Now, my lads, give way."

The boat was rowed rapidly from under the shadow of the mighty cliff, and the midshipman could not repress a shudder as he noticed how swiftly the current ran right out to sea, and fully realised what would have been the consequences to any one who had tried to swim along the coast if he had managed to descend in safety to the cliff foot.

Back on board the cutter there was a fair amount of bustle and excitement among the men, for, after months of unfruitful hanging about the coast, chasing luggers which proved to be empty, following false leads to get them off the scent or out of the way when contraband goods were to be landed, here was genuine information at last, the smugglers having, after such long immunity, placed themselves in the hands of the King's men.

Consequently cutlasses were being filed up, pistols carefully examined as to their flints and nicked off to see that they threw a good shower of sparks into the pans, and the men sat and talked together as eagerly as if they were about proceeding upon a pleasant jaunt, instead of upon a risky expedition which might result in death to several, and certainly would in serious injury.

"Yes," the lieutenant said, "rats will run away as long as they can, but when driven to the end of their holes they will fight."

"But will they dare, do you think, sir?" said Archy.

"Dare! Yes, my lad. You had a bit of a taste of it the other night when they were surprised in the lane. They will be more savage in their holes, and therefore, as you are so young, I should like you to go with the men, show them the way, and then leave them to do the work."

Archy stared at him.

"Yes: I mean it. Of course as an officer you cannot shrink from your duty, but, as you are a mere boy, it is not your duty to go and fight against strong men who are sure to get the better of you."

"But they are not all men there, sir," said the midshipman, with a look of disappointment getting heavier in his face. "There's a boy there—that young rascal who came after the cow. I owe him such a thrashing that I must have a turn at him."

"Ah, that's different," said the lieutenant; "and it will keep up appearances. But take care to confine yourself to fighting with him. And—er—I would not use my pistol, Raystoke."

"Not shoot, sir?"

"Well—no. I want to destroy this wasps' nest, but in as merciful a way as possible. I have given orders to the men, and I wish you to mind too—I don't want to kill the wasps, but to make them prisoners."

"Yes, sir, I see."

"They are not French wasps, or Dutch wasps, but English. You understand?"

"Quite, sir."

"That's right. Another hour and you may be off. You think you can find the place?"

"I do not feel a doubt about it, sir."

"Well, it's going to be a dark night, and you and Mr Gurr will have to be careful over your men. You had better keep as close to the cliff as you can, for, of course, the entrance must be somewhere near. I have given Mr Gurr full instructions. You are to search and find the place, and if found hold it, but if you do not find it you will be back on board by daybreak, and another expedition must be made by day. If we can surprise them by night, when they think all is safe, it may save bloodshed. If we are obliged to go by day, they will have good warning, and be prepared to receive us, though they may be now. I wish I was going with you, but that cannot be."

Chapter Thirty Six

Everything was arranged on board, so that no watcher armed with a glass who scanned the ship should suspect that an expedition was on hand; but as soon as it was dark the men were ordered into two boats, one commanded by Gurr, with whom was Archy, the other by the boatswain, only leaving a very small crew on board with the lieutenant. Then they pushed off, rowing with muffled oars, and keeping right away from the cliffs, so that any watcher there should have no indication of their passing.

The quiet little cove was still a couple of miles away, when Archy suddenly touched the master's arm as he sat there holding his cutlass.

"Yes; what is it?"

For answer the midshipman leaned forward, and pointed to where, far back and apparently opposite to the cutter, a couple of faint lights could be seen high up and away from the cliff.

"Humph! Lights," said Gurr; "but they may be up at some cottage. What do you think?"

"I thought they might be signals."

"Well, my lad, if they be, it's to bring the smugglers ashore, where we may have the luck to be in waiting for 'em. But before that the skipper may have seen them, and, though he's short-handed, they could manage to shake out a sail or two, and manage a gun."

"You would not put back, then, after seeing these lights?"

"Not likely, with the orders we've got, sir," said the master; and the men rowed on, and in due time reached the cove, where all was perfectly quiet, the tide falling, and as they landed quite a noisy tramp had to be made over the fine pebbles, in which the men's feet sank.

A couple of men were left in charge of the boats, the others were formed up, and, after passing the cottages of the few fishermen of the place, the party struck off for the top of the cliffs, to follow the rugged, faint track which was more often lost, and the arduous tramp was continued hour after hour, till, partly from the schooner's lights, partly from his idea of the run of the coast, the late prisoner began to calculate that they must be approaching the land side of the large cliff.

It had been a terrible walk in the darkness, for the cliff tops were as if a gigantic storm had taken place when that part of the coast was formed, and a series of mountainous—really mountainous—waves had run along and became suddenly congealed, leaving sharp-crested hill and deeply grooved valley, which had to be climbed and descended in turn, till the men vowed that the distance was double what it would have been by road, and they certainly were not exaggerating much.

It was only here and there that the party had been able to follow the edge of the cliff. For the most part prudence forced them to keep well in, but at times they had some arduous climbs, and walked along the sides of slopes of thin short grass, covered with tiny snails, whose shells crushed beneath their feet with a peculiar crisp sound; and had it been daylight, the probabilities were that they would have given these risky spots a wider berth.

"Call a halt, Gurr," whispered Archy at last; and it was done. Then, giving the master his ideas, the men were allowed a few minutes' breathing space before being formed in a line, with a space of a few yards between the men, one end of the line being close to the edge of the cliff, the other some distance inland.

In this way the men were instructed to walk slowly on, scanning every depression and clump of bared stone carefully, and at a word uttered by the man who felt that he had found any place likely to prove to be an entrance to a cave or quarry, all were to halt, the word was to be passed along, and the officers were to examine the place before the line went on again.

The plan was good, and the long line swept slowly along, the halt being called soon after they had started, but the stoppage was in vain, the midshipman and Gurr finding before them only a rough piled-up collection of stones from which the earth had in the course of ages crumbled or been washed away.

On again in the darkness, the officers pacing along portions of the line to urge on the men to be careful, and warning those near the cliff edge.

The advice was needed, for all at once, just as Archy was leaving the edge, there was a faint cry; the halt was called, and the young officer, closely followed by Dick, went quickly to the spot from whence the cry had come.

"It's Bob Harris, sir," said the last man they reached. "I see him a moment ago, and heard him cry out, and then he was gone."

With his blood seeming to chill, Archy crept in the darkness close to the cliff edge, to find that it sloped down where he stood.

"Give me your hand, Dick," he whispered.

"Lie down, my lad, and I'll go down too," said the sailor in a husky voice, which told of the horror he felt.

It was good advice, and the midshipman was putting it in force just as Gurr came tearing up.

"What is it?" he panted.

"Bob Harris gone over, sir," whispered Dick.

"And no rope with us!" exclaimed the master. "See anything, my lad?"

"Yes; he is just below here on a ledge. Hi! Are you hurt?"

"No, sir," came up faintly; "but I durstn't move, or I should go over."

"Lie still, then, till we pull you up. Mr Gurr, I can almost touch him. I could, if some one lowered me a little more."

"No, no, my lad, no, no!" whispered the master. "Here, Dick, and you," he said in short, quick, decisive tones, as he lay down and looked over. "Now, then, four more men here. Now, who'll volunteer to lean over and get a good grip of him, while we hold by your legs?"

"I will," said Dick.

"'Spose I'm as strong as any on 'em. But who's going to hold my legs?"

"Two men, my lad, and there'll be others to hold them."

"Right," said Dick shortly; and the men lay down, forming themselves into a human chain, the end of which Dick was lowered slowly down the slope and over the edge.

"Look here, my man," said Archy, as he lay with his head and chest over the edge of the awful precipice, listening to the faint beat of the waves, and involuntarily thinking of his adventure with Ram, "as soon as Dick grips you, get tight hold of him too."

"Ay," came up in a hoarse whisper. "Please be quick. I feel as if I was going."

"Now," said the master, "ready, lads? Steady! You, Dick, give the word yourself to lower away."

"Ay, ay, sir; lower away." Then again, "Lower away! Lower away!"

The suspense in the darkness seemed strained to breaking point, and Archy lay with his heart beating painfully, watching till it seemed as if the case was hopeless, and that if Dick, now nearly off the cliff, could grip hold of the fallen man, they would never be able to get him and his burden back.

"'Nother inch," came up out of the void. "Touched him. 'Nother inch!"

At each order, given in a hoarse, smothered way, the men shuffled themselves forward a little, and lowered Dick down.

"Just a shade more, my lads," came up.

"Can't!" said one of the men who held one of Dick's legs.

"Right. Got him," came up, as a thrill of horror ran along the chain at that word *can't*. "Haul away!"

How that hauling up was managed the midshipman hardly knew, but he had some consciousness of having joined in the efforts made, by seizing one man of the human chain, and dimly seeing Gurr and two other men of the group now gathered about them lend their aid. Then there was a scuffling and dragging, a loud panting, and, with a few adjurations to "hold on," and "haul," and "keep tight," Dick and the man he had been lowered down to save were dragged into safety.

"Phew!" panted Dick. "Look here, Bob Harris—never no more, my lad, never no more!"

"Bravely done, Dick," whispered Gurr.

"Thank ye, sir. But, never no more. I want to be a good mate to everybody, but this here's a shade too much."

"And I'd take it kindly, Master Raystoke, sir," said the man the midshipman had gripped, "if nex' time, sir, you wouldn't mind grappling my clothes only. You're tidy strong now, and I can't 'answer for my flesh', if you take hold like that."

"Hush! No talking," said the master. "Dick, take the outside now, and be careful. Form your line again. Bob Harris, take the far left."

"Well, Master Raystoke, sir," grumbled Dick, "I call that giving a fellow a prize. Saves that chap, and here am I."

"Post of honour, Dick. Go slowly, and not too near."

"Not too nigh it is, sir," said Dick, with a sigh; and a minute later the word was given, and they went on once more.

One hundred, two hundred, three hundred yards, but no sign.

Then a discovery was made, and by the midshipman.

They had come to the descent on the far side of the vast hill by whose top they had been searching. There was a stiff slope beyond, and another mass of cliff loomed up, rising dimly against the sky, in a way that made

Archy feel certain that, though so far their search had been in vain, they had now before them the huge cliff which held the smugglers' store.

The midshipman felt so assured of this, that he whispered his belief freely to Gurr, as he encountered him from time to time perambulating the line of men, but the old master received the communication rather surlily.

"All guess-work, my lad," he said. "We're working wrong way on. These great places would puzzle a monkey, and we shan't find the hole unless we come by daylight, and leave a boat off-shore to signal to us till we get over the spot."

"What's that?" cried Archy excitedly, as one of the men on his left uttered a sharp, "Look out!"

"Sheep, I think, sir."

"No, it was a dog," said another.

"Hi! Stop him!" cried a third. "Boy!"

There was a rush here and there in the darkness, the line being completely broken, and the men who composed it caught sight from time to time of a shadowy figure to which they gave chase as it dodged in and out of the bushes, doubling round masses of weather-worn stone, plunging into hollows, being lost in one place and found in another, but always proving too active for its pursuers, who stumbled about among the rough ground and dangerous slopes. Here for a moment it was lost in a damp hollow full of a high growth of mares-tail (*equisetum*), that curious whorled relic of ancient days; driven from that by a regular course of beating the ground, it led its pursuers upward among rough tumbled stones where the brambles tripped them, and here they lost it for a time. But, growing hotter in the chase, and delighted with the sport, which came like a relief from their monotonous toil, the Jacks put their quarry up again, to get a dim view of it, and follow it in full cry, like a pack of hounds, over the rounded top of the hill, down the other side into a damp hollow full of tall reeds, through which the men had to beat again, panting and regaining their breath, but too excited by the chase to notice the direction in which they had gone, and beyond hearing of the recall shouted by their officers.

The midshipman joined as eagerly in the chase as any of the men, forgetting at the moment all about discipline, formation, and matters of that kind, for in one glimpse which he had of the figure, he made certain that it was Ram, whom they had surprised just leaving the entrance to the cave; and it was not until he had been joined in the hunt for about a quarter of an hour, that he felt that the men ought instantly to have been stopped, and the place around thoroughly searched.

"How vexatious!" he cried to himself, as he panted on alone, always in dread of coming suddenly upon the edge of the cliff, and trembling lest in their excitement the men might go over.

All regrets were vain now, and he kept on following the cries he heard, first in one direction and then in another, till at last, after a weary struggle through a great patch of brambles and stones, he found himself quite alone and left behind.

But his vanity would not accept this last.

"I've quite out-run them," he said, half aloud, as he peered round through the gloom, listening intently the while, but not a sound could be heard, and in his angry impatience he stamped his foot upon the short dry grass.

"What an idiot I am for an officer!" he cried. "Leading men and letting them bolt off in all directions like this. Suppose the smugglers should turn upon us now!"

"They would not have any one to turn upon," he added, after a pause.

"Well, it's all over with anything like a surprise," he continued, after a time, "and we must get back to the place where we started from, if we can find it."

"I'll swear that was Ram," he said, as he trudged on up a steep hillside; "and if they have caught him, we'll make him show us the way. Stubborn brute! He was too much for me in the quarry, but out here with the men about, I'll make him sing a different tune."

"Where can they be?" he cried, after wandering about for quite half an hour. "Why! Ah!" he ejaculated. "I can see it all now. It was Ram, and he was playing peewit. The cunning rascal! Oh, if I only get hold of him!

"Yes; there's no doubt about it, and he has been too clever for us. He was watching by the entrance, and just as the men got up, and would have found it, he jumped up and dodged about, letting the men nearly catch him, and then running away and leading them farther and farther on."

"Never mind. I'll get the men together, and we'll go back to the place and soon find it. Oh, how vexatious! Which way does the sea lie?"

There was not a star to be seen, and the night was darker than ever.

He listened, but the night was too calm for the waves to be heard at the foot of the cliffs, and, gaze which way he would, there was nothing but dimly seen rugged ground with occasional slopes of smooth, short grass.

"Ahoy!" he cried at last, and "Ahoy!" came back faintly.

"Hurrah!" he said, after answering again, and walking in the direction from which the cry came, downward in one of the combe-like hollows of the district. "No one need be lost for long, if he has a voice. Don't hear any of the others though."

He shouted again and again, getting answers, and gradually diminishing the distance, till he saw dimly the figure of a stoutly built man, and the next minute he was saluted with, —

"Oh, it's you, is it, Mr Raystoke? Pretty run you've led me. Pray what sort of a game do you call this?"

"Game, sir!" said Archy ruefully; "it's horribly hard work!"

"Hard work! To you, sir—a mere boy! Then what do you suppose it is to me? I have hardly a breath left in me."

"But where are the men Mr Gurr?"

"The men, Mr Raystoke, sir? That's what I was going to ask you. Now just have the goodness to tell me what you mean by forgetting all the discipline you have been taught, and leading these poor chaps off on such a wild-goose chase."

"I, Mr Gurr?" said Archy in astonishment.

"Yes, sir, you, sir. What am I to say to Mr Brough when we get back? I am in command of this expedition, and you lead the men away like a pack of mad March hares, and now I find you here without them. Where are they?"

"I don't know, sir."

"You don't know!"

"I thought they were with you."

"And you took them away and left them?"

"I didn't take them away!" cried the midshipman angrily.

"Then where are they, sir?"

"I don't know. You were close by me when they rushed off after that boy."

"Sheep, sir."

"No, no, Mr Gurr; boy—Ram."

"Well, I said sheep, Mr Raystoke."

"No, no, boy; that's his name—Ram."

"Nonsense, sir; it was a sheep, and if it was not, it was a dog."

"I tell you, sir, it was the smuggler's boy, Ram,—the one who came aboard after the cow."

"Hang the cow, sir! I want my men. Do you think I can go back on board without them. Why, it's high treason for a naval officer to let one man slip away, and here you have let two boats' crews go. I say once more, how am I to face Mr Brough?"

"I don't know, Mr Gurr," said Archy, who was growing vexed now at the blame being thrown on his shoulders. "You were in command of the expedition, and the bosun was in charge of the second boat's crew. I don't see how I am to blame."

"But you led the men away, sir."

"Not I, Mr Gurr. I joined in the chase, and I tried to get the boys together, but they scattered everywhere."

"But it really is awkward, Mr Raystoke, isn't it?"

"Horribly, sir. Got anything to eat?"

"To eat? No, my lad. But—tut—tut—tut! I can't hear them anywhere."

"Nor I, sir."

"Well, we must not stand here. But what did you say?—I did not see what it was; they went off after a boy?"

The master spoke so civilly now that Archy forgot his anger, and entered into the trouble warmly.

"Yes," he said; "and it was a plan. That boy is as cunning as can be. We must have been close up to the way into the cave when he started out and led us all away from it."

"Eh?"

"I say he jumped up and dodged about, knowing the place by heart, and kept hiding and running off again, to get us right away from the entrance."

"That's it—that's it, Mr Raystoke. Don't try any more, sir. You've hit right in the bull's eye."

"You think so?"

"No, sir; I'm sure of it. A young fox. Now as soon as we've taken him prisoner, I'll put the matter before Mr Brough in such a way that the young scamp will be tied up, and get four dozen on the bare back."

"Hadn't we better catch him first, Mr Gurr?"

"Right, Mr Raystoke. Come on then; and the first thing is to get the men together. We shall catch him, never you fear that. These cunning ones generally get caught first. Now then, sir, let's listen."

They listened, but there was not a sound.

"'Pon my word! This is a pretty state of affairs!" cried the master. "What do you propose next?"

"Let's get right up to the top of this place and hail."

"That's good advice, Mr Raystoke, sir: so come on."

They started at once, and at the end of ten minutes they were at the top of a hill, but upon gazing round they could only dimly see other hills similar to the one on which they stood,—regular earth-waves of the great convulsion which had thrown the strata of the Freestone Shore into a state of chaos,—but nothing more.

"I'll hail," said Archy; and he shouted, but there was no reply.

"The scoundrels!" cried the master angrily. "They're all together in some public-house drinking, and glad to get away from us. Eh? What are you laughing at?"

"There are no public-houses out in this wild place, Mr Gurr."

"Eh? Well, no, I suppose not. I'll hail. Ahoy?"

A faint echo in reply. That was all.

"Which way shall we go?"

"I don't know, Mr Gurr."

"Can't make out which is the north, can you?"

"No, sir, nor the south neither."

"Humph! I think I could find the south if you told me which was the north," said the master drily. "Well, we must do the best we can. Let's strike along here. I seem to feel that this is the right direction."

Archy felt that it was the wrong direction, but, at he could not point out the right, he followed his leader for about a quarter of a mile, both pausing to shout and listen from time to time.

All at once Gurr came to a dead stop.

"I feel as if we're going wrong," he said. "You choose this time."

"Let's try this way," said Archy, selecting the route because it was down hill; but a quarter of an hour of this did not satisfy him, and he too stopped dead short.

"I feel just as much lost as I did in the dark in that cave, Mr Gurr," he said.

"Never mind, my lad," said the master good-humouredly. "It's all an accident, and nobody's fault. Wish I had my pipe."

"Ahoy!" shouted Archy, but there was no reply.

"I'd sit down and wait for morning, only conscience won't let me."

"Well, let's try this way," suggested Archy.

"Seems to me, my lad, that it don't matter which way we take, we only go wandering in and out among the stones and brambles and winding all sorts of ways. Never mind; we must keep moving, so come on."

They trudged on for how long they could not tell, but both were getting exceedingly weary, and as ignorant now ever as to their whereabouts; for, whether the direction they followed was east, west, south, or north, there was no indication in the sky; and they kept on, always cautiously, in dread and yet in hope that they might come upon the edge of the cliff, which would solve their difficulty at once, if they could see the cutter's lights.

"Though that aren't likely, Mr Raystoke. Strikes me that he'll lie there, and not show a light, on the chance of a smuggling lugger coming along, though that's hardly our luck."

"I don't know," said Archy bitterly. "Seems just the time for her to come when the skipper's so short-handed that he can't attack."

"Yes, we are an unlucky craft and no mistake, and I 'most wish sometimes I'd never sailed in her. Look here, for instance, here's a chance for us."

"Hist! Listen!" whispered Archy.

"What is it?"

"A hail right in the distance."

"No such luck, my lad. I don't know how I'm going to face Mr Brough. Hark!"

"Yes; there it is again, away to the left. Yes; there it goes. Ahoy!"

They stopped and listened after the midshipman had hailed as loudly as he could; and, to the intense delight of both, the hail was responded to.

Hurriedly changing their direction, they went on as rapidly as the rough ground would allow, getting an answering hail every time they shouted, and each time louder, as if those who called were also coming toward them.

Ten minutes later they heard voices, by degrees these became a murmur, and they knew that there must be several of the men together.

In another ten minutes they came upon a group steadily approaching.

Mutual inquiries took place.

No, the men had not captured the fugitive, but they were sure it was a boy; Dirty Dick was ready to take an oath to that effect, but he was not asked.

Then came the important question—Where were they?

The boatswain gave it as his opinion that they had been going westward, but he could give no reason why; and it was decided to continue in that direction, after Gurr had satisfied himself that the men were all present, though they learned that there had been a good deal of hailing before all were collected.

They trudged on almost in silence, for the whole party were wearied out, till an announcement galvanised them all, for suddenly Dick put an end to the question of their journeying west by suddenly shouting,—

"South ho!"

"Eh? What do you mean?" cried the master.

"I know yon hill," said Dick, pointing to an eminence dimly seen away before him. "That's just close to the cove, and if we keep straight on, we shall be in the road in less than half an hour, and at the boats ten minutes later."

"No, no, my lad," said the master; "I don't think that's right.—Yes, it is, my lad; I'm 'most sure of it now."

Right it was, as was proved a quarter of an hour later, by their striking the rough road at right angles, and there a halt was called.

"Don't seem any good to go searching along again in the dark, Mr Raystoke," said the master; and the boatswain shook his head decisively.

"All 'bout done up," he growled.

"We could do no good now," said Archy, "for of course I am not sure where the entrance is."

"Must be getting toward morning too, and time to be aboard, Mr Raystoke. There, sir, sometimes we win and many more times we lose. We've lost this time, so let's go back aboard, according to orders. Forward right, my lads, and let's make the best of it."

"Never mind, Mr Gurr," said Archy in a low voice. "I was regularly in despair as I was being taken from one prison to be shut up in another, when

I ran up against you. Perhaps we may run up against the smugglers after all."

"Wish we might," said the master. "Oh, how I could fight!"

But they ran up against no smugglers on their way to the boats, which they hailed from the strand, where the water was very low; and soon after they were passing in the lowest of low spirits, out of the cove to the open channel, when once more every one was thrilled with excitement, for right away in the offing they heard a gun.

Chapter Thirty Seven

"Can't be, sir," said Gurr, as he tried to pierce the darkness, "because the skipper must be lying at anchor where we left him."

"Hah! See that?" cried Archy, as the men bent to their oars and made the now phosphorescent water flash.

"Only the oars, lad. Water brimes."

Thud! came the report of a heavy gun.

"You're right, lad! 'Twas the flash from a gun. Some one's pursuing of something. Pull away, my lads, let's get aboard, and the skipper may join in. Bah! What's the good o' shore-going? Man's sure to get wrong there."

The men forgot their weariness in the excitement, as they realised that some vessel was in chase of a smuggler, but they murmured among themselves at their ill luck at being away from the cutter; for if they had been aboard at the first shot, the anchor would have been weighed or slipped, and the *White Hawk* gone to see what was going on, probably to help capture a heavily laden smuggler craft.

"And we should have took our share, lads," said Dick in a whisper. "Hey, boot we are out o' luck."

"Don't sit muttering and grumbling there, my lad, but pull hard, and let's get aboard," cried the master, and the oars dipped away in the dark sea, seeming to splash up so much pale lambent fire at every stroke.

But this was no novelty to the men, and the boats sped on, one in the other's wake, with the crew straining their heads over their left shoulders to catch a glimpse of the next flash which preceded the gun.

"Good six mile away from where we are now," said Gurr. "Oh, my lad, my lad, I wish we were aboard."

But it was a long pull from the cove to where the cutter lay, nearly a mile and a half from the shore, and, though the master and Archy kept straining their eyes to catch sight of their little vessel, she was invisible.

As they rowed on, they kept on increasing their distance from the shore, steering so as to pass along one side of a right-angled triangle, instead of along by the cliff and then straight off; but, as the cutter showed no lights, this was all guess-work, and made the task rather anxious.

The firing kept on, the dull thud of the gun being preceded by the flash, and at each notification of a shot the men gave such a tug at the stout ash blades that they bent, and the boat leaped through the water.

"Hurrah! Morning," cried Archy, and the men answered his remark with a cheer, for there was a grey light coming fast now in the east, but, to the utter astonishment of all, the cutter did not become visible.

They gazed round excitedly as the light broadened, but there was no cutter where they expected she would be, but ten minutes later, dimly seen as yet, they made her out miles away under full sail, in chase of a long, low, three-masted lugger, at which she was keeping up a slow and steady fire.

The men cheered as the direction of the boats' heads was changed.

"Pull, my lads, pull!" cried master and boatswain. The men responded with another cheer, and the water rattled under their bows.

"It's a long pull," cried the master; "but as soon as she sees us, she'll run down and pick us up."

"Hurrah!" shouted the men.

"Well done, Mr Brough, well done!" cried Gurr excitedly. "Think of him, with hardly a man to help him, sailing the cutter, and keeping up a steady fire like that. Oh, Mr Raystoke, why aren't we aboard?"

"Ah, why indeed? There she goes again. I say, Mr Gurr, won't she be able to knock some of her spars overboard."

"I wish I was aboard the lugger with an axe," growled Gurr, shading his eyes; and then, placing his foot against the stroke oar, he gave a regular thrust with the man's pull, a plan imitated by the boatswain on board the other boat.

The light increased rapidly now, and the soft grey sky gave promise of a glorious day, but this did not take the attention of those on board the boats, who could see nothing but the lugger trying to escape, and gradually growing more distant, while the cutter kept on slowly, sending a shot in her wake, evidently in the hope of bringing down one of her masts.

"What boat's that, Mr Gurr?" said Archy at last, drawing the master's attention to one in full sail in the opposite direction to that in which they were going.

"Dunno, my lad. Never mind her. Lobster, I should say."

"Looks fast and smart for a lobster-boat," thought Archy, as he kept glancing at the craft, whose aspect seemed to have a strange attraction for him alone. In fact, every eye was fixed upon the two vessels in the offing, while it seemed to Archy that the boat, which was sailing rapidly, had changed her course on seeing them, and was trying to get close up under the cliffs, apparently to reach the cove from which they had come.

There was nothing suspicious in a sailing-boat making for the cove, but, as the middy looked at it, the boat heeled over in a puff of wind, and he fancied that he caught sight of a familiar figure behind the sail.

It was only a momentary glance, and directly after he told himself it was nonsense, for the figure which had started up in the night, away on the cliff was Ram Shackle, and he could not be in two places at once.

"We shall never do it, my lads," said the master suddenly. "Easy—easy. It's of no use to break your backs, and your hearts too. She's sailing two knots to our one. Easy in that boat," he shouted. "We can't do it."

A low murmur arose from both crews.

"Silence there!" shouted Gurr. Then, more gently, "I don't want to give it up, but you can see for yourself, bo's'n, we can't do it."

"No," came back abruptly.

"It would only be hindering her too. No, Mr Raystoke, it's only our old bad luck, and common sense says it's of no use to fight again it."

"Mr Gurr," said Archy excitedly, speaking with his eyes fixed on the sailing-boat.

"Yes, my lad, what is it?"

"Do you think it possible that yonder boat has had anything to do with the lugger?"

"Eh? What?" cried the master sharply. "Haven't got a glass. I dunno. They're such a set of foxes about here that she might."

He shaded his eyes with his hand, and took a long look at her, and once more a puff of wind caught her sail and heeled her over, so that he could get a good look over her side.

She was about a mile away, and well in toward the shore, keeping far enough from the cliffs to catch the land breeze, and now, as the task of catching up the cutter was given up as impossible, the boat took the attention of all.

"Why, she's got a lot of men in her," cried Gurr excitedly; "nine or ten lying down in her bottom."

"Yes," cried Archy; "and it doesn't take ten men to catch a lobster."

"Ahoy, bo's'n!" cried Gurr; "pull off to the west'ard sharp, and cut off that boat if she makes for that way. Try and head her in under the cliff where there's no wind, if she tries to pass you. Look out! She has a lot of men on board."

The direction of the second boat was altered at once, the men began to pull hard; and just as a dull thud from seaward told that the *White Hawk* was still well on the heels of her quarry, the first boat turned smartly and began to chase.

"I hope you're right, Mr Raystoke," said the master. "I should like to have one little bit o' fun before we go back aboard. Ah, look at her! She don't mean us to overhaul her. Be smart, my lads. Don't cheer, but seem to be taking it coolly. You're right, Mr Raystoke," he added a minute later; "there's something wrong with that boat, or she would not want to run away."

For the direction of the little yawl they were making for was suddenly changed, and it was evident that, seeing how the second boat, commanded by the boatswain, was going to head her off from the west, she was being put on the other course, so as to run east.

But the first boat was going rapidly through the water now, and a turn of the helm changed her course, so that it would be easy to cut the yawl off from going in the new direction, while an attempt to pass between the boats and head straight for sea was also met by the steersmen of the pursuers.

"Why, what's she going to do?" said Gurr. "Ah, my lad, it's all a flam. Only a lobster-boat after all. She's going to run in under the cliffs where there's no wind, and of course it's to take up her lobster-pots."

"If she was only going to take up lobster-pots she wouldn't have tried to run," said Archy sharply. "I'd overhaul her, Mr Gurr."

"Going to, my lad. Don't you be scared about that. I'll overhaul her, if it's only to get some fresh lobsters for breakfast. There, I told you so," he continued, after a few minutes' interval, during which the boat was sailing straight in for the cliffs, about five hundred yards away from the landing ledge, away to the west; and as the master spoke the mainsail was rapidly lowered, the jib dropped, and those in the *White Hawk's* leading boat saw that there was a good deal of busy work on board; and before they had recovered from their surprise, several men rose up, oars were thrust over now that the wind had failed, and, with eight men pulling, they were going straight for the cliff.

"Smugglers!" shouted Gurr excitedly. "Jump up, Mr Raystoke, and signal the bo's'n to come on. We shall have a prize after all, though it's only a little one. Pull my lads, pull?"

The smugglers' boat was now about half a mile away, the men in her pulling with all their might, but the King's boat was the more swift, though after a few minutes' chase it was evident that the start was in the smugglers' favour.

"Hang them! They're going to run ashore. They've got a nook there, I'll be bound, and as soon as they're landed they'll be scuffling up the side of the cliff. Pull, my lads, and as we reach the rock, out with you and chase them; you can climb as well as they can. If they're getting away, cover them with your pistols, and tell 'em they shall have it if they don't surrender."

The excitement was now tremendous: the cutter's boat was going fast, and the second boat was closing up, so that it would be impossible for the smugglers to escape by sea. And now, as they drew nearer, Archy saw that his first surmise was right: Ram was in the boat, and right forward, his red cap showing out plainly in the morning light. Jemmy Dadd was there too, and Shackle, beside the big dark fellow who had tricked the lieutenant, while the rest of the crew were strong-looking fellows of the fisherman type.

"Now then there!" shouted Gurr, rising up, but retaining his hold of the tiller with one hand. "It's of no use. Surrender!"

A yell of derision came from the boat, and Ram jumped up and waved his red cap, with the effect that it seemed as if some of the dye had been transferred to Archy's face, which a minute sooner had been rather pale with excitement.

"Pull, my lads, pull, and you'll have them before they land!" cried the master, stamping his foot. "Here, take the tiller, Mr Raystoke;" and he shifted his position, passed the tiller to Archy, and stood up and drew his sword.

"Starboard a little—starboard!" he said. "Run her right alongside, my lad; and you, my men, never mind your oars, the others'll pick them up. The moment we touch, up with you, out with your cutlashes, and down with any man who does not surrender."

"Ay, ay, sir!" cheered the men.

"Now, then," shouted Gurr, "do you surrender?"

A derisive laugh came from the smugglers, who pulled their hardest, pretty closely followed by the king's boat, when, just as they seemed to be coming stem on to the rocks at the foot of the cliff, the four men on the starboard side suddenly plunged their oars down deep, backing water, while the men on the larboard pulled furiously, the result being that the head of the boat swung round, and she glided right out of sight behind a tall rock, which seemed part of the main cliff from a few yards out.

A fierce cry of rage came from the master, but he was quick at giving directions, checking the course of his boat, and then proceeding cautiously; and having no difficulty in following under a low archway for some twenty yards,—a passage evidently only possible at extreme low water,—and directly after they were out again in broad daylight, and at the bottom of a huge funnel-like hollow, from which the rocky cliffs rose up some three hundred feet.

It was a marvellously beautiful spot, but the occupants of the *White Hawk's* boat had only eyes then for the smugglers, who had run their boat into a nook just across the bottom of the pool, and they had had time to leap on to the rock, and were rapidly climbing a rough zigzag path.

"And us never to have been along here at the right time of the tide to find this hole!" thought Archy, as, in obedience to a sign, he steered the boat across the beautiful transparent pool, and laid her alongside the smugglers boat.

Then oars were thrown down, the men sprang across the smugglers' craft, and, headed by Archy and Gurr, began to climb rapidly after their enemies.

"It's of no use to call upon them to surrender," said Gurr rather breathlessly, as they toiled up the zigzag.

"We'll make them do it later on," cried Archy, whose youth and activity helped him to get on first.

"Steady, my lad, steady!"

"But I want to see which way they go."

"Right, but keep out of danger, my lad. If they show fight, keep back."

Archy heard, but made no reply, and toiled on up the rugged ascent, straining every nerve as he saw the last smuggler disappear over the top, and, at the next turn he made in the zigzag, he caught a glimpse of the ascent from top to bottom, with the sailors climbing up, and just then there was a fresh cheer, which made him turn swiftly again, to look round and see the second boat gliding through the rocky arch into the pool.

It was rather risky, for he was on a narrow slippery place at one of the turns of the *zigzag*, and nearly lost his footing, but, darting out a hand, he caught at the rock, recovered himself, and climbed on, to reach the top just in time to see Ram's red cap disappearing some four hundred yards away over a rounded eminence due west of where he stood.

He glanced down again, and then, breathless as he was, ran on over the down-like hillside till he reached the spot where he had seen Ram's red cap disappear, and here he stopped, to make sure of Mr Gurr seeing the direction he had taken, standing well up with his sword raised above his head in the bright sunshine.

There was nothing visible but soft green rolling cliff top, and he looked vainly for some sign of the enemy, eager to go on, but taught caution, and not knowing but what Ram might have taken one direction to lure the pursuers away, while the men were in hiding in another.

But, as he waited and scanned the place around, he suddenly caught sight of what seemed to be a rift against the sky in the edge of a cliff which rose up rapidly, and his heart gave a great throb.

"Let Ram play what tricks he likes," he said, "I know where I am now."

"Well, my lad, well!" panted Gurr, running up, followed by the men. "Don't say they've got away!"

"No," cried Archy excitedly. "I think I can lead you to the foxes' hole. This way."

And, as he spoke, there came in rapid succession a couple of dull thuds from seaward, and a cheer from the crew behind, as, led by Archy Raystoke, the men now went over the undulating cliff top at a trot.

Chapter Thirty Eight

The discovery of the way through the cliff made clear to Archy several matters connected with the appearance and disappearance of Ram and his companion with the boat, for upon more than one occasion it had seemed impossible that they could have rowed six miles to the cove and come back again. And, excited as the midshipman was, these ideas occurred to him while running along over the top of the down-like cliff.

On looking back beyond the first boat's crew, the head of the second crew could be seen as they reached the top of the zigzag path, where the boatswain waited till the last man was up, and then gave the word for them to double after their fellows.

Seeing that he was so well supported, the master felt that he was ready for any force the smugglers might have to back them up, and, turning to Archy, he suggested that the midshipman should point out the way into the smugglers' cave, and then leave them to do the work.

"It will be time enough to talk about that, Mr Gurr," said Archy rather breathlessly, "when we have found the place."

"But I thought you had found it, my lad!"

"After the tricks played us, I shall not be certain until I see you all right in the cave."

"But you think it's close here?"

"Yes; unless I am quite wrong, the old quarry is in that great cliff where the grass runs right up to the edge."

"Then if it's there, and those fellows have gone in, we'll find the way, and go in too."

"Oh!" ejaculated Archy, stopping short.

"What's the matter, lad?—hurt?"

"No. The place is dark as pitch, and we have no lights."

"Then we'll strike some with our pistol locks, and set fire to some wood. Never mind the lights. If it's light enough for them, it will be light enough for us, lad. Let's find the way in, and that will be enough. They won't show fight. Let's get on, and we shall be marching them all out tied two and two before they're much older."

The party kept on along the rugged undulating top of the cliffs, till, after a careful inspection in all directions, Archy declared that they must now be over the cavern.

The second boat's crew had overtaken them now, and, upon receiving this information, the master spread his men out a few yards apart, to sweep the ground after the fashion observed on the previous night.

"You must find it now, my lads," he said. "I should say what you've got to look for is a hole pretty well grown over with green stuff right up at the end of a bit of a gully, and looking as if no one had been there for a hundred years."

"Yes, something like the mouths of the old quarries we have seen," added Archy.

"Then there's something of the sort down yonder," cried Dick, pointing to a spot where the ground seemed to have sunk down.

"Yes," cried Archy eagerly; "and that's the place. Look here, Mr Gurr."

"What at, my lad?"

"The grass."

"Well, we want to find smugglers, not grass, my lad."

"Yes, but don't you see that some one has gone over here lately. The dew is all brushed off, and you can see the footmarks."

"I can't, my lad. Perhaps you can with your young eyes."

"Oh, it's all right," growled the boatswain.

"Keep a sharp look-out, then, and mind no one gets by."

The little force advanced, with the men spread out to right and left, the officers in the centre, following the trail which led right to the gully-like depression, once doubtless a well-worn track, but now completely smoothed over and grass-grown; and there, sure enough, as discovered only a short time before by Celia, was the scooped-out hollow filled with fern, bramble, and wild clematis, and the rough steps down, and the archway dimly seen beyond the loose stones.

"Halt!" cried the master; and, after a careful inspection had shown that the footprints in the dewy grass had gone no farther than the entrance, the men were called up, and stood round the pit.

There it all was, exactly as Archy had pictured it in his own mind: the loose stones at the bottom of the hole covering, he was sure, the trap-door he had so often heard opened and shut; but, as he went down a few steps in his eagerness, and scanned the place, he was puzzled and disappointed; for the trap-door, if that was the spot where it lay, was covered, and therefore the men could not be in the cave.

"Bad job we've got no lanthorns," said Gurr, who was looking over Archy's shoulder at the low-browed arch of the passage leading right in; "and it looks bad travelling, but in we've got to go if they won't surrender. Let me go first, my lad."

For answer the midshipman went down to the bottom of the rough steps, and stood over the trap-door on the loose stones.

"No, no, my lad," said Gurr kindly, as he joined him. "Too rough a job for you. I'll lead, and, hang it! I shall have to crawl. Not very good work for one's clothes. Come along, my lads. You, Mr Raystoke, and four men stop back, and form the reserve, to take prisoner any one who tries to escape."

The men descended till every step was occupied, the little force extending from top to bottom.

"Stop a minute, Mr Gurr. Let the bo's'n guard the entry here; I must go with you to act as guide."

"It aren't all passage, then, like this?"

"No; it's a great open place supported by pillars, big enough to lose yourselves in. But stop; that can't be the way, sir."

"Oh, hang it all, my lad!" cried the master in disappointed tones. "Don't say that."

"But I do," cried Archy. "There ought to be a trap-door covered with stones leading down a place like a well."

"Yes; that's what we've come down."

"No, no, another. I think it was down here."

He stamped his foot on the loose stones, and then uttered a cry of joy, for there was a curious hollow sound, and on stooping down he pulled away some of the great shaley fragments, and laid bare a rough plank with a bolt partly visible.

"Right! Got 'em at last," cried Gurr. "Clear off more stones, my lads. No; stop!" he said.

"Yes, I know what you are thinking, Mr Gurr," said Archy. "The men couldn't have shut themselves in there."

"Course not, my lad. But you are right, that's the way down to their curiosity shop, and they're hiding in this hole here."

Then, thrusting in his head, and holding on by the rugged stones, he shouted into the hollow passage,—

"Now then, my lads, out you come!"

A pause.

"D'yer hear? The game's up, and if you don't come out quietly, we shall have to fetch you out on the rough."

Still no reply.

"Come, come, my lads, no nonsense! Surrender. I don't want to use pistols and cutlashes to Englishmen. You know the game's up. Surrender."

Still no reply.

"I don't think that hole goes in far, Mr Raystoke," whispered the master. "There's no echo like, and it sounds smothered." Then aloud,—

"Now, then, is it surrender? Oh, very well; I've got some nice little round messengers to send in after you."

He drew a pistol from his belt and cocked it, winking at Archy as he did so. "Now, then, once—twice—fire!"

He pointed the mouth of the pistol downward, and drew the trigger, and in the semi-darkness below the overhanging brambles and clematis there was a dull flash, the report sounded smothered, and the place was filled with the dank, heavy-scented smoke.

"There's precious little room in there," whispered the master. "If there'd been much of it, we should have heard the sound go rolling along instead of coming back like a slap in the face. Here, one of you, reload that. You, Dick, follow me. If they show fight, you come on next, bo's'n, with the whole of your boat's crew."

"Ay, ay, sir."

"Hi! In there. Do you surrender?"

There was not a sound, and, after a momentary pause, the master spat in his fist, gripped his cutlass, went down on all fours, after driving his hat on tightly, and crawled into the hole, followed by Dick.

"Keep a cheery heart on it, lad," said one of the men just before to Dick. "We'll fetch you out and bury you at sea."

Dick drove his elbow into the man's chest for an answer, grinned as he felt the point of his cutlass, and dived into the hole, while the boatswain and his men stood waiting eagerly, ready to plunge forward at the first sound of a scuffle.

Archy peered in at the dark passage, his heart beating as he listened to the noise made by the two men crawling in, and the last of the two had hardly disappeared when there was a shout, a scuffle, and the boatswain plunged in.

"All right!" they heard Gurr say. "I've got him. Hold still, you varmint, or I'll cut your ears off. Here, Dick, get by me, and go forrard if you can."

There was more scuffling, and the rattle of a stone or two, as the listeners pictured in their own minds the man squeezing past the master and his prisoner, and then Dick's voice came out in a half smothered way:

"Can't get no farther. All choked-up."

"All right, then, but make sure."

"Oh, I'm sure enough," said Dick. "It's all a stopper here."

"Then out you come, my lad," said the master; and the next minute his legs were seed as he backed out, dragging evidently some one after him who was resisting.

"Here, Dick," came in smothered tones.

"Ay, ay, sir."

"Says he won't come. If he gives me any more of his nonsense, touch him up behind with the pynte of your cutlash."

"Ay, ay, sir."

"Yah! Cowards!" came in angry tones.

"Ram!" exclaimed Archy, as the boy, looking hot and fierce, was dragged out by the master, to stand looking round him as fiercely as a wild cat.

"Hullo!" cried Archy. "It's my turn now, Ram;" but he repented his words directly, as he saw the reproachful look the boy darted at him. Then he forgot all directly, as he exclaimed, —

"I see, Mr Gurr, I see! The smugglers are down here after all, and they left this boy behind to fasten the door, and cover it over with stones."

Unable to contain himself, Ram thoroughly endorsed the midshipman's words by giving an angry stamp upon the bottom of the hole.

"That's it!" cried Gurr. "Here, chuck these stones into the passage, my lads;" and the rough trap-door was laid bare, the two bolts by which it was secured were seen to be unfastened, and the lock unshot.

"No way out, Mr Raystoke, is there?"

"No."

"Then we've got 'em trapped safe this time," said Gurr, as the door was thrown open. "Bad job we've no lanthorns; but never mind, my lads. If they won't surrender, you must feel your way with the pyntes of your toothpicks."

There was a murmur of excitement among the men, and then Gurr leaned down over the hole, put his hand to his mouth, and shouted, —

"Below there! In the King's name — surrender!"

His words went rolling and echoing through the place, but there was no reply.

"Once more, my lads, to save bloodshed, will you surrender?"

No reply.

"Very well. It's your fault, my lads, and very onsensible. Bo's'n, it's a big place, and I shall want all my men. You're all right here; with one you ought to be able to hold this."

"And the prisoner?"

"No; we'll take him with us. Here, lash his hands behind him, and tie his legs together. We'll lay him down to have a nap somewhere yonder down below. That's right," he continued, as a man produced a piece of line, and firmly secured the boy, who was lowered down to one of the men who had descended, laid on the stones in a corner at the bottom; and then, after giving the word to be ready, Gurr braced himself up.

"You'll stop aside me, Mr Raystoke, and try and guide."

"Yes, sir."

"You understand, bo's'n, down with the first who tries to escape up the hole here."

"Ay, ay."

"Then, now, forward!" cried Gurr; and, closely followed by Archy and his men, he descended into the old quarry, and then stood listening at the top of the slope, before preparing to advance into the enemy-peopled darkness right ahead.

Chapter Thirty Nine

Archy felt his heart throb as he led the way down the slope, every step of which seemed so familiar that he advanced without hesitation, the knowledge of how many sturdy men he had at his back keeping away the natural shrinking which under other circumstances he might have felt.

"Halt!" said the master suddenly, and then in a whisper to his guide, "Strikes me as they'll have the best of it if they should fight, my lad."

"Not much," replied Archy; "it's as dark for them as it is for us, so that they can't take us at a disadvantage. Call on them to surrender again."

"Ay, to be sure," cried the master; and once more he summoned the smugglers to give in.

There was not a sound to suggest that his orders were heard.

"Don't know what to do, my lad," whispered the master again. "If we go forward, we're leaving the way open for the enemy to attack the watch at the entrance, and we don't want that. Are you sure they're here?"

"I feel certain of it," said Archy in the same low tone. "They must be, but they're hiding, so as to try to escape, or else to take us at a disadvantage."

"Well," said Gurr, "let them. So long as they come out and fight fair, I don't care what they do. Here, four of you stop here; Dick, take command. We'll go forward and turn the enemy, and try to take them in the rear. Stand fast if they come at you; no pistols, but use your cutlasses. We shall come up to you at the least sound, to help."

The men uttered a low, "Ay, ay, sir," speaking as if they were oppressed by the darkness, and the master whispered.

"Now, my lad," he said, "try and give us the shape of the place like."

Archy obeyed, and explained where the smugglers' stores lay, and the pile of little kegs, if they had not been moved, the place where he had slept, and the positions of the huge pillars and heaps of broken stones.

"And you was shut up here all that time, and didn't go mad!" said Gurr. "Well, you are a wonder! Tell you what, my lad, I should just like to make sure that those brandy kegs are still here, and then I think we'll be off, and come back with lights. There's no one here but ourselves. Place isn't big enough for any one to be hiding without our hearing them?"

"Plenty, Mr Gurr," said Archy firmly; "and I am sure they are here; but it is impossible to search without lights. They may be hiding behind the pillars or piles of stone. Have lights got as soon as possible, and then we can come and make them prisoners."

All this was said in a hurried whisper, as the two stood together in front of their men, and in absolute darkness, for they had advanced into the place far enough for the faint light which filtered down from the trap-door to be completely lost.

"Yes; but I'd like to be able to tell the skipper that we have got something in the way of a prize for the men. Can you lead us to it, my lad?"

"But you couldn't take it away."

"Well, we might carry one keg aboard, as a sample. Now then, where will it be from here?"

"Give me your hand, and I'll lead you right to it."

"There you are. Take care how you go. Can you keep close behind us, my lads? Better join hands. Now then, are you ready?"

"Ay, ay," came in a low murmur; and, grasping the master's hand, Archy led on, fully believing that the smugglers were still there, but feeling that they would keep in hiding, and try to escape when they were gone.

"Say, my lad," whispered the master, "I pity you—I do from my soul. Think of you being shut up all alone in a place like this! Hah! Look out!"

The order was needless, for the smugglers gave every one warning to do that.

One moment the King's men were advancing cautiously through the darkness, the next, without a sound to warn them, there was a rush; blows fell thick and fast, cudgel striking head, cutlass, shoulder, anything that opposed the advance; and in less time than it takes to describe the encounter, the sailors were beaten down or aside, and the party of four, who were warned of what to expect by the noise in their front, advanced to the help of their friends, but only to be beaten down or aside by the gang which rushed at them.

"Stop them, Dick. Down with them!" shouted the master, as soon as he could get on his feet. "Hi, Dick! Pass the word to the bo's'n to look out. Here, Mr Raystoke! Hi, bo's'n, down with that trap and make it fast. Mr Raystoke, I say, where are you? Which way is it? Who's this?"

"No, no, sir," cried one of them; "it's on'y me."

"Mr Gurr! Here!" cried Archy. "Where are you?"

"At last. Where were you, then?"

"On the stones, half stunned," cried Archy. "Here, all get together and follow me."

"What are you going to do?"

"Make for the trap-door—sharp! They're fighting there."

"Oh, dear, who'd have thought it was this way!" grumbled the master. "Talk about blind man's buff! Sure you're going right, lad? Shall I fire a pistol to make a flash?"

"No; I know."

"Hah!" cried Gurr, as an echoing bang ran through the great cavern. "Bravo, bo's'n!"

The bang was followed by a heavy rattling sound perfectly familiar to Archy, as he hurried the master along to the foot of the slope.

"Are you all there?" cried Archy.

"Yes,"—"No,"—"No," came from different directions.

"Then keep up this way, and be ready for another rush."

"Ay," cried the master loudly; "and I warn you fellows now, I'd have treated you easy; but if you will have it, the word's war, and a volley of bullets next time you come on."

"No, no, don't fire! You'll hit our own men," whispered Archy, as he reached the top of the slope. "Ah! Who's this?" he cried, as he nearly fell over a prostrate figure.

"Steady, my lad, steady!"

"Steady it is," said another voice.

"What, bo's'n?"

"Yes, sir, and me too. Oh, my head! How it bleeds!"

"Why, what are you doing here?"

"They came at us, sir, like mad bulls, and 'fore I knew where I was they had me. Pair o' hands pops up out of the hole, takes hold of my legs, and I was pulled down, had a crack of the head, was danced on, and here I am, sir."

"And me too, sir," said the other voice. "But, I'm much worse than him."

"But the smugglers?"

"All seemed to come over us, sir; banged the door down, and they've been rattling big stones on it. There, you can hear 'em now."

In corroboration of the boatswain's words, there was a dull thunderous sound overhead, as of great stones being thrown down over the trap-door, and all listened in silence for a time till the noise ceased.

The silence was broken by Gurr, who suddenly roared out, as if he had only just grasped the position,—

"Why, they've got away!"

"Every man jack of 'em, sir, and they all walked over me."

"And they've shut us in!"

"Yes, Mr Gurr," said Archy sadly; "they've shut us in."

"But if they were here," cried the master; "that's what I wanted to do to them. I say, Mr Raystoke, you've done it now."

Half angry, half amused, but all the while smarting with the pain caused by a blow he had received, Archy remained silent, listening to the heavy breathing and muttering of his companions in misfortune. The sounds above ground had ceased, and it was evident that the smugglers had made good their escape.

Again the silence was broken by the master, who raging with pain and mortification, exclaimed,—

"Well, Mr Raystoke, sir, you know all about this place; which is the way out?"

"Up above here, Mr Gurr, close to where we stand."

"Very well, sir; then why don't you lead on?"

"Because they have shut and fastened the trap, and heaped about a ton of stone upon it."

"Well, then, we must hack through the door with our cutlashes, and let the stone down."

"What's that?" cried Archy excitedly,—"a light!"

For there was a dull report and a flash of blue like lightning; and, running down the slope, the midshipman beheld that which sent a thrill of terror through him. For, away toward the far end of the cave, there was a great pool of flickering blue light; and, as it lit up the ceiling and the huge square stone supports of the place, he saw that which explained the meaning of what had seemed to be a wonderful phenomenon.

There, beyond the flickering pool of blue and yellow flame, which was rapidly spreading in every direction, he could dimly see quite a wall of piled-up kegs, one of which lay right in the edge of the pool of fire, and suddenly exploded with a dull report, which blew the tongues of fire in all directions, half extinguishing them for the moment, but instantaneously flashing out again in a volume of fire, which quadrupled the size of the pool, and began to lick the sides of the kegs.

"The wretches! They fired the spirits before they escaped," cried Archy, who realised to the full what had been done; and, for the sake of our common humanity, let us say it must have been an act of vindictive spite, aimed only at the destruction of the proof spirit, so that it might not fall into the sailors' hands—not intended to condemn them to a hideous death.

"Back quick to the entrance! We must hack down that door," roared Archy.

"Ay, ay," shouted the men, who the moment before were mad with terror, but who leaped at the command as if their safety were assured.

"No, no!" shouted the midshipman, as a fresh keg exploded; and in the flash of flame which followed, the place glowed with a ghastly light.

"Yes, sir, yes!" shouted the men.

"I tell you no," cried Archy; "we should be burned or suffocated long before we could get that open."

And, as in imagination he saw the men fighting and striving with one another to get to the trap-door, which remained obstinately closed, he clapped his hand on Mr Gurr's shoulder.

"I know another way," he cried. "Follow me."

"Hurrah!" yelled the men, and the lad had taken a dozen steps toward the pool of fire, when a wild shout came from near the entrance.

"All! Who's that?" cried Archy, as he mentally saw a wounded man being left behind.

"Don't leave a poor fellow to be burnt to death, Mr Raystoke," cried a familiar voice.

"Ram!" cried Archy, running back to where the boy lay bound behind a pile of stones, forgotten for the time, and unheeded by his companions.

"Yes, it's me," said the boy excitedly.

"Quick! Get up. Can you walk?" said Archy, cutting him free.

"Yes," cried the lad.

"Then come on!"

"For the top passage," whispered Ram. "That's the only way now."

"Yes. Follow me."

The midshipman had hardly given the command when there was another explosion, a fresh flash of fire, which nearly reached them, and he saw beyond the dancing tongues of flame the black opening he sought.

But this fresh explosion—one of which he knew scores must now rapidly follow—checked him for the moment, and he saw that Ram had disappeared.

"It's our only chance, my lads," cried Archy. "Are you all ready?"

"Ay, ay."

"Hold your breath, then, as you get to the fire, and follow me."

"Through that blaze, my lad?" whispered the master.

"Yes. Don't stop to talk. Now, then," roared Archy, "come on!"

"Hurrah!" cried the men wildly; and Archy dashed forward, but was thrown back, and had to retreat, as a fresh keg exploded and added to the size of the pool, now almost a river of fire many yards wide.

"It's now or never!" cried Archy frantically, and he rushed into the blue flames, which leaped about his feet and up as if to lick his face.

A dozen strides, splashing up blue fire at every step, and he was through it, and where a faint current of cold air seemed to be meeting him.

Almost as he reached the farther side, the men came leaping and yelling after him, to stand beating the tongues of fire from their feet and legs.

Bang—bang—a couple more explosions, and the men crowded up to Archy, the master included, as if to ask what next.

"Are you all here?"

"Ay, ay, sir."

"And that boy?"

"I'm here," cried Ram. "Quick, before they all go off."

"Yes," said Archy. "Forward!"

He led the way into the darkness once more, but into an atmosphere which he could breathe. Then up the familiar way, with its rugged steps, and on to the newly mortared wall, with its loophole, through which the glorious light of day streamed.

"Now, my lads, cutlasses here. That wall's new. Four of you work, and loosen the stones, the others take them and throw them back below."

The men cheered, and, headed by Mr Gurr and Dick, worked as they had never worked before.

The stones were hard to move at first, but it was child's play compared to the toil through which the young midshipman had gone when he attacked the wall. First one yielded, then another, and, as they were dragged out, the men cheered, and passed them back to those down the rough steps.

With every stone removed, hope strengthened the little party; but as the explosions followed fast, and the flames began to flicker and play up the passage in which they were penned, Archy closed his eyes for a few moments to mutter a prayer, for his thoughts were getting wild.

Just then, he knew that some one else thought as he did, for a hand touched his arm, and a voice whispered,—

"It wasn't my fault. It must have been Jemmy Dadd. I say—case they can't make a way out in time—shake hands once, mate. I do like you."

Something like a hysterical sob burst from the young midshipman's breast at this; and, facing death as he was just then,—a horrible death which might follow at any moment,—the lad's hand grasped that of his young gaoler—officer and smuggler, but both boys of one blood, who had fought each according to his lights.

"Hah!" sighed Ram, as he gripped hard, and then let go. "Now, then, tell 'em to shove the stones, sharp, and let 'em fall out. Quick! Before the powder ketches."

"Powder?" said Archy in an awe-stricken whisper. "Yes; there's a lot not far from the kegs." The men cheered, as the fresh order was given, and a new set took the places of those who were growing weary, sending the stones out rapidly, till there was room for a man to creep through.

"Here, Ram, you through first, and show them how to climb on the shelf."

"No, no, you lead, Mr Raystoke," cried the master. "Silence, sir! I know what I'm doing," yelled Archy. "Out with you, Ram."

The boy went through like a rabbit, passing something dark before him, and then rapidly one by one the men followed, with the flames roaring horribly now below, and explosion after explosion following quickly, the cave rapidly becoming a reservoir of fire.

"Hurrah! That's all," cried Mr Gurr. "Now, Mr Raystoke."

"No, sir, you."

"I say you."

"And I—"

Archy yielded to his superior in the expedition, crept out, and the master was following, and got stuck, but a fierce tug from a couple of the men set him free, and he had only just joined the two boats' crews standing side by side on the shelf of rock, when the whole cliff seemed to shake; and, as if the passage they had left were some vast cannon, the artificial wall left was blown right out by an awful burst of flame, the stones hurtling down as if the end of the cliffs had come, and falling with a mighty splash into the chasm.

The men stood white and awe-stricken, expecting the cliff to crumble away beneath them, but save that a stream of fire roared out of the opening, all was now still.

Then, in the midst of the awe-inspiring silence, Ram spoke, —

"I thought it wouldn't be long before the powder caught;" and then, before any one could reply, the lad said quietly, "I didn't want to be burnt to death. Better go to prison for smuggling. I say, I got this rope. Hadn't we better make it fast somewhere, and then you can all get down to the big shelf? I'll come last, and unfasten it."

"And then how will you get down?" said the master suspiciously.

"Oh," said Ram, laughing, "I can climb down; can't I, orficer?"

"Yes," said Archy quietly. "He can get down. You will not try to escape, will you, Ram?"

"No; not I. What's the good?" said Ram sadly. "It's all over now."

The rope was made fast, and by its help the men easily reached the great ledge, Ram coming down soon after with the coiled-up rope about his shoulder and under one arm.

"Couldn't have got away if I wanted to," he said, laughing frankly in Archy's face. "I say, I am hungry! Aren't you? Don't I wish I'd got one of mother's baskets full of good stuff!"

"Where's your mother?" asked Archy.

"Up at the farm."

"And your father?"

"Oh, he went off in the lugger this morning, after they'd tried to run a cargo. Your cutter was too quick for them though. We tried to get out to her, but the skipper sent a shot at us, and we came back here, only you saw us, and run us down."

"Where do you suppose your men are now?" asked Archy.

"Don't know, and if I did, I wouldn't tell," said the boy bluntly. "I say," he added, after a pause, "I give you a pretty good run last night, didn't I?"

"You young dog!" growled the master.

"Well, if I hadn't, you'd have found the way in yonder, and I wasn't going to let you if I could help it."

"Ah, you'll be hung, sir."

"Get out!" cried Ram. "Your skipper wouldn't hang a boy like me. Think the cutter will be long?" said the boy after a pause, during which all had been watching the flame which seemed to flow out of the opening far overhead.

"I don't know; why?" replied Archy.

"Because she'll have to come and take us off. This rope's long enough, and we shall have to slide down into a boat."

But the cutter was long. For the lugger had escaped to Holland consequent upon the *White Hawk* being so short-handed, and it was toward evening that she came close in to search for the crews, and all the party descended in safety to the boat, which rowed under in answer to the signals made by firing pistols.

As to the boats that passed under the archway, they were prisoned till the next low water.

"Satisfied?" said the lieutenant, after all were on board, and he had heard the report. "More than satisfied. I was horribly disappointed at losing the lugger, and I made a hard fight for it, but your news—my dear boy—my dear Mr Gurr, this is splendid! What a despatch I can write!"

"It will be the breaking up of the gang, will it not, sir?" asked Archy.

"Yes, my dear boy; and an end to this wretched work. They must promote me now, and draft you, too, into a good ship. If we can be together, Mr Raystoke, I shall be delighted."

That same night, as he was thinking about Ram Shackle, Archy went up to the lieutenant, who was walking up and down rubbing his hands.

"Beg pardon, sir, but may I ask a favour?"

"A dozen if you like, Raystoke, and I'll grant them if I can. Want a run ashore?"

"No, sir. I want you to be easy with that boy. He was very kind to me when I was a prisoner."

"Hum! Hah! Well, I don't know what to say to that. Here, my man, fetch that boy on deck."

Ram came up, whistling softly, and looking sharply from one to the other.

"Now, sir, take off your cap," said the lieutenant sternly.

Ram did not look a bit afraid, but he doffed his red cap.

"I suppose you know, sir, that you'll be sent to gaol?"

"Yes.—I knew you wouldn't hang me."

"And pray what have you to say for yourself?"

"Nothing that I knows on," said Ram. "Yes, I have. I say father's gone, and I dessay he won't come back for ever so long, and I don't want to go among the Dutchmen. May I stop here 'long of him? There won't be no more smuggling to do."

"You mean you want to volunteer for His Majesty's service?"

"Yes, that's it," said Ram cheerfully. "May I?"

"Yes," said Lieutenant Brough shortly. "There; you can go below."

Ram waved his red cap, tossed it in the air, and turned to Archy.

"I say, orficer," he said, "I know where your little sword is. You send one of your chaps to-morrow to mother, and tell her I'm aboard and going to be a sailor, and she's to give him your little sword as father put in the top drawer."

Archy's eyes sparkled, for the loss of his dirk was a bitter memory.

"Humph!" said the lieutenant, as Ram went below; "not a bad sort of boy. Well, Mr Raystoke, will that do?"

Archy shook the hand held out, and went aft to gaze at the cliff, feeling that somehow he liked Ram Shackle.

Then he turned, rather despondent, for he knew that the next day there would be an expedition ashore, when visits would be paid to the farm and to the Hoze, and he felt uncomfortable about the Graemes.

Chapter Forty

"Hullo, young fellow!"

"Hullo, orficer!"

"You must not speak like that," said Archy, as he encountered Ram on deck next morning, whistling softly as he neatly coiled down a rope. "And you must touch your cap."

"That way?" said Ram.

"Yes; that will do, but you must say 'Sir,' or 'Ay, ay sir.'"

"Ay, ay, sir."

"Well, you seem to be settling down very soon."

"Oh, yes, I'm all right. What's the good of making a fuss. Going ashore?"

"Yes. Do you want to go?"

Ram shook his head.

"No; I should only see some of our chaps, and it would look as if I'd been splitting on them; and I didn't, did I?"

"No; you behaved very bravely and well, Ram."

"Mean it—*sir*?"

"Yes, I do, indeed."

"Thank ye—sir," said Ram. "No, don't let the skipper send me ashore; and—I say—"

"Yes?"

"Tell mother I'm all right, and that I shan't have to go to prison, and that I'll get some one to tell her how I'm getting on now and then. She's a good one is mother, that she is."

"I'll tell her you have given up all smuggling, and that you are going to be a good sailor now."

"Yes, do, please—sir. She hates the smuggling, and used to beg father not, but he would do it. And I say, are you going up to the Hoze?"

"Yes; we shall search the farm and the Hoze too."

"Won't find nothing at the farm. Father never had nothing there, not even a keg. And you won't find nothing at the Hoze."

"Not in the cellar?"

"No," said Ram frankly.

"How long has that Sir Risdon Graeme been a smuggler?"

"Him? Never was one, poor old chap, only father good as made him lend us his cellar, because it was nice and handy, and nobody would think of going and searching there. Ha, ha, ha!" laughed Ram, showing his white teeth; "you people went up there one day and touched your hats to Sir Risdon, and were afraid to go close up to the house, when all the time the cellar was choke full."

"I remember," said the midshipman; "and I found it out. But look here, Ram, how could your father make Sir Risdon, who is a gentleman, lend him the cellar?"

"'Cause father and mother used to pretty well keep 'em. I had to be always going without father knowing, and taking 'em bread and butter and bacon and eggs. They just are poor. Mother used to send me, and she often used to tell me that they was 'most starved to death."

"Then Sir Risdon didn't get anything by the smuggling?"

"Him!" cried Ram. "Why, father sent me up one day with a keg of brandy for him, and a piece of silk for her ladyship; I did get hot that day carrying of 'em up the hill. It was last summer."

"Yes; and what did Sir Risdon say?"

"Say? He 'most shied 'em at me, and I had to carry 'em back. My! That was a hot day and no mistake."

Somehow Archy felt relieved about the Graemes, and, after a little consideration, he went and reported all he had heard to the lieutenant, who nodded his head, looked severe, and ordered the two boats to be manned.

The midshipman took the order on deck, and Ram stared.

"I say," he said, "what's the good of going now? You'll have to row all the way to the cove and walk all the way along by the cliffs. If you wait till the tide's right out, you can get in through Grabley's hole."

Archy reported this, and in due time Gurr was left in charge of the cutter, the lieutenant went off in one boat, and the other was in Archy's charge.

It all seemed very matter of fact now, as they rowed in through the opening, left the boats in the little pool, climbed the zigzag; and a halt was called, during which the little lieutenant wiped his streaming face, and recovered his breath.

Then the party marched for the farm, where, red-eyed, and her florid face mottled and troubled-looking, Mrs Shackle met them.

"Well, woman," said the lieutenant severely; "I have to search this place."

"If you please, sir," said the woman humbly.

"One moment. Answer me honestly. Is there any contraband article stored about the farm?"

"No, sir, and never was."

"Humph! That's what your son said."

"My son? Oh, pray, pray tell me, gentlemen, is he safe? I heard that he was burned to death."

"Your son is quite well, aboard my ship."

"Thank God! Oh, thank God!" cried the poor woman, sinking upon her knees to cover her face with her hands, sobbing violently, and rocking herself to and fro.

"There!" she cried, jumping up quickly, and wiping her eyes; "I've no cause to fret now."

"He has volunteered for the navy," continued the lieutenant; "and if he is a good lad, we shall make a man of him."

"Then you will, sir; for a better boy never stepped."

"For a smuggler, eh?" said the lieutenant drily.

"Well, sir, he was my husband's boy, and he did what his father told him."

"And your husband?"

"The men came and told me, sir, that he escaped in the lugger."

"And the men—where are they?"

"They got away yesterday, sir, those who were left. They felt that they must leave these parts for good."

"Yes, for *good*!" said the lieutenant emphatically. "Now, Mr Raystoke, have you anything to say?"

"Only to deliver my message. Mrs Shackle, Ram told me to tell you he was all right."

"Thank Heaven!" said the woman, wiping away a tear; "and you won't punish him, sir, and you'll keep him away from the smuggling?"

"Never fear," cried the lieutenant, laughing.

"You were to give me my dirk, Mrs Shackle."

"Oh, *yes*, sir!" cried the woman, crossing to an old bureau, and taking out the little weapon. "And I suppose, sir, all the old home will be taken and destroyed?"

"Oh, I don't know. We shall see. But, look here, my good woman; do you want to sail right or wrong now?"

"Oh, right, sir, please."

"Then tell me honestly where there are any more goods stored?"

"Everything left, sir, was put in the old quarry."

"Nothing up at that house on the hill?"

"No, sir, I think not. It's all over now, and my husband has gone, so I may as well speak out."

"Of course. It will be best for you—and for your son."

"They only stored cargoes up at Sir Risdon's because it was handy, sir, and then took them on afterwards to the big store in the old quarry that was burned last night. But pray tell me, sir, was any one hurt?"

"No, but we have no thanks to give your people. Now, Mr Raystoke."

He marched out, and Archy was following, but Mrs Shackle arrested him.

"God bless you, my dear!" she whispered. "I knew about you being there, but we couldn't help it, and Ram used to tell me all about it, and how he liked you; and we sent you everything we could to make you comfortable. Be kind now to my son."

"If Ram turns out a good lad, Mrs Shackle, he shall never want a—"

Archy was going to say friend, but he could not, for Mrs Shackle had thrown her arms about his neck in a big, motherly hug, from which the young officer escaped red-faced and vexed.

"I wish she hadn't kissed me," he said to himself, after making sure that no one had seen. "And she has made my face all wet with her crying."

They were on the march now to the Hoze, with the lieutenant in the highest of glee, and chatting merrily to Archy as a brother officer and a friend.

"If I could only have got the lugger too, Raystoke," he cried, "it would have been glorious! But I couldn't do impossibilities, could I?"

"I am sure you did wonders, Mr Brough," said Archy.

"Well, never mind what I did, sir. You and Gurr acted so that I'm proud of you both, and of the lads. Completely burned out the wasps' nest, eh? It—will be a glorious despatch, Raystoke. By the way, we must go straight down there and see if the place is cool enough to search. There may be a little of the wasps' comb left, eh?"

"I'm afraid the whole of the stores would be destroyed."

"Ah, well, we shall see, and—Who are these?"

"Sir Risdon and Lady Graeme and their daughter," whispered Archy, who coloured as he saw Celia looking at him defiantly.

They were outside the house, and Lieutenant Brough halted his men, marched forward with the midshipman, and raised his hat, his salute being formally returned.

"I regret to have to come in this unceremonious way, sir," said the lieutenant.

"Excuse me," interrupted the baronet. "I expected you, sir, and, while congratulating you and your men upon their success, I wish to humbly own that my place has unwillingly on my part, been made one of the stores for their nefarious transactions."

The lieutenant moved away with Sir Risdon, leaving Archy alone with Celia and her mother.

"Oh," cried the girl, taking a step nearer to the midshipman, "how I hate you!"

"Miss Graeme!"

"I thought you a nice frank boy, and that you would be our friend."

"Celia, my child," whispered Lady Graeme reproachfully.

"I can't help it, mamma. I wanted to help him, but he would keep saying that he must tell of papa because it was his duty."

"Yes," said Archy bluntly; "and so it was."

"Yes," said Lady Graeme, "it was."

"Oh, mamma dear, pray don't say that. And now he has come with his hateful men to take papa to prison, and—"

"Oh, yes, yes, yes, Sir Risdon, of course, I must write my despatch. But you have given me your word of honour as a gentleman that you never engaged in these contraband practices."

These words reached the little group, and also Sir Risdon's reply:

"I swear it, sir; and it was only—"

"Yes, yes. Never mind that. Word of honour's enough between gentlemen. Oh, no, I shall not search, sir. I am satisfied."

"Oh!" ejaculated Celia.

"Hah!" ejaculated Archy in a sigh of relief.

"Now, Mr Raystoke, midshipman," said the lieutenant merrily. "My chief officer, ladies! Come, we have a great deal to do. Good morning. If you will pay us a visit on the cutter, we shall be only too proud to see you."

A friendly salute was interchanged, and Archy emphasised his by holding out his hand to Celia.

"Good-bye," he said. "Don't hate me, please. I only did my duty."

"I don't hate you," she replied, giving him her hand. Only a boy and girl; but Archy looked back several times, as they marched downward to the cliff, and then up its steep, grassy slope, to see at a turn a white handkerchief being waved to him.

"Why—hullo, Mr Raystoke!" cried the lieutenant merrily. "Oh, I see. Well, wait till you become a post-captain, and I hope I shall be an admiral by then, and that you will ask me to honour the wedding."

"Hush, pray, sir!" said Archy. "Some of the men will hear."

But the men did not hear, for they were quietly trudging along over the short grass, chewing their quids, and discussing the fire in the cave; those who had escaped relating again to those who were on the cutter their terrible experiences before the powder caught.

In due time they reached the entrance to the quarry, and found that everything was as they had anticipated, the smugglers having piled quite a ton of stones over the trap-door. These were removed at length, and the door was thrown open, when a peculiar dim bluish mist slowly rose, and disappeared in the broad sunshine.

"Keep back, my lads," said the lieutenant. "The powder smells badly, and it would be very risky to go down now."

"Fire seems to be out," said Archy, as he held his hand in the bluish smoke, which was dank and cold.

"Not much to burn," said the lieutenant; and, giving the word, the men bivouacked on the short turf to eat the provender they had brought, quite alone, for not a soul from the cottages between the farm and the cave appeared.

So strong a current of air set through the old quarry, that by the time they had ended the air was good; but now another difficulty arose. There were no lights, and a couple of men had to be despatched to the farm, from whence they returned with four lanthorns which had often been used for signals.

Armed with these, the party descended, and explored the place, to find that, where the powder had exploded, the walls were blackened and grisly, and that scores of little barrel staves were lying about shattered in all directions and pretty well burned away. On the other hand, the staves of the brandy kegs were for the most part hardly scorched, and the stone floor showed no traces of fire having passed.

The spirits had burned vividly till the explosion took place, when the force of the powder seemed to have scattered everything, but it had been saving as well as destructive, separating the brandy kegs, some of which burst and added fuel to the flames, but many remained untouched.

In fact, to the great delight of all, it was found that, though a great deal of destruction had been done, there was an ample supply of the smugglers' stores left to well load the cutter twice; and, jubilant with the discovery, the men returned on board, dreaming of prize-money, but not until a strong guard had been left over the place, in case any of the wasps should return.

But they did not come back. The nest had been burned out, and the smuggling in that part of the Freestone Shore had received so heavy a blow, that only one or two of the men cared to return, and then only for a temporary stay.

Lieutenant Brough's despatch had of course been sent in, and he obtained praise and prize-money.

"But no promotion, Mr Raystoke," he cried; "and of course you can have none until you have passed. They have not even appointed you to another ship."

"Well, if you are going to stay in the *White Hawk*, sir, I don't know that I want to change. I'm very comfortable here."

"That's very good of you, Raystoke, very good," said the lieutenant. "And then it's of no use to complain. I shall never get my promotion. I'm too little and too fat."

"No, that's not it," said Archy boldly; "they think you do the work so well that they will not remove you from the station."

"No," said the lieutenant sadly; "it's because I am so stout. I shall never be lifted now."

Mr Brough was wrong, for two years later he was appointed to a frigate, and his first efforts were directed to getting Archy Raystoke and Ram berths in the same ship, where a long and successful career awaited them.

But with that we have at present nought to do. This is the chronicle of the expedition of the *White Hawk* to crush the smuggling on the Freestone Shore, the most famous place for the doings of those who set the King's laws at defiance.

It was some ten years later, when one of His Majesty King George's smartest frigates was homeward bound from the East Indies, where her captain had distinguished himself by many a gallant act, that, as she was making for Portsmouth, with the tall white cliffs of the Isle just in sight, a tall handsome young officer went to the side, where a sun-browned seaman was standing gazing shoreward, shading his eyes with his hand.

"Why, Ram," said the officer; "looking out for the scene of some of your old villainies?"

"No, sir," said the man, touching his cap. "I was wondering whether my old mother was down on the cliff yonder, looking after the cows."

"The cows!" cried the young lieutenant. "Ah, to be sure. Remember the cow falling off the cliff, Ram?"

"Ay, sir, that I do. But look yonder, sir. You could make out the shelf on the big cliff if you had your glass. Remember our tussle there?"

"To be sure I do," said Lieutenant Raystoke, sheltering his eyes in a very deceptive fashion, for he was trying to make out the old grove of trees amidst which stood the Hoze.

"Mr Raystoke!"

"Captain calling you, sir," said a rugged-looking sailor, with a very swarthy face, that looked as if it would be all the better for a wash, but only seemed.

"All right, Dick, my man," said the young officer; and he hurried to where a plump, rosy little man stood in full post-captain's uniform.

"Ah, there you are, Mr Raystoke," said the captain, handing the lieutenant his glass. "I've been sweeping the shore, and it brought back old days. Look there; you can easily make out the range of cliffs. That highest one is where you and Mr Gurr were at the burning out of the smugglers ten years ago. How time slips by!"

"Yes, sir," said Lieutenant Archy Raystoke, returning the glass; "that's where the wasps' nest was destroyed."

Then to himself,—

"I wonder whether Celia will be glad to see me."

She was: very glad indeed.

ABOUT THE AUTHOR

Dictionary of National Biography Calls Sir John Alexander Hammerton "the most successful creator of large-scale works of reference that Britain has known" (he was born on February 27, 1871, in Alexandria, Scotland and died on May 12, 1949, in London). Hammerton first job as a journalist was in Nottingham, where he met Arthur Mee, who would become his lifelong partner and friend. He joined Alfred Harmsworth's Amalgamated Press in 1905. The Harmsworth Self-Educator was made by him and Mee. Hammerton helped with the first version of Mee's Children's Encyclopaedia. It came out every two weeks from 1908 to 1910 and was later collected in eight big books. Hammerton contributed by putting together pieces about "Poetry" and "Famous Books." Harmsworth's Universal Encyclopaedia was Hammerton's most important work. It was first released every two weeks from 1920 to 1922. Twelve million books of the Encyclopedia were sold all over the English-speaking world. Other parts of the text were changed and published as articles in Hammerton's later six-volume self-help series called Practical Knowledge for All.

CONTENTS

JOSEPH ADDISON

The Spectator

"The Spectator," the most popular and elegant miscellany of English literature, appeared on the 1st of March, 1711. With an interruption of two years—1712 to 1714—during part of which time "The Guardian," a similar periodical, took its place, "The Spectator" was continued to the 20th of December, 1714. Addison's fame is inseparably associated with this periodical. He was the animating spirit of the magazine, and by far the most exquisite essays which appear in it are by him. Richard Steele, Addison's friend and coadjutor in "The Spectator," was born in Dublin in March, 1672, and died at Carmarthen on September 1, 1729. (Addison biography, see Vol. XVI, p. 1.)

The Essays and the Essayist

Addison's "Spectator" is one of the most interesting books in the English language. When Dr. Johnson praised Addison's prose, it was specially of "The Spectator" that he was speaking. "His page," he says, "is always luminous, but never blazes in unexpected splendour. His sentences have neither studied amplitude nor affected brevity; his periods, though not diligently rounded, are voluble and easy. Whoever wishes to attain an English style, familiar but not coarse, and elegant but not ostentatious, must give his days and nights to Addison."

Johnson's verdict has been upheld, for it is chiefly by "The Spectator" that Addison lives. None but scholars know his Latin verse and his voluminous translations now. His "Cato" survives only in some half-dozen occasional quotations. Two or three hymns of his, including "The spacious firmament on high," and "When all Thy mercies, O my God," find a place in church collections; and his simile of the angel who rides upon the whirlwind and directs the storm is used now and again by pressmen and public speakers. But, in the main, when we think of Addison, it is of "The Spectator" that we think.

Recall the time when it was founded. It was in the days of Queen Anne, the Augustan age of the essay. There were no newspapers then, no magazines or reviews, no Parliamentary reports, nothing corresponding to the so-called "light literature" of later days. The only centres of society that existed were the court, with the aristocracy that revolved about it, and the clubs and coffee-houses, in which the commercial and professional classes met to discuss matters of general interest, to crack their jokes, and to exchange small talk about this, that and the other person, man or woman, who might happen to figure, publicly or privately, at the time. "The Spectator" was one of the first organs to give form and consistency to the opinion, the humour and the gossip engendered by this social contact.

One of the first, but not quite the first; for the less famous, though still remembered, "Tatler" preceded it. And these two, "The Tatler" and "The Spectator," have an intimate connection from the circumstance that Richard Steele, who started "The Tatler" in April, 1709, got Addison to write for it, and then joined with Addison in "The Spectator" when his own paper stopped in January, 1711. Addison and Steele had been friends since boyhood. They were contemporaries at the Charterhouse, and Steele often spent his holidays in the parsonage of Addison's father.

The two friends were a little under forty years of age when "The Spectator" began in March, 1711. It was a penny paper, and was published daily, its predecessor having been published three times a week. It began with a circulation of 3,000 copies, and ran up to about 10,000 before it stopped its daily issue in December, 1712. Macaulay, writing in 1843, insists upon the sale as "indicating a popularity quite as great as that of the most successful works of Scott and Dickens in our time." The 555 numbers of the daily issue formed seven volumes; and then there was a final eighth volume, made up of triweekly issues: a total of 635 numbers, of which Addison wrote 274, and Steele 236.

To summarise the contents of these 635 numbers would require a volume. They are so versatile and so varied. As one of Addison's biographers puts it, to-day you have a beautiful meditation, brilliant in imagery and serious as a sermon, or a pious discourse on death, or perhaps an eloquent and scathing protest against the duel; while to-morrow the whole number is perhaps concerned with the wigs, ruffles, and shoe-buckles of the *macaroni*, or the hoops, patches, farthingales and tuckers of the ladies. If you wish to see the plays and actors of the time, "The Spectator" will always show them to you; and, moreover, point out the dress, manners, and mannerisms, affectations, indecorums, plaudits, or otherwise of the frequenters of the theatre.

For here is no newspaper, as we understand the term. "The Spectator" from the first indulged his humours at the expense of the quidnuncs. Says he:

"There is another set of men that I must likewise lay a claim to as being altogether unfurnished with ideas till the business and conversation of the day has supplied them. I have often considered these poor souls with an eye of great commiseration when I have heard them asking the first man they have met with whether there was any news stirring, and by that means gathering together materials for thinking. These needy persons do not know what to talk of till about twelve o'clock in the morning; for by that time they are pretty good judges of the weather, know which way the wind sets, and whether the Dutch mail be come in. As they lie at the mercy of the first man they meet, and are grave or impertinent all the day long, according to the notions which they have imbibed in the morning, I would earnestly entreat them not to stir out of their chambers till they have read this paper; and do promise them that I will daily instil into them such sound and wholesome sentiments as shall have a good effect on their conversation for the ensuing twelve hours."

Now, the essential, or at least the leading feature of "The Spectator" is this: that the entertainment is provided by an imaginary set of characters forming a Spectator Club. The club represents various classes or sections of the community, so that through its members a corresponding variety of interests and opinions is set before the reader, the Spectator himself acting as a sort of final censor or referee. Chief among the Club members is Sir Roger de Coverley, a simple, kindly, honourable, old-world country gentleman. Here is the description of this celebrated character:

"The first of our society is a gentleman of Worcestershire, of ancient descent, a baronet, his name Sir Roger de Coverley. His great-grandfather was inventor of that famous country dance which is called after him. All who know that shire are very well acquainted with the parts and merits of Sir Roger. He is a gentleman that is very singular in his behaviour, but his singularities proceed from his good sense, and are contradictions to the manners of the world only as he thinks the world is in the wrong. However, this humour creates him no enemies, for he does nothing with sourness or obstinacy; and his being unconfined to modes and forms makes him but the readier and more capable to please and oblige all who know him. When he is in town, he lives in Soho Square. It is said he keeps himself a bachelor by reason he was crossed in love by a perverse beautiful widow of the next county to him. Before this disappointment, Sir Roger was what you call a fine gentleman, had often supped with my Lord Rochester and Sir George

Etherege, fought a duel upon his first coming to town, and kicked Bully Dawson in a public coffee-house for calling him youngster. But being ill-used by the above-mentioned widow, he was very serious for a year and a half; and though, his temper being naturally jovial, he at last got over it, he grew careless of himself, and never dressed afterwards. He continues to wear a coat and doublet of the same cut that were in fashion at the time of his repulse, which, in his merry humours, he tells us, has been in and out twelve times since he first wore it. It is said Sir Roger grew humble in his desires after he had forgot this cruel beauty, insomuch that it is reported he was frequently offended with beggars and gipsies; but this is looked upon by his friends rather as matter of raillery than truth. He is now in his fifty-sixth year, cheerful, gay, and hearty; keeps a good house both in town and country; a great lover of mankind; but there is such a mirthful cast in his behaviour that he is rather beloved than esteemed."

Then there is Sir Andrew Freeport, "a merchant of great eminence in the City of London; a person of indefatigable industry, strong reason, and great experience." He is "acquainted with commerce in all its parts; and will tell you it is a stupid and barbarous way to extend dominion by arms; for true power is to be got by arts and industry. He will often argue that, if this part of our trade were well cultivated, we should gain from one nation; and if another, from another."

There is Captain Sentry, too, "a gentleman of great courage and understanding, but invincible modesty," who in the club speaks for the army, as the templar does for taste and learning, and the clergyman for theology and philosophy.

And then, that the club may not seem to be unacquainted with "the gallantries and pleasures of the age," there is Will Honeycomb, the elderly man of fashion, who is "very ready at that sort of discourse with which men usually entertain women." Will "knows the history of every mode, and can inform you from which of the French king's wenches our wives and daughters had this manner of curling their hair, that way of placing their hoods; whose frailty was covered by such a sort of petticoat; and whose vanity to show her foot made that part of the dress so short in such a year. In a word, all his conversation and knowledge have been in the female world. As other men of his age will take notice to you what such a minister said upon such and such an occasion, he will tell you when the Duke of Monmouth danced at court, such a woman was then smitten, another was taken with him at the head of his troop in the park. This way of talking of his very much enlivens the conversation among us of a more sedate turn; and I find there is not one of the company, but myself, who rarely speak at all, but speaks of him as that sort of man who is usually called a well-bred fine gentleman. To conclude his character, where women are not concerned, he is an honest, worthy man."

Nor must we forget Will Wimble, though he is really an outsider. Will is the younger son of a baronet: a man of no profession, looking after his father's game, training his dogs, shooting, fishing, hunting, making whiplashes for his neighbors, knitting garters for the ladies, and afterwards slyly inquiring how they wear: a welcome guest at every house in the county; beloved by all the lads and the children.

Besides these, and others, there is a fine little gallery of portraits in Sir Roger's country neighbours and tenants. We have, for instance, the yeoman who "knocks down a dinner with his gun twice or thrice a week, and by that means lives much cheaper than those who have not so good an estate as himself"; and we have Moll White, the reputed witch, who, if she made a mistake at church and cried "Amen!" in a wrong place, "they never failed to conclude that she was saying her prayers backwards." We have the diverting captain, "young, sound, and impudent"; we have a demure Quaker; we have Tom Touchy, a fellow famous for "taking the law" of everybody; and we have the inn-keeper, who, out of compliment to Sir Roger, "put him up in a sign-post before the door," and then, when Sir Roger objected, changed the figure into the Saracen's Head by "a little aggravation of the features" and the addition of a pair of whiskers!

Best of all is the old chaplain. Sir Roger was "afraid of being insulted with Latin and Greek at his own table"; so he got a university friend to "find him out a clergyman, rather of plain sense than much learning, of a good aspect, a clear voice, a sociable temper, and, if possible, a man that understood a little of backgammon." The genial knight "made him a present of all the good sermons printed in English, and only begged of him that every Sunday he would pronounce one of them in the pulpit." Thus, if Sir Roger happened to meet his chaplain on a Saturday evening, and asked who was to preach to-morrow, he would perhaps be answered: "The Bishop of St. Asaph in the morning, and Dr. South in the afternoon." About which arrangement "The Spectator" boldly observes: "I could heartily wish that more of our country clergy would follow this example; and, instead of wasting their spirits in laborious compositions of their own, would endeavour after a handsome elocution, and all those other talents that are proper to enforce what has been penned by greater masters. This would not only be more easy to themselves, but more edifying to the people."

There is no end to the subjects discussed by "The Spectator." They range from dreams to dress and duelling; from ghosts to gardening and goats' milk; from wigs to wine and widows; from religion to riches and riding; from servants to sign-posts and snuff-boxes; from love to lodgings and lying; from beards to bankruptcy and blank verse; and hundreds of other interesting themes. Correspondents often wrote to emphasise this variety, for letters from the outside public were always welcome. Thus one "Thomas Trusty":

"The variety of your subjects surprises me as much as a box of pictures did formerly, in which there was only one face, that by pulling some pieces of isinglass over it was changed into a senator or a merry-andrew, a polished lady or a nun, a beau or a blackamoor, a prude or a coquette, a country squire or a conjurer, with many other different representations very entertaining, though still the same at the bottom."

But perhaps, on the whole, woman and her little ways have the predominant attention. Indeed, Addison expressly avowed this object of engaging the special interests of the sex when he started. He says:

"There are none to whom this paper will be more useful than to the female world. I have often thought that there has not been sufficient pains taken in finding out proper employments and diversions for the fair ones. Their amusements seem contrived for them rather as they are women than as they are reasonable creatures; and are more adapted to the sex than to the species. The toilet is their great scene of business, and the right adjustment of their hair the principal employment of their lives. The sorting of a suit of ribands is reckoned a very good morning's work; and if they make an excursion to a mercer's or a toy-shop, so great a fatigue makes them unfit for anything else all the day after. Their more serious occupations are sewing and embroidery, and their greatest drudgery the preparations of jellies and sweetmeats. This, I say, is the state of ordinary women; though I know there are multitudes of those of a more elevated life and conversation, that move in an exalted sphere of knowledge and virtue, that join all the beauties of the mind to the ornaments of dress, and inspire a kind of awe and respect, as well as of love, into their male beholders. I hope to increase the number of these by publishing this daily paper, which I shall always endeavour to make an innocent, if not an improving, entertainment, and by that means, at least, divert the minds of my female readers from greater trifles."

These reflections on the manners of women did not quite please Swift, who wrote to Stella: "I will not meddle with 'The Spectator'; let him *fair sex* it to the world's end." But they pleased most other people, as the main contents of "The Spectator" still please. Here is one typical acknowledgment, signed "Leonora":

> Mr. Spectator,—Your paper is part of my tea-equipage; and
> my servant knows my humour so well that, calling for my

breakfast this morning (it being past my usual hour), she answered, "'the Spectator' was not yet come in, but the tea-kettle boiled, and she expected it every moment."

As an "abstract and brief chronicle of the time," this monumental work of Addison and Steele is without peer. In its pages may be traced the foundations of all that is noble and healthy in modern English thought; and its charming sketches may be made the open sesame to a period and a literature as rich as any our country has seen.

ÆSOP

Fables

It is in the fitness of things that the early biographies of Æsop, the great fabulist, should be entirely fabulous. Macrobius has distinguished between *fabula* and *fabulosa narratio*: "He would have a fable to be absolutely false, and a fabulous narration to be a number of fictions built upon a foundation of truth." The Lives of Æsop belong chiefly to the latter category. In the following pages what is known of the life of Æsop is set forth, together with condensed versions of some of his most characteristic fables, which have long passed into the wisdom of all nations, this being a subject that calls for treatment on somewhat different lines from the majority of the works dealt with in The World's Greatest Books.

Introductory

Pierre Bayle, in his judicious fashion, sums up what is said of Æsop in antiquity, resting chiefly upon Plutarch. "Plutarch affirms: (1) That Crœsus sent Æsop to Periander, the Tyrant of Corinth, and to the Oracle of Delphi; (2) that Socrates found no other expedient to obey the God of Dreams, without injuring his profession, than to turn the Fables of Æsop into verse; (3) that Æsop and Solon were together at the Court of Crœsus, King of Lydia; (4) that those of Delphi, having put Æsop to death cruelly and unjustly, and finding themselves exposed to several calamities on account of this injustice, made a public declaration that they were ready to make satisfaction to the memory of Æsop; (5) that having treated thereupon with a native of Samos, they were delivered from the evil that afflicted them."

To this summary Bayle added a footnote concerning "The Life of Æsop, composed by Meziriac": "It is a little book printed at Bourg-en-Bress, in 1632. It contains only forty pages in 16. It is becoming exceedingly scarce.... This is what I extract from it. It is more probable that Æsop was born at Cotiœum, a town of Phrygia, than that he was born at Sardis, or in the island of Samos, or at Mesembria in Thrace. The first master that he served was one Zemarchus, or Demarchus, surnamed Carasius, a native and inhabitant of Athens. Thus it is probable that it was there he learned the purity of the Greek tongue, as in its spring, and acquired the knowledge of moral philosophy which was then in esteem....

"In process of time he was sold to Xanthus, a native of the Isle of Samos, and afterwards to Idmon, or Iadmnon, the philosopher, who was a Samian also, and who enfranchised him. After he had recovered his liberty, he soon acquired a great reputation among the Greeks; so that the report of his singular wisdom having reached the ears of Crœsus, he sent to inquire after him; and having conceived an affection for him, he obliged him by his favours to engage himself in his service to the end of his life. He travelled through Greece—whether for his own pleasure or for the private affairs of Crœsus is uncertain—and passing by Athens, soon after Pisistratus had usurped the sovereign power there and had abolished the popular state, and seeing that the Athenians bore the yoke very impatiently, he told them the Fable of the Frogs that asked a King of Jupiter. Afterwards he met the Seven Wise Men in the City of Corinth at the Tyrant Periander's. Some relate that, in order to show that the life of man is full of miseries, and that one pleasure is attended with a thousand pains, Æsop used to say that when Prometheus took the clay to form man, he did not temper it with water, but with tears."

Concerning the death of this extraordinary man we read that Æsop went to Delphi, with a great quantity of gold and silver, being ordered by Crœsus to offer a great sacrifice to Apollo, and to give a considerable sum to each inhabitant. The quarrel which arose between the Delphians and him was the occasion, after his sending away the sacrifice, of his sending back the money to Crœsus; for he thought that those for whom this prince designed it had rendered themselves unworthy of it. The inhabitants of Delphi contrived an accusation of sacrilege against him, and, pretending that they had convicted him, cast him down from the top of a rock.

Bayle has a long line of centuries at his back when he says: "Æsop's lectures against the faults of men were the fullest of good sense and wit that can be imagined." He substantiates this affirmation in the following manner: "Can any inventions be more happy than the images Æsop made use of to instruct mankind? They are exceedingly fit for children, and no less proper for grown persons; they are all that is necessary to perfect a precept —I mean the mixture of the useful with the agreeable." He then quotes Aulus Gellius as saying: "Æsop the Phrygian fabulist was not without reason esteemed to be wise, since he did not, after the manner of the philosophers, severely and imperiously command such things as were fit to be advised and persuaded, but by feigning, diverting and entertaining apologues, he insinuates good and wholesome advice into the minds of men with a kind of willing attention."

Bayle continues: "At all times these have been made to succeed the homespun stories of nurses. 'Let them learn to tell the Fables of Æscop, which succeed the stories of the nursery, in pure and easy style, and afterwards endeavour to write in the same familiar manner.' They have never fallen into contempt. Our age, notwithstanding its pride and delicacy, esteems and admires them, and shows them in a hundred different shapes. The inimitable La Fontaine has procured them in our time a great deal of honour and glory; and great commendations are given to the reflections of an English wit, Sir Roger L'Estrange, on these very fables."

Since the period when Pierre Bayle composed his great biographical dictionary, the Fables of Æsop have perhaps suffered something of a relapse in the favour of grown persons; but if one may judge from the number of new editions illustrated for children, they are still the delight of modern nurseries. There is this, however, to be said of contemporary times—that the multitude of books in a nursery prevent children from acquiring the profound and affectionate acquaintance with Æsop which every child would naturally get when his fables were almost the only book provided by the Press for juvenile readers.

It is questionable whether the fables will any longer produce the really deep effect which they certainly have had in the past. But we may be certain that some of them will always play a great part in the wisdom of the common people, and that these particularly true and striking apologues are secure of an eternal place in the literature of nations. As an example of what we mean, we will tell as simply as possible some of the most characteristic fables.

The Dog and the Shadow

A Dog, with a piece of stolen meat between his teeth, was one day crossing a river by means of a plank, when he caught sight of another dog in the water carrying a far larger piece of meat. He opened his jaws to snap at the greater morsel, when the meat dropped in the stream and was lost even in the reflection.

The Dying Lion

A Lion, brought to the extremity of weakness by old age and disease, lay dying in the sunlight. Those whom he had oppressed in his strength now came round about him to revenge themselves for past injuries. The Boar ripped the flank of the King of Beasts with his tusks. The Bull came and gored the Lion's sides with his horns. Finally, the Ass drew near, and after carefully seeing that there was no danger, let fly with his heels in the Lion's face. Then, with a dying groan, the mighty creature exclaimed: "How much worse it is than a thousand deaths to be spurned by so base a creature!"

The Mountain in Labour

A Mountain was heard to produce dreadful sounds, as though it were labouring to bring forth something enormous. The people came and stood about waiting to see what wonderful thing would be produced from this labour. After they had waited till they were tired, out crept a Mouse.

Hercules and the Waggoner

A Waggoner was driving his team through a muddy lane when the wheels stuck fast in the clay, and the Horses could get no farther. The Man immediately dropped on his knees, and, crying bitterly, besought Hercules to come and help him. "Get up and stir thyself, thou lazy fellow!" replied Hercules. "Whip thy Horses, and put thy shoulder to the wheel. If thou art in need of my help, when thou thyself hast laboured, then shalt thou have it."

The Frogs that Asked for a King

The Frogs, who lived an easy, happy life in the ponds, once prayed to Jupiter that he should give them a King. Jupiter was amused by this prayer, and cast a log into the water, saying: "There, then, is a King for you." The Frogs, frightened by the great splash, regarded their King with alarm, until at last, seeing that he did not stir, some of them jumped upon his back and began to be merry there, amused at such a foolish King. However, King Log did not satisfy their ideas for very long, and so once again they petitioned Jupiter to send them a King, a real King who would rule over them, and not lie helpless in the water. Then Jupiter sent the Frogs a Stork, who caught them by their legs, tossed them in the air, and gobbled them up whenever he was hungry. All in a hurry the Frogs besought Jupiter to take away King Stork and restore them to their former happy condition. "No, no," answered Jupiter; "a King that did you no hurt did not please you; make the best of him you now have, lest a worse come in his place!"

The Gnat and the Lion

A lively and insolent Gnat was bold enough to attack a Lion, which he so maddened by stinging the most sensitive parts of his nose, eyes and ears that the beast roared with anguish and tore himself with his claws. In vain were the Lion's efforts to rid himself of his insignificant tormentor; again and again the insect returned and stung the furious King of Beasts, till at last the Lion fell exhausted on the ground. The triumphant Gnat, sounding his tiny trumpet, hovered over the spot exulting in his victory. But it happened that in his circling flight he got himself caught in the web of a Spider, which, fine and delicate as it was, yet had power enough to hold the tiny insect a prisoner. All the Gnat's efforts to escape only held him the more tightly and firmly a prisoner, and he who had conquered the Lion became in his turn the prey of the Spider.

The Wolf and the Stork

A Wolf ate his food so greedily that a bone stuck in his throat. This caused him such great pain that he ran hither and thither, promising to reward handsomely anyone who would remove the cause of his torture. A Stork, moved with pity by the Wolf's cry of pain, and tempted also by the reward, undertook the dangerous operation. When he had removed the bone, the Wolf moved away, but the Stork called out and reminded him of the promised reward. "Reward!" exclaimed the Wolf. "Pray, you greedy fellow, what reward can you expect? You dared to put your head in my mouth, and instead of biting it off, I let you take it out again unharmed. Get away with you! And do not again place yourself in my power."

The Frog who Wanted to Be as Big as an Ox

A vain Frog, surrounded by her children, looked up and saw an Ox grazing near by. "I can be as big as the Ox," she said, and began to blow herself out. "Am I as big now?" she inquired. "Oh, no; not nearly so big!" said the little frogs. "Now?" she asked, blowing herself out still more. "No, not nearly so big!" answered her children. "But now?" she inquired eagerly, and blew herself out still more. "No, not even now," they said; "and if you try till you burst yourself you will never be so big." But the Frog would not listen, and attempting to make herself bigger still, burst her skin and died.

The Dog in the Manger

A Dog lay in a manger which was full of hay. An Ox, being hungry, came near, and was about to eat when the Dog started up, and, with angry snarls, would not let the Ox approach. "Surly brute," said the Ox; "you cannot eat the hay yourself, and you will let no one else have any."

The Bundle of Faggots

An honest Man had the unhappiness to have a quarrelsome family of children. One day he called them before him, and bade them try to break a bundle of faggots. All tried, and all failed. "Now," said he, "unbind the bundle and take every stick by itself, and see if you cannot break them." They did his bidding, and snapped all the sticks one by one with the greatest possible ease. "This, my children," said the Father at last, "is a true emblem of your condition. Keep together and you are safe, divide and you are undone."

The Fox Without a Tail

A Fox was once caught in a trap by his tail, and in order to get free was obliged to leave it behind. He knew that his fellows would make fun of his tailless condition, so he made up his mind to induce them all to part with their tails. At the next assemblage of Foxes he made a speech on the uselessness of tails in general, and the inconvenience of a Fox's tail in particular, declaring that never in his whole life had he felt so comfortable as now in his tailless freedom. When he sat down, a sly old Fox rose, and, waving his brush, said, with a sneer, that if he had lost his tail, he would be convinced by the last speaker's arguments, but until such an accident occurred he fully intended to vote in favour of tails.

The Blind Man and the Paralytic

A blind man finding himself stopped in a rough and difficult road, met with a paralytic and begged his assistance. "How can I help you," replied the paralytic, "when I can scarcely move myself along?" But, regarding the blind man, he added: "However, you appear to have good legs and a broad back, and, if you will lift me and carry me, I will guide you safely through this difficulty, which is more than each one can surmount for himself. You shall walk for me, and I will see for you." "With all my heart," rejoined the blind man; and, taking the paralytic on his shoulders, the two went cheerfully forward in a wise partnership which triumphed over all difficulties.

MATTHEW ARNOLD

Essays in Criticism

Matthew Arnold, son of Dr. Arnold of Rugby (see Vol. X, p. 260), was born on December 24, 1822, and died on April 15, 1888. He was by everyday calling an inspector of schools and an educational expert, but by nature and grace a poet, a philosopher, a man of piety and of letters. Arnold almost ceased to write verse when he was forty-five, though not without having already produced some of the choicest poetry in the English language. Before that he had developed his theories of literary criticism in his "Essays in Criticism"; and about the time of his withdrawal from Oxford he published "Culture and Anarchy," in which his system of philosophy is broadly outlined. Later, in "St. Paul and Protestantism," "Literature and Dogma" and "God and the Bible," he tried to adjust Christianity according to the light of modern knowledge. In his "Lectures on Translating Homer," he had expressed views on criticism and its importance that were new to, and so were somewhat adversely discussed by the Press. Whereupon, in 1865, with a militant joy, he re-entered the fray and defined the province of criticism in the first of a series of "Essays in Criticism," showing the narrowness of the British conception. "The Literary Influence of Academies" was a subject that enabled him to make a further comparison between the literary genius of the French and of the English people, and a number of individual critiques that followed only enhanced his great and now undisputed position both as a poet and as a critic. The argument of the two general essays is given here.

I.—Creative Power and Critical Power

Many objections have been made to a proposition of mine about criticism: "Of the literature of France and Germany, as of the intellect of Europe in general, the main effort, for now many years, has been a critical effort—the endeavour, in all branches of knowledge, to see the object as in itself it really is." I added that "almost the last thing for which one would come to English literature was just that very thing which now Europe most desired—criticism," and that the power and value of English literature were thereby impaired. More than one rejoinder declared that the importance here again assigned to criticism was excessive, and asserted the inherent superiority of the creative effort of the human spirit over its critical effort. A reporter of Wordsworth's conversation quotes a judgment to the same effect: "Wordsworth holds the critical power very low; indeed, infinitely lower than the inventive."

The critical power is of lower rank than the inventive—true; but, in assenting to this proposition, we must keep in mind that men may have the sense of exercising a free creative activity in other ways than in producing great works of literature or art; and that the exercise of the creative power in the production of great works of literature or art is not at all epochs and under all conditions possible. This creative power works with elements, with materials—what if it has not those materials ready for its use? Now, in literature, the elements with which creative power works are ideas—the best ideas on every matter which literature touches, current at the time. The grand work of literary genius is a work of synthesis and exposition; its gift lies in the faculty of being happily inspired by a certain intellectual and spiritual atmosphere, by a certain order of ideas, when it finds itself in them; of dealing divinely with these ideas, presenting them in most effective and attractive combinations, making beautiful works with them, in short. But it must have the atmosphere, it must find itself amidst the order of the ideas, in order to work freely; and these it is not so easy to command. This is really why great creative epochs in literature are so rare—because, for the creation of a master-work of literature two powers must concur, the power of the man and the power of the moment; and the man is not enough without the moment.

The creative power has for its happy exercise appointed elements, and those elements are not in its control. Nay, they are more within the control of the critical power. It is the business of the critical power in all branches of knowledge to see the object as in itself it really is. Thus it tends at last to make an intellectual situation of which the creative power can avail itself. It tends to establish an order of ideas, if not absolutely true, yet true by comparison with that which it displaces—to make the best ideas prevail. Presently these new ideas reach society; the touch of truth is the touch of life; and there is a stir and growth everywhere. Out of this stir and growth come the creative epochs of literature.

II.—The Literary "Atmosphere"

It has long seemed to me that the burst of creative activity in our literature through the first quarter of the nineteenth century had about it something premature, and for this cause its productions are doomed to prove hardly more lasting than the productions of far less splendid epochs. And this prematureness comes from its having proceeded without having its proper data, without sufficient materials to work with. In other words, the English poetry of the first quarter of the nineteenth century, with plenty of energy, plenty of creative force, did not know enough. This makes Byron so empty of matter, Shelley so incoherent, Wordsworth, profound as he is, so wanting in completeness and variety.

It was not really books and reading that lacked to our poetry at this epoch. Shelley had plenty of reading, Coleridge had immense reading; Pindar and Sophocles had not many books; Shakespeare was no deep reader. True; but in the Greece of Pindar and Sophocles and the England of Shakespeare the poet lived in a current of ideas in the highest degree animating and nourishing to creative power.

Such an atmosphere the many-sided learning and the long and widely combined critical effort of Germany formed for Goethe when he lived and worked. In the England of the first quarter of the nineteenth century there was neither a national glow of life and thought, such as we had in the age of Elizabeth, nor yet a force of learning and criticism, such as was to be found in Germany. The creative power of poetry wanted, for success in the highest sense, materials and a basis—a thorough interpretation of the world was necessarily denied to it.

At first it seems strange that out of the immense stir of the French Revolution and its age should not have come a crop of works of genius equal to that which came out of the stir of the great productive time of Greece, or out of that of the Renaissance, with its powerful episode of the Reformation. But the truth is that the stir of the French Revolution took a character which essentially distinguished it from such movements as these. The French Revolution found, undoubtedly, its motive power in the intelligence of men, and not in their practical sense. It appeals to an order of ideas which are universal, certain, permanent. The year 1789 asked of a thing: Is it rational? That a whole nation should have been penetrated with an enthusiasm for pure reason is a very remarkable thing when we consider how little of mind, or anything so worthy or quickening as mind, comes into the motives which in general impel great masses of men. In spite of the crimes and follies in which it lost itself, the French Revolution derives, from the force, truth and universality of the ideas which it took for its law, a unique and still living power; and it is, and will probably long remain, the greatest, the most animating event in history.

But the mania for giving an immediate political and practical application to all these fine ideas of the reason was fatal. Here an Englishman is in his element: on this theme we can all go on for hours. Ideas cannot be too much prized in and for themselves, cannot be too much lived with; but to transport them abruptly into the world of politics and practice, violently to revolutionise this world to their bidding—that is quite another thing. "Force and right are the governors of the world; force till right is ready" Joubert has said. The grand error of the French Revolution was that it set at naught the second great half of that maxim—force till right is ready—and, rushing furiously into the political sphere, created in opposition to itself what I may call an epoch of concentration.

The great force of that epoch of concentration was England, and the great voice of that epoch of concentration was Burke. I will not deny that his writings are often disfigured by the violence and passion of the moment, and that in some directions Burke's view was bounded and his observations therefore at fault; but for those who can make the needful corrections what distinguishes these writings is their profound, permanent, fruitful, philosophical truth—they contain the true philosophy of an epoch of concentration. Now, an epoch of expansion seems to be opening in this country. In spite of the absorbing and brutalising influence of our passionate material progress, this progress is likely to lead in the end to an apparition of intellectual life. It is of the last importance that English criticism should discern what rule it ought to take, to avail itself of the field now opening to it. That rule may be summed up in one word—disinterestedness.

III.—The Virtue of Detachment

How is criticism to show disinterestedness? By keeping aloof from practice; by resolutely following the law of its own nature, which is to be a free play of the mind on all subjects which it touches. Its business is simply to know the best that is known and thought in the world, and by making this known to create a current of fresh and true ideas. What is at present the bane of criticism in this country? It is that our organs of criticism are organs of men and parties having practical ends to serve, and with them those practical ends are the first thing, and the play of the mind the second—so much play of mind as is compatible with the prosecution of these practical ends is all that is wanted.

An organ like the *Revue des Deux Mondes*, existing as just an organ for a free play of mind, we have not; but we have the "Edinburgh Review," existing as an organ of the old Whigs, and for as much play of mind as may suit its being that; we have the "Quarterly Review," existing as an organ of the Tories, and for as much play of mind as may suit its being that; we have the "British Quarterly Review," existing as an organ of the political Dissenters, and for as much play of mind as may suit its being that; we have "The Times," existing as an organ of the common, satisfied, well-to-do Englishman, and for as much play of mind as may suit its being that. And so on through all the various fractions, political and religious, of our society—every fraction has, as such, its organ of criticism, but the notion of combining all fractions in the common pleasure of a free, disinterested play of mind meets with no favour. Yet no other criticism will ever attain any real authority, or make any real way towards its end—the creating of a current of true and fresh ideas.

It will be said that, by embracing in this manner the Indian virtue of detachment, criticism condemns itself to a slow and obscure work; but it is the only proper work of criticism. Whoever sets himself to see things as they are will find himself one of a very small circle; but it is only by this small circle resolutely doing its work that adequate ideas will ever get current at all. For the practical man is not apt for fine distinctions, and yet in these distinctions truth and the highest culture greatly find their account. To act is so easy, as Goethe says, and to think is so hard. Criticism must maintain its independence of the practical spirit and its aims. Even with well meant efforts of the practical spirit it must express dissatisfaction if, in the sphere of the ideal, they seem impoverishing and limiting. It must be apt to study and praise elements that for the fulness of spiritual perfection are wanted, even though they belong to a power which, in the practical sphere, may be maleficent. It must be apt to discern the spiritual shortcomings of powers that in the practical sphere may be beneficent.

By the very nature of things much of the best that is known and thought in the world cannot be of English growth—must be foreign; by the nature of things, again, it is just this that we are least likely to know, while English thought is streaming in upon us from all sides, and takes excellent care that we shall not be ignorant of its existence. The English critic must dwell much on foreign thought, and with particular heed on any part of it, which, while significant and fruitful in itself, is for any reason specially likely to escape him.

Again, judging is often spoken of as the critic's business; and so in some sense it is. But the judgment which almost insensibly forms itself in a fair and clear mind, along with fresh knowledge, is the valuable one; and, therefore, knowledge, and ever fresh knowledge, must be the critic's great concern for himself. And it is by communicating fresh knowledge, and letting his own judgment pass along with it—as a sort of companion and clue—that he will generally do most good to his readers.

To get near the standard of the best that is known and thought in the world, every critic should possess one great literature at least beside his own; and the more unlike his own the better. For the criticism I am concerned with regards Europe as being for intellectual and spiritual purposes one great confederation, bound to a joint action and working to a common result.

I conclude with what I said at the beginning. To have the sense of creative activity is not denied to criticism; but then criticism must be sincere, simple, flexible, ardent, ever widening its knowledge. Then it may have, in no contemptible measure, a joyful sense of creative activity, a sense which a man of insight and conscience will prefer to that he might derive from a poor, starved, fragmentary, inadequate creation. And at some epochs no other creation is possible. Still, in full measure, the sense of creative activity belongs only to genuine creation; in literature we must never forget that. But what true man of letters ever can forget it? It is no such common matter for a gifted nature to come into possession of a current of true and living ideas, and to produce amidst the inspiration of them, that we are likely to underrate it. The glorious epochs of Æschylus and Shakespeare make us feel their pre-eminence. In an epoch like those is the true life of literature; there is the promised land towards which criticism can only beckon.

IV.—Should We Have an Academy?

It is impossible to put down a book like the history of the French Academy by Pellisson and D'Olivet without being led to reflect upon the absence in our own country of any institution like the French Academy, upon the probable causes of this absence, and upon its results. Improvement of the language was the declared grand aim for the operations of that academy. Its statutes of foundation say expressly that "the Academy's principal function shall be to work with all the care and all the diligence possible at giving sure rules to our language, and rendering it pure, eloquent and capable of treating the arts and sciences." It is said that Richelieu had it in his mind that French should succeed Latin in its general ascendancy, as Latin had succeeded Greek. If it were so, even this wish has to some extent been fulfilled. This was not all Richelieu had in his mind, however. The new academy was meant to be a literary tribunal, a high court of letters, and this is what it has really been.

Such an effort, to set up a recognised authority, imposing on us a high standard in matters of intellect and taste, has many enemies in human nature. We all of us like to go our own way, and not to be forced out of the atmosphere of commonplace habitual to most of us. We like to be suffered to lie comfortably on the old straw of our habits, especially of our intellectual habits, even though this straw may not be very fine and clean. But if this effort to limit the freedom of our lower nature finds enemies in human nature, it also finds auxiliaries in it. Man alone of living creatures, says Cicero, goes feeling after the discovery of an order, a law of good taste; other creatures submissively fulfil the law of their nature.

Now in France, says M. Sainte-Beuve, "the first consideration for us is not whether we are amused and pleased by a work of art or of mind, or is it whether we are touched by it. What we seek above all to learn is whether we were right in being amused with it, and in applauding it, and in being moved by it." A Frenchman has, to a considerable degree, what one may call a conscience in intellectual matters. Seeing this, we are on the road to see why the French have their Academy and we have nothing of the kind.

What are the essential characteristics of the spirit of our nation? Our greatest admirers would not claim for us an open and clear mind, a quick and flexible intelligence. Rather would they allege as our chief spiritual characteristics energy and honesty—most important and fruitful qualities in the intellectual and spiritual, as in the moral sphere, for, of what we call genius, energy is the most essential part. Now, what that energy, which is the life of genius, above everything demands and insists upon, is freedom—entire independence of authority, prescription and routine, the fullest power to extend as it will. Therefore, a nation whose chief spiritual characteristic is energy will not be very apt to set up in intellectual matters a fixed standard, an authority like an academy. By this it certainly escapes real inconveniences and dangers, and it can, at the same time, reach undeniably splendid heights in poetry and science. We have Shakespeare, and we have Newton. In the intellectual sphere there can be no higher names.

On the other hand, some of the requisites of intellectual work are specially the affair of quickness of mind and flexibility of intelligence. In prose literature they are of first-rate importance. These are elements that can, to a certain degree, be appropriated, while the free activity of genius cannot. Academies consecrate and maintain them, and therefore a nation with an eminent turn for them naturally establishes academies.

V.—Our Loss Through Provinciality

How much greater is our nation in poetry than prose! How much better do the productions of its spirit show in the qualities of genius than in the qualities of intelligence! But the question as to the utility of academies to the intellectual life of a nation is not settled when we say that we have never had an academy, yet we have, confessedly, a very great literature. It is by no means sure that either our literature or the general intellectual life of our nation has got already without academies all that academies can give. Our literature, in spite of the genius manifested in it, may fall short in form, method, precision, proportions, arrangement—all things where intelligence proper comes in. It may be weak in prose, full of haphazard, crudeness, provincialism, eccentricity, violence, blundering; and instead of always fixing our thoughts upon the points in which our literature is strong, we should, from time to time, fix them upon those in which it is weak. In France, the Academy serves as a sort of centre and rallying-point to educated opinion, and gives it a force which it has not got here. In the bulk of the intellectual work of a nation which has no centre, no intellectual metropolis like an academy, there is observable a note of provinciality. Great powers of mind will make a man think profoundly, but not even great powers of mind will keep his taste and style perfectly sound and sure if he is left too much to himself with no sovereign organ of opinion near him.

Even men like Jeremy Taylor and Burke suffer here. Theirs is too often extravagant prose; prose too much suffered to indulge its caprices; prose at too great a distance from the centre of good taste; prose with the note of provinciality; Asiatic prose, somewhat barbarously rich and overloaded. The note of provinciality in Addison is to be found in the commonplace of his ideas, though his style is classical. Where there is no centre like an academy, if you have genius and powerful ideas, you are apt not to have the best style going; if you have precision of style and not genius, you are apt not to have the best ideas going.

The provincial spirit exaggerates the value of its ideas for want of a high standard at hand by which to try them; it is hurried away by fancies; it likes and dislikes too passionately, too exclusively; its admiration weeps hysterical tears, and its disapprobation foams at the mouth. So we get the eruptive and aggressive manner in literature. Not having the lucidity of a large and centrally-placed intelligence, the provincial spirit has not its graciousness; it does not persuade, it makes war; it has not urbanity, the tone of the city, of the centre, the tone that always aims at a spiritual and intellectual effect. It loves hard-hitting rather than persuading. The newspaper, with its party spirit, its resolute avoidance of shades and distinctions, is its true literature. In England there needs a miracle of genius like Shakespeare to produce balance of mind, and a miracle of intellectual delicacy like Dr. Newman's to produce urbanity of style.

The reader will ask for some practical conclusion about the establishment of an academy in this country, and perhaps I shall hardly give him the one he expects. Nations have their own modes of acting, and these modes are not easily changed; they are even consecrated when great things have been done in them. When a literature has produced a Shakespeare and a Milton, when it has even produced a Barrow and a Burke, it cannot well abandon its traditions; it can hardly begin at this late time of day with an institution like the French Academy. An academy quite like the French Academy, a sovereign organ of the highest literary opinion, a recognised authority in matters of intellectual tone and taste, we shall hardly have, and perhaps ought not to wish to have. But then every one amongst us with any turn for literature at all will do well to remember to what shortcomings and excesses, which such an academy tends to correct, we are liable, and the more liable, of course, for not having it. He will do well constantly to try himself in respect of these, steadily to widen his culture, and severely to check in himself the provincial spirit.

VI.—Some Illustrative Criticisms

To try and approach Truth on one side after another, not to strive or cry, not to persist in pressing forward on any one side with violence and self-will—it is only thus that mortals may hope to gain any vision of the mysterious goddess whom we shall never see except in outline.

The grand power of poetry is the power of dealing with things so as to awaken in us a wonderfully full, new and intimate sense of them and of our relation with them, so that we feel ourselves to be in contact with the essential nature of those objects, to have their secret, and be in harmony with them, and this feeling calms and satisfies us as no other can. Maurice de Guérin manifested this magical power of poetry in singular eminence. His passion for perfection disdained all poetical work that was not perfectly adequate and felicitous.

His sister Eugénie de Guérin has the same characteristic quality— distinction. Of this quality the world is impatient; it chafes against it, rails at it, insults it, hates it, but ends by receiving its influence and by undergoing its law. This quality at last inexorably corrects the world's blunders, and fixes the world's ideals.

Heine claimed that he was "a brave soldier in the war of the liberation of humanity." That was his significance. He was, if not pre-eminently a brave, yet a brilliant soldier in the war of liberation of humanity. He was not an adequate interpreter of the modern world, but only a brilliant soldier.

Born in 1754, and dying in 1824, Joseph Joubert chose to hide his life; but he was a man of extraordinary ardour in the search for truth and of extraordinary fineness in the perception of it. He was one of those wonderful lovers of light who, when they have an idea to put forth, brood long over it first, and wait patiently till it shines.

GEORGE BRANDES

Main Currents of the Literature of the Nineteenth Century

George Brandes was born in Copenhagen on February 4, 1842, and was educated at the University of Copenhagen. The appearance of his "Æsthetic Studies" in 1868 established his reputation among men of letters of all lands. His criticism received a philosophic bent from his study of John Stuart Mill, Comte, and Renan. Complaint is often made of the bias exhibited by Brandes in his works, which is somewhat of a blemish on the breadth of his judgment. This bias finds its chief expression in his anti-clericalism. His publications number thirty-three volumes, and include works on history, literature, and criticism. He has written studies of Shakespeare, of Lord Beaconsfield, of Ibsen, and of Ferdinand Lassalle. His greatest work is the "Main Currents of the Literature of the Nineteenth Century." The field covered is so vast that any attempted synopsis of the volume is impossible here, so in this place we merely indicate the scope of Brandes's monumental work, and state his general conclusions.

The Man and the Book

This remarkable essay in literary criticism is limited to the first half of the nineteenth century; it concludes with the historical turning-point of 1848. Within this period the author discovers, first, a reaction against the literature of the eighteenth century; and then, the vanquishment of that reaction. Or, in other words, there is first a fading away and disappearance of the ideas and feelings of the preceding century, and then a return of the ideas of progress in new and higher waves.

"Literary history is, in its profoundest significance, psychology, the study, the history of the soul"; and literary criticism is, with our author, nothing less than the interior history of peoples. Whether we happen to agree or to disagree with his personal sympathies, which lie altogether with liberalism and whether his interpretation of these complex movements be accepted or rejected by future criticism, it is at least unquestionable that his estimate of his science is the right one, and that his method is the right one, and that no one stands beside Brandes as an exponent.

The historical movement of the years 1800 to 1848 is here likened to a drama, of which six different literary groups represent the six acts. The first three acts incorporate the reaction against progress and liberty. They are, first, the French Emigrant Literature, inspired by Rousseau; secondly, the semi-Catholic Romantic school of Germany, wherein the reaction has separated itself more thoroughly from the contemporary struggle for liberty, and has gained considerably in depth and vigour; and, thirdly, the militant and triumphant reaction as shown in Joseph de Maistre, Lamennais, Lamartine and Victor Hugo, standing out for pope and monarch. The drama of reaction has here come to its climax; and the last three acts are to witness its fall, and the revival, in its place, of the ideas of liberty and of progress.

"It is one man, Byron, who produces the revulsion in the great drama." And Byron and his English contemporaries, Wordsworth, Coleridge, Scott, Keats and Shelley, hold the stage in the fourth act, "Naturalism in England." The fifth act belongs to the Liberal movement in France, the "French Romantic School," including the names of Lamennais, Lamartine and Hugo in their second phase; and also those of De Musset and George Sand. The movement passes from France into "Young Germany," where the sixth act is played by Heine, Ruge, Feuerbach and others; and the ardent revolutionary writers of France and of Germany together prepare for the great political transformation of 1848.

I.—The Emigrant Literature

At the beginning of our period, France was subjected to two successive tyrannies: those, namely, of the Convention and of the Empire, both of which suppressed all independent thought and literature. Writers were, perforce, emigrants beyond the frontiers of French power, and were, one and all, in opposition to the Reign of Terror, or to the Napoleonic tyranny, or to both; one and all they were looking forward to the new age which should come.

There was, therefore, a note of expectancy in this emigrant literature, which had also the advantage of real knowledge, gained in long exile, of foreign lands and peoples. Although it reacts against the dry and narrow rationalism of the eighteenth century, it is not as yet a complete reaction against the Liberalism of that period; the writers of the emigrant group are still ardent in the cause of Liberty. They are contrary to the spirit of Voltaire; but they are all profoundly influenced by Rousseau.

Chateaubriand's romances, "Atala" and "René," Rousseau's "The New Héloïse" and Goethe's "Werther" are the subjects of studies which lead our critic to a consideration of that new spiritual condition of which they are the indications. "All the spiritual maladies," he says, "which make their appearance at this time may be regarded as the products of two great events—the emancipation of the individual and the emancipation of thought."

Every career now lies open, potentially, to the individual. His opportunities, and therefore his desires, but not his powers, have become boundless; and "inordinate desire is always accompanied by inordinate melancholy." His release from the old order, which limited his importance, has set him free for self-idolatry; the old laws have broken down, and everything now seems permissible. He no longer feels himself part of a whole; he feels himself to be a little world which reflects the great world. The belief in the saving power of enlightenment had been rudely shaken, and the minds of men were confused like an army which receives contradictory orders in the midst of a battle. Sénancour, Nodier and Benjamin Constant have left us striking romances picturing the human spirit in this dilemma; they show also a new feeling for Nature, new revelations of subjectivity, and new ideas of womanhood and of passion.

But of the emigrant literature Madame de Staël is the chief and central figure. The lawless savagery of the Revolution did not weaken her fidelity to personal and political freedom. "She wages war with absolutism in the state and hypocrisy in society. She teaches her countrymen to appreciate the characteristics and literature of the neighbouring nations; she breaks down with her own hands the wall of self-sufficiency with which victorious France had surrounded itself. Barante, with his perspective view of eighteenth-century France, only continues and completes her work."

II.—The Romantic School in Germany

German Romanticism continues the growing reaction against the eighteenth century; yet, though it is essentially reaction, it is not mere reaction, but contains the seeds of a new development. It is intellectual, poetical, philosophical and full of real life.

This literary period, marked by the names of Hölderlin, A. W. Schlegel, Tieck, Jean Paul Richter, Schleiermacher, Wackenroder, Novalis, Arnim, Brentano, resulted in little that has endured. It produced no typical forms; the character of its literature is musical rather than plastic; its impulse is not a clear perception or creation, but an infinite and ineffable aspiration.

An intenser spiritual life was at once the impulse and the goal of the Romanticists, in whom wonder and infinite desire are born again. A sympathetic interest in the fairy tale and the legend, in the face of Nature and in her creatures, in history, institutions and law, and a keener emotional sensitiveness in poetry, were the result of this refreshed interior life. In religion, the movement was towards the richly-coloured mystery and child-like faith of Catholicism; and in respect of human love it was towards freedom, spontaneity, intensity, and against the hard bonds of social conventions.

But its emotions became increasingly morbid, abnormal and ineffectual. Romanticism tended really, not to the spiritual emancipation that was its avowed aim, but to a refinement of sensuality; an indolent and passive enjoyment is its actual goal; and it repudiates industry and utility as the philistine barriers which exclude us from Paradise. Retrogression, the going back to a fancied Paradise or Golden Age, is the central idea of Romanticism, and is the secret of the practical ineffectiveness of the movement.

Friedrich Schlegel's romance, "Lucinde," is a very typical work of this period. It is based on the Romantic idea that life and poetry are identical, and its aim is to counsel the transformation of our actual life into a poem or work of art. It is a manifesto of self-absorption and of subjectivity; the reasoned defence of idleness, of enjoyment, of lawlessness, of the arbitrary expression of the Self, supreme above all.

The mysticism of Novalis, who preferred sickness to health, night to day, and invested death itself with sensual delights, is described by himself as voluptuousness. It is full of a feverish, morbid desire, which becomes at last the desire for nothingness. The "blue flower," in his story "Heinrich von Ofterdingen," is the ideal, personal happiness, sought for in all Romanticism, but by its very nature never attainable.

III. — The Reaction in France

Herein we have the culmination of the reactionary movement. Certain authors are grouped together as labouring for the re-establishment of the fallen power of authority; and by the principle of authority is to be understood "the principle which assumes the life of the individual and of the nation to be based upon reverence for inherited tradition." Further, "the principle of authority in general stood or fell with the authority of the Church. When that was undermined, it drew all other authorities with it in its fall."

After a study of the Revolution in its quality as a religious movement, and the story of the Concordat, our author traces the genesis of this extreme phase of the reaction. Its promoters were all of noble birth and bound by close ties to the old royal families; their aim was political rather than religious; "they craved for religion as a panacea for lawlessness." Their ruling idea was the principle of externality, as opposed to that of inward, personal feeling and private investigation; it was the principle of theocracy, as opposed to the sovereignty of the people; it was the principle of power, as opposed to the principles of human rights and liberties.

Chateaubriand's famous book, "Le Génie du Christianisme," devoid of real feeling, attempts to vindicate authority by means of an appeal to sentiment, as if taking for granted that a reasoned faith was now impossible. His point of view is romantic, and therefore, religiously, false; his reasoning is of the "how beautiful!" style.

But the principle was enthroned by Count Joseph de Maistre, a very different man. The minister of the King of Sardinia at the court of Russia, he gained the emperor's confidence by his strong and pure character, his royalist principles, and his talents. His more important works, "Du Pape," "De l'Eglise Gallicane," and "Soirées de St. Pétersbourg," are the most uncompromising defence of political and religious autocracy. The fundamental idea of his works is that "there is no human society without government, no government without sovereignty, and no sovereignty without infallibility." Beside De Maistre stands Bonald, a man of the same views, but without the other's daring and versatile wit. Chateaubriand's prose epic "Les Martyrs," the mystically sensual writings of Madame Krüdener, and the lyric poetry of Lamartine and Victor Hugo further popularised the reaction, which reached its breaking point in Lamennais.

It was at this moment, April, 1824, that the news came of Byron's death in Greece. The illusion dissolved; the reaction came to an end. The principle of authority fell, never to rise again; and the Immanuelistic school was succeeded by the Satanic.

IV.—Naturalism in England

The distinguishing character which our author discovers in the English poets is a love of Nature, of the country and the sea, of domestic animals and vegetation. This Naturalism, common to Wordsworth, Coleridge, Scott, Keats, Moore, Shelley and Byron, becomes, when transferred to social interests, revolutionary; the English poet is a Radical. Literary questions interest him not; he is at heart a politician.

The political background of English intellectual life at this period is painted forcibly and in the darkest tones. It was "dark with terror produced in the middle classes by the excesses of the liberty movement in France, dark with the tyrannic lusts of proud Tories and the Church's oppressions, dark with the spilt blood of Irish Catholics and English artisans." In the midst of all this misery, Wordsworth and Coleridge recalled the English mind to the love of real Nature and to the love of liberty. Wordsworth's conviction was that in town life and its distractions men had forgotten Nature, and had been punished for it; constant social intercourse had dissipated their talents and impaired their susceptibility to simple and pure impressions. His naturalism is antagonistic to all official creeds; it is akin to the old Greek conception of Nature, and is impregnated with pantheism.

The separate studies which follow, dealing with the natural Romanticism of Coleridge, Southey's Oriental Romanticism, the Lake school's conception of Liberty, the Historic Naturalism of Scott, the sensuous poetry of Keats, the poetry of Irish opposition and revolt, Thomas Campbell's poetry of freedom, the Republican Humanism of Landor, Shelley's Radical Naturalism, and like subjects, are of the highest importance to every English reader who would understand the time in which he lives. But Byron's is the heroic figure in this act. "Byron's genius takes possession of him, and makes him great and victorious in his argument, directing his aim with absolute certainty to the vital points." Byron's whole being burned with the profoundest compassion for the immeasurable sufferings of humanity. It was liberty that he worshipped, and he died for liberty.

V.—The Romantic School in France

During the Revolution the national property had been divided into twenty times as many hands as before, and with the fall of Napoleon the industrial period begins. All restrictions had been removed from industry and commerce, and capital became the moving power of society and the object of individual desires. The pursuit of money helps to give to the literature of the day its romantic, idealistic stamp. Balzac alone, however, made money the hero of his epic. Other great writers of the period, Victor Hugo, Alfred de Musset, George Sand, Beyle, Mérimée, Théophile Gautier, Sainte-Beuve, kept as far as possible from the new reality.

The young Romanticists of 1830 burned with a passion for art and a detestation of drab bourgeoisie. A break with tradition was demanded in all the arts; the original, the unconscious, the popular, were what they aimed at. It was now, as in Hugo's dramas, that the passionate plebeian appeared on the scene as hero; Mérimée, as in "Carmen," painted savage emotions;

Nodier's children spoke like real children; George Sand depicted, in woman, not conscious virtue and vice, but the innate nobility and natural goodness of a noble woman's heart. The poet was no longer looked on as a courtier, but as the despised high-priest of humanity.

The French Romantic school is the greatest literary school of the nineteenth century. It displayed three main tendencies—the endeavour to reproduce faithfully some real piece of past history or some phase of modern life; the endeavour after perfection of form; and enthusiasm for great religious or social reformatory ideas. These three tendencies are traced out in the ideals and work of the brilliant authors of the period; in George Sand, for instance, who proclaimed that the mission of art is a mission of sentiment and love; and in Balzac, who views society as the scientist investigates Nature—"he never moralises and condemns; he never allows himself to be led by disgust or enthusiasm to describe otherwise than truthfully; nothing is too small, nothing is too great to be examined and explained."

The impressions which our author gives of Sainte-Beuve, Gautier, George Sand, Balzac and Mérimée are vivid and concrete; they are high achievements in literary portraiture, set in a real historic background.

VI. — Young Germany

The personality, writings, and actions of Byron had an extraordinary influence upon "Young Germany," a movement initiated by Heine and Börne, and characterised by a strong craving for liberty. "Byron, with his contempt for the real negation of liberty that lay concealed beneath the 'wars of liberty' against Napoleon, with his championship of the oppressed, his revolt against social custom, his sensuality and spleen, his passionate love of liberty in every domain, seemed to the men of that day to be an embodiment of all that they understood by the modern spirit, modern poetry."

The literary group known as Young Germany has no creative minds of the highest, and only one of very high rank, namely, Heine. "It denied, it emancipated, it cleared up, it let in fresh air. It is strong through its doubt, its hatred of thraldom, its individualism." The Germany of those days has been succeeded by a quite new Germany, organised to build up and to put forth material strength, and the writers of the first half of the nineteenth century, who were always praising France and condemning the sluggishness of their own country, are but little read.

The literary figures of this period who are painted by our author, are Börne, Heine, Immermann, Menzel, Gutzkow, Laube, Mundt,

Rahel Varnhagen von Ense, Bettina von Arnim, Charlotte Stieglitz, and many others, to whose writings, in conjunction with those of the French Romanticists, Brandes ascribes the general revolt of the oppressed peoples of Europe in 1848. Of the men of that date he says: "They had a faith that could remove mountains, and a hope that could shake the earth. Liberty, parliament, national unity, liberty of the Press, republic, were to them magic words, at the very sound of which their hearts leaped like the heart of a youth who suddenly sees his beloved."

ROBERT BURTON

The Anatomy of Melancholy

Robert Burton was born on February 8, 1576, of an old family, at Lindley, Leicestershire, England; was educated at the free school of Sutton Coldfield, Warwickshire, and at Brasenose College, Oxford, and in 1599 was elected student of Christ Church. In 1616 he was presented with the vicarage of St. Thomas, Oxford, and in 1636 with the rectory of Segrave, in Leicestershire, and kept both these livings until his death. But he lived chiefly in his rooms at Christ Church, Oxford, where, burrowing in the treasures of the Bodleian Library, he elaborated his learned and whimsical book. He died on January 25, 1639, and was buried in Christ Church Cathedral. The "Anatomy of Melancholy" is an enormous compendium of sound sense, sly humour, universal erudition, mediæval science, fantastic conceits, and noble sentiments, arranged in the form of a most methodical treatise, divided, and subdivided again, into sections dealing with every conceivable aspect of this fell disorder. It is an intricate tissue of quotations and allusions, and its interest lies as much in its texture as in its argument. The "Anatomy" consists of an introduction, "Democritus Junior to the Reader," and then of three "Partitions," of which the first treats of the Causes of Melancholy, the second of its Cure, and the third of Love-Melancholy, wherewith is included the Melancholy of Superstition.

I.—Democritus Junior to the Reader

Gentle reader, I presume thou wilt be very inquisitive to know what antic or personate actor this is that so insolently intrudes upon this common theatre to the world's view, arrogating another man's name; whence he is, why he doth it, and what he hath to say. Seek not after that which is hid; if the contents please thee, suppose the man in the moon, or whom thou wilt, to be the author; I would not willingly be known.

I have masked myself under this visard because, like Democritus, I have lived a silent, sedentary, solitary, private life in the university, penned up most part in my study. Though by my profession a divine, yet, out of a running wit, an unconstant, unsettled mind, I had a great desire to have some smattering in all subjects; which Plato commends as fit to be imprinted in all curious wits, not to be a slave of one science, as most do, but to rove abroad, to have an oar in every man's boat, to taste of every dish, and to sip of every cup; which, saith Montaigne, was well performed by Aristotle.

I have little, I want nothing; all my treasure is in Minerva's tower. Though I lead a monastic life, myself my own theatre, I hear and see what is done abroad, how others run, ride, turmoil, in court and country. Amid the gallantry and misery of the world, jollity, pride, perplexities and cares, simplicity and villainy, subtlety, knavery, candour, and integrity, I rub on in private, left to a solitary life and mine own domestic discontents.

So I call myself Democritus, to assume a little more liberty of speech, or, if you will needs know, for that reason which Hippocrates relates, how, coming to visit him one day, he found Democritus in his garden at Abdera, under a shady bower, with a book on his knees, busy at his study, sometimes writing, sometimes walking. The subject of his book was melancholy and madness. About him lay the carcasses of many several beasts, newly by him cut up and anatomised; not that he did contemn God's creatures, but to find out the seat of this black bile, or melancholy, and how it is engendered in men's bodies, to the intent he might better cure it in himself, and by his writings teach others how to avoid it; which good intent of his Democritus Junior is bold to imitate, and because he left it imperfect and it is now lost, to revive again, prosecute, and finish in this treatise. I seek not applause; I fear good men's censures, and to their favourable acceptance I submit my labours. But as the barking of a dog I contemn those malicious and scurrile obloquies, flouts, calumnies of railers and detractors.

Of the necessity of what I have said, if any man doubt of it, I shall desire him to make a brief survey of the world, as Cyprian adviseth Donate; supposing himself to be transported to the top of some high mountain, and thence to behold the tumults and chances of this wavering world, he cannot choose but either laugh at, or pity it. St. Hierom, out of a strong imagination, being in the wilderness, conceived that he saw them dancing in Rome; and if thou shalt climb to see, thou shalt soon perceive that all the world is mad, that it is melancholy, dotes; that it is a common prison of gulls, cheats, flatterers, etc., and needs to be reformed. Kingdoms and provinces are melancholy; cities and families, all creatures vegetal, sensible and rational, all sorts, sects, ages, conditions, are out of tune; from the highest to the lowest have need of physic. Who is not brain-sick? Oh, giddy-headed age! Mad endeavours! Mad actions!

If Democritus were alive now, and should but see the superstition of our age, our religious madness, so many professed Christians, yet so few imitators of Christ, so much talk and so little conscience, so many preachers and such little practice, such variety of sects—how dost thou think he might have been affected? What would he have said to see, hear, and read so many bloody battles, such streams of blood able to turn mills, to make sport for princes, without any just cause? Men well proportioned, carefully brought up, able in body and mind, led like so many beasts to the slaughter in the flower of their years, without remorse and pity, killed for devils' food, 40,000 at once! At once? That were tolerable; but these wars last always; and for many ages, nothing so familiar as this hacking and hewing, massacres, murders, desolations! Who made creatures, so peaceable, born to love, mercy, meekness, so to rave like beasts and run to their own destruction?

How would our Democritus have been affected to see so many lawyers, advocates, so many tribunals, so little justice; so many laws, yet never more disorders; the tribunal a labyrinth; to see a lamb executed, a wolf pronounce sentence? What's the market but a place wherein they cozen one another, a trap? Nay, what's the world itself but a vast chaos, a theatre of hypocrisy, a shop of knavery, a scene of babbling, the academy of vice? A warfare, in which you must kill or be killed, wherein every man is for himself; no charity, love, friendship, fear of God, alliance, affinity, consanguinity, can contain them. Our goddess is Queen Money, to whom we daily offer sacrifice. It's not worth, virtue, wisdom, valour, learning, honesty, religion, for which we are respected, but money, greatness, office, honour. All these things are easy to be discerned, but how would Democritus have been moved had he seen the secrets of our hearts! All the world is mad, and every member of it, and I can but wish myself and them a good physician, and all of us a better mind.

II.—The Causes of Melancholy

The impulsive cause of these miseries in man was the sin of our first parent, Adam; and this, belike, is that which our poets have shadowed unto us in the tale of Pandora's Box, which, being opened through her curiosity, filled the world full of all manner of diseases. But as our sins are the principal cause, so the instrumental causes of our infirmities are as diverse as the infirmities themselves. Stars, heavens, elements, and all those creatures which God hath made, are armed against sinners. But the greatest enemy to man is man, his own executioner, a wolf, a devil to himself and others. Again, no man amongst us so sound that hath not some impediment of body or mind. There are diseases acute and chronic, first and secondary, lethal, salutary, errant, fixed, simple, compound, etc. Melancholy is the most eminent of the diseases of the phantasy or imagination; and dotage, phrensy, madness, hydrophobia, lycanthropy, St. Vitus' dance, and ecstasy are forms of it.

Melancholy is either in disposition or habit. In disposition it is that transitory melancholy which comes and goes upon every small occasion of sorrow; we call him melancholy that is dull, sad, sour, lumpish, ill-disposed, and solitary; and from these dispositions no man living is free; none so wise, patient, happy, generous, or godly, that can vindicate himself.

Melancholy is a cold and dry, thick, black, and sour humour, purged from the spleen; it is a bridle to the other two hot humours, blood and choler, preserving them in the blood and nourishing the bones. Such as have the Moon, Saturn, Mercury, misaffected in their genitures; such as live in over-cold or over-hot climates; such as are solitary by nature; great students, given to much contemplation; such as lead a life out of action; all are most subject to melancholy.

Six things are much spoken of amongst physicians as principal causes of this disease; if a man be melancholy, he hath offended in one of the six. They are diet, air, exercise, sleeping, and walking, and perturbations of the mind.

Idleness, the badge of gentry, or want of exercise, the bane of body and mind, the nurse of naughtiness, the chief author of all mischief, one of the seven deadly sins, and a sole cause of this and many other maladies, the devil's cushion and chief reposal, begets melancholy sooner than anything else. Such as live at ease, and have no ordinary employment to busy themselves about, cannot compose themselves to do aught; they cannot abide work, though it be necessary, easy, as to dress themselves, write a letter, or the like. He or she that is idle, be they never so rich, fortunate, happy, let them have all that heart can desire, they shall never be pleased, never well in body and mind, but weary still, sickly still, vexed still, loathing still, weeping, sighing, grieving, suspecting, offended with the world, with every object, wishing themselves gone or dead, or else carried away with some foolish phantasy or other.

Others, giving way to the passions and perturbations of fear, grief, shame, revenge, hatred, malice, etc., are torn in pieces, as Actæon was with his dogs, and crucify their own souls. Every society and private family is full of envy; it takes hold of all sorts of men, from prince to ploughman; scarce three in a company, but there is siding, faction, emulation, between two of them, some jar, private grudge, heart-burning in the midst. Scarce two great scholars in an age, but with bitter invectives they fall foul one on the other. Being that we are so peevish and perverse, insolent and proud, so factious and seditious, malicious and envious, we do maul and vex one another, torture, disquiet, and precipitate ourselves into that gulf of woes and cares, aggravate our misery and melancholy, and heap upon us hell and eternal damnation.

III.—The Cure of Melancholy

"It matters not," saith Paracelsus, "whether it be God or the devil, angels or unclean spirits, cure him, so that he be eased." Some have recourse to witches; but much better were it for patients that are troubled with melancholy to endure a little misery in this life than to hazard their souls' health for ever. All unlawful cures are to be refused, and it remains to treat of those that are admitted.

These are such as God hath appointed, by virtue of stones, herbs, plants, meats, and the like, which are prepared and applied to our use by the art and industry of physicians, God's intermediate ministers. We must begin with prayer and then use physic; not one without the other, but both together.

Diet must be rectified in substance and in quantity; air rectified; for there is much in choice of place and of chamber, in opportune opening and shutting of windows, and in walking abroad at convenient times. Exercise must be rectified of body and mind. Hawking, hunting, fishing are good, especially the last, which is still and quiet, and if so be the angler catch no fish, yet he hath a wholesome walk and pleasant shade by the sweet silver streams. But the most pleasant of all pastimes is to make a merry journey now and then with some good companions, to visit friends, see cities, castles, towns, to walk amongst orchards, gardens, bowers, to disport in some pleasant plain. St. Bernard, in the description of his monastery, is almost ravished with the pleasures of it. "Good God," saith he, "what a company of pleasures hast Thou made for man!" But what is so fit and proper to expel idleness and melancholy as study? What so full of content as to read, and see maps, pictures, statues, jewels, and marbles, so exquisite to be beheld that, as Chrysostom thinketh, "if any man be sickly or troubled in mind, and shall but stand over against one of Phidias's images, he will forget all care in an instant?"

If thou receivest wrong, compose thyself with patience to bear it. Thou shalt find greatest ease to be quiet. I say the same of scoffs, slanders, detractions, which tend to our disgrace; 'tis but opinion; if we would neglect or contemn them, they would reflect disgrace on them that offered them.

"Yea, but I am ashamed, disgraced, degraded, exploded; my notorious crimes and villainies are come to light!" Be content; 'tis but a nine days' wonder; 'tis heavy, ghastly, fearful news at first, but thine offence will be forgotten in an instant. Thou art not the first offender, nor shalt thou be the last. If he alone should accuse thee that were faultless, how many executioners, how many accusers, would thou have? Shall every man have his desert, thou wouldst peradventure be a saint in comparison. Be not dismayed; it is human to err. Be penitent, ask forgiveness, and vex thyself no more. Doth the moon care for the barking of a dog?

IV.—Love-Melancholy

There will not be wanting those who will much discommend this treatise of love-melancholy, and object that it is too light for a divine, too phantastical, and fit only for a wanton poet. So that they may be admired for grave philosophers, and staid carriage, they cannot abide to hear talk of love-toys; in all their outward actions they are averse; and yet, in their cogitations, they are all but as bad, if not worse than others. I am almost afraid to relate the passions which this tyrant love causeth among men; it hath wrought such stupendous and prodigious effects, such foul offences.

As there be divers causes of this heroical love, so there be many good remedies, among which good counsel and persuasion are of great moment, especially if it proceed from a wise, fatherly, discreet person. They will lament and howl for a while; but let him proceed, by foreshewing the miserable dangers that will surely happen, the pains of hell, joys of paradise, and the like; and this is a very good means, for love is learned of itself, but hardly left without a tutor.

In sober sadness, marriage is a bondage, a thraldom, a hindrance to all good enterprises; "he hath married a wife, and therefore cannot come"; a rock on which many are saved, many are cast away. Not that the thing is evil in itself, or troublesome, but full of happiness, and a thing which pleases God; but to indiscreet, sensual persons, it is a feral plague, many times an hell itself. If thy wife be froward, all is in an uproar; if wise and learned, she will be insolent and peevish; if poor, she brings beggary; if young, she is wanton and untaught. Say the best, she is a commanding servant; thou hadst better have taken a good housewifely maid in her smock. Since, then, there is such hazard, keep thyself as thou art; 'tis good to match, much better to be free. Consider withal how free, how happy, how secure, how heavenly, in respect, a single man is.

But when all is said, since some be good, some bad, let's put it to the venture. Marry while thou mayest, and take thy fortune as it falls. Be not so covetous, so distrustful, so curious and nice, but let's all marry; to-morrow is St. Valentine's Day. Since, then, marriage is the last and best cure of heroical love, all doubts are cured and impediments removed; God send us all good wives!

Take this for a corollory and conclusion; as thou tenderest thine own welfare in love-melancholy, in the melancholy of religion, and in all other melancholy; observe this short precept—Be not solitary; be not idle.

THOMAS CARLYLE

On Heroes and Hero-Worship

This is the last of four series of lectures which Carlyle (see Vol. IX, p. 99) delivered in London in successive years, and is the only series which was published. The "Lectures on Heroes" were given in May, 1840, and were published, with emendations and additions, from the reporter's notes in 1841. The preceding series were on "German Literature," 1837; "The Successive Periods of European Culture," 1838; and "The Revolutions of Modern Europe," 1839. Carlyle's profound and impassioned belief in the quasi-divine inspiration of great men, in the authoritative nature of their "message," and in their historical effectiveness, was a reaction against a way of writing history which finds the origin of events in "movements," "currents," and "tendencies" neglecting or minimising the power of personality. For Carlyle, biography was the essential element in history; his view of events was the dramatic view, as opposed to the scientific view. It is idle to inquire which is the better or truer view, where both are necessary. But Carlyle is here specially tilting against a prejudice which has so utterly passed away that it is difficult even to imagine it. This was to the effect that eminent historical figures have been in some sense impostors. This work suffers a good deal from its origin, but, like others of Carlyle's writings, it has had great effect in discrediting a barren and flippant rationalism.

I.—The Hero as Divinity

We have undertaken to discourse on great men, their manner of appearance in our world's business, how they shaped themselves in the world's history, what ideas men formed of them, and what work they did. We are to treat of hero-worship and the heroic in human affairs. The topic is as wide as universal history itself, for the history of what man has accomplished in this world is, at bottom, the history of the great men who have worked here.

It is well said that a man's religion is the chief fact with regard to him. I do not mean the Church creed which he professes, but the thing that he does practically believe, the manner in which he feels himself to be spiritually related to the unseen world. Was it heathenism, a plurality of gods, a mere sensuous representation of the mystery of life, and for chief recognised element therein physical force? Was it Christianism; faith in an Invisible as the only reality; time ever resting on eternity; pagan empire of force displaced by the nobler supremacy of holiness? Was it scepticism, uncertainty, and inquiry whether there was an unseen world at all, or perhaps unbelief and flat denial? The answer to these questions gives us the soul of the history of the man or nation.

Odin, the central figure of Scandinavian paganism, shall be our emblem of the hero as divinity. And in the first place I protest against the theory that this paganism or any other religion has consisted of mere quackery, priestcraft, and dupery. Quackery gives birth to nothing; gives death to all. Man everywhere is the born enemy of lies, and paganism, to its followers, was at one time earnestly true. Nor can we admit that other theory, which attributed these mythologies to allegory, or to the play of poetic minds. Pagan religion, like every other, is indeed a symbol of what men felt about the universe, but a practical guiding knowledge of this mysterious life of theirs, and not a perfect poetic symbol of it, has been the want of men. The "Pilgrim's Progress" is a just and beautiful allegory, but it could never have preceded the faith which it symbolises. Men never risked their soul's life on allegories; there was a kind of fact at the heart of paganism.

To the primitive pagan thinker, who was simple as a child, yet had a man's depth and strength, nature had as yet no name. It stood naked, flashing in on him, beautiful, awful, unspeakable; nature was preternatural. The world, which is now divine only to the gifted, was then divine to whosoever would turn his eye upon it. Still more was the body of man, and the mystery of his consciousness, an emblem to them of God, and truly worshipful.

How much more, then, was the worship of a hero reasonable—the transcendent admiration of a great man! For great men are still admirable. At bottom there is nothing else admirable. Admiration for one higher than himself is to this hour the vivifying influence in man's life, and is the germ of Christianity itself. The greatest of all heroes is One whom we do not name here.

Without doubt there was a first teacher and captain of these northern peoples, an Odin palpable to the sense, a real hero of flesh and blood. Tradition calls him inventor of the Runes, or Scandinavian alphabet, and again of poetry. To the wild Norse souls this noble-hearted man was hero, prophet, god. That the man Odin, speaking with a hero's voice and heart, as with an impressiveness out of Heaven, told his people the infinite importance of valour, how man thereby became a god; and that his people believed this message of his, and thought it a message out of Heaven, and believed him a divinity for telling it to them—this seems to me the primary seed-grain of the Norse religion. For that religion was a sternly impressive consecration of valour.

II.—The Hero as Prophet

We turn now to Mohammedanism among the Arabs for the second phase of hero-worship, wherein the hero is not now regarded as a god, but as one God-inspired, a prophet. Mohammed is not the most eminent prophet, but is the one of whom we are freest to speak. Nor is he the truest of prophets but I do esteem him a true one. Let us try to understand what he meant with the world; what the world meant and means with him will then be more answerable.

Certainly he was no scheming impostor, no falsehood incarnate; theories of that kind are the product of an age of scepticism, and indicate the saddest spiritual paralysis. A false man found a religion? Why, a false man cannot build a brick house! No Mirabeau, Napoleon, Burns, Cromwell, no man adequate to do anything, but is first of all in right earnest about it. Sincerity is the great characteristic of all men in any way heroic.

The Arabs are a notable people; their country itself is notable. Consider that wide, waste horizon of sand, empty, silent like a sea; you are all alone there, left alone with the universe; by day a fierce sun blazing down with intolerable radiance; by night the great deep heaven, with its stars—a fit country for a swift-handed, deep-hearted race of men. The Arab character is agile, active, yet most meditative, enthusiastic. Hospitable, taciturn, earnest, truthful, deeply religious, the Arabs were a people of great qualities, waiting for the day when they should become notable to all the world.

Here, in the year 570 of our era, the man Mohammed was born, and grew up in the bosom of the wilderness, alone with Nature and his own thoughts. From an early age he had been remarked as a thoughtful man, and his companions named him "The Faithful." He was forty before he talked of any mission from Heaven. All this time living a peaceful life, he was looking through the shows of things into things themselves.

Then, having withdrawn to a cavern near Mecca for a month of prayer and meditation, he told his wife Kadijah that, by the unspeakable favour of Heaven, he was in doubt and darkness no longer, but saw it all. That all these idols and formulas were nothing; that there was one God in and over all; that God is great and is the reality. *Allah akbar*, "God is great"; and then *Islam*, "we must submit to Him."

This is yet the only true morality known. A man is right and invincible, while he joins himself to the great deep law of the world, in spite of all superficial laws, temporary appearances, profit-and-loss calculations. This is the soul of Islam, and is properly also the soul of Christianity. We are to receive whatever befalls us as sent from God above. Islam means in its way the denial of self, annihilation of self. This is yet the highest wisdom that Heaven has revealed to our earth. In Mohammed, and in his Koran, I find first of all sincerity, the total freedom from cant. For these twelve centuries his religion has been the guidance of a fifth part of mankind, and, above all, it has been a religion heartily believed.

The Arab nation was a poor shepherd people; a hero-prophet was sent down to them; within one century afterwards Arabia is at Grenada on this hand, at Delhi on that!

III. — The Hero as Poet

The hero as divinity and as prophet are productions of old ages, not to be repeated in the new. We are now to see our hero in the less ambitious, but also less questionable, character of poet. For the hero can be poet, prophet, king, priest, or what you will, according to the kind of world he finds himself born into. I have no notion of a truly great man that could not be all sorts of men.

Indeed, the poet and prophet, participators in the open secret of the universe, are one; though the prophet has seized the sacred mystery rather on its moral side, and the poet on the æsthetic side. Poetry is essentially a song; its thoughts are musical not in word only, but in heart and in substance.

Shakespeare and Dante are our two canonised poets; they dwell apart, none equal, none second to them. Dante's book was written, in banishment, with his heart's blood. His great soul, homeless on earth, made its home more and more in that awful other world. The three kingdoms— *Inferno, Purgatorio, Paradiso*—are like compartments of a great supernatural world-cathedral, piled up there, stern, solemn, awful; Dante's world of souls. It is the sincerest of all poems. Sincerity here, too, we find to be the measure of worth. Intensity is the prevailing character of his genius; his greatness lies in fiery emphasis and depth; it is seen even in the graphic vividness of his painting. Dante burns as a pure star, fixed in the firmament, at which the great and high of all ages kindle themselves.

As Dante embodies musically the inner life of the Middle Ages, so Shakespeare embodies for us its outer life, its chivalries, courtesies, humours, ambitions. Dante gave us the soul of Europe; Shakespeare gave us its body. Of this Shakespeare of ours, the best judgment of Europe is slowly pointing to the conclusion that he is the chief of all poets, the greatest intellect who has left record of himself in the way of literature.

It is in portrait-painting, the delineation of men, that the greatness of Shakespeare comes out most decisively. His calm, creative perspicacity is unexampled. The word that will describe the thing follows of itself from such clear intense sight of the thing. He takes in all kinds of men—a Falstaff, Othello, Juliet, Coriolanus; sets them all forth to us in their rounded completeness, loving, just, the equal brother of all.

The degree of vision that dwells in a man is a correct measure of the man, and Shakespeare's is the greatest of intellects. Novalis beautifully remarks of him that those dramas of his are products of nature, too, deep as nature herself. Shakespeare's art is not artifice; the noblest worth of it is not there by plan or pre-contrivance. The latest generations of men will find new meanings in Shakespeare, new elucidations of their own human being.

Shakespeare, too, was a prophet, in his way, of an insight analogous to the prophetic, though he took it up in another strain. Nature seemed to this man also divine, unspeakable, deep as Tophet, high as heaven. "We are such stuff as dreams are made of." There rises a kind of universal psalm out of Shakespeare, not unfit to make itself heard among the still more sacred psalms.

England, before long, this island of ours, will hold but a small fraction of the English; east and west to the antipodes there will be a Saxondom covering great spaces of the globe. What is it that can keep all these together into virtually one nation, so that they do not fall out and fight, but live at peace? Here, I say, is an English king whom no time or chance can dethrone! King Shakespeare shines over us all, as the noblest, gentlest, yet strongest of rallying-signs; we can fancy him as radiant aloft over all the nations of Englishmen, a thousand years hence. Truly it is a great thing for a nation that it gets an articulate voice.

IV.—The Hero as Priest

The priest, too, is a kind of prophet. In him, also, there is required to be a light of inspiration. He presides over the worship of the people, and is the uniter of them with the unseen Holy. He is their spiritual captain, as the prophet is their spiritual king with many captains.

Luther and Knox were by express vocation priests, yet it will suit us better here to consider them chiefly in their historical character as reformers. The battling reformer is from time to time a needful and inevitable phenomenon. Obstructions are never wanting; the very things that were once indispensable furtherances become obstructions, and need to be shaken off and left behind us—a business often of enormous difficulty.

We are to consider Luther as an idol-breaker, a bringer back of men to reality, for that is the function of great men and teachers. Thus it was that Luther said to the Pope, "This thing of yours that you call a pardon of sins, is a bit of rag-paper with ink. It, and so much like it, is nothing else. God alone can pardon sins. God's Church is not a semblance, Heaven and Hell are not semblances. Standing on this, I, a poor German monk, am stronger than you all."

The most interesting phase which the Reformation anywhere assumes is that of Puritanism, which even got itself established as a Presbyterianism and National Church among the Scotch, and has produced in the world very notable fruit. Knox was the chief priest and founder of that faith which became the faith of Scotland, of New England, of Oliver Cromwell; and that which Knox did for his nation we may really call a resurrection as from death. The people began to live. Scotch literature and thought, Scotch industry, James Watt, David Hume, Walter Scott, Robert Burns—I find Knox and the Reformation acting in the heart's core of every one of these persons and phenomena; I find that without the Reformation they would not have been.

Knox could not live but by fact. He is an instance to us how a man, by sincerity itself, becomes heroic. We find in Knox a good, honest, intellectual talent, no transcendent one; he was a narrow, inconsiderable man as compared with Luther; but in heartfelt, instinctive adherence to truth, in real sincerity, he has no superior. His heart is of the true prophet cast. "He lies there," said the Earl of Morton, at his grave, "who never feared the face of man."

V.—The Hero as Man of Letters

The hero as man of letters is a new and singular phenomenon. Living in his squalid garret and rusty coat; ruling from his grave after death whole nations and generations; he must be regarded as our most important modern person. Such as he may be, he is the soul of all. Intrinsically it is the same function which the old generations named a prophet, priest, or divinity for doing.

The three great prophets of the eighteenth century, that singular age of scepticism, were Johnson, Rousseau, and Burns; they were not, indeed, heroic bringers of the light, but heroic seekers of it, struggling under mountains of impediment.

As for Johnson, I have always considered him to be, by nature, one of our great English souls. It was in virtue of his sincerity, of his speaking still in some sort from the heart of nature, though in the current artificial dialect, that Johnson was a prophet. The highest gospel he preached was a kind of moral prudence, coupled with this other great gospel, "Clear your mind of cant!" These two things, joined together, were, perhaps, the greatest gospel that was possible at that time.

Of Rousseau and his heroism I cannot say so much. He was not a strong man; but a morbid, excitable, spasmodic man; at best, intense rather than strong. Yet, at least he was heartily in earnest, if ever man was; his ideas possessed him like demons.

The fault and misery of Rousseau was egoism, which is the source and summary of all faults and miseries whatsoever. He had not perfected himself into victory over mere desire; a mean hunger was still his motive principle. He was a very vain man, hungry for the praises of men. The whole nature of the man was poisoned; there was nothing but suspicion, self-isolation, and fierce, moody ways.

And yet this Rousseau, with his celebrations of nature, even of savage life in nature, did once more touch upon reality and struggle towards reality. Strangely through all that defacement, degradation, and almost madness, there is in the inmost heart of poor Rousseau a spark of real heavenly fire. Out of all that withered, mocking philosophism, scepticism, and persiflage of his day there has arisen in this man the ineradicable feeling and knowledge that this life of ours is true, not a theorem, but a fact.

The French Revolution found its evangelist in Rousseau. His semi-delirious speculations on the miseries of civilised life, and such like, helped to produce a delirium in France generally. It is difficult to say what the governors of the world could do with such a man. What he could do with them is clear enough—guillotine a great many of them.

The tragedy of Burns's life is known to all. The largest soul of all the British lands appeared under every disadvantage; uninstructed, poor, born only to hard manual toil; and writing, when it came to that, in a rustic special dialect, known only to a small province of the country he lived in.

We find in Burns a noble, rough genuineness, the true simplicity of strength, and a deep and earnest element of sunshine and joyfulness; yet the chief quality, both of his poetry and of his life, is sincerity—a wild wrestling with the truth of things.

VI.—The Hero as King

The commander over men, to whose will our wills are to be subordinated and loyally surrender themselves, and find their welfare in doing so, may be reckoned the most important of great men. He is called *Rex*, "Regulator"; our own name is still better—king, which means "can-ning," "able-man."

In rebellious ages, when kingship itself seems dead and abolished, Cromwell and Napoleon step forth again as kings. The old ages are brought back to us; the manner in which kings were made, and kingship itself first took rise, is again exhibited in the history of these two.

The war of the Puritans was a section of that universal war which alone makes up the true history of the world—the war of Belief against Unbelief; the struggle of men intent on the real essence of things, against men intent on the semblances and forms of things. And among these Puritans Cromwell stood supreme, grappling like a giant, face to face, heart to heart, with the naked truth of things. Yet Cromwell alone finds no hearty apologist anywhere. Selfish ambition, dishonesty, duplicity; a fierce, coarse, hypocritical Tartuffe; turning all that noble struggle for constitutional liberty into a sorry farce played for his own benefit. This, and worse, is the character they give him.

From of old, this theory of Cromwell's falsity has been incredible to me. All that we know of him betokens an earnest, hearty sincerity. Everywhere we have to note his decisive, practical eye, how he drives towards the practicable, and has a genuine insight into what is fact. Such an intellect does not belong to a false man; the false man sees false shows, plausibilities, expediences; the true man is needed to discern even practical truth.

Napoleon by no means seems to me so great a man as Cromwell. His enormous victories which reached over all Europe, while Cromwell abode mainly in our little England, are but as the high stilts on which the man is seen standing; the stature of the man is not altered thereby. I find in him no such sincerity as in Cromwell; only a far inferior sort.

"False as a bulletin," became a proverb in Napoleon's time. Yet he had a sincerity, a certain instinctive, ineradicable feeling for reality; and did base himself upon fact, so long as he had any basis. He had an instinct of Nature better than his culture was. His companions, we are told, were one evening busily occupied arguing that there could be no God; they had proved it by all manner of logic. Napoleon, looking up into the stars, answers, "Very ingenious, Messieurs; but who made all that?" The atheistic logic runs off from him like water; the great fact stares him in the face. So, too, in practice; he, as every man that can be great, sees, through all entanglements, the practical heart of the matter, and drives straight towards that.

Accordingly, there was a faith in him, genuine so far as it went. That this new, enormous democracy is an insuppressible fact, which the whole world cannot put down—this was a true insight of his, and took his conscience and enthusiasm along with it. And did he not interpret the dim purport of it well? *La carrière ouverte aux talents*—"the implements to him who can handle them"—this actually is the truth, and even the whole truth; it includes whatever the French Revolution or any revolution could mean. It is a great, true message from our last great man.

Sartor Resartus

"Sartor Resartus," first published in "Frazer's Magazine" in 1833–34, is Thomas Carlyle's most popular work, and is largely autobiographical.

I.—*The Philosophy of Clothes*

Considering our present advanced state of culture, and how the torch of science has now been brandished and borne about, with more or less effect, for five thousand years and upwards, it is surprising that hitherto little or nothing of a fundamental character, whether in the way of philosophy or history, has been written on the subject of clothes. Every other tissue has been dissected, but the vestural tissue of woollen or other cloth, which man's soul wears as its outmost wrappage, has been quite overlooked. All speculation has tacitly figured man as a clothed animal, whereas he is by nature a naked animal, and only in certain circumstances, by purpose and device, masks himself in clothes.

But here, as in so many other cases, learned, indefatigable, deep-thinking Germany comes to our aid. The editor of these sheets has lately received a new book from Professor Teufelsdröckh, of Weissnichtwo, treating expressly of "Clothes, their Origin and Influence" (1831). This extensive volume, a very sea of thought, discloses to us not only a new branch of philosophy, but also the strange personal character of Professor Teufelsdröckh, which is scarcely less interesting. We were just considering how the extraordinary doctrines of this book might best be imparted to our own English nation, when we received a letter from Herr Hofrath Heuschrecke, our professor's chief associate, offering us the requisite documents for a biography of Teufelsdröckh. This was the origin of our "Sartor Resartus," now presented in the vehicle of "Frazer's Magazine."

Professor Teufelsdröckh, when we knew him at Weissnichtwo, lived a still and self-contained life, devoted to the higher philosophies and to a certain speculative radicalism. The last words that he spoke in our hearing were to propose a toast in the coffee-house—"The cause of the poor, in heaven's name and the devil's." But we looked for nothing moral from him, still less anything didactico-religious.

Brave Teufelsdröckh, who could tell what lurked in thee? In thine eyes, deep under thy shaggy brows, and looking out so still and dreamy, have we not noticed gleams of an ethereal or else a diabolic fire? Our friend's title was that of Professor of Things in General, but he never delivered any course. We used to sit with him in his attic, overlooking the town; he would contemplate that wasp-nest or bee-hive spread out below him, and utter the strangest thoughts. "That living flood, pouring through these streets, is coming from eternity, going onward to eternity. These are apparitions. What else?" Thus he lived and meditated with Heuschrecke as Boswell for his Johnson.

"As Montesquieu wrote a 'Spirit of Laws,'" observes our professor, "so could I write a 'Spirit of Clothes,' for neither in tailoring nor in legislating does man proceed by mere accident, but the hand is ever guided by the mysterious operations of the mind." And so he deals with Paradise and fig-leaves, and proceeds to view the costumes of all mankind, in all countries, in all times.

The first purpose of clothes, he imagines, was not warmth or decency, but ornament. "Yet what have they not become? Increased security and pleasurable heat soon followed; divine shame or modesty, as yet a stranger to the anthropophagous bosom, arose there mysteriously under clothes, a mystic shrine for the holy in man. Clothes gave us individuality, distinctions, social polity; clothes have made men of us; they are threatening to make clothes-screens of us."

Teufelsdröckh dwells chiefly on the seams, tatters, and unsightly wrong-side of clothes, but he has also a superlative transcendentalism. To him, man is a soul, a spirit, and divine apparition, whose flesh and senses are but a garment. He deals much in the feeling of wonder, insisting that wonder is the only reasonable temper for the denizen of our planet. "Wonder," he says, "is the basis of worship," and that progress of science, which is to destroy wonder and substitute mensuration and numeration, finds small favour with him. "Clothes, despicable as we think them, are unspeakably significant."

II.—Biography of Teufelsdröckh

So far as we can gather from the disordered papers which have been placed in our hands, the genesis of Diogenes Teufelsdröckh is obscure. We see nothing but an exodus out of invisibility into visibility. In the village of Entepfuhl we find a childless couple, verging on old age. Andreas Futteral, who has been a grenadier sergeant under Frederick the Great, is now cultivating a little orchard. To him and Gretchen his wife there entered one evening a stranger of reverend aspect, who deposited a silk-covered basket, saying, "Good people, here is an invaluable loan; take all heed thereof; with high recompense, or else with heavy penalty, will it one day be required back." Therein they found, as soon as he had departed, a little infant in the softest sleep. Our philosopher tells us that this story, told him in his twelfth year, produced a quite indelible impression. Who was his unknown father, whom he was never able to meet?

We receive glimpses of his childhood, schooldays, and university life, and then meet with him in that difficulty, common to young men, of "getting under way." "Not what I have," he says, "but what I do, is my kingdom; and we should grope throughout our lives from one expectation and disappointment to another were we not saved by one thing—our hunger." He had thrown up his legal profession, and found himself without landmark of outward guidance; whereby his previous want of decided belief, or inward guidance, is frightfully aggravated. So he sets out over an unknown sea; but a certain Calypso Island at the very outset falsifies his whole reckoning.

"Nowhere," he says, "does Heaven so immediately reveal itself to the young man as in the young maiden. The feeling of our young forlorn towards the queens of this earth was, and indeed is, altogether unspeakable. A visible divinity dwelt in them; to our young friend all women were holy, were heavenly. And if, on a soul so circumstanced, some actual air-maiden should cast kind eyes, saying thereby, 'Thou too mayest love and be loved,' and so kindle him—good Heaven, what an all-consuming fire were probably kindled!"

Such a fire of romance did actually burst forth in Herr Diogenes. We know not who "Blumine" was, nor how they met. She was young, hazel-eyed, beautiful, high-born, and of high spirit, but unhappily dependent and insolvent, living perhaps on the bounty of moneyed relatives. "To our friend the hours seemed moments; holy was he and happy; the words from those sweetest lips came over him like dew on thirsty grass. At parting, the Blumine's hand was in his; in the balmy twilight, with the kind stars above them, he spoke something of meeting again, which was not contradicted; he pressed gently those soft, small fingers, and it seemed as if they were not hastily, not angrily withdrawn."

Poor Teufelsdröckh, it is clear to demonstration thou art smit! Flame-clad, thou art scaling the upper Heaven, and verging towards insanity, for prize of a high-souled brunette, as if the earth held but one and not several of these! "One morning, he found his morning-star all dimmed and dusky-red; doomsday had dawned; they were to meet no more!" Their lips were joined for the first time and the last, and Teufelsdröckh was made immortal by a kiss. And then—"thick curtains of night rushed over his soul, and he fell, through the ruins as of a shivered universe, towards the abyss."

He quietly lifts his pilgrim-staff, and begins a perambulation and circumambulation of the terraqueous globe. We find him in Paris, in Vienna, in Tartary, in the Sahara, flying with hunger always parallel to him, and a whole infernal chase in his rear. He traverses mountains and valleys with aimless speed, writing with footprints his sorrows, that his spirit may free herself, and he become a man. Vain truly is the hope of your swiftest runner to escape from his own shadow! We behold him, through these dim years, in a state of crisis, of transition; his aimless pilgrimings are but a mad fermentation, wherefrom, the fiercer it is, the clearer product will one day evolve itself.

Man has no other possession but hope; this world of his is emphatically the "Place of Hope"; yet our professor, for the present, is quite shut out from hope. As he wanders wearisomely through this world he has now lost all tidings of another and higher. "Doubt," says he, "had darkened into unbelief." It is all a grim desert, this once fair world of his; and no pillar of cloud by day, and no pillar of fire by night, any longer guides the pilgrim. "Invisible yet impenetrable walls, as of enchantment, divided me from all living; was there, in the wide world, any true bosom I could press trustfully to mine? O Heaven, no, there was none! To me the universe was all void of life, of purpose, of volition, even of hostility; it was one huge, dead, immeasurable steam-engine, rolling on, in its dead indifference, to grind me limb from limb. O, the vast, gloomy, solitary Golgotha, and mill of death!

"Full of such humour, and perhaps the miserablest man in the whole French capital or suburbs, was I, one sultry dog-day, after much perambulation, toiling along the dirty little Rue Saint Thomas de l'Enfer, among civic rubbish enough, in a close atmosphere, and over pavements hot as Nebuchadnezzar's furnace; whereby doubtless my spirits were a little cheered; when, all at once, there rose a thought in me, and I asked myself, 'What *art* thou afraid of? Wherefore, like a coward, dost thou forever pip and whimper, and go cowering and trembling? Despicable biped! what is the sum-total of the worst that lies before thee? Death? Well, death; and say the pangs of Tophet too, and all that the devil and man may, will, or can do against thee! Hast thou not a heart; canst thou not suffer whatever it be; and, as a child of freedom, though outcast, trample Tophet itself under thy feet, while it consumes thee? Let it come, then; I will meet it and defy it!' And, as I so thought, there rushed like a stream of fire over my whole soul; and I shook base fear away from me for ever. Ever from that time, the temper of my misery was changed; not fear or whining sorrow was it, but indignation and grim fire-eyed defiance.

"Thus had the *Everlasting No* pealed authoritatively through all the recesses of my being, of my *Me*; and then was it that my whole *Me* stood up, in native God-created majesty, and with emphasis recorded its protest. The Everlasting No had said, 'Behold, thou art fatherless, outcast, and the universe is mine, the devil's'; to which my whole *Me* now made answer, 'I am not thine, but free, and for ever hate thee!'

"It is from this hour that I incline to date my spiritual new-birth, or Baphometic Fire-baptism; perhaps I directly thereupon began to be a man."

Our wanderer's unrest was for a time but increased. "Indignation and defiance are not the most peaceable inmates," yet it was no longer a quite hopeless unrest. He looked away from his own sorrows, over the many-coloured world, and few periods of his life were richer in spiritual culture than this. He had reached the Centre of Indifference wherein he had accepted his own nothingness. "I renounced utterly, I would hope no more and fear no more. To die or to live was to me alike insignificant. Here, then, as I lay in that Centre of Indifference, cast by benignant upper influence into a healing sleep, the heavy dreams rolled gradually away, and I awoke to a new heaven and a new earth. I saw that man can do without happiness and instead thereof find blessedness. Love not pleasure; love God. This is the *Everlasting Yea*, wherein all contradiction is solved; wherein whoso walks and works, it is well with him. In this poor, miserable, hampered, despicable Actual, wherein thou even now standest, here or nowhere is thy Ideal; work it out therefrom; and working, believe, live, be free! Produce! produce! Work while it is called to-day."

III. — The Volume on Clothes

In so capricious a work as this of the professor's, our course cannot be straightforward, but only leap by leap, noting significant indications here and there. Thus, "perhaps the most remarkable incident in modern history," he says, "is George Fox's making to himself a suit of leather, when, desiring meditation and devout prayer to God, he took to the woods, chose the hollow of a tree for his lodging and wild berries for his food, and for clothes stitched himself one perennial suit of leather. Then was there in broad Europe one free man, and Fox was he!"

Under the title "Church-Clothes," by which Teufelsdröckh signifies the forms, the vestures, under which men have at various periods embodied and represented for themselves the religious principle, he says, "These are unspeakably the most important of all the vestures and garnitures of human existence. Church-clothes are first spun and woven by society; outward religion originates by society; society becomes possible by religion."

Of "symbols," as means of concealment and yet of revelation, thus uniting in themselves the efficacies at once of speech and of silence, our professor writes, "In the symbol proper there is ever, more or less distinctly and directly, some embodiment and revelation of the Infinite; the Infinite is made to blend itself with the finite; to stand visible, and, as it were, attainable there. Of this sort are all true works of art; in them, if thou know a work of art from a daub of artifice, wilt thou discern eternity looking through time; the God-like rendered visible. But nobler than all in this kind are the lives of heroic God-inspired men, for what other work of art is so divine?" And again, "Of this be certain, wouldst thou plant for eternity, then plant into the deep infinite faculties of man, his fantasy and heart; wouldst thou plant for year and day, then plant into his shallow superficial faculties, his self-love and arithmetical understanding."

As for Helotage, or that lot of the poor wherein no ray of heavenly nor even of earthly knowledge visits him, Teufelsdröckh says, "That there should one man die ignorant who had capacity for knowledge, this I call a tragedy, were it to happen more than twenty times in the minute."

In another place, our professor meditates upon the awful procession of mankind. "Like a God-created, fire-breathing spirit-host, we emerge from the inane; haste stormfully across the astonished earth; then plunge again into the inane. But whence?—O Heaven, whither? Sense knows not; Faith knows not; only that it is through mystery to mystery, from God and to God.

> "We are such stuff
> As dreams are made of, and our little life
> Is rounded with a sleep!"

MARCUS TULLIUS CICERO

Concerning Friendship

The dialogue "Concerning Friendship" was composed immediately after the assassination of Julius Cæsar, and was suggested by the conduct of certain friends of the mighty dead, who were trying, in the name of friendship, to inflame the populace against the cause of the conspirators. (Cicero biography, see Vol. IX, p. 155, and also p. 274 of the present volume.)

A Dialogue

Fannius: I agree with you, Lælius; never was man better known for justice or for glory than Scipio Africanus. That is why everyone in Rome is looking to you; everyone is asking me, and Scævola here, how the wise Lælius is bearing the loss of his dead friend. For they call you wise, you know, in the same sense as the oracle called Socrates wise, because you believe that your happiness depends on yourself alone, and that virtue can fortify the soul against every calamity. May we know, then, how you bear your sorrow?

Scævola: He says truly; many have asked me the same question. I tell them that you are composed and patient, though deeply touched by the death of your dearest friend, and one of the greatest of men.

Lælius: You have answered well. True it is that I sorrow for a friend whose like I shall never see again; but it is also true that I need no consolations, since I believe that no evil has befallen Scipio. Whatever misfortune there is, is my misfortune, and any immoderate distress would show self-love, not love for him. What a man he was! Well, he is in heaven; and I sometimes hope that the friendship of Scipio and Lælius may live in human memory.

Fannius: Yes—your friendship: what do you believe about friendship?

Scævola: That's what we want to know.

Lælius: Who am I, to speak on such a subject all on a sudden? You should go to these Greek professionals, who can spin you a discourse on anything at a moment's notice. For my part, I can only advise this—prize friendship above all earthly things. We seem to be made for friendship; it is our great stand-by whether in weal or woe. Yet I can say this too: friendship cannot be except among the good. I don't mean a fantastical and unattainable pitch of goodness such as the philosophers prate about; I mean the genuine, commonplace goodness of flesh and blood, that actually exists. I mean such men as live in honour, justice, and liberality, and are consistent, and are neither covetous nor licentious, nor brazen-faced; such men are good enough for us, because they follow Nature as far as they can.

Friendship consists of a perfect conformity of opinion upon all subjects, divine and human, together with a feeling of kindness and attachment. And though some prefer riches, health, power, honours, or even pleasure, no greater boon than friendship, with the single exception of wisdom, has been given by the gods to man. It is quite true that our highest good depends on virtue; but virtue inevitably begets and nourishes friendship. What a part, for instance, friendship has played in the lives of the good men we have known—the Catos, the Galli, the Scipios, and the like!

How manifold, again, are its benefits! What greater delight is there than to have one with whom you may talk as if with yourself? One who will joy in your good fortune, and bear the heaviest end of your burdens! Other things are good for particular purposes, friendship for all; neither water nor fire has so many uses. But in one respect friendship transcends everything else: it throws a brilliant gleam of hope over the future, and banishes despondency. Whoever has a true friend sees in him a reflection of himself; and each is strong in the strength and rich in the wealth of the other.

If you consider that the principle of harmony and benevolence is necessary to the very existence of families and states, you will understand how high a thing is friendship, in which that harmony and benevolence reach their perfect flower. There was a philosopher of Agrigentum who explained the properties of matter and the movements of bodies in terms of affection and repulsion; and however that may be, everyone knows that these are the real forces in human life. Who does not applaud the friendship that shares in mortal dangers, whether in real life or in the play?

Scævola: You speak highly of friendship. What are its principles and duties?

Lælius: Do we desire a friend because of our own weakness and deficiency, in order that we may obtain from him what we lack ourselves, repaying him by reciprocal service? Or is all that only an incident of friendship, and does the bond derive from a remoter and more beautiful origin, in the heart of Nature herself? For my part, I take the latter view. Friendship is a natural emotion, and not an arrangement of convenience.

Its character may be recognised even in the lower animals, and much more plainly in the love of human parents for their children, and, most of all, in our affection for a congenial friend, whom we see in an atmosphere of virtue and worth.

The other is not an ignoble theory, but it leaves us in the difficulty that if it were true, the weakest, meanest, and poorest of humanity would be the most inclined to friendship. But it is the strong, rich, independent, and self-reliant man, deeply founded in wisdom and dignity, who makes great friendships. What did Africanus need of me, or I of him? Advantages followed, but they did not lead. But there are people who will always be referring everything to the one principle of self-advantage; they have no eyes for anything great and god-like. Let us leave such theorists alone; the plain fact is, that whenever worth is seen, love for it is enkindled. Associations founded upon interest presently dissolve, because interest changes; but Nature never changes, and therefore true friendships are imperishable.

Scipio used to say that it was exceedingly difficult to carry on a friendship to the end of life, because the paths of interest so often diverge. There may be competition for office, or a dishonorable request may be refused, or some other accident may be fatal to the bond. This refusal to join in a nefarious course of action is often the end of a friendship, and it is worth inquiring how far the claims of affection ought to extend. Tiberius Gracchus, when he troubled the state, was deserted by almost all his friends; one of them who had assisted him told me that he had such high regard for Gracchus that he could refuse him nothing. "But what," said I, "if he had asked you to set fire to the capitol?" "I would have done it!"

What an infamous confession! No degree of friendship can justify a crime; and since virtue is the foundation of friendship, crime must inevitably undermine it. Let this, then, be the rule of friendship—never to make disgraceful requests, and never to grant them when they are made.

Among the perverse, over-subtle ideas of certain Greek philosophers is the maxim that we should be very cool in the matter of friendship. They say that we have enough to do with our own affairs, without taking on other people's affairs too; and that our minds cannot be serenely at leisure if we are liable to be tortured by the sorrows of a friend. They advise, also, that friendships should be sought for the sake of protection, and not for the sake of kindliness. O noble philosophy! They put out the sun in the heavens, and offer us instead a freedom from care that is worse than worthless. Virtue has not a heart of stone, but is gentle and compassionate, rejoicing with the joyful and weeping with those who mourn. True virtue is never unsocial, never haughty.

With regard to the limits of friendship, I have heard three several maxims, but disapprove them all. First, that we ought to feel towards our friend exactly as we feel towards ourselves. That would never do; for we do many things for our friends that we should never think of doing for ourselves. We ask favours and reprehend injuries for a friend, where we would not solicit for, or defend, ourselves. Secondly, that our kindness to a friend should be meted out in precise equipoise to his kindness to us. This is too miserable a theory: friendship is opulent and generous. The third is, that we should take our friend's own estimate of himself, and act upon it. This is the worst principle of the three; for if our friend is over-humble, diffident or despondent, it is the very business of friendship to cheer him and urge him on. But Scipio used to condemn yet another principle that is worse still. Some one—he thought it must have been a bad man—once said that we ought to remember in friendship that some day the friend might be an enemy. How, in that state of mind, could one be a friend at all?

A sound principle, I think, is this. In the friendship of upright men there ought to be an unrestricted communication of every interest, every purpose, every inclination. Then, in any matter of importance to the life or reputation of your friend, you may deviate a little from the strictest line of conduct so long as you do not do anything that is actually infamous. Then, with regard to the choice of friends, Scipio used to say that men were more careful about their sheep and goats than about their friends. Choose men of constancy, solidity, and firmness; and until their trustworthiness has been tested, be moderate in your affection and confidence. Seek first of all for sincerity. Your friend should also have an open, genial, and sociable temper, and his sympathies should be the same as yours. He must not be ready to believe accusations. Lastly, his talk and manner should be debonair; we don't want austerities and solemnities in friendship.

I have heard it suggested that we ought perhaps to prefer new friends to old, as we prefer a young horse to an old one. Satiety should have no place in friendship. Old wines are the best, and so are the friends of many years. Do not despise the acquaintance that promises to ripen into something better; but do not sacrifice for it the deeply rooted intimacy. Even inanimate things take hold of our hearts by long custom; we love the mountains and forests of our youth.

There is often a great disparity in respect of rank or talent between intimate friends. Whenever that is so, let the superior place himself on the level of the inferior; let him share all his advantages with his friend. The best way to reap the full harvest of genius, or of merit, or of any other excellence, is to encourage all one's kindred and associates to enjoy it too. But if the superior ought to condescend to the inferior, so the inferior ought to be free from envy. And let him not make a fuss about such services as he has been able to render.

To pass from the noble friendships of the wise to more commonplace intimacies, we cannot leave out of account the necessity that sometimes arises of breaking off a friendship. A man falls into scandalous courses, his disgrace is reflected on his companions, and their relation must come to an end. Well, the end had best come gradually and gently, unless the offence is so detestable that an abrupt and final cutting of the acquaintance is absolutely inevitable. Disengage, if possible, rather than cut. And let the matter end with estrangement; let it not proceed to active animosity and hostility. It is very unbecoming to engage in public war with a man who has been known as one's friend. On two separate occasions Scipio thought it right to withdraw his confidence from certain friends. In each case he kept his dignity and self-command; he was grieved, but never bitter. Of course, the best way to guard against such unfortunate occurrences is to take the greatest care in forming friendships. All excellence is rare, and that moral excellence which makes fit objects for friendship is as rare as any.

On the other hand, it would be unreasonable and presumptuous in anyone to expect to find a friend of a quality to which he himself can never hope to attain, or to demand from his friend an indulgence which he is not prepared himself to offer. Friendship was given us to be an incentive to virtue, and not as an indulgence to vice or to mediocrity; in order that, since a solitary virtue cannot scale the peaks, it may do so with the loyal help of a comrade. A comradeship of this kind includes within it all that men most desire.

Think nobly of friendship, and conduct yourselves wisely in it, for in one way or another it enters into the life of every man. Even Timon of Athens, whose one impulse was a brutal misanthropy, must needs seek a confidant into whose mind he may instil his detestable venom. I have heard, and I agree with it, that though a man should contemplate from the heavens the universal beauty of creation, he would soon weary of it without a companion for his admiration.

Of course, there are rubs in friendship which a sensible man will learn to avoid, or to ignore, or to bear them cheerfully. Admonitions and reproofs must have their part in true amity, and it is as difficult to utter them tactfully as it is to receive them in good part. Complaisance seems more propitious to friendship than are these naked truths. But though truth may be painful, complaisance is more likely in the long run to prove disastrous. It is no kindness to allow a friend to rush headlong to ruin. Let your remonstrances be free from bitterness and from insult; let your complaisance be affable, but never servile. As for adulation, there are no words bad enough for it. Even the populace have only contempt for the politician who flatters them. Despise the insinuations of the sycophant, for what is more shameful than to be made a fool of?

I tell you, sirs, that it is virtue that lasts; that begets real friendships and maintains them. Lay, therefore, while you are young, the foundations of a virtuous life.

WILLIAM COBBETT

Advice to Young Men

William Cobbett, the celebrated English political writer, was born in March, 1762, at Farnham in Surrey. He took a dislike to rural occupations, and at an early age went to London, where he was employed for a few months as a copying clerk. This work was distasteful to him, and he enlisted in the army, and went with his regiment to Nova Scotia. On returning to England in 1791, he obtained his discharge, married, and went to America. In Philadelphia he commenced his career as a political writer. Cobbett's "Advice to Young Men" was published in 1830. It has always been the most popular of his books, partly because of its subject, and partly because it illustrates so well the bold and forceful directness of his style. An intensely egotistical and confident man, Cobbett believed that his own strangely inconsistent life was a model for all men. Yet, contrary to what might have been expected, he was a delightful man in the domestic circle, and the story of his marriage—which has been narrated in his "Rural Rides"—is one of the romances of literary life. The original introduction to the "Advice" contained personal reference incredible in anyone except Cobbett. Said he, "Few will be disposed to question my fitness for the task. If such a man be not qualified to give advice, no man is qualified." And he went on to claim for himself "genius and something more." He certainly had a remarkable fund of commonsense, except when his subject was himself. Cobbett died June 18, 1835.

I.—To a Youth

You are arrived, let us suppose, at the age of from fourteen to nearly twenty, and I here offer you my advice towards making you a happy man, useful to all about you, and an honour to those from whom you sprang. Start, I beseech you, with a conviction firmly fixed in your mind that you have no right to live in this world without doing work of some sort or other. To wish to live on the labour of others is to contemplate a fraud.

Happiness ought to be your great object, and it is to be found only in independence. Turn your back on what is called interest. Write it on your heart that you will depend solely on your own merit and your own exertions, for that which a man owes to favour or to partiality, that same favour or partiality is constantly liable to take from him.

The great source of independence the French express in three words, "*Vivre de peu.*" "To live upon little" is the great security against slavery; and this precept extends to dress and other things besides food and drink. Extravagance in dress arises from the notion that all the people in the street will be looking at you as you walk out; but all the sensible people that happen to see you will think nothing at all about you. Natural beauty of person always will and must have some weight, even with men, and great weight with women; but this does not want to be set off by expensive clothes.

A love of what is called "good eating and drinking," if very unamiable in a grown-up person, is perfectly hateful in a youth. I have never known such a man worthy of respect.

Next, as to amusements. Dancing is at once rational and healthful; it is the natural amusement of young people, and none but the most grovelling and hateful tyranny, or the most stupid and despicable fanaticism, ever raised its voice against it. As to gaming, it is always criminal, either in itself or in its tendency. The basis of it is covetousness; a desire to take from others something for which you have given, and intend to give, no equivalent.

Be careful in choosing your companions; and lay down as a rule never to be departed from that no youth or man ought to be called your friend who is addicted to indecent talk.

In your manners be neither boorish nor blunt, but even these are preferable to simpering and crawling. Be obedient where obedience is due; for it is no act of meanness to yield implicit and ready obedience to those who have a right to demand it at your hands. None are so saucy and disobedient as slaves; and, when you come to read history, you will find that in proportion as nations have been free has been their reverence for the laws.

Let me now turn to the things which you ought to do. And, first of all, the husbanding of your time. Young people require more sleep than those that are grown up, and the number of hours cannot well be, on an average, less than eight. An hour in bed is better than an hours spent over the fire in an idle gossip.

Money is said to be power; but superior sobriety, industry, and activity are still a more certain source of power. Booklearning is not only proper, but highly commendable; and portions of it are absolutely necessary in every case of trade or profession. One of these portions is distinct reading, plain and neat writing, and arithmetic. The next thing is the grammar of your own language, for grammar is the foundation of all literature. Excellence in your own calling is the first thing to be aimed at. After this may come general knowledge. Geography naturally follows grammar; and you should begin with that of this kingdom. When you come to history, begin also with that of your own country; and here it is my bounded duty to put you well on your guard. The works of our historians are, as far as they relate to former times, masses of lies unmatched by any others that the world has ever seen.

II. — To a Young Man

To be poor and independent is very nearly an impossibility; though poverty is, except where there is an actual want of food and raiment, a thing much more imaginary than real. Resolve to set this false shame of being poor at defiance. Nevertheless, men ought to take care of their names, ought to use them prudently and sparingly, and to keep their expenses always within the bounds of their income, be it what it may.

One of the effectual means of doing this is to purchase with ready money. Innumerable things are not bought at all with ready money which would be bought in case of trust; it is so much easier to order a thing than to pay for it. I believe that, generally speaking, you pay for the same article a fourth part more in the case of trust than you do in the case of ready money. The purchasing with ready money really means that you have more money to purchase with.

A great evil arising from the desire not to be thought poor is the destructive thing honoured by the name of "speculation," but which ought to be called gambling. It is a purchasing of something to be sold again with a great profit at a considerable hazard. Your life, while you are thus engaged, is the life of a gamester: a life of general gloom, enlivened now and then by a gleam of hope or of success.

In all situations of life avoid the trammels of the law. If you win your suit and are poorer than you were before, what do you accomplish? Better to put up with the loss of one pound than with two, with all the loss of time and all the mortification and anxiety attending a law suit.

Unless your business or your profession be duly attended to there can be no real pleasure in any other employment of a portion of your time. Men, however, must have some leisure, some relaxation from business; and in the choice of this relaxation much of your happiness will depend.

Where fields and gardens are at hand, they present the most rational scenes for leisure. Nothing can be more stupid than sitting, sotting over a pot and a glass, sending out smoke from the head, and articulating, at intervals, nonsense about all sorts of things.

Another mode of spending the leisure time is that of books. To come at the true history of a country you must read its laws; you must read books treating of its usages and customs in former times; and you must particularly inform yourselves as to prices of labour and of food. But there is one thing always to be guarded against, and that is not to admire and applaud anything you read merely because it is the fashion to admire and applaud it. Read, consider well what you read, form your own judgments, and stand by that judgment until fact or argument be offered to convince you of your error.

III.—To a Lover

There are two descriptions of lovers on whom all advice would be wasted, namely, those in whose minds passion so wholly overpowers reason as to deprive the party of his sober senses, and those who love according to the rules of arithmetic, or measure their matrimonial expectations by the claim of the land-surveyor.

I address myself to the reader whom I suppose to be a real lover, but not so smitten as to be bereft of reason. You should never forget that marriage is a thing to last for life, and that, generally speaking, it is to make life happy or miserable.

The things which you ought to desire in a wife are chastity, sobriety, industry, frugality, cleanliness, knowledge of domestic affairs, good temper and beauty.

Chastity, perfect modesty, in word, deed, and even thought, is so essential that without it no female is fit to be a wife. If prudery mean false modesty, it is to be despised; but if it mean modesty pushed to the utmost extent, I confess that I like it. The very elements of jealousy ought to be avoided, and the only safeguard is to begin well and so render infidelity and jealousy next to impossible.

By sobriety I mean sobriety of conduct. When girls arrive at that age which turns their thoughts towards the command of a house it is time for them to cast away the levity of a child. Sobriety is a title to trustworthiness, and that is a treasure to prize above all others. But in order to possess this precious trustworthiness you must exercise your reason in the choice of a partner. If she be vain, fond of flattery, given to gadding about, coquettish, she will never be trustworthy, and you will be unjust if you expect it at her hands. But if you find in her that innate sobriety of which I have been speaking, there requires on your part confidence and trust without any limit.

An ardent-minded young man may fear that sobriety of conduct in a young woman argues a want of warmth; but my observation and experience tell me that levity, not sobriety, is, ninety-nine times out of a hundred, the companion of a want of ardent feeling.

There is no state in life in which industry in the wife is not necessary to the happiness and prosperity of the family. If she be lazy there will always be a heavy arrear of things unperformed, and this, even among the wealthy, is a great curse. But who is to tell whether a girl will make an industrious woman? There are certain outward signs, which, if attended to with care, will serve as pretty sure guides.

If you find the tongue lazy you may be nearly certain that the hands and feet are the same. The pronunciation of an industrious person is generally quick, distinct, and firm. Another mark of industry is a quick step and a tread showing that the foot comes down with a hearty good will.

Early rising is another mark of industry. It is, I should imagine, pretty difficult to keep love alive towards a woman who never sees the dew, never beholds the rising sun.

Frugality. This means the contrary of extravagance. It does not mean stinginess; it means an abstaining from all unnecessary expenditure. The outward and vulgar signs of extravagance are all the hardware which women put upon their persons. The girl who has not the sense to perceive that her person is disfigured, and not beautified by parcels of brass, tin, and other hardware stuck about her body, is too great a fool to be trusted with the purse of any man.

Cleanliness is a capital ingredient. Occasional cleanliness is not the thing that an English or American husband wants; he wants it always. A sloven in one thing is a sloven in all things. Make up your mind to a rope rather than to live with a slip-shod wife.

Knowledge of domestic affairs is so necessary in every wife that the lover ought to have it continually in his eye. A wife must not only know how things ought to be done, but how to do them. I cannot form an idea of a more unfortunate being than a girl with a mere boarding-school education and without a future to enable her to keep a servant when married. Of what use are her accomplishments?

Good temper is a very difficult thing to ascertain beforehand—smiles are so cheap. By "good temper" I do not mean easy temper—a serenity which nothing disturbs is a mark of laziness. Sulkiness, querulousness, cold indifference, pertinacity in having the last word, are bad things in a young woman, but of all the faults of temper your melancholy ladies are the worst. Most wives are at times misery-makers, but the melancholy carry it on as a regular trade.

The great use of female beauty is that it naturally tends to keep the husband in good humour with himself, to make him pleased with his bargain.

As to constancy in lovers, even when marriage has been promised, and that, too, in the most solemn manner, it is better for both parties to break off than to be coupled together with the reluctant assent of either.

IV.—To a Husband

It is as a husband that your conduct will have the greatest effect on your happiness. All in a wife, beyond her own natural disposition and education, is, nine times out of ten, the work of her husband.

First convince her of the necessity of moderation in expense; make her clearly see the justice of beginning to act upon the presumption that there are children coming. The great danger of all is beginning with a servant. The wife is young, and why is she not to work as well as her husband? If the wife be not able to do all the work to be done in the house, she ought not to have been able to marry.

The next thing to be attended to is your demeanour towards a young wife. The first frown that she receives from you is a dagger to her heart. Let nothing put you out of humour with her.

Every husband who spends his leisure time in company other than that of his wife and family tells her and them that he takes more delight in other company than in theirs. Resolve from the very first never to spend an hour from home unless business or some necessary and rational purpose demand it. If you are called away your wife ought to be fully apprised of the probable duration of the absence and of the time of return. When we consider what a young woman gives up on her wedding day, how can a just man think anything a trifle that affects her happiness?

Though these considerations may demand from us the kindest possible treatment of a wife, the husband is to expect dutiful deportment at her hands. A husband under command is the most contemptible of God's creatures. Am I recommending tyranny? Am I recommending disregard of the wife's opinions and wishes? By no means. But the very nature of things prescribes that there must be a head of every house, and an undivided authority. The wife ought to be heard, and patiently heard; she ought to be reasoned with, and, if possible, convinced; but if she remain opposed to the husband's opinion, his will must be obeyed.

I now come to that great bane of families—jealousy. One thing every husband can do in the way of prevention, and that is to give no ground for it. Few characters are more despicable than that of a jealous-headed husband, and that, not because he has grounds, but because he has not grounds.

If to be happy in the married state requires these precautions, you may ask: Is it not better to remain single? The cares and troubles of the married life are many, but are those of the single life few? Without wives men are poor, helpless mortals.

As to the expense, I firmly believe that a farmer married at twenty-five, and having ten children during the first ten years, would be able to save more money during these years than a bachelor of the same age would be able to save, on the same farm, in a like space of time. The bachelor has no one on whom he can in all cases rely. To me, no being in this world appears so wretched as he.

V.—To a Father

It is yourself that you see in your children. They are the great and unspeakable delight of your youth, the pride of your prime of life, and the props of old age. From the very beginning ensure in them, if possible, an ardent love for their mother. Your first duty towards them is resolutely to prevent their drawing the means of life from any breast but hers. That is their own; it is their birthright.

The man who is to gain a living by his labour must be drawn away from home; but this will not, if he be made of good stuff, prevent him from doing his share of the duty due to his children. There ought to be no toils, no watchings, no breakings of rest, imposed by this duty, of which he ought not to perform his full share, and that, too, without grudging. The working man, in whatever line, and whether in town or country, who spends his day of rest away from his wife and children is not worthy of the name of father.

The first thing in the rearing of children who have passed from the baby state is, as to the body, plenty of good food; and, as to the mind, constant good example in the parents. There is no other reason for the people in the American states being generally so much taller and stronger than the people in England are, but that, from their birth, they have an abundance of good food; not only of food, but of rich food. Nor is this, in any point of view, an unimportant matter, for a tall man is worth more than a short man. Good food, and plenty of it, is not more necessary to the forming of a stout and able body than to the forming of an active and enterprising spirit. Children should eat often, and as much as they like at a time. They will never take, of plain food, more than it is good for them to take.

The next thing after good and plentiful and plain food is good air. Besides sweet air, children want exercise. Even when they are babies in arms they want tossing and pulling about, and talking and singing to. They will, when they begin, take, if you let them alone, just as much exercise as nature bids them, and no more.

I am of opinion that it is injurious to the mind to press book-learning upon a child at an early age. I must impress my opinion upon every father that his children's happiness ought to be his first object; that book-learning, if it tend to militate against this, ought to be disregarded. A man may read books for ever and be an ignorant creature at last, and even the more ignorant for his reading.

And with regard to young women, everlasting book-reading is absolutely a vice. When they once get into the habit they neglect all other matters, and, in some cases, even their very dress. Attending to the affairs of the house—to the washing, the baking, the brewing, the cooking of victuals, the management of the poultry and the garden, these are their proper occupations.

VI.—To the Citizen

Having now given my advice to the youth, the man, the lover, the husband, and the father, I shall tender it to the citizen. To act well our part as citizens we ought clearly to understand what our rights are; for on our enjoyment of these depend our duties, rights going before duties, as value received goes before payments. The great right of all is the right of taking a part in the making of the laws by which we are governed.

It is the duty of every man to defend his country against an enemy, a duty imposed by the law of nature as well as by that of civil society. Yet how are you to maintain that this is the duty of every man if you deny to some men the enjoyment of a share in making the laws? The poor man has a body and a soul as well as the rich man; like the latter, he has parents, wife, and children; a bullet or a sword is as deadly to him as to the rich man; yet, notwithstanding this equality, he is to risk all, and, if he escape, he is still to be denied an equality of rights! Why are the poor to risk their lives? To uphold the laws and to protect property—property of which they are said to possess none? What! compel men to come forth and risk their lives for the protection of property, and then in the same breath tell them that they are not allowed to share in the making of the laws, because, and only because, they have no property!

Here, young man of sense and of spirit, here is the point on which you are to take your stand. There are always men enough to plead the cause of the rich, and to echo the woes of the fallen great; but be it your part to show compassion for those who labour, and to maintain their rights.

If the right to have a share in making the laws were merely a feather, if it were a fanciful thing, if it were only a speculative theory, if it were but an abstract principle, it might be considered as of little importance. But it is none of these; it is a practical matter. Who lets another man put his hand into his purse when he pleases? It is the first duty of every man to do all in his power to maintain this right of self-government where it exists, and to restore it where it has been lost. Men are in such a case labouring, not for the present day only, but for ages to come. If life should not allow them time to see their endeavours crowned, their children will see it.

DANIEL DEFOE

A Journal of the Plague Year

"A Journal of the Plague Year" appeared in 1722. In its second edition it received the title of "A History of the Plague." This book was suggested by the public anxiety caused by a fearful visitation of the plague at Marseilles in the two preceding years. As an account of the epidemic in London, it has all the vividness of Defoe's fiction, while it is acknowledged to be historically accurate. (Defoe biography, see Vol. III, p. 26.)

I.—A Stricken City

It was about the beginning of September, 1664, that I, among the rest of my neighbours, heard that the plague was returned again in Holland. We had no such thing as printed newspapers in those days to spread rumours and reports of things; but such things as these were gathered from the letters of merchants, and from them were handed about by word of mouth only. In December, two Frenchmen died of the plague in Long Acre, or, rather, at the upper end of Drury Lane. The secretaries of state got knowledge of it, and two physicians and a surgeon were ordered to go to the house and make inspection. This they did, and, finding evident tokens of the sickness upon both the bodies, they gave their opinions publicly, that they died of the plague; whereupon it was given in to the parish clerk, and he also returned them to the Hall; and it was printed in the weekly bill of mortality in the usual manner, thus:

Plague, 2; Parishes infected, 1.

The distemper spread slowly, and in the beginning of May, the city being healthy, we began to hope that as the infection was chiefly among the people at the other end of the town, it might go no further. We continued in these hopes for a few days, but it was only for a few, for the people were no more to be deceived thus; they searched the houses, and found that the plague was really spread every way, and that many died of it every day; and accordingly, in the weekly bill for the next week, the thing began to show itself. There was, indeed, but fourteen set down of the plague, but this was all knavery and collusion.

Now the weather set in hot, and from the first week in June the infection spread in a dreadful manner, and the bills rose high. Yet all that could conceal their distempers did it to prevent their neighbours shunning them, and also to prevent authority shutting up their houses.

I lived without Aldgate, midway between Aldgate church and Whitechapel Bars, and our neighbourhood continued very easy. But at the other end of the town their consternation was very great, and the richer sort of people, especially the nobility and gentry, from the west part of the city, thronged out of town with their families and servants. In Whitechapel, where I lived, nothing was to be seen but waggons and carts, with goods, women, servants, children, etc., all hurrying away. This was a very terrible and melancholy thing to see, and it filled me with very serious thoughts of the misery that was coming upon the city.

I now began to consider seriously how I should dispose of myself, whether I should resolve to stay in London, or shut up my house and flee. I had two important things before me: the carrying on of my business and shop, and the preservation of my life in so dismal a calamity. My trade was a saddler, and though a single man, I had a family of servants and a house and warehouses filled with goods, and to leave them all without any overseer had been to hazard the loss of all I had in the world.

I had resolved to go; but, one way or other, I always found that to appoint to go away was always crossed by some accident or other, so as to disappoint and put it off again; and I advise every person, in such a case, to keep his eye upon the particular providences which occur at that time, and take them as intimations from Heaven of what is his unquestioned duty to do in such a case. Add to this, that, turning over the Bible which lay before me, I cried out, "Well, I know not what to do; Lord, direct me!" and at that juncture, casting my eye down, I read: "Thou shalt not be afraid for the pestilence that walketh in darkness.... A thousand shall fall at thy side, and ten thousand at thy right hand; but it shall not come nigh thee." I scarce need tell the reader that from that moment I resolved that I would stay in the town, casting myself entirely upon the protection of the Almighty.

The court removed in the month of June, and went to Oxford, where it pleased God to preserve them; for which I cannot say they showed any great token of thankfulness, and hardly anything of reformation, though they did not want being told that their crying voices might, without breach of charity, have gone far in bringing that terrible judgment upon the whole nation.

A blazing star or comet had appeared for several months before the plague, and there had been universal melancholy apprehensions of some dreadful calamity. The people were at this time more addicted to prophecies, dreams, and old wives' fables, than ever they were before or since. Some ran about the streets with oral predictions, one crying, "Yet forty days, and London shall be destroyed!" Another poor naked creature cried, "Oh, the great and dreadful God!" repeating these words continually, with voice and countenance full of horror, and a swift pace, and nobody could ever find him to stop. Some saw a flaming sword in a hand coming out of a cloud; others, hearses and coffins in the air; others, heaps of dead bodies unburied. But those who were really serious and religious applied themselves in a truly Christian manner to the proper work of repentance and humiliation. Many consciences were awakened, many hard hearts melted into tears. People might be heard in the streets as we passed along, calling upon God for mercy, and saying, "I have been a thief," or "a murderer," and the like; and none dared stop to make the least inquiry into such things, or to comfort the poor creatures that thus cried out. The face of London was now strangely altered; it was all in tears; the shrieks of women and children at the windows and doors, where their dearest relations were dead, were enough to pierce the stoutest heart.

About June, the lord mayor and aldermen began more particularly to concern themselves for the regulation of the city, by the shutting up of houses. Examiners were appointed in every parish to order the house to be shut up wherever any person sick of the infection was found. A night watchman and a day watchman were appointed to each infected house to prevent any person from coming out or going into the same. Women searchers were appointed in each parish to examine the bodies of such as were dead, to see if they had died of the infection, and over these were appointed physicians and chirurgeons. Other orders were made with regard to giving notice of sickness, sequestration of the sick, airing the goods and bedding of the infected, burial of the dead, cleansing of the streets, forbidding wandering beggars, loose persons, and idle assemblages, and the like. One of these orders was—"That every house visited be marked with a red cross of a foot long, in the middle of the door, with these words, 'Lord have mercy upon us,' to be set close over the same cross." Many got out of their houses by stratagem after they were shut up, and thus spread the plague; in one place they blowed up their watchman with gunpowder and burnt the poor fellow dreadfully, and while he made hideous cries, the whole family got out at the windows; others got out by bribing the watchman, and I have seen three watchmen publicly whipped through the streets for suffering people to go out.

II.—How the Dead Were Buried

I went all the first part of the time freely about the streets, and when they dug the great pit in the churchyard of Aldgate I could not resist going to see it. A terrible pit it was, forty feet long, about sixteen wide, and in one part they dug it to near twenty feet deep, until they could go no deeper for the water. It was filled in just two weeks, when they had thrown into it 1,114 bodies from our own parish.

I got admittance into the churchyard by the sexton, who at first refused me, but at last said: "Name of God, go in; depend upon it, 'twill be a sermon to you, it may be the best that ever you heard. It is a speaking sight," says he; and with that he opened the door and said, "Go, if you will." I stood wavering for a good while, but just at that interval I saw two links come over from the end of the Minories, and heard the bellman, and then appeared a dead-cart coming over the streets, so I went in.

The scene was awful and full of terror. The cart had in it sixteen or seventeen bodies; some were wrapped in sheets or rugs, some little other than naked, or so loose that what covering they had fell from them in the shooting out of the cart, and they fell quite naked among the rest. But the matter was not much to them, seeing they were all dead, and were to be huddled together into the common grave of mankind, as we may call it; for here was no difference made, but poor and rich went together. The cart was turned round, and the bodies shot into the pit promiscuously.

There was following the cart a poor unhappy gentleman who fell down in a swoon when the bodies were shot into the pit. The buriers ran to him and took him up, and after he had come to himself, they led him away to the Pye tavern, over against the end of Houndsditch. His case lay so heavy on my mind that after I had gone home I must go out again into the street and go to the Pye tavern, to inquire what became of him.

It was by this time one in the morning, and yet the poor gentleman was there. The people of the house were civil and obliging, but there was a dreadful set of fellows that used their house, and who, in the middle of all this horror, met there every night, and behaved with revelling and roaring extravagances, so that the master and mistress of the house were terrified at them. They sat in a room next the street, and as often as the dead-cart came along, they would open the windows and make impudent mocks and jeers at the sad lamentations of the people, especially if they heard the poor people call upon God to have mercy upon them.

They were at this vile work when I came to the house, ridiculing the unfortunate man, and his sorrow for his wife and children, taunting him with want of courage to leap into the pit and go to Heaven with them, and adding profane and blasphemous expressions.

I gently reproved them, being not unknown to two of them. But I cannot call to mind the abominable raillery which they returned to me, making a jest of my calling the plague the Hand of God. They continued this wretched course three or four days; but they were, every one of them, carried into the great pit before it was quite filled up.

In my walks I had daily many dismal scenes before my eyes, as of persons falling dead in the streets, terrible shrieks and screechings of women, and the like. Passing through Tokenhouse Yard, in Lothbury, of a sudden a casement violently opened just over my head, and a woman gave three frightful screeches, and then cried: "Oh Death! Death! Death!" in a most inimitable tone, which struck me with horror and a chillness in my very blood. There was nobody to be seen in the whole street, neither did any other window open; for people had no curiosity now, nor could anybody help another. I went on into Bell Alley.

Just in Bell Alley, at the right hand of the passage, there was a more terrible cry than that, and I could hear women and children run screaming about the rooms distracted. A garret window opened, and somebody from a window on the other side of the alley called and asked, "What is the matter?" upon which, from the first window it was answered: "O Lord, my old master has hanged himself!" The other asked again: "Is he quite dead?" And the first answered, "Ay, ay, quite dead—quite dead and cold."

It is scarce credible what dreadful things happened every day, people in the rage of the distemper, or in the torment of their swellings, which was indeed intolerable, oftentimes laying violent hands on themselves, throwing themselves out at their windows, etc.; mothers murdering their own children in their lunacy; some dying of mere fright, without any infection; others frightened into despair, idiocy, or madness.

There were a great many robberies and wicked practices committed even in this dreadful time. The power of avarice was so strong in some that they would run any hazard to steal and to plunder; and in houses where all the inhabitants had died and been carried out, they would break in without regard to the danger of infection, and take even the bedclothes.

III.—Universal Desolation

For about a month together, I believe there did not die less than 1,500 or 1,700 a day, one day with another; and in the beginning of September good people began to think that God was resolved to make a full end of the people in this miserable city. Whole families, and, indeed, whole streets of families were swept away together, and the infection was so increased that at length they shut up no houses at all. People gave themselves up to their fears, and thought that nothing was to be hoped for but an universal desolation. It was even in the height of this despair that it pleased God to stay His hand, and to slacken the fury of the contagion.

When the people despaired of life and abandoned themselves, it had a very strange effect for three or four weeks; it made them bold and venturous; they were no more shy of one another, nor restrained within doors, but went anywhere and everywhere, and ran desperately into any company. It brought them to crowd into the churches; looking on themselves as all so many dead corpses, they behaved as if their lives were of no consequence, compared to the work which they came about there.

The conduct of the lord mayor and magistrates was all the time admirable, so that bread was always to be had in plenty, and cheap as usual; provisions were never wanting in the markets; the streets were kept free from all manner of frightful objects—dead bodies, or anything unpleasant; and for a time fires were kept burning in the streets to cleanse the air of infection.

Many remedies were tried; but it is my opinion, and I must leave it as a prescription, that the best physic against the plague is to run away from it. I know people encourage themselves by saying, "God is able to keep us in the midst of danger," and this kept thousands in the town, whose carcasses went into the great pits by cart-loads. Yet of the pious ladies who went about distributing alms to the poor, and visiting infected families, though I will not undertake to say that none of those charitable people were suffered to fall under the calamity, yet I may say this, that I never knew any of them to fall under it.

Such is the precipitant disposition of our people, that no sooner had they observed that the distemper was not so catching as formerly, and that if it was catched it was not so mortal, and that abundance of people who really fell sick recovered again daily, than they made no more of the plague than of an ordinary fever, nor indeed so much. They went into the very chambers where others lay sick. This rash conduct cost a great many their lives, who had been preserved all through the heat of the infection, and the bills of mortality increased again four hundred in the first week of November.

But it pleased God, by the continuing of wintry weather, so to restore the health of the city that by February following we reckoned the distemper quite ceased. The time was not far off when the city was to be purged with fire, for within nine months more I saw it all lying in ashes.

I shall conclude the account of this calamitous year with a stanza of my own:

> A dreadful plague in London was
> In the year sixty-five,
> Which swept an hundred thousand souls
> Away; yet I alive!

DEMOSTHENES

The Philippics

Demosthenes, by universal consensus of opinion the greatest orator the world has known, was born at Athens 385 B.C. and died 322 B.C. His birth took place just nineteen years after the conclusion of the Peloponnesian War. Losing his father when he was yet a child, his wealth was frittered away by three faithless guardians, whom he prosecuted when he came of age. This dispute, and some other struggles, led him into public life, and by indomitable perseverance he overcame the difficulty constituted by certain physical disqualifications. Identifying himself for life entirely with the interests of Athens, he became the foremost administrator in the state, as well as its most eloquent orator. His stainless character, his matchless powers of advocacy, his fervent patriotism, and his fine diplomacy, render him altogether one of the noblest figures of antiquity. His fame rests mainly on "The Philippics"; those magnificent orations delivered during a series of several years against the aggressions of Philip of Macedon; though the three "Olynthiacs," and the oration "De Coronâ," and several other speeches are monumental of the genius of Demosthenes, more especially the "De Coronâ." He continued to resist the Macedonian domination during the career of Alexander the Great, and was exiled, dying, it is supposed, by poison administered by himself, at Calauria. (Cf. also p. 273 of this volume.) This epitome has been prepared from the original Greek.

I.—"Men of Athens, Arouse Yourselves!"

The subject under discussion on this occasion, men of Athens, is not new, and there would be no need to speak further on it if other orators deliberated wisely. First, I advise you not to regard the present aspect of affairs, miserable though it truly is, as entirely hopeless. For the primary cause of the failure is your own mismanagement. If any consider it difficult to overcome Philip because of the power that he has attained, and because of our disastrous loss of many fortresses, they should remember how much he has gained by achieving alliances.

If, now, you will emulate his policy, if every citizen will devote himself assiduously to the service of his country, you will assuredly recover all that has been lost, and punish Philip. For he has his enemies, even among his pretended friends. All dread him because your inertia has prevented you from providing any refuge for them. Hence the height of arrogance which he now displays and the constantly expanding area of his conquests.

When, men of Athens, will you realise that your attitude is the cause of this situation? For you idle about, indulging in gossip over circumstances, instead of grappling with the actualities. Were this antagonist to pass away, another enemy like him would speedily be produced by your policy, for Philip is what he is not so much through his own prowess as through your own indifference.

As to the plan of action to be initiated, I say that we must inaugurate it by providing fifty triremes, also the cavalry and transports and boats needed for the fleet. Thus we should be fully prepared to cope with the sudden excursions of Philip to Thermopylæ or any other point. Besides this naval force, you should equip an army of 2,000 foot soldiers, of whom 500 should be Athenians, the remainder mercenaries, together with 250 cavalry, including 50 Athenians. Lastly, we should have an auxiliary naval contingent of ten swift galleys.

We are now conducting affairs farcically. For we act neither as if we were at peace, nor as if we had entered on a war. You enlist your soldiers not for warfare, but for religious pageants, and for parades and processions in the market-place. We must consolidate our resources, embody permanent forces, not temporary levies hastily enlisted, and we must secure winter quarters for our troops in those islands which possess harbours and granaries for the corn.

No longer, men of Athens, must you continue the mere discussion of measures without ever executing any of your projects. Remember that Philip sustains his power by drawing on the resources of your own allies.

But by adopting my plan you will at one and the same time deprive him of his chief sources of supply, and place yourselves out of the reach of danger. The policy he has hitherto pursued will be effectually thwarted. No longer will he be able to capture your citizens, as he did by attacking Lemnos and Imbros, or to seize your Paralus, as he did on his descent at Marathon.

But, men of Athens, you spend far larger sums of money on the splendid Panathenaic and Dionysian festivals than on your naval and military armaments. Moreover, those festivals are always punctually celebrated, while your preparations for war are always behindhand. Then, when a critical juncture arrives, we find our forces are totally inadequate to the emergency.

Having larger resources than any other state, you, Athenians, have never adequately availed yourselves of them. You never anticipate the movements of Philip, but simply drift after him, sending forces to Thermopylæ if you hear he is there, or to any other quarter where he may happen to be. Such policy might formerly be excused, but now it is as disgraceful as it is intolerable. Are we to wait for Philip's aggressiveness to cease? It never will do so unless we resist it. Shall we not assume the offensive and descend on his coast with some of our forces?

Nothing will result from mere oratory and from mutual recrimination among ourselves. My own conviction is that Philip is encouraged by our inertia, and that he is carried away by his own successes, but that he has no fixed plan of action that can be guessed by foolish chatterers. Men of Athens, let us for the future abandon such an attitude, and let us bear in mind that we must depend not on the help of others, but on ourselves alone. Unless we go to attack Philip where he is, Philip will come to attack us where we are.

II. — Beware the Guile of Philip

Nothing, men of Athens, is done as a sequel to the speeches which are delivered and approved concerning the outrageous proceedings of Philip. You are earnest in discussion; he is earnest in action. If we are to be complacently content because we employ the better arguments, well and good; but if we are successfully to resist this formidable and increasing power, we must be prepared to entertain advice that is salutary, however unpalatable, rather than counsel which is easy and pleasant.

If you give me any credit for clear perception, I beg you to attend to what I plead. After subduing Thermopylæ and the Phocians, Philip quickly apprehended that you could not be induced by any selfish considerations to abandon other Greek states to him. The Thebans, Messenians, and Argives he lured by bribes. But he knew how, in the past, your predecessors scorned the overtures of his ancestor, Alexander of Macedon, sent by Mardonius the Persian to induce the Athenians to betray the rest of the Greeks. It was not so with the Argives and the Thebans, and thus Philip calculates that their successors will care nothing for the interests of the Greeks generally. So he favours them, but not you.

Everything demonstrates Philip's animosity against Athens. He is instinctively aware that you are conscious of his plots against you, and ascribes to you a feeling of hatred against him. Eager to be beforehand with us, he continues to negotiate with Thebans and Peloponnesians, assuming that they may be beguiled with ease.

I call to mind how I addressed the Messenians and the Argives, reminding them how Philip had dishonourably given certain of their territories to the Olynthians. Would the Olynthians then have listened to any disparagements of Philip? Assuredly not. Yet they were soon shamefully betrayed and cheated by him. It is unsafe for commonwealths to place confidence in despots. In like manner were the Thessalians deceived when he had ejected their tyrants and had restored to them Nicasa and Magnesia, for he instituted the new tyranny of the Decemvirate. Philip is equally ready with gifts and promises on the one hand, and with fraud and deceit on the other.

"By Jupiter," said I to those auditors, "the only infallible defence of democracies against despots is the absolute refusal of all confidence in them. Always to mistrust them is the only safeguard. What is it that you seek to secure? Liberty? Then do you not perceive that the very titles worn by Philip prove him to be adverse to this? For every king and tyrant is an enemy to freedom and an opponent to laws."

But though my speeches and those of other emissaries were received with vociferous applause, all the same those who thus manifested profound approbation will never be able to resist the blandishments and overtures of Philip. It may well be so with those other Greeks. But you, O Athenians, surely should understand your own interests better. For otherwise irreparable disaster must ensue.

In justice, men of Athens, you should summon the men who communicated to you the promises which induced you to consent to peace. Their statements misled us; otherwise, neither would I have gone as ambassador, nor would you have ceased hostilities. Also, you should call those who, after my return from my second embassy, contradicted my report. I then protested against the abandonment of Thermopylæ and of the Phocians.

They ridiculed me as a water-drinker, and they persuaded you that Philip would cede to you Oropus and Eubœa in exchange for Amphipolis, and also that he would humble the Thebans and at his own charges cut through the Chersonese. Your anger will be excited in due time when you realise what you have hitherto disregarded, namely, that these projects on the part of Philip are devised against Athens.

Though all know it only too well, let me remind you who it was, even Æschines himself, who induced you by his persuasion to abandon Thermopylæ and Phocis. By possessing control over these, Philip now commands also the road to Attica and Peloponnesus.

Hence the present situation is this, that you must now consider, not distant affairs, but the means of defending your homes and of conducting a war in Attica, that war having become inevitable through those events, grievous though it will be to every citizen when it begins. May the gods grant that the worst fears be not fully confirmed!

III.—Athens Must Head the War

Various circumstances, men of Athens, have reduced our affairs to the worst possible state, this lamentable crisis being due mainly to the specious orators who seek rather to please you than wisely to guide you. Flattery has generated perilous complacency, and now the position is one of extreme danger. I am willing either to preserve silence, or to speak frankly, according to your disposition. Yet all may be repaired if you awaken to your duty, for Philip has not conquered you; you have simply made no real effort against him.

Strange to say, while Philip is actually seizing cities and appropriating various portions of our territory, some among us affirm that there is really no war. Thus, caution is needed in speech, for those who suggest defensive measures may afterwards be indicted for causing hostilities. Now, let those who maintain that we are at peace propose a resolution for suitable plans. But if you are invaded by an armed aggressor, who pretends to be at peace with you, what can you do but initiate measures of defence?

Both sides may profess to be at peace, and I do not demur; but it is madness to style that a condition of peace which allows Philip to subjugate all other states and then to assail you last of all. His method of proceeding is to prepare to attack you, while securing immunity from the danger of being attacked by you.

If we wait for him to declare war, we wait in vain. For he will treat us as he did the Olynthians and the Phocians. Professing to be their ally, he appropriated territories belonging to them. Do you imagine he would declare war against you before commencing operations of encroachment? Never, so long as he knows that you are willing to be deceived.

By a series of operations he has been infringing the peace: by his attempt to seize Megara, by his intervention in Euboea, by his excursion into Thrace. I reckon that the virtual beginnings of hostilities must be dated from the day that he completed the subjugation of the Thracians. From your other orators I differ in deeming any discussion irrelevant respecting the Chersonese or Byzantium. Aid these, indeed; but let the safety of all Greece alike be the subject of your deliberations.

What I would emphasise is that to Philip have been conceded liberties of encroachment and aggression, by you first of all, such as in former days were always contested by war. He has attacked and enslaved city after city of the Greeks. You Athenians were for seventy-three years the supreme leaders in Hellas, as were the Spartans for twenty-nine years. Then after the battle of Leuctra the Thebans acquired paramount influence. But neither you nor these others ever arrogated the right to act according to your pleasure.

If you appeared to act superciliously towards any state, all the other states sided with that one which was aggrieved. Yet all the errors committed by our predecessors and by those of the Spartans during the whole of that century were trivial compared with the wrongs perpetrated by Philip during these thirteen years. Cruel has been his destruction of Olynthus, of Methone, of Apollonia, and of thirty-two cities on the borders of Thrace, and also the extermination of the Phocians. And now he domineers ruthlessly over Thessaly and Euboea. Yet all we Greeks of various nationalities are in so abjectly miserable a condition that, instead of arranging embassies and declaring our indignation, we entrench ourselves in isolation in our several cities.

It must be reflected that when wrongs were inflicted by other states, by us or the Spartans, these faults were at any rate committed by genuine sons of Greece. How much more hateful is the offence when perpetrated against a household by a slave or an alien than by a son or other member of the family! But Philip is not only no son of Hellas; he is not even a reputable barbarian, but only a vile fellow of Macedon, a country from which formerly even a respectable slave could not be purchased!

What is lacking to his unspeakable arrogance? Does he not assemble the Pythian games, command Thermopylæ, garrison the passes, secure prior access to the oracle at Delphi, and dictate the form of government for Thessaly? All this the Greeks look upon with toleration; they seem to regard it as they would some tempest, each hoping it will fall on someone else. We are all passive and despondent, mutually distrusting each other instead of the common foe.

How different the noble spirit of former days! How different that old passion for liberty which is now superseded by the love of servitude! Then corruption was so deeply detested that there was no pardon for the guilt of bribery. Now venality is laughed at and bribery goes unpunished. In ships, men, equipment, and revenues our resources are larger than ever before, but corruption neutralises them all.

But preparations for war are not sufficient. You must not only be ready to encounter the foes without, but must punish those who among you are the creatures of Philip, like those who caused the ruin of Olynthus by betraying the cavalry and by securing the banishment of Apollonides. Similar treachery brought about the downfall of other cities. The same fate may befall us. What, then, must be done?

When we have done all that is needful for our own defence, let us next send our emissaries to all the other states with the intelligence that we are ready. If you imagine that others will save Greece while you avoid the conflict, you cherish a fatal delusion. This enterprise devolves on you; you inherit it from your ancestors.

IV.—Exterminate the Traitors!

Men of Athens, your chief misfortune is that, though for the passing moment you heed important news, you speedily scatter and forget what you have just heard. You have become fully acquainted with the doings of Philip, and you well know how great is his ambition; and yet, so profound has been our indifference that we have earned the contempt of several other states, which now prefer to undertake their defence separately rather than in alliance with us.

You must become more deeply convinced than you have been hitherto that our destruction is the supreme anxiety of Philip. The special object of his hatred is your democratic constitution. Our mode of procedure is a mockery, for we are always behind in the execution of our schemes. You must form a permanent army with a regular organisation, and with funds sufficient for its maintenance.

Most of all, money is needed to meet coming requirements. There was a time when money was forthcoming and everything necessary was performed. Why do we now decline to do our duty? In a time of peril to the commonwealth the affluent should freely contribute of their possessions for the welfare of the country; but each class has its obligations to the state and should observe them.

Many and inveterate are the causes of our present difficulties. You, O Athenians, have surrendered the august position which your predecessors bequeathed you, and have indolently permitted a stranger to usurp it. The present crisis involves peril for all the states, but to Athens most of all; and that not so much on account of Philip's schemes of conquest, as of your neglect.

How is it, Athenians, that none affirm concerning Philip that he is guilty of aggression, even while he is seizing cities, while those who advise resistance are indicated as inciting to war? The reason is that those who have been corrupted believe that if you do resist him you will overcome him, and they can no longer secure the reward of treachery.

Remember what you have at stake. Should you fall under the dominion of Philip, he will show you no pity, for his desire is not merely to subdue Athens, but to destroy it. The struggle will be to the death; therefore, those who would sell the country to him you must exterminate without scruple. This is the only city where such treacherous citizens can dare to speak in his favour. Only here may a man safely accept a bribe and openly address the people.

RALPH WALDO EMERSON

English Traits

In 1847 Emerson (see Vol. XIII, p. 339) made his second visit to England, this time on a lecturing tour. An outcome of the visit was "English Traits," which was first published in 1856. "I leave England," he wrote on his return home, "with an increased respect for the Englishman. His stuff or substance seems to be the best in the world." "English Traits" deals with a series of definite subjects which do not admit of much philosophic digression, and there is, therefore, an absence of the flashes of spiritual and poetic insight which gave Emerson his charm.

I.—*The Anchorage of Britain*

I did not go very willingly to England. I am not a good traveller, nor have I found that long journeys yield a fair share of reasonable hours. I find a sea-life an acquired taste, like that for tomatoes and olives. The sea is masculine, the type of active strength. Look what egg-shells are drifting all over it, each one filled with men in ecstasies of terror alternating with cockney conceit, as it is rough or smooth. But to the geologist the sea is the only firmament; it is the land that is in perpetual flux and change. It has been said that the King of England would consult his dignity by giving audience to foreign ambassadors in the cabin of a man-of-war; and I think the white path of an Atlantic ship is the right avenue to the palace-front of this seafaring people.

England is a garden. Under an ash-coloured sky, the fields have been combed and rolled till they appear to have been finished with a pencil instead of a plough. Rivers, hills, valleys, the sea itself, feel the hand of a master. The problem of the traveller landing in Liverpool is, Why England is England? What are the elements of that power which the English hold over other nations? If there be one test of national genius universally accepted, it is success; and if there be one successful country in the universe that country is England.

The culture of the day, the thoughts and aims of men, are English thoughts and aims. A nation considerable for a thousand years has in the last centuries obtained the ascendant, and stamped the knowledge, activity, and power of mankind with its impress.

The territory has a singular perfection. Neither hot nor cold, there is no hour in the whole year when one cannot work. The only drawback to industrial conveniency is the darkness of the sky. The night and day are too nearly of a colour.

England resembles a ship in shape, and, if it were one, its best admiral could not have anchored it in a more judicious or effective position. The shop-keeping nation, to use a shop word, has a good stand. It is anchored at the side of Europe, and right in the heart of the modern world.

In variety of surface Britain is a miniature of Europe, as if Nature had given it an artificial completeness. It is as if Nature had held counsel with herself and said: "My Romans are gone. To build my new empire I will choose a rude race, all masculine, with brutish strength. Sharp and temperate northern breezes shall blow to keep them alive and alert. The sea shall disjoin the people from others and knit them by a fierce nationality. Long time will I keep them on their feet, by poverty, border-wars, seafaring, sea-risks, and stimulus of gain." A singular coincidence to this geographic centrality is the spiritual centrality which Emanuel Swedenborg ascribes to the people: "The English nation are in the centre of all Christians, because they have an interior intellectual light. This light they derive from the liberty of speaking and writing, and thereby of thinking."

II.—Racial Characteristics

The British Empire is reckoned to contain a fifth of the population of the globe; but what makes the British census proper important is the quality of the units that compose it. They are free, forcible men in a country where life has reached the greatest value. They have sound bodies and supreme endurance in war and in labour. They have assimilating force, since they are imitated by their foreign subjects; and they are still aggressive and propagandist, enlarging the dominion of their arts and liberty.

The English composite character betrays a mixed origin. Everything English is a fusion of distant and antagonistic elements. The language is mixed; the currents of thought are counter; contemplation and practical skill; active intellect and dead conservatism; world-wide enterprise and devoted use and wont; a country of extremes—nothing in it can be praised without damning exceptions, and nothing denounced without salvos of cordial praise.

The sources from which tradition derives its stock are mainly three: First, the Celtic—a people of hidden and precarious genius; second, the Germans, a people about whom, in the old empire, the rumour ran there was never any that meddled with them that repented it not; and, third, the Norsemen and the children out of France. Twenty thousand thieves landed at Hastings. These founders of the House of Lords were greedy and ferocious dragoons, sons of greedy and ferocious pirates. Such, however, is the illusion of antiquity and wealth that decent and dignified men now existing actually boast their descent from these filthy thieves.

As soon as this land, thus geographically posted, got a hardy people into it, they could not help becoming the sailors and factors of the world. The English, at the present day, have great vigour of body. They are round, ruddy, and handsome, with a tendency to stout and powerful frames. It is the fault of their forms that they grow stocky, but in all ages they are a handsome race, and please by an expression blending good nature, valour, refinement, and an uncorrupt youth in the face of manhood.

The English are rather manly than warlike. They delight in the antagonism which combines in one person the extremes of courage and tenderness. Nelson, dying at Trafalgar, says, "Kiss me, Hardy," and turns to sleep. Even for their highwaymen this virtue is claimed, and Robin Hood is the gentlest thief. But they know where their war-dogs lie, and Cromwell, Blake, Marlborough, Nelson, and Wellington are not to be trifled with.

They have vigorous health and last well into middle and old age. They have more constitutional energy than any other people. They box, run, shoot, ride, row, and sail from Pole to Pole. They are the most voracious people of prey that have ever existed, and they have written the game-books of all countries.

These Saxons are the hands of mankind—the world's wealth-makers. They have that temperament which resists every means employed to make its possessor subservient to others. The English game is main force to main force, the planting of foot to foot, fair play and an open field—a rough tug without trick or dodging till one or both comes to pieces. They hate craft and subtlety; and when they have pounded each other to a poultice they will shake hands and be friends for the remainder of their lives.

Their realistic logic of coupling means to ends has given them the leadership of the modern world. Montesquieu said: "No people have true commonsense but those who are born in England." This commonsense is a perception of laws that cannot be stated, or that are learned only by practice, with allowance for friction. The bias of the nation is a passion for utility. They are heavy at the fine arts, but adroit at the coarse. The Frenchman invented the ruffle, the Englishman added the shirt. They think him the best-dressed man whose dress is so fit for his use that you cannot notice or remember to describe it.

In war the Englishman looks to his means; but, conscious that no better race of men exists, they rely most on the simplest means. They fundamentally believe that the best stratagem in naval war is to bring your ship alongside of the enemy's ship, and bring all your guns to bear on him until you or he go to the bottom. This is the old fashion which never goes out of fashion.

Tacitus said of the Germans: "Powerful only in sudden efforts, they are impatient of toil and labour." This highly destined race, if it had not somewhere added the chamber of patience to its brain, would not have built London. I know not from which of the tribes and temperaments that went to the composition of the people this tenacity was supplied, but they clinch every nail they drive. "To show capacity," a Frenchman described as the end of speech in a debate. "No," said an Englishman, "but to advance the business."

The nation sits in the immense city they have builded—a London extended into every man's mind. The modern world is theirs. They have made and make it day by day. In every path of practical ability they have gone even with the best. There is no department of literature, of science, or of useful art in which they have not produced a first-rate book. It is England whose opinion is waited for. English trade exists to make well everything which is ill-made elsewhere. Steam is almost an Englishman.

One secret of the power of this people is their mutual good understanding. Not only good minds are born among them, but all the people have good minds. An electric touch by any of their national ideas melts them into one family. The chancellor carries England on his mace, the midshipman at the point of his dirk, the smith on his hammer, the cook in the bowl of his spoon, and the sailor times his oars to "God save the King!"

I find the Englishman to be him of all men who stands firmest in his shoes. The one thing the English value is pluck. The word is not beautiful, but on the quality they signify by it the nation is unanimous. The cabmen have it, the merchants have it, the bishops have it, the women have it, the journals have it. They require you to dare to be of your own opinion, and they hate the practical cowards who cannot answer directly Yes or No.

Their vigour appears in the incuriosity and stony neglect each of the other. Each man walks, eats, drinks, shaves, dresses, gesticulates, and in every manner acts and suffers, without reference to the bystanders— he is really occupied with his own affairs, and does not think of them.

In short, every one of these islanders is an island himself, safe, tranquil, incommunicable.

Born in a harsh and wet climate, which keeps him indoors whenever he is at rest, and, being of an affectionate and loyal temper, the Englishman dearly loves his home. If he is rich he builds a hall, and brings to it trophies of the adventures and exploits of the family, till it becomes a museum of heirlooms. England produces, under favourable conditions of ease and culture, the finest women in the world. Nothing can be more delicate without being fantastical, than the courtship and mutual carriage of the sexes. Domesticity is the taproot which enables the nation to branch wide and high. In an aristocratical country like England, not the trial by jury, but the dinner is the capital institution. It is the mode of doing honour to a stranger to ask him to eat.

The practical power of the English rests on their sincerity. Alfred, whom the affection of the nation makes the type of their race, is called by a writer at the Norman Conquest, the "truth-speaker." The phrase of the lowest of the people is "honour-bright," and their praise, "his word is as good as his bond." They confide in each other—English believes in English. Madame de Staël says that the English irritated Napoleon mainly because they have found out how to unite success with honesty. The ruling passion of an Englishman is a terror of humbug.

The English race are reputed morose. They have enjoyed a reputation for taciturnity for six or seven hundred years. Cold, repressive manners prevail, and there is a wooden deadness in certain Englishmen which surpasses all other countrymen. In the power of saying rude truth no men rival them. They are proud and private, and even if disposed to recreation will avoid an open garden. They are full of coarse strength, butcher's meat, and sound sleep. They are good lovers, good haters, slow but obstinate admirers, and very much steeped in their temperament, like men hardly awaked from deep sleep which they enjoy.

The English have a mild aspect, and ringing, cheerful voice. Of absolute stoutness of spirit, no nation has more or better examples. They are good at storming redoubts, at boarding frigates, at dying in the last ditch, or any desperate service which has daylight and honour in it. They stoutly carry into every nook and corner of the earth their turbulent sense of inquiry, leaving no lie uncontradicted, no pretension unexamined.

They are very conscious of their advantageous position in history. I suppose that all men of English blood in America, Europe, or Asia, have a secret feeling of joy that they are not Frenchmen. They only are not foreigners. In short, I am afraid that the English nature is so rank and aggressive as to be a little incompatible with any other. The world is not wide enough for two. More intellectual than other races, when they live with other races they do not take their language, but bestow their own. They subsidise other nations, and are not subsidised. They proselytise and are not proselytised. They assimilate other nations to themselves and are not assimilated.

III. — Wealth, Aristocracy, and Religion

There is no country in which so absolute a homage is paid to wealth. There is a mixture of religion in it. The Englishman esteems wealth a final certificate. He believes that every man has himself to thank if he does not mend his condition. To pay their debts is their national point of honour. The British armies are solvent, and pay for what they take. The British empire is solvent. It is their maxim that the weight of taxes must be calculated not by what is taken but by what is left. They say without shame: "I cannot afford it." Such is their enterprise, that there is enough wealth in England to support the entire population in idleness one year. The proudest result of this creation of wealth is that great and refined forces are put at the disposal of the private citizen, and in the social world the Englishman to-day has the best lot. I much prefer the condition of an English gentleman of the better class to that of any potentate in Europe.

The feudal character of the English state, now that it is getting obsolete, glares a little in contrast with democratic tendencies. But the frame of society is aristocratic. Every man who becomes rich buys land, and does what he can to fortify the nobility, into which he hopes to rise. The taste of the people is conservative. They are proud of the castles, language, and symbols of chivalry. English history is aristocracy with the doors open. Who has courage and faculty, let him come in.

All nobility in its beginnings was somebody's natural superiority. The things these English have done were not done without peril of life, nor without wisdom of conduct, and the first hands, it may be presumed, were often challenged to show their right to their honours, or yield them to better men.

Comity, social talent, and fine manners no doubt have had their part also. The lawyer, the farmer, the silk mercer lies *perdu* under the coronet, and winks to the antiquary to say nothing. They were nobody's sons who did some piece of work at a nice moment.

The English names are excellent—they spread an atmosphere of legendary melody over the land. Older than epics and histories, which clothe a nation, this undershirt sits close to the body. What stores of primitive and savage observation it infolds! Cambridge is the bridge of the Cam;

Sheffield the field of the river Sheaf; Leicester the camp of Lear; Waltham is Strong Town; Radcliffe is Red Cliff, and so on—a sincerity and use in naming very striking to an American, whose country is whitewashed all over with unmeaning names, the cast-off clothes of the country from which the emigrants came, or named at a pinch from a psalm tune.

In seeing old castles and cathedrals I sometimes say: "This was built by another and a better race than any that now look on it." Their architecture still glows with faith in immortality. Good churches are not built by bad men; at least, there must be probity and enthusiasm somewhere in society.

England felt the full heat of the Christianity which fermented Europe, and, like the chemistry of fire, drew a firm line between barbarism and culture. When the Saxon instinct had secured a service in the vernacular tongue the Church was the tutor and university of the people.

Now the Anglican Church is marked by the grace and good sense of its forms; by the manly grace of its clergy. The gospel it preaches is "By taste are ye saved." The religion of England is part of good breeding. When you see on the Continent the well-dressed Englishman come into his ambassador's chapel and put his face for silent prayer into his well-brushed hat, you cannot help feeling how much national pride prays with him, and the religion of a gentleman.

At this moment the Church is much to be pitied. If a bishop meets an intelligent gentleman and reads fatal interrogation in his eyes, he has no resource but to take wine with him.

But the religion of England—is it the Established Church? No. Is it the sects? No. Where dwells the religion? Tell me first where dwells electricity, or motion, or thought? They do not dwell or stay at all. Electricity is passing, glancing, gesticular; it is a traveller, a newness, a secret. Yet, if religion be the doing of all good, and for its sake the suffering of all evil, that divine secret has existed in England from the days of Alfred to the days of Florence Nightingale, and in thousands who have no fame.

Representative Men

Some of the lectures delivered by Emerson during his lecturing tour in England were published in 1850 under the title of "Representative Men," and the main trend of their thought and opinion is here followed in Emerson's own words. It will be noted that the use of the term "sceptic," as applied to Montaigne, is not the ordinary use of the word, but signifies a person spontaneously given to free inquiry rather than aggressive disbelief. The estimate of Napoleon is original. In "Representative Men" Emerson is much more consecutive in his thought than is customary with him. His pearls are as plentiful here as elsewhere, but they are not scattered disconnectedly.

Plato

Among secular books, Plato only is entitled to Omar's fanatical compliment to the Koran: "Burn all books, for their value is in this book." Out of Plato come all things that are still written and debated among men of thought. Plato is philosophy, and philosophy Plato. No wife, no children had he, but the thinkers of all civilised nations are his posterity, and are tinged with his mind.

Great geniuses have the shortest biographies. They lived in their writings, and so their house and street life is commonplace. Their cousins can tell you nothing about them. Plato, especially, has no external biography.

Plato stands between the truth and every man's mind, and has almost impressed language and the primary forms of thought with his name and seal.

The first period of a nation, as of an individual, is the period of unconscious strength. Children cry, scream, and stamp with fury, unable to express their desires. As soon as they can speak and tell their wants they become gentle. With nations he is as a god to them who can rightly divide and define. This defining is philosophy. Philosophy is the account which the human mind gives to itself of the constitution of the world.

Two cardinal facts lie ever at the base of thought: Unity and Variety — oneness and otherness.

To this partiality the history of nations corresponds. The country of unity, faithful to the idea of a deaf, unimplorable, immense fate, is Asia; on the other side, the genius of Europe is active and creative. If the East loves infinity, the West delights in boundaries. Plato came to join and enhance the energy of each. The excellence of Europe and Asia is in his brain. No man ever more fully acknowledged the Ineffable; but having paid his homage, as for the human race, to the illimitable, he then stood erect, and for the human race affirmed: "And yet things are knowable!" Full of the genius of Europe, he said "Culture," he said "Nature," but he failed not to add, "There is also the divine."

This leads us to the central figure which he has established in his academy. Socrates and Plato are the double-star which the most powerful instrument will not entirely separate. Socrates, in his traits and genius, is the best example of that synthesis which constitutes Plato's extraordinary power.

Socrates, a man of humble stem, and a personal homeliness so remarkable as to be a cause of wit in others, was a cool fellow, with a knowledge of his man, be he whom he might whom he talked with, which laid the companion open to certain defeat in debate; and in debate he immoderately delighted. He was what in our country people call "an old one." This hard-headed humorist, whose drollery diverted the young patricians, turns out in the sequel to have a probity as invincible as his logic, and to be, under cover of this play, enthusiastic in his religion. When accused before the judges, he affirmed the immortality of the soul and a future reward and punishment, and, refusing to recant, was condemned to die; he entered the prison and took away all ignominy from the place. The fame of this prison, the fame of the discourses there, and the drinking of the hemlock, are one of the most precious passages in the history of the world.

The rare coincidence in one ugly body of the droll and the martyr, the keen street debater with the sweetest saint known to any history at that time, had forcibly struck the mind of Plato, and the figure of Socrates placed itself in the foreground of the scene as the fittest dispenser of the intellectual treasures he had to communicate.

It remains to say that the defect of Plato is that he is literary, and never otherwise. His writings have not the vital authority which the screams of prophets and the sermons of unlettered Arabs and Jews possess.

And he had not a system. The acutest German, the lovingest disciple could never tell what Platonism was. No power of genius has ever yet had the smallest success in explaining existence. The perfect enigma remains.

Montaigne

The philosophers affirm disdainfully the superiority of ideas. To men of this world the man of ideas appears out of his reason. The abstractionist and the materialist thus mutually exasperating each other, there arises a third party to occupy the middle ground between the two, the sceptic. He labours to be the beam of the balance. There is so much to say on all sides. This is the position occupied by Montaigne.

In 1571, on the death of his father, he retired from the practice of the law, at Bordeaux, and settled himself on his estate. Downright and plain dealing, and abhorring to be deceived or to deceive, he was esteemed in the country for his sense and probity. In the civil wars of the League, which converted every house into a fort, Montaigne kept his gates open, and his house without defence. All parties freely came and went, his courage and honor being universally esteemed.

Montaigne is the frankest and honestest of all writers. The essays are an entertaining soliloquy on every random topic that comes into his head, treating everything without ceremony, yet with masculine sense. I know not anywhere the book that seems less written. It is the language of conversation transferred to a book. Montaigne talks with shrewdness, knows the world, and books, and himself; never shrieks, or protests, or prays. He keeps the plain; he rarely mounts or sinks; he likes to feel solid ground and the stones underneath.

We are natural believers. We are persuaded that a thread runs through all things, and all worlds are strung on it as beads. But though we reject a sour, dumpish unbelief, to the sceptical class, which Montaigne represents, every man at some time belongs. The ground occupied by the sceptic is the vestibule of the temple. The interrogation of custom at all points is an inevitable stage in the growth of every superior mind. It stands in the mind of the wise sceptic that our life in this world is not quite so easy of interpretation as churches and school books say. He does not wish to take ground against these benevolences, but he says: "There are doubts. Shall we, because good nature inclines us to virtue's side, say, 'There are no doubts—and lie for the right?' Is not the satisfaction of the doubts essential to all manliness?"

I may play with the miscellany of facts, and take those superficial views which we call scepticism; but I know they will presently appear to me in that order which makes scepticism impossible. For the world is saturated with deity and law. Things seem to tend downward, to justify despondency, to promote rogues, to defeat the just; but by knaves as by martyrs the just cause is carried forward, and general ends are somewhat answered. The world-spirit is a good swimmer, and storms and waves cannot drown him. Through the years and the centuries, through evil agents, through toys and atoms, a great and beneficent tendency irresistibly streams. So let a man learn to look for the permanent in the mutable and fleeting; let him learn to bear the disappearance of things he was wont to reverence without losing his reverence.

Shakespeare

Shakespeare is the only biographer of Shakespeare. So far from Shakespeare being the least known, he is the one person in all modern history known to us. What point of morals, of manners, of economy, of philosophy, of taste, of conduct of life has he not settled? What district of man's work has he not remembered? What king has he not taught statecraft? What maiden has not found him finer than her delicacy? What lover has he not outloved?

Some able and appreciating critics think no criticism on Shakespeare valuable that does not rest purely on the dramatic merit; that he is falsely judged as poet and philosopher. I think as highly as these critics of his dramatic merit, but still think it secondary. He was a full man who liked to talk; a brain exhaling thoughts and images, which, seeking vent, found the drama next at hand.

Shakespeare is as much out of the category of eminent authors as he is out of the crowd. He is inconceivably wise; the others, conceivably. With this wisdom of life is the equal endowment of imaginative and lyric power. An omnipresent humanity co-ordinates all his faculties. He has no peculiarity, no importunate topic, but all is duly given. No mannerist is he; he has no discoverable egotism—the great he tells greatly, the small subordinately. He is wise without emphasis or assertion; he is strong as Nature is strong, who lifts the land into mountain slopes without effort, and by the same rule as she floats a bubble in the air, and likes as well to do the one as the other. This power of transferring the inmost truth of things into music and verse makes him the type of the poet.

One royal trait that belongs to Shakespeare is his cheerfulness. He delights in the world, in man, in woman, for the lovely light that sparkles from them. Beauty, the spirit of joy, he sheds over the universe. If he appeared in any company of human souls, who would not march in his troop? He touches nothing that does not borrow health and longevity from his festal style. He was master of the revels to mankind.

Napoleon

Among the eminent persons of the nineteenth century, Bonaparte owes his predominance to the fidelity with which he expresses the aim of the masses of active and cultivated men. If Napoleon was Europe, it was because the people whom he swayed were little Napoleons. He is the representative of the class of industry and skill. "God has granted," says the Koran, "to every people a prophet in its own tongue." Paris, London, and New York, the spirit of commerce, of money, of material power, were also to have their prophet—and Bonaparte was qualified and sent. He was the idol of common men because he, in transcendent degree, had the qualities and powers of common men. He came to his own and they received him.

An Italian proverb declares that if you would succeed you must not be too good. Napoleon renounced, once for all, sentiments and affections, and helped himself with his hands and his head. The art of war was the game in which he exerted his arithmetic. He had a directness of action never before combined with so much comprehension. History is full of the imbecility of kings and governors. They are a class of persons to be much pitied, for they know not what they should do. But Napoleon understood his business. He knew what to do, and he flew to his mark. He put out all his strength; he risked everything; he spared nothing; he went to the edge of his possibilities.

This vigour was guarded and tempered by the coldest prudence and punctuality. His very attack was never the inspiration of courage, but the result of calculation. The necessity of his position required a hospitality to every sort of talent, and his feeling went along with this policy. In fact, every species of merit was sought and advanced under his government. Seventeen men in his time were raised from common soldiers to the rank of king, marshal, duke, or general. I call Napoleon the agent or attorney of the middle class of modern society.

His life was an experiment, under the most favourable conditions, of the powers of intellect without conscience. All passed away, like the smoke of his artillery, and left no trace. He did all that in him lay to live and thrive without moral principle.

Goethe

I find a provision in the constitution of the world for the writer or secretary who is to report the doings of the miraculous spirit of life that everywhere throbs and works. Nature will be reported. All things are engaged in writing their history. The planet goes attended by its shadow. The air is full of sounds, the sky of tokens; the ground is all memoranda and signatures.

Society has really no graver interest than the well-being of the literary class. Still, the writer does not stand with us on any commanding ground. I think this to be his own fault. There have been times when he was a sacred person; he wrote Bibles; the first hymns; the codes; the epics; tragic songs; Sibylline verses; Chaldæan oracles. Every word was true, and woke the nations to new life. How can he be honoured when he is a sycophant ducking to the giddy opinion of a reckless public?

Goethe was the philosopher of the nineteenth century multitude, hundred-handed, Argus-eyed, able and happy to cope with the century's rolling miscellany of facts and sciences, and by his own versatility dispose of them with ease; and what he says of religion, of passion, of marriage, of manners, of property, of paper-money, of periods of belief, of omens, of luck, of whatever else, refuses to be forgotten.

What distinguishes Goethe, for French and English readers, is an habitual reference to interior truth. But I dare not say that Goethe ascended to the highest grounds from which genius has spoken. He is incapable of self-surrender to the moral sentiment. Goethe can never be dear to men. His is a devotion to truth for the sake of culture. But the idea of absolute eternal truth, without reference to my own enlargement by it is higher; and the surrender to the torrent of poetic inspiration is higher.

ERASMUS

Familiar Colloquies

Desiderius Erasmus, the most learned ecclesiastic of the fifteenth century, and the friend of Luther and other reformers, was born at Rotterdam on October 28, 1466, and died at Basel on July 12, 1536. He was the son of a Dutchman named Gerard, and, according to the fashion of the age, changed his family name into its respective Latin and Greek equivalents, Desiderius and Erasmus, meaning "desired," or "loved." Entering the priesthood in 1492, he pursued his studies at Paris, and became so renowned a scholar that he was, on visiting England, received with distinction, not only at the universities, but also by the king. For some time Erasmus settled in Italy, brilliant prospects being held out to him at Rome; but his restless temperament impelled him to wander again, and he came again to England, where he associated with the most distinguished scholars, including Dean Colet and Sir Thomas More. Perhaps nothing in the whole range of mediæval literature made a greater sensation immediately on its appearance, in 1521, than the "Colloquia," or "Familiar Colloquies Concerning Men, Manners, and Things," of Erasmus. As its title indicates, it consists of dialogues, and its author intended it to make youths more proficient in Latin, that language being the chief vehicle of intercommunication in the Middle Ages. But Erasmus claims, in his preface, that another purpose of the book is to make better men as well as better Latinists, for he says: "If the ancient teachers of children are commended who allured the young with wafers, I think it ought not to be charged on me that by the like reward I allure youths either to the elegancy of the Latin tongue or to piety." This selection is made from the Latin text.

Concerning Men, Manners and Things

Erasmus issued his first edition of the "Colloquies" in 1521. Successive editions appeared with great rapidity. Its popularity wherever Latin was read was immense, but it was condemned by the Sarbonne, prohibited in France, and devoted to the flames publicly in Spain. The reader of its extraordinary chapters will not fail to comprehend that such a fate was inevitable in the case of such a production in those times. For, as the friend of the reformers who were "turning the world upside down," Erasmus in this treatise penned the most audacious, sardonic, and withering onslaught ever delivered by any writer on ecclesiastical corruption of religion. He never attacks religion itself, but extols and defends it; his aim is to launch a series of terrific innuendoes on ecclesiasticism as it had developed and as he saw it. He satirically, and even virulently, attacks monks and many of their habits, the whole system of cloister-life, the festivals and pilgrimages which formed one of the chief features of religious activity, and the grotesque superstitions which his peculiar genius for eloquent irony so well qualified him to caricature.

This great work, one of the epoch-making books of the world, consists of sixty-two "Colloquies," of very varying length. They treat of the most curiously diverse topics, as may be imagined from such titles of the chapters as "The Youth's Piety," "The Lover and the Maiden," "The Shipwreck," "The Epithalamium of Peter Egidius," "The Alchemist," "The Horse Cheat," "The Cyclops, or the Gospel Carrier," "The Assembly or Parliament of Women," "Concerning Early Rising."

A sample of the style of the "Colloquies" in the more serious sections may be taken from the one entitled "The Religious Banquet."

Nephew: How unwillingly have I seen many Christians die. Some put their trust in things not to be confided in; others breathe out their souls in desperation, either out of a consciousness of their lewd lives, or by reason of scruples that have been injected into their minds, even in their dying hours, by some indiscreet men, die almost in despair.

Chrysoglottus: It is no wonder to find them die so, who have spent their lives in philosophising all their lives about ceremonies.

Nephew: What do you mean by ceremonies?

Chrysoglottus: I will tell you, but with protestation beforehand, over and over, that I do not find fault with the rites and sacraments of the Church, but rather highly approve of them; but I blame a wicked and superstitious sort of people who teach people to put their confidence in these things, omitting those things that make them truly Christians. If you look into Christians in common, do they not live as if the whole sum of religion consisted in ceremonies? With how much pomp are the ancient rites of the Church set forth in baptism? The infant waits without the church door, the exorcism is performed, the catechism is performed, vows are made, Satan is abjured with all his pomps and pleasures; then the child is anointed, signed, seasoned with salt, dipped, a charge given to its sureties to see it well brought up; and the oblation money being paid, they are discharged, and by this time the child passes for a Christian, and in some sense is so. A little time after it is anointed again, and in time learns to confess, receive the sacrament, is accustomed to rest on holy days, to hear divine service, to fast sometimes, to abstain from flesh; and if he observes all these he passes for an absolute Christian. He marries a wife, and then comes on another sacrament; he enters into holy orders, is anointed again and consecrated, his habit is changed, and then to prayers.

Now, I approve of the doing of all this well enough, but the doing of them more out of custom than conscience I do not approve. But to think that nothing else is requisite for the making of a Christian I absolutely disapprove. For the greater part of the men in the world trust to these things, and think they have nothing else to do but get wealth by right or wrong, to gratify their passions of lust, rage, malice, ambition. And this they do till they come on their death-bed. And then follow more ceremonies—confession upon confession more unction still, the eucharists are administered; tapers, the cross, the holy water are brought in; indulgences are procured, if they are to be had for love or money; and orders are given for a magnificent funeral. Now, although these things may be well enough, as they are done in conformity to ecclesiastical customs, yet there are some more internal impressions which have an efficacy to fortify us against the assaults of death by filling our hearts with joy, and helping us to go out of the world with a Christian assurance.

Eusebius: When I was in England I saw St. Thomas' tomb all over bedecked with a vast number of jewels of an immense price, besides other rich furniture, even to admiration. I had rather that these superfluities should be applied to charitable uses than to be reserved for princes that shall one time or other make a booty of them. The holy man, I am confident, would have been better pleased to have had his tomb adorned with leaves and flowers.... Rich men, nowadays, will have their monuments in churches, whereas in time past they could hardly get room for their saints there. If I were a priest or a bishop, I would put it into the head of these thick-skulled courtiers or merchants that if they would atone for their sins to Almighty God they should privately bestow their liberality on the relief of the poor.

*****

A wonderful plea for peace, in shape of an exquisite satire, is the "Colloquy" entitled "Charon." It is a dialogue between Charon, the ghostly boatman on the River Styx, and Genius Alastor. Its style may be gathered from the following excerpt.

Charon: Whither are you going so brisk, and in such haste, Alastor?

Alastor: O Charon, you come in the nick of time; I was coming to you.

Charon: Well, what news do you bring?

Alastor: I bring a message to you and Prosperine that you will be glad to hear. All the Furies have been no less diligent than they have been successful in gaining their point. There is not one foot of ground upon earth that they have not infected with their hellish calamities, seditions, wars, robberies, and plagues. Do you get your boat and your oars ready; you will have such a vast multitude of ghosts come to you anon that I am afraid you will not be able to carry them all over yourself.

Charon: I could have told you that.

Alastor: How came you to know it?

Charon: Ossa brought me that news about two days ago!

Alastor: Nothing is more swift than that goddess. But what makes you loitering here, having left your boat?

Charon: My business brought me hither. I came hither to provide myself with a good strong three-oared boat, for my boat is so rotten and leaky with age that it will not carry such a burden, if Ossa told me true.

Alastor: What was it that Ossa told you?

Charon: That the three monarchs of the world were bent upon each other's destruction with a mortal hatred, and that no part of Christendom was free from the rage of war; for these three have drawn in all the rest to be engaged in the war with them. They are all so haughty that not one of them will in the least submit to the other. Nor are the Danes, the Poles, the Scots, nor the Turks at quiet, but are preparing to make dreadful havoc. The plague rages everywhere: in Spain, Britain, Italy, France; and, more than all, there is a new fire sprung out of the variety of opinions, which has so corrupted the minds of all men that there is no such thing as sincere friendship anywhere; but brother is at enmity with brother, and husband and wife cannot agree. And it is to be hoped that this distraction will be a glorious destruction of mankind, if these controversies, that are now managed by the tongue and pen, come once to be decided by arms.

Alastor: All that fame has told you is true; for I myself, having been a constant companion of the Furies, have with these eyes seen more than all this, and that they never at any time have approved themselves more worthy of their name than now.

Charon: But there is danger lest some good spirit should start up and of a sudden exhort them to peace. And men's minds are variable, for I have heard that among the living there is one Polygraphus who is continually, by his writing, inveighing against wars, and exhorting to peace.

Alastor: Ay, ay, but he has a long time been talking to the deaf. He once wrote a sort of hue and cry after peace, that was banished or driven away; after that an epitaph upon peace defunct. But then, on the other hand, there are others that advance our cause no less than do the Furies themselves. They are a sort of animals in black and white vestments, ash-coloured coats, and various other dresses, that are always hovering about the courts of the princes, and are continually instilling into their ears the love of war, and exhorting the nobility and common people to it, haranguing them in their sermons that it is a just, holy, and religious war. And that which would make you stand in admiration at the confidence of these men is the cry of both parties. In France they preach it up that God is on the French side, and that they can never be overcome that has God for their protector. In England and Spain the cry is, "The war is not the king's, but God's"; therefore, if they do but fight like men, they depend on getting the victory, and if anyone should chance to fall in the battle, he will not die, but fly directly up into heaven, arms and all.

In Praise of Folly

"The Praise of Folly" was written in Latin, and the title, "Encomium Moriæ," is a pun on the name of his friend, the Greek word *moria* (folly) curiously corresponding with his host's family name. The purpose of this inimitable satire is to cover every species of foolish men and women with ridicule. Yet through all the biting sarcasm runs an unbroken vein of religious seriousness, the contrast greatly enhancing the impression produced by this masterpiece.

I.—Stultitia's Declamation

In whatever manner I, the Goddess of Folly, may be generally spoken of by mortals, yet I assert it emphatically that it is from me, Stultitia, and from my influence only, that gods and men derive all mirth and cheerfulness. You laugh, I see. Well, even that is a telling argument in my favour. Actually now, in this most numerous assembly, as soon as ever I have opened my mouth, the countenances of all have instantly brightened up with fresh and unwonted hilarity, whereas but a few moments ago you were all looking demure and woebegone.

On my very brow my name is written. No one would take me, Stultitia, for Minerva. No one would contend that I am the Goddess of Wisdom. The mere expression of my countenance tells its own tale. Not only am I incapable of deceit, but even those who are under my sway are incapable of deceit likewise. From my illustrious sire, Plutus [Wealth], I glory to be sprung, for he, and no other, was the great progenitor of gods and men, and I care not what Hesiod, or Homer, or even Jupiter himself may maintain to the contrary. Everything, I affirm, is subjected to the control of Plutus. War, peace, empires, designs, judicial decisions, weddings, treaties, alliances, laws, arts, things ludicrous and things serious, are all administered in obedience to his sovereign will.

Now notice the admirable foresight which nature exercises, in order to ensure that men shall never be destitute of folly as the principal ingredient in their constitution. Wisdom, as your divines and moralists put it, consists in men being guided by their reason; and folly, in their being actuated by their passions. See then here what Jupiter has done. In order to prevent the life of man from being utterly intolerable, he has endowed him with reason in singularly small proportion to his passions—only, so to speak, as a half-ounce is to a pound. And whereas he has dispersed his passions over every portion of his body, he has confined his reason to a narrow little crevice in his skull.

And yet, of these silly human beings, the male sex is born under the necessity of transacting the business of the world. When Jupiter was taking counsel with me I advised him to add a woman to the man—a creature foolish and frivolous, but full of laughter and sweetness, who would season and sweeten by her folly the sadness of his manly intelligence.

When Plato doubted whether or not he should place women in the class of rational animals, he really only wished to indicate the remarkable silliness of that sex. Yet women will not be so absolutely senseless as to be offended if I, a woman myself, the goddess Stultitia, tell them thus plainly that they are fools. They will, if they look at the matter aright, be flattered by it. For they are by many degrees more favoured creatures than men. They have beauty—and oh, what a gift is that! By its power they rule the rulers of the world.

The supreme wish of women is to win the admiration of men, and they have no more effectual means to this end than folly. Men, no doubt, will contend that it is the pleasure they have in women's society, and not their folly, that attracts them. I answer that their pleasure is folly, and nothing but folly, in which they delight. You see, then, from what fountain is derived the highest and most exquisite enjoyment that falls to man's lot in life. But there are some men (waning old crones, most of them) who love their glasses better than the lasses, and place their chief delight in tippling. Others love to make fools of themselves to raise a laugh at a feast, and I beg to say that of laughter, fun, and pleasantry, I—Folly—am the sole purveyor.

II.—The Mockery of Wisdom

So much for the notion that wisdom is of any use in the pleasures of life. Well, the next thing that our gods of wisdom will assert is that wisdom is necessary for affairs of state. Says Plato, "Those states will prosper whose rulers are guided by the spirit of philosophy." With this opinion I totally disagree. Consult history, and it will tell you that the two Catos, Brutus, Cassius, the Gracchi, Cicero, and Marcus Antoninus all disturbed the tranquillity of the state and brought down on them by their philosophy the disgust and disfavour of the citizens. And who are the men who are most prone, from weariness of life, to seek to put an end to it? Why, men of reputed wisdom. Not to mention Diogenes, the Catos, the Cassii, and the Bruti, there is the remarkable case of Chiron, who, though he actually had immortality conferred on him, voluntarily preferred death.

You see, then, that if men were universally wise, the world would be depopulated, and there would be need of a new creation. But, since the world generally is under the influence of folly and not of wisdom, the case is, happily, different. I, Folly, by inspiring men with hopes of good things they will never get, so charm away their woes that they are far from wishing to die. Nay, the less cause there is for them to desire to live, the more, nevertheless, do they love life. It is of my bounty that you see everywhere men of Nestorean longevity, mumbling, without brains, without teeth, whose hair is white, whose heads are bald, so enamoured of life, so eager to look youthful, that they use dyes, wigs, and other disguises, and take to wife some frisky heifer of a creature; while aged and cadaverous-looking women are seen caterwauling, and, as the Greeks express it, behaving goatishly, in order to induce some beauteous Phaon to pay court to them.

As to the wisdom of the learned professions, the more empty-headed and the more reckless any member of any one of them is, the more he will be thought of. The physician is always in request, and yet medicine, as it is now frequently practised, is nothing but a system of pure humbug. Next in repute to the physicians stand the pettifogging lawyers, who are, according to the philosophers, a set of asses. And asses, I grant you that, they are.

Nevertheless, it is by the will and pleasure of these asses that the business of the world is transacted, and they make fortunes while the poor theologians starve.

By the immortal gods, I solemnly swear to you that the happiest men are those whom the world calls fools, simpletons, and blockheads. For they are entirely devoid of the fear of death. They have no accusing consciences to make them fear it. They are, happily, without the experience of the thousands of cares that lacerate the minds of other men. They feel no shame, no solicitude, no ambition, no envy, no love. And, according to the theologians, they are free from any imputation of the guilt of sin! Ah, ye besotted men of wisdom, you need no further evidence than the ills you have gone through to convince you from what a mass of calamities I have delivered my idiotic favourites.

To be deceived, people say, is wretched. But I hold that what is most wretched is not to be deceived. They are in great error who imagine that a man's happiness consists in things as they are. No; it consists entirely in his opinion of what they are. Man is so constituted that falsehood is far more agreeable to him than truth.

Does anyone need proof of this? Let him visit the churches, and assuredly he will find it. If solemn truth is dwelt on, the listeners at once become weary, yawn, and sleep; but if the orator begins some silly tale, they are all attention. And the saints they prefer to appeal to are those whose histories are most made up of fable and romance. Though to be deceived adds much more to your happiness than not to be deceived, it yet costs you much less trouble.

And now to pass to another argument in my favour. Among all the praises of Bacchus this is the chief, that he drives away care; but he does it only for a short time, and then all your care comes again. How much more complete are the benefits mankind derive from me! I also afford them intoxication, but an intoxication whose influence is perennial, and all, too, without cost to them. And my favours I deny to nobody. Mars, Apollo, Saturn, Phœbus, and Neptune are more chary of their bounties and dole them out to their favourites only but I confine my favours to none.

III.—Classification of Fools

Of all the men whose doings I have witnessed, the most sordid are men of trade, and appropriately so, for they handle money, a very sordid thing indeed. Yet, though they lie, pilfer, cheat, and impose on everybody, as soon as they grow rich they are looked up to as princes. But as I look round among the various classes of men, I specially note those who are esteemed to possess more than ordinary sagacity. Among these a foremost place is occupied by the schoolmasters. How miserable would these be were it not that I, Folly, of my benevolence, ameliorate their wretchedness and render them insanely happy in the midst of their drudgery! Their lot is one of semi-starvation and of debasing slavery. In the schools, those bridewells of uproar and confusion, they grow prematurely old and broken down, Yet, thanks to my good services, they know not their own misery. For in their own estimation they are mighty fine fellows, strutting about and striking terror into the hearts of trembling urchins, half scarifying the little wretches with straps, canes, and birches. They are, apparently, quite unconscious of the dust and dirt with which their schoolrooms are polluted. In fact, their own most wretched servitude is to them a kingdom of felicity.

The poets owe less to me. Yet they, too, are enthusiastic devotees of mine, for their entire business consists in tickling the ears of fools with silly ditties and ridiculously romantic tales. Of the services of my attendants, Philautia [Self-approbation] and Kolakia [Flattery], they never fail to avail themselves, and really I do not know that there is any other class of men in the world amongst whom I should find more devoted and constant followers.

Moreover, there are the rhetoricians. Quintilian, the prince of them all, has written an immense chapter on no more serious subject than how to excite a laugh. Those, again, who hunt after immortal fame in the domain of literature unquestionably belong to my fraternity. Poor fellows! They pass a wretched existence poring over their manuscripts, and for what reward? For the praise of the very, very limited few who are capable of appreciating their erudition.

Very naturally, the barristers merit our attention next. Talk of female garrulity! Why, I would back any one of them to win a prize for chattering against any twenty of the most talkative women that you could pick out. And well indeed would it be if they had no worse fault than that. I am bound to say that they are not only loquacious, but pugnacious. Their quarrelsomeness is astounding.

After these come the bearded and gowned philosophers. Their insane self-deception as to their sagacity and learning is very delightful. They beguile their time with computing the magnitude of the sun, moon, and stars, and they assign causes for all the phenomena of the universe, as if nature had initiated them into all her secrets. In reality they know nothing, but profess to know everything.

IV.—On Princes and Pontiffs

It is high time that I should say a few words to you about kings and the royal princes belonging to their courts. Very different are they from those whom I have just been describing, who pretend to be wise when they are the reverse, for these high personages frankly and openly live a life of folly, and it is just that I should give them their due, and frankly and openly tell them so. They seem to regard it to be the duty of a king to addict himself to the chase; to keep up a grand stud of horses; to extract as much money as possible from the people; to caress by every means in his power the vulgar populace, in order to win their good graces, and so make them the subservient tools of his tyrannical behests.

As for the grandees of the court, a more servile, insipid, empty-headed set than the generality of them you will fail to find anywhere. Yet they wish to be regarded as the greatest personalities on earth. Not a very modest wish, and yet, in one respect, they are modest enough. For instance, they wish to be bedecked with gold and gems and purple, and other external symbols of worth and wisdom, but nothing further do they require.

These courtiers, however, are superlatively happy in the belief that they are perfectly virtuous. They lie in bed till noon. Then they summon their chaplain to their bedside to offer up the sacrifice of the mass, and as the hireling priest goes through his solemn farce with perfunctory rapidity, they, meanwhile, have all but dropped off again into a comfortable condition of slumber. After this they betake themselves to breakfast; and that is scarcely over when dinner supervenes. And then come their pastimes—their dice, their cards, and their gambling—their merriment with jesters and buffoons, and their gallantries with court favourites.

Next let us turn our attention to popes, cardinals, and bishops, who have long rivalled, if they do not surpass, the state and magnificence of princes. If bishops did but bear in mind that a pastoral staff is an emblem of pastoral duties, and that the cross solemnly carried before them is a reminder of the earnestness with which they should strive to crucify the flesh, their lot would be one replete with sadness and solicitude. As things are, a right bonny time do they spend, providing abundant pasturage for themselves, and leaving their flocks to the negligent charge of so-called friars and vicars.

Fortune favours the fool. We colloquially speak of him and such as him as "lucky birds," while, when we speak of a wise man, we proverbially describe him as one who has been "born under an evil star," and as one whose "horse will never carry him to the front." If you wish to get a wife, mind, above all things, that you beware of wisdom; for the girls, without exception, are heart and soul so devoted to fools, that you may rely on it a man who has any wisdom in him they will shun as they would a vampire.

And now, to sum up much in a few words, go among what classes of men you will, go among popes, princes, cardinals, judges, magistrates, friends, foes, great men, little men, and you will not fail to find that a man with plenty of money at his command has it in his power to obtain everything that he sets his heart upon. A wise man, however, despises money. And what is the consequence? Everyone despises him!

GESTA ROMANORUM

A Story-Book of the Middle Ages

The "Gesta Romanorum," or "Deeds of the Romans," a quaint collection of moral tales compiled by the monks, was used in the Middle Ages for pulpit instruction. Hence the curious "Applications" to the stories, two of which are here given as examples. Wynkyn de Worde was the first to print the "Gesta" in English, about 1510. His version is based on Latin manuscripts of English origin, and differs from the first edition, and from the Latin text printed abroad about 1473. The stories have little to do with authentic Roman history, and abound in amusing confusions, contradictions, and anachronisms. But their interest is undeniable, and they form the source of many famous pieces of English literature. In the English "Gesta" occur the originals of the bond and casket incidents in "The Merchant of Venice."

I.—Of Love

Pompey was a wise and powerful king. He had one well-beloved daughter, who was very beautiful. Her he committed to the care of five soldiers, who were to guard her night and day. Before the door of the princess's chamber they hung a burning lamp, and, moreover, they kept a loud-barking dog to rouse them from sleep. But the lady panted for the pleasures of the world, and one day, looking abroad, she was espied by a certain amorous duke, who made her many fair promises.

Hoping much from these, the princess slew the dog, put out the light, and fled by night with the duke. Now, there was in the palace a certain doughty champion, who pursued the fugitives and beheaded the duke. He brought the lady home again; but her father would not see her, and thenceforward she passed her time bewailing her misdeeds.

Now, at court there was a wise and skilful mediator, who, being moved with compassion, reconciled the lady with her father and betrothed her to a powerful nobleman. The king then gave his daughter diverse gifts. These were a rich, flowing tunic inscribed with the words, "Forgiven. Sin no more"; and a golden coronet with the legend, "Thy dignity is from me." Her champion gave her a ring, engraved, "I have loved thee; learn thou to love." Likewise the mediator bestowed a ring, saying, "What have I done? How much? Why?" A third ring was given by the king's son, with the words: "Despise not thy nobility." A fourth ring, from her brother, bore the motto: "Approach! Fear not. I am thy brother." Her husband gave a golden coronet, confirming his wife in the inheritance of his possessions, and superscribed: "Now thou are espoused, sin no more."

The lady kept these gifts as long as she lived. She regained the affections of those whom her folly had estranged, and closed her days in peace.

APPLICATION

My beloved, the king is our Heavenly Father; the daughter is the soul; the guardian soldiers are the five senses; the lamp is the will; the dog is conscience; the duke is the Evil One. The mediator is Christ. The cloak is our Lord's wounded body. The champion and the brother are likewise Christ; the coronet is His crown of thorns; the rings are the wounds in His hands and feet. He is also the Spouse. Let us study to keep these gifts uninjured.

II.—Of Fidelity

The subject of a certain king, being captured by pirates, wrote to his father for ransom; but the father refused, and the youth was left wasting in prison. Now, his captor had a beautiful and virtuous daughter, who came to comfort the prisoner. At first he was too disconsolate to listen to her, but at length he begged her to try to set him free. The lady feared her father's wrath, but at last, on promise of marriage, she freed the young man, and fled with him to his own country. His father said, "Son, I am overjoyed at thy return, but who is the lady under thy escort?"

When his son told him, he charged him, on pain of losing his inheritance, not to marry her.

"But she released me from deadly peril," said the youth.

The father answered, "Son, thou mayest not confide in her, for she hath deceived her own father; and, furthermore, although she indeed set thee free, it was but to oblige thee to marry her. And since it was an unworthy passion that was the source of thy liberty, I think that she ought not to be thy wife."

When the lady heard these reasons, she answered thus, "I have not deceived my parent. He that deceives diminishes a certain good. But my father is so rich that he needs not any addition. Wherefore, your son's ransom would have left him but little richer, while you it would have utterly impoverished. I have thus served you, and done my father no injury. As for unworthy passion, that arises from wealth, honours, or a handsome appearance, none of which your son possessed, for he had not even enough to procure his ransom, and imprisonment had destroyed his beauty. Therefore, I freed him out of compassion."

When the father heard this, he could object nothing more. So the son married the lady with great pomp, and closed his life in peace.

APPLICATION

My beloved, the son is the human race, led captive by the devil. The father is the world, that will not redeem the sinner, but loves to detain him. The daughter is Christ.

III.—O Venial Sin

Julian, a noble soldier, fond of the chase, was one day pursuing a stag, which turned and addressed him thus, "Thou who pursuest me so fiercely shalt one day destroy thy parents."

In great alarm, Julian sought a far country, where he enlisted with a certain chieftain. For his renowned services in war and peace he was made a knight, and wedded to the widow of a castellan, with her castle as a dowry.

Meanwhile, his parents sought him sorrowing, and coming at length to Julian's castle in his absence, they told his wife their story. The lady, for the love she bore her husband, put them into her own bed, and early in the morning went forth to her devotions. Julian returned, and softly entering his wife's apartment, saw two persons therein, and was filled with terrible alarm for his lady's fealty.

Without pause, he slew both, and hurried out. Meeting his wife in the church porch, he fell into amazement, and asked who they might be. Hearing the truth, he was shaken with an agony of tears, and cried, "Accursed that I am! Dearest wife, forgive, and receive my last farewell!"

"Nay," she replied. "Wilt thou abandon me, beloved, and leave me widowed? I, that have shared thy happiness will now share thy grief!"

Together they departed to a great and dangerous river, where many had perished. There they built a hospital, where they abode in contrition, ferrying over such as wished to cross the river, and cherishing the poor. After many years, Julian was aroused at midnight by a dolorous voice calling his name. He found and ferried over a leper, perishing with cold. Failing to warm the wretch by other means, Julian placed him in his own bed, and strove by the heat of his own body to restore him. After a while he who seemed sick and cold and leprous appeared robed in immortal splendour, and, waving his light wings, seemed ready to mount up into heaven. Turning upon his wondering host a look of the utmost benignity, the visitant exclaimed, "Julian, the Lord hath sent me to thee to announce the acceptance of thy contrition. Ere long thou and thy partner will sleep in Him."

So saying, the angelic messenger disappeared, and Julian and his wife, after a short time occupied in good works, died in peace.

IV.—Of the End of Sinners

Dionysius records that Perillus, wishing to become the artificer of Phalaris, the cruel tyrant of Agrigentum, presented him with a brazen bull. In its side was a secret door, for the entry of those who should be burned to death within. The idea was that the agonised cries of the victim, resembling the roaring of a bull and nothing human, should arouse no feeling of mercy. The king, highly applauding the invention, said, "Friend, the value of thy industry is still untried; more cruel even than the people account me, thou thyself shalt be the first victim."

There is no law more equitable than that "the artificer of death should perish by his own devices," as Ovid hath observed.

V.—Of Too Much Pride

As the Emperor Jovinian lay abed, reflecting on his power and possessions, he impiously asked, "Is there any other god than I?"

Amid such thoughts he fell asleep.

Now, on the morrow, as he followed the chase, he separated himself from his followers in order to bathe in a stream. And as he bathed, one like him in all respects took the emperor's dress, and arraying himself in them, mounted the monarch's horse, and joined the royal retinue, who knew him not from their master. Jovinian, horseless and naked, was vexed beyond measure.

"Miserable that I am," he exclaimed, "I will to a knight who lives hard by. Him have I promoted; haply he will befriend me." But when he declared himself to be Jovinian, the knight ordered him to be flogged. "Oh, my God!" exclaimed the emperor, "is it possible that one whom I have loaded with honours should use me thus?"

Next he sought out a certain duke, one of his privy counsellors, and told his tale.

"Poor, mad wretch," said the duke. "I am but newly returned from the palace, where I left the emperor."

He therefore had Jovinian flogged, and imprisoned. Contriving to escape, he went to the palace. "Surely," he reflected, "my servants will know me." But his own porter denied him. Nevertheless, he persuaded the man to take a secret sign to the empress, and to demand his imperial robes. The empress, sitting at table with the feigned emperor, was much disturbed, and said, "Oh, my lord, there is a vile fellow at the gate who declares the most hidden passages of our life, and says he is my husband."

Being condemned to be dragged by a horse's tail, Jovinian, in despair, sought his confessor's cell. But the holy man would not open to him, although at last, being adjured by the name of the Crucified, he gave him shrift at the window. Thereupon he knew the emperor, and giving him some clothes, bade him show himself again at the palace. This he did, and was received with due obeisance. Still, none knew which was the emperor, and which the impostor, until the feigned emperor spake.

"I," said he, "am the guardian angel of the king's soul. He has now purged his pride by penance; let your obedience wait on him."

So saying, he disappeared. The emperor gave thanks to God, lived happily after, and finished his days in peace.

VI.—Of Avarice

A covetous and wicked carpenter placed all his riches in a log, which he hid by his fireside. Now, the sea swept away that part of his house, and drifted the log to a city where lived a generous man. He found the log, cleft it, and laid the gold in a secure place until he should discover the owner.

Now, the carpenter, seeking his wealth with lamentations, came by chance to the house of him that had found it. Mentioning his loss, his host said to himself, "I will prove if God will that I return his money to him." He then made three cakes, one filled with earth, the second with dead men's bones, and the third with some of the lost gold. The carpenter, being invited to choose, weighed the cakes in his hand, and finding that with earth heaviest, took it.

"And if I want more, my worthy host," said he, "I will choose that," laying his hand on the cake containing the bones. "The third you may keep for yourself."

"Thou miserable varlet," cried the host. "It is thine own gold, which plainly the Lord wills not that I return to thee."

So saying, he distributed all the treasure among the poor, and drove the carpenter away from his house in great tribulation.

VII.—Of Temporary Tribulation

Antiochus, king of Antioch, had one lovely daughter, who was much courted. But her father, seeking to withhold her from marriage, proposed a riddle to every suitor, and each one who failed to guess the answer was put to death. Among the suitors came Apollonius, the young Prince of Tyre, who guessed the riddle, the answer to which revealed a shameful secret of the king's life. Antiochus, loudly denying that the young man had hit upon the truth, sent him away for thirty days, and bade him try again, on pain of death. So Apollonius departed.

Now, Antiochus sent his steward, Taliarchus, to Tyre, with orders to destroy Apollonius; but by the time the steward arrived the prince had put to sea in a fleet laden with treasure, corn, and many changes of raiment. Hearing this, Antiochus set a price on the head of Apollonius, and pursued him with a great armament. The prince, arriving at Tharsus, saved that city from famine by the supplies he brought, and a statue was raised in his honour. Then, by the advice of one Stranguilio and his wife, Dionysias, he sailed to Pentapolis. On the way he suffered shipwreck, and reached that city on a plank. There, by his skill in athletics and music, he won the favour of Altistrates, the king, who gave him his daughter to wife.

Some time after, hearing that the wicked Antiochus and his daughter had been killed by lightning, Apollonius and his wife set sail to take up the sovereignty of Antioch, which had fallen to him. On the way the lady died, leaving a new-born daughter. The prince placed his wife's body in a coffin smeared with pitch, and committed it to the deep. In the coffin he put money and a tablet, instructing anyone who found the body to bury it sumptuously. Apollonius returned to Pentapolis and gave his infant daughter into the care of Stranguilio and Dionysias. Then he himself sailed away and wandered the world in deep grief. In the meantime, his wife's body was cast up at Ephesus, and was found by the physician Cerimon, one of whose pupils revived the lady, who became a vestal of Diana.

Years passed, and the child, who was called Tharsia, incurred the jealousy of Dionysias, because she was fairer than her own child Philomatia. Dionysias sought to kill Tharsia, who, at the critical moment, was carried away by pirates, and sold into slavery at Machylena. There her beauty and goodness protected her, so that none who came to her master's evil house would do her wrong. She persuaded her owner to let her earn her bread by her accomplishments in music and the unravelling of hard sayings. Thus she won the love of the prince of that place, Athanagoras, who protected her.

Some time afterwards a strange fleet came to Machylena. Athanagoras, struck by the beauty of one of the ships, went on board, and asked to see the owner. He found a rugged and melancholy man, who was none other than Apollonius. In due time that prince was joyfully reunited with his child, who was given in marriage to her perserver. Speedy vengeance overtook Tharsia's cruel owner, and later Stranguilio and Dionysias suffered for their misdeeds. Being warned by a dream to return to Ephesus, Apollonius found his wife in the precinct of the vestals, and, together with her, he reigned long and happily over Antioch and Tyre. After death he went into everlasting life. To which may God, of His infinite mercy, lead us all.

OLIVER GOLDSMITH

The Citizen of the World

"The Citizen of the World," after appearing in the "Public Ledger" newspaper in 1760–61, was published in two volumes in 1762, with the sub-title, "Letters from a Chinese Philosopher, Residing in London, to his Friends in the East." It established Goldsmith's literary reputation (see Vol. IV, p. 275). The author's main purpose was to indulge in a keen, but not ill-natured, satire upon Western, and especially upon English, civilisation; but sometimes the satiric manner yields place to the philosophical.

The Troubles of the Great
FROM LIEN CHI ALTANGI TO FUM HOAM, FIRST PRESIDENT OF THE CEREMONIAL ACADEMY AT PEKIN

The princes of Europe have found out a manner of rewarding their subjects who have behaved well, by presenting them with about two yards of blue ribbon, which is worn over the shoulder. They who are honoured with this mark of distinction are called knights, and the king himself is always the head of the order. This is a very frugal method of recompensing the most important services, and it is very fortunate for kings that their subjects are satisfied with such trifling rewards. Should a nobleman happen to lose his leg in battle, the king presents him with two yards of ribbon, and he is paid for the loss of his limb. Should an ambassador spend all his paternal fortunes in supporting the honour of his country abroad, the king presents him with two yards of ribbon, which is to be considered as an equivalent to his estate. In short, while a European king has a yard of blue or green ribbon left, he need be under no apprehension of wanting statesmen, generals, and soldiers.

I cannot sufficiently admire those kingdoms in which men with large patrimonial estates are willing thus to undergo real hardships for empty favours. A person, already possessed of a competent fortune, who undertakes to enter the career of ambition feels many real inconveniences from his station, while it procures him no real happiness that he was not possessed of before. He could eat, drink, and sleep before he became a courtier, as well, perhaps better, than when invested with his authority.

What real good, then, does an addition to a fortune already sufficient procure? Not any. Could the great man, by having his fortune increased, increase also his appetite, then precedence might be attended with real amusement. But, on the contrary, he finds his desire for pleasure often lessen as he takes pains to be able to improve it; and his capacity of enjoyment diminishes as his fortune happens to increase.

Instead, therefore, of regarding the great with envy, I generally consider them with some share of compassion. I look upon them as a set of good-natured, misguided people, who are indebted to us, and not to themselves, for all the happiness they enjoy. For our pleasure, and not their own, they sweat under a cumbrous heap of finery; for our pleasure, the hackneyed train, the slow-parading pageant, with all the gravity of grandeur, moves in review; a single coat, or a single footman, answers all the purposes of the most indolent refinement as well; and those who have twenty may be said to keep one for their own pleasure, and the other nineteen for ours. So true is the observation of Confucius, "That we take greater pains to persuade others that we are happy than in endeavouring to think so ourselves."

But though this desire of being seen, of being made the subject of discourse, and of supporting the dignities of an exalted station, be troublesome to the ambitious, yet it is well that there are men thus willing to exchange ease and safety for danger and a ribbon. We lose nothing by their vanity, and it would be unkind to endeavour to deprive a child of its rattle.... Adieu.

The Folly of the Recluse
FROM LIEN CHI ALTANGI TO HINGPO, HIS SON

Books, my son, while they teach us to respect the interests of others, often make us unmindful of our own; while they instruct the youthful reader to grasp at social happiness, he grows miserable in detail. I dislike, therefore, the philosopher, who describes the inconveniences of life in such pleasing colours that the pupil grows enamoured of distress, longs to try the charms of poverty, meets it without dread, nor fears its inconveniences till he severely feels them.

A youth who has thus spent his life among books, new to the world, and unacquainted with man but by philosophic information, may be considered as a being whose mind is filled with the vulgar errors of the wise. He first has learned from books, and then lays it down as a maxim that all mankind are virtuous or vicious in excess; warm, therefore, in attachments, and steadfast in enmity, he treats every creature as a friend or foe. Upon a closer inspection of human nature he perceives that he should have moderated his friendship, and softened his severity; he finds no character so sanctified that has not its failings, none so infamous but has somewhat to attract our esteem; he beholds impiety in lawn, and fidelity in fetters.

He now, therefore, but too late, perceives that his regards should have been more cool, and his hatred less violent; that the truly wise seldom court romantic friendships with the good, and avoid, if possible, the resentment even of the wicked; every movement gives him fresh instances that the bonds of friendship are broken if drawn too closely, and that those whom he has treated with disrespect more than retaliate the injury; at length, therefore, he is obliged to confess that he has declared war upon the vicious half of mankind, without being able to form an alliance among the virtuous to espouse his quarrel.

Our book-taught philosopher, however, is now too far advanced to recede; and though poverty be the just consequence of the many enemies his conduct has created, yet he is resolved to meet it without shrinking. "Come, then, O Poverty! for what is there in thee dreadful to the Wise? Temperance, Health, and Frugality walk in thy train; Cheerfulness and Liberty are ever thy companions. Come, then, O Poverty, while kings stand by, and gaze with admiration at the true philosopher's resignation!"

The goddess appears, for Poverty ever comes at the call; but, alas! he finds her by no means the charming figure books and his warm imagination had painted. All the fabric of enthusiasm is at once demolished, and a thousand miseries rise upon its ruins, while Contempt, with pointing finger, is foremost in the hideous procession.

The poor man now finds that he can get no kings to look at him while he is eating; he finds that, in proportion as he grows poor, the world turns its back upon him, and gives him leave to act the philosopher in all the majesty of solitude. Spleen now begins to take up the man; not distinguishing in his resentments, he regards all mankind with detestation, and commencing man-hater, seeks solitude to be at liberty to rail.

It has been said that he who retires to solitude is either a beast or an angel. The censure is too severe, and the praise unmerited; the discontented being who retires from society is generally some good-natured man, who has begun life without experience, and knew not how to gain it in his intercourse with mankind. Adieu.

On Mad Dogs
FROM LIEN CHI ALTANGI TO FUM HOAM

Indulgent Nature seems to have exempted this island from many of those epidemic evils which are so fatal in other parts of the world. But though the nation be exempt from real evils, think not, my friend, that it is more happy on this account than others. They are afflicted, it is true, with neither famine nor pestilence, but then there is a disorder peculiar to the country, which every season makes strange ravages among them; it spreads with pestilential rapidity, and infects almost every rank of people; what is still more strange, the natives have no name for this peculiar malady, though well enough known to foreign physicians by the name of epidemic terror.

A season is never known to pass in which the people are not visited by this cruel calamity in one shape or another, seemingly different, though ever the same. The people, when once infected, lose their relish for happiness, saunter about with looks of despondence, ask after the calamities of the day, and receive no comfort but in heightening each other's distress. A dread of mad dogs is the epidemic terror which now prevails, and the whole nation is at present actually groaning under the malignity of its influence.

It is pleasant enough for a neutral being like me, who have no share in these ideal calamities, to mark the stages of this national disease. The terror at first feebly enters with a little dog that had gone through a neighbouring village, that was thought to be mad by several who had seen him. The next account comes that a mastiff ran through a certain town, and had bit five geese, which immediately ran mad, foamed at the bill, and died in great agonies soon after. Then comes an affecting history of a little boy bit in the leg, and gone down to be dipped in the salt water; when the people have sufficiently shuddered at that, they are next congealed with a frightful account of a man who was said lately to have died from a bite he had received some years before.

My landlady, a good-natured woman, but a little credulous, waked me some mornings ago, before the usual hour, with horror and astonishment in her looks; she desired me, if I had any regard for my safety, to keep within, for a few days ago so dismal an accident had happened as to put all the world upon their guard. A mad dog down in the country, she assured me, had bit a farmer who, soon becoming mad, ran into his own yard, and bit a fine brindled cow; the cow quickly became as mad as the man, began to foam at the mouth, and raising herself up, walked about on her hind legs, sometimes barking like a dog, and sometimes attempting to talk like the farmer.

Were most stories of this nature thoroughly examined, it would be found that numbers of such as have been said to suffer were in no way injured; and that of those who have been actually bitten, not one in a hundred was bit by a mad dog. Such accounts in general, therefore, only serve to make the people miserable by false terrors.

Of all the beasts that graze the lawn or hunt the forest, a dog is the only animal that, leaving his fellows, attempts to cultivate the friendship of man; no injuries can abate his fidelity; no distress induce him to forsake his benefactor; studious to please and fearing to offend, he is still an humble, steadfast dependent, and in him alone fawning is not flattery. How unkind, then, to torture this faithful creature who has left the forest to claim the protection of man! How ungrateful a return to the trusty animal for all his services! Adieu.

On Elections
FROM LIEN CHI ALTANGI TO FUM HOAM

The English are at present employed in celebrating a feast, which becomes general every seventh year: the parliament of the nation being then dissolved, and another appointed to be chosen. This solemnity falls infinitely short of our Feast of the Lanterns in magnificence and splendour; it is also surpassed by others of the East in unanimity and pure devotion; but no festival in the world can compare with it for eating.

To say the truth, eating seems to make a grand ingredient in all English parties of zeal, business, or amusement. When a church is to be built, or an hospital endowed, the directors assemble, and instead of consulting upon it, they eat upon it, by which means the business goes forward with success. When the poor are to be relieved, the officers appointed to dole out public charity assemble and eat upon it. Nor has it ever been known that they filled the bellies of the poor till they had satisfied their own. But in the election of magistrates the people seem to exceed all bounds.

What amazes me is that all this good living no way contributes to improve their good humour. On the contrary, they seem to lose their temper as they lose their appetites; every morsel they swallow, and every glass they pour down, serves to increase their animosity. Upon one of these occasions I have actually seen a bloody-minded man-milliner sally forth at the head of a mob, to face a desperate pastrycook, who was general of the opposite party.

I lately made an excursion to a neighbouring village, in order to be a spectator of the ceremonies practised. Mixing with the crowd, I was conducted to the hall where the magistrates are chosen; but what tongue can describe this scene of confusion! The whole crowd seemed equally inspired with anger, jealousy, politics, patriotism, and punch. I remarked one figure that was carried up by two men upon this occasion. I at first began to pity his infirmities as natural, but soon found the fellow so drunk that he could not stand; another made his appearance to give his vote, but though he could stand, he actually lost the use of his tongue, and remained silent; a third, who, though excessively drunk, could both stand and speak, being asked the candidate's name for whom he voted, could be prevailed upon to make no other answer but "Tobacco and brandy!" In short, an election-hall seems to be a theatre, where every passion is seen without disguise; a school where fools may readily become worse, and where philosophers may gather wisdom. Adieu.

Opinions and Anecdotes

The most ignorant nations have always been found to think most highly of themselves.

It may sound fine in the mouth of a declaimer, when he talks of subduing our appetites, of teaching every sense to be content with a bare sufficiency, and of supplying only the wants of nature; but is there not more satisfaction in indulging these appetites, if with innocence and safety, than in restraining them? Am I not better pleased in enjoyment, than in the sullen satisfaction of thinking that I can live without enjoyment?

When five brethren had set upon the great Emperor Guisong, alone with his sabre he slew four of them; he was struggling with the fifth, when his guards, coming up, were going to cut the conspirator into a thousand pieces. "No, no!" cried the emperor, with a placid countenance. "Of all his brothers he is the only one remaining; at least let one of the family be suffered to live, that his aged parents may have somebody left to feed and comfort them."

It was a fine saying of Nangfu the emperor, who, being told that his enemies had raised an insurrection in one of the distant provinces, said: "Come, then, my friends, follow me, and I promise you that we shall quickly destroy them." He marched forward, and the rebels submitted upon his approach. All now thought that he would take the most signal revenge, but were surprised to see the captives treated with mildness and humanity. "How!" cries his first minister, "is this the manner in which you fulfil your promise? Your royal word was given that your enemies should be destroyed, and behold, you have pardoned all, and even caressed some!" "I promised," replied the emperor, with a generous air, "to destroy my *enemies*; I have fulfilled my word, for see, they are enemies no longer; I have made *friends* of them."

Well it were if rewards and mercy alone could regulate the commonwealth; but since punishments are sometimes necessary, let them at least be rendered terrible, by being executed but seldom; and let justice lift her sword rather to terrify than revenge.

HENRY HALLAM

Introduction to the Literature of Europe

The full volume of this work, "Introduction to the Literature of Europe in the Fifteenth, Sixteenth, and Seventeenth Centuries," was published about 1837, and is a vast accumulation of facts, but is lacking in organic unity, in vigour, and vitality. Hallam's spelling of proper names has been followed throughout this epitome. (Henry Hallam, biography; see Vol. XI, p. 255.)

I. — *Before the Fifteenth Century*

The establishment of the barbarian nations on the ruins of the Roman Empire in the West was followed by an almost universal loss of classical learning. The last of the ancients, and one who forms a link with the Middle Ages, is Boëthius, whose "Consolation of Philosophy" mingles a Christian sanctity with the lessons of Greek and Roman sages. But after his death, in 524, the downfall of learning and eloquence was inconceivably rapid, and a state of general ignorance, except here and there within the ecclesiastical hierarchy, lasted for five centuries.

The British islands led the way in the slow restoration of knowledge. The Irish monasteries, in the seventh century, were the first to send out men of comparative eminence, and the Venerable Bede, in the eighth century, was probably superior to any other man whom the world at that time possessed. Then came the days when Charlemagne laid in his vast dominions the foundations of learning.

In the tenth century, when England and Italy alike were in the most deplorable darkness, France enjoyed an age of illumination, and a generation or two later we find many learned and virtuous churchmen in Germany. But it is not until the twelfth century that we enter on a new epoch in European literary history, when universities were founded, modern languages were cultivated, the study of Roman law was systematically taken up, and a return was made to a purer Latinity.

Next, we observe the rise of the scholastic theology and philosophy, with their strenuous attempt at an alliance between faith and reason. The dry and technical style of these enquiries, their minute subdivisions of questions, and their imposing parade of accuracy, served indeed to stimulate subtlety of mind, but also hindered the revival of polite literature and the free expansion of the intellect.

Dante and Petrarch are the morning stars of the modern age. They lie outside our period, and we must pass them over with a word. It is sufficient to notice that, largely by their influence, we find, in the year 1400, a national literature existing in no less than seven European languages—three in the Spanish peninsula, the French, the Italian, the German, and the English.

II.—The Fifteenth Century

We now come to a very important event—the resuscitation of the study of Greek in Italy. In 1423, Giovanni Aurispa, of Sicily, brought over two hundred manuscripts from Greece, including Plato, Plotinus, Diodorus, Pindar, and many other classics. Manuel Chrysoloras, teacher of Greek in Florence, had trained a school of Hellenists; and copyists, translators, and commentators set to work upon the masterpieces of the ancient world. We have good reason to doubt whether, without the Italians of those times, the revival of classical learning would ever have occurred. The movement was powerfully aided by Nicolas V., pope in 1447, who founded the Vatican library, supported scholars, and encouraged authors.

Soon after 1450, the art of printing began to be applied to the purposes of useful learning, and Bibles, classical texts, collections of fables; and other works were rapidly given to the world. The accession to power of Lorenzo de Medici in 1464 marks the revival of native Italian genius in poetry, and under his influence the Platonic academy, founded by his grandfather Cosmo, promoted a variety of studies. But we still look in vain to England for either learning or native genius. The reign of Edward IV. is one of the lowest points in our literary annals.

In France, the "Cent Nouvelles Nouvelles," 1486, and the poems of Villon, 1489, show a marked advance in style. Many French "mysteries," or religious dramas, belong to this period, and this early form of the dramatic art had also much popularity in Germany and in Italy. Literary activity, in France and in Germany, had become regularly progressive by the end of the century.

Two men, Erasmus and Budæus, were now devoting incessant labour, in Paris, to the study of Greek; and a gleam of light broke out even in England, where William Grocyn began, in 1491, to teach that language in Oxford.

On his visit to England, in 1497, Erasmus was delighted with everything he found, and gave unbounded praise to the scholarship of Grocyn, Colet, Linacre, and the young Thomas More.

The fifteenth century was a period of awakening and of strenuous effort. But if we ask what monuments of its genius and erudition still receive homage, we can give no very triumphant answer. Of the books then written, how few are read now!

III. — The Sixteenth Century (1500–1550)

In the early years of this century the press of Aldus Manutius, who had settled in Venice in 1489, was publishing many texts of the classics, Greek as well as Latin.

It was at this time that the regular drama was first introduced into Europe. "Calandra," the earliest modern comedy, was presented at Venice in 1508, and about the same time the Spanish tragi-comedy of "Calisto and Meliboea" was printed. The pastoral romance, also, made its appearance in Portugal; and the "Arcadia," 1502, by the Italian Sannazaro, a work of this class, did much to restore the correctness and elegance of Italian prose. Peter Bembo's "Asolani," 1505, a dialogue on love, has also been thought to mark an epoch in Italian literature. At the same time, William Dunbar, with his "Thistle and Rose," 1503, and his allegorical "Golden Targe," was leading the van of British poetry.

The records of voyages of discovery begin to take a prominent place. The old travels of Marco Polo, as well as those of Sir John Mandeville, and the "Cosmography" of Ptolemy, had been printed in the previous century; but the stupendous discoveries of the close of that age now fell to be told. The voyages of Cadamosto, a Venetian, in Western Africa, appeared in 1507; and those of Amerigo Vespucci, entitled "Mondo Nuovo," in the same year. An epistle of Columbus himself had been printed in Germany about 1493.

Leo X., who became pope in 1513, placed men of letters in the most honourable stations of his court, and was the munificent patron of poets, scholars, and printers. Rucellai's "Rosmunda," a tragedy played before Leo in 1515, was the earliest known trial of blank verse. The "Sophonisba" of Trissino, published in 1524, a play written strictly on the Greek model, had been acted some years before. Two comedies by Ariosto were presented about 1512.

Meanwhile, the printing press became very active in Paris, Basle, and Germany, chiefly in preparing works for the use of students in universities. But in respect of learning, we have the testimony of Erasmus that neither France, nor Germany, stood so high as England. In Scotland, boys were being taught Latin in school; and the translation of the Æneid by Gawin Douglas, completed about 1513, shows, by its spirit and fidelity, the degree of scholarship in the north. The only work of real genius which England can claim in this age is the "Utopia" of Sir Thomas More, first printed in 1516.

Erasmus diffuses a lustre over his age, which no other name among the learned supplies. About 1517, he published an enlarged edition of his "Adages," which displays a surprising intimacy with Greek and Roman literature. The most remarkable of them, in every sense, are those which reflect with excessive bitterness on kings and priests. Erasmus knew that the regular clergy were not to be conciliated, and resolved to throw away the scabbard; and his invectives against kings proceeded from a just sense of the oppression of Europe in that age by ambitious and selfish rulers.

We are now brought by necessary steps to the great religious revolution known as the Reformation, with which we are only concerned in so far as it modified the history of literature. In all his dispute, Luther was sustained by a prodigious force of popular opinion; and the German nation was so fully awakened to the abuses of the Church that, if neither Luther nor Zwingli had ever been born, a great religious schism was still at hand. Erasmus, who had so manifestly prepared the way for the new reformers, continued, beyond the year 1520, favourable to their cause. But some of Luther's tenets he did not and could not approve; and he was already disgusted by that intemperance of language which soon led him to secede entirely from the Protestant side.

The laws of synchronism bring strange partners together, and we may pass at once from Luther to Ariosto, whose "Orlando Furioso" was printed at Ferrara in 1516. Ariosto has been, after Homer, the favourite poet of Europe. His grace and facility, his clear and rapid stream of language, his variety of invention, left him no rival.

No edition of "Amadis de Gaul" has been proved to exist before that printed at Seville in 1519. This famous romance was translated into French between 1540 and 1557, and into English by Munday in 1619.

A curious dramatic performance was represented in Paris in 1511, and published in 1516. It is entitled "Le Prince des Sots et la Mère sotte," by Peter Gringore; its chief aim was to ridicule the Pope and the court of Rome. Hans Sachs, a shoemaker of Nuremberg, produced his first carnival play in 1517. The English poets Hawes and Skelton fall within this period.

From 1520 to 1550, Italy, where the literature of antiquity had been first cultivated, still retained her superiority in the fine perception of its beauties, but the study was proceeding also elsewhere in Europe. Few books of that age give us more insight into its literary history and the public taste than the "Circeronianus" of Erasmus, against which Scaliger wrote with unmannerly invective. The same period of thirty years is rich with poets, among whom are the Spanish Mendoza, the Portuguese Ribero, Marot in France, many hymn-writers in Germany; and in England, Wyatt and Surrey. At this time also, Spain was forming its national theatre, chiefly under the influence of Lope de Rueda and of Torres Naharro, the inventor of Spanish comedy. The most celebrated writer of fiction in this age is Rabelais, than whom few have greater fertility of language and imagination.

IV.—The Sixteenth Century (1550–1600)

Montaigne's "Essays," which first appeared at Bordeaux in 1580, make an epoch in literature, being the first appeal from the academy to the haunts of busy and idle men; and this delightful writer had a vast influence on English and French literature in the succeeding age.

Turning now to the Italian poets of our period, we find that most of them are feeble copyists of Petrarch, whose style Bembo had rendered so popular. Casa, Costanzo, Baldi, Celio Magno, Bernardino Rota, Gaspara Stampa, Bernado Tasso, father of the great Tasso, Peter Aretin, and Firenzuola, flourished at this time. The "Jerusalem" of Torquato Tasso is the great epic of modern times; it is read with pleasure in almost every canto, though the native melancholy of Tasso tinges all his poem. It was no sooner published than it was weighed against the "Orlando Furioso," and Europe has not yet agreed which scale inclines.

Spanish poetry is adorned by Luis Ponce de Leon, born in 1527, a religious and mystical lyric poet. The odes of Herrera have a lyric elevation and richness of phrase, derived from the study of Pindar and of the Old Testament. Castillejo, playful and witty, attempted to revive the popular poetry, and ridiculed the imitators of Petrarch.

The great Camoens had now arisen in Portugal; his "Lusiad," written in praise of the Lusitanian people, is the mirror of his loving, courageous, generous, and patriotic heart. Camoens is the chief Portuguese poet in this age, and possibly in every other.

This was an age of verse in France. Pierre Ronsard, Amadis Jamyn his pupil, Du Bartas, Pibrac, Desportes, and many others, were gradually establishing the rules of metre, and the Alexandrine was displacing the old verse of ten syllables.

Of German poetry there is little to say; but England had Lord Vaux's short pieces in "The Paradise of Dainty Devices"; Sackville, with his

"Induction" to the "Mirrour of Magistrates," 1559; George Gascoyne, whose "Steel Glass," 1576, is the earliest English satire; and, above all, Spenser, whose "Shepherd's Kalendar" appeared in 1579. This work was far more natural and more pleasing than the other pastorals of the age. Shakespeare's "Venus and Adonis," and his "Rape of Lucrece," were published in 1593–94. Sir Philip Sidney, Raleigh, Lodge, Breton, Marlowe, Green, Watson, Davison, Daniel, and Michael Drayton were now writing poems, and Drake has a list of more than two hundred English poets of this time.

The great work of the period is, however, the "Faëry Queen," the first three books of which were published in 1590, and the last three in 1596. Spenser excels Ariosto in originality, force, and variety of character, and in depth of reflection, but especially in the poetical cast of feeling.

Of dramatic literature, between 1550 and 1600, we have many Italian plays by Groto, Decio da Orto, and Tasso. The pastoral drama originating with Agostino Beccari in 1554, reached its highest perfection in Tasso's "Aminta," which was followed by Guarini's "Pastor Fido."

Lope de Vega is the great Spanish dramatist of this time. His astonishing facility produced over two thousand original dramas, of which three hundred have been preserved. Jodelle, the father of the French theatre, presented his "Cléopatre" in 1552. In 1598 the foundations were laid of the Comédie Française.

In England, Sackville led the way with his tragedy of "Gorboduc," played at Whitehall before Elizabeth in 1562. In 1576, the first public theatre was erected in Blackfriars. Several young men of talent appeared, Marlowe, Peele, Greene, Kyd, and Nash, as the precursors of Shakespeare; and in 1587, being then twenty-three years old, the greatest of dramatists settled in London, and several of his plays had been acted before the close of the century.

Among English prose writings of this time may be mentioned Ascham's "Schoolmaster," 1570, Puttenham's "Art of English Poesie," 1586, and, as a curiosity of affectation, Lilly's "Euphues." But the first good prose-writer is Sir Philip Sidney, whose "Arcadia" appeared in 1590; and the finest master of prose in the Elizabethan period is Hooker. The first book of the "Ecclesiastical Polity" is one of the masterpieces of English eloquence.

V.—The Seventeenth Century (1600–1650)

The two great figures in philosophy of this period are Bacon and Descartes. At its beginning the higher philosophy had been little benefited by the labours of any modern enquirer. It was become, indeed, no strange thing to question the authority of Aristotle, but his disciples could point with scorn at the endeavours made to supplant it.

In the great field of natural jurisprudence, the most eminent name in this period is that of Hugo Grotius, whose famous work "De Jure Belli et Pacis" was published in Paris in 1625. This treatise made an epoch in the philosophical, and, we might almost say, in the political history of Europe.

In the history of poetry, between 1600 and 1650, we have the Italians Marini, Tassoni, and Chiabrera, the last being the founder of a school of lyric poetry known as "Pindaric." Among Spanish poets are Villegas and Gongora; in France, Malherbe, Regnier, Racan, Maynard, Voiture, and Sarrazin; Opitz, in Germany, was the founder of German poetic literature; and this, the golden age of Dutch literature, included the poets Spiegel, Hooft, Cats, and Vondel. The English poets of these fifty years are very numerous, but for the most part not well known. Spenser was imitated by Phineas and Giles Fletcher. Sir John Denham, Donne, Crashaw, Cowley, Daniel, Michael Drayton, William Browne, and Sir William Davenant wrote at this time, to which also belong the sonnets of Shakespeare. Drummond of Hawthornden, Carew, Ben Jonson, Wither, Habington, Suckling, and Herrick, were all in the first half of the seventeenth century. John Milton was born in 1609, and in 1634 wrote "Comus," which was published in 1637; "Lycidas," the "Allegro" and "Penseroso," the "Ode on the Nativity," and Milton's sonnets followed.

The Italian drama was weak at this period, but in Spain Lope de Vega and Calderon were at the height of their glory. In France, Corneille's "Mélite," his first play, was produced in 1629, and was followed by "Clitandre," "La Veuve," "Medea," "Cid," and others. The English drama was exceedingly popular, and the reigns of James and Charles were the glory of our theatre. Shakespeare—the greatest name in all literature—Ben Jonson, Beaumont and Fletcher, Massinger, Shirley, Heywood, Webster, and many other dramatists contributed to its fame.

In prose writings, Italian and Spanish works of this time show a great decline in taste; but in France, the letters of the moralist Balzac and of Voiture, from 1625, have ingenuity and sprightliness. English prose writings of the period include the works of Knolles, Raleigh, Daniel, Bacon, Milton, Clarendon; Burton's "Anatomy of Melancholy," Earle's "Microcosmographia" and Overbury's "Characters."

Fiction was represented by "Don Quixote," of which the first part was published in 1605—almost the only Spanish book which is popularly read in every country; by the French heroic romance, and by the English Godwin's "Man in the Moon."

VI.—The Seventeenth Century (1650–1700)

Among the greatest writers of this period are Bossuet and Pascal, in theology; Gassendi, Malebranche, Spinoza, and Locke, in philosophy; and Cumberland, Puffendorf, La Rochefoucauld, and La Bruyère, in morals. Leibnitz wrote on jurisprudence before he passed on to philosophy, and the same subject was treated also by Godefroy, Domat, and Noodt.

Italian poetry had now improved in tone. Filicaja, a man of serious and noble spirit, wrote odes of deep patriotic and religious feeling. Guidi, a native of Pavia, raised himself to the highest point that any lyric poet of Italy has attained. Spain and Portugal were destitute of poets; but in France La Fontaine, Boileau, Benserade, Chaulieu, Segrais, Deshoulières, and Fontenelle, were famous. In England at this time there were Waller, Milton, Butler, and Dryden, as well as Marvell and other minor poets.

Neither Italy nor Spain was now producing dramatic works of any importance, but it was very different in France. Corneille continued to write for the stage, and Racine's first play, the "Andromaque," was presented in 1667. This was followed by "Britannicus," "Bérénice," "Mithridate," "Iphigénie," and others. Racine's style is exquisite; he is second only to Virgil among all poets. Molière, the French writer whom his country has most uniformly admired, began with "L'Étourdi" in 1653, and his pieces followed rapidly until his death, in 1673. The English Restoration stage was held by Dryden, Otway, Southern, Lee, Congreve, Wycherley, Farquhar, and Vanbrugh.

In prose literature Italy is deficient; but this period includes the most distinguished portion of the great age in France, the reign of Louis XIV. Bossuet, Malebranche, Arnauld, and Pascal are among the greatest of French writers.

English writing now became easier and more idiomatic, sometimes even to the point of vulgarity. The best masters of prose were Cowley, Evelyn, Dryden, and Walton in the "Complete Angler."

Among novels of the period may be named those of Quevedo in Spain; of Scarron, Bergerac, Perrault, and Hamilton, in France; and the "Pilgrim's Progress"—for John Bunyan may pass for the father of our novelists—in England. Swift's "Tale of a Tub," than which Rabelais has nothing superior, was indeed not published till 1704, but was written within the seventeenth century.

WILLIAM HAZLITT

Lectures on the English Poets

William Hazlitt, critic and essayist, was born on April 10, 1778, and was educated in London for the Unitarian ministry. But his talents for painting and for writing diverted him from that career, and soon, though he showed great promise as a painter, he devoted himself to authorship, contributing largely to the "Morning Chronicle," the "Examiner," and the "Edinburgh Review." His wide, genial interests, his ardent temperament, and his admirable style, have given Hazlitt a high place among English critics. He is no pedant or bookworm; he is always human, always a man of the world. His "Characters of Shakespeare's Plays," 1817, gave him a reputation which was confirmed by his "Lectures on the English Poets," delivered next year at the Surrey Institute. Further lectures, on the English comic writers and on the Elizabethan dramatists, followed. His essays, on all kinds of subjects, are collected in volumes under various titles. All are the best of reading. Hazlitt's later works include "Liber Amoris," 1823; "Spirit of the Age," 1825, consisting of character studies; and the "Life of Napoleon" (Hazlitt's hero), 1828–30. The essayist was twice married, and died on September 18, 1830.

What Is Poetry?

The best general notion which I can give of poetry is that it is the natural impression of any object or event by its vividness exciting an involuntary movement of imagination and passion, and producing, by sympathy, a certain modulation of the voice or sounds expressing it. Poetry is the universal language which the heart holds with Nature and itself. He who has a contempt for poetry cannot have much respect for himself or for anything else. It is not a mere frivolous accomplishment; it has been the study and delight of mankind in all ages.

Nor is it found only in books; wherever there is a sense of beauty, or power, or harmony, as in a wave of the sea, or in the growth of a flower, there is poetry in its birth. It is not a branch of authorship; it is the "stuff of which our life is made." The rest is "mere oblivion," for all that is worth remembering in life is the poetry of it. If poetry is a dream, the business of life is much the same. If it is a fiction, made up of what we wish things to be, and fancy that they are because we wish them so, there is no other or better reality.

The light of poetry is not only a direct, but also a reflected light, that, while it shows us the object, throws a sparkling radiance on all around it; the flame of the passions communicated to the imagination reveals to us, as with a flash of lightning, the inmost recesses of thought, and penetrates our whole being. Poetry represents forms chiefly as they suggest other forms; feelings, as they suggest forms, or other feelings. Poetry puts a spirit of life and motion into the universe. It describes the flowing, not the fixed. The poetical impression of any object is that uneasy, exquisite sense of beauty or power that cannot be contained within itself, that is impatient of all limit; that—as flame bends to flame—strives to link itself to some other image of kindred beauty or grandeur, to enshrine itself, as it were, in the highest forms of fancy, and to relieve the aching sense of pleasure by expressing it in the boldest manner, and by the most striking examples of the same quality in other instances.

As in describing natural objects poetry impregnates sensible impressions with the forms of fancy, so it describes the feelings of pleasure or pain by blending them with the strongest movements of passion and the most striking forms of Nature. Tragic poetry, which is the most impassioned species of it, strives to carry on the feeling to the utmost point of sublimity or pathos by all the force of comparison or contrast, loses the sense of present suffering in the imaginary exaggeration of it, exhausts the terror or pity by an unlimited indulgence of it, and lifts us from the depths of woe to the highest contemplations of human life.

The use and end of poetry, "both at the first and now, was and is to hold the mirror up to Nature," seen through the medium of passion and imagination, not divested of that medium by means of literal truth or abstract reason. Those who would dispel the illusions of imagination, to give us their drab-coloured creation in their stead, are not very wise. It cannot be concealed, however, that the progress of knowledge and refinement has a tendency to clip the wings of poetry. The province of the imagination is principally visionary, the unknown and undefined; we can only fancy what we do not know. There can never be another Jacob's dream. Since that time the heavens have gone farther off, and grown astronomical.

Poetry combines the ordinary use of language with musical expression. As there are certain sounds that excite certain movements, and the song and dance go together, so there are, no doubt, certain thoughts that lead to certain tones of voice, or modulations of sound. The jerks, the breaks, the inequalities and harshnesses of prose are fatal to the flow of a poetical imagination, as a jolting road disturbs the reverie of an absent-minded man. But poetry makes these odds all even. The musical in sound is the sustained and continuous; the musical in thought is the sustained and continuous also. An excuse may be made for rhyme in the same manner.

Chaucer and Spenser

These are two out of the four greatest English poets; but they were both much indebted to the early poets of Italy, and may be considered as belonging, in some degree, to that school. Spenser delighted in luxurious enjoyment; Chaucer in severe activity of mind. Spenser was the most romantic and visionary of all great poets; Chaucer the most practical, the most a man of business and the world.

Chaucer does not affect to show his power over the reader's mind, but the power which his subject has over his own. The readers of Chaucer's poetry feel more nearly what the persons he describes must have felt, than perhaps those of any other poet. There is no artificial, pompous display; but a strict parsimony of the poet's materials, like the rude simplicity of the age in which he lived. His words point as an index to the objects, like the eye or finger. There were none of the commonplaces of poetic diction in his time, no reflected lights of fancy, no borrowed roseate tints; he was obliged to inspect things narrowly for himself, so that his descriptions produce the effect of sculpture.

His descriptions of natural scenery possess a characteristic excellence which may be termed gusto. They have a local truth and freshness which give the very feeling of the air, the coolness or moisture of the ground. Inanimate objects are thus made to have a fellow-feeling in the interest of the story, and render the sentiment of the speaker's mind.

It was the same trust in Nature and reliance on his subject which enabled Chaucer to describe the grief and patience of Griselda and the faith of Constance. Chaucer has more of this deep, internal, sustained sentiment than any other writer, except Boccaccio. In depth of simple pathos and intensity of conception, never swerving from his subject, I think no other writer comes near him, not even the Greek tragedians.

The poetry of Chaucer has a religious sanctity about it, connected with the manners and superstitions of the age. It has all the spirit of martyrdom.

It has also all the extravagance and the utmost licentiousness of comic humour, equally arising out of the manners of the time. He excelled in both styles, and could pass at will from the one to the other; but he never confounded the two styles together.

Of all the poets, Spenser is the most poetical. There is an originality, richness, and variety in his allegorical personages and fictions which almost vie with the splendours of the ancient mythology. His poetry is all fairyland; he paints Nature not as we find it, but as we expected to find it, and fulfils the delightful promise of our youth. His ideas, indeed, seem more distinct than his perceptions. The love of beauty, however, and not of truth, is the moving principle of his mind; and he is guided in his fantastic delineations by no rule but the impulse of an inexhaustible imagination.

Some people will say that Spenser's poetry may be very fine, but that they cannot understand it, on account of the allegory. They are afraid of the allegory. This is very idle. If they do not meddle with the allegory, the allegory will not meddle with them. Without minding it at all, the whole is as plain as a pikestaff.

Spenser is the poet of our waking dreams, and he has invented not only a language, but a music of his own for them. The undulations are infinite, like those of the waves of the sea; but the effect is still the same, lulling the senses into a deep oblivion of the jarring noises of the world, from which we have no wish ever to be recalled.

Shakespeare and Milton

Those arts which depend on individual genius and incommunicable power have always leaped at once from infancy to manhood, from the first rude dawn of invention to their meridian height and dazzling lustre, and have in general declined ever after. Homer, Chaucer, Spenser, Shakespeare, Dante, and Ariosto—Milton alone was of a later age, and not the worse for it—Raphael, Titian, Michael Angelo, Correggio, Cervantes, and Boccaccio, the Greek sculptors and tragedians, all lived near the beginning of their arts, perfected, and all but created them. They rose by clusters, never so to rise again.

The four greatest names in English poetry are almost the four first we come to—Chaucer, Spenser, Shakespeare, and Milton. There are no others that can really be put into competition with these. Of these four, Chaucer excels as the poet of manners, or of real life; Spenser as the poet of romance; Shakespeare as the poet of Nature, in the largest use of the term; and Milton as the poet of morality. Chaucer describes things as they are; Spenser, as we wish them to be; Shakespeare, as they would be; and Milton, as they ought to be. The characteristic of Chaucer is intensity; of Spenser, remoteness; of Milton, elevation; of Shakespeare, everything.

The peculiarity of Shakespeare's mind was its generic quality; its power of communication with all other minds, so that it contained a universe of thought and feeling within itself. He was just like any other man, but he was like all other men. He was the least of an egotist that it was possible to be. He was nothing in himself; but he was all that others were, or that they could become. His genius shone equally on the evil and on the good, on the wise and the foolish, the monarch and the beggar. The world of spirits lay open to him, like the world of real men and women; and there is the same truth in his delineations of the one as of the other. Each of his characters is as much itself, and as absolutely independent of the rest, as well as of the author, as if they were living persons, not fictions of the mind. His plays alone are properly expressions of the passions, not descriptions of them.

Chaucer's characters are narrative; Shakespeare's, dramatic; Milton's, epic. In Chaucer we perceive a fixed essence of character. In Shakespeare there is a continual composition and decomposition of its elements, a fermentation of every particle in the whole mass, by its alternate affinity or antipathy to other principles which are brought in contact with it. Milton took only a few simple principles of character, and raised them to the utmost conceivable grandeur.

The passion in Shakespeare is full of dramatic fluctuation. In Chaucer it is like the course of a river—strong, full, and increasing; but in Shakespeare it is like the sea, agitated this way and that, and loud-lashed by furious storms. Milton, on the other hand, takes only the imaginative part of passion, that which remains after the event, and abstracts it from the world of action to that of contemplation.

The great fault of a modern school of poetry [the Lake poets] is that it would reduce poetry to a mere effusion of natural sensibility; or, what is worse, would divest it both of imaginary splendour and human passion, to surround the meanest objects with the morbid feelings and devouring egotism of the writers' own minds. Milton and Shakespeare did not so understand poetry. They gave a more liberal interpretation both to Nature and art. They did not do all they could to get rid of the one and the other, to fill up the dreary void with the moods of their own minds.

Shakespeare's imagination is of the same plastic kind as his conception of character or passion. Its movement is rapid and devious, and unites the most opposite extremes. He seems always hurrying from his subject, even while describing it; but the stroke, like the lightning's, is as sure as it is sudden. His language and versification are like the rest of him. He has a magic power over words; they come winged at his bidding, and seem to know their places. His language is hieroglyphical. It translates thoughts into visible images. He had an equal genius for comedy and tragedy; and his tragedies are better than his comedies, because tragedy is better than comedy. His female characters are the finest in the world. Lastly, Shakespeare was the least of a coxcomb of anyone that ever lived, and much of a gentleman.

Shakespeare discovers in his writings little religious enthusiasm, and an indifference to personal reputation; in these respects, as in every other, he formed a direct contrast to Milton. Milton's works are a perpetual invocation to the muses, a hymn to Fame. He had his thoughts constantly fixed on the contemplation of the Hebrew theocracy, and of a perfect commonwealth; and he seized the pen with a hand warm from the touch of the ark of faith. The spirit of the poet, the patriot, and the prophet vied with each other in his breast. He thought of nobler forms and nobler things than those he found about him. He strives hard to say the finest things in the world, and he does say them. In Milton there is always an appearance of effort; in Shakespeare, scarcely any.

Milton has borrowed more than any other writer, and exhausted every source of imitation; yet he is perfectly distinct from every other writer. The power of his mind is stamped on every line. He describes objects of which he could only have read in books with the vividness of actual observation.

Milton's blank verse is the only blank verse in the language, except Shakespeare's, that deserves the name of verse. The sound of his lines is moulded into the expression of the sentiment, almost of the very image.

Dryden and Pope

These are the great masters of the artificial style of poetry, as the four poets of whom I have already treated were of the natural, and they have produced a kind and degree of excellence which existed equally nowhere else.

Pope was a man of exquisite faculties and of the most refined taste; he was a wit and critic, a man of sense, of observation, and the world. He was the poet not of Nature, but of art. He saw Nature only dressed by art; he judged of beauty by fashion; he sought for truth in the opinions of the world; he judged of the feelings of others by his own. His muse never wandered with safety but from his library to his grotto, or from his grotto into his library back again. That which was the nearest to him was the greatest; the fashion of the day bore sway in his mind over the immutable laws of Nature. He had none of the enthusiasm of poetry; he was in poetry what the sceptic is in religion. Yet within this narrow circle how much, and that how exquisite, was contained! The wrong end of the magnifier is held to everything, but still the exhibition is highly curious. If I had to choose, there are one or two persons—and but one or two—that I should like to have been better than Pope!

Dryden was a bolder and more various versifier than Pope; he had greater strength of mind, but he had not the same delicacy of feeling. Pope describes the thing, and goes on describing his own descriptions, till he loses himself in verbal repetitions; Dryden recurs to the object often, and gives us new strokes of character as well as of his pencil.

Thomson and Cowper

Thomson is the best of our descriptive poets; the colours with which he paints still seem wet. Nature in his descriptions is seen growing around us, fresh and lusty as in itself. He puts his heart into his subject, and it is for this reason that he is the most popular of all our poets. But his verse is heavy and monotonous; it seems always labouring uphill.

Cowper had some advantages over Thomson, particularly in simplicity of style, in a certain precision of graphical description, and in a more careful choice of topics. But there is an effeminacy about him which shrinks from and repels common and hearty sympathy. He shakes hands with Nature with a pair of fashionable gloves on; he is delicate to fastidiousness, and glad to get back to the drawing-room and the ladies, the sofa, and the tea-urn. He was a nervous man; but to be a coward is not the way to succeed either in poetry, in war, or in love. Still, he is a genuine poet, and deserves his reputation.

Robert Burns

Burns was not like Shakespeare in the range of his genius; but there is something of the same magnanimity, directness, and unaffected character about him. He was as much of a man, not a twentieth part as much of a poet, as Shakespeare. He had an eye to see, a heart to feel—no more. His pictures of good fellowship, of social glee, of quaint humour, are equal to anything; they come up to Nature, and they cannot go beyond it. His strength is not greater than his weakness; his virtues were greater than his vices. His virtues belonged to his genius; his vices to his situation.

Nothing could surpass Burns's love-songs in beauty of expression and in true pathos, except some of the old Scottish ballads themselves. There is in these a still more original cast of thought, a more romantic imagery; a closer intimacy with Nature, a more infantine simplicity of manners, a greater strength of affection, "thoughts that often lie too deep for tears." The old English ballads are of a gayer turn. They are adventurous and romantic; but they relate chiefly to good living and good fellowship, to drinking and hunting scenes.

Some Contemporary Poets

Tom Moore is heedless, gay, and prodigal of his poetical wealth. Everything lives, moves, and sparkles in his poetry, while, over all, love waves his purple light. His levity at last oppresses; his variety cloys, his rapidity dazzles and distracts the sight.

Lord Byron's poetry is as morbid as Moore's is careless and dissipated. His passion is always of the same unaccountable character, at once violent and sullen, fierce and gloomy. It is the passion of a mind preying upon itself, and disgusted with, or indifferent to, all other things. There is nothing less poetical or more repulsive. But still there is power; and power forces admiration. In vigour of style and force of conception he surpasses every writer of the present day.

Walter Scott is deservedly the most popular of living poets. He differs from his readers only in a greater range of knowledge and facility of expression. The force of his mind is picturesque rather than moral. He is to the great poet what an excellent mimic is to a great actor.

Mr. Wordsworth is the most original poet now living. His poetry is not external, but internal; he furnishes it from his own mind, and is his own subject. He is the poet of mere sentiment. Many of the "Lyrical Ballads" are of inconceivable beauty, of perfect originality and pathos. But his powers have been mistaken by the age. He cannot form a whole. He has not the constructive faculty. His "Excursion" is a proof of this; the line labours, the sentiment moves slowly, but the poem stands stock-still.

The Lake school of poetry had its origin in the French Revolution, or rather in the sentiments and opinions which produced that event. The world was to be turned topsy-turvy, and poetry was to share its fate. The paradox they set out with was that all things are by Nature equally fit subjects for poetry, or rather, that the meanest and most unpromising are best. They aimed at exciting attention by reversing the established standards of estimation in the world. An adept in this school of poetry is jealous of all excellence but his own. He is slow to admire anything admirable, feels no interest in what is most interesting to others, no grandeur in anything grand. He sees nothing but himself and the universe. His egotism is, in some respects, a madness. The effect of this has been perceived as something odd;

but the cause or principle has never been traced to its source before. The proofs are to be found throughout many of the poems of Mr. Southey, Mr. Coleridge, and Mr. Wordsworth.

I may say of Mr. Coleridge that he is the only person I ever knew who answered to the idea of a man of genius. But his "Ancient Mariner" is the only work that gives an adequate idea of his natural powers. In it, however, he seems to "conceive of poetry but as a drunken dream, reckless, careless, and heedless of past, present, and to come."

I have thus gone through my task. I have felt my subject sinking from under me as I advanced, and have been afraid of ending in nothing. The interest has unavoidably decreased at almost every step of the progress, like a play that has its catastrophe in the first or second act. This, however, I could not help.

OLIVER WENDELL HOLMES

The Autocrat of the Breakfast-Table

In 1857 Oliver Wendell Holmes (see Vol. V, p. 87) leapt into fame by his "Autocrat of the Breakfast-Table" papers in the "Atlantic Monthly," then edited by Lowell. His "Professor" and "Poet" series of papers followed, with hardly less success. In these writings a robust idealism, humour, fancy, and tenderness are so gently mixed as to amount to genius.

Every Man His Own Boswell

"All generous minds have a horror of what are commonly called 'facts.' They are the brute beasts of the intellectual domain. Who does not know fellows that always have an ill-conditioned fact or two that they lead after them into decent company like so many bulldogs, ready to let them slip at every ingenious suggestion, or convenient generalisation, or pleasant fancy? I allow no 'facts' at this table."

I continued, for I was in the talking vein, "This business of conversation is a very serious matter. There are men that it weakens one to talk with an hour more than a day's fasting would do. They are the talkers that have what may be called jerky minds. After a jolting half-hour with one of these jerky companions talking with a dull friend affords great relief. It is like taking the cat in your lap after holding a squirrel."

"Do not dull people bore you?" said one of the lady boarders.

"Madam," said I, "all men are bores except when we want them. Talking is like playing on the harp; there is as much in laying the hand on the strings to stop the vibrations as in twanging them to bring out the music. There is this, too, about talking," I continued; "it shapes our thoughts for us; the waves of conversation roll them as the surf rolls the pebbles on the shore. Writing or printing is like shooting with a rifle; you may hit your reader's mind, or miss it, but talking is like playing at a mark with the pipe of an engine—if it is within reach, and you have time enough, you can't help hitting it."

The company agreed that this last illustration was of superior excellence.

The Ageing of Ideas

"I want to make a literary confession now, which I believe nobody has made before me. I never wrote a 'good' line in my life, but the moment after it was written it seemed a hundred years old. The rapidity with which ideas grow old in our memories is in a direct ratio to the squares of their importance. A great calamity, for instance, is as old as the trilobites an hour after it has happened. It stains backward through all the leaves we have turned over in the book of life, before its blot of tears or of blood is dry on the page we are turning."

I wish I had not said all this then and there. The pale schoolmistress, in her mourning dress, was looking at me with a wild sort of expression; and all at once she melted away from her seat like an image of snow; a sling shot could not have brought her down better. God forgive me!

The Confusion of Personality

"We must remember that talking is one of the fine arts—the noblest, the most important, and the most difficult. It is not easy at the best for two persons talking together to make the most of each other's thoughts, there are so many of them."

The company looked as if they wanted an explanation.

"When John and Thomas, for instance, are talking together," I continued, "it is natural that among the six there should be more or less confusion and misapprehension."

Our landlady turned pale. No doubt she thought there was a screw loose in my intellect, and that it involved the probable loss of a boarder. Everybody looked up, and the old gentleman opposite slid the carving-knife to one side, as it were, carelessly.

"I think," I said, "I can make it plain that there are at least six personalities distinctly to be recognised as taking part in that dialogue between John and Thomas.

THREE JOHNS

1. The real John; known only to his Maker.

2. John's ideal John; never the real one, and often very unlike him.

3. Thomas's ideal John; never the real John, nor John's John, but often very unlike either.

THREE THOMASES

1. The real Thomas.
2. Thomas's ideal Thomas.
3. John's ideal Thomas.

"It follows that until a man can be found who knows himself as his Maker knows him, or who sees himself as others see him, there must be at least six persons engaged in every dialogue between two. No wonder two disputants often get angry when there are six of them talking and listening all at the same time."

A very unphilosophical application of the above remarks was made by a young fellow, answering to the name of John, who sits near me at table. A certain basket of peaches, a rare vegetable, little known to boarding-houses, was on its way to me *viâ* this unlettered Johannes. He appropriated the three that remained in the basket, remarking that there was just one apiece for him. I convinced him that his practical inference was hasty and illogical—but in the meantime he had eaten the peaches.

More on Books

"Some of you boarders ask me why I don't write a novel, or something of that kind. Well, there are several reasons against it. In the first place I should tell all my secrets, and I maintain that verse is the proper medium for such revelations. Again, I am terribly afraid I should show up all my friends, and I am afraid all my friends would not bear showing up very well. And sometimes I have thought I might be too dull to write such a story as I should wish to write. And, finally, I think it is very likely I *shall* write a story one of these days.

"I saw you smiled when I spoke about the possibility of my being too dull to write a good story. When one arrives at the full and final conclusion that he or she is really dull, it is one of the most tranquillising and blessed convictions that can enter a mortal's mind.

"How sweetly and honestly one said to me the other day, 'I hate books!' I did not recognise in him inferiority of literary taste half so distinctly as I did simplicity of character, and fearless acknowledgment of his inaptitude for scholarship. In fact, I think there are a great many who read, with a mark to keep their place, that really 'hate books,' but never had the wit to find it out, or the manliness to own it."

Dual Consciousness

I am so pleased with my boarding-house that I intend to remain here, perhaps for years.

"Do thoughts have regular cycles? Take this: All at once a conviction flashes through us that we have been in the same precise circumstances as at the present instant once or many times before."

When I mentioned this the Schoolmistress said she knew the feeling well, and didn't like to experience it; it made her think she was a ghost, sometimes.

The young fellow whom they call John said he knew all about it. He had just lighted a cheroot the other day when a tremendous conviction came over him that he had done just that same thing ever so many times before.

"How do I account for it? Well, some think that one of the hemispheres of the brain hangs fire, and the small interval between the perceptions of the nimble and the sluggish half seems an indefinitely long period, and therefore the second perception appears to be the copy of another, ever so old."

The Race of Life

"Nothing strikes one more in the race of life than to see how many give out in the first half of the course. 'Commencement day' always reminds me of the start of the 'Derby.' Here we are at Cambridge and a class is first 'graduating.' Poor Harry! he was to have been there, but he has paid forfeit.

"*Ten years gone.* First turn in the race. A few broken down; two or three bolted. 'Cassock,' a black colt, seems to be ahead of the rest. 'Meteor' has pulled up.

"*Twenty years.* Second corner turned. 'Cassock' has dropped from the front, and 'Judex,' an iron-grey, has the lead. But look! how they have thinned out! Down flat—five—six—how many? They will not get up again in this race be very sure!

"*Thirty years.* Third corner turned. 'Dives,' bright sorrel, ridden by the fellow in a yellow jacket, begins to make play fast—is getting to be the favourite with many. But who is that other one that now shows close up to the front? Don't you remember the quiet brown colt 'Asteroid,' with the star in his forehead? That is he; he is one of the sort that lasts. 'Cassock' is now taking it easily in a gentle trot.

"*Forty years.* More dropping off, but places much as before.

"*Fifty years*. Race over. All that are on the course are coming in at a walk; no more running. Who is ahead? Ahead? What! and the winning-post a slab of white or gray stone standing out from that turf where there is no more jockeying, or straining for victory! Well, the world marks their places in its betting-book; but be sure that these matter very little, if they have run as well as they knew how!

"I will read you a few lines, if you do not object, suggested by looking at a section of one of those chambered shells to which is given the name of Pearly Nautilus.

THE CHAMBERED NAUTILUS

This is the ship of pearl, which, poets feign,
Sails the unshadowed main—
The venturous bark that flings
On the sweet summer wind its purpled wings
In gulfs enchanted, where the siren sings,
And coral reefs lie bare,
Where the cold sea-maids rise to sun their streaming hair.

Its webs of living gauze no more unfurl;
Wrecked is the ship of pearl!
And every chambered cell,
Where its dim, dreaming life was wont to dwell,
As the frail tenant shaped his growing shell,
Before thee lies revealed—
Its irised ceiling rent, its sunless crypt unsealed!

Year after year beheld the silent toil187
That spread his lustrous coil;
Still, as the spiral grew,
He left the past year's dwelling for the new,
Stole with soft step its shining archway through,
Built up its idle door,
Stretched in his last found home, and knew the old no
more.

Thanks for the heavenly message brought by thee,
Child of the wandering sea,
Cast from her lap forlorn!
From thy dead lips a clearer note is born
Than ever Triton blew from wreathed horn!
While on mine ear it rings,
Through the deep caves of thought I hear a voice that sings:

Build thee more stately mansions, O my soul,
As the swift seasons roll!
Leave thy low-vaulted past!
Let each new temple, nobler than the last,
Shut thee from heaven with a dome more vast,
Till thou at length art free,
Leaving thine outgrown shell by life's unresting sea!

Sensibility and Scholarship

"Every person's feelings have a front-door and a side-door by which they may be entered. The front-door is on the street. The side-door opens at once into the sacred chambers. There is almost always at least one key to this side-door. This is carried for years hidden in a mother's bosom. Be very careful to whom you entrust one of these keys of the side-door. Some of those who come in at the side-door have a scale of your whole nervous system, and can play on all the gamut of your sensibilities in semi-tones. Married life is the school in which the most accomplished artists in this department are found. Be very careful to whom you give the side-door key.

"The world's great men have not commonly been great scholars, nor its great scholars great men. The Hebrew patriarchs had small libraries, if any; yet they represent to our imaginations a very complete idea of manhood, and I think if we could ask Abraham to dine with us men of letters next Saturday we should feel honoured by his company."

A Growing Romance

"I should like to make a few intimate revelations relating especially to my early life, if I thought you would like to hear them."

The schoolmistress turned in her chair and said, "If we should *like* to hear them—we should *love* to."

So I drew my chair a shade nearer her, and went on to speak of voices that had bewitched me.

"I wish you could hear my sister's voice," said the schoolmistress.

"If it is like yours it must be a pleasant one," said I.

Lately she has been walking early and has brought back roses in her cheeks. I love the damask rose best of all flowers.

Our talk had been of trees, and I had been comparing the American and the English elms in the walk we call the Mall. "Will you walk out and look at those elms with me after breakfast?" I said to the schoolmistress.

I am not going to tell lies about it, and say that she blushed. On the contrary, she turned a little bit pale, but smiled brightly, and said, "Yes, with pleasure." So she went to fetch her bonnet, and the old gentleman opposite followed her with his eyes, and said he wished he was a young fellow.

"This is the shortest way," she said, as we came to the corner.

"Then we won't take it," said I.

When we reached the school-room door the damask roses were so much heightened in colour by exercise that I felt sure it would be useful to her to take a stroll like this every morning.

I have been low-spirited and listless lately. It is coffee, I think. I notice that I tell my secrets too easily when I am downhearted. There are inscriptions on our hearts never seen except at dead low-tide. And there is a woman's footstep on the sand at the side of my deepest ocean-buried inscription.

I am not going to say which I like best, the seashore or the mountains. The one where your place is, is the best for you; but this difference there is—you can domesticate mountains. The sea is feline. It licks your feet, its huge flanks purr very pleasantly for you; but it will crack your bones and eat you for all that, and wipe the crimsoned foam from its jaws as if nothing had happened. The mountains have a grand, stupid, lovable tranquillity; the sea has a fascinating, treacherous intelligence.

"If I thought I should ever see the Alps!" said the schoolmistress.

"Perhaps you might some time or other," I said.

"It is not very likely," she answered.

Tableau. Chamouni. Mont Blanc in full view. Figures in the foreground, two of them standing apart; one of them a gentleman—oh—ah—yes!— the other a lady, leaning on his shoulder. (The reader will understand this was an internal, private, subjective diorama, seen for one instant on the background of my own consciousness.)

*****

I can't say just how many walks she and I had taken together. I found the effect of going out every morning was decidedly favourable on her health. I am afraid I did the greater part of the talking. Better too few words from the woman we love than too many; while she is silent, Nature is working for her; while she talks she works for herself. Love is sparingly soluble in the words of men, therefore they speak much of it; but one syllable of woman's speech can dissolve more of it than a man's heart can hold.

Nature's Patient Advance

I don't know anything sweeter than the leaking in of Nature through all the cracks in the walls and floors of cities. You heap a million tons of hewn rocks on a square mile or so of earth which was green once. The trees look down from the hill-tops and ask each other, as they stand on tiptoe, "What are these people about?" And the small herbs look up and whisper back, "We will go and see." So the small herbs pack themselves up in the least possible bundles, and wait until the night wind steals to them and whispers, "Come with me." Then they go softly with it into the great city—one to a cleft in the pavement, one to a spout on the roof, one to a seam in the marble over a rich gentleman's bones, and one to the grave without a stone, where nothing but a man is buried—and there they grow, looking down on the generations of men from mouldy roofs, looking up from between the less-trodden pavements, looking out through iron cemetery railings.

Listen to them when there is only a light breath stirring, and you will hear them saying to each other, "Wait awhile." The words run along the telegraph of those narrow green lines that border the roads leading from the city, until they reach the slope of the hills, and the trees repeat in low murmurs, "Wait awhile." By and by the flow of life in the streets ebbs, and the old leafy inhabitants—the smaller tribes always in front—saunter in, one by one, very careless seemingly, but very tenacious, until they swarm so that the great stones gape from each other with the crowding of their roots, and the feldspar begins to be picked out of the granite to find them food. At last the trees take up their solemn line of march, and never rest until they have camped in the market-place. Wait long enough, and you will find an old doting oak hugging in its yellow underground arms a huge worn block that was the cornerstone of the State-house. Oh, so patient she is, this imperturbable Nature!

The Long Path

It was in talking of life that the schoolmistress and I came nearest together. I thought I knew something about that. The schoolmistress had tried life, too. Once in a while one meets with a single soul greater than all the living pageant that passes before it. This was one of them. Fortune had left her, sorrow had baptised her. Yet as I looked upon her tranquil face, gradually regaining a cheerfulness that was often sprightly, as she became interested in the various matters we talked about and places we visited, I saw that eye and lip and every shifting lineament were made for love.

I never addressed a word of love to the schoolmistress in the course of these pleasant walks. It seemed as if we talked of everything but love on that particular morning. There was, perhaps, a little more timidity and hesitancy on my part than I have commonly shown among our people at the boarding-house. In fact, I considered myself the master at the breakfast-table; but somehow I could not command myself just then so well as usual. The truth is, I had secured a passage to Liverpool in the steamer which was to leave at noon—with the condition of being released if circumstances occurred to detain me. The schoolmistress knew nothing about this, of course, as yet.

It was on the Common that we were walking. The boulevard of the Common, you know, has various branches leading from it in different directions. One of these runs across the whole length of the Common. We called it the "long path," and were fond of it.

I felt very weak indeed—though of a tolerably robust habit—as we came opposite to the head of this path on that morning. I think I tried to speak twice, without making myself distinctly audible. At last I got out the question, "Will you take the long path with me?" "Certainly," said the schoolmistress, "with much pleasure." "Think," I said, "before you answer. If you take the long path with me now, I shall interpret it that we are to part no more."

The schoolmistress stepped back with a sudden movement, as if an arrow had struck her. One of the long granite blocks used as seats was hard by—the one you may still see close by the gingko-tree. "Pray sit down," I said.

"No, no," she answered softly; "I will walk the *long path* with you!"

The old gentleman who sits opposite met us walking, arm-in-arm, about the middle of the long path, and said very charmingly to us, "Good-morning, my dears!"

LA BRUYÈRE

Characters

Jean de la Bruyère was born in Paris, in August, 1645. He studied law and became a barrister, but at the age of twenty-eight gave up that profession, which did not agree with his tendencies to meditation and his scrupulous mind. In 1673, he bought the office of Treasurer of the Finances, and led an independent and studious life. In 1684, he became a tutor to the Duc de Bourbon, grandson of the great Condé, and continued to reside in the Condé household until his death in 1696. In the "Caractères," which first appeared in 1688, La Bruyère has recorded his impressions of men. In 1687 the manuscript was handed to Michallet, a publisher in whose shop La Bruyère spent many hours every week. "Will you print this?" asked the author. "I don't know whether it will be to your advantage; but should it prove a success, the money will be for my dear friend, your little daughter." The sale of the book produced over $40,000. When La Bruyère was elected a member of the French Academy, his enemies declared that the "Characters" consisted of satirical portraits of leading personalities, and "keys" to the portraits were widely circulated. The pen sketches, however, are not only applicable to that period, but to every age.

I.—On Men and Books

All has been said, and one comes too late after the seven thousand years during which men have existed—and thought. All that one can do is to think and speak rightly, without attempting to force one's tastes and feelings upon others.

Mediocrity in poetry, music, painting, and oratory is unbearable.

There is in art a certain degree of perfection, as there is in Nature an ideal point of matureness. To go beyond, or to remain below that degree is faulty.

The ability of a writer consists mainly in giving good definitions and apt descriptions. The superiority of Moses, Homer, Plato, Virgil, and Horace resides in the beauty of their expressions and images. One has to express the truth to write in a natural, powerful, and refined manner.

It has taken centuries for men to return to the ideal of the ancients and to all that is simple and natural.

We feed on the classics and the able, modern authors. Then, when we become authors ourselves, we ill-use our masters, like those children who, strengthened by the milk they have suckled, beat their nurses.

Read your works to those who are able to criticise and appreciate them. A good and careful writer often finds that the expression he had so long looked for was most simple and natural, and one which ought to have occurred to him at once and without effort.

The pleasure there is in criticising takes from us the joy of being moved by that which is really beautiful.

Arsène, from the top of his mind, looks down upon humanity; and, owing to the distance from which he sees men, is almost frightened at their smallness. He is so filled with his own sublime thoughts that he hardly finds time to deliver a few precious oracles.

Théocrine knows things which are rather useless; his ideas are always strange, his memory always at work. He is a supercilious dreamer, and always seems to laugh at those whom he considers as his inferiors. I read my book to him; he listens. Afterwards, he speaks to me about his own book. What does he think of mine? I told you so before: he speaks to me of his own work!

What an amazing difference there is between a beautiful book and a perfect book!

When a book elevates your mind, and inspires you with noble thoughts, you require nothing else to judge it; it is a good and masterly work.

The fools do not understand what they read. The mediocre think they understand thoroughly. Great minds do not always understand every page of a book; they think obscure that which is obscure, and clear that which is clear. The pedantic find obscure that which is not, and refuse to understand that which is perfectly clear.

Molière would have been a perfect writer had he only avoided jargon and barbarisms, and written more purely.

Ronsard had in him enough good and bad to form great disciples in prose and verse.

Corneille, at his best, is original and inimitable, but he is uneven. He had a sublime mind, and has written a few verses which are among the best ever written.

Racine is more human. He has imitated the Greek classics, and in his tragedies there is simplicity, clearness, and pathos.

Corneille paints men as they ought to be; Racine paints them as they are. Corneille is more moral; Racine is more natural. The former, it seems, owes much to Sophocles; the latter, to Euripides.

How is it that people at the theatre laugh so freely, and yet are ashamed to weep? Is it less natural to be moved by all that is worthy of pity than to burst out laughing at all that is ridiculous? Is it that we consider it weak to cry, especially when the cause of our emotion is an artificial one? But the cause of our laughter at the theatre is also artificial. Some persons think it is as childish to laugh excessively as to sob.

Not only should plays not be immoral; they should be elevating.

Logic is the art of convincing oneself of some truth. Eloquence is a gift of the soul which makes one capable of conquering the hearts and minds of the listeners and of making them believe anything one pleases.

He who pays attention only to the taste of his own century thinks more of himself than of his writings. One should always aim at perfection. If our contemporaries fail to do us justice, posterity may do so.

Horace and Boileau have said all this before. I take your word for it; but may I not, after them, "think a true thought," which others will think after me?

There are more tools than workers, and among the latter, more bad than good ones.

There is, in this world, no task more painful than that of making a name for oneself; we die before having even sketched our work. It takes, in France, much firmness of purpose and much broadmindedness to be indifferent to public functions and offices, and to consent to remain at home and do nothing.

Hardly anyone has enough merit to assume that part in a dignified manner, or enough brains to fill the gap of time without what is generally called business.

All that is required is a better name for idleness; and that meditation, conversation, reading, and repose should be called work.

You tell me that there is gold sparkling on Philémon's clothes. So there is on the clothes at the draper's. He is covered with the most gorgeous fabrics.

I can see those fabrics in the shops. But the embroidery and ornaments on Philémon's clothes further increase their magnificence. If so, I praise the embroiderer's workmanship. If someone asks him the time, he takes from his pocket a jewelled watch; the hilt of his sword is made of onyx; he displays a dazzling diamond on his finger and wears all the curious and pretty trifles of fashion and vanity. You arouse my interest at last. I ought to see those precious things. Send me the clothes and jewels of Philémon; I don't require to see *him*.

It is difficult to tell the hero from the great man at war. Both have military virtues. However, the former is generally young, enterprising, gifted, self-controlled even in danger, and courageous; the latter has much judgment, foresees events, and is endowed with much ability and experience. Perhaps one might say that Alexander was only a hero and that Cæsar was a great man.

Ménippe is a bird adorned with feathers which are not his own. He has nothing to say; he has no feelings, no thoughts. He repeats what others have said, and uses their ideas so instinctively that he deceives himself, and is his first victim. He often believes that he is expressing his own thoughts, while he is only an echo of someone whom he has just left. He believes childishly that the amount of wit he possesses is all that man ever possessed. He therefore looks like a man who has nothing to desire.

II.—On Women and Wealth

From the age of thirteen to the age of twenty-one, a girl wishes she were beautiful; afterwards she wishes she were a man.

An unfaithful woman is a woman who has ceased to love.

A light-hearted woman is a woman who already loves another.

A fickle woman is a woman who does not know whether she loves or not, and who does not know what or whom she loves.

An indifferent woman is a woman who loves nothing.

There is a false modesty which is vanity; a false glory which is light-mindedness; a false greatness which is smallness; a false virtue which is hypocrisy; a false wisdom which is prudishness.

Why make men responsible for the fact that women are ignorant? Have any laws or decrees been issued forbidding them to open their eyes, to read, to remember what they have read, and to show that they understood it in their conversations and their works? Have they not themselves decided to know little or nothing, because of their physical weakness, or the sluggishness of their minds; because of the time their beauty requires; because of their light-mindedness which prevents them from studying; because they have only talent and genius for needlework or house-managing; or because they instinctively dislike all that is earnest and demands some effort?

Women go to extremes. They are better or worse than men.

Women go farther than men in love; but men make better friends.

It is because of men that women dislike one another.

It is nothing for a woman to say what she does not mean; it is easier still for a man to say all what he thinks.

Time strengthens the ties of friendship and loosens those of love.

There is less distance between hatred and love than between dislike and love.

One can no more decide to love for ever than decide never to love at all.

One comes across men who irritate one by their ridiculous expressions, the strangeness and unfitness of the words they use. Their weird jargon becomes to them a natural language. They are delighted with themselves and their wit. True, they have some wit, but one pities them for having so little of it; and, what is more, one suffers from it.

Arrias has read and seen everything, and he wants people to know it. He is a universal man; he prefers to lie rather than keep silent or appear ignorant about something. The subject of the conversation is the court of a certain northern country. He at once starts talking, and speaks of it as if he had been born in that country; he gives details on the manners and customs, the women and the laws: he tells anecdotes and laughs loudly at his own wit. Someone ventures to contradict him and proves to him that he is not accurate in his statements. Arrias turns to the interrupter: "I am telling nothing that is not exact," he says. "I heard all those details from Sethon, ambassador of France to that court. Sethon returned recently; I know him well, and had a long conversation with him on this matter." Arrias was resuming his story with more confidence than ever, when one of the guests said to him: "I am Sethon, and have just returned from my mission."

Cléante is a most honest man. His wife is the most reasonable person in the world. Both make everybody happy wherever they go, and it were impossible to find a more delightful and refined couple. Yet they separate to-morrow!

At thirty you think about making your fortune; at fifty you have not made it; when you are old, you start building, and you die while the painters are still at work.

Numberless persons ruin themselves by gambling, and tell you coolly they cannot live without gambling. What nonsense! Would it be allowed to say that one cannot live without stealing, murdering, or leading a riotous existence?

Giton has a fresh complexion, and an aggressive expression. He is broad-shouldered and corpulent. He speaks with confidence. He blows his nose noisily, spits to a great distance, and sneezes loudly. He sleeps a great deal, and snores whenever he pleases. When he takes a walk with his equals he occupies the centre; when he stops, they stop; when he advances again, they do the same. No one ever interrupts him. He is jovial, impatient, haughty, irritable, independent. He believes himself witty and gifted. He is rich.

Phédon has sunken eyes. He is thin, and his cheeks are hollow. He sleeps very little. He is a dreamer, and, although witty, looks stupid. He forgets to say what he knows, and when he does speak, speaks badly. He shares the opinion of others; he runs, he flies to oblige anyone; he is kind and flattering. He is superstitious, scrupulous, and bashful. He walks stealthily, speaks in a low voice, and takes no room. He can glide through the densest crowd without effort. He coughs, and blows his nose inside his hat, and waits to sneeze until he is alone. He is poor.

III.—On Men and Manners

Paris is divided into a number of small societies which are like so many republics. They have their own customs, laws, language, and even their own jokes.

One grows up, in towns, in a gross ignorance of all that concerns the country. City-bred men are unable to tell hemp from flax, and wheat from rye. We are satisfied as long as we can feed and dress.

When we speak well of a man at court, we invariably do so for two reasons: firstly, in order that he may hear that we spoke well of him; secondly, in order that he may speak well of us in his turn.

To be successful and to secure high offices there are two ways: the highroad, on which most people pass; and the cross-road, which is the shorter.

The youth of a prince is the origin of many fortunes.

Court is where joys are evident, but artificial; where sorrows are concealed, but real.

A slave has one master; an ambitious man has as many as there are persons who may be useful to him in his career.

With five or six art terms, people give themselves out as experts in music, painting, and architecture.

The high opinions people have of the great and mighty is so blind, and their interest in their gestures, features, and manners so general, that if the mighty were only good, the devotion of the people to them would amount to worship.

Lucile prefers to waste his life as the protégé of a few aristocrats than to live on familiar terms with his peers.

It is advisable to say nothing of the mighty. If you speak well of them, it is flattery. It is dangerous to speak ill of them during their lifetime, and it is cowardly to do so after they are dead.

Life is short and annoying. We spend life wishing.

When life is wretched, it is hard to bear; when it is happy, it is dreadful to lose it. The one alternative is as bad as the other.

Death occurs only once, but makes itself felt at every moment of our life. It is more painful to fear it than to suffer it.

There are but three events for man: birth, life, and death. He does not realise his birth, he suffers when he dies, and he forgets to live.

We seek our happiness outside ourselves. We seek it in the opinions of men whom we know are flatterers, and who lack sincerity. What folly! Most men spend half their lives making the other half miserable.

It is easier for many men to acquire one thousand virtues than to get rid of one defect.

It is as difficult to find a conceited man who believes himself really happy as to discover a modest man who thinks himself too unhappy.

The birch is necessary to children. Grown-up men need a crown, a sceptre, velvet caps and fur-lined robes. Reason and justice devoid of ornaments would not be imposing or convincing. Man, who is a mind, is led by his eyes and his ears!

IV.—On Customs and Religion

Fashion in matters of food, health, taste and conscience is utterly foolish. Game is at present out of fashion, and condemned as a food. It is to-day a sin against fashion to be cured of the ague by blood-letting.

The conceited man thinks every day of the way in which he will be able to attract attention on the following day. The philosopher leaves the matter of his clothes to his tailor. It is just as childish to avoid fashion as to follow its decrees too closely.

Fashion exists in the domain of religion.

There have been young ladies who were virtuous, healthy and pious, who wished to enter a convent, but who were not rich enough to take in a wealthy abbey the vows of poverty.

How many men one sees who are strong and righteous, who would never listen to the entreaties of their friends, but who are easily influenced and corrupted by women.

I would like to hear a sober, moderate, chaste, righteous man declare that there is no God. At least he would be speaking in a disinterested manner. But there is no such man to be found.

The fact that I am unable to prove that God does not exist establishes for me the fact that God does exist.

Atheism does not exist. If there were real atheists, it would merely prove that there are monsters in this world.

Forty years ago I didn't exist, and it was not within my power to be born. It does not depend upon me who now exist to be no more. Consequently, I began being and am going on being, thanks to something which is beyond me, which will last after me, which is mightier than I am. If that something is not God, pray tell me what it is.

Everything is great and worthy of admiration in Nature.

O you vain and conceited man, make one of these worms which you despise! You loathe toads; make a toad if you can!

Kings, monarchs, potentates, sacred majesties, have I given you all your supreme names? We, mere men, require some rain for our crops or even some dew; make some dew, send to the earth a drop of water!

A certain inequality in the destinies of men, which maintains order and obedience, is the work of God. It suggests a divine law.

If the reader does not care for these "characters," it will surprise me; if he does care for them, it will also surprise me.

WALTER SAVAGE LANDOR

Imaginary Conversations

Walter Savage Landor, writer, scholar, poet, and, it might almost be said, quarreller, said of his own fame, "I shall dine late, but the dining-room will be well lighted, the guests few and select." A powerful, turbulent spirit, he attracted great men. Emerson, Browning, Dickens, and Swinburne travelled to sit at his feet, and he knew Byron, Shelley, Wordsworth, Lamb, and Southey. Born at Warwick, on January 30, 1775, he was dismissed from Rugby School at the age of fifteen, and from Oxford at the age of nineteen; was estranged from his father; several times left the wife whom he had married for her golden hair, and spent the last years of his life, lonely but lionised, at Florence. To the last—which came on September 17, 1864—he wrote both prose and verse. Landor appears, to the average appreciator of English literature, an interesting personality rather than a great writer, though his epic, "Gebir" (1798), and his tragedy, "Count Julian" (1812), like some of his minor verse, contain passages of great beauty. But it was in the "Imaginary Conversations," written between 1821 and 1829, and first sampled by the public in review form in 1823, that he endowed the English language with his most permanent achievement. Nearly 150 of these "Conversations" were written in all, and we epitomise here five of the best-known.

I.—Peter the Great and Alexis

Peter: And so, after flying from thy father's house, thou hast returned again from Vienna. After this affront in the face of Europe, thou darest to appear before me?

Alexis: My emperor and father! I am brought before your majesty not at my own desire.

Peter: I believe it well. What hope hast thou, rebel, in thy flight to Vienna?

Alexis: The hope of peace and privacy; the hope of security, and, above all things, of never more offending you.

Peter: Didst thou take money?

Alexis: A few gold pieces. Hitherto your liberality, my father, hath supplied my wants of every kind.

Peter: Not of wisdom, not of duty, not of spirit, not of courage, not of ambition. I have educated thee among my guards and horses, among my drums and trumpets, among my flags and masts. I have rolled cannon balls before thee over iron plates; I have shown thee bright new arms, bayonets, and sabres. I have myself led thee forth to the window when fellows were hanged and shot; and I have made thee, in spite of thee, look steadfastly upon them, incorrigible coward! Thy intention, I know, is to subvert the institutions it has been the labour of my lifetime to establish. Thou hast never rejoiced at my victories.

Alexis: I have rejoiced at your happiness and your safety.

Peter: Liar! Coward! Traitor! When the Polanders and the Swedes fell before me, didst thou congratulate me? Didst thou praise the Lord of Hosts? Wert thou not silent and civil and low-spirited?

Alexis: I lamented the irretrievable loss of human life, I lamented that the bravest and noblest were swept away the first, that order was succeeded by confusion, and that your majesty was destroying the glorious plans you alone were capable of devising.

Peter: Of what plans art thou speaking?

Alexis: Of civilising the Muscovites. The Polanders in parts were civilised; the Swedes more than any other nation.

Peter: Civilised, forsooth? Why the robes of the metropolitan, him at Upsal, are not worth three ducats. But I am wasting my words. Thine are tenets that strike at the root of politeness and sound government.

Alexis: When I hear the God of Mercy invoked to massacres, and thanked for furthering what He reprobates and condemns—I look back in vain on any barbarous people for worse barbarism.

Peter: Malignant atheist! Am I Czar of Muscovy, and hear discourse on reason and religion—from my own son, too? No, by the Holy Trinity! thou art no son of mine. Unnatural brute, I have no more to do with thee. Ho there! Chancellor! What! Come at last! Wert napping, or counting thy ducats?

Chancellor: Your majesty's will, and pleasure!

Peter: Is the senate assembled?

Chancellor: Every member, sire.

Peter: Conduct this youth with thee, and let them judge him; thou understandest?

Chancellor: Your majesty's commands are the breath of our nostrils.

Peter: If these rascals are amiss, I will try my new cargo of Livonian hemp upon 'em.

Chancellor (*returning*): Sire! Sire!

Peter: Speak, fellow! Surely they have not condemned him to death without giving themselves time to read the accusation, that thou comest back so quickly.

Chancellor: No, sire! Nor has either been done.

Peter: Then thy head quits thy shoulders.

Chancellor: O sire! he fell.

Peter: Tie him up to thy chair, then. Cowardly beast! What made him fall?

Chancellor: The hand of death.

Peter: Prythee speak plainlier.

Chancellor: He said calmly, but not without sighing twice or thrice, "Lead me to the scaffold; I am weary of life. My father says, too truly, I am not courageous, but the death that leads me to my God shall never terrify me." When he heard your majesty's name accusing him of treason and attempts at parricide, he fell speechless. We raised him up: he was dead!

Peter: Inconsiderate and barbarous varlet as thou art, dost thou recite this ill accident to a father—and to one who has not dined? Bring me a glass of brandy. Away and bring it: scamper! Hark ye! bring the bottle with it: and—hark ye! a rasher of bacon on thy life! and some pickled sturgeon, and some krout and caviar.

II.—*Joseph Scaliger and Montaigne*

Montaigne: What could have brought you, M. de l'Escale, other than a good heart? You rise early, I see; you must have risen with the sun, to be here at this hour. I have capital white wine, and the best cheese in Auvergne. Pierre, thou hast done well; set it upon the table, and tell Master Matthew to split a couple of chickens and broil them.

Scaliger: This, I perceive, is the ante-chamber to your library; here are your every-day books.

Montaigne: Faith! I have no other. These are plenty, methinks.

Scaliger: You have great resources within yourself, and therefore can do with fewer.

Montaigne: Why, how many now do you think here may be?

Scaliger: I did not believe at first that there could be above fourscore.

Montaigne: Well! are fourscore few? Are we talking of peas and beans?

Scaliger: I and my father (put together) have written well-nigh as many.

Montaigne: Ah! to write them is quite another thing. How do you like my wine? If you prefer your own country wine, only say it. I have several bottles in my cellar. I do not know, M. de l'Escale, whether you are particular in these matters?

Scaliger: I know three things—wine, poetry, and the world.

Montaigne: You know one too many, then. I hardly know whether I know anything about poetry; for I like Clem Marot better than Ronsard.

Scaliger: It pleases me greatly that you like Marot. His version of the Psalms is lately set to music, and added to the New Testament of Geneva.

Montaigne: It is putting a slice of honeycomb into a barrel of vinegar, which will never grow the sweeter for it.

Scaliger: Surely, you do not think in this fashion of the New Testament?

Montaigne: Who supposes it? Whatever is mild and kindly is there. But Jack Calvin has thrown bird-lime and vitriol upon it, and whoever but touches the cover dirties his fingers or burns them.

Scaliger: Calvin is a very great man.

Montaigne: I do not like your great men who beckon me to them, call me their begotten, their dear child, and their entrails; and, if I happen to say on any occasion, "I beg leave, sir, to dissent a little from you," stamp and cry, "The devil you do!" and whistle to the executioner.

Scaliger: John Calvin is a grave man, orderly, and reasonable.

Montaigne: In my opinion he has not the order nor the reason of my cook. Mat never twitched God by the sleeve and swore He should not have his own way.

Scaliger: M. de Montaigne, have you ever studied the doctrine of predestination?

Montaigne: I should not understand it if I had; and I would not break through an old fence merely to get into a cavern. Would it make me honester or happier, or, in other things, wiser?

Scaliger: I do not know whether it would materially.

Montaigne: I should be an egregious fool, then, to care about it. Come, walk about with me; after a ride you can do nothing better to take off fatigue. I can show you nothing but my house and my dairy.

Scaliger: Permit me to look a little at those banners. They remind me of my own family, we being descended from the great Cane della Scala, Prince of Verona, and from the House of Hapsburg, as you must have heard from my father.

Montaigne: What signifies it to the world whether the great Cane was tied to his grandmother or not? As for the House of Hapsburg, if you could put together as many such houses as would make up a city larger than Cairo, they would not be worth his study, or a sheet of paper on the table of it.

III.—Bossuet and the Duchesse de Fontanges

Bossuet: Mademoiselle, it is the king's desire that I compliment you on the elevation you have attained.

Fontanges: O monseigneur, I know very well what you mean. His majesty is kind and polite to everybody. The last thing he said to me was, "Angélique! do not forget to compliment monseigneur the bishop on the dignity I have conferred upon him, of almoner to the dauphiness. I desired the appointment for him only that he might be of rank sufficient to confess you, now you are duchess." You are so agreeable a man, monseigneur, I will confess to you, directly.

Bossuet: Have you brought yourself to a proper frame of mind, young lady?

Fontanges: What is that?

Bossuet: Do you hate sin?

Fontanges: Very much.

Bossuet: Do you hate the world?

Fontanges: A good deal of it; all Picardy, for example, and all Sologne; nothing is uglier—and, oh my life! what frightful men and women!

Bossuet: I would say in plain language, do you hate the flesh and the devil?

Fontanges: Who does not hate the devil? If you will hold my hand the while, I will tell him so—"I hate you, beast!" There now. As for flesh, I never could bear a fat man. Such people can neither dance nor hunt, nor do anything that I know of.

Bossuet: Mademoiselle Marie Angélique de Scoraille de Rousille, Duchesse de Fontanges! Do you hate titles, and dignities, and yourself?

Fontanges: Myself! Does anyone hate me? Why should I be the first? Hatred is the worst thing in the world; it makes one so very ugly.

Bossuet: We must detest our bodies if we would save our souls.

Fontanges: That is hard. How can I do it? I see nothing so detestable in mine. Do you? As God hath not hated me, why should I? As for titles and dignities, I am glad to be a duchess. Would not you rather be a duchess than a waiting-maid if the king gave you your choice?

Bossuet: Pardon me, mademoiselle. I am confounded at the levity of your question. If you really have anything to confess, and desire that I should have the honour of absolving you, it would be better to proceed.

Fontanges: You must first direct me, monseigneur. I have nothing particular. What was it that dropped on the floor as you were speaking?

Bossuet: Leave it there!

Fontanges: Your ring fell from your hand, my lord bishop! How quick you are! Could not you have trusted me to pick it up?

Bossuet: Madame is too condescending. My hand is shrivelled; the ring has ceased to fit it. A pebble has moved you more than my words.

Fontanges: It pleases me vastly. I admire rubies. I will ask the king for one exactly like it. This is the time he usually comes from the chase. I am sorry you cannot be present to hear how prettily I shall ask him. I am sure he will order the ring for me, and I will confess to you with it upon my finger. But, first, I must be cautious and particular to know of him how much it is his royal will that I should say.

IV.—The Empress Catharine and Princess Dashkof

Catharine: Into his heart! Into his heart! If he escapes, we perish! Do you think, Dashkof, they can hear me through the double door? Yes, hark! they heard me. They have done it! What bubbling and gurgling! He groaned but once. Listen! His blood is busier now than it ever was before. I should not have thought it could have splashed so loud upon the floor. Put you ear against the lock.

Dashkof: I hear nothing.

Catharine: My ears are quicker than yours, and know these notes better. Let me come. There! There again! The drops are now like lead. How now? Which of these fools has brought his dog with him? What trampling and lapping! The creature will carry the marks all about the palace with his feet! You turn pale, and tremble. You should have supported me, in case I had required it.

Dashkof: I thought only of the tyrant. Neither in life nor in death could any one of these miscreants make me tremble. But the husband slain by his wife! What will Russia—what will Europe say?

Catharine: Russia has no more voice than a whale. She may toss about in her turbulence, but my artillery (for now, indeed, I can safely call it mine) shall stun and quiet her.

Dashkof: I fear for your renown.

Catharine: Europe shall be informed of my reasons, if she should ever find out that I countenanced the conspiracy. She shall be persuaded that her repose made the step necessary; that my own life was in danger; that I fell upon my knees to soften the conspirators; that only when I had fainted, the horrible deed was done.

Dashkof: Europe may be more easily subjugated than duped.

Catharine: She shall be both, God willing! Is the rouge off my face?

Dashkof: It is rather in streaks and mottles, excepting just under the eyes, where it sits as it should do.

Catharine: I am heated and thirsty. I cannot imagine how. I think we have not yet taken our coffee. I could eat only a slice of melon at breakfast— my duty urged me *then*—and dinner is yet to come. Remember, I am to faint at the midst of it, when the intelligence comes in, or, rather, when, in despite of every effort to conceal it from me, the awful truth has flashed upon my mind. Remember, too, you are to catch me, and to cry for help, and to tear those fine flaxen hairs which we laid up together on the toilet; and we are both to be as inconsolable as we can be for the life of us.

Come, sing. I know not how to fill up the interval. Two long hours yet! How stupid and tiresome! I wish all things of the sort could be done and be over in a day. They are mightily disagreeable when by nature one is not cruel. People little know my character. I have the tenderest heart upon earth. Ivan must follow next; he is heir to the throne. But not now. Another time. Two such scenes together, and without some interlude, would perplex people.

I thought we spoke of singing. Do not make me wait. Cannot you sing as usual, without smoothing your dove's throat with your handkerchief, and taking off your necklace? Sing, sing! I am quite impatient!

V. — Bacon and Richard Hooker

Bacon: Hearing much of your worthiness and wisdom, Master Richard Hooker, I have besought your comfort and consolation in this my too heavy affliction, for we often do stand in need of hearing what we know full well, and our own balsams must be poured into our breasts by another's hand. Withdrawn, as you live, from court and courtly men, and having ears occupied by better reports than such as are flying about me, yet haply so hard a case as mine, befalling a man heretofore not averse from the studies in which you take delight, may have touched you with some concern.

Hooker: I do think, my lord of Verulam, that the day which in his wisdom he appointed for your trial was the very day on which the king's majesty gave unto your ward and custody the great seal of his English realm. And—let me utter it without offence—your features and stature were from that day forward no longer what they were before. Such an effect do rank and power and office produce even on prudent and religious men. You, my lord, as befits you, are smitten and contrite; but I know that there is always a balm which lies uppermost in these afflictions.

Bacon: Master Richard, it is surely no small matter to lose the respect of those who looked up to us for countenance; and the favour of a right learned king, and, O Master Hooker, such a power of money! But money is mere dross. I should always hold it so, if it possessed not two qualities—that of making men treat us reverently, and that of enabling us to help the needy.

Hooker: The respect, I think, of those who respect us for what a fool can give and a rogue can take away, may easily be dispensed with; but it is indeed a high prerogative to help the needy, and when it pleases the Almighty to deprive us of it, he hath removed a most fearful responsibility.

Bacon: Methinks it beginneth to rain, Master Richard. What if we comfort our bodies with a small cup of wine, against the ill-temper of the air. Pledge me; hither comes our wine.(*To the servant*) Dolt! Is not this the beverage I reserve for myself?

Bear with me, good Master Hooker, but verily I have little of this wine, and I keep it as a medicine for my many and growing infirmities. You are healthy at present: God, in His infinite mercy, long maintain you so! Weaker drink is more wholesome for you. But this Malmsey, this Malmsey, flies from centre to circumference, and makes youthful blood boil.

Hooker: Of a truth, my knowledge in such matters is but sparse. My lord of Canterbury once ordered part of a goblet, containing some strong Spanish wine, to be taken to me from his table when I dined by sufferance with his chaplains, and, although a most discreet, prudent man, as befitteth his high station, was not so chary of my health as your lordship. Wine is little to be trifled with; physic less. The Cretans, the brewers of this Malmsey, have many aromatic and powerful herbs among them. On their mountains, and notably on Ida, grows that dittany which works such marvels, and which perhaps may give activity to this hot medicinal drink of theirs. I would not touch it knowingly; an unregarded leaf dropped into it above the ordinary might add such puissance to the concoction as almost to break the buckles in my shoes.

Bacon: When I read of such things I doubt them: but if I could procure a plant of dittany I would persuade my apothecary and my gamekeeper to make experiments.

Hooker: I dare not distrust what grave writers have declared in matters beyond my knowledge.

Bacon: Good Master Hooker, I have read many of your reasonings, and they are admirably well sustained. Yet forgive me, in God's name my worthy master, if you descried in me some expression of wonder at your simplicity. You would define to a hair's breadth the qualities, states, and dependencies of principalities, dominations, and powers; you would be unerring about the apostles and the churches, and 'tis marvellous how you wander about a pot-herb!

Hooker: I know my poor, weak intellects, most noble lord, and how scantily they have profited by my hard painstaking. Wisdom consisteth not in knowing many things, nor even in knowing them thoroughly, but in choosing and in following what conduces the most certainly to our lasting happiness and true glory.

Bacon: I have observed among the well-informed and the ill-informed nearly the same quantity of infirmities and follies; those who are rather the wiser keep them separate, and those who are wisest of all keep them better out of sight. I have persuaded men, and shall persuade them for ages, that I possess a wide range of thought unexplored by others, and first thrown open by me, with many fair enclosures of choice and abstruse knowledge. One subject, however, hath almost escaped me, and surely one worth the trouble.

Hooker: Pray, my lord, if I am guilty of no indiscretion, what may it be?

Bacon: Francis Bacon.

LA ROCHEFOUCAULD

Reflections and Moral Maxims

Rochefoucauld's "Reflections, or Sentences and Moral Maxims," were published in 1665. In them his philosophy of life is expressed with a perfection of form which still remains unrivalled and unequalled. The original work contains only 314 short sentences; the last edition he published contains 541; but when one examines the exquisite workmanship of his style, one does not wonder that it represents the labour of twenty years. La Rochefoucauld (see Vol. X, p. 203) is one of the greatest masters of French prose, as well as one of the great masters of cynicism. He has exerted a deep influence both on English and French literature, and Swift and Byron were among his disciples.

I. — Of Love and of Women

To judge love by most of its effects, it seems more like hatred than kindness.

In love we often doubt of what we most believe.

As long as we love, we forgive.

Love is like fire, it cannot be without continual motion; as soon as it ceases to hope or fear it ceases to exist.

Many persons would never have been in love had they never heard talk of it.

Agreeable and pleasant as love is, it pleases more by the manners in which it shows itself than by itself alone.

We pass on from love to ambition; we seldom return from ambition to love.

Those who have had a great love affair find themselves all their life happy and unhappy at being cured of it.

In love the one who is first cured is best cured.

The reason why lovers are never weary of talking of each other is that they are always talking of themselves.

Constancy in love is a perpetual inconstancy which makes our heart attach itself in succession to all the qualities of our beloved, and prefer, now this trait and now that; so that this constancy is only a kind of inconstancy fixed and enclosed in a single object.

If there is a love pure and exempt from all mixture with our other passions, it is that which is hidden in the depth of our heart and unknown to ourselves.

The pleasure of love consists in loving, and our own passion gives us more happiness than the feelings which our beloved has for us.

The grace of novelty is to love like the fine bloom on fruit; it gives it a lustre which is easily effaced and never recovered.

We are nearer loving those who hate us than those who love us more than we desire.

Women often fancy themselves to be in love when they are not. Their natural passion for being beloved, their unwillingness to give a denial, the excitement of mind produced by an affair of gallantry, all these make them imagine they are in love when they are in fact only coquetting.

All women are flirts. Some are restrained by timidity and some by reason.

The greatest miracle of love is the reformation of a coquette.

A coquette pretends to be jealous of her lover, in order to conceal her envy of other women.

Most women yield more from weakness than from passion, hence an enterprising man usually succeeds with them better than an amiable man.

It is harder for women to overcome their coquetry than their love. No woman knows how much of a coquette she is.

Women who are in love more readily forgive great indiscretions than small infidelities.

Some people are so full of themselves that even when they become lovers they find a way of being occupied with their passion without being interested in the person whom they love.

It is useless to be young without being beautiful, or beautiful without being young.

In their first love affairs women love their lover; in all others they love love.

In the old age of love, as in the old age of life, we continue to live to pain long after we have ceased to live to pleasure.

There is no passion in which self-love reigns so powerfully as in love; we are always more ready to sacrifice the repose of a person we love than to lose our own.

There is a certain kind of love which, as it grows excessive, leaves no room for jealousy.

Jealousy is born with love, but it does not always die with it.

Jealousy is the greatest of all afflictions, and that which least excites pity in the persons that cause it.

In love and in friendship we are often happier by reason of the things that we do not know than by those that we do.

There are few women whose merit lasts longer than their beauty.

The reason why most women are little touched by friendship is that friendship is insipid to those who have felt what love is.

II. — Friendship

In the misfortunes of our best friends we always find something that does not displease us.

Rare as true love is, it is less rare than true friendship.

What makes us so changing in our friendships is that it is difficult to discern the qualities of the soul, and easy to recognize the qualities of the mind.

It is equally difficult to have a friendship for those whom we do not esteem as for those we esteem more than ourselves.

We love those who admire us, not those whom we admire.

Most of the friendships of the world ill deserve the name of friendship; still, a man may make occasional use of them, as in a business where the profits are uncertain and it is usual to be cheated.

It is more dishonourable to mistrust a friend than to be deceived by him.

We are fond of exaggerating the love our friends bear us, but it is less from a feeling of gratitude than from a desire to advertise our own merits.

What usually hinders us from revealing the depths of our hearts to our friends is not so much the distrust which we have of them as the distrust that we have of ourselves.

We confess our little defects merely to persuade our friends that we have no great failings.

The greatest effort of friendship is not to show our defects to a friend, but to make him see his own.

Sincerity is an opening of the heart. It is found in exceedingly few people, and what passes for it is only a subtle dissimulation used to attract confidence.

We can love nothing except in relation to ourselves, and we merely follow our own bent and pleasure when we prefer our friends to ourselves; yet it is only by this preference that friendship can be made true and perfect.

It seems as if self-love is the dupe of kindness and that it is forgotten while we are working for the benefit of other men. In this case, however, our self-love is merely taking the safest road to arrive at its ends; it is lending at usury under the pretext of giving, it is aiming at winning all the world by subtle and delicate means.

The first impulses of joy excited in us by the good fortune of our friends proceed neither from our good nature nor from the friendship we have for them; it is an effect of self-love that flatters us with the hope either of being fortunate in our turn or of drawing some advantage from their prosperity.

What makes us so eager to form new acquaintances is not the mere pleasure of change or a weariness of old friendships, so much as a disgust at not being enough admired by those who know us too well, and a hope of winning more admiration from persons who do not know much about us.

III. — Things of the Mind

The mind is always the dupe of the heart. Those who are acquainted with their own mind are not acquainted with their own heart.

The mind is more indolent than the body.

It is the mark of fine intellects to explain many things in a few words; little minds have the gift of speaking much and saying nothing.

We speak but little when vanity does not make us speak.

A spirit of confidence helps on conversation more than brilliance of mind does.

True eloquence consists of saying all that is necessary, and nothing more.

A man may be witty and still be a fool; judgment is the source of wisdom.

A man does not please for very long when he has but one kind of wit.

It is a mistake to imagine that wit and judgment are two distinct things; judgment is only the perfection of wit, which pierces into the recesses of things and there perceives what from the outside seems to be imperceptible.

A man of intelligence would often be at a loss were it not for the company of fools.

It is not so much fertility of mind that leads us to discover many expedients in regard to a single matter, as a defect of intelligence, that makes us stop at everything presented to our imagination, and hinders us from discerning at once which is the best course.

Some old men like to give good advice to console themselves for being no longer in a state to give a bad example.

No man of sound good sense strikes us as such unless he is of our way of thinking.

Stiffness of opinion comes from pettiness of mind; we do not easily believe in anything that is beyond our range of vision.

Good taste is based on judgment rather than on intelligence.

It is more often through pride than through any want of enlightenment that men set themselves stubbornly to oppose the most current opinions; finding all the best places taken on the popular side, they do not want those in the rear.

In order to understand things well one must know the detail of them; and as this is almost infinite, our knowledge is always superficial and imperfect.

It is never so difficult to talk well as when we are ashamed of our silence.

The excessive pleasure we feel in talking about ourselves ought to make us apprehensive that we afford little to our listeners.

Truth has not done so much good in the world as the false appearances of it have done harm.

Man's chief wisdom consists in being sensible of his follies.

IV.—*Human Life and Human Nature*

Youth is a continual intoxication; it is the fever of reason.

The passions of youth are scarcely more opposed to salvation than the lukewarmness of old persons.

There is not enough material in a fool to make a good man out of him.

We have more strength than will, and it is often to excuse ourselves to ourselves that we imagine things are impossible.

There are few things impossible in themselves; it is the application to achieve them that we lack more than the means.

It is a mistake to imagine that only the more violent passions, such as ambition and love, can triumph over the rest. Idleness often masters them all. It indeed influences all our designs and actions, and insensibly destroys both our vices and our virtues.

Idleness is of all our passions that which is most unknown to ourselves. It is the most ardent and the most malign of all, though we do not feel its working, and the harm which it does is hidden. If we consider its power attentively, we shall see that in every struggle it triumphs over our feelings, our interests, and our pleasures. To give a true idea of this passion it is necessary to add that idleness is like a beatitude of the soul which consoles it for all its losses and serves in place of all its wealth.

The gratitude of most men is only a secret desire to receive greater favours.

We like better to see those on whom we confer benefits than those from whom we receive them.

It is less dangerous to do harm to most men than to do them too much good.

If we had no defects ourselves we should not take so much pleasure in observing the failings of others.

One man may be more cunning than another man, but he cannot be more cunning than all the world.

Mankind has made a virtue of moderation in order to limit the ambition of great men and to console mediocre people for their scanty fortune and their scanty merit.

We should often be ashamed of our finest actions if the world saw all the motives that produced them.

Our desire to speak of ourselves, and to reveal our defects in the best light in which we can show them, constitutes a great part of our sincerity.

The shame that arises from undeserved praise often leads us to do things which we should not otherwise have attempted.

The labours of the body free us from the pains of the mind. It is this that constitutes the happiness of the poor.

It is more necessary to study men than to study books.

The truly honest man is he who sets no value on himself.

Censorious as the world is, it is oftener favourable to false merit than unjust to true.

It is not enough to possess great qualities; we must know how to use them.

He who lives without folly is not so wise as he fancies.

Good manners are the least of all laws and the most strictly observed.

Everybody complains of a lack of memory, nobody of a lack of judgment.

The love of justice is nothing more than a fear of injustice.

Passion often makes a fool of a man of sense, and sometimes it makes a fool a man of sense.

Nature seems to have hidden in the depth of our minds a skill and a talent of which we are ignorant; only our passions are able to bring them out and to give us sometimes surer and more complete views than we could arrive at by thought and study.

Our passions are the only orators with an unfailing power of persuasion. They are an art of nature with infallible rules, and the simplest man who is possessed by passion is far more persuasive than the most eloquent speaker who is not moved by feeling.

As we grow old we grow foolish as well as wise.

Few people know how to grow old.

Death and the sun are things one cannot look at steadily.

V. — Virtues and Vices

Hypocrisy is a homage that vice pays to virtue.

Our vices are commonly disguised virtues.

Virtue would not go far if vanity did not go with her.

Prosperity is a stronger test of virtue than misfortune is.

Men blame vice and praise virtue only through self-interest.

Great souls are not those which have less passions and more virtues than common souls, but those which have larger ambitions.

Of all our virtues one might say what an Italian poet has said of the honesty of women, "that it is often nothing but an art of pretending to be honest."

Virtues are lost in self-interest, as rivers are in the sea.

To the honour of virtue it must be acknowledged that the greatest misfortunes befall men from their vices.

When our vices leave us, we flatter ourselves that we have left them.

Feebleness is more opposed to vice than virtue is.

What makes the pangs of shame and jealousy so sharp is that our vanity cannot help us to support them.

What makes the vanity of other persons so intolerable is that it hurts our own.

We have not the courage to say in general that we have no defects, and that our enemies have no good qualities; but in matters of detail we are not very far from believing it.

If we never flattered ourselves the flattery of others Would not injure us.

We sometimes think we dislike flattery; we only dislike the way in which we are flattered.

Flattery is a kind of bad money to which our vanity gives currency.

Self-love, as it happens to be well or ill-conducted, constitutes virtue and vice.

We are so prepossessed in our own favour that we often mistake for virtues those vices that bear some resemblance to them, and are artfully disguised by self-love.

Nothing is so capable of lessening our self-love as the observation that we disapprove at one time what we approve at another.

Self-love is the love of self, and of everything for the sake of self. When fortune gives the means, self-love makes men idolise themselves and tyrannise over others. It never rests or fixes itself anywhere outside its home. If it settle on external things, it is only as the bee does on flowers, to extract what may be serviceable. Nothing is so impetuous as its desires, nothing so secret as its designs, nothing so adroit as its conduct. We can neither fathom the depth, nor penetrate the obscurity of its abyss. There, concealed from the most piercing eye, it makes numberless turnings and windings; there is it often invisible even to itself; there it conceives, breeds, and cherishes, without being aware of it, an infinity of likings and hatreds; some of which are so monstrous that, having given birth to them, self-love either does not recognize them, or cannot bear to own them. From the darkness which covers self-love spring the ridiculous notions which it entertains of itself; thence its errors, ignorance, and silly mistakes; thence it imagines that its feelings are dead when they are but asleep; and thinks that it has lost all appetite when it is for the moment sated.

But the thick mist which hides it from itself does not hinder it from seeing perfectly whatever is without; and thus it resembles the eye, that sees all things except itself. In great concerns and important affairs, where the violence of its desire excites its whole attention, it sees, perceives, understands, invents, suspects, penetrates, and divines all things; so that one is tempted to believe that each of its passions has its peculiar magic.

Its desires are inflamed by itself rather than by the beauty and merit of the objects; its own taste heightens and embellishes them; itself is the game it pursues, and its own inclination is what is followed rather than the things which seem to be the objects of its inclination. Composed of contrarieties, it is imperious and obedient, sincere and hypocritical, merciful and cruel, timid and bold. Its desires tend, according to the diverse moods that direct it, sometimes to glory, sometimes to wealth, sometimes to pleasure. These are changed as age and experience alter; and whether it has many inclinations or only one is a matter of indifference, because it can split itself into many or collect itself into one just as is convenient or agreeable.

It is inconstant; and numberless are the changes, besides those which happen from external causes, which proceed from its own nature. Inconstant through levity, through love, through novelty, through satiety, through disgust, through inconstancy itself. Capricious; and sometimes labouring with eagerness and incredible pains to obtain things that are in no way advantageous, nay, even hurtful, but which are pursued merely as a passion. Whimsical, and often exerting intense application in the most trifling employments; taking delight in the most insipid things, and preserving all its haughtiness in the most contemptible pursuits. Attendant on all ages and conditions; living everywhere; living on everything; living on nothing. Easy in either the enjoyment, or privation of things. Going over to those who are at variance with it; even entering into their schemes; and, wonderful! joining with them, it hates itself; conspires its own destruction; labours to be undone; desires only to exist; and, that granted, consents to be its own enemy.

We are not therefore to be surprised if sometimes, uniting with the most rigid austerity, it enters boldly into a combination against itself; because what is lost in one respect is regained in another. When we think it relinquishes pleasures, it only suspends or changes them; and even when discomforted, and we seem to be rid of it, we find it triumphant in its own defeat. Such is self-love! —of which man's whole life is only a strong, a continued agitation. The sea is a striking image of it, and in the flux and reflux of the waves, self-love may find a lively expression of the turbulent succession of its thoughts, and of its eternal agitation.

LEONARDO DA VINCI

Treatise on Painting

Leonardo Da Vinci was born in 1452 at Anchiano, near Vinci, in Tuscany, the son of a Florentine notary. Trained in the workshop of Andrea Verrocchio, he became one of the greatest and most versatile artists of the Renaissance. Indeed, he must be considered one of the master-minds of all times, for there was scarcely a sphere of human knowledge in which he did not excel and surpass his contemporaries. He was not only preeminent as painter, sculptor, and architect, but was an accomplished musician, poet, and improvisatore, an engineer—able to construct canals, roads, fortifications, ships, and war-engines of every description—an inventor of rare musical instruments, and a great organiser of fêtes and pageants. Few of his artistic creations have come down to us; but his profound knowledge of art and science, and the wide range of his intellect are fully revealed in the scattered leaves of his notebooks, which are now preserved in the British Museum, the Bibliothèque Nationale in Paris, the Ambrosiani in Milan, and other collections. The first edition of the "Treatise on Painting" was a compilation from these original notes, published at Paris in 1651. Leonardo died at Cloux on May 2, 1519.

From Da Vinci's Notebooks

The eye, which is called the window of the soul, is the principal means whereby our intelligence may most fully and splendidly comprehend the infinite works of nature; and the ear comes next, by gaining importance through hearing the things that have been perceived by the eye. If you historians or poets, or mathematicians, had not seen things with your eyes, badly would you describe them in your writings. If you, O poet, call painting dumb poetry, the painter might say of the poet's writing blind painting. Now consider, which taunt is more mordant—to be called blind or dumb?

If the poet is as free in invention as the painter, yet his fiction is not as satisfying to mankind as is painting, for whereas poetry endeavours with words to represent forms, actions, and scenes, the painter's business is to imitate forms with the images of these very forms. Take the case of a poet, describing the beauties of a woman to her lover, and that of a painter depicting her; you will soon see whither nature will attract the enamoured judge. And should not the proof of things be the verdict of experience?

If you say that poetry is more enduring, I may reply that the works of a coppersmith are more enduring still, since time has preserved them longer than your works or ours; yet they are less imaginative, and painting, if done with enamels on copper, can be made far more enduring. We, in our art, may be said to be grandsons unto God. If you despise painting, which is the sole imitator of all the visible works of nature, then you certainly despise a subtle invention which, with philosophical and ingenious reflection, considers all the properties of forms, airs, and scenes, trees, animals, grasses and flowers, which are surrounded by light and shade.

And this is a science and the true-born daughter of nature, since painting is born of this self-same nature. But, in order to speak more correctly, let us call it the grandchild of nature, because all visible things are produced by nature, and from these same things is born painting. Wherefore we may rightly call it the grandchild of nature, related to God Himself.

How Sculpture is Less Intellectual

Being sculptor no less than painter, and practising both arts in the same degree, it seems to me that I may without arrogance pronounce how one of them is more intellectual, difficult, and perfect than the other.

Firstly, sculpture is subject to a certain light—namely, from above—and painting carries everywhere with it light and shade. Light and shade are, therefore, the essentials in sculpture. In this respect the sculptor is aided by the nature of the relief, which produces these of its own accord; the painter introduces them by his art where nature would reasonably place them. The sculptor cannot reproduce the varying nature of the colours of objects; painting lacks nothing in this respect. The sculptor's perspectives never seem true, but the painter's lead the eye hundreds of miles into the work. Aerial perspective is alien to their work. They can neither represent transparent nor luminous bodies, neither reflected rays nor shiny surfaces like mirrors and similar glittering bodies; no mist, no dull sky, nor countless other things, which I refrain from mentioning to avoid getting wearisome. It has the advantage that it offers greater resistance to time, although enamels on copper fused in fire have equal power of resistance. Thus painting surpasses sculpture even in durability.

Were you to speak only of painting on panels, I should be content to give the verdict against sculpture by saying: Whilst painting is more beautiful, more imaginative, and more resourceful, sculpture is more durable; and this is all that can be said for it. It reveals with little effort what it is. Painting seems a miraculous thing, making things intangible appear tangible, presenting flat objects in relief, and distant near at hand. Indeed, painting is adorned with endless possibilities that are not used by sculpture.

Painters fight and compete with nature.

Of the Ten Offices of the Eye

Painting extends over all the ten offices of the eye—namely, darkness, light, body and colour, figure and scenery, distance and nearness, movement and repose—all of which offices will be woven through this little work of mine. For I will remind the painter by what rule and in what manner he shall use his art to imitate all these things, the work of nature and the ornament of the world.

Rule for Beginners in Painting

We know clearly that sight is one of the swiftest actions in existence, perceiving in one moment countless forms. Nevertheless, it cannot comprehend more than one thing at a time. Suppose, for instance, you, reader, were to cast a single glance upon this entire written page and were to decide at once that it is full of different letters; but you will not be able to recognize in this space of time either what letters they are or what they purport to say. Therefore, you must take word by word, verse by verse, in order to gain knowledge from these letters. Again, if you want to reach the summit of a building, you must submit to climbing step by step, else it would be impossible for you to reach the top. And so I say to you, whom nature inclines to this art, if you would have a true knowledge of the form of things, begin with their details, and don't pass on to the second before the first is well fixed in your memory, else you will waste your time.

Perspective is the rein and rudder of painting.

I say whatever is forced within a border is more difficult than what is free. Shadows have in certain degrees their borders, and he who ignores them cannot obtain roundness, which roundness is the essence and soul of painting. Drawing is free, since, if you see countless faces, they will all be different—the one has a long, the other a short nose. Thus the painter may take this liberty, and where is liberty, is no rule.

Precepts for Painting

The painter should endeavour to be universal, because he is lacking in dignity if he do one thing well and another thing badly, like so many who only study the well-proportionate nude and not its variations, because a man may be proportionate and yet be short and stout, or long and thin. And he who does not bear in mind these variations will get his figures stereotyped, so that they all seem to be brothers and sisters, which deserves to be censured severely.

Let the sketching of histories be swift and the articulation not too perfect. Be satisfied with suggesting the position of the limbs, which you may afterwards carry to completion at your leisure and as you please.

Methinks it is no small grace in a painter if he give a pleasing air to his figures, a grace which, if it be not one's own by nature, may be acquired by study, as follows. Try to take the best parts from many beautiful faces, whose beauty is affirmed by public fame rather than by your own judgment, for you may deceive yourself by taking faces which resemble your own. For it would often seem that such similarities please us; and if you were ugly you would not select beautiful faces, and you would make ugly ones, like many painters whose types often resemble their master. Therefore, take beautiful features, as I tell you, and commit them to your memory.

Monstrous is he who has a very large head and short legs, and monstrous he who with rich garments has great poverty; therefore we shall call him well proportioned whose every part corresponds with his whole.

On the Choice of Light

If you had a courtyard, which you could cover at will with a canvas awning, this light would be good; or when you wish to paint somebody, paint him in bad weather, or at the hour of dusk, placing the sitter with his back to one of the walls of this courtyard.

Observe in the streets at the fall of the evening the faces of men and women when it is bad weather, what grace and sweetness then appear to be theirs.

Therefore, you should have a courtyard, prepared with walls painted in black, and with the roof projecting a little over the said wall. And it should be ten *braccia* [ten fathoms] in width, and twenty in length and ten in height; and when the sun shines you should cover it over with the awning, or you should paint an hour before evening, when it is cloudy or misty. For this is the most perfect light.

Of the Gesture of Figures

You should give your figures such movement as will suffice to show what is passing in the mind of the figure; else your art would not be praiseworthy. A figure is not worthy of praise if it do not express by some gesture the passion of the soul. That figure is most worthy of praise which best expresses by its gesture the passion of its nature.

If you have to represent an honest man talking, see that his action be companion to his good words; and again, if you have to depict a bestial man, give him wild movements—his arms thrown towards the spectator, and his head pressed towards his chest, his legs apart.

The Judgment of Painting

We know well that mistakes are more easily detected in the works of others than in one's own, and often, while censuring the small faults of others, you do not recognise your own great faults. In order to escape such ignorance, have a care that you be, above all, sure of your perspective; then acquire full knowledge of the proportions of man and other animals. And, moreover, be a good architect; that is, in so far as it is necessary for the form of the buildings and other things that are upon the earth, and that are infinitely varied in form.

The more knowledge you have of these, the more worthy of praise will be your work. And for those things in which you have no practice, do not disdain to copy from nature. When you are painting, you should take a flat mirror and often look at your work within it. It will be seen in reverse, and will appear to be by some other master, and you will be better able to judge of its faults than in any other way. It is also a good plan every now and then to go away and have a little relaxation, for then, when you come back to the work, your judgment will be surer, since to remain constantly at work will cause you to lose the power of judgment.

Surely, while one paints one should not reject any man's judgment; for we know very well that a man, even if he be no painter, has knowledge of the forms of another man, and will judge aright whether he is hump-backed, or has one shoulder too high or too low, or whether he has too large a mouth or nose, or other faults; and if we are able rightly to judge the work of nature in men, how much more is it fit to admit that they are able to judge our mistakes.

You know how much man may be deceived about his own works, and if you do not know it of yourself, observe it in others, and you will derive benefit from other people's mistakes. Therefore, you should be eager to listen patiently to the views of other men and consider and reflect carefully whether he who finds fault is right or not in blaming you. If you find that he is right, correct your work; but if not, pretend not to have understood him; or show him, if he be a man whom you respect, by sound argument, why it is that he is mistaken in finding fault.

Do Not Disdain to Work from Nature

A master who let it be understood that his mind could retain all the forms and effects of nature, I should certainly hold to be endowed with great ignorance, since the said effects are infinite, and our memory is not of such capacity as to suffice thereto. Therefore, O painter, see that the greed for gain do not outweigh within you the honour of art, for to gain in honour is a far greater thing than to be honoured for wealth.

For these and other reasons that might be adduced, you should endeavour first to demonstrate to the eye, by means of drawing, a suggestion of the intention and of the invention originated first by your imagination. Then proceed, taking from it or adding to it, until you are satisfied with it. Then have men arranged as models, draped or nude, in the manner in which they are disposed in your work, and make the proportions and size in accordance with perspective, so that no part of the work remains that is not counselled by reason as well as by nature.

And this will be the way to make you honoured through your art. First of all, copy drawings by a good master made by his art from nature, and not as exercises; then from a relief, keeping by you a drawing done from the same relief; then from a good model, and of this you ought to make a general practice.

Of the Painter's Life in His Study

The painter or draughtsman should be solitary, so that physical comfort may not injure the thriving of the mind, especially when he is occupied with the observations and considerations which ever offer themselves to his eye and provide material to be treasured up by the memory. If you are alone, you belong wholly to yourself; and if you are accompanied even by one companion, you belong only half to yourself; and if you are with several of them, you will be even more subject to such inconveniences.

And if you should say, "I shall take my own course, I shall keep apart, so that I may be the better able to contemplate the forms of natural objects," then I reply, this cannot well be, because you cannot help frequently lending your ear to their gossip; and since nobody can serve two masters at once, you will badly fulfil your duties as companion, and you will have worse success in artistic contemplation. And if you should say, "I shall keep so far apart that their words cannot reach me or disturb me," then I reply in this case that you will be looked upon as mad. And do you not perceive that, in acting thus, you would really be solitary?

Of Ways to Represent Various Scenes

A man in despair you should make turning his knife against himself. He should have rent his garments, and he should be in the act of tearing open his wound with one hand. And you should make him with his feet apart and his legs somewhat bent, and the whole figure likewise bending to the ground, with dishevelled and untidy hair.

As a rule, he whom you wish to represent talking to many people will consider the subject of which he has to treat, and will fit his gestures to this subject—that is to say, if the subject is persuasion, the gestures should serve this intention; if the subject is explanation by various reasons, he who speaks should take a finger of his left hand between two fingers of his right, keeping the two smaller ones pressed together; his face should be animated and turned towards the people, his mouth slightly opened, so that he seems to be talking. And if he is seated, let him seem to be in the act of slightly raising himself, with his head forward; and if he is standing, make him lean forward a little, with his head towards the people, whom you should represent silent and attentive, all watching, with gestures of admiration, the orator's face. Some old men should have their mouths drawn down at the corners in astonishment at what they hear, drawing back the cheeks in many furrows, and raising their eyebrows where they meet, so as to produce many wrinkles on their foreheads. Some who are seated should hold their tired knees between the interlaced fingers of their hands, and others should cross one knee over the other, and place upon it one hand, so that its hollow supports the other elbow, whose hand again supports the bearded chin.

Whatever is wholly deprived of light is complete darkness. Night being in this condition, if you wish to represent a scene therein, you must contrive to have a great fire in this night, and everything that is in closer proximity to this fire will assume more of its colour, because the nearer a thing is to another object, the more it partakes of its nature. And since you will make the fire incline towards a red colour, you will have to give a reddish tinge to all things lighted by it, and those which are farther away from the fire will have to hold more of the black colour of night. The figures which are between you and the fire appear dark against the brightness of the flame, for that part of the object which you perceive is coloured by the darkness of night, and not by the brightness of the fire; and those which flank the fire will be half dark and half reddish. Those which are behind the flames will be altogether illuminated by a reddish light against the black background.

If you wish to represent a tempest properly, observe and set down the effects of the wind blowing over the face of the sea and of the land, raising and carrying away everything that is not firmly rooted in the general mass. And in order properly to represent this tempest, you should first of all show the riven and torn clouds swept along by the wind, together with the sandy dust blown up from the seashore, and with branches and leaves caught up and scattered through the air, together with many other light objects, by the power of the furious wind. The trees and shrubs, bent to the ground, seem to desire to follow the direction of the wind, with branches twisted out of their natural growth, and their foliage tossed and inverted.

Of the men who are present, some who are thrown down and entangled with their garments and covered with dust should be almost unrecognisable; and those who are left standing may be behind some tree which they embrace, so that the storm should not carry them off. Others, bent down, their garments and hair streaming in the wind, should hold their hands before their eyes because of the dust.

Let the turbulent and tempestuous sea be covered with eddying foam between the rising waves, and let the wind carry fine spray into the stormy air to resemble a thick and all-enveloping mist. Of the ships that are there, show some with rent sails, whose shreds should flap in the air, together with some broken halyards; masts splintered, tumbled, with the ship itself broken by the fury of the waves; some human beings, shrieking, and clinging to the wreckage of the vessel. You should show the clouds, chased by the impetuous wind, hurled against the high tops of the mountains, wreathing and eddying like waves that beat against the cliffs. The air should strike terror through the murky darkness caused by the dust, the mist, and the heavy clouds.

To Learn to Work from Memory

If you want properly to commit to your memory something that you have learnt, proceed in this manner—namely, when you have drawn one object so often that you believe you can remember it, try to draw it without the model, after having traced your model on a thin sheet of glass. This glass you will then lay upon the drawing which you have made without model. Observe well where the tracing does not tally with your drawing, and wherever you find that you have gone wrong, you must remember not to go wrong again. You should even return to the model, in order again to draw the wrong passage until it shall be fixed in your memory. And if you have no level sheet of glass for tracing, take a very thin sheet of goat-parchment, well oiled, and then dried. And after the tracing has done service for your drawing, you can efface it with a sponge and use it again for another tracing.

On Studying in Bed

I have experienced upon myself that it is of no small benefit if, when you are in bed, you apply your imagination to repeating the superficial lines of the forms which you have been studying, or to other remarkable things which are comprehensible to a fine intellect. This is a praiseworthy and useful action which will help you to fix things in your memory.

GOTTHOLD EPHRAIM LESSING

Laocoon

In 1766, while acting as secretary to the governor of Breslau, Lessing wrote his celebrated "Laocoon," a critical treatise defining the limits of poetry and the plastic arts. The epitome given here has been prepared from the German text. A short biographical sketch of Lessing appears in the introduction to his play, "Nathan the Wise," appearing in Volume XVII of The World's Greatest Books.

I.—On the Limits of Painting and Poetry

Winkelman has pronounced a noble simplicity and quiet grandeur, displayed in the posture no less than in the expression, to be the characteristic feature common to all the Greek masterpieces of painting and sculpture. "As," says he, "the depths of the sea always remain calm, however violently the surface may rage, so the expression in the figures of the Greeks, under every form of passion, shows a great and self-collected soul.

"This spirit is portrayed in the countenance of Laocoon, but not in the countenance alone. Even under the most violent suffering the pain discovers itself in every muscle and sinew of his body, and the beholder, while looking at the agonised conditions of the stomach, without viewing the face and other parts, believes that he almost feels the pain himself. The pain expresses itself without any violence, both in the features and in the whole posture. Laocoon suffers, but he suffers as the Philoctetes of Sophocles. His misery pierces us to the very soul, but inspires us with a wish that we could endure misery like that great man.

"The expressing of so great a soul is far higher than the painting of beautiful nature. The artist must feel within himself that strength of spirit which he would imprint on his marble. Greece had philosophers and artists in one person. Philosophy gave her hand to art, and inspired its figures with no ordinary souls."

The above remarks are founded on the argument that "the pain in the face of Laocoon does not show itself with that force which its intensity would have led us to expect." This is correct. But I confess I differ from Winkelman as to what, in his opinion, is the basis of this wisdom, and as to the universality of the rule which he deduces from it. I acknowledge I was startled, first by the glances of disapproval which he casts on Virgil, and, secondly, by the comparison with Philoctetes. From this point I shall begin, writing down my thoughts as they were developed in me.

"Laocoon suffers as does the Philoctetes of Sophocles." But how does this last suffer? It is curious that his sufferings should leave such a different impression behind them. The cries and mild imprecations with which he filled the camp and interrupted the sacrifices echoed through the desolate island. The same sounds of despair fill the theatre in the poet's imitation.

A cry is the natural expression of bodily pain. Homer's wounded heroes frequently fall to the ground with cries. They are in their actions beings of higher order; in their feelings, true men.

We more civilised and refined Europeans of a wiser and later age are forbidden to cry and weep, and even our ancestors were taught to suppress lamentation at loss, and to die laughing under the bites of adders. Not so the Greeks. They felt and feared, and gave utterance to pain and sorrow, only nothing must hold them back from duty.

Now for my inference. If it be true that, a cry at the sensation of bodily pain, according to the old Greek way of thinking, is quite compatible with greatness of soul, it cannot have been for the sake of expressing such greatness that the artist avoided imitating his shriek in marble. Another reason must be found for his deviation from his rival, the poet, who has expressed it with the happiest results.

Be it fable or history, it is love that made the first essay in the plastic arts, and never wearied of guiding the hands of the masters of old. Painting now may be defined generally as "the imitation of bodies of matter on a level surface"; but the wise Greek allotted for it narrower limits, and confined it to imitations of the beautiful only; his artists painted nothing else. It was the perfection of their work that absorbed them. Among the ancients beauty was the highest law of the plastic arts. To beauty everything was subordinated. There are passions by which all beautiful physical lines are lost through the distortion of the body, but from all such emotions the ancient masters abstained entirely. Rage and despair disgrace none of their productions, and I dare maintain that they never painted a fury.

Indignation was softened down to seriousness. Grief was lessened into mournfulness. All know how Timanthes in his painting of the sacrifice of Iphigenia shows the sorrow of the bystanders, but has concealed the face of the father, who should show it more than all. He left to conjecture what he might not paint. This concealment is a sacrifice to beauty by the artist, and it shows how art's first law is the law of beauty.

Now apply this to Laocoon. The master aimed at the highest beauty compatible with the adopted circumstances of bodily pain. He must soften shrieks into sighs. For only imagine the mouth of Laocoon to be forced open, and then judge.

But art in modern times has been allowed a far wider sphere. It has been affirmed that its limitations extend over the whole of visible nature, of which the beautiful is but a small part. And as nature is ever ready to sacrifice beauty to higher aims, so should the artist render it subordinate to his general design. But are there not other considerations which compel the artist to put certain limits to expression, and prevent him from ever drawing it at its highest intensity?

I believe that the fact that it is to a single moment that the material limits of art confine all its limitations, will lead us to similar views.

If the artist out of ever-varying nature can only make use of a single moment, while his works are meant to stand the test not only of a passing glance, but of a long and repeated contemplation, it is clear that this moment cannot be chosen too happily. Now that only is a happy choice which allows the imagination free scope. In the whole course of a feeling there is no moment which possesses this advantage so little as its highest stage. There is nothing beyond this, and the presentation of extremes to the eye clips the wings of fancy, prevents her from soaring beyond the impression of the senses, and compels her to occupy herself with weaker images. Thus if Laocoon sighs, the imagination can hear him shriek; but if he shrieks, it can neither rise above nor descend below this representation without seeing him in a condition which, as it will be more endurable, becomes less interesting. It either hears him merely moaning, or sees him already dead.

Of the frenzied Ajax of Timomachus we can form some judgment from the account of Philoctetes. Ajax does not appear raging among herds and slaughtering cattle instead of men; but the master exhibits him sitting wearied with these deeds of insanity, and that is really the raging Ajax. We can form the most lively idea of the extremity of his frenzy from the shame and despair which he himself feels at the thought of it. We see the storm in the wrecks and corpses which it had strewn on the beach.

II.—The Poet

Perhaps hardly any of the above remarks concerning the necessary limits of the artist would be found equally applicable to poetry. It is undeniable that the whole realm of the perfectly excellent lies open to the imitation of the poet, that excellence of outward form which we call beauty being only one of the least of the means by which he can interest us in his characters.

Moreover, the poet is not compelled to concentrate his picture into a single moment. He can take up every action of his hero at its source, and pursue it to its issue through all possible variations. Each of these, which would cost the artist a separate work, costs the poet but a single trait. What wonderful skill has Sophocles shown in strengthening and enlarging, in his tragedy of Philoctetes, the idea of bodily pain! He chose a wound, and not an internal malady, because the former admits of a more lively representation than the latter. This wound was, moreover, a punishment divinely decreed. But to the Greeks a wound from a poisoned arrow was but an ordinary incident. Why, then, in the case of Philoctetes only was it followed by such dreadful consequences?

Sophocles felt full well that, however great he made the bodily pain to his hero, it would not have sufficed of itself to excite any remarkable degree of sympathy. He therefore combined it with other evils—the complete lack of society, hunger, and all the hardships to which such a man under terrible privations is exposed when cast on a wild, deserted isle of the Cyclades.

Imagine, now, a man in these conditions, but give him health and strength and industry, and he becomes a Crusoe, whose lot, though not indifferent to us, has no great claim on our sympathy. On the other hand, imagine a man afflicted by a painful and incurable disease, but at the same time surrounded by kind friends. For him we should feel sympathy, yet this would not endure throughout. Only when both cases are combined do we see nothing but despair, which excites our amazement and horror. Typical beauty arises from the harmonious effect of numerous parts, all of which the sight is capable of comprehending at the same time. It requires, therefore, that these parts should lie near each other; and since things whose parts lie near each other are the peculiar objects of plastic beauty, these it is, and these only, which can imitate typical beauty. The poet, since he can only exhibit in succession its component parts, entirely abstains from the description of typical beauty. He feels that these parts, ranged one after the other, cannot possibly have the effect they produce when closely arranged together.

In this respect Homer is a pattern of patterns. He says Nireus was beautiful, Achilles still more so, Helen was endowed with divine beauty. But nowhere does he enter on a detailed sketch of these beauties, and yet the whole Iliad is based on the loveliness of Helen.

In this point, in which he can imitate Homer by merely doing nothing, Virgil is also tolerably happy. His heroine Dido, too, is never anything more than *pulcherrima* Dido (loveliest Dido). When he wishes to be more circumstantial, he is so in the description of her rich dress and apparel.

Lucian, also, was too acute to convey any idea of the body of Panthea otherwise than by reference to the most lovely female statues of the old artists.

Yet what is this but the acknowledgment that language by itself is here without power; that poetry falters and eloquence grows speechless unless art in some measure serve them as an interpreter?

But, it will be said, does not poetry lose too much if we deprive her of all objects of typical beauty? Who would deprive her of them? Because we would debar her from wandering among the footsteps of her sister art, without ever reaching the same goal as she, do we exclude her from every other, where art in her turn must gaze after her steps with fruitless longings?

Even Homer, who so pointedly abstains from all detailed descriptions of typical beauties, from whom we but just learn that Helen had white arms and lovely hair, even he, with all this, knew how to convey to us an idea of her beauty which far exceeds anything that art is able to accomplish.

III. — Beauty and Charm

Again, another means which poetry possesses of rivalling art in the description of typical beauty is the change of beauty into charm. Charm is beauty in motion, and is for this very reason less suitable to the painter than to the poet. The painter can only leave motion to conjecture, while in fact his figures are motionless. Consequently, with him charm becomes grimace.

But in poetry it remains what it is, a transitory beauty which we would gladly see repeated. It comes and goes, and since we can generally recall to our minds a movement more easily and vividly than forms or colours, charm necessarily in the same circumstances produces a stronger effect than beauty.

Zeuxis painted a Helen, and had the courage to write below the picture those renowned lines of Homer in which the enraptured elders confess their sensations. Never had painting and poetry been engaged in such contest. The contest remained undecided, and both deserved the crown.

For just as a wise poet showed us the beauty which he felt he could not paint according to its constituent parts, but merely in its effect, so the no less wise painter showed us that beauty by nothing but those parts, deeming it unbecoming for his art to resort to any other means for aid. His picture consisted of a single figure, undraped, of Helen, probably the one painted for the people of Crotona.

In beauty a single unbecoming part may disturb the harmonious effect of many, without the object necessarily becoming ugly. For ugliness, too, requires several unbecoming parts, all of which we must be able to comprehend at the same view before we experience sensations the opposite of those which beauty produces.

According to this, therefore, ugliness in its essence could be no subject of poetry; yet Homer has painted extreme ugliness in Thersites, and this ugliness is described according to its parts near each other. Why in the case of ugliness did he allow himself the license from which he had abstained in that of beauty? A successive enumeration of the elements of beauty will annihilate its effects. Will not a similar cause produce a similar effect in the case of ugliness?

Undoubtedly it will; but it is in this very fact that the justification of Homer lies. The poet can only take advantage of ugliness so far as it is reduced in his description into the less repugnant appearance of bodily imperfection, and ceases, as it were, in point of effect, to be ugliness. Thus, what he cannot make use of by itself he can use as the ingredient for the purpose of producing and strengthening certain mixed sensations.

These mixed feelings are the ridiculous and the horrible. Homer makes Thersites ugly in order to make him ridiculous. He is not made so, however, merely by his ugliness, for ugliness is an imperfection, and the contrast of perfection with imperfections is required to produce the ridiculous. To this I may add that the contrast must not be too sharp and glaring, and that the contrasts must blend into each other.

The wise and virtuous Æsop does not become ridiculous because of ugliness attributed to him. For his misshapen body and beautiful mind are as oil and vinegar; however much you shake them together, they always remain distinct to the taste. They will not amalgamate to produce a third quality. The body produces annoyance; the soul, pleasure; each has its own effect.

It is only when the deformed body is also fragile and, sickly, when it impedes the soul, that the annoyance and pleasure melt into each other.

For, let us suppose that the instigations of the malicious and snarling Thersites had resulted in mutiny, that the people had forsaken their leaders and departed in the ships, and that these leaders had been massacred by a revengeful foe. How would the ugliness of Thersites appear then? If ugliness, when harmless, may be ridiculous, when hurtful it is always horrible. In Shakespeare's "King Lear," Edmund, the bastard Count of Gloucester, is no less a villain than Richard, Duke of Gloucester, in "King Richard III." How is it, then, that the first excites our loathing so much less than the second? It is because when I hear the former, I listen to a devil, but see him as an angel of light; but in listening to Richard I hear a devil and see a devil.

JOHN STUART MILL

Essay on Liberty

Ten years elapsed between the publication of "Political Economy" (see Vol. XIV, p. 294) and the "Essay on Liberty," Mill in the meantime (1851) having married Mrs. John Taylor, a lady who exercised no small influence on his philosophical position. The seven years of his married life saw little or nothing from his pen. The "Essay on Liberty," in many respects the most carefully prepared of all his books, appeared in 1859, the year following the death of his wife, in collaboration with whom it was thought out and partly written. The treatise goes naturally with that on "Utilitarianism." Both are succinct and incisive in their reasoning, and both are grounded on similar sociological principles. Perhaps the primary problem of politics in all ages has been the reconciliation of individual and social interests; and at the present day, when the problem appears to be particularly troublesome, Mill's view of the situation is of especial value. In recent time, legislation has certainly tended to become more socialistic, and the doctrine of individual liberty promulgated in this "Essay" has a most interesting relevancy to modern social movements.

I. —*Liberty of Thought and Discussion*

Protection against popular government is as indispensable as protection against political despotism. The people may desire to oppress a part of their number, and precautions are needed against this as against any other abuse of power. So much will be readily granted by most, and yet no attempt has been made to find the fitting adjustment between individual independence and social control.

The object of this essay is to assert the simple principle that the sole end for which mankind are warranted, individually or collectively, in interfering with the liberty of action of any of their number is self-protection—that the only purpose for which power can be rightfully exercised over any member of a civilised community, against his will, is to prevent harm to others, either by his action or inaction. The only part of the conduct of anyone for which he is amenable to society is that which concerns others. In the part which merely concerns himself, his independence is, of right, absolute. Over himself, over his own body and mind, the individual is sovereign.

This principle requires, firstly, liberty of conscience in the most comprehensive sense, liberty of thought and feeling; absolute freedom of opinion and sentiment on all subjects, practical or speculative, scientific, moral, or theological—the liberty even of publishing and expressing opinions. Secondly, the principle requires liberty of tastes and pursuits; of framing the plan of our life to suit our own character; of doing as we like, so long as we do not harm our fellow-creatures. Thirdly, the principle requires liberty of combination among individuals for any purpose not involving harm to others, provided the persons are of full age and not forced or deceived.

The only freedom which deserves the name is that of pursuing our own good in our own way, so long as we do not attempt to deprive others of theirs, or impede their efforts to obtain it. Mankind gains more by suffering each other to live as seems good to themselves than by compelling each to live as seems good to the rest.

Coercion in matters of thought and discussion must always be illegitimate. If all mankind save one were of one opinion, mankind would be no more justified in silencing the solitary individual than he, if he had the power, would be justified in silencing mankind. The peculiar evil of silencing the expression of opinion is that it is robbing the whole human race, present and future—those who dissent from the opinion even more than those who hold it. For if the opinion is right, they are deprived of the opportunity of exchanging error for truth; and if wrong, they lose the clear and livelier impression of truth produced by its collision with error.

All silencing of discussion is an assumption of infallibility, and, as all history teaches, neither communities nor individuals are infallible. Men cannot be too often reminded of the condemnation of Socrates and of Christ, and of the persecution of the Christians by the noble-minded Marcus Aurelius.

Enemies of religious freedom maintain that persecution is a good thing, for, even though it makes mistakes, it will root out error while it cannot extirpate truth. But history shows that even if truth cannot be finally extirpated, it may at least be put back centuries.

We no longer put heretics to death; but we punish heresies with a social stigma almost as effective, since it may debar men from earning their bread. Social intolerance does not actually eradicate heresies, but it induces men to hide unpopular opinions. The result is that new and heretical opinions smoulder in the narrow circles of thinking and studious persons who originate them, and never light up the general affairs of mankind with either a true or deceptive light. The price paid for intellectual pacification is the sacrifice of the entire moral courage of the human race. Who can compute what the world loses in the multitude of promising intellects too timid to follow out any bold, independent train of thought lest it might be considered irreligious or immoral? No one can be a great thinker who does not follow his intellect to whatever conclusions it may lead. In a general atmosphere of mental slavery a few great thinkers may survive, but in such an atmosphere there never has been, and never will be, an intellectually active people; and all progress in the human mind and in human institutions may be traced to periods of mental emancipation.

Even if an opinion be indubitably true and undoubtingly believed, it will be a dead dogma, and not a living truth, if it be not fully, frequently, and fearlessly discussed. If the cultivation of the understanding consists of one thing more than another, it is surely in learning the grounds of one's own opinions, and these can only be fully learned by facing the arguments that favour the opposite opinions. He who knows only his own side of the case knows little of that. Unless he knows the difficulties which his truth has to encounter and conquer, he knows little of the force of his truth. Not only are the grounds of an opinion unformed or forgotten in the absence of discussion, but too often the very meaning of the opinion. When the mind is not compelled to exercise its powers on the questions which its belief presents to it, there is a progressive tendency to forget all of the belief except the formularies, until it almost ceases to connect itself at all with the inner life of the human being. In such cases a creed merely stands sentinel at the entrance of the mind and heart to keep them empty, as is so often seen in the case of the Christian creed as at present professed.

So far we have considered only two possibilities—that the received opinion may be false and some other opinion consequently true, or that, the received opinion being true, a conflict with the opposite error is essential to a clear apprehension and deep feeling of the truth. But there is a commoner case still, when conflicting doctrines share the truth, and when the heretical doctrine completes the orthodox. Every opinion which embodies somewhat of the portion of the truth which the common opinion omits, ought to be considered precious with whatever amount of error and confusion it may be conjoined. In politics, again, it is almost a commonplace that a party of order or stability, and a party of progress or reform, are both necessary factors in a healthy political life. Unless opinions favourable to democracy and to aristocracy, to property, and to equality, to co-operation and to competition, to sociality and to individuality, to liberty and to discipline, and all the other standing antagonisms of practical life are expressed with equal freedom, and enforced and defended with equal talent and energy, there is no chance of both elements obtaining their due. Truth is usually reached only by the rough process of a struggle between combatants fighting under hostile banners.

It may be objected, "But *some* received principles, especially on the highest and most vital subjects, are more than half-truths." This objection is not sound. Even the Christian morality is, in many important points, incomplete and one-sided, and unless ideas and feelings not sanctioned by it had constituted to the formation of European life and character, human affairs would have been in a worse condition than they now are.

II.—Individuality as One of the Elements of Well-Being

We have seen that opinions should be freely formed and freely expressed. How about *actions*? If a man refrains from molesting others in what concerns him, and merely acts according to his own inclination and judgment in things which concern himself, the same reasons which show that opinion should be free prove also that he should be allowed to carry his opinions into action. As it is useful that while mankind are imperfect there should be different opinions, so it is useful that there should be different experiments of living, that free scope should be given to varieties of character short of injury to others, and that the worth of different modes of life should be proved practically. It is desirable, in short, that in things which do not primarily concern others, individuality should assert itself. When, not the person's own character, but the traditions or customs of other people are the rule of conduct, there is wanting one of the principal ingredients of human happiness and quite the chief ingredient of individual and social progress.

No one's idea of excellence in conduct is that people should do absolutely nothing but copy one another. On the other hand, it would be absurd to pretend that people ought to live as if experience had as yet done nothing towards showing that one mode of existence or of conduct is preferable to another. No one denies that people should be so taught and trained in youth as to know and benefit by the results of human experience. But it is the privilege of a mature man to use and interpret experience in his own way. He who lets the world, or his own portion of it, choose his plan of life for him has no need of any other faculty than the ape-like one of imitation. He, on the other hand, who chooses his plan for himself, employs all his faculties—reasoning, foresight, activity, discrimination, resolution, self-control. We wish not automatons, but living, originating men and women.

So much will be readily conceded, but nevertheless it may be maintained that strong desires and passions are a peril and a snare. Yet it is desires and impulses which constitute character, and one with no desires and impulses of his own has no more character than a steam-engine. An energetic character implies strong, spontaneous impulses under the control of a strong will; and such characters are desirable, since the danger which threatens modern society is not excess but deficiency of personal impulses and preferences. Everyone nowadays asks: what is usually done by persons of my station and pecuniary circumstances, or (worse still) what is usually done by persons of a station and circumstances superior to mine? The consequence is that, through failure to follow their own nature, they have no nature to follow; their human capacities are withered and starved, and are incapable of any strong pleasures or opinions properly their own.

It is not by pruning away the individual but by cultivating it wisely that human beings become valuable to themselves and to others, and that human life becomes rich, diversified, and interesting. Individuality is equivalent to development, and in proportion to the latitude given to individuality an age becomes noteworthy or the reverse.

Unfortunately, the general tendency of things is to render mediocrity the ascendant power. At present, individuals are lost in the crowd, and it is almost a triviality to say that public opinion now rules the world. And public opinion is the opinion of collective mediocrity, and is expressed by mediocre men. The initiation of all wise and noble opinions must come from individuals, and the individuality of those who stand on the higher eminences of thought is necessary to correct the tendency that makes mankind acquiesce in customary and popular opinions.

III.—The Limits of the Authority of Society Over the Individual

Where, then, does the authority of society begin? How much of human life should be assigned to individuality, and how much to society?

To individuality should belong that part of life in which it is chiefly the individual that is interested; to society, the part which chiefly interests society.

Society, in return for the protection it affords its members, and as a condition of its existence, demands, firstly, that its members respect the rights of one another; and, secondly, that each person bear his share of the labours and sacrifices incurred in defending society for its members. Further, society may punish acts of an individual hurtful to others, even if not a violation of rights, by the force of public opinion.

But in all cases where a person's conduct affects or need only affect himself, society may not interfere. Society may help individuals in their personal affairs, but neither one person, nor any number of persons, is warranted in saying to any human creature that he may not use his own life, so far as it concerns himself, as he pleases. He himself is the final judge of his own concerns, and the inconveniences which are strictly inseparable from the unfavourable judgment of others are the only ones to which a person should ever be subjected for that portion of his conduct and character which affects his own good, but which does not affect the interests of others.

But how, it may be asked, can any part of the conduct of a member of society be a matter of indifference to the other members?

I fully confess that the mischief which a person does to himself may seriously affect those nearly connected with him, and even society at large. But such contingent and indirect injury should be endured by society for the sake of the greater good of human freedom, and because any attempt at coercion in private conduct will merely produce rebellion on the part of the individual coerced. Moreover, when society interferes with purely personal conduct, the odds are that it interferes wrongly, and in the wrong places, as the pages of history and the records of legislation abundantly demonstrate.

Closely connected with the question of the limitations of the authority of society over the individual is the question of government participation in industrial and other enterprises generally undertaken by individuals.

There are three main objections to the interference of the state in such matters. In the first place, the matter may be better managed by individuals than by the government. In the second place, though individuals may not do it so well as government might, yet it is desirable that they should do it, as a means of their own mental education. In the third place, it is undesirable to add to the power of the government. If roads, railways, banks, insurance offices, great joint-stock companies, universities, public charities, municipal corporations, and local boards were all in the government service, and if the employees in these look to the government for promotion, not all the freedom of the Press and the popular constitution of the legislature would make this or any other country free otherwise than in name. And, for various reasons, the better qualified the heads and hands of the government officials, the more detrimental would the rule of the government be. Such a government would inevitably degenerate into a pedantocracy monopolising all the occupations which form and cultivate the faculties required for the government of mankind.

To find the best compromise between individuals and the state is difficult, but I believe the ideal must combine the greatest possible dissemination of power consistent with efficiency, and the greatest possible centralisation and diffusion of information.

JOHN MILTON

Areopagitica

It has been said of "Areopagitica, a Speech of Mr. John Milton
for the Liberty of Unlicensed Printing to the Parliament of
England," that it is "the piece that lies more surely than any
other at the very heart of our prose literature." In 1637 the Star
Chamber issued a decree regulating the printing, circulation,
and importation of books, and on June 14, 1643, the Long
Parliament published an order in the same spirit. Milton
(see Vol. XVII) felt that what had been done in the days of
repression and tyranny was being continued under the reign
of liberty, and that the time for protest had arrived. Liberty
was the central principle of Milton's faith. He regarded it
as the most potent, beneficent, and sacred factor in human
progress; and he applied it all round — to literature, religion,
marriage, and civic life. His "Areopagitica," published
in November, 1644, was an application of the principle
to literature that has remained unanswered. The word
"Areopagitica" is derived from Areopagus, the celebrated
open-air court in Athens, whose decision in matters of public
importance was regarded as final.

I. — The Right of Appeal

It is not a liberty which we can hope, that no grievance ever should
arise in the Commonwealth — that let no man in this world expect; but when
complaints are freely heard, deeply considered, and speedily reformed,
then is the utmost bound of civil liberty attained that wise men look for. To
which we are already in good part arrived; and this will be attributed first
to the strong assistance of God our Deliverer, next to your faithful guidance
and undaunted wisdom, Lords and Commons of England.

If I should thus far presume upon the meek demeanour of your civil and
gentle greatness, Lords and Commons, as to gainsay what your published
Order hath directly said, I might defend myself with ease out of those ages
to whose polite wisdom and letters we owe that we are not yet Goths and

Jutlanders. Such honour was done in those days to men who professed the study of wisdom and eloquence that cities and signiories heard them gladly, and with great respect, if they had aught in public to admonish the state.

When your prudent spirit acknowledges and obeys the voice of reason from what quarter soever it be heard speaking, I know not what should withhold me from presenting ye with a fit instance wherein to show, both that love of truth which ye eminently profess, and that uprightness of your judgment which is not wont to be partial to yourselves, by judging over again that Order which ye have ordained to regulate printing: that no book, pamphlet, or paper shall be henceforth printed unless the same be first approved and licensed by such, or at least one of such, as shall be thereto appointed.

I shall lay before ye, first, that the inventors of licensing books be those whom ye will be loth to own; next, what is to be thought in general of reading, whatever sort the books be; last, that it will be primely to the discouragement of all learning and the stop of truth. I deny not that it is of greatest concernment in the Church and commonwealth to have a vigilant eye how books demean themselves, as well as men. For books are not absolutely dead things, but do contain a potency of life in them to be as active as that soul was whose progeny they are.

Nay, they do preserve as in a vial the purest efficacy and extraction of that living intellect that bred them. I know they are as lively and as vigorously productive as those fabulous dragon's teeth; and, being sown up and down, may chance to spring up armed men. And yet, on the other hand, unless wariness be used, as good almost kill a man as kill a good book. Many a man lives a burden to the earth; but a good book is the precious life-blood of a master spirit, embalmed and treasured up on purpose to life beyond life. 'Tis true, no age can restore a life, whereof perhaps there is no great loss; and revolutions of ages do not oft recover the loss of a rejected truth, for the want of which whole nations fare the worse.

We should be wary, therefore, how we spill that seasoned life of man, preserved and stored up in books, since we see a kind of homicide may be thus committed, that strikes at that ethereal essence, the breath of reason itself, and slays an immortality rather than a life.

II.—*The History of Repression*

In Athens, where books and wits were ever busier than in any other part of Greece, I find but only two sorts of writings which the magistrate cared to take notice of—those either blasphemous and atheistical, or libellous. The Romans, for many ages trained up only to a military roughness, knew of learning little. There libellous authors were quickly cast into prison, and the like severity was used if aught were impiously written. Except in these two points, how the world went in books the magistrate kept no reckoning.

By the time the emperors were become Christians, the books of those whom they took to be grand heretics were examined, refuted, and condemned in the general councils, and not till then were prohibited.

As for the writings of heathen authors, unless they were plain invectives against Christianity, they met with no interdict that can be cited till about the year 400. The primitive councils and bishops were wont only to declare what books were not commendable, passing no further till after the year 800, after which time the popes of Rome extended their dominion over men's eyes, as they had before over their judgments, burning and prohibiting to be read what they fancied not, till Martin V. by his Bull not only prohibited, but was the first that excommunicated the reading of heretical books; for about that time Wickliffe and Huss, growing terrible, drove the papal court to a stricter policy of prohibiting. To fill up the measure of encroachment, their last invention was to ordain that no book, pamphlet, or paper should be printed (as if St. Peter had bequeathed them the keys of the press also out of Paradise), unless it were approved and licensed under the hands of two or three glutton friars.

Not from any ancient state or polity or church, nor by any statute left us by our ancestors, but from the most tyrannous Inquisition have ye this book-licensing. Till then books were as freely admitted into the world as any other birth. No envious Juno sat cross-legged over the nativity of any man's intellectual offspring. That ye like not now these most certain authors of this licensing Order, all men who know the integrity of your actions will clear ye readily.

III.—The Futility of Prohibition

But some will say, "What though the inventors were bad, the thing, for all that, may be good?" It may be so, yet I am of those who believe it will be a harder alchemy than Lullius ever knew to sublimate any good use out of such an invention.

Good and evil in the field of this world grow up together almost inseparably. As the state of man now is, what wisdom can there be to choose, what continence to forbear, without the knowledge of evil? I cannot praise a fugitive and cloistered virtue, unexercised and unbreathed, that never sallies out and sees her adversary, but slinks out of the race, where that immortal garland is to be run for, not without dust and heat. That which purifies us is trial, and trial is by what is contrary. And how can we more safely, and with less danger scout into the regions of sin and falsity than by reading all manner of tractates and hearing all manner of reason? And this is the benefit which may be had of books promiscuously read.

'Tis next alleged we must not expose ourselves to temptations without necessity, and next to that, not employ our time in vain things. To both these objections one answer will serve—that to all men such books are not temptations, nor vanities, but useful drugs and materials wherewith to temper and compose effective and strong medicines. The rest, as children and childish men, who have not the art to qualify and prepare these working minerals, well may be exhorted to forbear, but hindered forcibly they cannot be by all the licensing that sainted Inquisition could ever yet contrive.

This Order of licensing conduces nothing to the end for which it was framed. If we think to regulate printing, thereby to rectify manners, we must regulate all recreations and pastimes, all that is delightful to man. No music must be heard, no song be set or sung, but what is grave and Doric. There must be licensing dancers, that no gesture, motion, or deportment be taught our youth but what by their allowance shall be thought honest. Our garments, also, should be referred to the licensing of some more sober workmasters to see them cut into a less wanton garb. Who shall regulate all the mixed conversation of our youth? Who shall still appoint what shall be discoursed, what presumed, and no further? Lastly, who shall forbid and separate all idle resort, all evil company? If every action which is good or evil in man at ripe years were to be under pittance and prescription and compulsion, what were virtue but a name?

When God gave Adam reason, he gave him reason to choose, for reason is but choosing. Wherefore did he create passions within us, pleasures round about us, but that these rightly tempered are the very ingredients of virtue?

Why should we then affect a rigour contrary to the manner of God and of nature, by abridging or scanting those means which books freely permitted are both to the trial of virtue and the exercise of truth?

IV.—An Indignity to Learning

I lastly proceed from the no good it can do to the manifest hurt it causes in being, first, the greatest discouragement and affront that can be offered to learning and to learned men. If ye be loth to dishearten utterly and discontent the free and ingenuous sort of such as were born to study, and love learning for itself, not for lucre or any other end but the service of God and of truth, and perhaps that lasting fame and perpetuity of praise which God and good men have consented shall be the reward of those whose published labours advance the good of mankind, then know that so far to distrust the judgment and the honesty of one who hath but a common repute in learning, and never yet offended, as not to count him fit to print his mind without a tutor and examiner, is the greatest displeasure and indignity to a free and knowing spirit that can be put upon him.

When a man writes to the world he summons up all his reason and deliberation to assist him; he searches, meditates, is industrious, and likely consults and confers with his judicious friends. If in this, the most consummate act of his fidelity and ripeness, no years, no industry, no former proof of his abilities can bring him to that state of maturity as not to be still mistrusted and suspected, unless he carry all his considerate diligence to the hasty view of an unleisured licenser, perhaps much his younger, perhaps far his inferior in judgment, perhaps one who never knew the labour of book-writing, and if he be not repulsed or slighted, must appear in print with his censor's hand on the back of his title, to be his bail and surety that he is no idiot or seducer, it cannot be but a dishonour and derogation to the author, to the book, to the privilege and dignity of learning.

And, further, to me it seems an undervaluing and vilifying of the whole nation. I cannot set so light by all the invention, the art, the wit, the grave and solid judgment which is in England, as that it can be comprehended in any twenty capacities how good soever, much less that it should not pass except their superintendence be over it, except it be sifted and strained with their strainers, that it should be uncurrent without their manual stamp. Truth and understanding are not such wares as to be monopolised and traded in by tickets and statutes and standards.

Lords and Commons of England, consider what nation it is whereof ye are, and whereof ye are the governors—a nation not slow and dull, but of a quick, ingenious and piercing spirit, acute to invent, subtle and sinewy to discourse, not beneath the reach of any point the highest that human capacity can soar to. Is it for nothing that the grave and frugal Transylvanian sends out yearly from as far as the mountainous borders of Russia, and beyond the Hercynian wilderness, not their youth, but their staid men, to learn our language and our theologic arts? By all concurrence of signs, and by the general instinct of holy and devout men, God is decreeing to begin some new and great period in His Church, even to the reforming of Reformation itself. What does He, then, but reveal Himself to His servants, and as His manner is, first to His Englishmen?

Behold now this vast city—a city of refuge, the mansion house of liberty, encompassed and surrounded with His protection. The shop of war hath not there more anvils and hammers waking to fashion out the plates and instruments of armed justice in defence of beleaguered truth than there be pens and heads there, sitting by their studious lamps, musing, searching, revolving new notions and ideas wherewith to present, as with their homage and their fealty, the approaching Reformation; others as fast reading, trying all things, assenting to the force of reason and convincement. What could a man require more from a nation so pliant and so prone to seek after knowledge? Where there is much desire to learn, there, of necessity, will be much arguing, much writing, many opinions; for opinion in good men is but knowledge in the making. A little generous prudence, a little forbearance of one another, and some grain of charity might win all these diligencies to join and unite in one general search after truth, could we but forego this prelatical tradition of crowding free consciences and Christian liberties into canons and precepts of men.

Methinks I see in my mind a noble and puissant nation rousing herself like a strong man after sleep, and shaking her invincible locks. Methinks I see her as an eagle mewing her mighty youth, and kindling her undazzled eyes at the full midday beam; purging and unsealing her long-abused sight at the fountain itself of heavenly radiance; while the whole noise of timorous and flocking birds, with those also that love the twilight, flutter about, amazed at what she means, and in their envious gabble would prognosticate a year of sects and schisms.

What should ye do then? Should ye suppress all this flowery crop of knowledge and new light? Should ye set an oligarchy of twenty engrossers over it, to bring a famine upon our minds again, when we shall know nothing but what is measured to us by their bushel? Believe it, Lords and Commons, they who counsel ye to such a suppressing do as good as bid ye suppress yourselves. If it be desired to know the immediate cause of all this free writing and free speaking, there cannot be assigned a truer than your own mild, and free, and humane government. It is the liberty, Lords and Commons, which our own valorous and happy counsels have purchased us, liberty, which is the nurse of all great wits. Give me the liberty to know, to utter, and to argue freely according to conscience above all liberties. And though all the winds of doctrine were let loose to play upon the earth, so Truth be in the field, we do injuriously, by licensing and prohibiting, to misdoubt her strength. Let her and Falsehood grapple. Whoever knew Truth put to the worse in a free and open encounter? For who knows not that Truth is strong, next to the Almighty? She needs no policies, nor stratagems, nor licensing to make her victorious. Those are the shifts and defences that error uses against her power. Give her but room, and do not bind her when she sleeps.

PLUTARCH

Parallel Lives

Little is known of the life of Plutarch, greatest of biographers. He was born about 50 A.D., at Chæronea, in Bœotia, Greece, the son of a learned and virtuous father. He studied philosophy under Ammonius at Delphi, and on his return to his native city became a priest of Apollo, and archon, or chief magistrate. Plutarch wrote many philosophical works, which are enumerated by his son Lamprias, but are no longer extant. We have about fifty biographies, which are called "parallel" because of the method by which Plutarch, after giving separately the lives of two or more people, proceeds to compare them with one another. The "Lives" were translated into French in Henry II.'s reign, and into English in the time of Elizabeth. They have been exceedingly popular at every period, and many authors, including Shakespeare, have owed much to them. Plutarch died about 120 A.D.

I.—*Lycurgus and Numa*

According to the best authors, Lycurgus, the law-giver, reigned only for eight months as king of Sparta, until the widow of the late king, his brother, had given birth to a son, whom he named Charilaus. He then travelled for some years in Crete, Asia, and possibly also in Egypt, Libya, Spain, and India, studying governments and manners; and returning to Sparta, he set himself to alter the whole constitution of that kingdom, with the encouragement of the oracles and the favour of Charilaus.

The first institution was a senate of twenty-eight members, whose place it was to strengthen the throne when the people encroached too far, and to support the people when the king should attempt to become absolute. Occasional popular assemblies, in the open air, were to be called, not to propose any subject of debate, but only to ratify or reject the proposals of the senate and the two kings.

His second political enterprise was a new division of the lands, for he found a prodigious inequality, wealth being centred in the hands of a few; and by this reform Laconia became like an estate newly divided among many brothers. Each plot of land was sufficient to maintain a family in health, and they wanted nothing more.

Then, desiring also to equalise property in movable objects, he resorted to the device of doing away with gold and silver currency, and establishing an iron coinage, of which great bulk and weight went to but little value. He excluded all unprofitable and superfluous arts; and the Spartans soon had no means of purchasing foreign wares, nor did any merchant ship unlade in their harbours. Luxury died away of itself, and the workmanship of their necessary and useful furniture rose to great excellence.

Public tables were now established, where all must eat in common of the same frugal meal; whereby hardiness and health of body and mutual benevolence of mind were alike promoted. There were about fifteen to a table, to which each contributed in provisions or in money; the conversation was liberal and well-informed, and salted with pleasant raillery.

Lycurgus left no law in writing; he depended on principles pervading the customs of the people; and he reduced the whole business of legislation into the bringing up of the young. And in this matter he began truly at the beginning, by regulating marriages. The man unmarried after the prescribed age was prosecuted and disgraced; and the father of four children was immune from taxation.

Lycurgus considered the children as the property of the state rather than of the parents, and derided the vanity of other nations, who studied to have horses of the finest breed, yet had their children begotten by ordinary persons rather than by the best and healthiest men. At birth, the children were carried to be examined by the oldest men in council, who had the weaklings thrown away into a cavern, and gave orders for the education of the sturdy.

As for learning, they had just what was necessary and no more, their education being directed chiefly to making them obedient, laborious, and warlike. They went barefoot, and for the most part naked. They were trained to steal with astuteness, to suffer pain and hunger, and to express themselves without an unnecessary word. Dignified poetry and music were encouraged. To the end of his life, the Spartan was kept ever in mind that he was born, not for himself, but for his country; the city was like one great camp, where each had his stated allowance and his stated public charge.

Let us turn now to Numa Pompilius, the great law-giver of the Romans. A Sabine of illustrious virtue and great simplicity of life, he was elected to be king after the interregnum which followed on the disappearance of Romulus. He had spent much time in solitary wanderings in the sacred groves and other retired places; and there, it is reported, the goddess Egeria communicated to him a happiness and knowledge more than mortal.

Numa was in his fortieth year, and was not easily persuaded to undertake the Roman kingdom. But his disinclination was overcome, and he was received with loud acclamations as the most pious of men and most beloved of the gods. His first act was to discharge the body-guard provided for him, and to appoint a priest for the cult of Romulus. But his great task was to soften the Romans, as iron is softened by fire, and to bring them from a violent and warlike disposition to a juster and more gentle temper. For Rome was composed at first of most hardy and resolute men, inveterate warriors.

To reduce this people to mildness and peace, he called in the assistance of religion. By sacrifices, solemn dances, and processions, wherein he himself officiated, he mixed the charms of festal pleasure with holy ritual.

He founded the hierarchy of priests, the vestal virgins, and several other sacred orders; and passed most of his time in performing some religious function or in conversing with the priests on some divine subject. And by all this discipline the people became so tractable, and were so impressed with Numa's power, that they would believe the most fabulous tales, and thought nothing impossible which he undertook. Numa further introduced agriculture, and fostered it as an incentive to peace; he distributed the citizens of Rome into guilds, or companies, according to their several arts and trades; he reformed the calendar, and did many other services to his people.

Comparing, now, Lycurgus and Numa, we find that their resemblances are obvious—their wisdom, piety, talent for government, and their deriving their laws from a divine source. Of their distinctions, the chief is that Numa accepted, but Lycurgus relinquished, a crown; and as it was an honour to the former to attain royal dignity by his justice, so it was an honour to the latter to prefer justice to that dignity. Again, Lycurgus tuned up the strings of Sparta, which he found relaxed with luxury, to a keener pitch; Numa, on the contrary, softened the high and harsh tone of Rome. Both were equally studious to lead their people to sobriety, but Lycurgus was more attached to fortitude and Numa to justice.

Though Numa put an end to the gain of rapine, he made no provision against the accumulation of great fortunes, nor against poverty, which then began to spread within the city. He ought rather to have watched against these dangers, for they gave birth to the many troubles that befell the Roman state.

II.—Aristides and Cato

Aristides had a close friendship with Clisthenes, who established popular government in Athens after the expulsion of the tyrants; yet he had at the same time a great veneration for Lycurgus of Sparta, whom he regarded as supreme among law-givers; and this led him to be a supporter of aristocracy, in which he was always opposed by Themistocles, the democrat. The latter was insinuating, daring, artful, and impetuous, but Aristides was solid and steady, inflexibly just, and incapable of flattery or deceit.

Neither elated by honour nor disheartened by ill success, Aristides became deeply founded in the estimation of the best citizens. He was appointed public treasurer, and showed up the peculations of Themistocles and of others who had preceded him. When the fleet of Darius was at Marathon, with a view to subjugating Greece, Miltiades and Aristides were the Greek generals, who by custom were to command by turns, day about; and Aristides freely gave up his command to the other, to promote unity of discipline, and to give example of military obedience. The next year he became archon. Though a poor man and a commoner, Aristides won the royal and divine title of "the Just." At first loved and respected for his surname "the Just," Aristides came to be envied and dreaded for so extraordinary an honour, and the citizens assembled from all the towns in Attica and banished him by ostracism, cloaking their envy of his character under the pretence of guarding against tyranny. Three years later they reversed this decree, fearing lest Aristides should join the cause of Xerxes. They little knew the man; even before his recall he had been inciting the Greeks to defend their liberty.

In the great battle of Platæa, Aristides was in command of the Athenians; Pausanias, commander-in-chief of all the confederates, joined him there with the Spartans. The opposing Persian army covered an immense area. In the engagements which took place the Greeks behaved with the utmost firmness, and at last stormed the Persian camp, with a prodigious slaughter of the enemy. When, later, Aristides was entrusted with the task of assessing the cities of the allies for a tax towards the war, and was thus clothed with an authority which made him master of Greece, though he set out poor he returned yet poorer, having arranged the burden with equal justice and humanity. In fact, he esteemed his poverty no less a glory than all the laurels he had won.

The Roman counterpart of Aristides was Cato; which name he received for his wisdom, for Romans call wise men Catos. Marcus Cato, the censor, came of an obscure family, yet his father and grandfather were excellent soldiers. He lived on an estate which his father left him near the Sabine country. With red hair and grey eyes, his appearance was such, says an epigram, as to scare the spirits of the departed. Inured to labour and temperance, he had the sound constitution of one brought up in camps; and he had practised eloquence as a necessary instrument for one who would mix with affairs. While still a lad he had fought in so many battles that his breast was covered with scars; and all who spoke with him noted a gravity of behaviour and a dignity of sentiment such as to fit him for high responsibilities.

A powerful nobleman, Valerius Flaccus, whose estate was near Cato's home, heard his servants praise their neighbour's laborious life. He sent for Cato, and, charmed with his sweet temper and ready wit, persuaded him to go to Rome and apply himself to political affairs. His rise was rapid; he became tribune of the soldiers, then quæstor, and at last was the colleague of Valerius both as consul and as censor.

Cato's eloquence brought him the epithet of the Roman Demosthenes, but he was even more celebrated for his manner of living. Few were willing to imitate him in the ancient custom of tilling the ground with his own hands, in eating a dinner prepared without fire, and a spare, frugal supper; few thought it more honourable not to want superfluities than to possess them. By reason of its vast dominions, the commonwealth had lost its pristine purity and integrity; the citizens were frightened at labour and enervated by pleasure. But Cato never wore a costly garment nor partook of an elaborate meal; even when consul he drank the same wine as his servants. He thought nothing cheap that is superfluous. Some called him mean and narrow, others thought that he was setting an object-lesson to the growing luxury of the age. For my part, I think that his custom of using his servants like beasts of burden, and of turning them off or selling them when grown old, was the mark of an ungenerous spirit, which thinks that the sole tie between man and man is interest or necessity. For my own part, I would not sell even an old ox that had laboured for me.

However that may be, his temperance was wonderful. When governor of Sardinia, where his predecessors had put the province to great expense, he did not even use a carriage, but walked from town to town with one attendant. He was inexorable in everything that concerned public justice. He proved himself a brave general in the field; and when he became censor, which was the highest dignity of the republic, he waged an uncompromising campaign against luxury, by means of an almost prohibitive tax on the expenditure of ostentatious superfluity. His style in speaking was at once humorous, familiar, and forcible, and many of his wise and pregnant sayings are remembered.

When we compare Aristides and Cato, we are at once struck by many resemblances; and examining the several parts of their lives distinctly, as we examine a poem or a picture, we find that they both rose to great honour without the help of family connections, and merely by their own virtue and abilities. Both of them were equally victorious in war; but in politics Aristides was less successful, being banished by the faction of Themistocles; while Cato, though his antagonists were the most powerful men in Rome, kept his footing to the end like a skilled wrestler.

Again, Cato was no less attentive to the management of his domestic affairs than he was to affairs of state, and not only increased his own fortune, but became a guide to others in finance and in agriculture. But Aristides, by his indigence, brought disgrace upon justice itself, as if it were the ruin and impoverishment of families; it is even said that he left not enough for the portions of his daughters nor for the expenses of his own funeral. So Cato's family produced prætors and consuls to the fourth generation; but of the descendants of Aristides some were conjurors and paupers, and not one of them had a sentiment worthy of his illustrious ancestor.

III.—Demosthenes and Cicero

That these two great orators were originally formed by nature in the same mould is shown by the similarity of their dispositions. They had the same ambition, the same love of liberty, and the same timidity in war and danger. Their fortunes also were similar; both raised themselves from obscure beginnings to authority and power; both opposed kings and tyrants; both of them were banished, then returned with honour, were forced to fly again, and were taken by their enemies; and with both of them expired the liberties of their countries.

Demosthenes, while a weakly child of seven years, lost his father, and his fortune was dissipated by unworthy guardians. But his ambition was fired in early years by hearing the pleadings of the orator Callistratus, and by noting the honours which attended success in that profession. He at once applied himself to the practice of declamation, and studied rhetoric under Isæus; and as soon as he came of age he appeared at the Bar in the prosecution of his guardians for their embezzlements. Though successful in this claim, Demosthenes had much to learn, and his earlier speeches provoked the amusement of his audience. His manner was at once violent and confused, his voice weak and stammering, and his delivery breathless;

but these faults were overcome by an arduous and protracted course of exercise in the subterraneous study which he had built, where he would remain for two or three months together. He corrected the stammering by speaking with pebbles in his mouth; strengthened his voice by running uphill and declaiming while still unbreathed; and his attitude and gestures were studied before a mirror.

Demosthenes was rarely heard to speak extempore, and though the people called upon him in the assembly, he would sit silent unless he had come prepared. He wrote a great part, if not the whole, of each oration beforehand, so that it was objected that his arguments "smelled of the lamp"; yet, on exceptional occasions, he would speak unprepared, and then as if from a supernatural impulse.

His nature was vindictive and his resentment implacable. He was never a time-server in word or in action, and he maintained to the end the political standpoint with which he had begun. The glorious object of his ambition was the defence of the cause of Greece against Philip; and most of his orations, including these Philippics, are written upon the principle that the right and worthy course is to be chosen for its own sake. He does not exhort his countrymen to that which is most agreeable, or easy, or advantageous, but to that which is most honourable. If, besides this noble ambition of his and the lofty tone of his orations, he had been gifted also with warlike courage and had kept his hands clean from bribes, Demosthenes would have deserved to be numbered with Cimon, Thucydides, and Pericles.

Cicero's wonderful genius came to light even in his school-days; he had the capacity and inclination to learn all the arts, but was most inclined to poetry, and the time came when he was reputed the best poet as well as the greatest orator in Rome. After a training in law and some experience of the wars, he retired to a life of philosophic study, but being persuaded to appear in the courts for Roscius, who was unjustly charged with the murder of his father, Cicero immediately made his reputation as an orator.

His health was weak; he could eat but little, and that only late in the day; his voice was harsh, loud, and ill regulated; but, like Demosthenes, he was able by assiduous practice to modulate his enunciation to a full, sonorous, and sweet tone, and his studies under the leading rhetoricians of Greece and Asia perfected his eloquence.

His diligence, justice, and moderation were evidenced by his conduct in public offices, as quæstor, prætor, and then as consul. In his attack on Catiline's conspiracy, he showed the Romans what charms eloquence can add to truth, and that justice is invincible when properly supported. But his immoderate love of praise interrupted his best designs, and he made himself obnoxious to many by continually magnifying himself.

Demosthenes, by concentrating all his powers on the single art of speaking, became unrivalled in the power, grandeur, and accuracy of his eloquence. Cicero's studies had a wider range; he strove to excel not only as an orator, but as a philosopher and a scholar also. Their difference of temperament is reflected in their styles. Demosthenes is always grave and serious, an austere man of thought; Cicero, on the other hand, loves his jest, and is sometimes playful to the point of buffoonery. The Greek orator never touches upon his own praise except with some great point in view, and then does it modestly and without offence; the Roman does not seek to hide his intemperate vanity.

Both of these men had high political abilities; but while the former held no public office, and lies under the suspicion of having at times sold his talent to the highest bidder, the latter ruled provinces as a pro-consul at a time when avarice reigned unbridled, and became known only for his humanity and his contempt of money.

MADAME DE STAËL

On Germany

Madame de Staël's book "On Germany" (De l'Allemagne) was finished in 1810. The manuscript was passed by the censor, and partly printed, when the whole impression was seized by the order of the Emperor and destroyed. Madame de Staël herself escaped secretly, and came eventually to London, where, in 1813, the work was published. She did not long survive the fall of her tremendous enemy, Napoleon, but died in her beloved Paris on July 14, 1817. When it is considered that "On Germany" was written by other than an inhabitant of the country, and that Madame de Staël did not travel far beyond her own residences at Mainz, Frankfort, Berlin, and Vienna, the work may be reckoned the most remarkable performance of its kind in literature or biography (Mme. de Staël, biography: see Vol. VIII, p. 89).

I.—Germany, Its People and Customs

The multitude and extent of the forests indicate a still new civilisation. Germany still shows traces of uninhabited nature. It is a sad country, and time is needed to discover what there is to love in it. The ruined castles on the hills, the narrow windows of the houses, the long stretches of snow in winter, the silence of nature and men, all contribute towards the sadness. Yet the country and its inhabitants are interesting and poetical. You feel that human souls and imagination have embellished this land.

The only remarkable monuments in Germany are the Gothic ones which recall the age of chivalry. Modern German architecture is not worth mentioning, but the towns are well built, and the people try to make their houses look as cheerful and pleasing as possible. The gardens in some parts of Germany are almost as beautiful as in England, which denotes love of nature. Often, in the midst of the superb gardens of the German princes, æolian harps are placed; the breezes waft sound and scent at once. Thus northern imagination tries to construct Italian nature.

The Germans are generally sincere and faithful; they scarcely ever break their word and are strangers to deception. Power of work and thought is another of their national traits. They are naturally literary and philosophical, but their pride of class affects in some ways their *esprit* adversely. The nobles are lacking in ideas, and the men of letters know too little about business. The Germans have imagination rather than *esprit*.

The town dwellers and the country folk, the soldiers and the workmen, nearly all have some knowledge of music. I have been to some poor houses, blackened with tobacco smoke, and not only the mistress, but also the master of the house, improvise on the piano, just as the Italians improvise in verse. Instrumental music is as generally fostered in Germany as vocal music is in Italy. Italy has the advantage, because instrumental music requires work, whilst the southern sky suffices to produce beautiful voices.

Peasant women and servants, who are too poor to put on finery, decorate their hair with a few flowers, so that imagination may at least enter into their attire.

One is constantly struck in Germany with the contrast between sentiment and custom, between talent and taste; civilisation and nature do not seem to have properly amalgamated yet. Enthusiasm for art and poetry goes with very vulgar habits in social life. Nothing could be more bizarre than the combination of the warlike aspect of Germany, where soldiers are met at every step, with the indoor life led by the people. There is a dread of fatigue and change of air, as if the nation were composed only of shopkeepers and men of letters; and yet all the institutions tend towards giving the nation military habits.

Stoves, beer, and tobacco-smoke crate around the German people a kind of heavy and hot atmosphere which they do not like to leave. This atmosphere is injurious to activity, which is at least as necessary in war as in courage; resolutions are slow, discouragement is easy, because a generally sad existence does not engender much confidence in fortune.

Three motive powers lead men to fight: love of the fatherland and of liberty, love of glory, and religious fanaticism. There is not much love of the fatherland in an Empire that has been divided for centuries, where Germans fought against Germans; love of glory is not very lively where there is no centre, no capital, no society. The Germans are much more apt to get roused by abstract ideas than by the interests of life.

The love of liberty is not developed with the Germans; they have learnt neither by enjoyment, nor by privation, the prize that may be attached to it. The very independence enjoyed by Germany in all respects made the

Germans indifferent to liberty; independence is a possession, liberty a guarantee, and just because nobody was crossed in Germany either in his rights or in his pleasures, nobody felt the need for an order of things that would maintain this happiness.

The Germans, with few exceptions, are scarcely capable of succeeding in anything that requires cleverness and skill; everything troubles them, makes them nervous, and they need method in action as well as independence in thought.

German women have a charm of their own, a touching quality of voice, fair hair, and brilliant complexion; they are modest, but not as shy as the English. One can see that they have often met men who were superior to them, and that they have less cause to fear the severity of public judgment. They try to please by their sensibility, and to arouse interest by the imagination. The language of poetry and of the fine arts is known to them; they flirt with enthusiasm, just as one flirts in France with *esprit* and wit.

Love is a religion in Germany, but a poetic religion, which willingly tolerates all that may be excused by sensibility. The facility of divorce in the Protestant provinces certainly affects the sanctity of marriage. Husbands are changed as peacefully as if it were merely a question of arranging the incidents of a play. The good-nature of men and women prevents any bitterness entering these easy ruptures.

Some German women are ever in a state of exaltation that amounts to affectation, and the sweet expressions of which efface whatever there may be piquant or pronounced in their mind and character. They are not frank, and yet not false either; but they see and judge nothing with truth, and the real events pass before their eyes like phantasmagoria.

But these women are the exception. Many German women have true sentiment and simple manners. Their careful education and natural purity of soul renders their dominion gentle and moderate; every day they inspire you with increased interest for all that is great and noble, with increased confidence in every kind of hope. What is rare among German women is real *esprit* and quick repartee. Conversation, as a talent, exists only in France; in other countries it only serves for polite intercourse, for discussion and for friendship; in France it is an art.

II.—On Southern Germany and Austria

Franconia, Suabia, and Bavaria were, before the foundation of the Munich Academy, strangely heavy and monotonous countries; no arts except music, little literature; an accent that did not lend itself well to the pronunciation of the Latin languages, no society; great parties that resembled ceremonies rather than amusement; obsequious politeness towards an unelegant aristocracy; kindness and loyalty in all classes, but a certain smiling stiffness which is neither ease nor dignity. In a country where society counts for nothing, and nature for little, only the literary towns can be really interesting.

A temperate climate is not favourable for poetry. Where the climate is neither severe nor beautiful, one lives without fearing or hoping anything from heaven, and one only takes interest in the positive facts of existence. Southern Germany, temperate in every respect, keeps up a state of monotonous well-being which is as bad for business activity as it is for the activity of the mind. The keenest wish of the inhabitants of that peaceful and fertile country is to continue the same existence. And what can one do with that one desire? It is not even enough to preserve that with which one is contented.

There are many excellent things in Austria, but few really superior men, because in that country it is not much use to excel one's neighbour; one is not envied for it, but forgotten, which is still more discouraging. Ambition turns in the direction of obtaining good posts.

Austria, embracing so many different peoples, Bohemians, Hungarians, etc., has not the unity necessary for a monarchy. Yet the great moderation of the heads of the state has for a long time constituted a strong link.

Industry, good living and domestic pleasures are Austria's principal interests. In spite of the glory she gained by the perseverance and valour of her troops, the military spirit has really never got hold of all classes of the nation.

In a country where every movement is difficult, and where everything inspires tranquility, the slightest obstacle is an excuse for complete idleness of action and thought. One might say that this is real happiness; but does happiness consist of the faculties which one develops, or of those which one chokes?

Vienna is situated in a plain amid picturesque hills. It is an old town, very small, but surrounded by very spacious suburbs. It is said that the city proper within the fortifications is no larger than it was when Richard Cœur-de-Lion was put into prison not far from its gates. The streets are as narrow as in Italy; the palaces recall a little those of Florence; in fine, nothing here resembles the rest of Germany except a few Gothic buildings, which bring back the Middle Ages to the imagination. First among these is the tower of St. Stephen's, around which somehow centres the whole history of Austria. No building can be as patriotic as a church—the only one in which all classes of the population meet, the only one which recalls not only the public events, but also the secret thoughts, the intimate affections which the rulers and the citizens have brought within its precincts.

Every great city has some building, or promenade, some work of art or nature, to which the recollections of childhood are attached. It seems to me that the *Prater* should have this charm for the Viennese. No other city can match this splendid promenade through woods and deer-stocked meadows. The daily promenade at a fixed hour is an Italian custom. Such regularity would be impossible in a country where the pleasures are as varied as in Paris; but the Viennese could never do without it. Society folk in their carriages and the people on their feet assemble here every evening. It is in the Prater that one is most struck with the easy life and the prosperity of the Viennese. Vienna has the uncontested reputation of consuming more food than any other equally populous city. You can see whole families of citizens and artisans starting for the Prater at five o'clock for a rustic meal as substantial as dinner in any other country, and the money they are able to spend on it proves their industry and kindly rule.

At night thousands of people return, without disorder, without quarrel. You can scarcely hear a voice, so silently do they take their pleasures. It is not due to sadness, but to laziness and physical well-being. Society is here with magnificent horses and carriages. Their whole amusement is to recognise in a Prater avenue the friends they have just left in a drawing-room. The emperor and his brothers take their place in the long row of carriages, and prefer to be considered just as ordinary private people. They only use their rights when they are performing their duties. You never see a beggar: the charity institutions are admirably managed. And there are very few mortal crimes in Austria. Everything in this country bears the impress of a paternal, wise, and religious government.

III.—On the German Language

Germany is better suited for prose than for poetry, and the prose is better written than spoken; it is an excellent instrument if you wish to describe or to say everything; but you cannot playfully pass from subject to subject as you can in French. If you would adapt the German words to the French style of conversation you would rob them altogether of grace and dignity. The merit of the Germans is to fill their time well; the talent of the French is to make us forget time.

Although the sense of German sentences is frequently only revealed at the very end, the construction does not always permit to close a phrase with the most piquant expression, which is one of the great means to make conversation effective. You rarely hear among the Germans what is known as a *bon-mot*; you have to admire the thought and not the brilliant way in which it is expressed.

Brilliant expression is considered a kind of charlatanism by the Germans, who take to abstract expression because it is more conscientious and approaches more closely to the very essence of truth. But conversation ought not to cause any trouble either to the listener or to the speaker. As soon as conversation in Germany departs from the ordinary interests of life it becomes too metaphysical; there is nothing between the common and the sublime; and it is just this intermediate region that is the proper sphere for the art of conversation.

WEIMAR

Of all the German principalities, Weimar makes one best realise the advantages of a small country, if the ruler is a man of fine intellect who may try to please his subjects without losing their obedience. The Duchess Louise of Saxe-Weimar is the true model of a woman destined for high rank. The duke's military talents are highly esteemed; his conversation is pointed and well considered; his intellect and his mother's have attracted the most distinguished men of letters to Weimar. Germany had for the first time a literary capital.

Herder had just died when I arrived at Weimar, but Wieland, Goethe, and Schiller were still there. They can be judged from their works, for their books bear a striking resemblance to their character and conversation.

Life in small towns has never appealed to me. Man's intellect seems to become narrow and woman's heart cold. One feels oppressed by the close proximity of one's equals. All the actions of your life are minutely examined in detail, until the ensemble of your character is no longer understood. And the more your spirit is independent and elevated, the less you can breathe within the narrow confines. This disagreeable discomfort did not exist at Weimar, which was not a little town, but a large castle. A chosen circle took a lively interest in every new art production. Imagination, constantly stimulated by the conversation of the poets, felt less need for those outside distractions which lighten the burden of existence but often dissipates its forces. Weimar has been called the Athens of Germany, and rightly so. It was the only place where interest in the fine arts was, so to speak, rational and served as fraternal link between the different ranks.

IV.—*Prussia*

To know Prussia, one has to study the character of Frederick II. A man has created this empire which had not been favoured by nature, and which has only become a power because a soldier has been its master. There are two distinct men in Frederick II.: a German by nature, and a Frenchman by education. All that the German did in a German kingdom has left lasting traces; all that the Frenchman tried has been fruitless.

Frederick's great misfortune was that he had not enough respect for religion and customs. His tastes were cynical. Frederick, in liberating his subjects of what he called prejudices, stifled in them their patriotism, for in order to get attached to a naturally sombre and sterile country one must be ruled by very stern opinions and principles. Frederick's predilection for war may be excused on political grounds. His realm, as he took it over from his father, could not exist, and aggrandisement was necessary for its preservation. He had two and a half million subjects when he ascended the throne, and he left six millions on his death.

One of his greatest wrongs was his share in the division of Poland. Silesia was acquired by force of arms. Poland by Macchiavellian conquest, "and one could never hope that subjects thus robbed should be faithful to the juggler who called himself their sovereign."

Frederick II. wanted French literature to rule alone in his country, and had no consideration for German literature, which, no doubt, was then not as remarkable as it is to-day; but a German prince should encourage all that is German. Frederick wanted to make Berlin resemble Paris, and he flattered himself to have found among the French refugees some writers of sufficient distinction to have a French literature. Such hope was bound to be deceptive. Artificial culture never prospers; a few individuals may fight against the natural difficulties, but the masses will always follow their natural leaning. Frederick did a real wrong to his country when he professed to despise German genius.

BERLIN

Berlin is a large town, with wide, long, straight streets, beautiful houses, and an orderly aspect; but as it has only recently been rebuilt, it contains nothing to recall the past. No Gothic monument exists among the modern dwellings, and this newly-formed country is in no way interfered with by the past. But modern Berlin, with all its beauty, does not impress me seriously. It tells nothing of the history of the country or the character of its inhabitants; and these beautiful new houses seem to be destined only for the comfortable gatherings of business or industry. The most beautiful palaces of Berlin are built of brick. Prussia's capital resembles Prussia herself; its buildings and institutions have the age of one generation, and no more, because one man alone is their creator.

THE "GERMANIA" OF TACITUS

Customs and Peoples of Germany

"Germania," the full title of which is "Concerning the Geography, the Manners and Customs, and the Peoples of Germany," consists of forty-six sections, the first twenty-seven describing the characteristics of the peoples, their customs, beliefs, and institutions; the remaining nineteen dealing with the individual peculiarities of each separate tribe. As a record of the Teutonic tribes, written purely from an ethical and rhetorical standpoint, the work is of the utmost importance, and, on the whole, is regarded as trustworthy. Its weak point is its geography, details of which Tacitus (see Vol. XI, p. 156) no doubt gathered from hearsay. The main object of the work was not so much to compose a history of Germany, as to draw a comparison between the independence of the Northern peoples and the corrupt civilisation of contemporary Roman life. Possibly, also, Tacitus intended to sound a note of alarm.

I.—Germany and the German Tribes

The whole of Germany is thus bounded. It is separated from Gaul, Rhætia, and Pannonia by the rivers Rhine and Danube; from Sarmatia and Dacia by mutual fear, or by high mountains; the rest is encompassed by the ocean, which forms vast bays and contains many large islands. The Rhine, rising from a rocky summit in the Rhætian Alps, winds westward, and is lost in the northern ocean. The Danube, issuing from Mount Abnoba, traverses several countries and finally falls into the Euxine.

I believe that the population is indigenous to Germany, and that the nation is free from foreign admixture. They affirm Germany to be a recent word, lately bestowed on those who first passed the Rhine and repulsed the Gauls. From one tribe the whole nation has thus been named. They cherish a tradition that Hercules had been in their country, and him they extol in their battle songs. Some are of opinion that Ulysses also, during his long wanderings, was carried into this ocean and entered Germany, and that he founded the city Asciburgium, which stands at this day upon the bank of the Rhine. Such traditions I purpose myself neither to confirm nor to refute; but I agree with those who maintain that the Germans have never intermingled by marriages with other nations, but have remained a pure, independent people, resembling none but themselves.

With whatever differences in various districts, their territory mainly consists of gloomy forests or insalubrious marshes, lower and more humid towards Gaul, more hilly and bleak towards Noricum and Pannonia. The soil is suited to the production of grain, but less so for the cultivation of fruits. Flocks and herds abound, but the cattle are somewhat small. Their herds are their most valued possessions. Silver and gold the gods have denied them, whether in mercy or in wrath I cannot determine. Nor is iron plentiful with them, as may be judged from their weapons. Swords or long spears they rarely use, for they fight chiefly with javelins and shields. Their strength lies mainly in their foot, and such is the swiftness of the infantry that it can suit and match the motions and engagements of the cavalry.

Generals are chosen for their courage, kings are elected through distinction of race. The power of the rulers is not unlimited or arbitrary, and the generals secure obedience mainly by force of the example of their own enterprise and bravery.

Therefore, when going on a campaign, they carry with them sacred images taken from the sacred groves. It is their custom also to flock to the field of war not merely in battalions, but with whole families and tribes of relations. Thus, close to the scene of conflict are lodged the most cherished pledges of nature, and the cries of wives and infants are heard mingling with the echoes of battle. Their wounds and injuries they carry to their mothers and wives, and the women administer food and encouragement to their husbands and sons even while these are engaged in fighting.

II.—Customs of Government and War

Mercury is the god most generally worshipped. To him at certain times it is lawful to offer even human sacrifices. Hercules, Mars, and Isis are also recognised as deities. From the majesty of celestial beings, the Germans judge it to be unsuitable to hold their shrines within walls, or to represent them under any human likeness. They therefore consecrate whole woods and groves, and on these sylvan retreats they bestow the names of the deities, thus beholding the divinities only in contemplation and mental reverence.

Although the chiefs regulate affairs of minor import, the whole nation deliberates concerning matters of higher consequence, the chiefs afterwards discussing the public decision. The assemblies gather leisurely, for sometimes many do not arrive for two or three days. The priests enjoin silence, and on them is devolved the prerogative of correction. The chiefs are heard according to precedence, or age, or nobility, or warlike celebrity, or eloquence. Ability to persuade has more influence than authority to command. Inarticulate murmurs express displeasure at a proposition, pleasure is indicated by the brandishing of javelins and the clashing of arms.

Punishments vary with the character of crime. Traitors and deserters are hanged on trees; cowards, sluggards, and vicious women are smothered in bogs. Fines, to be paid in horses or cattle, are exacted for lighter offences, part of the mulct being awarded to the party wronged, part to the chief.

The Germans transact no business without carrying arms, but no man thus bears weapons till the community has tested his capacity to wield them. When the public approval has been signified, the youth is invested in the midst of the assembly by his father or other relative with a shield and javelin.

Their chief distinction is to be constantly surrounded by a great band of select young men, for their honour in peace and their help in warfare.

In battle it is disgraceful to a chief to be surpassed in feats of bravery, and it is an indelible reproach to his followers to return alive from a conflict in which their prince has been slain. The chief fights for victory, his followers fight for him. The Germans are so restless that they cannot endure repose, and thus many of the young men of rank, if their own tribe is tranquil, quit it for a community which happens to be engaged in war. In place of pay the retainers are supplied with daily repasts, grossly prepared, but always profuse.

III.—Domestic Customs of the Germans

Intervals of peace are not much devoted to the chase by the Germans, but rather to indolence, to sleep, and to feasting. Many surrender themselves entirely to sloth and gluttony, the cares of house, lands, and possessions being left to the wives. It is an astonishing paradox that in the same men should co-exist so much delight in idleness and so great a repugnance to tranquil life.

The Germans do not dwell in cities, and endure no contiguity in their abodes, inhabiting spots distinct and apart, just as they fancy, a fountain, a grove, or a field. Their villages consist of houses arranged in opposite rows, not joined together as are ours. Each is detached, with space around, and mortar and tiles are unknown. Many, in winter, retreat to holes dug in the ground, to which they convey their grain.

The laws of matrimony are strictly observed, and polygamy is rarely practised among the Germans. The dowry is not brought by the wife, but by the husband. Conjugal infidelity is exceedingly rare, and is instantly punished. In all families the children are reared without clothing, and thus grow into those physical proportions which are so wonderful to look upon. They are invariably suckled by their mothers, never being entrusted to nursemaids. The young people do not hasten to marry, and thus the robust vigour of the parents is inherited by their offspring.

No nation was ever more noted for hospitality. It is esteemed inhuman to refuse to admit to the home any stranger whatever. Every comer is willingly received and generously feasted. Hosts and guests delight in exchanging gifts. To continue drinking night and day is no reproach to any man. Quarrels through inebriety are very frequent, and these often result in injuries and in fatalities. But likewise, in these convivial feasts they usually deliberate about effecting reconciliation between those who are at enmity, and also about forming affinities, the election of chiefs, and peace and war.

Slaves gained in gambling with dice are exchanged in commerce to remove the shame of such victories. Of their other slaves each has a dwelling of his own, his lord treating him like a tenant, exacting from him an amount of grain, or cattle, or cloth. Thus their slaves are not subservient as are ours. For they do not perform services in the households of their masters, these duties falling to the wives and children of the family. Slaves are rarely seen in chains or punished with stripes, though in the heat of passion they may sometimes be killed.

Usury and borrowing at interest are unknown. The families every year shift on the spacious plains, cultivating fresh allotments of the soil. Only corn is grown, for there is no inclination to expend toil proportionate to the capacity of the lands by planting orchards, or enclosing meadows, or watering gardens.

Their funerals are not ostentatious, neither apparel nor perfumes being accumulated on the pile, though the arms of the deceased are thrown into the fire. Little demonstration is made in weeping or wailing, but the grief endures long. So much concerning the customs of the whole German nation.

IV.—Tribes of the West and North

I shall now describe the institutions of the several tribes, as they differ from one another, giving also an account of those who from thence removed, migrating to Gaul. That the Gauls were more powerful in former times is shown by that prince of authors, the deified Julius Cæsar. Hence it is probable that they have passed into Germany.

The region between the Hercynian forest and the rivers Maine and Rhine was occupied by the Helvetians, as was that beyond it by the Boians, both Gallic tribes. The Treveri and Nervii fervently aspire to the reputation of descent from the Germans, and the Vangiones, Triboci, and Nemetes, all dwelling by the Rhine, are certainly all Germans. The Ubii are ashamed of their origin and delight to be called Agrippinenses, after the name of the founder of the Roman colony which they were judged worthy of being constituted.

The Batavi are the bravest of all these nations. They inhabit a little territory by the Rhine, but possess an island on it. Becoming willingly part of the Roman empire, they are free from all impositions and pay no tribute, but are reserved wholly for wars, precisely like a magazine of weapons and armour. In the same position are the Mattiaci, living on the opposite banks and enjoying a settlement and limits of their own, while they are in spirit and inclination attached to us.

Beginning at the Hercynian forest are the Catti, a robust and vigorous people, possessed also of much sense and ability. They are not only singularly brave, but are more skilled in the true art of war than other Germans.

Near the Catti were formerly dwelling the Bructeri, in whose stead are now settled the Chamani and the Angrivarii, by whom the Bructeri were expelled and almost exterminated, to the benefit of us Romans. May the gods perpetuate among these nations their mutual hatred, since fortune befriends our empire by sowing strife amongst our foes!

The country of the Frisii, facing that of the Angrivarii and the Chamani, is divided into two sections, called the greater and the lesser, which both extend along the Rhine to the ocean.

Hitherto I have been describing Germany towards the west. Northward it stretches with an immense compass. The great tribe of the Chauci occupy the whole region between the districts of the Frisii and of the Catti. These Chauci are the noblest people of all the Germans. They prefer to maintain their greatness by justice rather than by violence, seeking to live in tranquillity, and to avoid quarrels with others.

By the side of the Chauci and the Catti dwell the Cherusci, a people who have degenerated in both influence and character. Finding no enemy to stimulate them, they were enfeebled by too lasting a peace, and whereas they were formerly styled good and upright, they are now called cowards and fools, having been subdued by the Catti. In the same winding tract live the Cimbri, close to the sea, a tribe now small in numbers but great in fame for many monuments of their old renown. It was in the 610th year of Rome, Cæcilius Metellus and Papirius Carbo being consuls, that the first mention was made of the arms of the Cimbri. From that date to the second consulship of the Emperor Trajan comprehends an interval of nearly 210 years; so long a period has our conquest of Germany occupied. In so great an interval many have been the disasters on both sides.

Indeed, not from the Samnites, or from the Carthaginians, or from the people of Spain, or from all the tribes of Gaul, or even from the Parthians, have we received more checks or encountered more alarms. For the passion of the Germans for liberty is more indomitable than that of the Arsacidæ. What has the power of the East to lay to our dishonour? But the overthrow and abasement of Crassus, and the loss by the Romans of five great armies, all commanded by consuls, have to be laid to the account of the Germans. By the Germans, also, even the Emperor Augustus was deprived of Varus and three legions.

Only with great difficulty and the loss of many men were the Germans defeated by Caius Marius in Italy, or by the deified Julius Cæsar in Gaul, or by Drusus, or Tiberius, or Germanicus in their native territories. And next, the strenuous menaces of Caligula against these foes ended in mockery and ridicule. Afterwards, for a season they were quiet, till, tempted to take advantage of our domestic schisms and civil wars, they stormed and seized the winter entrenchments of our legions, and attempted the conquest of Gaul. Though they were once more repulsed, our success was rather a triumph than an overwhelming victory.

V.—The Great Nation of the Suevi

Next I must refer to the Suevi, who are not, like the Catti, a homogeneous people, but are divided into several tribes, all bearing distinct names, although they likewise are called by the generic title of Suevi. They occupy the larger part of Germany. From other Germans they are distinguished by their peculiar fashion of twisting their hair into a knot, this also marking the difference between the freemen and their slaves. Of all the tribes of the Suevi, the Semnones esteem themselves to be the most ancient and the noblest, their faith in their antiquity being confirmed by the mysteries of their religion. Annually in a sacred grove the deputies of each family clan assemble to repeat the rites practised by their ancestors. The horrible ceremonies commence with the sacrifice of a man. Their tradition is that at this spot the nation originated, and that here the supreme deity resides. The Semnones inhabit a hundred towns, and by their superior numbers and authority dominate the rest of the Suevi.

On the contrary, the Langobardi are ennobled by the paucity of their number, for, though surrounded by powerful tribes, they assert their superiority by their valour and skill instead of displaying obsequiousness. Next come the Reudigni, the Aviones, the Angli, the Varini, the Eudoses, the Suardones and the Nuithones, all defended by rivers or forests.

These are marked by no special characteristics, excepting the common worship of the goddess Nerthum, or Mother Earth, of whom they believe that she not only intervenes in human affairs, but also visits the nations. In a certain island of the sea is a wood called Castum. Here is kept a chariot sacred to the goddess, covered with a curtain, and permitted to be touched only by her priest, who perceives her whenever she enters the holy vehicle, and with deepest veneration attends the motion of the chariot, which is always drawn by yoked cows. Till the same priests re-conducts the goddess to her shrine, after she has grown weary of intercourse with mortals, feasts and games are held with great rejoicings, no arms are touched, and none go to war. Slaves wash the chariot and curtains in a sacred lake, and, if you will believe it, the goddess herself; and forthwith these unfortunate beings are doomed to be swallowed up in the same lake.

This portion of the Suevian territory stretches to the centre of Germany. Next adjoining is the district of the Hermunduri (I am now following the course of the Danube as I previously did that of the Rhine), a tribe faithful to the Romans. To them, accordingly, alone of all the Germans, is commerce permitted. They travel everywhere at their own discretion. When to others we show nothing more than our arms and our encampments, to this people we open our houses, as to men who are not longing to possess them. The Elbe rises in the territory of the Hermunduri.

VI.—The Tribes of the Frontier

Near the Hermunduri reside the Narisci, and next the Marcomanni and the Quadi, the former being the more famed for strength and bravery, for it was by force that they acquired their location, expelling from it the Boii. Now, here is, as it were, the frontier of Germany, as far as it is washed by the Danube. Not less powerful are several tribes whose territories enclose the lands of those just named—the Marsigni, the Gothini, the Osi, and the Burii. The Marsigni in speech and dress resemble the Suevi; but as the Gothini speak Gallic, and the Osi the Pannonian language, and as they endure the imposition of tribute, it is manifest that neither of these peoples are Germans.

Upon them, as aliens, tribute is imposed, partly by the Sarmatæ, partly by the Quadi, and, to deepen their disgrace, the Gothini are forced to labour in the iron mines. Little level country is possessed by all these several tribes, for they are located among mountainous forest regions, Suevia being parted by a continuous range of mountains, beyond which live many nations. Of these, the most numerous and widely spread are the Lygii. Among others, the most powerful are the Arii, the Helveconæ, the Manimi, the Elysii, and the Naharvali.

The Arii are the most numerous, and also the fiercest of the tribes just enumerated. They carry black shields, paint their bodies black, and choose dark nights for engaging in battle. The ghastly aspect of their army strikes terror into their foes, for in all battles the eyes are vanquished first. Beyond the Lygii dwell the Gothones, ruled by a king, and thus held in stricter subjection than the other German tribes, yet not so that their liberties are extinguished. Immediately adjacent are the Rugii and the Lemovii, dwelling by the coast. The characteristic of both is the use of a round shield and a short sword.

Next are the Suiones, a seafaring community with very powerful fleets. The ships differ in form from ours in possessing prows at each end, so as to be always ready to row to shore without turning. They are not propelled by sails, and have no benches of oars at the sides. The rowers ply in all parts of the ship alike, and change their oars from place to place according as the course is shifted hither and thither. Great homage is paid among them to wealth; they are governed by a single chief, who exacts implicit obedience. Arms are not used by these people indiscriminately, as by other German tribes. Weapons are shut up under the care of a slave. The reason is that the ocean always protects the Suiones from their foes, and also that armed bands, when not employed, grow easily demoralised.

Beyond the Suiones is another sea, dense and calm. It is thought that by this the whole globe is bounded, for the reflection of the sun, after his setting, continues till he rises, and that so radiantly as to obscure the stars. Popular opinion even adds that the tumult is heard of his emerging from the ocean, and that at sunrise forms divine are seen, and also the rays about his head. Only thus far extend the limits of Nature, if what fame reports be true.

The Æstii reside on the right of the Suevian Sea. Their dress and customs resemble those of the Suevi, but the language is akin to that of Britain. They worship the Mother of gods, and wear images of boars, without any weapons, superstitiously trusting the goddess and the images to safeguard them. But they cultivate the soil with much greater zeal than is usual with Germans, and they even search the ocean, and are the only people who gather amber, which they find in the shallows and along the shore. It lay long neglected till it gained value from our luxury.

Bordering on the Suiones are the Sitones, agreeing with them in all things excepting that they are governed by a woman. So emphatically have they degenerated, not merely from liberty, but even below a condition of bondage. Here end the territories of the Suevi. Whether I ought to include the Peucini, the Venedi, and the Fenni among the Sarmatæ or the Germani I cannot determine, although the Peucini speak the same language with the Germani, dress, build, and live like them, and resemble them in dirt and sloth.

What further accounts we have are fabulous, and these I leave untouched.

HIPPOLYTE ADOLPHE TAINE

History of English Literature

Two years before the appearance of his "Histoire de la Littérature Anglaise" Taine had aroused a lively interest in England by his "Notes sur l'Angleterre," a work showing much wayward sympathy for the English character, and an irregular understanding of English institutions. The same mixed impression was produced by the laboriously conceived and brilliantly written "History of English Literature." Taine (see Vol. XXIV, p. 177) wrote to a theory that often worked out into curious contradictions. His method was to show how men have been shaped by the environments and tendencies of their age. Unfortunately, having formed an idea of the kind of literature our age should produce according to his theory, he had eyes for nothing except what he expected to find. He went to literature for his confirmations of his reading of history. Taine's criticism, in consequence, is often incomplete, and more piquant than trustworthy. The failure to appreciate some of the great English writers—notably Shakespeare and Milton—is patent. Still, the critic always had the will to be just, and no foreigner has devoted such complimentary labour to the formation of a complete estimate of English literature. The book was published in 1863–4.

Saxon and Norman

History has been revolutionised by the study of literatures. A work of literature is now perceived, not to be a solitary caprice, but a transcript of contemporary manners, from which we may read the style of man's feelings for centuries back. By the study of a literature, one may construct a moral history, the psychology of a people. To find a complete literature is rare. Only ancient Greece, and modern France and England offer a complete series of great literary monuments. I have chosen England because it is alive, and one can see it with more detachment than one can see France.

Huge white bodies, cool-blooded, with fierce blue eyes, reddish flaxen hair; ravenous stomachs filled with meat and cheese and heated by strong drinks; a cold temperament, slow to love, home-staying, prone to drunkenness—these are to this day the features which descent and climate preserve to the English race. The heavy human brute gluts himself with sensations and noise, and this appetite finds a grazing-ground in blows and battle. Strife for strife's sake such is their pleasure. A race so constituted was predisposed to Christianity by its gloom, and beyond Christianity foreign culture could not graft any fruitful branch on this barbarous stock. The Norman conquerors of France had by intermarriage become a Latin race, and nimbly educated themselves from the Gauls, who boasted of "talking with ease." When they crossed to England, they introduced new manners and a new spirit. They taught the Saxon how ideas fall in order, and which ideas are agreeable; they taught him how to be clear, amusing, and pungent. At length, after long impotence of Norman literature, which was content to copy, and of Saxon literature, which bore no fruit, a definite language was attained, and there was room for a great writer.

Chaucer

Then Geoffrey Chaucer appeared, inventive though a disciple, original though a translator, and by his genius, education, and life was enabled to know and depict a whole world, but above all to satisfy the chivalric world and the splendid courts which shone upon the heights. He belonged to it, and took such part in it that his life from end to end was that of a man of the world and a man of action.

Two motives raised the middle age above the chaos of barbarism, one religious, which fashioned the gigantic cathedrals, the other secular, which built the feudal fortresses. The one produced the adventurous hero, the other the mystical monk. These master-passions gave way at last to monotony of habit and taste for worldliness. Something was then needed to make the evening hours flow sweetly. The lords at table have finished dinner; the poet arrives; they ask him for his subject, and he answers "Love."

There is something more pleasant than a fine narrative, and that is a collection of fine narratives, especially when the narratives are all of different colouring. This collection Chaucer gave us, and more. If over-excited, he is always graceful, polished, full of light banter, half-mockeries, somewhat gossipy. An elegant speaker, facile, every ready to smile, he makes of love not a passion but a gay feast. But if he was romantic and gay after the fashion of his age, he also had a fashion of his own. He observes characters, notes their differences, studies the coherence of their parts, brings forward living and distinct persons—a thing unheard of in his time. It is the English positive good sense and aptitude for seeing the inside of things beginning to appear. Chaucer ceases to gossip, and thinks. Each tale is suited to the teller. Instead of surrendering himself to the facility of glowing improvisation, he plans. All his tales are bound together by veritable incidents which spring from the characters of the personages, and are such as we light upon in our travels. He advanced beyond the threshold of his art, but he paused in the vestibule. He half-opens the door of the temple, but does not take his seat there; at most he sat down at intervals. His voice is like that of a boy breaking into manhood. He sets out as if to quit the middle ages; but in the end he is still there.

The Renaissance

For seventeen centuries a deep and sad thought had weighed upon the spirit of man—the idea of his impotence and decadence. Greek corruption, Roman oppression, and the dissolution of the old world had given it birth; it, in its turn, had produced a stoical resignation, an epicurean indifference, Alexandrian mysticism, and the Christian hope in the Kingdom of God. At last invention makes another start. All was renewed, America and the Indies were added to the map. The system of the universe was propounded, the experimental sciences were set on foot, art and literature shot forth like a harvest, and religion was transformed. It seems as though men had suddenly opened their eyes and seen. They attained a new and superior kind of intelligence which produced extraordinary warmth of soul, a super-abundant and splendid imagination, reveries, visions, artists, believers, founders, creators. This was Europe's grand age, and the most notable epoch of human growth. To this day we live from its sap. To vent the feelings, to set free boldly on all the roads of existence the pack of appetites and instincts, this was the craving which the manners of the time betrayed. It was "merry England," as they called it then. It was not yet stern and constrained. It extended widely, freely, and rejoiced to find itself so expanded. A few sectarians, chiefly in the towns, clung gloomily to the Bible; but the Court, and the men of the world sought their teachers and their heroes from Pagan Greece and Rome. Nearer still was another Paganism, that of Italy, and civilisation was drawn thence as from a spring. Transplanted into different races and climates, this paganism received from each a distinct character—in England it becomes English. Here Surrey—the English Petrarch—introduced a new style, a manly style, which marks a great transformation of the mind. He looks forward to the last line while writing the first, and keeps the strongest word for the last. He collects his phrases in harmonious periods, and by his inversions adds force to his ideas. Every epithet contains an idea, every metaphor a sentiment. Those who have ideas now possess in the new-born art an instrument capable of expressing them. In half a century English writers had introduced every artifice of language, period, and style.

Luxuriance and irregularity were the two features of the new literature. Sir Philip Sydney may be selected as exhibiting the greatness and the folly of the prevailing taste. How can his pastoral epic, "The Arcadia," be described? It is but a recreation, a poetical romance written in the country for the amusement of a sister, a work of fashion, a relic, but it shows the best of the general spirit, the jargon of the world of culture, fantastic imagination, excessive sentiment, a medley of events which suited men scarcely recovered from barbarism. At his period men's heads were full of tragical images, and Sydney's "Arcadia" contains enough of them to supply half a dozen epics. And Sydney was only a soldier in an army; there is a multitude about him, a multitude of poets. How happens it that when this generation was exhausted true poetry ended in England as true painting in Italy and Flanders? It was because an epoch of the mind came and passed away. These men had new ideas and no theories in their heads. Their emotions were not the same as ours. For them all things had a soul, and though they had no more beauty then than now, men found them more beautiful.

Spenser

Among all the poems of this time there is one truly divine—Spenser's "Faërie Queene." Everything in his life was calculated to lead Spenser to ideal poetry; but the heart within is the true poet. Before all, his was a soul captivated by sublime and chaste beauty. Philosophy and landscapes, ceremonies and ornaments, splendours of the country and the court, on all which he painted or thought he impressed his inward nobleness. Spenser remains calm in the fervour of invention. He is epic, that is, a narrator. No modern is more like Homer. Like Homer, he is always simple and clear; he makes no leap, he omits no argument, he preserves the natural sequence of ideas while presenting noble classical images. Like Homer, again, he is redundant, ingenuous: even childish. He says everything, and repeats without limit his ornamental epithets.

To expand in epic faculties in the region where his soul is naturally borne, he requires an ideal stage, situated beyond the bounds of reality, in a world which could never be. His most genuine sentiments are fairy-like. Magic is the mould of his mind. He carries everything that he looks upon into an enchanted land. Only the world of chivalry could have furnished materials for so elevated a fancy. It is the beauty in the poet's heart which his whole works try to express, a noble yet laughing beauty, English in sentiment, Italian in externals, chivalric in subject, representing a unique epoch, the appearance of Paganism in a Christian race, and the worship of form by an imagination of the North.

Among the prose writers of the Pagan renaissance, two may be singled out as characteristic, namely, Robert Burton—an ecclesiastic and university recluse who dabbled in all the sciences, was gifted with enthusiasm and spasmodically gay, but as a rule sad and morose, and according to circumstances a poet, an eccentric, a humorist, a madman, or a Puritan— and Francis Bacon, the most comprehensive, sensible, originative mind of the age; a great and luminous intellect. After more than two centuries it is still to Bacon that we go to discover the theory of what we are attempting and doing.

The Theatre

The theatre was a special product of the English Renaissance. If ever there was a living and natural work, it is here. There were already seven theatres in Shakespeare's time, so great and universal was the taste for representations. The inborn instincts of the people had not been tamed, nor muzzled, nor diminished. We hear from the stage as from the history of the times, the fierce murmur of all the passions. Not one of them was lacking. The poets who established the drama, carried in themselves the sentiments which the drama represents. Greene, Marlowe, and the rest, were ill-regulated, passionate, outrageously vehement and audacious. The drama is found in Marlowe as the plant in the seed, and Marlowe was a primitive man, the slave of his passions, the sport of his dreams. Shakespeare, Beaumont, Fletcher, Jonson, Webster, Massinger, Ford, appear close upon each other, a new and favoured generation, flourishing in the soil fertilised by the efforts of the generation which preceded them. The characters they produced were such as either excite terror by their violence, or pity by their grace. Passion ravages all around when their tragic figures are on the stage; and contrasted with them is a troop of sweet and timid figures, tender before everything, and the most loveworthy it has been given to man to depict. The men are warlike, imperious, unpolished; the women have sweetness, devotion, patience, inextinguishable affection—a thing unknown in distant lands, and in France especially. With these women love becomes almost a holy thing. They aim not at pleasure but at devotion. When a new civilisation brings a new art to light there are about a dozen men of talent who express the general idea surrounding one or two men of genius who express it thoroughly. The first constitute the chorus, the others the leaders. The leaders in this movement are Shakespeare and Ben Jonson.

Ben Jonson was a genuine Englishman, big and coarsely framed, combative, proud, often morose, prone to strain splenitic imaginations. His knowledge was vast. In an age of great scholars he is one of the best classics of his time. Other poets for the most part are visionaries; Jonson is all but a logician. Whatever he undertakes, whatever be his faults, haughtiness, rough-handling, predilection for morality and the past, he is never little or commonplace. Nearly all his work consists of comedies, not sentimental and fanciful as Shakespeare's, but satirical, written to represent and correct follies and vices. Even when he grew old his imagination remained abundant and fresh. He is the brother of Shakespeare.

Shakespeare

Only this great age could have cradled such a child as Shakespeare. What soul! What extent of action, and what sovereignty of an unique faculty! What diverse creations, and what persistence of the same impress! Look now. Do you not see the poet behind the crowd of his creations? They have all shown somewhat of him. Ready, impetuous, impassioned, delicate, his genius is pure imagination, touched more vividly and by slighter things than ours. Hence, his style, blooming with exuberant images, loaded with exaggerated metaphors. An extraordinary species of mind, all-powerful, excessive, equally master of the sublime and the base, the most creative that ever engaged in the exact copy of the details of actual existence, in the dazzling caprice of fancy, in the profound complications of superhuman passions; a nature inspired, superior to reason, extreme in joy and pain, abrupt of gait, stormy and impetuous in its transports!

Shakespeare images with copiousness and excess; he spreads metaphors profusely over all he writes; it is a series of painting which is unfolded in his mind, picture on picture, image on image, he is forever copying the strange and splendid visions which are heaped up within him. Such an imagination must needs be vehement. Every metaphor is a convulsion. Shakespeare's style is a compound of curious impressions. He never sees things tranquilly. Like a fiery and powerful horse, he bounds but cannot run. He flies, we creep. He is obscure and original beyond all the poets of his or any other age—the most immoderate of all violaters of language, the most marvellous of all creators of souls. The critic is lost in Shakespeare as in an immense town. He can only describe a few monuments and entreat the reader to imagine the city.

The Christian Renaissance

Following the pagan came the Christian Renaissance born of the Reformation, a new birth in harmony with the genius of the Germanic peoples. It must be admitted that the Reformation entered England by a side door. It was established when Henry VIII. permitted the English Bible to be published. England had her book. Hence have sprung much of the English language and half of the English manners; to this day the country is Biblical. After the Bible the book most widely-read in England is the Pilgrim's Progress by John Bunyan. It is a manual of devotion for the use of simple folk. In it we hear a man of the people speaking to the people, who would render intelligible to all the terrible doctrine of damnation and salvation. Allegory is natural to Bunyan. He employs it from necessity. He only grasps truth when it is made simple by images. His work is allegorical, that it may be intelligible. Bunyan is a poet because he is a child. He has the freedom, the tone, the ease, the clearness of Homer; he is as close to Homer as an Anabaptist tinker could be to a heroic singer. He and Milton survived as the two last poets of the Reformation, oppressed and insulted, but their work continues without noise, for the ideal they raised was, after all, that which the time suggested and the race demanded.

Milton

John Milton was not one of those fevered souls whose rapture takes them by fits, and whose inquietude condemns them to paint the contradictions of passion. His mind was lucid, his imagination limited. He does not create souls but constructs arguments. Emotions and arguments are arranged beneath a unique sentiment, that of the sublime, and the broad river of lyric poetry streams from him with even flow, splendid as a cloth of gold.

Against external fluctuations he found a refuge in himself; and the ideal city which he had built in his soul endured impregnable to all assaults. He believed in the sublime with the whole force of his nature, and the whole authority of his logic. When after a generous education he returned from his travels he threw himself into the strife of the times heartily, armed with logic, indignation and learning, and protected by conviction and conscience. I have before me the formidable volume in which his prose works were collected. What a book! The chairs creak when you place it upon them. How we cannot fix our attention on the same point for a page at a time. We require manageable ideas; we have disused the big two-handed sword of our forefathers. If Michael Angelo's prophets could speak, it would be in Milton's style. Overloaded with ornaments, infinitely prolonged, these periods are triumphant choruses of angelic Alleluias sung by deep voices to the accompaniment of ten thousand harps of gold. But is he truly a prose-writer? Entangled dialectics, a heavy and awkward mind, fanatical and ferocious provincialism, the blast and temerities of implacable passion, the sublimity of religious and lyric exaltation—we do not recognize in these features a man born to explain, persuade, and prove.

As a poet Milton wrote not by impulse but like a man of letters with the assistance of books, seeing objects as much through previous writings as in themselves, adding to his images the images of others, borrowing and recasting their inventions. He made thus for himself a composite and brilliant style, less natural than that of his precursors, less fit for effusions, less akin to the lively first glow of sensation, but more solid, more regular, more capable of concentrating in one large patch of light all their sparklings and splendours. He compacted and ennobled the poets' domain.

When, however, after seventeen years of fighting and misfortune had steeped his soul in religious ideas, mythology yielded to theology, the habit of discussion subdued the lyric light. The poet no longer sings sublime verse, he harangues in grave verse, he gives us correct solemn discourses. Adam and Eve the first pair! I listen and hear two reasoners of the period— Colonel Hutchinson and his wife. Heavens! dress them at once. Folks so cultivated should have invented before all a pair of trousers and modesty. This Adam enters Paradise via England. There he learnt respectability and moral speechifying. Adam was your true *pater familias* with a vote, an old Oxford man, consulted at need by his wife, and dealing out to her with prudent measure the scientific explanations which she requires. The flow of dissertations never pauses. From Paradise it gets into Heaven. Milton's Jehovah is a grave king who maintains a suitable state something like Charles I. The finest thing in connection with Paradise is Hell; and in this history of God, the chief part is taken by the devil. No poetic creation equals in horror and grandeur the spectacle that greeted Satan on leaving his dungeon.

But what a heaven! One would rather enter Charles I's troops of lackeys, or Cromwell's Ironsides. What a gap between this monarchical frippery and the visions of Dante! To the poet of the Apocalypse the voice of the deity was "as the sound of many waters; and he had in his right hand seven stars; and his countenance was as the sun shining in his strength; and when I saw him I fell at his feet as dead." When Milton arranged his celestial show, he did not fall at his feet as dead.

When we take in, in one view, the vast literary region of England, extending from the restoration of the Stuarts to the French Revolution, we perceive that all the productions bear a classical impress, such as is met with neither in the preceding nor in the succeeding time. This classical art finds its centre in the labours of Pope, and above all in Pope, whose favourite author is Dryden, of all English poets the least inspired and the most classical. Pope gave himself up to versification. He did not write because he thought, but he thought in order to write. I wish I could admire his works of imagination, but I cannot. I know the machinery. There is, however, a poet in Pope, and to discover him we have only to read him in fragments. Each verse in Pope is a masterpiece if taken alone. There is a classical architecture of ideas, and of all the masters who have practised it in England Pope is the most skilled.

The Modern Spirit

The spirit of the modern revolution broke out first in a Scotch peasant, Robert Burns. Scarcely ever was seen together more of misery and talent. Burns cries out in favour of instinct and joy. Love was his main business. In him for the first time a poet spoke as men speak, or, rather, as they think, without premeditation, with a mixture of all styles. Burns was much in advance of his age, and the life of men in advance of their age is not wholesome. He died worn out at 37. In him old narrow moralities give place to the wide sympathy of the modern man.

Now appeared the English romantic school. Among the multitude of its writers we may distinguish Southey, a clever man, a producer of decorative poems to suit the fashion; Coleridge, a poor fellow who had steeped himself in mystical theories; Thomas More, a witty railer; and Walter Scott, the favourite of his age, who was read over the whole of Europe, was almost equal to Shakespeare, had more popularity than Voltaire, earned about £200,000, and taught us all history. Scott gave to Scotland a citizenship of literature. Scott loves men from the bottom of his heart. By his fundamental honesty and wide humanity he was the Homer of modern life.

When the philosophical spirit passed from Germany to England, transformed itself and became Anglican, deformed itself and became revolutionary, it produced a Wordsworth, a Byron, a Shelley. Wordsworth, a new Cowper, with less talent and more ideas, was essentially an interior man, engrossed by the concerns of the soul. To such men life becomes a grave business on which we must incessantly and scrupulously reflect. Wordsworth was a wise and happy man, a thinker and dreamer, who read and walked and listened in deep calm to his own thoughts. The peace was so great within him and around him that he could perceive the imperceptible. He saw grandeur and beauty in the trivial events which weave the woof of our most commonplace days. His "Excursion" is like a Protestant temple — august though bare and monstrous.

Shelley, one of the greatest poets of the age, beautiful as an angel, of extraordinary precocity, sweet, generous, tender, overflowing with gifts of heart, mind, birth, and fortune, marred his life by introducing into his conduct the enthusiastic imagination he should have kept for his verse. His world is beyond our own. We move in it between heaven and earth, in abstraction, dreamland, symbolism. Shelley loved desert and solitary places, where man enjoys the pleasure of believing infinite what he sees —

infinite as his soul. Verily there is a soul in everything; in the universe is a soul; even beyond the sensible form shines a secret essence and something divine which we catch sight of by sublime illuminations, never reaching or penetrating it. The poets hear the great heart of nature beat; they would reach it. One alone, Byron, succeeds.

I have reserved for the last the greatest and most English artist, from whom we may learn more truths of his country and of his age than from all the rest. All styles appear dull, and all souls sluggish by the side of Byron's. No such great poet has had so narrow an imagination. They are his own sorrows, his own revolts, his own travels, which, hardly transformed and modified, he introduces into his verses. He never could make a poem save of his own heart. If Goethe was the poet of the universe, Byron was the poet of the individual; and if the German genius found its interpretation in the one, the English genius found its interpretation in the other.

HENRY DAVID THOREAU

"Walden"

Henry David Thoreau, America's poet-naturalist, as he might be called, was born at Concord, Mass., on July 12, 1817. His great-grandparents were natives of the Channel Islands, whence his grandfather emigrated. Thoreau was educated at Hartford, and began work as a teacher, but under the influence of Emerson, in whose house he lived at intervals, made writing his hobby and a study of the outdoor world his occupation. In 1845, as related in "Walden," he built himself a shanty near Walden Pond, on land belonging to Emerson. There he busied himself with writing his "Week on the Concord and Merrimac Rivers," and in recording his observations in the woods. After the Walden experiment he mingled the pursuit of literature and the doing of odd jobs for a living. His books, "The Maine Woods," "A Yankee in Canada," "Excursions in Field and Wood," were mostly published after his death. He died on May 6, 1862, from consumption. Emerson, Hawthorne, and Alcott were his warm friends in life, and helped the world to appreciate his genius. A poet in heart, Thoreau was only successful in giving his poetry a prose setting, but that setting is harmonised with the utmost delicacy. No one has produced more beautiful effects in English prose with simpler words.

The Simple Life

When I wrote the following pages, I lived alone, in the woods, a mile from any neighbour, in a house I had built for myself, on the shore of Walden Pond, in Concord, Massachusetts, and earned my living by the labour of my hands only. I lived there two years and two months. At present I am a sojourner in civilized life again.

Men labour under a mistake. By a seeming fate, commonly called necessity, they are employed laying up treasures which moth and rust will corrupt. It is a fool's life, as they will find when they get to the end of it if not before.

But it is never too late to give up our prejudices. What old people say you cannot do, you try and find that you can. I have lived some thirty years and I have yet to hear the first syllable of valuable advice from my seniors.

To many creatures, there is but one necessity of life—food. None of the brute creation require more than food and shelter. The necessaries of life for man in this climate may be distributed under the several heads of food, shelter, clothing, and fuel. I find by my own experience a few implements, a knife, an axe, a spade, a wheelbarrow, etc., and for the studious, lamplight, stationery, and access to a few books, rank next to necessaries, and can all be obtained at a trifling cost. Most of the luxuries, and many of the so-called comforts of life, are positive hindrances to the elevation of mankind. None can be an impartial or wise observer of human life but from the vantage ground of voluntary poverty.

Ideals

If I should attempt to tell how I have desired to spend my life in years past it would probably astonish those who know nothing about it.

I long ago lost a hound, a bay horse, and a turtle dove, and am still on their trail. Many are the travellers I have spoken, concerning them, describing their tracks and what calls they answered to. I have met one or two who had heard the hound, and the tramp of the horse, and even seen the dove disappear behind a cloud, and they seemed as anxious to recover them as if they had lost them themselves.

How many mornings, summer and winter, before any neighbour was stirring about his business, have I been about mine! So many autumn, aye, and winter days, spent outside the town trying to hear what was in the wind, to hear and carry it. At other times waiting at evening on the hill-tops for the sky to fall that I might catch something, though I never caught much, and that, manna-wise, would dissolve again in the sun.

For many years I was self-appointed inspector of snow storms and rain storms, and did my duty faithfully; surveyor, if not of highways, then of forest paths. I looked after the wild stock of the town. I have watered the red huckleberry, the sand cherry and the nettle tree, the red pine and the black ash, the white grape and the yellow violet, which might have withered else in dry seasons.

My purpose in going to Walden Pond was not to live cheaply nor to live dearly there, but to transact some private business with the fewest obstacles.

House Building

When I consider my neighbours, the farmers of Concord, I find that for the most part they have been toiling twenty, thirty, or forty years, that they may become the real owners of their farms; and we may regard one-third of that toil as the cost of their houses. And when the farmer has got his house he may not be the richer but the poorer for it, and it be the house that has got him. The very simplicity and nakedness of men's life in the primitive ages imply that they left him still a sojourner in nature. When he was refreshed with food and sleep he contemplated his journey again. He dwelt as it were in the tent of this world. We now no longer camp as for a night, but have settled down on earth and forgotten Heaven.

Near the end of March, 1845, I borrowed an axe and went down to the woods by Walden Pond, nearest to where I intended to build my house, and began to cut down some tall, arrowy, white pines, still in their youth, for timber. It was a pleasant hillside where I worked, covered with pine woods, through which I looked out on the pond, and a small open field in the woods where pines and hickories were springing up. Before I had done I was more the friend than the foe of the pine tree, having become better acquainted with it.

By the middle of April my house was framed and ready for raising. At length, in the beginning of May, with the help of some of my acquaintances, rather to improve so good an occasion for neighbourliness than from any necessity, I set up the frame of my house. I began to occupy it on the 4th of July, as soon as it was boarded and roofed, for the boards were carefully feather-edged and lapped, so that it was perfectly impervious to rain, but before boarding I laid the foundation of a chimney. I built the chimney after my hoeing in the fall, before a fire became necessary for warmth, doing my cooking in the meantime out of doors on the ground, early in the morning. When it stormed before my bread was baked I fixed a few boards over the fire, and sat under them to watch my loaf, and passed some pleasant hours in that way.

The exact cost of my house, not counting the work, all of which was done by myself, was just over twenty-eight dollars. I thus found that the student who wishes for a shelter can obtain one for a lifetime at an expense not greater than the rent which he now pays annually.

Farming

Before I finished my house, wishing to earn ten or twelve dollars by some honest and agreeable method, in order to meet my unusual expenses, I planted about two acres and a half of light and sandy soil near it, chiefly with beans, but also a small part with potatoes, corn, peas, and turnips. I was obliged to hire a team and a man for the ploughing, though I held the plough myself. My farm outgoes for the first season were, for employment, seed, work, etc., 14 dollars 72½ cents. I got twelve bushels of beans and eighteen bushels of potatoes, besides some peas and sweet corn. My whole income from the farm was 23 dollars 43 cents, a profit of 8 dollars 71½ cents, besides produce consumed.

The next year I did better still, for I spaded up all the land that I required, about a third of an acre, and I learned from the experience of both years, not being in the least awed by many celebrated works on husbandry, that if one would live simply and eat only the crop which he raised, he would need to cultivate only a few rods of ground, and that it would be cheaper to spade up that than to use oxen to plough it, and he could do all his necessary farm work, as it were, with his left hand at odd hours in the summer.

My food for nearly two years was rye and Indian meal without yeast, potatoes, rice, a very little salt pork, molasses and salt, and my drink water. I learned from my two years' experience that it would cost incredibly little trouble to obtain one's necessary food even in this latitude, and that a man may use as simple a diet as the animals and yet retain health and strength.

Bread I at first made of pure Indian meal and salt, genuine hoe-cakes, which I baked before my fire out of doors, but at last I found a mixture of rye and Indian meal most convenient and agreeable. I made a study of the ancient and indispensable art of bread-making, going back to the primitive days. Leaven, which some deem to be the soul of bread, I discovered was not indispensable.

Thus I found I could avoid all trade and barter, so far as my food was concerned, and having a shelter already, it would only remain to get clothing and fuel. My furniture, part of which I made myself, consisted of a bed, a table, a desk, three chairs, a looking-glass, three inches in diameter, a pair of tongs and andirons, a kettle, a skillet, and a frying pan, a dipper, a wash bowl, two knives and forks, three plates, one cup, one spoon, a jug for oil, a jug for molasses, and a japanned lamp. When I have met an immigrant tottering under a bundle which contained his all, I have pitied him, not because it was his all, but because he had all that to carry.

Earning a Living

For more than five years I maintained myself solely by the labour of my hands, and I found that by working for about six weeks in the year I could meet all the expenses of living. The whole of my winters, as well as most of my summers, I had free and clear for study. I have thoroughly tried school-keeping, and found that my expenses were out of proportion to my income, for I was obliged to dress and train, not to say think and believe accordingly; and I lost my time into the bargain. I have tried trade; but I have learned that trade curses everything it handles; and though you trade in messages from Heaven, the whole curse of trade attaches to the business. I found that the occupation of day-labourer was the most independent of any, especially as it required only thirty or forty days in the year to support me. The labourer's day ends with the going down of the sun, and he is then free to devote himself to his chosen pursuit, independent of his labour; but his employer, who speculates from month to month, has no respite from one end of the year to the other.

But all this is very selfish, I have heard some of my townsmen say. I confess that I have hitherto indulged very little in philanthropic enterprises. However, when I thought to indulge myself in this respect by maintaining certain poor persons as comfortably as I maintain myself, and even ventured so far as to make them the offer, they one and all unhesitatingly preferred to remain poor.

The Life with Nature

When I took up my abode in the woods I found myself suddenly neighbour to the birds, not by having imprisoned one, but having caged myself near them. I was not only nearer to some of those which commonly frequent the garden and orchard, but to those wilder and more thrilling songsters of the forest which never, or rarely, serenade a villager.

Every morning was a cheerful invitation to make my life of equal simplicity, and I may say, innocence, with Nature herself. I have been as sincere a worshipper of Aurora as the Greeks. Morning brings back the heroic ages. Then, for an hour at least, some part of us awakes which slumbers all the rest of the day and night.

Why should we live with such hurry and waste of life? As for work, we haven't any of any consequence. We have the Saint Vitus' dance, and cannot possibly keep our heads still. Hardly a man takes a half hour's nap after dinner, but when he wakes he holds up his head and asks: "What's the news?" as if the rest of mankind had stood his sentinels. "Pray tell me anything new that has happened to a man anywhere on this globe." And he reads over his coffee and rolls that a man has had his eyes gouged out this morning on the Wachito River, never dreaming the while that he lives in the dark, unfathomed mammoth cave of this world, and has but the rudiment of an eye himself.

Let us spend our day as deliberately as Nature. Let us rise early and fast, or break fast, gently and without perturbation. Let us not be upset and overwhelmed in that terrible rapid and whirlpool called a dinner situated in the meridian shadows.

Time is but the stream I go a-fishing in. I drink at it, but while I drink I see the sandy bottom, and detect how shallow it is. Its thin current glides away, but eternity remains. I would drink deeper, fish in the sky, whose bottom is pebbly with stars.

Reading

My residence was more favourable, not only to thought but to serious reading, than a university; and though I was beyond the range of the morning circulating library I had more than ever come within the influence of those books which circulate round the world. I kept Homer's "Iliad" on my table through the summer, though I looked at his pages only now and then. To read well—that is to read true books in a true spirit—is a noble exercise and one that will task the reader more than any exercise which the customs of the day esteem. Books must be read as deliberately and reservedly as they were written. No wonder that Alexander carried the "Iliad" with him on his expeditions in a precious casket. A written word is the choicest of relics.

In the Sun

I did not read books the first summer; I hoed beans. Nay, I often did better than this. There were times when I could not afford to sacrifice the bloom of the present moment to any work, whether of the head or hands. I love a broad margin to my life. Sometimes on a summer morning, having taken my accustomed bath, I sat in my sunny doorway from sunrise till noon, rapt in a reverie, amidst the pines and hickories and sumachs in undisturbed solitude and stillness, while the birds sang around or flitted noiseless through the house, until by the sun falling in at my west window, or the noise of some traveller's waggon on the distant highway, I was reminded of the lapse of time. I grew in those seasons like corn in the night, and they were far better than any work of the hands would have been. They were not time subtracted from my life, but so much over and above my usual allowance. I realised what the Orientals mean by contemplation and the forsaking of works. Instead of singing like the birds I silently smiled at my incessant good fortune. This was sheer idleness to my fellow townsmen, no doubt, but if the birds and flowers had tried me by their standard I should not have been found wanting.

Night Sounds

Regularly at half past seven, in one part of the summer, the whip-poor-wills chanted their vespers for half an hour, sitting on a stump by my door, or upon the ridge pole of the house. When other birds were still the screech owls took up the strain, like mourning women their ancient u-lu-lu. Wise midnight hags! I love to hear their wailing, their doleful responses, trilled along the woodside. They give me a new sense of the variety and capacity of that nature which is our common dwelling. *Oh-o-o-o-o that I had never been bor-r-r-r-n!* sighs one on this side of the pond, and circles, with the restlessness of despair to some new perch on the gray oaks. Then: *That I had never been bor-r-r-r-n!* echoes another on the further side with tremulous sincerity, and *bor-r-r-r-n!* comes faintly from far in the Lincoln woods. I require that there are owls. They represent the stark twilight and unsatisfied thoughts which all have.

I am not sure that ever I heard the sound of cock crowing from my clearing, and I thought that it might be worth the while to keep a cockerel for his music merely, as a singing bird. The note of this once wild Indian pheasant is certainly the most remarkable of any bird's, and if they could be naturalised without being domesticated it would soon become the most famous sound in our woods.

I kept neither dog, cat, cow, pig, nor hens, so that you would have said there was a deficiency of domestic sounds, neither the churn nor the spinning wheel, nor even the singing of the kettle, nor the hissing of the urn, nor children crying, to comfort me; only squirrels on the roof, a whip-poor-will on the ridge pole, a bluejay screaming beneath the window, a woodchuck under the house, a laughing loon on the pond, and a fox to bark in the night.

This is a delicious evening, when the whole body is one sense and imbibes delight through every pore. I go and come with a strange liberty in Nature, a part of herself. Sympathy with the fluttering alder and poplar leaves almost takes away my breath; yet, like the lake, my serenity is rippled, but not ruffled. Though it is now dark the wind still blows and roars in the woods, the waves still dash, and some creatures lull the rest with their notes. The repose is never complete. The wildest animals do not repose but seek their prey now. They are Nature's watchmen—links which connect the days of animated life.

I find it wholesome to be alone the greater part of the time. I never found the companion that was never so companionable as solitude. A man thinking or working is always alone, let him be where he will. I am no more lonely than the loon in the pond that laughs so loud. God is alone, but the devil, he is far from being alone; he sees a great deal of company; he is legion. I am no more lonely than a single dandelion in a pasture, or a humble bee, or the North Star, or the first spider in a new house.

Visitors

In my house I have three chairs: one for solitude, two for friendship, three for society. My best room, however—my withdrawing room—always ready for company, was the pine wood behind my house. Thither in Summer days, when distinguished guests came, I took them, and a priceless domestic swept the floor and kept the things in order.

I could not but notice some of the peculiarities of my visitors. Girls and boys, and young women generally, seemed glad to be in the woods. They looked in the pond and at the flowers, and improved their time. Men of business, even farmers, thought only of solitude and employment, and of the great distance at which I dwelt from something or other; and though they said that they loved a ramble in the woods occasionally, it was obvious that they did not. Restless, committed men, whose time was all taken up in getting a living, or keeping it, ministers, who spoke of God as if they enjoyed a monopoly of the subject, and who could not bear all kinds of opinions, doctors, lawyers, and uneasy housekeepers, who pried into my cupboard and bed when I was out, young men who had ceased to be young, and had concluded that it was safest to follow the beaten track of the professions— all these generally said that it was not possible to do as much good in my position.

Interference

After hoeing, or perhaps reading and writing in the forenoon, I usually bathed again in the pond, washed the dust of labour from my person, and for the afternoon was absolutely free. Every day or two I strolled to the village. As I walked in the woods to see the birds and the squirrels, so I walked in the village to see the men and the boys. Instead of the wind among the pines I heard the carts rattle.

One afternoon near the end of the first summer, when I went to the village to get a shoe from the cobbler's, I was seized and put into jail, because I did not pay a tax to, or recognise the authority of, the State. I had gone down to the woods for other purposes. But wherever a man goes men will pursue and paw him with their dirty institutions, and, if they can, constrain him to belong to their desperate Odd Fellows society. However, I was released the next day, obtained my mended shoe, and returned to the woods in season to get my dinner of huckleberries on Fair Haven Hill. I was never molested by any person but those who represented the State. I had no lock nor bolt but for the desk which held my papers, not even a nail to put over my latch or window. I never fastened my door night or day, and though I was absent several days my house was more respected than if it had been surrounded by a file of soldiers.

Exhausted Experience

I left the woods for as good a reason as I went there. Perhaps it seemed to me that I had several more lives to live and could not spare any more time for that one. It is remarkable how easily and insensibly we fall into a particular route, and make a beaten track for ourselves. I had not lived there a week before my feet wore a path from my door to the pond side, and though it is five or six years since I trod it, it is still quite distinct. So with the paths which the mind travels. How worn and dusty then must be the highways of the world—how deep the ruts of tradition and conformity. I learned this, at least by my experiment, that if one advances confidently in the direction of his dreams, and endeavours to live the life which he has imagined, he will meet with a success unexpected in common hours. In proportion as he simplifies his life the laws of the Universe will appear less complex, and solitude will not be solitude, nor poverty poverty, nor weakness weakness.

ALEXIS DE TOCQUEVILLE

Democracy in America

Alexis de Tocqueville (see Vol. XII, p. 117), being commissioned at the age of twenty-six to investigate and report on American prisons, made use of his residence in the United States to gain a thorough insight into the political institutions and social conditions of the great Republic. The results of his observations and reflections were given to the world in 1835, in the two famous volumes *De la Démocratie en Amérique*, which were followed in 1840 by a third and fourth volume under the same title. As an analysis of American political institutions De Tocqueville's work has been superseded by Mr. Bryce's admirable study of the same subject; but as one of the great classics of political philosophy it can never be superseded, and has rarely been rivalled. With all a Frenchman's simplicity and lucidity he traces the manifold results of the democratic spirit; though sometimes an excessive ingenuity, which is also French, leads him to over-speculative conclusions. The work was received with universal applause.

I.—Equality

The most striking impression which I received during my residence in the United States was that of the equality which reigns there. This equality gives a peculiar character to public opinion and to the laws of that country, and influences the entire structure of society in the most profound degree. Realising that equality, or democracy, was rapidly advancing in the Old World also, I determined to make a thorough study of democratic principles and of their consequences, as they are revealed in the western continent.

We have only to review the history of European countries from the days of feudalism, to understand that the development of equality is one of the great designs of Providence; inasmuch as it is universal, inevitable, and lasting, and that every event and every individual contributes to its advancement.

It is impossible to believe that a social movement which has proceeded so far as this movement towards equality has done, can be arrested by human efforts, or that the democracy which has bearded kings and barons can be successfully resisted by a wealthy bourgeoisie. We know not whither we are moving; we only know that greater equality is found to-day among Christian populations than has been known before in any age or in any country.

I confess to a kind of religious terror in the presence of this irresistible revolution, which has defied every obstacle for the last ten centuries. A new political science is awaited by a world which is wholly new; but the most immediate duties of the statesman are to instruct the democracy, if possible to revive its beliefs, to purify its morals, to enlighten its inexperience by some knowledge of political principles, and to substitute for the blind instincts which sway it, the consciousness of its true interests.

In the Old World, and in France especially, the more powerful, intelligent, and moralised classes have held themselves apart from democracy, and the latter has, therefore, been abandoned to its own savage instincts. The democratic revolution has permeated the whole substance of society, without those concomitant changes in laws, ideas, habits, and manners which ought to have embodied and clothed it. So it is that we indeed have democracy, but without those features which should have mitigated its vices and liberated its advantages. The prestige of royal power is gone, without being replaced by the majesty of law, and our people despise authority as much as they fear it. Our poor have the prejudices of their fathers without their beliefs, their ignorance, without their virtues; they have taken self-interest for a principle without knowing what their interests are. Our society is tranquil, not in the consciousness of strength and of well-being, but a sense of decrepitude and despair. That is why I have studied America, in order that we may ourselves profit by her example. I have no intention of writing a panegyric on the United States. I have seen more in America than America herself; I have sought a revelation of Democracy, with all its characters and tendencies, its prejudices and its passions.

II.—Religion and Liberty

Our first consideration is of great importance, and must never be lost sight of. The Anglo-American civilisation which we find in the United States is the product of two perfectly distinct elements, which elsewhere are often at war with one another, but have here been merged and combined in the most wonderful way; I mean the spirit of religion and the spirit of liberty. The founders of New England were at the same time ardent secretaries and enthusiastic radicals; they were bound by the narrowest religious beliefs, but were free from all political prejudice.

Thus arose two tendencies which we may trace everywhere in American manners, as well as in their lives. All political principles, laws, and human institutions seem to have become plastic in the hands of the early colonists. The bonds which fettered the society in which they had been born fell from their limbs; ancient opinions which had dominated the world for ages simply disappeared; a new career opened for the human race; a world without horizons was before them, and they exulted in liberty. But outside the limits of the political world, they made no ventures of this kind. They abjured doubt, renounced their desire for innovation, left untouched the veil of the sanctuary, and knelt with awe before the truths of religion.

So, in their world of morals, everything was already classed, arranged, foreseen, and determined; but in their world of politics, everything was agitated, debated, and uncertain. In the former they were ruled by a voluntary obedience, but in all political affairs they were inspired by independence, contempt for experience, and jealous of every authority.

Far from impeding one another, these two tendencies, which appear so radically opposed, actually harmonise and seem even to support each other. Religion sees in civil liberty a noble field for the exercise of human faculties. Free and powerful in her own sphere, and satisfied with the part reserved for her, she knows that her sovereignty is all the more securely established when she depends only on her own strength and is founded in the hearts of men. And liberty, on the other hand, recognises in religion the comrade of its struggles and triumphs, the cradle of its rights. It knows that religion is the safeguard of morals, and that morals are the safeguard of the laws, and the judge of the continuance of liberty itself.

III.—Omnipotence of the Majority

The greatest danger to liberty in America lies in the omnipotence of the majority. A democratic power is never likely to perish for lack of strength or of resources, but it may very well fall because of the misdirection of its strength and the abuse of its resources. If ever liberty is lost in America, it will be due to an oppression of minorities which may drive them to an appeal to arms. The anarchy which must then result will be due only to despotism.

This danger has not escaped the notice of American statesmen. Thus, President James Madison said, "It is of great importance to republics, not only that society should be defended from the oppression of those who govern it, but also that one section of society should be protected against the injustice of another section; for justice is the end towards which all government must be directed." Again, Jefferson said that "The tyranny of legislators is at present, and will be for many years, our most formidable danger. The tyranny of the executive will arise in its turn, but at a more distant period." Jefferson's words are of great importance, for I consider him to have been the most powerful apostle that democracy has ever had.

But there are certain factors in the United States which moderate this tyranny of the majority. Chief among these is the absence of any administrative centralisation; so that the majority, which has often the tastes and instincts of a despot, lacks the instruments and the means of tyranny. The local administrative bodies constitute so many reefs and breakwaters to retard or divide the stream of the popular will.

Not less important, as a counterpoise to the danger of democracy, is the strong legal spirit which pervades the United States. Lawyers have great influence and authority in matters of government. But lawyers are strongly imbued with the tasks and habits of mind which are most characteristic of aristocracy; they have an instinctive liking for forms and for order, a native distaste for the will of the multitude, and a secret contempt for popular government. Of course, their own personal interest may and often does over-ride this professional bias. But lawyers will always be, on the whole, friends of order and of precedent, and enemies of change. And in America, where there are neither nobles nor able political writers, and where the people are suspicious of the wealthy, the lawyers do, in fact, form the most powerful order in politics, and the most intellectual class of society. They therefore stand to lose by any innovation, and their conservative tendency is reinforced by their interests as a class.

A third safeguard against the tyranny of the majority is to be found in the institution of a jury. Almost everyone is called at one time or another to sit on a jury, and thus learns at least something of the judicial spirit. The civil jury has saved English freedom in past times, and may be expected to maintain American liberties also. It is true that there are many cases, and those often the most important, in which the American judge pronounces sentence without a jury. Under those circumstances, his position is similar to that of a French judge, but his moral power is far greater; for the memory and the influence of juries are all about him, and he speaks with the authority of one who habitually rests upon the jury system. In no other countries are the judges so powerful as in those where the people are called in to share judicial privileges and responsibilities.

IV.—Equality of Men and Women

Inasmuch as democracy destroys or modifies the various inequalities which social traditions have made, it is natural to ask whether it has had any effect on that great inequality between men and women which is elsewhere so conspicuous. We are driven to the conclusion that the social movement which places son and father, servant and master, and in general, the inferior and superior, more nearly on the same level, must raise woman more and more to an equality with man.

Let us guard, however, against misconceptions. There are people in Europe who confuse the natural qualities of the two sexes, and desire that men and women should be, not only equal, but also similar to one another. That would give them both the same functions, the same duties and the same rights, and would have them mingle in everything, in work, in pleasures, and in business. But the attempt to secure this kind of equality between the two sexes, only degrades them both, and must result in unmanly men, and unwomanly women.

The Americans have not thus mistaken the kind of democratic equality which ought to hold between man and woman. They know that progress does not consist in forcing these dissimilar temperaments and faculties into the same mould, but in securing that each shall fulfil his or her task in the best possible way. They have most carefully separated the functions of man and woman, in order that the great work of social life may be most prosperously carried on.

In America, far more than elsewhere, the lines of action of the two sexes have been clearly divided. You do not find American women directing the external affairs of the family, or entering into business or into politics; but neither do you find them obliged to undertake the rough labours of the field, or any other work requiring physical strength. There are no families so poor as to form an exception to this rule.

So it is that American women often unite a masculine intelligence and a virile energy with an appearance of great refinement and altogether womanly manners.

One has often noticed in Europe a certain tinge of contempt even in the flatteries which men lavish on women; and although the European often makes himself a slave of a woman, it is easy to see that he never really regards her as his equal. But in the United States men rarely praise women, though they show their esteem for them every day.

Americans show, in fact, a full confidence in woman's reason, and a profound respect for her liberty. They realise that her mind is just as capable as that of man to discover truth, and that her heart is just as courageous in following it; and they have never tried to shelter or to guide her by means of prejudice, ignorance, or fear.

For my part I do not hesitate to say that the singular prosperity and the evergrowing power of the American people is due to the superiority of American women.

V.—The Perfectibility of Man

Equality suggests many ideas which would never have arisen without it, and among others the notion that humanity can reach perfection—a theory which has practical consequences of great interest.

In countries where the population is classed according to rank, profession, and birth, and everyone has to follow the career to which he happens to be born, each is conscious of limits to his power, and does not attempt to struggle against an inevitable destiny. Aristocratic peoples do not deny that man may be improved, but they think of this as an amelioration of the individual, and not as a change in social circumstances, and while they admit that humanity has made great progress, they believe in certain limits which it cannot pass. They do not think, for instance, that we shall arrive at sovereign good or at absolute truth.

But in proportion as caste and class-distinction disappear, the vision of an ideal perfection arises before the human mind. Continual changes are ever taking place, some of them to his disadvantage, but the majority to his advantage, and the democrat concludes that man in general is capable of arriving at perfection. His reverses teach him that no one has yet discovered absolute good, and his frequent successes excite him to pursue it. Always seeking, falling, and rising again, often deceived, but never discouraged, he hastens towards an immense grandeur which he dimly conceives as the goal of humanity. This theory of perfectibility exercises prodigious influence even on those who have never thought of it. For instance, I ask an American sailor why the ships of his country are built to last only a few years; and he tells me without hesitation that the art of shipbuilding makes such rapid progress every day, that the finest ship constructed to-day must be useless after a very short time. From these words, spoken at random by an uneducated man, I can perceive the general and systematic idea which guides this great people in every matter.

VI.—American Vanity

All free people are proud of themselves, but national pride takes different forms. The Americans, in their relations with strangers, are impatient of the least criticism, and absolutely insatiable for praise. The slightest congratulation pleases them, but the most extravagant eulogium is not enough to satisfy them; they are all the time touting for your praise, and if you are slow to give it they begin praising themselves. It is as if they were doubtful of their own merit. Their vanity is not only hungry, but anxious and envious. It gives nothing, and asks insistently. It is both supplicant and pugnacious. If I tell an American that his country is a fine one, he replies, "It is the finest in the world." If I admire the liberty which it enjoys, he answers, "There are few people worthy of such liberty." I remark on the purity of manners in the United States, and he says, "Yes, a stranger who knows the corruption of other nations must indeed be astonished at us." At length I leave him to the contemplation of his country and of himself, but he presently runs after me, and will not go away until I have repeated it all over again. It is a kind of patriotism that worries even those who honour it.

The Englishman, on the contrary, tranquilly enjoys the real or imaginary advantages which his country affords. He cares nothing for the blame nor for the praise of strangers. His attitude towards the whole world is one of disdainful and ignorant reserve. His pride seeks no nourishment; it lives on itself. It is very remarkable that the two people who have arisen from the same stock should differ so radically in their way of feeling and speaking.

In aristocratic countries, great families possess enormous privileges, on which their pride rests. They consider these privileges as a natural right inherent in their person, and their feeling of superiority is therefore a peaceful one. They have no reason to boast of the prerogatives which everyone concedes to them without question. So, when public affairs are directed by an aristocracy, the national pride tends to take this reserved, haughty, and independent form.

Under democratic conditions, on the contrary, the least advantage which anyone gains has great importance in his eyes; for everyone is surrounded by millions very nearly his equal. His pride therefore becomes anxious and insatiable; he founds it on miserable trifles and defends it obstinately. Again, most Americans have recently acquired the advantages which they possess, and therefore have inordinate pleasure in contemplating these advantages, and in showing them to others; and as these advantages may escape at any moment, they are always uneasy about them, and look at them again and again to see that they still have them. Men who live in democracies love their country as they love themselves, and model their national vanity upon their private vanity. The close dependence of this anxious and insatiable vanity of democratic peoples upon the equality and fragility of their conditions is seen from the fact that the members of the proudest nobility show exactly the same passionate jealousy for the most trifling circumstances of their life when these become unstable or are contested.

IZAAK WALTON

The Compleat Angler

Izaak Walton, English author and angler, was born at Stafford on August 9, 1593, and until about his fiftieth year lived as a linen-draper in London. He then retired from business and lived at Stafford for a few years; but returned to London in 1650, and spent his closing years at Winchester, where he died on December 15, 1683, and was buried in the cathedral there. Walton was thrice married, his second wife being sister of the future Bishop Ken. He had a large acquaintance with eminent clergymen, and among his literary friends were Ben Jonson and Michael Drayton. He was author of several charming biographies, including those of the poet Donne, 1640, of Sir Henry Wotton, 1651, of Richard Hooker, 1652, and of George Herbert, 1670. But by far his most famous work is "The Compleat Angler; or, the Contemplative Man's Recreation," published in 1653. There were earlier books on the subject in English, such as Dame Juliana Berner's "Treatise pertaining to Hawking, Hunting, and Fishing with an Angle," 1486; the "Book of Fishing with Hook and Line," 1590; a poem, "The Secrets of Angling," by John Denny, 1613; and several others. The new thing in Walton's book, and the secret of its unfading popularity, is the charm of temperament. Charles Lamb well said that it "breathes the very spirit of innocence, purity, and simplicity of heart." A sequel to the book, entitled the "Second Part of the Compleat Angler," was written by Charles Cotton, and published in 1676.

The Virtues of Angling

PISCATOR, VENATOR, AND AUCEPS

Piscator. You are well overtaken, gentlemen! A good morning to you both! I have stretched my legs up Tottenham Hill to overtake you, hoping your business may occasion you towards Ware, whither I am going this fine fresh May morning.

Venator. Sir, I, for my part, shall almost answer your hopes, for my purpose is to drink my morning's draught at the Thatched House. And, sir, as we are all so happy to have a fine morning, I hope we shall each be the happier in each other's company.

Auceps. Sir, I shall, by your favour, bear you company as far as Theobald's, for then I turn up to a friend's house, who mews a hawk for me. And as the Italians say, good company in a journey maketh the way to seem the shorter, I, for my part, promise you that I shall be as free and open-hearted as discretion will allow with strangers.

Piscator. I am right glad to hear your answers. I shall put on a boldness to ask you, sir, whether business or pleasure caused you to be up so early, for this other gentleman hath declared he is going to see a hawk that a friend mews for him.

Venator. Sir, I intend to go hunting the otter.

Piscator. Those villainous vermin, for I hate them perfectly, because they love fish so well, or rather destroy so much. For I, sir, am a brother of the angle.

Auceps. And I profess myself a falconer, and have heard many grave, serious men scoff at anglers and pity them, as it is a heavy, contemptible, dull recreation.

Piscator. You know, gentlemen, it is an easy thing to scoff at any art or recreation; a little wit mixed with all nature, confidence, and malice will do it; but though they often venture boldly, yet they are often caught, even in their own trap.

There be many men that are by others taken to be serious, and grave men, which we contemn and pity: men that are taken to be grave because nature hath made them of a sour complexion—money-getting men, men that are condemned to be rich; for these poor, rich men, we anglers pity them most perfectly. No, sir! We enjoy a contentedness above the reach of such dispositions.

Venator. Sir, you have almost amazed me; for though I am no scoffer, yet I have—I pray let me speak it without offence—always looked upon anglers as more patient and simple men than, I fear, I shall find you to be.

Piscator. Sir, I hope you will not judge my earnestness to be impatience! As for my simplicity, if by that you mean a harmlessness which was usually found in the primitive Christians, who were, as most anglers are, followers of peace—then myself and men of my profession will be glad to be so understood. But if, by simplicity, you mean to express a general defect, I hope in time to disabuse you.

But, gentlemen, I am not so unmannerly as to engross all the discourse to myself; I shall be most glad to hear what you can say in the commendation of your several recreations.

Auceps. The element I use to trade in, the air, is an element of more worth than weight; an element that doubtless exceeds both the earth and water; in it my noble falcon ascends to such a height as the dull eye of man is not able to reach to; my troop of hawks soars up on high, so that they converse with the gods.

And more, the worth of this element of air is such that all creatures whatsoever stand in need of it. The waters cannot preserve their fish without air; witness the not breaking of ice and the result thereof.

Venator. Well, sir, I will now take my turn. The earth, that solid, settled element, is the one on which I drive my pleasant, wholesome, hungry trade. What pleasure doth man take in hunting the stately stag, the cunning otter! The earth breeds and nourishes the mighty elephant, and also the least of creatures! It puts limits to the proud and raging seas, and so preserves both man and beast; daily we see those that are shipwrecked and left to feed haddocks; but, Mr. Piscator, I will not be so uncivil as not to allow you time for the commendation of angling; I doubt we shall hear a watery discourse—and I hope not a long one.

Piscator. Gentlemen, my discourse is likely to prove suitable to my recreation—calm and quiet.

Water is the eldest daughter of the creation, the element upon which the spirit of God did first move. There be those that profess to believe that all bodies are water, and may be reduced back into water only.

The water is more productive than the earth. The increase of creatures that are bred in the water is not only more miraculous, but more advantageous to man for the preventing of sickness. It is observed that the casting of Lent and other fish days hath doubtless been the cause of these many putrid, shaking agues, to which this country of ours is now more subject.

To pass by the miraculous cures of our known baths the Romans have made fish the mistress of all their entertainments; and have had music to usher in their sturgeons, lampreys, and mullets.

Auceps. Sir, it is with such sadness that I must part with you here, for I see Theobald's house. And so I part full of good thoughts. God keep you both.

Venator. Sir, you said angling was of great antiquity, and a perfect art, not easily attained to. I am desirous to hear further concerning those particulars.

Piscator. Is it not an art to deceive a trout with an artificial fly? A trout! more sharp-sighted than any hawk! Doubt not, angling is an art worth your learning. The question is rather, whether you be capable of learning it? Angling is like poetry—men are to be born so. Some say it is as ancient as Deucalion's flood, and Moses makes mention of fish-hooks, which must imply anglers.

But as I would rather prove myself a gentleman by being learned, and humble, valiant, and inoffensive, virtuous, and communicable, than by any fond ostentation of riches, or, wanting those virtues, boast these were in my ancestors, so if this antiquity of angling shall be an honour to this art, I shall be glad I made mention of it.

I shall tell you that in ancient times a debate hath arisen, whether the happiness of man doth consist more in contemplation or action?

Some have endeavoured to maintain their opinion of the first by saying that the nearer we mortals approach to God by way of imitation, the more happy we are. And they say God enjoys Himself only by a contemplation of His own infiniteness, eternity, power, goodness and the like.

On the contrary, there want not men of equal authority that prefer action to be the more excellent, such as experiments in physics for the ease and prolongation of man's life. Concerning which two opinions I shall forbear to add a third, and tell you, my worthy friend, that both these meet together and do most properly belong to the most honest, quiet, and harmless art of angling.

An ingenious Spaniard says that "rivers and the inhabitants thereof were made for wise men to contemplate, and fools to pass by without consideration."

There be many wonders reported of rivers, as of a river in Epirus, that puts out any lighted torch, and kindles any torch that was not lighted; the river Selarus, that in a few hours turns a rod to stone, and mention is made of the like in England, and many others on historical faith.

But to tell you something of the monsters, or fish, call them what you will, Pliny says the fish called the Balæna is so long and so broad as to take up more length and breadth than two acres of ground; and in the river Ganges there be eels thirty feet long.

I know we islanders are averse to the belief of these wonders, but there are many strange creatures to be now seen. Did not the Prophet David say, "They that occupy themselves in deep water see the wonderful works of God"; and the apostles of our Saviour, were not they four simple fishermen; He found that the hearts of such men, by nature, were fitted for contemplation and quietness—men of sweet and peaceable spirits, as indeed most anglers are.

Venator. Sir, you have angled me on with much pleasure to the Thatched House, for I thought we had three miles of it. Let us drink a civil cup to all lovers of angling, of which number I am now willing to count myself, and if you will but meet me to-morrow at the time and place appointed, we two will do nothing but talk of fish and fishing.

Piscator. 'Tis a match, sir; I will not fail you, God willing, to be at Amwell Hill to-morrow before sun-rising.

Master and Pupil

Piscator. Sir, I am right glad to meet you. Come, honest Venator, let us be gone; I long to be doing.

Venator. Well, let's to your sport of angling.

Piscator. With all my heart. But we are not yet come to a likely place. Let us walk on. But let us first to an honest alehouse, where my hostess can give us a cup of her best drink.

Seneca says that the ancients were so curious in the newness of their fish, that they usually did keep them living in glass-bottles in their dining-rooms, and did glory much in the entertaining of their friends, to have the fish taken from under their tables alive that was instantly to be fed upon. Our hostess shall dress us a trout, that we shall presently catch, and we, with brother Peter and Goridon, will sup on him here this same evening.

Venator. And now to our sport.

Piscator. This is not a likely place for a trout; the sun is too high. But there lie upon the top of the water twenty Chub. Sir, here is a trial of my skill! I'll catch only one, and he shall be the big one, that has some bruise upon his tail.

Venator. I'll sit down and hope well; because you seem so confident.

Piscator. Look you, sir! The very one! Oh, 'tis a great logger-headed Chub! I'll warrant he will make a good dish of meat.

Under that broad beech tree yonder, I sat down when I was last a-fishing; and the birds in the adjoining grove seemed to have a friendly contention with the echo that lives in a hollow near the brow of that primrose-hill. There I sat viewing the silver stream slide away, and the lambs sporting harmlessly. And as I sat, these sights so possessed my soul, that I thought as the poet hath it:

"I was for that time lifted above earth;
And possess'd joys not promised at my birth."

But, let us further on; and we will try for a Trout. 'Tis now past five of the clock.

Venator. I have a bite! Oh me! He has broke all; and a good hook lost! But I have no fortune! Sure yours is a better rod and tackling.

Piscator. Nay, then, take mine, and I will fish with yours. Look you, scholar, I have another. I pray, put that net under him, but touch not my line. Well done, scholar, I thank you.

And now, having three brace of Trouts, I will tell you a tale as we walk back to our hostess.

A preacher that was to procure the approbation of a parish got from a fellow preacher the copy of a sermon that was preached with great commendation by him that composed it; and though the borrower preached it, word for word, yet it was utterly disliked; and on complaining to the lender of it, was thus answered: "I lent you indeed my fiddle, but not my fiddlestick; for you are to know, everyone cannot make music with my words, which are fitted for my own mouth." And though I lend you my very rod and tacklings, yet you have not my fiddlestick, that is, the skill wherewith I guide it.

Venator. Master, you spoke very true. Yonder comes mine hostess to call us to supper; and when we have supped we will sing songs which shall give some addition of mirth to the company.

Piscator. And so say I; for to-morrow we meet again up the water towards Waltham.

Fish of English Streams

Piscator. Indeed, my good scholar, we may say of angling, as Dr. Boteler said of strawberries, "Doubtless God could have made a better berry, but doubtless God never did"; and so, God never did make a more calm, quiet, innocent recreation than angling.

And when I see how pleasantly that meadow looks; and the earth smells so sweetly too; I think of them as Charles the Emperor did of the City of Florence; "that they were too pleasant to be looked on, but on holidays."

To speak of fishes; the Salmon is accounted the king of fresh-water fish. He breeds in the rivers in the month of August, and then hastes to the sea before winter; where he recovers his strength and comes the next summer to the same river; for like persons of riches, he has his summer and winter house, to spend his life in, which is, as Sir Francis Bacon hath observed, not above ten years.

The Pike, the tyrant of the fresh-waters, is said to be the longest-lived of any fresh-water fish, but not usually above forty years. Gesner relates of a man watering his mule in a pond, where the Pike had devoured all the fish, had the Pike bite his mule's lips; to which he hung so fast, the mule did draw him out of the water. And this same Gesner observes, that a maid in Poland washing clothes in a pond, had a Pike bite her by the foot. I have told you who relate these things; and shall conclude by telling you, what a wise-man hath observed: "It is a hard thing to persuade the belly, because it has no ears."

Besides being an eater of great voracity, the Pike is observed to be a solitary, melancholy and a bold fish. When he is dressed with a goodly, rich sauce, and oysters, this dish of meat is too good for any man, but an angler, or a very honest man.

The Carp, that hath only lately been naturalised in England, is said to be the queen of rivers, and will grow to a very great bigness; I have heard, much above a yard long.

The stately Bream, and the Tench, that physician of fishes, love best to live in ponds. In every Tench's head are two little stones which physicians make great use of. Rondeletius says, at his being in Rome, he saw a great cure done by applying a Tench to the feet of a sick man.

But I will not meddle more with that; there are too many meddlers in physic and divinity that think fit to meddle with hidden secrets and so bring destruction to their followers.

The Perch is a bold, biting fish, and carries his teeth in his mouth; and to affright the Pike and save himself he will set up his fins, like as a turkey-cock will set up his tail. If there be twenty or forty in a hole, they may be catched one after the other, at one standing; they being, like the wicked of this world, not afraid, though their fellows and companions perish in their sight.

And now I think best to rest myself, for I have almost spent my spirits with talking.

Venator. Nay, good master, one fish more! For it rains yet; you know our angles are like money put to usury; they may thrive, though we sit still. Come, the other fish, good master!

Piscator. But shall I nothing from you, that seem to have both a good memory and a cheerful spirit?

Venator. Yes, master; I will speak you a copy of verses that allude to rivers and fishing:

> Come, live with me, and be my love,
> And we will some new pleasures prove;
> Of golden sands, and crystal brooks,
> With silken lines, and silver hooks.
>
> When thou wilt swim in that live bath,
> Each fish, which every channel hath,
> Most amorously to thee will swim,
> Gladder to catch thee, than thou him.
>
> Let others freeze with angling reeds,
> And cut their legs with shells and weeds,
> Or treacherously poor fish beget
> With trangling snare or windowy net;
>
> For thee, thou need'st no such deceit,
> For thou, thyself, art thine own bait,
> That fish, that is not catched thereby
> Is wiser far, alas, than I!

Piscator. I thank you for these choice verses. And I will now tell you of the Eel, which is a most dainty fish. The Romans have esteemed her the Helena of their feasts. Sir Francis Bacon will allow the Eel to live but ten years; but he mentions a Lamprey, belonging to the Roman Emperor, that was made tame and kept for three-score years; so that when she died, Crassus, the orator, lamented her death.

I will tell you next how to make the Eel a most excellent dish of meat.

First, wash him in water and salt, then pull off his skin and clean him; then give him three or four scotches with a knife; and then put into him sweet herbs, an anchovy and a little nutmeg. Then pull his skin over him, and tie him with pack-thread; and baste him with butter, and what he drips, be his sauce. And when I dress an Eel thus, I wish he were a yard and three-quarters long. But they are not so proper to be talked of by me because they make us anglers no sport.

The Barbel, so called by reason of his barb or wattles, and the Gudgeon, are both fine fish of excellent shape.

My further purpose was to give you directions concerning Roach and Dace, but I will forbear. I see yonder, brother Peter. But I promise you, to-morrow as we walk towards London, if I have forgotten anything now I will not then keep it from you.

Venator. Come, we will all join together and drink a cup to our jovial host, and so to bed. I say good-night to everybody.

Piscator. And so say I.

Walking Homewards

Piscator. I will tell you, my honest scholar, I once heard one say, "I envy not him that eats better meat, or wears better clothes than I do; I envy him only that catches more fish than I do."

And there be other little fish that I had almost forgot, such as the Minnow or Penk; the dainty Loach; the Miller's-Thumb, of no pleasing shape; the Stickle-bag, good only to make sport for boys and women anglers.

Well, scholar, I could tell you many things of the rivers of this nation, the chief of which is the Thamisis; of fish-ponds, and how to breed fish within them, and how to order your lines and baits for the several fishes; but, I will tell you some of the thoughts that have possessed my soul since we met together. And you shall join with me in thankfulness to the Giver of every good and perfect gift for our happiness; which may appear the greater when we consider how many, even at this very time, lie under the torment, and the stone, the gout, and tooth-ache; and all these we are free from.

Since we met, others have met disasters, some have been blasted, and we have been free from these. What is a far greater mercy, we are free from the insupportable burden of an accusing conscience.

Let me tell you, there be many that have forty times our estates, that would give the greatest part of it to be healthful and cheerful like us; who have eat, and drank, and laughed, and angled, and sung, and slept; and rose next day, and cast away care, and sung, and laughed, and angled again.

I have a rich neighbour that is always so busy that he has no leisure to laugh. He says that Solomon says, "The diligent man makest rich"; but, he considers not what was wisely said by a man of great observation, "That there be as many miseries beyond riches, as on this side them."

Let me tell you, scholar, Diogenes walked one day through a country fair, where he saw ribbons, and looking-glasses, and nut-crackers, and fiddles, and many other gimcracks; and said to his friend, "Lord, how many things are there in this world Diogenes hath no need!"

All this is told you to incline you to thankfulness: though the prophet David was guilty of murder and many other of the most deadly sins, yet he was said to be a man after God's own heart, because he abounded with thankfulness.

Well, scholar, I have almost tired myself, and I fear, more than tired you.

But, I now see Tottenham High Cross, which puts a period to our too long discourse, in which my meaning was to plant that in your mind with which I labour to possess my own soul—that is, a meek and thankful heart. And, to that end, I have showed you that riches without them do not make a man happy. But riches with them remove many fears and cares. Therefore, my advice is, that you endeavour to be honestly rich, or contentedly poor; but be sure your riches be justly got; for it is well said by Caussin, "He that loses his conscience, has nothing left that is worth the keeping." So look to that. And in the next place, look to your health, for health is a blessing that money cannot buy. As for money, neglect it not, and, if you have a competence, enjoy it with a cheerful, thankful heart.

Venator. Well, master, I thank you for all your good directions, and especially for this last, of thankfulness. And now being at Tottenham High Cross, I will requite a part of your courtesies with a drink composed of sack, milk, oranges, and sugar, which, all put together, make a drink like nectar indeed; and too good for anybody, but us anglers. So, here is a full glass to you.

Piscator. And I to you, sir.

Venator. Sir, your company and discourse have been so pleasant that I truly say, that I have only lived since I enjoyed it an turned angler, and not before.

I will not forget the doctrines Socrates taught his scholars, that they should not think to be honoured for being philosophers, so much as to honour philosophy by the virtue of their lives. You advised me to the like concerning angling, and to live like those same worthy men. And this is my firm resolution.

And when I would beget content, I will walk the meadows, by some gliding stream, and there contemplate the lilies that take no care. That is my purpose; and so, "let the blessing of St. Peter's Master be with mine."

Piscator. And upon all that are lovers of virtue, and be quiet, and go a-angling.

Index

In the following Index the Roman Numerals refer to the *Volumes*, and the Arabic Numerals to *Pages*. The numerals in heavy, or **black-faced** type, indicate the place where the *biographical* notice will be found.

Mexico

Peru

United States

see also Washington, Franklin, etc.

— —, Democracy in

— —, Wanderings in South

Anabasis, The

Anatomy of Melancholy, The

— — of Vertebrates

Andersen, Hans Christian

Angler, The Complete

Animal Chemistry

Anna Karenina

Annals of the Parish

— — of Tacitus

Antigone

Antiquary, The

Antiquities of the Jews

Apocrypha, The

Apologia Pro Vita Sua

Apology, or Defence of Socrates

Apuleius

Arabian Nights

Arcadia

Areopagitica

Ariosto, Ludovico

Aristophanes*seq.*

Aristotle

Arne

Arnold, Matthew

Arnold, Life of Thomas

Bentham, Jeremy

Bérénice

Bergerac, Cyrano de

Berkeley, George

Bernard, Life of Saint

Betrothed, The

Beyle, Henri: see Stendhal

Bible in Spain, The

Biographia Literaria

Biology, Principles of

Birds, The

Björnson, Björnstjerne*seq.*

Black, William

Black Prophet, The

—— Tulip, The

Blackmore, R. D.

Bleak House

Bloch, Jean

Blot in the 'Scutcheon, A

Boccaccio, Giovanni

Book of the Dead

Borrow, George *seq.; seq.*

Boswell, James

Bothwell

Braddon, M. E.

Bradley, Edward ("Cuthbert Bede")

Brahmanism, Books of

Bramwell, John Milne

Brandes, George

Brewster, Sir Davis

Brontë, Charlotte *seq.;*

—— and Italy, Sentimental Journey Through

Frankenstein

Franklin, Benjamin

Frederick the Great

Freeman, Edward A.

Friendship, Concerning

Frogs, The

Froude, James Anthony

Future of War, The

Gaboriau, Émile

Galileo Galilei

Gallic War, Cæsar's Commentaries on the

Galt, John

Galton, Sir Francis

Garden of Allah, The

Gargantua and Pantagruel

Gaskell, Mrs. *seq.*;

Geoffry Hamlyn

Geology, Principles of

George, Henry

Germania

Germany, On

Gesta Romanorum

Gibbon, Edward (Memoirs); *seq.*;

Gil Blas

Girondists, History of the

Godwin, William

Goethe, Johann Wolfgang Von *seq.*; *seq.*; ; *seq.*

Goetz von Berlichingen

Gogol, Nicolai

Golden Ass, The

Goldsmith, Oliver *seq.*;

Goncourt, Edmond and Jules de

Götterdämmerung

Grace Abounding

Grammont, Memoirs of the Count de

Grant, James

Gray, Maxwell

Gray, Thomas

Great Expectations

—— Lone Land, The

Greece, History of *seq.*;

(modern)

Griffin, Gerald

Grote, George

Guizot, François Pierre Guillame

Gulliver's Travels

Guy Mannering

Habberton, John

Haeckel, Ernst

Hajji Baba of Ispahan, The Adventures of

Hakluyt, Richard

Halevy, Ludovic

Hallam, Henry

Hamilton, Anthony

Hamlet

Handy Andy

Hard Cash

—— Times

Harvey, William

Hawthorne, Nathaniel *seq.*;

Hazlitt, William

Jane Eyre

Jerusalem Delivered

Jesus, Life of

Jews:

History and Antiquities of *seq.*;

Religion (Talmud)

John Halifax, Gentleman

Johnson, Samuel

"Life of"

Jokai, Maurice

Jonathan Wild

Jonson, Ben

Joseph Andrews

Josephus, Flavius

Joshua Davidson

Journal of George Fox

—— of the Plague Year, A

—— to Stella

—— of a Tour to the Hebrides

—— of John Wesley

—— of John Woolman

Journey Round My Room, A

Juvenal

Kant, Immanuel*seq.*

Kempis, Thomas à

Kenilworth

Kernahan, Coulson

King Amuses Himself, The

—— of the Mountains, The

Kinglake, A. W.

Kingsley, Charles*seq.*

Mackenzie, Henry

Macpherson, James

Magic Skin, The

Magnetism, Treatise on Electricity and

Main Currents of Nineteenth Century Literature

Maistre, Xavier De

Malory, Sir Thomas

Malthus, T. R.

Man, Essay on

— —, Evolution of

— —, Nature of

— —, The Rights of

— — of Feeling, The

— — Who Laughs, The

Mandeville, Sir John

Manning, Anne

Mansfield Park

Mansie Wauch

Manzoni, Alessandro

Marguerite de Valois

Marion de Lorme

Marlowe, Christopher

Marmion

Marriage of Figaro, The

Marryat, Captain*seq.*

Martial

Martin Chuzzlewit

Mary Barton

— — Queen of Scots, Love Affairs of

Marx, Karl

Maspero, Gaston*seq.*

Mill on the Floss, The

Miller, Hugh

Milman, Henry

Milton, John

Mirabeau, Honoré Gabriel Comte de

Misanthrope, The

Misérables, Les

Missionary Travels and Researches

Mitford, Mary Russell

Modern Régime

Moir, David

Molière *seq.*

Mommsen, Theodor

Montaigne

Monte Cristo, The Count of

Montesquieu

Moore, Thomas

Moral Maxims, Reflections and

Morals and Legislation, Principles of

More, Sir Thomas

"Household of"

Morier, James

Morison, J. A. C.

Morley, John

Morte D'Arthur

Motley, John Lothrop*seq.*

Mourning Bride, The

Murray, David Christie

My Confession (Tolstoy)

Mysteries of Paris, The

Nathan the Wise

Senses of Insects, The

Sentimental Journey through France and Italy

Sévigné, Mme. de

Shadow of the Sword, The

Shakespeare, William*seq.*

Shelley, Mary Wollstonecraft

Shelley, Percy Bysshe

Sheridan, Richard Brinsley

She Stoops to Conquer

Shirley

Sidney, Sir Philip

Siegfried

Silas Marner

Silence of Dean Maitland, The

Simple Story, A

Sir Charles Grandison

Smith, Adam

Smoke

Smollett, Tobias*seq.*

Social Contract, The

Sociology, Principles of

Socrates, Apology or Defence of

Some Fruits of Solitude

Sophocles

Sorrows of Young Werther

Southey, Robert

Spain: (Reign of Ferdinand and Isabella)

Spectator, The

Speke, John Hanning

Spencer, Herbert*seq.*

Spinoza, Benedict de